THE
BRUTAL
TELLING
& BURY
YOUR DEAD

THE
BRUTAL
TELLING

& BURY
YOUR DEAD

LOUISE PENNY

~

MINOTAUR BOOKS ✹ NEW YORK

THE BRUTAL TELLING. Copyright © 2009 by Louise Penny. BURY YOUR DEAD. Copyright © 2010 by Three Pines Creations, Inc. All rights reserved. Printed in the United States of America. For information, address St. Martin's Press, 175 Fifth Avenue, New York, N.Y. 10010.

www.minotaurbooks.com

Grateful acknowledgment is given for permission to reprint the following in *The Brutal Telling*:

"The Bells of Heaven" by Ralph Hodgson is used by kind permission of Bryn Mawr College.

Excerpts from "Cressida to Troilius: A Gift" and "Sekhmet, the Lion-Headed Goddess of War" from *Morning in the Burned House: New Poems* by Margaret Atwood. Copyright © 1995 by Margaret Atwood. Reprinted by permission of Houghton Mifflin Harcourt Publishing Company. All rights reserved.

Excerpt from "Gravity Zero" from *Bones* by Mike Freeman. Copyright © 2007 by Mike Freeman. Reproduced with kind permission of the author.

Grateful acknowledgment is given for permission to reprint the following in *Bury Your Dead*:

"Morning in the Burned House" by Margaret Atwood © 1995. Published by McClelland & Stewart Ltd. Used with permission of the publisher.

"Vapour Trails" by Marylyn Plessner © 2000. Published by Stephen Jarislowsky. Used with permission of the publisher.

The Library of Congress Cataloging-in-Publication Data is available upon request.

ISBN 978-1-250-14095-1 (trade paperback)

Our books may be purchased in bulk for promotional, educational, or business use. Please contact your local bookseller or the Macmillan Corporate and Premium Sales Department at 1-800-221-7945, extension 5442, or by email at Macmillan SpecialMarkets@macmillan.com.

The Brutal Telling first published in Great Britain by Headline Publishing Group

First Edition: June 2017

10 9 8 7 6 5 4 3 2 1

THE BRUTAL TELLING

For the SPCA Monteregie, and all the people
who would "ring the bells of Heaven."

And, for Maggie,
who finally gave all her heart away.

ACKNOWLEDGMENTS

—

Once again, this book is the result of a whole lot of help from a whole lot of people. I want and need to thank Michael, my husband, for reading and rereading the manuscript, and always telling me it was brilliant. Thank you to Lise Page, my assistant, for her tireless and cheery work and great ideas. To Sherise Hobbs and Hope Dellon for their patience and editorial notes.

I want to thank, as always, the very best literary agent in the world, Teresa Chris. She sent me a silver heart when my last book made the *New York Times* bestseller list (I also thought I'd just mention that!). Teresa is way more than an agent. She's also a lovely, thoughtful person.

I'd also like to thank my good friends Susan McKenzie and Lili de Grandpré, for their help and support.

And finally I want to say a word about the poetry I use in this book, and the others. As much as I'd love not to say anything and hope you believe I wrote it, I actually need to thank the wonderful poets who've allowed me to use their works and words. I adore poetry, as you can tell. Indeed, it inspires me—with words and emotions. I tell aspiring writers to read poetry, which I think for them is often the literary equivalent of being told to eat Brussels sprouts. They're none too enthusiastic. But what a shame if a writer doesn't at least try to find poems that speak to him or her. Poets manage to get into a couplet what I struggle to achieve in an entire book.

I thought it was time I acknowledged that.

In this book I use, as always, works from Margaret Atwood's slim volume *Morning in the Burned House*. Not a very cheerful title, but brilliant poems. I've also quoted from a lovely old work called *The Bells of*

Heaven by Ralph Hodgson. And a wonderful poem called "Gravity Zero" from an emerging Canadian poet named Mike Freeman, from his book *Bones*.

I wanted you to know that. And I hope these poems speak to you, as they speak to me.

ONE

"All of them? Even the children?" The fireplace sputtered and crackled and swallowed his gasp. "Slaughtered?"

"Worse."

There was silence then. And in that hush lived all the things that could be worse than slaughter.

"Are they close?" His back tingled as he imagined something dreadful creeping through the woods. Toward them. He looked around, almost expecting to see red eyes staring through the dark windows. Or from the corners, or under the bed.

"All around. Have you seen the light in the night sky?"

"I thought those were the Northern Lights." The pink and green and white shifting, flowing against the stars. Like something alive, glowing, and growing. And approaching.

Olivier Brulé lowered his gaze, no longer able to look into the troubled, lunatic eyes across from him. He'd lived with this story for so long, and kept telling himself it wasn't real. It was a myth, a story told and repeated and embellished over and over and over. Around fires just like theirs.

It was a story, nothing more. No harm in it.

But in this simple log cabin, buried in the Quebec wilderness, it seemed like more than that. Even Olivier felt himself believing it. Perhaps because the Hermit so clearly did.

The old man sat in his easy chair on one side of the stone hearth with Olivier on the other. Olivier looked into a fire that had been alive for more than a decade. An old flame not allowed to die, it mumbled and popped in the grate, throwing soft light into the log cabin. He gave the embers a shove with the simple iron poker, sending sparks up the chimney. Candlelight twinkled off shiny objects like eyes in the darkness, found by the flame.

"It won't be long now."

The Hermit's eyes were gleaming like metal reaching its melting point. He was leaning forward as he often did when this tale was told.

Olivier scanned the single room. The dark was punctuated by flickering candles throwing fantastic, grotesque shadows. Night seemed to have seeped through the cracks in the logs and settled into the cabin, curled in corners and under the bed. Many native tribes believed evil lived in corners, which was why their traditional homes were rounded. Unlike the square homes the government had given them.

Olivier didn't believe evil lived in corners. Not really. Not in the daylight, anyway. But he did believe there were things waiting in the dark corners of this cabin that only the Hermit knew about. Things that set Olivier's heart pounding.

"Go on," he said, trying to keep his voice steady.

It was late and Olivier still had the twenty-minute walk through the forest back to Three Pines. It was a trip he made every fortnight and he knew it well, even in the dark.

Only in the dark. Theirs was a relationship that existed only after nightfall.

They sipped Orange Pekoe tea. A treat, Olivier knew, reserved for the Hermit's honored guest. His only guest.

But now it was story time. They leaned closer to the fire. It was early September and a chill had crept in with the night.

"Where was I? Oh, yes. I remember now."

Olivier's hands gripped the warm mug even tighter.

"The terrible force has destroyed everything in its way. The Old World and the New. All gone. Except . . ."

"Except?"

"One tiny village remains. Hidden in a valley, so the grim army hasn't seen it yet. But it will. And when it does their great leader will stand at the head of his army. He's immense, bigger than any tree, and clad in armor made from rocks and spiny shells and bone."

"Chaos."

The word was whispered and disappeared into the darkness, where it curled into a corner. And waited.

"Chaos. And the Furies. Disease, Famine, Despair. All are swarming. Searching. And they'll never stop. Not ever. Not until they find it."

"The thing that was stolen."

The Hermit nodded, his face grim. He seemed to see the slaughter, the destruction. See the men and women, the children, fleeing before the merciless, soulless force.

"But what was it? What could be so important they had to destroy everything to get it back?"

Olivier willed his eyes not to dart from the craggy face and into the darkness. To the corner, and the thing they both knew was sitting there in its mean little canvas sack. But the Hermit seemed to read his mind and Olivier saw a malevolent grin settle onto the old man's face. And then it was gone.

"It's not the army that wants it back."

They both saw then the thing looming behind the terrible army. The thing even Chaos feared. That drove Despair, Disease, Famine before it. With one goal. To find what was taken from their Master.

"It's worse than slaughter."

Their voices were low, barely scraping the ground. Like conspirators in a cause already lost.

"When the army finally finds what it's searching for it will stop. And step aside. And then the worst thing imaginable will arrive."

There was silence again. And in that silence lived the worst thing imaginable.

Outside a pack of coyotes set up a howl. They had something cornered.

Myth, that's all this is, Olivier reassured himself. Just a story. Once more he looked into the embers, so he wouldn't see the terror in the Hermit's face. Then he checked his watch, tilting the crystal toward the fireplace until its face glowed orange and told him the time. Two thirty in the morning.

"Chaos is coming, old son, and there's no stopping it. It's taken a long time, but it's finally here."

The Hermit nodded, his eyes rheumy and runny, perhaps from the wood smoke, perhaps from something else. Olivier leaned back, surprised to feel his thirty-eight-year-old body suddenly aching, and realized he'd sat tense through the whole awful telling.

"I'm sorry. It's getting late and Gabri will be worried. I have to go."

"Already?"

Olivier got up and pumping cold, fresh water into the enamel sink he cleaned his cup. Then he turned back to the room.

"I'll be back soon," he smiled.

"Let me give you something," said the Hermit, looking around the log cabin. Olivier's gaze darted to the corner where the small canvas sack sat. Unopened. A bit of twine keeping it closed.

A chuckle came from the Hermit. "One day, perhaps, Olivier. But not today."

He went over to the hand-hewn mantelpiece, picked up a tiny item and held it out to the attractive blond man.

"For the groceries." He pointed to the tins and cheese and milk, tea and coffee and bread on the counter.

"No, I couldn't. It's my pleasure," said Olivier, but they both knew the pantomime and knew he'd take the small offering. "*Merci*," Olivier said at the door.

In the woods there was a furious scrambling, as a doomed creature raced to escape its fate, and coyotes raced to seal it.

"Be careful," said the old man, quickly scanning the night sky. Then, before closing the door, he whispered the single word that was quickly devoured by the woods. Olivier wondered if the Hermit crossed himself and mumbled prayers, leaning against the door, which was thick but perhaps not quite thick enough.

And he wondered if the old man believed the stories of the great and grim army with Chaos looming and leading the Furies. Inexorable, unstoppable. Close.

And behind them something else. Something unspeakable.

And he wondered if the Hermit believed the prayers.

Olivier flicked on his flashlight, scanning the darkness. Gray tree trunks crowded round. He shone the light here and there, trying to find the narrow path through the late summer forest. Once on the trail he hurried. And the more he hurried the more frightened he became, and the more fearful he grew the faster he ran until he was stumbling, chased by dark words through the dark woods.

He finally broke through the trees and staggered to a stop, hands on his bent knees, heaving for breath. Then, slowly straightening, he looked down on the village in the valley.

Three Pines was asleep, as it always seemed to be. At peace with itself and the world. Oblivious of what happened around it. Or perhaps aware of everything, but choosing peace anyway. Soft light glowed at some of the windows. Curtains were drawn in bashful old homes. The sweet scent of the first autumn fires wafted to him.

And in the very center of the little Quebec village there stood three great pines, like watchmen.

Olivier was safe. Then he felt his pocket.

The gift. The tiny payment. He'd left it behind.

Cursing, Olivier turned to look into the forest that had closed behind him. And he thought again of the small canvas bag in the corner of the cabin. The thing the Hermit had teased him with, promised him, dangled before him. The thing a hiding man hid.

Olivier was tired, and fed up and angry at himself for forgetting the trinket. And angry at the Hermit for not giving him the other thing. The thing he'd earned by now.

He hesitated, then turning he plunged back into the forest, feeling his fear growing and feeding the rage. And as he walked, then ran, a voice followed, beating behind him. Driving him on.

"Chaos is here, old son."

TWO

⸺

"You get it."

Gabri pulled up the covers and lay still. But the phone continued to ring and beside him Olivier was dead to the world. Out the window Gabri could see drizzle against the pane and he could feel the damp Sunday morning settling into their bedroom. But beneath the duvet it was snug and warm, and he had no intention of moving.

He poked Olivier. "Wake up."

Nothing, just a snort.

"Fire!"

Still nothing.

"Ethel Merman!"

Nothing. Dear Lord, was he dead?

He leaned in to his partner, seeing the precious thinning hair lying across the pillow and across the face. The eyes closed, peaceful. Gabri smelled Olivier, musky, slightly sweaty. Soon they'd have a shower and they'd both smell like Ivory soap.

The phone rang again.

"It's your mother," Gabri whispered in Olivier's ear.

"What?"

"Get the phone. It's your mother."

Olivier sat up, fighting to get his eyes open and looking bleary, as though emerging from a long tunnel. "My mother? But she's been dead for years."

"If anyone could come back from the dead to screw you up, it'd be her."

"You're the one screwing me up."

"You wish. Now get the phone."

Olivier reached across the mountain that was his partner and took the call.

"*Oui, allô?*"

Gabri snuggled back into the warm bed, then registered the time on the glowing clock. Six forty-three. On Sunday morning. Of the Labor Day long weekend.

Who in the world would be calling at this hour?

He sat up and looked at his partner's face, studying it as a passenger might study the face of a flight attendant during takeoff. Were they worried? Frightened?

He saw Olivier's expression change from mildly concerned to puzzled, and then, in an instant, Olivier's blond brows dropped and the blood rushed from his face.

Dear God, thought Gabri. We're going down.

"What is it?" he mouthed.

Olivier was silent, listening. But his handsome face was eloquent. Something was terribly wrong.

"What's happened?" Gabri hissed.

They rushed across the village green, their raincoats flapping in the wind. Myrna Landers, fighting with her huge umbrella, came across to meet them and together they hurried to the bistro. It was dawn and the world was gray and wet. In the few paces it took to get to the bistro their hair was plastered to their heads and their clothes were sodden. But for once neither Olivier nor Gabri cared. They skidded to a stop beside Myrna outside the brick building.

"I called the police. They should be here soon," she said.

"Are you sure about this?" Olivier stared at his friend and neighbor. She was big and round and wet and wearing bright yellow rubber boots under a lime green raincoat and gripping her red umbrella. She looked as though a beachball had exploded. But she also had never looked more serious. Of course she was sure.

"I went inside and checked," she said.

"Oh, God," whispered Gabri. "Who is it?"

7

"I don't know."

"How can you not know?" Olivier asked. Then he looked through the mullioned glass of his bistro window, bringing his slim hands up beside his face to block out the weak morning light. Myrna held her brilliant red umbrella over him.

Olivier's breath fogged the window but not before he'd seen what Myrna had also seen. There was someone inside the bistro. Lying on the old pine floor. Face up.

"What is it?" asked Gabri, straining and craning to see around his partner.

But Olivier's face told him all he needed to know. Gabri focused on the large black woman next to him.

"Is he dead?"

"Worse."

What could be worse than death? he wondered.

Myrna was as close as their village came to a doctor. She'd been a psychologist in Montreal before too many sad stories and too much good sense got the better of her, and she'd quit. She'd loaded up her car intending to take a few months to drive around before settling down, somewhere. Any place that took her fancy.

She got an hour outside Montreal, stumbled on Three Pines, stopped for *café au lait* and a croissant at Olivier's Bistro, and never left. She unpacked her car, rented the shop next door and the apartment above and opened a used bookstore.

People wandered in for books and conversation. They brought their stories to her, some bound, and some known by heart. She recognized some of the stories as real, and some as fiction. But she honored them all, though she didn't buy every one.

"We should go in," said Olivier. "To make sure no one disturbs the body. Are you all right?"

Gabri had closed his eyes, but now he opened them again and seemed more composed. "I'm fine. Just a shock. He didn't look familiar."

And Myrna saw on his face the same relief she'd felt when she'd first rushed in. The sad fact was, a dead stranger was way better than a dead friend.

They filed into the bistro, sticking close as though the dead man might reach out and take one of them with him. Inching toward him they stared down, rain dripping off their heads and noses onto his worn clothes and puddling on the wide-plank floor. Then Myrna gently pulled them back from the edge.

And that's how both men felt. They'd woken on this holiday weekend in their comfortable bed, in their comfortable home, in their comfortable life, to find themselves suddenly dangled over a cliff.

All three turned away, speechless. Staring wide-eyed at each other.

There was a dead man in the bistro.

And not just dead, but worse.

As they waited for the police Gabri made a pot of coffee, and Myrna took off her raincoat and sat by the window, looking into the misty September day. Olivier laid and lit fires in the two stone hearths at either end of the beamed room. He poked one fire vigorously and felt its warmth against his damp clothing. He felt numb, and not just from the creeping cold.

When they'd stood over the dead man Gabri had murmured, "Poor one."

Myrna and Olivier had nodded. What they saw was an elderly man in shabby clothing, staring up at them. His face was white, his eyes surprised, his mouth slightly open.

Myrna had pointed to the back of his head. The puddled water was turning pink. Gabri leaned tentatively closer, but Olivier didn't move. What held him spellbound and stunned wasn't the shattered back of the dead man's head, but the front. His face.

"*Mon Dieu*, Olivier, the man's been murdered. Oh, my God."

Olivier continued to stare, into the eyes.

"But who is he?" Gabri whispered.

It was the Hermit. Dead. Murdered. In the bistro.

"I don't know," said Olivier.

Chief Inspector Armand Gamache got the call just as he and Reine-Marie finished clearing up after Sunday brunch. In the dining room of their apartment in Montreal's Outremont *quartier* he could hear his second in command, Jean Guy Beauvoir, and his daughter Annie. They weren't talking. They never talked. They argued. Especially when Jean Guy's wife, Enid, wasn't there as a buffer. But Enid had to plan school courses and had begged off brunch. Jean Guy, on the other hand, never turned down an invitation for a free meal. Even if it came at a price. And the price was always Annie.

It had started over the fresh-squeezed orange juice, coursed through the scrambled eggs and Brie, and progressed across the fresh fruit, croissants and *confitures*.

"But how can you defend the use of stun guns?" came Annie's voice from the dining room.

"Another great brunch, *merci*, Reine-Marie," said David, placing dishes from the dining room in front of the sink and kissing his mother-in-law on the cheek. He was of medium build with short, thinning dark hair. At thirty he was a few years older than his wife, Annie, though he often appeared younger. His main feature, Gamache often felt, was his animation. Not hyper, but full of life. The Chief Inspector had liked him from the moment, five years earlier, his daughter had introduced them. Unlike other young men Annie had brought home, mostly lawyers like herself, this one hadn't tried to out-macho the Chief. That wasn't a game that interested Gamache. Nor did it impress him. What did impress him was David's reaction when he'd met Armand and Reine-Marie Gamache. He'd smiled broadly, a smile that seemed to fill the room, and simply said, "*Bonjour.*"

He was unlike any other man Annie had ever been interested in. David wasn't a scholar, wasn't an athlete, wasn't staggeringly handsome. Wasn't destined to become the next Premier of Quebec, or even the boss of his legal firm.

No, David was simply open and kind.

She'd married him, and Armand Gamache had been delighted to walk with her down the aisle, with Reine-Marie on the other side of their only daughter. And to see this nice man wed his daughter.

For Armand Gamache knew what not-nice was. He knew what cruelty, despair, horror were. And he knew what a forgotten, and precious, quality "nice" was.

"Would you rather we just shoot suspects?" In the dining room Beauvoir's voice had risen in volume and tone.

"Thank you, David," said Reine-Marie, taking the dishes. Gamache handed his son-in-law a fresh dish towel and they dried as Reine-Marie washed up.

"So," David turned to the Chief Inspector, "do you think the Habs have a chance at the cup this year?"

"No," yelled Annie. "I expect you to learn how to apprehend someone without having to maim or kill them. I expect you to genuinely see suspects as just that. Suspects. Not sub-human criminals you can beat up, electrocute or shoot."

"I think they do," said Gamache, handing David a plate to dry and taking one himself. "I like their new goalie and I think their forward line has matured. This is definitely their year."

"But their weakness is still defense, don't you think?" Reine-Marie asked. "The Canadiens always concentrate too much on offense."

"You try arresting an armed murderer. I'd love to see you try. You, you . . ." Beauvoir was sputtering. The conversation in the kitchen stopped as they listened to what he might say next. This was an argument played out every brunch, every Christmas, Thanksgiving, birthday. The words changed slightly. If not tasers they were arguing about daycare or education or the environment. If Annie said blue, Beauvoir said orange. It had been this way since Inspector Beauvoir had joined the Sûreté du Québec's homicide division, under Gamache, a dozen years earlier. He'd become a member of the team, and of the family.

"You what?" demanded Annie.

"You pathetic piece of legal crap."

Reine-Marie gestured toward the back door of the kitchen that gave onto a small metal balcony and fire escape. "Shall we?"

"Escape?" Gamache whispered, hoping she was serious, but suspecting she wasn't.

"Maybe you could just try shooting them, Armand?" David asked.

"I'm afraid Jean Guy is a faster draw," said the Chief Inspector. "He'd get me first."

"Still," said his wife, "it's worth a try."

"Legal crap?" said Annie, her voice dripping disdain. "Brilliant. Fascist moron."

"I suppose I could use a taser," said Gamache.

"Fascist? Fascist?" Jean Guy Beauvoir almost squealed. In the kitchen Gamache's German shepherd, Henri, sat up in his bed and cocked his head. He had huge oversized ears which made Gamache think he wasn't purebred but a cross between a shepherd and a satellite dish.

"Uh-oh," said David. Henri curled into a ball in his bed and it was clear David would join him if he could.

All three looked wistfully out the door at the rainy, cool early September day. Labor Day weekend in Montreal. Annie said something unintelligible. But Beauvoir's response was perfectly clear.

"Screw you."

"Well, I think this debate's just about over," said Reine-Marie. "More coffee?" She pointed to their espresso maker.

"*Non, pas pour moi, merci*," said David, with a smile. "And please, no more for Annie."

"Stupid woman," muttered Jean Guy as he entered the kitchen. He grabbed a dish towel from the rack and began furiously drying a plate. Gamache figured that was the last they'd see of the India Tree design. "Tell me she's adopted."

"No, homemade." Reine-Marie handed the next plate to her husband.

"Screw you." Annie's dark head shot into the kitchen then disappeared.

"Bless her heart," said Reine-Marie.

Of their two children, Daniel was the more like his father. Large, thoughtful, academic. He was kind and gentle and strong. When Annie had been born Reine-Marie thought, perhaps naturally, this would be the child most like her. Warm, intelligent, bright. With a love of books so strong Reine-Marie Gamache had become a librarian, finally taking over a department at the *Bibliothèque nationale* in Montreal.

But Annie had surprised them both. She was smart, competitive, funny. She was fierce, in everything she did and felt.

They should have had an inkling about this. As a newborn Armand would take her for endless rides in the car, trying to soothe her as she howled. He'd sing, in his deep baritone, Beatles songs, and Jacques Brel songs. "*La Complainte du phoque en Alaska*" by Beau Dommage. That was Daniel's favorite. It was a soulful lament. But it did nothing for Annie.

One day, as he'd strapped the shrieking child into the car seat and turned on the ignition, an old Weavers tape had been in.

As they sang, in falsetto, she'd settled.

At first it had seemed a miracle. But after the hundredth trip around the block listening to the laughing child and the Weavers singing "*Wimoweh, a-wimoweh*," Gamache yearned for the old days and felt like shrieking himself. But as they sang the little lion slept.

Annie Gamache became their cub. And grew into a lioness. But sometimes, on quiet walks together, she'd tell her father about her fears and her disappointments and the everyday sorrows of her young life. And Chief Inspector Gamache would be seized with a desire to hold her to him, so that she needn't pretend to be so brave all the time.

She was fierce because she was afraid. Of everything.

The rest of the world saw a strong, noble lioness. He looked at his daughter and saw Bert Lahr, though he'd never tell her that. Or her husband.

"Can we talk?" Annie asked her father, ignoring Beauvoir. Gamache nodded and handed the dish towel to David. They walked down the hall and into the warm living room where books were ranged on shelves in orderly rows, and stacked under tables and beside the sofa in not-so-orderly piles. *Le Devoir* and the *New York Times* were on the coffee table and a gentle fire burned in the grate. Not the roaring flames of a bitter winter fire, but a soft almost liquid flame of early autumn.

They talked for a few minutes about Daniel, living in Paris with his wife and daughter, and another daughter due before the end of the month. They talked about her husband David and his hockey team, about to start up for another winter season.

Mostly Gamache listened. He wasn't sure if Annie had something specific to say, or just wanted to talk. Henri jogged into the room and plunked his head on Annie's lap. She kneaded his ears, to his grunts and moans. Eventually he lay down by the fire.

Just then the phone rang. Gamache ignored it.

"It's the one in your office, I think," said Annie. She could see it on the old wooden desk with the computer and the notebook, in the room that was filled with books, and smelled of sandalwood and rosewater and had three chairs.

She and Daniel would sit in their wooden swivel chairs and spin each other around until they were almost sick, while their father sat in his armchair, steady. And read. Or sometimes just stared.

"I think so too."

The phone rang again. It was a sound they knew well. Somehow different from other phones. It was the ringing that announced a death.

Annie looked uncomfortable.

"It'll wait," he said quietly. "Was there something you wanted to tell me?"

"Should I get that?" Jean Guy looked in. He smiled at Annie but his eyes went swiftly to the Chief Inspector.

"Please. I'll be there in a moment."

He turned back to his daughter, but by then David had joined them and Annie had once again put on her public face. It wasn't so different from her private one. Just, perhaps, a bit less vulnerable. And her father wondered briefly, as David sat down and took her hand, why she needed her public face in front of her husband.

"There's been a murder, sir," whispered Inspector Beauvoir. He stood just inside the room.

"*Oui*," said Gamache, watching his daughter.

"Go on, Papa." She waved her hand at him, not to dismiss him, but to free him of the need to stay with her.

"I will, eventually. Would you like to go for a walk?"

"It's pelting down outside," said David with a laugh. Gamache genuinely loved his son-in-law, but sometimes he could be oblivious. Annie also laughed.

"Really, Papa, not even Henri would go out in this."

Henri leaped up and ran to get his ball. The fatal words, "Henri" and "out," had been combined unleashing an undeniable force.

"Well," said Gamache as the German shepherd bounded back into the room. "I have to go to work."

He gave Annie and David a significant look, then glanced over at Henri. His meaning even David couldn't miss.

"Christ," whispered David good-humoredly, and getting off the comfortable sofa he and Annie went to find Henri's leash.

By the time Chief Inspector Gamache and Inspector Beauvoir arrived in Three Pines the local force had cordoned off the bistro, and villagers milled about under umbrellas and stared at the old brick building. The scene of so many meals and drinks and celebrations. Now a crime scene.

As Beauvoir drove down the slight slope into the village Gamache asked him to pull over.

"What is it?" the Inspector asked.

"I just want to look."

The two men sat in the warm car, watching the village through the lazy arc of the wipers. In front of them was the village green with its pond and bench, its beds of roses and hydrangea, late flowering phlox and hollyhocks. And at the end of the common, anchoring it and the village, stood the three tall pines.

Gamache's gaze wandered to the buildings that hugged the village green. There were weathered white clapboard cottages, with wide porches and wicker chairs. There were tiny fieldstone houses built centuries ago by the first settlers, who'd cleared the land and yanked the stones from the earth. But most of the homes around the village green were made of rose-hued brick, built by United Empire Loyalists fleeing the American Revolution. Three Pines sat just kilometers from the Vermont border and while relations now with the States were friendly and affectionate, they weren't back then. The people who created the village had been desperate for sanctuary, hiding from a war they didn't believe in.

The Chief Inspector's eyes drifted up du Moulin, and there, on the side of the hill leading out of the village, was the small white chapel. St. Thomas's Anglican.

Gamache brought his eyes back to the small crowd standing under umbrellas chatting, pointing, staring. Olivier's bistro was smack-dab in the center of the semicircle of shops. Each shop ran into the next. Monsieur Béliveau's general store, then Sarah's Boulangerie, then Olivier's Bistro and finally Myrna's new and used bookstore.

"Let's go," Gamache nodded.

Beauvoir had been waiting for the word and now the car moved slowly forward. Toward the huddled suspects, toward the killer.

But one of the first lessons the Chief had taught Beauvoir when he'd joined the famed homicide department of the Sûreté du Québec was that to catch a killer they didn't move forward. They moved back. Into the past. That was where the crime began, where the killer began. Some event, perhaps long forgotten by everyone else, had lodged inside the murderer. And he'd begun to fester.

What kills can't be seen, the Chief had warned Beauvoir. That's what makes it so dangerous. It's not a gun or a knife or a fist. It's not anything you can see coming. It's an emotion. Rancid, spoiled. And waiting for a chance to strike.

The car slowly moved toward the bistro, toward the body.

"*Merci,*" said Gamache a minute later as a local Sûreté officer opened the bistro door for them. The young man was just about to challenge the stranger, but hesitated.

Beauvoir loved this. The reaction of local cops as it dawned on them that this large man in his early fifties wasn't just a curious citizen. To the young cops Gamache looked like their fathers. There was an air of courtliness about him. He always wore a suit, or the jacket and tie and gray flannels he had on that day.

They'd notice the mustache, trimmed and graying. His dark hair was also graying around the ears, where it curled up slightly. On a rainy day like this the Chief wore a cap, which he took off indoors, and when he did the young officers saw the balding head. And if that wasn't enough they'd notice this man's eyes. Everyone did. They were deep brown, thoughtful, intelligent and something else. Something that distinguished the famous head of homicide for the Sûreté du Québec from every other senior officer.

His eyes were kind.

It was both his strength, Beauvoir knew, and his weakness.

Gamache smiled at the astonished officer who found himself face to face with the most celebrated cop in Quebec. Gamache offered his hand and the young agent stared at it for a moment before putting out his own. "*Patron*," he said.

"Oh, I was hoping it would be you." Gabri hurried across the room, past the Sûreté officers bending over the victim. "We asked if the Sûreté could send you but apparently it's not normal for suspects to order up a specific officer." He hugged the Chief Inspector then turned to the roomful of agents. "See, I do know him." Then he whispered to Gamache, "I think it would be best if we didn't kiss."

"Very wise."

Gabri looked tired and stressed, but composed. He was disheveled, though that wasn't unusual. Behind him, quieter, almost eclipsed, stood Olivier. He was also disheveled. That was very unusual. He also looked exhausted, with dark rings under his eyes.

"Coroner's just arriving now, Chief." Agent Isabelle Lacoste walked across the room to greet him. She wore a simple skirt and light sweater and managed to make both look stylish. Like most Québécoises, she was petite and confident. "It's Dr. Harris, I see."

They all looked out the window and the crowd parted to let a woman with a medical bag through. Unlike Agent Lacoste, Dr. Harris managed to make her simple skirt and sweater look slightly frumpy. But comfortable. And on a miserable day like this "comfortable" was very attractive.

"Good," said the Chief, turning back to Agent Lacoste. "What do we know?"

Lacoste led Gamache and Inspector Beauvoir to the body. They knelt, an act and ritual they'd performed hundreds of times. It was surprisingly intimate. They didn't touch him, but leaned very close, closer than they'd ever get to anyone in life, except a loved one.

"The victim was struck from behind by a blunt object. Something clean and hard, and narrow."

"A fireplace poker?" Beauvoir asked, looking over at the fires Olivier had set. Gamache also looked. It was a damp morning, but not all that cool. A fire wasn't necessary. Still, it was probably made to comfort more than to heat.

"If it was a poker it would be clean. The coroner will take a closer look, of course, but there's no obvious sign of dirt, ash, wood, anything, in the wound."

Gamache was staring at the gaping hole in the man's head. Listening to his agent.

"No weapon, then?" asked Beauvoir.

"Not yet. We're searching, of course."

"Who was he?"

"We don't know."

Gamache took his eyes off the wound and looked at the woman, but said nothing.

"We have no ID," Agent Lacoste continued. "We've been through his pockets and nothing. Not even a Kleenex. And no one seems to know him. He's a white male, mid-seventies I'd say. Lean but not malnourished. Five seven, maybe five eight."

Years ago, when she'd first joined homicide, it had seemed bizarre to Agent Lacoste to catalog these things the Chief could see perfectly well for himself. But he'd taught them all to do it, and so she did. It was only years later, when she was training someone else, that she recognized the value of the exercise.

It made sure they both saw the same things. Police were as fallible and subjective as anyone else. They missed things, and misinterpreted things. This catalog made it less likely. Either that or they'd reinforce the same mistakes.

"Nothing in his hands and it looks like nothing under his fingernails. No bruising. Doesn't appear to have been a struggle."

They stood up.

"The condition of the room verifies that."

They looked around.

Nothing out of place. Nothing tipped over. Everything clean and orderly.

It was a restful room. The fires at either end of the beamed bistro took the gloom out of the day. Their light gleamed off the polished wood floors, darkened by years of smoke and farmers' feet.

Sofas and large inviting armchairs sat in front of each fireplace, their fabric faded. Old chairs were grouped around dark wooden dining tables. In front of the mullioned bay windows three or four wing chairs waited for villagers nursing steaming *café au lait* and croissants, or Scotches, or burgundy wine. Gamache suspected the people milling outside in the rain could do with a good stiff drink. He thought Olivier and Gabri certainly could.

Chief Inspector Gamache and his team had been in the bistro many times, enjoying meals in front of the roaring fire in winter or a quiet cool drink on the *terrasse* in summer. Almost always discussing murder. But never with an actual body right there.

Sharon Harris joined them, taking off her wet raincoat then smiling at Agent Lacoste and shaking hands solemnly with the Chief Inspector.

"Dr. Harris," he said, bowing slightly. "I'm sorry about disturbing your long weekend."

She'd been sitting at home, flipping through the television channels, trying to find someone who wasn't preaching at her, when the phone had rung. It had seemed a godsend. But looking now at the body, she knew that this had very little to do with God.

"I'll leave you to it," said Gamache. Through the windows he saw the villagers, still there, waiting for news. A tall, handsome man with gray hair bent down to listen as a short woman with wild hair spoke. Peter and Clara Morrow. Villagers and artists. Standing like a ramrod beside them and staring unblinking at the bistro was Ruth Zardo. And her duck, looking quite imperious. Ruth wore a sou'wester that glistened in the rain. Clara spoke to her, but was ignored. Ruth Zardo, Gamache knew, was a drunken, embittered old piece of work. Who also happened to be his favorite poet in the world. Clara spoke again and this time Ruth did respond. Even through the glass Gamache knew what she'd said.

"Fuck off."

Gamache smiled. While a body in the bistro was certainly different, some things never changed.

"Chief Inspector."

The familiar, deep, singsong voice greeted him. He turned and saw Myrna Landers walking across the room, her electric yellow boots clumping on the floor. She wore a pink tracksuit tucked into her boots.

She was a woman of color, in every sense.

"Myrna," he smiled and kissed her on both cheeks. This drew a surprised look from some of the local Sûreté officers, who didn't expect the Chief Inspector to kiss suspects. "What're you doing in here when everyone else is out there?" He waved toward the window.

"I found him," she said, and his face grew grave.

"Did you? I'm sorry. That must've been a shock." He guided her to a chair by the fire. "I imagine you've given someone your statement?"

She nodded. "Agent Lacoste took it. Not much to tell, I'm afraid."

"Would you like a coffee, or a nice cup of tea?"

Myrna smiled. It was something she'd offered him often enough. Something she offered everyone, from the kettle that bubbled away on her woodstove. And now it was being offered to her. And she saw how comforting it actually was.

"Tea, please."

While she sat warming herself by the fire Chief Inspector Gamache went to ask Gabri for a pot of tea, then returned. He sat in the armchair and leaned forward.

"What happened?"

"I go out every morning for a long walk."

"Is this something new? I've never known you to do that before."

"Well, yes. Since the spring anyway. I decided since I turned fifty I needed to get into shape." She smiled fully then. "Or at least, into a different shape. I'm aiming for pear rather than apple." She patted her stomach. "Though I suspect my nature is to be the whole orchard."

"What could be better than an orchard?" he smiled, then looked at his own girth. "I'm not exactly a sapling myself. What time do you get up?"

"Set my alarm for six thirty and I'm out the door by quarter to seven. This morning I'd just left when I noticed Olivier's door was open a little, so I looked in and called. I know Olivier doesn't normally open until later on a Sunday so I was surprised."

"But not alarmed."

"No." She seemed surprised by the question. "I was about to leave when I spotted him."

Myrna's back was to the room, and Gamache didn't glance over to the body. Instead he held her gaze and encouraged her with a nod, saying nothing.

Their tea arrived and while it was clear Gabri wanted to join them he, unlike Gamache's son-in-law David, was intuitive enough to pick up the unspoken signals. He put the teapot, two bone china cups and saucers, milk, sugar and a plate of ginger cookies on the table. Then left.

"At first I thought it was a pile of linen left by the waiters the night before," Myrna said when Gabri was out of earshot. "Most of them're quite young and you never know. But then I looked closer and saw it was a body."

"A body?"

It was the way someone describes a dead man, not a living one.

"I knew he was dead right away. I've seen some, you know."

Gamache did know.

"He was exactly as you see him now." Myrna watched as Gamache poured their tea. She indicated milk and sugar then accepted her cup, with a biscuit. "I got up close but didn't touch him. I didn't think he'd been killed. Not at first."

"What did you think?" Gamache held the cup in his large hands. The tea was strong and fragrant.

"I thought he'd had a stroke or maybe a heart attack. Something sudden, by the look on his face. He seemed surprised, but not afraid or in pain."

That was, thought Gamache, a good way of putting it. Death had surprised this man. But it did most people, even the old and infirm. Almost no one really expected to die.

"Then I saw his head."

Gamache nodded. It was hard to miss. Not the head, but what was missing from it.

"Do you know him?"

"Never seen him before. And I suspect he'd be memorable."

Gamache had to agree. He looked like a vagrant. And while easily ignored they were hard to forget. Armand Gamache put his delicate cup on its delicate saucer. His mind kept going to the question that had struck him as soon as he'd taken the call and heard about the murder. In the bistro in Three Pines.

Why here?

He looked quickly over to Olivier who was talking to Inspector Beauvoir and Agent Lacoste. He was calm and contained. But he couldn't be oblivious of how this appeared.

"What did you do then?"

"I called 911 then Olivier, then went outside and waited for them."

She described what happened, up to the moment the police arrived.

"*Merci*," said Gamache and rose. Myrna took her tea and joined Olivier and Gabri across the room. They stood together in front of the hearth.

Everyone in the room knew who the three main suspects were. Everyone, that was, except the three main suspects.

THREE

Dr. Sharon Harris stood, brushed her skirt clean and smiled thinly at the Chief Inspector.

"Not much finesse," she said.

Gamache stared down at the dead man.

"He looks like a tramp," said Beauvoir, bending down and examining the man's clothing. It was mismatched and worn.

"He must be living rough," said Lacoste.

Gamache knelt down and looked closely at the old man's face again. It was weathered and withered. An almanac face, of sun and wind and cold. A seasoned face. Gamache gently rubbed his thumb across the dead man's cheek, feeling stubble. He was clean shaven, but what might have grown in would've been white. The dead man's hair was white and cut without enthusiasm. A snip here, a snip there.

Gamache picked up one of the victim's hands, as though comforting him. He held it for an instant, then turned it over, palm up. Then he slowly rubbed his own palm over the dead man's.

"Whoever he was he did hard work. These are calluses. Most tramps don't work."

Gamache shook his head slowly. So who are you? And why are you here? In the bistro, and in this village. A village few people on earth even knew existed. And even fewer found.

But you did, thought Gamache, still holding the man's cold hand. You found the village and you found death.

"He's been dead between six and ten hours," the doctor said. "Sometime after midnight but before four or five this morning."

Gamache stared at the back of the man's head and the wound that killed him.

It was catastrophic. It looked like a single blow by something extremely hard. And by someone extremely angry. Only anger accounted for this sort of power. The power to pulverize a skull. And what it protected.

Everything that made this man who he was was kept in this head. Someone bashed that in. With one brutal, decisive blow.

"Not much blood." Gamache got up and watched the Scene of Crime team fanning out and collecting evidence around the large room. A room now violated. First by murder and now by them. The unwanted guests.

Olivier was standing, warming himself by the fire.

"That's a problem," said Dr. Harris. "Head wounds bleed a lot. There should be more blood, lots more."

"It might've been cleaned up," said Beauvoir.

Sharon Harris bent over the wound again then straightened up. "With the force of the blow the bleeding might have been massive and internal. And death almost instantaneous."

It was the best news Gamache ever heard at a murder scene. Death he could handle. Even murder. It was suffering that disturbed him. He'd seen a lot of it. Terrible murders. It was a great relief to find one swift and decisive. Almost humane.

He'd once heard a judge say the most humane way to execute a prisoner was to tell him he was free. Then kill him.

Gamache had struggled against that, argued against it, railed against it. Then finally, exhausted, had come to believe it.

Looking at this man's face he knew he hadn't suffered. The blow to the back of the head meant he probably hadn't even seen it coming.

Almost like dying in your sleep.

But not quite.

They placed him in a bag and took the body away. Outside men and women stood somberly aside to let it pass. Men swept off their damp caps and women watched, tight-lipped and sad.

Gamache turned away from the window and joined Beauvoir, who was sitting with Olivier, Gabri and Myrna. The Scene of Crime team had moved into the back rooms of the bistro, the private dining room, the staff room, the kitchen. The main room now seemed almost normal. Except for the questions hanging in the air.

"I'm sorry this has happened," Gamache said to Olivier. "How're you doing?"

Olivier exhaled deeply. He looked drained. "I think I'm still stunned. Who was he? Do you know?"

"No," said Beauvoir. "Did anyone report a stranger in the area?"

"Report?" said Olivier. "To whom?"

All three turned perplexed eyes on Beauvoir. The Inspector had forgotten that Three Pines had no police force, no traffic lights, no sidewalks, no mayor. The volunteer fire department was run by that demented old poet Ruth Zardo, and most would rather perish in the flames than call her.

The place didn't even have crime. Except murder. The only criminal thing that ever happened in this village was the worst possible crime.

And here they were with yet another body. At least the rest had had names. This one seemed to have dropped from the sky, and fallen on his head.

"It's a little harder in the summer, you know," said Myrna, taking a seat on the sofa. "We get more visitors. Families come back for vacation, kids come home from school. This is the last big weekend. Everyone goes home after this."

"The weekend of the Brume County Fair," said Gabri. "It ends tomorrow."

"Right," said Beauvoir, who couldn't care less about the fair. "So Three Pines empties out after this weekend. But the visitors you describe are friends and family?"

"For the most part," said Myrna, turning to Gabri. "Some strangers come to your B and B, don't they?"

He nodded. "I'm really an overflow if people run out of space in their homes."

"What I'm getting at," said an exasperated Beauvoir, "is that the people who visit Three Pines aren't really strangers. I just want to get this straight."

"Straight we don't specialize in. Sorry," said Gabri. This brought a smile to even Olivier's tired face.

"I heard something about a stranger," said Myrna, "but I didn't really pay any attention."

"Who said it?"

"Roar Parra," she said, reluctantly. It felt a bit like informing, and no one had much stomach for that. "I heard him talking to Old Mundin and The Wife about seeing someone in the woods."

Beauvoir wrote this down. It wasn't the first time he'd heard about the Parras. They were a prominent Czech family. But Old Mundin and The Wife? That must be a joke. Beauvoir's lips narrowed and he looked at Myrna without amusement. She looked back, also without amusement.

"Yes," Myrna said, reading his mind. It wasn't hard. The teapot could read it. "Those are their names."

"Old and The Wife?" he repeated. No longer angry, but mystified. Myrna nodded. "What're their real names?"

"That's it," said Olivier. "Old and The Wife."

"Okay, I'll give you Old. It's just possible, but no one looks at a new-born and decides to call her The Wife. At least I hope not."

Myrna smiled. "You're right. I'm just so used to it I never thought. I have no idea what her real name is."

Beauvoir wondered just how pathetic a woman had to be to allow herself to be called The Wife. It actually sounded slightly biblical, Old Testament.

Gabri put some beers, Cokes and a couple of bowls of mixed nuts on the table. Outside the villagers had finally gone home. It looked wet and bleak, but inside they were snug and warm. It was almost possible to forget this wasn't a social occasion. The Scene of Crime agents seemed to have dissolved into the woodwork, only evident when a slight scratching or mumbling could be heard. Like rodents, or ghosts. Or homicide detectives.

"Tell us about last night," said Chief Inspector Gamache.

"It was a madhouse," said Gabri. "Last big weekend of the summer so everyone came by. Most had been to the fair during the day so they were tired. Didn't want to cook. It's always like that on Labor Day weekend. We were prepared."

"What does that mean?" asked Agent Lacoste, who'd joined them.

"I brought in extra staff," said Olivier. "But it went smoothly. People were pretty relaxed and we closed on time. At about one in the morning."

"What happened then?" asked Lacoste.

Most murder investigations appeared complex but were really quite simple. It was just a matter of asking "And then what happened?" over and over and over. And listening to the answers helped too.

"I usually do the cash and leave the night staff to clean up, but Saturdays are different," said Olivier. "Old Mundin comes after closing and delivers the things he's repaired during the week and picks up any furniture that's been broken in the meantime. Doesn't take long, and he does it while the waiters and kitchen staff are cleaning up."

"Wait a minute," said Beauvoir. "Mundin does this at midnight on Saturdays? Why not Sunday morning, or any other reasonable time? Why late at night?"

It sounded furtive to Beauvoir, who had a nose for things secretive and sly.

Olivier shrugged. "Habit, I guess. When he first started doing the work he wasn't married to The Wife so he'd hang around here Saturday nights. When we closed he'd just take the broken furniture then. We've seen no reason to change."

In a village where almost nothing changed this made sense.

"So Mundin took the furniture. What happened then?" asked Beauvoir.

"I left."

"Were you the last in the place?"

Olivier hesitated. "Not quite. Because it was so busy there were a few extra things to do. They're a good bunch of kids, you know. Responsible."

Gamache had been listening to this. He preferred it that way. His agents asked the questions and it freed him up to observe, and to hear what was said, how it was said, and what was left out. And now he heard a defensiveness creep into Olivier's calm and helpful voice. Was he defensive about his own behavior, or was he trying to protect his staff, afraid they'd fall under suspicion?

"Who was the last to leave?" Agent Lacoste asked.

"Young Parra," said Olivier.

"Young Parra?" asked Beauvoir. "Like Old Mundin?"

Gabri made a face. "Of course not. His name isn't 'Young.' That'd be weird. His name's Havoc."

Beauvoir's eyes narrowed and he glared at Gabri. He didn't like being mocked and he suspected this large, soft man was doing just that. He then looked over at Myrna, who wasn't laughing. She nodded.

"That's his name. Roar named his son Havoc."

Jean Guy Beauvoir wrote it down, but without pleasure or conviction.

"Would he have locked up?" asked Lacoste.

It was, Gamache and Beauvoir both knew, a crucial question, but its significance seemed lost on Olivier.

"Absolutely."

Gamache and Beauvoir exchanged glances. Now they were getting somewhere. The murderer had to have had a key. A world full of suspects had narrowed dramatically.

"May I see your keys?" asked Beauvoir.

Olivier and Gabri fished theirs out and handed them to the Inspector. But a third set was also offered. He turned and saw Myrna's large hand dangling a set of keys.

"I have them in case I get locked out of my place or if there's an emergency."

"*Merci*," said Beauvoir, with slightly less confidence than he'd been feeling. "Have you lent them to anyone recently?" he asked Olivier and Gabri.

"No."

Beauvoir smiled. This was good.

"Except Old Mundin, of course. He'd lost his and needed to make another copy."

"And Billy Williams," Gabri reminded Olivier. "Remember? He normally uses the one under the planter at the front but he didn't want to have to bend down while he carried the wood. He was going to take it to get more copies made."

Beauvoir's face twisted into utter disbelief. "Why even bother to lock up?" he finally asked.

"Insurance," said Olivier.

Well, someone's premiums are going up, thought Beauvoir. He looked at Gamache and shook his head. Really, they all deserved to be murdered in their sleep. But, of course, as irony would have it, it was the ones who locked and alarmed who were killed. In Beauvoir's experience Darwin was way wrong. The fittest didn't survive. They were killed by the idiocy of their neighbors, who continued to bumble along oblivious.

FOUR

—

"You didn't recognize him?" asked Clara as she sliced some fresh bread from Sarah's Boulangerie.

There was only one "him" Myrna's friend could be talking about. Myrna shook her head and sliced tomatoes into the salad, then turned to the shallots, all freshly picked from Peter and Clara's vegetable garden.

"And Olivier and Gabri didn't know him?" asked Peter. He was carving a barbecued chicken.

"Strange, isn't it?" Myrna paused and looked at her friends. Peter—tall, graying, elegant and precise. And beside him his wife Clara. Short, plump, hair dark and wild, bread crust scattered into it like sparkles. Her eyes were blue and usually filled with humor. But not today.

Clara was shaking her head, perplexed. A couple of crumbs fell to the counter. She picked them up absently, and ate them. Now that the initial shock of discovery was receding, Myrna was pretty sure they were all thinking the same thing.

This was murder. The dead man was a stranger. But was the killer?

And they probably all came to the same conclusion. Unlikely.

She'd tried not to think about it, but it kept creeping into her head. She picked up a slice of baguette and chewed on it. The bread was warm, soft and fragrant. The outer crust was crispy.

"For God's sake," said Clara, waving the knife at the half-eaten bread in Myrna's hand.

"Want some?" Myrna offered her a piece.

The two women stood at the counter eating fresh warm bread. They'd normally be at the bistro for Sunday lunch but that didn't seem likely today, what with the body and all. So Clara, Peter and Myrna had gone next door to Myrna's loft apartment. Downstairs the door to her shop was armed with an alarm, should anyone enter. It wasn't really so much an alarm as a small bell that tinkled when the door opened. Sometimes Myrna went down, sometimes not. Almost all her customers were local, and they all knew how much to leave by the cash register. Besides, thought Myrna, if anyone needed a used book so badly they had to steal it then they were welcome to it.

Myrna felt a chill. She looked across the room to see if a window was open and cool, damp air pouring in. She saw the exposed brick walls, the sturdy beams and the series of large industrial windows. She walked over to check, but all of them were closed, except for one open a sliver to let in some fresh air.

Walking back across the wide pine floors, she paused by the black pot-bellied woodstove in the center of the large room. It was crackling away. She lifted a round lid and slipped another piece of wood in.

"It must have been horrible for you," said Clara, going to stand by Myrna.

"It was. That poor man, just lying there. I didn't see the wound at first."

Clara sat with Myrna on the sofa facing the woodstove. Peter brought over two Scotches then quietly retired to the kitchen area. From there he could see them, could hear their conversation, but wouldn't be in the way.

He watched as the two women leaned close, sipping their drinks, talking softly. Intimately. He envied them that. Peter turned away and stirred the Cheddar and apple soup.

"What does Gamache think?" asked Clara.

"He seems as puzzled as the rest of us. I mean really," Myrna turned to face Clara, "why was a strange man in the bistro? Dead?"

"Murdered," said Clara and the two thought about that for a moment.

Clara finally spoke. "Did Olivier say anything?"

"Nothing. He seemed just stunned."

Clara nodded. She knew the feeling.

The police were at the door. Soon they'd be in their homes, in their kitchens and bedrooms. In their heads.

"Can't imagine what Gamache thinks of us," said Myrna. "Every time he shows up there's a body."

"Every Quebec village has a vocation," said Clara. "Some make cheese, some wine, some pots. We produce bodies."

"Monasteries have vocations, not villages," said Peter with a laugh. He placed bowls of rich-scented soup on Myrna's long refectory table. "And we don't make bodies."

But he wasn't really so sure.

"Gamache is the head of homicide for the Sûreté," said Myrna. "It must happen to him all the time. In fact, he'd probably be quite surprised if there wasn't a body."

Myrna and Clara joined Peter at the table and as the women talked Peter thought of the man in charge of the investigation. He was dangerous, Peter knew. Dangerous to whoever had killed that man next door. He wondered whether the murderer knew what sort of man was after him. But Peter was afraid the murderer knew all too well.

Inspector Jean Guy Beauvoir looked around their new Incident Room and inhaled. He realized, with some surprise, how familiar and even thrilling the scent was.

It smelled of excitement, it smelled of the hunt. It smelled of long hours over hot computers, piecing together a puzzle. It smelled of teamwork.

It actually smelled of diesel fuel and wood smoke, of polish and concrete. He was again in the old railway station of Three Pines, abandoned by the Canadian Pacific Railway decades ago and left to rot. But the Three Pines Volunteer Fire Department had taken it over, sneaking in and hoping no one noticed. Which, of course, they didn't, the CPR having long forgotten the village existed. So now the small station was home to their fire trucks, their bulky outfits, their equipment. The walls retained the tongue-in-groove wood paneling, and were papered with posters for scenic trips through the Rockies and life-saving techniques. Fire safety tips, volunteer rotation and old railway timetables competed for space, along with a huge poster announcing the winner of the Governor General's Prize for Poetry. There, staring out at them in perpetuity, was a madwoman.

She was also staring at him, madly, in person.

"What the fuck are you doing here?" Beside her a duck stared at him too.

Ruth Zardo. Probably the most prominent and respected poet in the country. And her duck Rosa. He knew that when Chief Inspector Gamache looked at her he saw a gifted poet. But Beauvoir just saw indigestion.

"There's been a murder," he said, his voice he hoped full of dignity and authority.

"I know there's been a murder. I'm not an idiot."

Beside her the duck shook its head and flapped its wings. Beauvoir had grown so used to seeing her with the bird it was no longer surprising. In fact, though he'd never admit it, he was relieved Rosa was still alive. Most things, he suspected, didn't last long around this crazy old fart.

"We need to use this building again," he said and turned away from them.

Ruth Zardo, despite her extreme age, her limp, and her diabolical temperament, had been elected head of the volunteer fire department. In hopes, Beauvoir suspected, that she'd perish in the flames one day. But he also suspected she wouldn't burn.

"No." She whacked her cane on the concrete floor. Rosa didn't jump but Beauvoir did. "You can't have it."

"I'm sorry, Madame Zardo, but we need it and we plan to take it."

His voice was no longer as gracious as it had been. The three stared at each other, only Rosa blinking. Beauvoir knew the only way this nutcase could triumph was if she started reciting her dreary, unintelligible verse. Nothing rhymed. Nothing even made sense. She'd break him in an instant. But he also knew that of all the people in the village, she was the least likely to quote it. She seemed embarrassed, even ashamed, by what she created.

"How's your poetry?" he asked and saw her waver. Her short, shorn hair was white and thin and lay close to her head, as though her bleached skull was exposed. Her neck was scrawny and ropy and her tall body, once sturdy he suspected, was feeble. But nothing else about her was.

"I saw somewhere that you'll soon have another book out."

Ruth Zardo backed up slightly.

"The Chief Inspector is here too, as you probably know." His voice was kind now, reasonable, warm. The old woman looked as though she was seeing Satan. "I know how much he's looking forward to talking to you about it. He'll be here soon. He's been memorizing your verses."

Ruth Zardo turned and left.

He'd done it. He'd banished her. The witch was dead, or at least gone.

He got to work setting up their headquarters. He ordered desks and communications equipment, computers and printers, scanners and faxes. Corkboards and fragrant Magic Markers. He'd stick a corkboard right on top of that poster of the sneering, mad old poet. And over her face he'd write about murder.

The bistro was quiet.

The Scene of Crime officers had left. Agent Isabelle Lacoste was kneeling on the floor where the body had been found, thorough as ever. Making absolutely sure no clues were missed. From what Chief Inspector Gamache could see Olivier and Gabri hadn't stirred: they still sat on the faded old sofa facing the large fireplace, each in his own world, staring at the fire, mesmerized by the flames. He wondered what they were thinking.

"What are you thinking?" Gamache went over and sat in the large armchair beside them.

"I was thinking about the dead man," said Olivier. "Wondering who he was. Wondering what he was doing here, and about his family. Wondering if anyone was missing him."

"I was thinking about lunch," said Gabri. "Anyone else hungry?"

From across the room Agent Lacoste looked up. "I am."

"So am I, *patron*," said Gamache.

When they could hear Gabri clanking pots and pans in the kitchen, Gamache leaned forward. It was just him and Olivier. Olivier looked at him blankly. But the Chief Inspector had seen that look before. It was, in fact, almost impossible to look blank. Unless the person wanted to. A blank face to the Chief Inspector meant a frantic mind.

From the kitchen came the unmistakable aroma of garlic and they could hear Gabri singing, "What shall we do with a drunken sailor?"

"Gabri thought the man was a tramp. What do you think?"

Olivier remembered the eyes, glassy, staring. And he remembered the last time he'd been in the cabin.

Chaos is coming, old son. It's taken a long time, but it's finally here.

"What else could he've been?"

"Why do you think he was killed here, in your bistro?"

"I don't know." And Olivier seemed to sag. "I've been racking my brains trying to figure it out. Why would someone kill a man here? It makes no sense."

"It does make sense."

"Really?" Olivier sat forward. "How?"

"I don't know. But I will."

Olivier stared at the formidable, quiet man who suddenly seemed to fill the entire room without raising his voice.

"Did you know him?"

"You've asked me that before," snapped Olivier, then gathered himself. "I'm sorry, but you have, you know, and it gets annoying. I didn't know him."

Gamache stared. Olivier's face was red now, blushing. But from anger, from the heat of the fire, or did he just tell a lie?

"Someone knew him," said Gamache at last, leaning back, giving Olivier the impression of pressure lifted. Of breathing room.

"But not me and not Gabri." His brow pulled together and Gamache thought Olivier was genuinely upset. "What was he doing here?"

"'Here' meaning Three Pines, or 'here' meaning the bistro?"

"Both."

But Gamache knew Olivier had just lied. He meant the bistro, that was obvious. People lied all the time in murder investigations. If the first victim of war was the truth, some of the first victims of a murder investigation were people's lies. The lies they told themselves, the lies they told each other. The little lies that allowed them to get out of bed on cold, dark mornings. Gamache and his team hunted the lies down and exposed them. Until all the small tales told to ease everyday lives disappeared. And people were left naked. The trick was distinguishing the important fibs from the rest. This one appeared tiny. In which case, why bother lying at all?

Gabri approached carrying a tray with four steaming plates. Within minutes they were sitting around the fireplace eating fettuccine with shrimp and scallops sautéed in garlic and olive oil. Fresh bread was produced and glasses of dry white wine poured.

As they ate they talked about the Labor Day long weekend, about the chestnut trees and conkers. About kids returning to school and the nights drawing in.

The bistro was empty, except for them. But it seemed crowded to the Chief Inspector. With the lies they'd been told, and the lies being manufactured and waiting.

FIVE

———

After lunch, while Agent Lacoste made arrangements for them to stay overnight at Gabri's B and B, Armand Gamache walked slowly in the opposite direction. The drizzle had stopped for the moment but a mist clung to the forests and hills surrounding the village. People were coming out of their homes to do errands or work in their gardens. He walked along the muddy road and turning left made his way over the arched stone bridge that spanned the Rivière Bella Bella.

"Hungry?" Gamache opened the door to the old train station and held out the brown paper bag.

"Starving, *merci*." Beauvoir almost ran over, and taking the bag he pulled out a thick sandwich of chicken, Brie and pesto. There was also a Coke and *pâtisserie*.

"What about you?" asked Beauvoir, his hand hesitating over the precious sandwich.

"Oh, I've eaten," the Chief said, deciding it would really do no good describing his meal to Beauvoir.

The men drew a couple of chairs up to the warm pot-bellied stove and as the Inspector ate they compared notes.

"So far," said Gamache, "we have no idea who the victim was, who killed him, why he was in the bistro and what the murder weapon was."

"No sign of a weapon yet?"

"No. Dr. Harris thinks it was a metal rod or something like that. It was smooth and hard."

"A fireplace poker?"

"Perhaps. We've taken Olivier's in for tests." The Chief paused.

"What is it?" Beauvoir asked.

"It just strikes me as slightly odd that Olivier would light fires in both grates. It's rainy but not that cold. And for that to be just about the first thing he'd do after finding a body . . ."

"You're thinking the weapon might be one of those fireplace pokers? And that Olivier lit the fires so that he could use them? Burn away evidence on them?"

"I think it's possible," said the Chief, his voice neutral.

"We'll have them checked," said Beauvoir. "But if one turns out to be the weapon it doesn't mean Olivier used it. Anyone could've picked it up and smashed the guy."

"True. But only Olivier lit the fires this morning, and used the poker."

It was clear as Chief Inspector he had to consider everyone a suspect. But it was also clear he wasn't happy about it.

Beauvoir waved to some large men at the door to come in. The Incident Room equipment had arrived. Lacoste showed up and joined them by the stove.

"I've booked us into the B and B. By the way, I ran into Clara Morrow. We're invited to dinner tonight."

Gamache nodded. This was good. They could find out more at a social event than they ever could in an interrogation.

"Olivier gave me the names of the people who worked in the bistro last night. I'm off to interview them," she reported. "And there are teams searching the village and the surrounding area for the murder weapon, with a special interest in fireplace pokers or anything like that."

Inspector Beauvoir finished his lunch and went to direct the setup of the Incident Room. Agent Lacoste left to conduct interviews. A part of Gamache always hated to see his team members go off. He warned them time and again not to forget what they were doing, and who they were looking for. A killer.

The Chief Inspector had lost one agent, years ago, to a murderer. He was damned if he was going to lose another. But he couldn't protect them all, all the time. Like Annie, he finally had to let them go.

It was the last interview of the day. So far Agent Lacoste had spoken to five people who'd worked at the bistro the night before, and gotten the same answers. No, nothing unusual happened. The place was full all evening, it being both a Saturday night and the long Labor Day weekend. School was back on Tuesday and anybody down for the summer would be heading back to Montreal on Monday. Tomorrow.

Four of the waiters were returning to university after the summer break the next day. They really weren't much help since all they seemed to have noticed was a table of attractive girls.

The fifth waiter was more helpful, since she hadn't simply seen a roomful of breasts. But it was, by all accounts, a normal though hectic evening. No dead body that anyone mentioned, and Lacoste thought even the breast boys would have noticed that.

She drove up to the home of the final waiter, the young man nominally in charge once Olivier had left. The one who'd done the final check of the place and locked up.

The house was set back from the main road down a long dirt driveway. Maples lined the drive and while they hadn't yet turned their brilliant autumn colors, a few were just beginning to show oranges and reds. In a few weeks this approach, Lacoste knew, would be spectacular.

Lacoste got out of the car and stared, amazed. Facing her was a block of concrete and glass. It seemed so out of place, like finding a tent pitched on Fifth Avenue. It didn't belong. As she walked toward it she realized something else. The house intimidated her and she wondered why. Her own tastes ran to traditional but not stuffy. She loved exposed brick and beams, but hated clutter, though she'd given up all semblance of being house-proud after the kids came. These days it was a triumph if she walked across a room and didn't step on something that squeaked.

This place was certainly a triumph. But was it a home?

The door was opened by a robust middle-aged woman who spoke very good, though perhaps slightly precise, French. Lacoste was surprised and realized she'd been expecting angular people to live in this angular house.

"Madame Parra?" Agent Lacoste held up her identification. The woman nodded, smiled warmly and stepped back for them to enter.

"*Entrez*. It's about what happened at Olivier's," said Hanna Parra.

"*Oui*." Lacoste bent to take off her muddy boots. It always seemed so awkward and undignified. The world famous homicide team of the Sûreté du Québec interviewing suspects in their stockinged feet.

Madame Parra didn't tell her not to. But she did give her slippers from a wooden box by the door, jumbled full of old footwear. Again, this surprised Lacoste, who'd expected everything to be neat and tidy. And rigid.

"We're here to speak to your son."

"Havoc."

Havoc. The name had amused Inspector Beauvoir, but Agent Lacoste found nothing funny about it. And, strangely, it seemed to fit with this cold, brittle place. What else could contain Havoc?

Before driving out she'd done some research on the Parras. Just a thumbnail sketch, but it helped. The woman leading her out of the mudroom was a councillor for the township of Saint-Rémy, and her husband, Roar, was a caretaker, working on the large properties in the area. They'd escaped Czechoslovakia in the mid-80s, come to Quebec and settled just outside Three Pines. There was, in fact, a large and influential Czech community in the area, composed of escapees, people running until they found what they were looking for. Freedom and safety. Hanna and Roar Parra had stopped when they found Three Pines.

And once there, they'd created Havoc.

"Havoc!" his mother cried, letting the dogs slip out as she called into the woods.

After a few more yells a short, stocky young man appeared. His face was flushed from hard work and his curly dark hair was tousled. He smiled and Lacoste knew the other waiters at the bistro hadn't stood a chance with the girls. This boy would take them all. He also stole a sliver of her heart, and she quickly did the figures. She was twenty-eight, he was twenty-one. In twenty-five years that wouldn't matter so much, although her husband and children might disagree.

"What can I do for you?" He bent and took off his green Wellington boots. "Of course, it is that man they found in the bistro this morning. I'm sorry. I should have known."

As he talked they walked into a quite splendid kitchen, unlike any Lacoste had seen in real life. Instead of the classic, and mandatory as far as Lacoste knew, triangle of fitments, the entire kitchen was ranged along one wall at the back of the bright room. There was one very long concrete counter, stainless steel appliances, open floating shelves with pure white dishes in a regimented line. The lower cabinets were dark laminate. It felt at once very retro and very modern.

There was no kitchen island but instead a frosted glass dining table, and what looked like vintage teak chairs stood in front of the counter. As Lacoste sat in one, and found it surprisingly comfortable, she wondered if these were antiques brought from Prague. Then she wondered if people really slipped across borders with teak chairs.

At the other end of the room was a wall of windows, floor to ceiling, that wrapped around the sides giving a spectacular view of fields and forest and a mountain beyond. She could just see a white church spire and a plume of smoke in the distance. The village of Three Pines.

In the living area by the huge windows two sofas lined up perfectly to face each other, with a low coffee table between them.

"Tea?" Hanna asked and Lacoste nodded.

These two Parras seemed at odds in the almost sterile environment and as they waited for the tea to brew Lacoste found herself wondering about the missing Parra. The father, Roar. Perhaps it was his angular, hard stamp on this house. Was he the one who yearned for cool certainty, straight lines, near empty rooms, and uncluttered shelves?

"Do you know who the dead man was?" asked Hanna as she placed a cup of tea in front of Agent Lacoste. A white plate piled with cookies was also put on the spotless table.

Lacoste thanked her and took one. It was soft and warm and tasted of raisin and oatmeal, with a hint of brown sugar and cinnamon. It tasted of home. She noticed the teacup had a smiling and waving snowman in a red suit. Bonhomme Carnaval. A character from the annual Quebec City winter carnival. She took a sip. It was strong and sweet.

Like Hanna herself, Lacoste suspected.

"No, we don't know who he was yet," she said.

"We've heard," Hanna hesitated, "that it wasn't natural. Is that right?"

Lacoste remembered the man's skull. "No, it wasn't natural. He was murdered."

"Dear God," said Hanna. "How awful. And you have no idea who did it?"

"We will, soon. For now I want to hear about last night." She turned to the young man sitting across from her.

Just then a voice called from the back door in a language Lacoste couldn't understand, but took to be Czech. A man, short and square, walked into the kitchen, whacking his knit hat against his coat.

"Roar, can't you do that in the mudroom?" Hanna spoke in French, and despite the slight reprimand she was clearly pleased to see him. "The police are here. About the body."

"What body?" Roar also switched to French, lightly accented. He sounded concerned. "Where? Here?"

"Not here, Dad. They found a body in the bistro this morning. He was killed."

"You mean murdered? Someone was murdered in the bistro last night?"

His disbelief was clear. Like his son he was stocky and muscular. His hair was curly and dark, but unlike his son's it was graying. He'd be in his late forties, Lacoste reckoned.

She introduced herself.

"I know you," he said, his gaze keen and penetrating. His eyes were disconcertingly blue and hard. "You've been in Three Pines before."

He had a good memory for faces, Lacoste realized. Most people re-membered Chief Inspector Gamache. Maybe Inspector Beauvoir. But few remembered her, or the other agents.

This man did.

He poured himself tea then sat down. He also seemed slightly out of place in this pristine modern room. And yet he was completely comfort-able. He looked a man who'd be comfortable most places.

"You didn't know about the body?"

Roar Parra took a bite of his cookie and shook his head. "I've been working all day in the woods."

"In the rain?"

He snorted. "What? A little rain won't kill you."

"But a blow to the head would."

"Is that how he died?" When Lacoste nodded Parra went on. "Who was he?"

"No one knows," said Hanna.

"But perhaps you do," said Lacoste. She brought a photograph out of her pocket and placed it face down on the hard, cold table.

"Me?" said Roar with a snort. "I didn't even know there was a dead man."

"But I hear you saw a stranger hanging around the village this sum-mer."

"Who told you that?"

"Doesn't matter. You were heard talking about it. Was it a secret?"

Parra hesitated. "Not really. It was just the once. Maybe twice. Not important. It was stupid, just some guy I thought I saw."

"Stupid?"

He gave a smile suddenly, the first one she'd seen from him, and it transformed his stern face. It was as though a crust had broken. Lines creased his cheeks and his eyes lit momentarily.

"Trust me, this is stupid. And I know stupid, having raised a teenage son. I'll tell you, but it can't mean anything. There're new owners at the old Hadley house. A couple bought it a few months ago. They're doing renovations and hired me to build a barn and clear some trails. They also wanted the garden cleaned up. Big job."

The old Hadley house, she knew, was a rambling old Victorian wreck on the hill overlooking Three Pines.

"I think I saw someone in the woods. A man. I'd felt someone looking at me when I worked there, but I thought I was imagining things. It's easy with that place. Sometimes I'd look around fast, to see if someone really was there, but there never was anyone. Except once."

"What happened?"

"He disappeared. I called out and even ran into the woods a little way after him, but he'd gone." Parra paused. "Maybe he was never there at all."

"But you don't believe that, do you? You believe there really was someone there."

Parra looked at her and nodded.

"Would you recognize him?" Lacoste asked.

"I might."

"I have a photograph of the dead man, taken this morning. It might be upsetting," she warned. Parra nodded and she turned the photograph face up. All three looked at it, staring intently, then shook their heads. She left it on the table, beside the cookies.

"Everything was normal last night? Nothing unusual?" she asked Havoc.

What followed was the same description as the other waiters had provided. Busy, lots of tips, no time to think.

Strangers?

Havoc thought about it and shook his head. No. Some summer people, and weekenders, but he knew everyone.

"And what did you do after Olivier and Old Mundin left?"

"Put away the dishes, did a quick look round, turned off the lights and locked up."

"Are you sure you locked up? The door was found unlocked this morning."

"I'm sure. I always lock up."

A note of fear had crept into the handsome young man's voice. But Lacoste knew that was normal. Most people, even innocent ones, grew fearful when examined by homicide detectives. But she'd noticed something else.

His father had looked at him, then quickly looked away. And Lacoste wondered who Roar Parra really was. He worked in the woods now. He cut grass and planted gardens. But what had he done before that? Many men were drawn to the tranquility of a garden only after they'd known the brutality of life.

Had Roar Parra known horrors? Had he created some?

SIX

———

"Chief Inspector? It's Sharon Harris."

"*Oui*, Dr. Harris," said Gamache into the receiver.

"I haven't done the complete autopsy but I have a couple of pieces of information from my preliminary work."

"Go on." Gamache leaned on the desk and brought his notebook closer.

"There were no identifying marks on the body, no tattoos, no operation scars. I've sent his dental work out."

"What shape were his teeth in?"

"Now that's an interesting point. They weren't as bad as I expected. I bet he didn't go to the dentist very often, and he'd lost a couple of molars to some gum disease, but overall, not bad."

"Did he brush?"

There was a small laugh. "Unbelievably, he did. He also flossed. There's some receding, some plaque and disease, but he took care of his teeth. There's even evidence he once had quite a bit of work done. Cavities filled, root canal."

"Expensive stuff."

"Exactly. This man had money at one time."

He wasn't born a tramp, thought Gamache. But then no one was.

"Can you tell how long ago the work was done?"

"I'd say twenty years at least, judging by the wear and the materials used, but I've sent a sample along to the forensic dentist. Should hear by tomorrow."

"Twenty years ago," mused Gamache, doing the math, jotting figures in his notebook. "The man was in his seventies. That would mean he had the work done sometime in his fifties. Then something happened. He lost his job, drank, had a breakdown; something happened that pushed him over the edge."

"Something happened," agreed Dr. Harris, "but not in his fifties. Something happened in his late thirties or early forties."

"That long ago?" Gamache looked down at his notes. He'd written *20 ans* and circled it. He was confused.

"That's what I wanted to tell you, Chief," the coroner continued. "There's something wrong about this body."

Gamache sat up straighter and took his half-moon reading glasses off. Across the room Beauvoir saw this and walked over to the Chief's desk.

"Go on," said Gamache, nodding to Beauvoir to sit. Then he punched a button on the phone. "I've put you on the speaker. Inspector Beauvoir's here."

"Good. Well, it struck me as strange that this man who seemed a derelict should brush his teeth and even floss. But homeless people can do odd things. They're often mentally unwell, as you know, and can be obsessive about certain things."

"Though not often hygiene," said Gamache.

"True. It was strange. Then when I undressed him I found he was clean. He'd had a bath or a shower recently. And his hair, while wild, was also clean."

"There're halfway homes," said Gamache. "Maybe he was in one of those. Though an agent called all the local social services and he's not known to them."

"How d'you know?" The coroner rarely questioned Chief Inspector Gamache, but she was curious. "We don't know his name and surely his description would sound like any number of homeless men."

"That's true," admitted Gamache. "She described him as a slim, older man in his seventies with white hair, blue eyes and weathered skin. None of the men who match that description and use shelters in this area is missing. But we're having someone take his photo around."

There was a pause on the line.

"What is it?"

"Your description is wrong."

"What do you mean?" Surely Gamache had seen him as clearly as everyone else.

"He wasn't an elderly man. That's what I called to tell you. His teeth were a clue; then I went looking. His arteries and blood vessels have very little plaque, and almost no atherosclerosis. His prostate isn't particularly enlarged and there's no sign of arthritis. I'd say he was in his mid-fifties."

My age, thought Gamache. Was it possible that wreck on the floor was the same age?

"And I don't think he was homeless."

"Why not?"

"Too clean for one thing. He took care of himself. Not *GQ* material, it's true, but not all of us can look like Inspector Beauvoir."

Beauvoir preened slightly.

"On the outside he looked seventy but on the inside he was in good physical condition. Then I looked at his clothes. They were clean too. And mended. They were old and worn, but *propres*."

She used the Québécois word that was rarely used anymore, except by elderly parents. But it seemed to fit here. *Propre*. Nothing fancy. Nothing fashionable. But sturdy and clean and presentable. There was a worn dignity about the word.

"I have to do more work, but that's my preliminary finding. I'll e-mail all this to you."

"*Bon*. Can you guess what sort of work he did? How'd he keep himself in shape?"

"Which gym did he belong to, you mean?" He could hear the smile in her voice.

"That's right," said Gamache. "Did he jog or lift weights? Was he in a spinning class or maybe Pilates?"

Now the coroner laughed. "At a guess I'd say it wasn't much walking, but a lot of lifting. His upper body is slightly more toned than his lower. But I'll keep that question in mind as I go."

"*Merci, docteur*," said Gamache.

"One more thing," said Beauvoir. "The murder weapon. Any further clues? Any ideas?"

"I'm just about to do that part of the autopsy, but I've taken a quick look and my assessment stays the same. Blunt instrument."

"A fireplace poker?" asked Beauvoir.

"Possibly. I did notice something white in the wound. Might be ash."

"We'll have the lab results from the pokers by tomorrow morning," said Gamache.

"I'll let you know when I have more to tell you."

Dr. Harris rung off just as Agent Lacoste arrived back. "Clearing up outside. It's going to be a nice sunset."

Beauvoir looked at her, incredulous. She was supposed to be scouring Three Pines for clues, trying to find the murder weapon and the murderer, interviewing suspects, and the first thing out of her mouth was about the nice sunset?

He noticed the Chief drift over to a window, sipping his coffee. He turned round and smiled. "Beautiful."

A conference table had been set up in the center of their Incident Room with desks and chairs placed in a semicircle at one end. On each desk was a computer and phone. It looked a little like Three Pines, with the conference table as the village green and their desks as the shops. It was an ancient and tested design.

A young Sûreté agent from the local detachment hovered, looking as if he wanted to say something.

"Can I help you?" Chief Inspector Gamache asked.

The other agents from the local detachment stopped and stared. Some exchanged knowing smiles.

The young man squared his shoulders.

"I'd like to help with your investigation."

There was dead silence. Even the technicians stopped what they were doing, as people do when witnessing a terrible calamity.

"I'm sorry?" said Inspector Beauvoir, stepping forward. "What did you just say?"

"I'd like to help." By now the young agent could see the truck hurtling toward him and could feel his vehicle spin out of control. Too late, he realized his mistake.

He saw all this, and stood firm, from either terror or courage. It was hard to tell. Behind him four or five large agents crossed their arms and did nothing to help.

"Aren't you supposed to be setting up desks and telephone lines?" asked Beauvoir, stepping closer to the agent.

"I have. That's all done." He voice was smaller, weaker, but still there.

"And what makes you think you can help?"

Behind Beauvoir stood the Chief Inspector, quietly watching. The young agent looked at Inspector Beauvoir when answering his questions, but then his eyes returned to Gamache.

"I know the area. I know the people."

"So do they." Beauvoir waved at the wall of police behind the agent. "If we needed help why would we choose you?"

This seemed to throw him and he stood silent. Beauvoir waved his hand to dismiss the agent and walked away.

"Because," the agent said to the Chief Inspector, "I asked."

Beauvoir stopped and turned round, looking incredulous. *"Pardon? Pardon?* This is homicide, not a game of Mother May I. Are you even in the Sûreté?"

It wasn't a bad question. The agent looked about sixteen and his uniform hung loosely on him, though an effort had obviously been made to make it fit. With him in the foreground and his *confrères* behind it looked like an evolutionary scale, with the young agent on the extinction track.

"If you have no more work to do, please leave."

The young agent nodded, turned to get back to work, met the wall of other officers, and stopped. Then he walked around them, watched by Gamache and his homicide team. Their last view of the young officer before they turned away was of his back, and a furiously blushing neck.

"Join me please," Gamache said to Beauvoir and Lacoste, who took their seats at the conference table.

"What do you think?" Gamache asked quietly.

"About the body?"

"About the boy."

"Not again," said Beauvoir, exasperated. "There are perfectly good officers already in homicide if we need someone. If they're busy with cases there's always the wait-list. Agents from other divisions are dying to get into homicide. Why choose an untested kid from the boonies? If we need another investigator let's call one down from headquarters."

It was their classic argument.

The homicide division of the Sûreté du Québec was the most prestigious posting in the province. Perhaps in Canada. They worked on the worst of all crimes in the worst of all conditions. And they worked with the best, the most respected and famous, of all investigators. Chief Inspector Gamache.

So why pick the dregs?

"We could, certainly," admitted the Chief.

But Beauvoir knew he wouldn't. Gamache had found Isabelle Lacoste sitting outside her Superintendent's office, about to be fired from traffic division. Gamache had asked her to join him, to the astonishment of everyone.

He'd found Beauvoir himself reduced to guarding evidence at the Sûreté outpost of Trois Rivières. Every day Beauvoir, Agent Beauvoir then, had suffered the ignominy of putting on his Sûreté uniform then stepping into the evidence cage. And staying there. Like an animal. He'd so pissed off his colleagues and bosses this was the only place left to put him. Alone. With inanimate objects. Silence all day, except when other agents came to put something in or take something out. They wouldn't even meet his eye. He'd become untouchable. Unmentionable. Invisible.

But Chief Inspector Gamache saw. He'd come one day on a case, had himself gone to the cage with evidence, and there he'd found Jean Guy Beauvoir.

The agent, the man no one wanted, was now the second in command in homicide.

But Beauvoir couldn't shake the certainty that Gamache had simply gotten lucky so far, with a few notable exceptions. The reality was, un-tested agents were dangerous. They made mistakes. And mistakes in homicide led to death.

He turned and looked at the slight young agent with loathing. Was this the one who'd finally make that blunder? The magnificent mistake that would lead to another death? It could be me who gets it, thought Beauvoir. Or worse. He glanced at Gamache beside him.

"Why him?" Beauvoir whispered.

"He seems nice," said Lacoste.

"Like the sunset," Beauvoir sneered.

"Like the sunset," she repeated. "He was standing all alone."

There was silence.

"That's it?" asked Beauvoir.

"He doesn't fit in. Look at him."

"You'd choose the runt of the litter? For homicide detail? For God's sake, sir," he appealed to Gamache. "This isn't the Humane Society."

"You think not?" said Gamache with a small smile.

"We need the best for this team, for this case. We don't have time to train people. And frankly, he looks as though he needs help tying his shoes."

It was true, Gamache had to admit, the young agent was awkward. But he was something else as well.

"We'll take him," said the Chief to Beauvoir. "I know you don't approve, and I understand your reasons."

"Then why take him, sir?"

"Because he asked," said Gamache, rising up. "And no one else did."

"But they'd join us in a second," Beauvoir argued, getting up as well. "Anyone would."

"What do you look for in a member of our team?" asked Gamache.

Beauvoir thought. "I want someone smart and strong."

Gamache tipped his head toward the young man. "And how much strength do you think that took? How much strength do you think it takes him to go to work every day? Almost as much as it took you, in Trois Rivières, or you," he turned to Lacoste, "in traffic division. The others might want to join us, but they either didn't have the brains or lacked the courage to ask. Our young man had both."

Our, thought Beauvoir. Our young man. He looked at him across the room. Alone. Coiling wires carefully and placing them in a box.

"I value your judgment, you know that, Jean Guy. But I feel strongly about this."

"I understand, sir." And he did. "I know this is important to you. But you're not always right."

Gamache stared at his Inspector and Beauvoir recoiled, afraid he'd gone too far. Presumed too much on their personal relationship. But then the Chief smiled.

"Happily, I have you to tell me when I make a mistake."

"I think you're making one now."

"Noted. Thank you. Will you please invite the young man to join us."

Beauvoir walked purposefully across the room and stopped at the young agent.

"Come with me," he said.

The agent straightened up. He looked concerned. "Yes, sir."

Behind them an officer snickered. Beauvoir stopped and turned back to the young officer following him.

"What's your name?"

"Paul Morin. I'm with the Cowansville detachment of the Sûreté, sir."

"Agent Morin, will you please take a seat at the table. We'd like your thoughts on this murder investigation."

Morin looked astonished. But not quite as astonished as the burly men behind him. Beauvoir turned back and walked slowly toward the conference table. It felt good.

"Reports, please," said Gamache and glanced at his watch. It was five thirty.

"Results are beginning to come in on some of the evidence we collected this morning in the bistro," said Beauvoir. "The victim's blood was found on the floor and between some of the floorboards, though there wasn't much."

"Dr. Harris will have a fuller report soon," said Gamache. "She thinks the lack of blood is explained by internal bleeding."

Beauvoir nodded. "We do have a report on his clothing. Still nothing to identify him. His clothes were old but clean and of good quality once. Merino wool sweater, cotton shirt, corduroy pants."

"I wonder if he'd put on his best clothes," said Agent Lacoste.

"Go on," said Gamache, leaning forward and taking off his glasses.

"Well." She picked her way through her thoughts. "Suppose he was going to meet someone important. He'd have a shower, shave, clip his nails even."

"And he might pick up clean clothes," said Beauvoir, following her thoughts. "Maybe at a used clothing store, or a Goodwill depot."

"There's one in Cowansville," said Agent Morin. "And another in Granby. I can check them."

"Good," said the Chief Inspector.

Agent Morin looked over at Inspector Beauvoir, who nodded his approval.

"Dr. Harris doesn't think this man was a vagrant, not in the classic sense of the word," said Chief Inspector Gamache. "He appeared in his seventies, but she's convinced he was closer to fifty."

"You're kidding," said Agent Lacoste. "What happened to him?"

That was the question, of course, thought Gamache. What happened to him? In life, to age him two decades. And in death.

Beauvoir stood up and walked to the fresh, clean sheets of paper pinned to the wall. He picked out a new felt pen, took off the cap and instinctively wafted it under his nose. "Let's go through the events of last night."

Isabelle Lacoste consulted her notes and told them about her interviews with the bistro staff.

They were beginning to see what had happened the night before. As he listened Armand Gamache could see the cheerful bistro, filled with villagers having a meal or drinks on Labor Day weekend. Talking about the Brume County Fair, the horse trials, the judging of livestock, the crafts tent. Celebrating the end of summer and saying good-bye to family and friends. He could see the stragglers leaving and the young waiters clearing up, banking the fires, washing the dishes. Then the door opening and Old Mundin stepping in. Gamache had no idea what Old Mundin looked like, so he placed in his mind a character from a painting by Bruegel the Elder. A stooped and cheery peasant. Walking through the bistro door, a young waiter perhaps helping to bring in the repaired chairs. Mundin and Olivier would have conferred. Money would have changed hands and Mundin would have left with new items needing fixing.

Then what?

According to Lacoste's interviews the waiters had left shortly before Olivier and Mundin. Leaving just one person in the bistro.

"What did you think of Havoc Parra?" Gamache asked.

"He seemed surprised by what had happened," said Lacoste. "It might've been an act, of course. Hard to tell. His father told me something interesting, though. He confirmed what we heard earlier. He saw someone in the woods."

"When?"

"Earlier in the summer. He's working at the old Hadley house for the new owners and thinks he saw someone up there."

"Thinks? Or did?" asked Beauvoir.

"Thinks. He chased him, but the guy disappeared."

They were silent for a moment, then Gamache spoke. "Havoc Parra says he locked up and left by one in the morning. Six hours later the man's body was found by Myrna Landers, who was out for a walk. Why would a stranger be murdered in Three Pines, and in the bistro?"

"If Havoc really did lock up, then the murderer had to be someone who knew where to find a key," said Lacoste.

"Or already had one," said Beauvoir. "Do you know what I wonder? I wonder why the murderer left him there."

"What do you mean?" asked Lacoste.

"Well, no one was there. It was dark. Why not pick up the body and take it into the forest? You wouldn't have to take him far, just a few hundred feet. The animals would do the rest and chances are he'd never be found. We'd never know a murder had been committed."

"Why do you think the body was left?" asked Gamache.

Beauvoir thought for a minute. "I think someone wanted him to be found."

"In the bistro?" asked Gamache.

"In the bistro."

SEVEN

Olivier and Gabri strolled across the village green. It was seven in the evening and lights were beginning to glow in windows, except at the bistro, which was dark and empty.

"Christ," came a growl through the dusk. "The fairies are out."

"*Merde*," said Gabri. "The village idiot's escaped from her attic." Ruth Zardo limped toward them followed by Rosa.

"I hear you finally killed someone with your rapier wit," said Ruth to Gabri, falling into step.

"Actually, I hear he read one of your poems and his head exploded," said Gabri.

"Would that that were true," said Ruth, slipping her bony arms into each of theirs, so that they walked across to Peter and Clara's arm in arm. "How are you?" she asked quietly.

"Okay," said Olivier, not glancing at the darkened bistro as they passed.

The bistro had been his baby, his creation. All that was good about him, he put in there. All his best antiques, his finest recipes, great wines. Some evenings he'd stand behind the bar, pretending to polish glasses, but really just listening to the laughter and looking at the people, who'd come to his bistro. And were happy to be there. They belonged, and so did he.

Until this.

Who'd want to come to a place where there'd been a murder?

And what if people found out he actually knew the Hermit? What if they found out what he'd done? No. Best to say nothing and see what happened. It was bad enough as it was.

They paused on the walk just outside Peter and Clara's house. Inside they saw Myrna putting her effusive flower arrangement on the kitchen table, already set for supper. Clara was exclaiming at its beauty and artistry. They couldn't hear the words, but her delight was obvious. In the living room Peter tossed another log on the fire.

Ruth turned from the comforting domestic scene to the man beside her. The old poet leaned in to whisper in his ear, so that not even Gabri could hear. "Give it time. It'll be all right, you know that, don't you?"

She turned to glance again through the glow at Clara hugging Myrna and Peter walking into the kitchen and exclaiming over the flowers as well. Olivier bent and kissed the old, cold cheek and thanked her. But he knew she was wrong. She didn't know what he knew.

Chaos had found Three Pines. It was bearing down upon them and all that was safe and warm and kind was about to be taken away.

Peter had poured them all drinks, except Ruth who'd helped herself and was now sipping from a vase filled with Scotch and sitting in the middle of the sofa facing the fire. Rosa was waddling around the room, barely noticed by anyone anymore. Even Lucy, Peter and Clara's golden retriever, barely looked at Rosa. The first time the poet had shown up with Rosa they'd insisted she stay outside, but Rosa set up such a quacking they were forced to let her in, just to shut the duck up.

"*Bonjour.*"

A deep, familiar voice was heard from the mudroom.

"God, you didn't invite Clouseau, did you?" asked Ruth, to the empty room. Empty except for Rosa, who raced to stand beside her.

"It's lovely," said Isabelle Lacoste as they walked from the mudroom into the airy kitchen. The long wooden table was set for dinner with baskets of sliced baguette, butter, jugs of water and bottles of wine. It smelled of garlic and rosemary and basil, all fresh from the garden.

And in the center of the table was a stunning arrangement of hollyhocks and climbing white roses, clematis and sweet pea and fragrant pink phlox.

More drinks were poured and the guests wandered into the living room and milled around nibbling soft runny Brie or orange and pistachio caribou pâté on baguette.

Across the room Ruth was interrogating the Chief Inspector.

"Don't suppose you know who the dead man was."

"Afraid not," said Gamache evenly. "Not yet."

"And do you know what killed him?"

"*Non.*"

"Any idea who did it?"

Gamache shook his head.

"Any idea why it happened in the bistro?"

"None," admitted Gamache.

Ruth glared at him. "Just wanted to make sure you're as incompetent as ever. Good to know some things can be relied upon."

"I'm glad you approve," said Gamache, bowing slightly before wandering off toward the fireplace. He picked up the poker, and examined it.

"It's a fireplace poker," said Clara, appearing at his elbow. "You use it to poke the fire."

She was smiling and watching him. He realized he must have looked a little odd, holding the long piece of metal to his face as though he'd never seen one before. He put it down. No blood on it. He was relieved.

"I hear your solo show is coming up in a few months." He turned to her, smiling. "It must be thrilling."

"If putting a dentist's drill up your nose is thrilling. Yes."

"That bad?"

"Oh, well, you know. It's only torture."

"Have you finished all the paintings?"

"They're all done, at least. They're crap, of course, but at least they're finished. Denis Fortin is coming down himself to discuss how they'll be hung. I have a specific order in mind. And if he disagrees I have a plan. I'll cry."

Gamache laughed. "That's how I got to be Chief Inspector."

"I told you so," Ruth hissed at Rosa.

"Your art is brilliant, Clara. You know that," said Gamache, leading her away from the crowd.

"How'd you know? You've only seen one piece. Maybe the others suck. I wonder if I made a mistake going with the paint by numbers."

Gamache made a face.

"Would you like to see them?" Clara asked.

"Love to."

"Great. How about after dinner? That gives you about an hour to practice saying, 'My God, Clara, they're the best works of art ever produced by anyone, anywhere.'"

"Sucking up?" smiled Gamache. "That's how I made Inspector."

"You're a Renaissance Man."

"I see you're good at it too."

"*Merci*. Speaking of your job, do you have any idea who that dead man is?" She'd lowered her voice. "You told Ruth you didn't, but is that true?"

"You think I'd lie?" he asked. But why not, he thought. Everyone else does. "You mean, how close are we to solving the crime?"

Clara nodded.

"Hard to say. We have some leads, some ideas. It makes it harder to know why the man was killed not knowing who he was."

"Suppose you never find out?"

Gamache looked down at Clara. Was there something in her voice? An imperfectly hidden desire that they never find out who the dead man was?

"It makes our job harder," he conceded, "but not impossible."

His voice, while relaxed, became momentarily stern. He wanted her to know they'd solve this case, one way or another. "Were you at the bistro last night?"

"No. We'd gone to the fair with Myrna. Had a disgusting dinner of fries, burgers and cotton candy. Went on a few rides, watched the local talent show, then came back here. I think Myrna might've gone in, but we were tired."

"We know the dead man wasn't a villager. He seems to have been a stranger. Have you seen any strangers around?"

"People come through backpacking or bicycling," said Clara, sipping her red wine and thinking. "But most of them are younger. I understand this was quite an old man."

Gamache didn't tell her what the coroner had said that afternoon.

"Roar Parra told Agent Lacoste he'd seen someone lurking in the woods this summer. Does that sound familiar?" He watched her closely.

"Lurking? Isn't that a bit melodramatic? No, I haven't seen anyone and neither has Peter. He'd have told me. And we spend a lot of time outside in the garden. If there was someone there we'd have seen him."

She waved toward their backyard, in darkness now, but Gamache knew it was large and sloped gently toward the Rivière Bella Bella.

"Mr. Parra didn't see him there," said Gamache. "He saw him there."

He pointed to the old Hadley house, on the hill above them. The two of them took their drinks and walked out the door to the front veranda. Gamache was wearing his gray flannels, shirt, tie and jacket. Clara had a sweater, and needed it. In early September the nights grew longer and cooler. All around the village lights shone in homes, and even in the house on the hill.

The two looked at the house in silence for a few moments.

"I hear it's sold," said Gamache, finally.

Clara nodded. They could hear the murmur of conversation from the living room, and light spilled out so that Gamache could see Clara's face in profile.

"Few months ago," she said. "What are we now? Labor Day? I'd say they bought it back in July and have been doing renovations ever since. Young couple. Or at least, my age, which seems young to me."

Clara laughed.

It was hard for Gamache to see the old Hadley house as just another place in Three Pines. For one thing, it never seemed to belong to the village. It seemed the accusation, the voyeur on the hill, that looked down on them. Judged them. Preyed on them. And sometimes took one of the villagers, and killed them.

Horrible things had happened in that place.

Earlier in the year he and his wife Reine-Marie had come down and helped the villagers repaint and repair the place. In the belief that everything deserved a second chance. Even houses. And the hopes someone would buy it.

And now someone had.

"I know they hired Roar to work on the grounds," said Clara. "Clean up the gardens. He's even built a barn and started reopening the trails. There must have been fifty kilometers of bridle paths in those woods in Timmer Hadley's time. Grown over, of course. Lots of work for Roar to do."

"He said he saw the stranger in the woods while he worked. Said he'd felt himself being watched for a while but only caught sight of someone once. He'd tried to run after him but the guy disappeared."

Gamache's gaze shifted from the old Hadley house down to Three Pines. Kids were playing touch football on the village green, eking out every last moment of their summer vacation. Snippets of voices drifted to them from villagers sitting on other porches, enjoying the early evening. The main topic of conversation, though, wouldn't be the ripening tomatoes, the cooler nights, or getting in the winter wood.

Into the gentle village something rotten had crawled. Words like "murder," "blood," "body," floated in the night air, as did something else. The soft scent of rosewater and sandalwood from the large, quiet man beside Clara.

Back inside Isabelle Lacoste was pouring herself another watereddown Scotch from the drinks tray on the piano. She looked around the room. A bookcase covered an entire wall, crammed with books, broken only by a window and the door to the veranda through which she could see the Chief and Clara.

Across the living room Myrna was chatting with Olivier and Gabri while Peter worked in the kitchen and Ruth drank in front of the fireplace. Lacoste had been in the Morrow home before, but only to conduct interviews. Never as a guest.

It was as comfortable as she'd imagined. She saw herself going back to her husband in Montreal and convincing him they could sell their home, take the kids out of school, chuck their jobs and move here. Find a cottage just off the village green and get jobs at the bistro or Myrna's bookshop.

She subsided into an armchair and watched as Beauvoir came in from the kitchen, a pâté-smeared piece of bread in one hand and a beer in the other, and started toward the sofa. He halted suddenly, as though repelled, changed course, and went outside.

Ruth rose and limped to the drinks tray, a malevolent sneer on her face. Scotch replenished she returned to the sofa, like a sea monster slipping beneath the surface once again, still waiting for a victim.

"Any idea when we can reopen the bistro?" Gabri asked as he, Olivier and Myrna joined Agent Lacoste.

"Gabri," said Olivier, annoyed.

"What? I'm just asking."

"We've done what we need to," she told Olivier. "You can open up whenever you'd like."

"You can't stay closed long, you know," said Myrna. "We'd all starve to death."

Peter put his head in and announced, "Dinner!"

"Though perhaps not immediately," said Myrna, as they headed for the kitchen.

Ruth hauled herself out of the sofa and went to the veranda door.

"Are you deaf?" she shouted at Gamache, Beauvoir and Clara. "Dinner's getting cold. Get inside."

Beauvoir felt his rectum spasm as he hurried past her. Clara followed Beauvoir to the dinner table, but Gamache lingered.

It took him a moment to realize he wasn't alone. Ruth was standing beside him, tall, rigid, leaning on her cane, her face all reflected light and deep crevices.

"A strange thing to give to Olivier, wouldn't you say?"

The old voice, sharp and jagged, cut through the laughter from the village green.

"I beg your pardon?" Gamache turned to her.

"The dead man. Even you can't be that dense. Someone did this to Olivier. The man's greedy and shiftless and probably quite weak, but he didn't kill anyone. So why would someone choose his bistro for murder?"

Gamache raised his eyebrows. "You think someone chose the bistro on purpose?"

"Well, it didn't happen by accident. The murderer chose to kill at Olivier's Bistro. He gave the body to Olivier."

"To kill both a man and a business?" asked Gamache. "Like giving white bread to a goldfish?"

"Fuck you," said Ruth.

"*Nothing I ever gave was good for you*," quoted Gamache. "*It was like white bread to a goldfish.*"

Beside him Ruth Zardo stiffened, then in a low growl she finished her own poem.

> "*They cram and cram, and it kills them,*
> *and they drift in the pool, belly up,*
> *making stunned faces*
> *and playing on our guilt*
> *as if their own toxic gluttony*
> *was not their fault.*"

Gamache listened to the poem, one of his favorites. He looked across at the bistro, dark and empty on a night when it should have been alive with villagers.

Was Ruth right? Had someone chosen the bistro on purpose? But that meant Olivier was somehow implicated. Had he brought this on himself? Who in the village hated the tramp enough to kill him, and Olivier enough to do it there? Or was the tramp merely a convenient tool? A poor man in the wrong place? Used as a weapon against Olivier?

"Who do you think would want to do this to Olivier?" he asked Ruth.

She shrugged, then turned to leave. He watched her take her place among her friends, all of them moving in ways familiar to each other, and now to him.

And to the killer?

EIGHT

The meal was winding down. They'd dined on corn on the cob and sweet butter, fresh vegetables from Peter and Clara's garden and a whole salmon barbecued over charcoal. The guests chatted amicably as warm bread was passed and salad served.

Myrna's exuberant arrangement of hollyhock, sweet pea and phlox sat in the center, so that it felt as though they were eating in a garden. Gamache could hear Lacoste asking her dinner companions about the Parras, and then segueing into Old Mundin. The Chief Inspector wondered if they realized they were being interrogated.

Beauvoir was chatting to his neighbors about the Brume County Fair, and visitors. Across the table from Beauvoir sat Ruth, glaring at him. Gamache wondered why, though with Ruth that was pretty much her only form of expression.

Gamache turned to Peter, who was serving arugula, frizzy lettuce and fresh ripe tomatoes.

"I hear the old Hadley house has been sold. Have you met the new owners?"

Peter passed him the salad bowl of deep-burled wood.

"We have. The Gilberts. Marc and Dominique. His mother lives with them too. Came from Quebec City. I think she was a nurse or something. Long retired. Dominique was in advertising in Montreal and Marc was an investment dealer. Made a fortune then retired early before the market went sour."

"Lucky man."

"Smart man," said Peter.

Gamache helped himself to the salad. He could smell the delicate dressing of garlic, olive oil and fresh tarragon. Peter poured them another glass of red wine and handed the bottle down the long table. Gamache watched to see if Peter's comment held a sting, a subtext. By "smart" did Peter mean "shrewd," "cunning," "sly"? But no, Gamache felt Peter meant what he said. It was a compliment. While Peter Morrow rarely insulted anyone, he rarely complimented them either. But he seemed impressed by this Marc Gilbert.

"Do you know them well?"

"Had them around for dinner a few times. Nice couple." For Peter that was an almost effusive comment.

"Interesting that with all that money they'd buy the old Hadley house," said Gamache. "It's been abandoned for a year or more. Presumably they could've bought just about any place around here."

"We were a little surprised as well, but they said they wanted a clean canvas, some place they could make their own. Practically gutted the house, you know. It also has loads of land and Dominique wants horses."

"Roar Parra's been clearing the trails, I hear."

"Slow job."

As he was talking Peter's voice had dropped to a whisper, so that the two men were leaning toward each other like co-conspirators. Gamache wondered what they were conspiring about.

"It's a lot of house for three people. Do they have children?"

"Well, no."

Peter's eyes shifted down the table, then back to Gamache. Whom had he just looked at? Clara? Gabri? It was impossible to say.

"Have they made friends in the community?" Gamache leaned back and spoke in a normal tone, taking a forkful of salad.

Peter looked down the table again and lowered his voice even more. "Not exactly."

Before Gamache could pursue it Peter got up and began clearing the table. At the sink he looked back at his friends, chatting. They were close. So close they could reach out and touch each other, which they occasionally did.

And Peter couldn't. He stood apart, and watched. He missed Ben, who'd once lived in the old Hadley house. Peter had played there as a child. He knew its nooks and crannies. All the scary places where ghosts and spiders lived. But now someone else lived there and had turned it into something else.

Thinking of the Gilberts, Peter could feel his own heart lift a little. "What're you thinking about?"

Peter started as he realized Armand Gamache was right beside him. "Nothing much."

Gamache took the mixer from Peter's hand and poured whipping cream and a drop of vanilla into the chilled bowl. He turned it on and leaned toward Peter, his voice drowned out by the whirring machine, lost to all but his companion.

"Tell me about the old Hadley house, and the people there."

Peter hesitated but knew Gamache wasn't going to let it go. And this was as discreet as it was going to get. Peter talked, his words whipped and mixed and unintelligible to anyone more than six inches away.

"Marc and Dominique plan to open a luxury inn and spa."

"At the old Hadley house?"

Gamache's astonishment was so complete it almost made Peter laugh. "It's not the same place you remember. You should see it now. It's fantastic."

The Chief Inspector wondered whether a coat of paint and new appliances could exorcise demons, and whether the Catholic Church knew about that.

"But not everyone's happy about it," Peter continued. "They've interviewed a few of Olivier's workers and offered them jobs at higher wages. Olivier's managed to keep most of his staff, but he's had to pay more. The two barely speak."

"Marc and Olivier?" Gamache asked.

"Won't be in the same room."

"That must be awkward, in a small village."

"Not really."

"Then why are we whispering?" Gamache shut the mixer off and spoke in a normal tone. Peter, flustered, looked over at the table again.

"Look, I know Olivier'll get over it, but for now it's just easier not to bring it up."

Peter handed Gamache a shortcake, which he cut in half, and Peter piled sliced ripe strawberries in their own brilliant red juice on top of it.

Gamache noticed Clara getting up and Myrna going with her. Olivier came over and put the coffee on to perk.

"Can I help?" asked Gabri.

"Here, put cream on. The cake, Gabri," said Peter as Gabri approached Olivier with a spoonful of whipped cream. Soon a small conga line of men assembling strawberry shortcakes was formed. When they'd finished they turned around to take the desserts to the table but stopped dead.

There, lit only by candles, was Clara's art. Or at least three large canvases, propped on easels. Gamache felt suddenly light-headed, as though he'd traveled back to the time of Rembrandt, da Vinci, Titian. Where art was viewed either by daylight or candlelight. Was this how the *Mona Lisa* was first seen? The Sistine Chapel? By firelight? Like cave drawings.

He wiped his hands on a dish towel and walked closer to the three easels. He noticed the other guests did the same thing, drawn to the paintings. Around them the candles flickered and threw more light than Gamache had expected, though it was possible Clara's paintings produced their own light.

"I have others, of course, but these'll be the centerpieces of the exhibition at the Galerie Fortin."

But no one was really listening. Instead they were staring at the easels. Some at one, some at another. Gamache stood back for a moment, taking in the scene.

Three portraits, three elderly women, stared back at him.

One was clearly Ruth. The one that had first caught Denis Fortin's eye. The one that had led him to his extraordinary offer of a solo show. The one that had the art world, from Montreal to Toronto, to New York and London, buzzing. About the new talent, the treasure, found buried in Quebec's Eastern Townships.

And there it was, in front of them.

Clara Morrow had painted Ruth as the elderly, forgotten Virgin Mary. Angry, demented, the Ruth in the portrait was full of despair, of bitterness. Of a life left behind, of opportunities squandered, of loss and betrayals real and imagined and created and caused. She clutched at a rough blue shawl with emaciated hands. The shawl had slipped off one bony shoulder and the skin was sagging, like something nailed up and empty.

And yet the portrait was radiant, filling the room from one tiny point of light. In her eyes. Embittered, mad Ruth stared into the distance, at something very far off, approaching. More imagined than real.

Hope.

Clara had captured the moment despair turned to hope. The moment life began. She'd somehow captured Grace.

It took Gamache's breath away and he could feel a burning in his eyes. He blinked and turned from it, as though from something so brilliant it blinded. He saw everyone else in the room also staring, their faces soft in the candlelight.

The next portrait was clearly Peter's mother. Gamache had met her, and once met, never forgotten. Clara had painted her staring straight at the viewer. Not into the distance, like Ruth, but at something very close. Too close. Her white hair in a loose bun, her face a web of soft lines, as though a window had just shattered but not yet fallen. She was white and pink and healthy and lovely. She had a quiet, gentle smile that reached her tender blue eyes. Gamache could almost smell the talcum powder and cinnamon. And yet the portrait made him deeply uneasy. And then he saw it. The subtle turn of her hand, outward. The way her fingers seemed to reach beyond the canvas. At him. He had the impression this gentle, lovely elderly woman was going to touch him. And if she did, he'd know sorrow like never before. He'd know that empty place where nothing existed, not even pain.

She was repulsive. And yet he couldn't help being drawn to her, like a person afraid of heights drawn to the edge.

And the third elderly woman he couldn't place. He'd never seen her before and he wondered if she was Clara's mother. There was something vaguely familiar about her.

He looked at it closely. Clara painted people's souls, and he wanted to know what this soul held.

She looked happy. Smiling over her shoulder at something of great interest. Something she cared about deeply. She too had a shawl, this of old, rough, deep red wool. She seemed someone who was used to riches but suddenly poor. And yet it didn't seem to matter to her.

Interesting, thought Gamache. She was heading in one direction but looking in the other. Behind her. From her he had an overwhelming feeling of yearning. He realized all he wanted to do was draw an armchair up to that portrait, pour a cup of coffee and stare at it for the rest of the evening. For the rest of his life. It was seductive. And dangerous.

With an effort he pulled his eyes away and found Clara standing in the darkness, watching her friends as they looked at her creations.

Peter was also watching. With a look of unmarred pride.

"*Bon Dieu*," said Gabri. "*C'est extraordinaire.*"

"*Félicitations*, Clara," said Olivier. "My God, they're brilliant. Do you have more?"

"Do you mean, have I done you?" she asked with a laugh. "*Non, mon beau*. Only Ruth and Peter's mother."

"Who's this one?" Lacoste pointed to the painting Gamache had been staring at.

Clara smiled. "I'm not telling. You have to guess."

"Is it me?" asked Gabri.

"Yes, Gabri, it's you," said Clara.

"Really?" Too late he saw her smiling.

The funny thing was, thought Gamache, it almost could have been Gabri. He looked again at the portrait in the soft candlelight. Not physically, but emotionally. There was happiness there. But there was also something else. Something that didn't quite fit with Gabri.

"So which one's me?" asked Ruth, limping closer to the paintings.

"You old drunk," said Gabri. "It's this one."

Ruth peered at her exact double. "I don't see it. Looks more like you."

"Hag," muttered Gabri.

"Fag," she mumbled back.

"Clara's painted you as the Virgin Mary," Olivier explained.

Ruth leaned closer and shook her head.

"Virgin?" Gabri whispered to Myrna. "Obviously the mind fucks don't count."

"Speaking of which," Ruth looked over at Beauvoir, "Peter, do you have a piece of paper? I feel a poem coming on. Now, do you think it's too much to put the words 'asshole' and 'shithead' in the same sentence?"

Beauvoir winced.

"Just close your eyes and think of England," Ruth advised Beauvoir, who had actually been thinking of her English.

Gamache walked over to Peter, who continued to stare at his wife's works.

"How are you?"

"You mean, do I want to take a razor to those and slash them to bits, then burn them?"

"Something like that."

It was a conversation they'd had before, as it became clear that Peter might soon have to cede his place as the best artist in the family, in the village, in the province, to his wife. Peter had struggled with it, not always successfully.

"I couldn't hold her back even if I tried," said Peter. "And I don't want to try."

"There's a difference between holding back and actively supporting."

"These are so good even I can't deny it anymore," admitted Peter. "She amazes me."

Both men looked over at the plump little woman looking anxiously at her friends, apparently unaware of the masterpieces she'd created.

"Are you working on something?" Gamache nodded toward the closed door to Peter's studio.

"Always am. It's a log."

"A log?" It was hard to make that sound brilliant. Peter Morrow was one of the most successful artists in the country and he'd gotten there by taking mundane, everyday objects and painting them in excruciating detail. So that they were no longer even recognizable as the object they were. He zoomed in close, then magnified a section, and painted that.

His works looked abstract. It gave Peter huge satisfaction to know they weren't. They were reality in the extreme. So real no one recognized them. And now it was the log's turn. He'd picked it up off the pile beside their fireplace and it was waiting for him in his studio.

The desserts were served, coffee and cognac poured; people wandered about, Gabri played the piano, Gamache kept being drawn to the paintings. Particularly the one of the unknown woman. Looking back. Clara joined him.

"My God, Clara, they're the best works of art ever produced by anyone, anywhere."

"Do you mean it?" she asked in mock earnestness.

He smiled. "They are brilliant, you know. You have nothing to be afraid of."

"If that was true I'd have no art."

Gamache nodded toward the painting he'd been staring at. "Who is she?"

"Oh, just someone I know."

Gamache waited, but Clara was uncharacteristically closed, and he decided it really didn't matter. She wandered off and Gamache continued to stare. And as he did so the portrait changed. Or perhaps, he thought, it was a trick of the uncertain light. But the more he stared the more he got the sense Clara had put something else in the painting. Where Ruth's was of an embittered woman finding hope, this portrait also held the unexpected.

A happy woman seeing in the near and middle distance things that pleased and comforted her. But her eyes seemed to just be focusing on, registering, something else. Something far off. But heading her way.

Gamache sipped his cognac and watched. And gradually it came to him what she was just beginning to feel.

Fear.

NINE

⁓

The three Sûreté officers said their good-byes and walked across the village green. It was eleven o'clock and pitch-black. Lacoste and Gamache paused to stare at the night sky. Beauvoir, a few paces ahead as always, eventually realized he was alone and stopped as well. Reluctantly he looked up and was quite surprised to see so many stars. Ruth's parting words came back to him.

"'Jean Guy' and 'bite me' actually rhyme, don't they?"

He was in trouble.

Just then a light went on above Myrna's bookstore, in her loft. They could see her moving about, making herself tea, putting cookies on a plate. Then the light went out. "We just saw her pour a drink and put cookies on a plate," said Beauvoir.

The others wondered why he'd just told them the obvious.

"It's dark. To do anything inside you need light," said Beauvoir.

Gamache thought about this string of obvious statements, but it was Lacoste who got there first.

"The bistro, last night. Wouldn't the murderer need to put on the lights? And if he did, wouldn't someone have seen?"

Gamache smiled. They were right. A light at the bistro must have been noticed.

He looked around to see which houses were the most likely to have seen anything. But the homes fanned out from the bistro like wings. None would have a perfect view, except the place directly opposite. He turned to look. The three majestic pines on the village green were there. They'd have seen a man take another man's life. But there was something else directly opposite the bistro. Opposite and above.

The old Hadley house. It was a distance away, but at night, with a light on in the bistro, it was just possible the new owners could have witnessed a murder.

"There's another possibility," said Lacoste. "That the murderer didn't put the lights on. He'd know he could be seen."

"He'd use a flashlight, you mean?" asked Beauvoir, imagining the murderer in there the night before, waiting for his victim, turning a flashlight on to make his way around.

Lacoste shook her head. "That could also be seen from outside. He wouldn't want to risk even that, I think."

"So he'd leave the lights off," said Gamache, knowing where this was leading. "Because he wouldn't need lights. He'd know his way around in the dark."

The next morning dawned bright and fresh. There was some warmth in the sun again and Gamache soon took off his sweater as he walked around the village green before breakfast. A few children, up before parents and grandparents, did some last-minute frog hunting in the pond. They ignored him and he was happy to watch them from a distance then continue his solitary and peaceful stroll. He waved at Myrna, cresting the hill on her own solitary walk.

This was the last day of summer vacation, and while it had been decades since he'd gone to school, he still felt the tug. The mix of sadness at the end of summer, and excitement to see his chums again. The new clothes, bought after a summer's growth. The new pencils, sharpened over and over, and the smell of the shavings. And the new notebooks. Always strangely thrilling. Unmarred. No mistakes yet. All they held was promise and potential.

A new murder investigation felt much the same. Had they marred their books yet? Made any mistakes?

As he slowly circled the village green, his hands clasped behind his back and his gaze far off, he thought about that. After a few leisurely circuits he went inside to breakfast.

Beauvoir and Lacoste were already down, with frothy *café au lait* in front of them. They stood up as he entered the room, and he motioned them down. The aroma of maple-cured back bacon and eggs and coffee came from the kitchen. He'd barely sat down when Gabri swept out of the kitchen with plates of eggs Benedict, fruit and muffins.

"Olivier's just left for the bistro. He's not sure if he'll open today," said the large man, who looked and sounded a great deal like Julia Child that morning. "I told him he should, but we'll see. I pointed out he'd lose money if he didn't. That usually does the trick. Muffin?"

"*S'il vous plaît*," said Isabelle Lacoste, taking one. They looked like nuclear explosions. Isabelle Lacoste missed her children and her husband. But it amazed her how this small village seemed able to heal even that hole. Of course, if you stuff in enough muffins even the largest hole is healed, for a while. She was willing to try.

Gabri brought Gamache his *café au lait* and when he left Beauvoir leaned forward.

"What's the plan for today, Chief?"

"We need background checks. I want to know all about Olivier, and I want to know who might have a grudge against him."

"*D'accord*," said Lacoste.

"And the Parras. Make inquiries, here and in the Czech Republic."

"Will do," said Beauvoir. "And you?"

"I have an appointment with an old friend."

Armand Gamache climbed the hill leading out of Three Pines. He carried his tweed jacket over his arm and kicked a chestnut ahead of him. The air smelled of apples, sweet and warm on the trees. Everything was ripe, lush, but in a few weeks there'd be a killing frost. And it would all be gone.

As he walked the old Hadley house grew larger and larger. He steeled himself against it. Prepared for the waves of sorrow that rolled from it, flowing over and into anyone foolish enough to get close.

But either his defenses were better than he'd expected, or something had changed.

Gamache stopped in a spot of sunshine and faced the house. It was a rambling Victorian trophy home, turreted, shingles like scales, wide swooping verandas and black wrought-iron rails. Its fresh paint gleamed in the sun and the front door was a cheery glossy red. Not like blood, but like Christmas. And cherries. And crisp autumn apples. The path had been cleared of brambles and solid flagstones laid. He noticed the hedges had been clipped and the trees trimmed, the deadwood removed. Roar Parra's work.

And Gamache realized, to his surprise, that he was standing outside the old Hadley house with a smile. And was actually looking forward to going inside.

The door was opened by a woman in her mid-seventies.

"*Oui?*"

Her hair was steel gray and nicely cut. She wore almost no makeup, just a little around the eyes, which looked at him now with curiosity, then recognition. She smiled and opened the door wider.

Gamache offered her his identification. "I'm sorry to bother you, madame, but my name is Armand Gamache. I'm with the Sûreté du Québec."

"I recognize you, monsieur. Please, come in. I'm Carole Gilbert."

Her manner was friendly and gracious as she showed him into the vestibule. He'd been there before. Many times. But it was almost unrecognizable. Like a skeleton that had been given new muscles and sinew and skin. The structure was there, but all else had changed.

"You know the place?" she asked, watching him.

"I knew it," he said, swinging his eyes to hers. She met his look steadily, but without challenge. As a chatelaine would, confident in her place and without need to prove it. She was friendly and warm, and very, very observant, Gamache guessed. What had Peter said? She'd been a nurse once? A very good one, he presumed. The best ones were observant. Nothing got past them.

"It's changed a great deal," he said and she nodded, drawing him farther into the house. He wiped his feet on the area rug protecting the gleaming wooden floor and followed her. The vestibule opened into a large hall with crisp new black and white tiles on the floor. A sweeping staircase faced them and archways led through to various rooms. When he'd last been here it had been a ruin, fallen into disrepair. It had seemed as though the house, disgusted, had turned on itself. Pieces were thrown off, wallpaper hung loose, floorboards heaved, ceilings warped. But now a huge cheerful bouquet sat on a polished table in the center of the hall, filling it with fragrance. The walls were painted a sophisticated tawny color, between beige and gray. It was bright and warm and elegant. Like the woman in front of him.

"We're still working on the house," she said, leading him through the archway to their right, down a couple of steps and into the large living room. "I say 'we' but it's really my son and daughter-in-law. And the workers, of course."

She said it with a small self-deprecating laugh. "I was foolish enough to ask if I could do anything the other day and they gave me a hammer and told me to put up some drywall. I hit a water pipe and an electrical cord."

Her laugh was so unguarded and infectious Gamache found himself laughing too.

"Now I make tea. They call me the tea lady. Tea?"

"*Merci, madame,* that would be very nice."

"I'll tell Marc and Dominique you're here. It's about that poor man in the bistro, I presume?"

"It is."

She seemed sympathetic, but not concerned. As though it had nothing to do with her. And Gamache found himself hoping it didn't.

As he waited he looked around the room and drifted toward the floor-to-ceiling windows, where sun streamed in. The room was comfortably furnished with sofas and chairs that looked inviting. They were upholstered in expensive fabrics giving them a modern feel. A couple of Eames chairs framed the fireplace. It was an easy marriage of contemporary and old world. Whoever had decorated this room had an eye for it.

The windows were flanked by tailored silk curtains that touched the hardwood floor. Gamache suspected the curtains were almost never closed. Why shut out that view?

It was spectacular. From its position on the hill the house looked over the valley. He could see the Rivière Bella Bella wind its way through the village and out around the next mountain toward the neighboring valley. The trees at the top of the mountain were changing color. It was autumn up there already. Soon the reds and auburns and pumpkin oranges would march down the slopes until the entire forest was ablaze. And what a vantage point to see it all. And more.

Standing at the window he could see Ruth and Rosa walking around the village green, the old poet tossing either stale buns or rocks at the other birds. He could see Myrna working in Clara's vegetable garden and Agent Lacoste walking over the stone bridge toward their makeshift Incident Room in the old railway station. He watched as she stopped on the bridge and looked into the gently flowing water. He wondered what she was thinking. Then she moved on. Other villagers were out doing their morning errands, or working in their gardens, or sitting on their porches reading the paper and drinking coffee.

From there he could see everything. Including the bistro.

Agent Paul Morin had arrived before Lacoste and was standing outside the railway station, making notes.

"I was thinking about the case last night," he said, watching her unlock the door then following her into the chilly, dark room. She flipped on the lights and walked over to her desk. "I think the murderer must've turned on the lights of the bistro, don't you? I tried walking around my house at two o'clock this morning, and I couldn't see anything. It was pitch-black. In the city you might get streetlights through the window, but not out here. How'd he know who he was killing?"

"I suppose if he'd invited the victim there, then it was pretty clear. He'd kill the only other person in the bistro."

"I realize that," said Morin, drawing his chair up to her desk. "But murder's a serious business. You don't want to get it wrong. It was a massive hit to the head, right?"

Lacoste typed her password into her computer. Her husband's name. Morin was so busy consulting his notes and talking she was sure he hadn't noticed.

"I don't think that's as easy as it looks," he continued, earnestly. "I tried it last night too. Hit a cantaloupe with a hammer."

Now he had her full attention. Not only because she wanted to know what had happened, but because anyone who'd get up at two in the morning to smack a melon in the dark deserved attention. Perhaps even medical attention.

"And?"

"The first time I just grazed it. Had to hit it a few times before I got it just right. Pretty messy."

Morin wondered, briefly, what his girlfriend would think when she got up and noticed the fruit with holes smashed in it. He'd left a note, but wasn't sure that helped.

I did this, he'd written. *Experimenting.*

He perhaps should have been more explicit.

But the significance wasn't lost on Agent Lacoste. She leaned back in her chair and thought. Morin had the brains to be quiet.

"So what do you think?" she finally asked.

"I think he must have turned the lights on. But it'd be risky." Morin seemed dissatisfied. "It doesn't make sense to me. Why kill him in the bistro when you have thick forests just feet away? You could slaughter tons of people in there and no one would notice. Why do it where the body would be found and you could be seen?"

"You're right," said Lacoste. "It doesn't make sense. The Chief thinks it might have something to do with Olivier. Maybe the murderer chose the bistro on purpose."

"To implicate him?"

"Or to ruin his business."

"Maybe it was Olivier himself," said Morin. "Why not? He'd be just about the only one who could find his way around without lights. He had a key to the place—"

"Everyone had a key to the place. Seems there were sets floating all over the township, and Olivier kept one under the urn at the front door," said Lacoste.

Morin nodded and didn't seem surprised. It was still the country way, at least in the smaller villages.

"He's certainly a main suspect," said Lacoste. "But why would he kill someone in his own bistro?"

"Maybe he surprised the guy. Maybe the tramp broke in and Olivier found him and killed him in a fight," said Morin.

Lacoste was silent, waiting to see if he'd work it all the way through. Morin steepled his hands and leaned his face into them, staring into space. "But it was the middle of the night. If he saw someone in the bistro wouldn't he have called the cops, or at least woken his partner? Olivier Brulé doesn't strike me as the kind of guy who'd grab a baseball bat and rush off alone."

Lacoste exhaled and looked at Agent Morin. If the light was just right, catching this slight young man's face just so, he looked like an idiot. But he clearly wasn't.

"I know Olivier," said Lacoste, "and I'd swear he was stunned by what he'd found. He was in shock. Hard to fake and I'm pretty sure he wasn't faking it. No. When Olivier Brulé woke up yesterday morning he didn't expect to find a body in his bistro. But that doesn't mean he isn't involved somehow. Even unwittingly. The Chief wants us to find out more about Olivier. Where he was born, his background, his family, his schools, what he did before coming here. Anyone who might have a grudge against him. Someone he pissed off."

"This is more than being pissed off."

"How do you know?" asked Lacoste.

"Well, I get pissed off, and I don't kill people."

"No, you don't. But I presume you're fairly well balanced, except for that melon incident." She smiled and he reddened. "Look, it's a huge mistake to judge others by ourselves. One of the first things you learn with Chief Inspector Gamache is that other people's reactions aren't ours. And a murderer's are even more foreign. This case didn't begin with the blow to the head. It started years ago, with another sort of blow. Something happened to our murderer, something we might consider insignificant, trivial even, but was devastating to him. An event, a snub, an argument that most people would shrug off. Murderers don't. They ruminate; they gather and guard resentments. And those resentments grow. Murders are about emotions. Emotions gone bad and gone wild. Remember that. And don't ever think you know what someone else is thinking, never mind feeling."

It was the first lesson she'd been taught by Chief Inspector Gamache, and the first one she'd now passed on to her own protégé. To find a murderer you followed clues, yes. But you also followed emotions. The ones that stank, the foul and putrid ones. You followed the slime. And there, cornered, you'd find your quarry.

There were other lessons, lots of others. And she'd teach him them as well.

That's what she'd been thinking on the bridge. Thinking and worrying about. Hoping she'd be able to pass to this young man enough wisdom, enough of the tools necessary to catch a killer.

"Nathaniel," said Morin, getting up and going over to his own computer. "Your husband's name or your son's?"

"Husband," said Lacoste, a little nonplussed. He'd seen after all.

The phone rang. It was the coroner. She had to speak to Chief Inspector Gamache urgently.

TEN

At the Chief Inspector's request Marc and Dominique Gilbert were giving him a tour of their home, and now they stood in front of a room Gamache knew well. It had been the master bedroom of the old Hadley house, Timmer Hadley's room.

Two murders had happened there.

Now he looked at the closed door, with its fresh coat of gleaming white paint, and wondered what lay beyond. Dominique swung the door open and sunlight poured out. Gamache couldn't hide his surprise.

"Quite a change," said Marc Gilbert, clearly pleased with his reaction.

The room was, quite simply, stunning. They'd removed all the fretwork and googahs added over the generations. The ornate moldings, the dark mantel, the velvet drapes that kept the light at bay with their weight of dust and dread and Victorian reproach. All gone. The heavy, foreboding four-poster bed was gone.

They'd taken the room back to its basic structure, clean lines that showed off its gracious proportions. The curtains had wide stripes of of sage and gray and let the light stream through. Along the top of each of the large windows was a lintel of stained glass. Original. More than a century old. It spilled playful colors into the room. The floors, newly stained, glowed. The king-size bed had an upholstered headboard and simple, fresh, white bed linen. A fire was laid in the hearth, ready for the first guest.

"Let me show you the en suite," said Dominique.

She was tall and willowy. Mid-forties, Gamache thought, she wore jeans, a simple white shirt and her blonde hair loose. She had an air of quiet confidence and well-being. Her hands were flecked with white paint and her nails cut short.

Beside her Marc Gilbert smiled, happy to be showing off their creation. And Gamache, of all people, knew this resurrection of the old Hadley house was an act of creation.

Marc was also tall, over six feet. Slightly taller than Gamache, and about twenty pounds lighter. His hair was short, almost shaved, and it looked as though if he grew it in he'd be balding. His eyes were a piercing, buoyant blue and his manner welcoming and energetic. But while his wife was relaxed there was something edgy about Marc Gilbert. Not nervous so much as needy.

He wants my approval, thought Gamache. Not unusual really when showing off a project this important to them. Dominique pointed out the features of the bathroom, with its aqua mosaic-glass tiles, spa bath and separate walk-in shower. She was proud of their work, but she didn't seem to need him to exclaim over it.

Marc did.

It was easy to give him what he wanted. Gamache was genuinely impressed.

"And we just put this door in last week," said Marc. Opening a door from the bathroom they stepped onto a balcony. It looked out over the back of the house, across the gardens and a field beyond.

Four chairs were drawn around a table.

"I thought you could use these," a voice said from behind them and Marc hurried to take the tray from his mother. On it were four glasses of iced tea and some scones.

"Shall we?" Dominique indicated the table and Gamache held a chair for Carole.

"*Merci*," the older woman said, and sat.

"To second chances," said the Chief Inspector. He lifted his iced tea and as they toasted he watched them. The three people who'd been drawn to this sad, violated, derelict house. Who'd given it new life.

And the house had returned the favor.

"Well, there's more to do," said Marc. "But we're getting there."

"We're hoping to have our first guests by Thanksgiving," said Dominique. "If Carole would just get off her *derrière* and do some work. But so far she's refused to dig the fence posts or pour concrete."

"Perhaps this afternoon," said Carole Gilbert with a laugh.

"I noticed some antiques. Did you bring them from your home?" Gamache asked her.

Carole nodded. "We combined our belongings, but there was still a lot to buy."

"From Olivier?"

"Some." It was the most curt answer he'd received so far. He waited for more.

"We got a lovely rug from him," said Dominique. "The one in the front hall, I think."

"No, it's in the basement," said Marc, his voice sharp. He tried to soften it with a smile, but it didn't quite work.

"And a few chairs, I think," said Carole, quickly.

That would account for about one one-hundredth of the furnishings in the rambling old place. Gamache sipped his tea, looking at the three of them.

"We picked up the rest in Montreal," said Marc. "On rue Notre Dame. Do you know it?"

Gamache nodded and then listened as Marc described their treks up and down the famed street, which was packed with antique shops. Some were not much more than junk shops but some contained real finds, near priceless antiques.

"Old Mundin's repairing a few items we picked up in garage sales. Don't tell the guests," said Dominique with a laugh.

"Why didn't you get more from Olivier?"

The women concentrated on their scones and Marc poked at the ice in his drink.

"We found his prices a little high, Chief Inspector," said Dominique at last. "We'd have preferred to buy from him, but . . ."

It was left hanging, and still Gamache waited. Eventually Marc spoke.

"We were going to buy tables and beds from him. Made all the arrangements, then discovered he'd charged us almost double what he'd originally asked for them."

"Now, Marc, we don't know that for sure," said his mother.

"Near enough. Anyway, we canceled the order. You can imagine how that went down."

Dominique had been silent for most of this exchange. Now she spoke.

"I still think we should have paid it, or spoken to him quietly about it. He is our neighbor, after all."

"I don't like being screwed," said Marc.

"No one does," said Dominique, "but there are ways of handling it. Maybe we should have just paid. Now look what's happened."

"What's happened?" asked Gamache.

"Well, Olivier's one of the forces in Three Pines," said Dominique. "Piss him off and you pay a price. We don't really feel comfortable going into the village, and we sure don't feel welcome in the bistro."

"I hear you approached some of Olivier's staff," said Gamache.

Marc colored. "Who told you that? Did Olivier?" he snapped.

"Is it true?"

"What if it is? He pays them practically slave wages."

"Did any agree to come?"

Marc hesitated then admitted they hadn't. "But only because he increased their pay. We at least did that for them."

Dominique had been watching this, uncomfortable, and now she took her husband's hand. "I'm sure they were also loyal to Olivier. They seem to like him."

Marc snorted and clamped down on his anger. A man, Gamache realized, ill-equipped for not getting his own way. His wife, at least, appreciated how all this might look and had tried to appear reasonable.

"Now he's bad-mouthed us to the whole village," said Marc, not letting it go.

"They'll come around," said Carole, looking at her son with concern. "That artist couple have been nice."

"Peter and Clara Morrow," said Dominique. "Yes. I like them. She says she'd like to ride, once the horses arrive."

"And when will that be?" asked Gamache.

"Later today."

"*Vraiment?* That must be fun for you. How many?"

"Four," said Marc. "Thoroughbreds."

"Actually, I believe you've changed that slightly, haven't you?" Carole turned to her daughter-in-law.

"Really? I thought you wanted thoroughbreds," said Marc to Dominique.

"I did, but then I saw some hunters and thought since we lived in the country that seemed appropriate." She looked at Gamache once again. "Not that I plan to hunt. It's a breed of horse."

"Used for jumping," he said.

"You ride?"

"Not at that level, but I enjoyed it. Haven't been on a horse in years now."

"You'll have to come," said Carole, though they all knew he almost certainly wasn't going to squeeze himself into a pair of jodhpurs and climb onto a hunter. But he did smile as he imagined what Gabri would make of that invitation.

"What're their names?" asked Marc.

Dominique hesitated and her mother-in-law jumped in. "It's so hard to remember, isn't it? But wasn't one called Thunder?"

"Yes, that's right. Thunder, Trooper, Trojan and what was the other one?" She turned back to Carole.

"Lightning."

"Really? Thunder and Lightning?" asked Marc.

"Brothers," said Dominique.

Their iced teas finished and the scones only crumbs they got to their feet and walked back into the house.

"Why did you move here?" Gamache asked, as they walked down to the main floor.

"*Pardon?*" asked Dominique.

"Why did you move to the country and to Three Pines in particular? It's not exactly easy to find."

"We like that."

"You don't want to be found?" asked Gamache. His voice held humor, but his eyes were sharp.

"We wanted peace and quiet," said Carole.

"We wanted a challenge," said her son.

"We wanted a change. Remember?" Dominique turned to her husband then back to Gamache. "We both had fairly high-powered jobs in Montreal, but were tired. Burned out."

"That's not really true," protested Marc.

"Well, pretty close. We couldn't go on. Didn't want to go on."

She left it at that. She could understand Marc's not wanting to admit what'd happened. The insomnia, the panic attacks. Having to pull the car over on the Ville Marie Expressway to catch his breath. Having to pry his hands off the steering wheel. He was losing his grip.

Day after day he'd gone into work like that. Weeks, months. A year. Until he'd finally admitted to Dominique how he felt. They'd gone away for a weekend, their first in years, and talked.

While she wasn't having panic attacks, she was feeling something else. A growing emptiness. A sense of futility. Each morning she woke up and had to convince herself that what she did mattered. Advertising.

It was a harder and harder sell.

Then Dominique had remembered something long buried and forgotten. A dream since childhood. To live in the country and have horses.

She'd wanted to run an inn. To welcome people, to mother them. They had no children of their own, and she had a powerful need to nurture. So they'd left Montreal, left the demands of jobs too stressful, of lives too callow. They'd come to Three Pines, with their bags of money, to heal first themselves. Then others.

They'd certainly healed this wound of a house.

"We saw an ad for this place in the *Gazette* one Saturday, drove down and bought it," said Dominique.

"You make it sound simple," said Gamache.

"It was, really, once we decided what we wanted."

And looking at her, Gamache could believe it. She knew something powerful, something most people never learned. That people made their own fortune.

It made her formidable.

"And you, madame?" Gamache turned to Carole Gilbert.

"Oh, I've been retired for a while."

"In Quebec City, I understand."

"That's correct. I quit work and moved there after my husband died."

"*Désolé.*"

"No need to be. It was many years ago. But when Marc and Dominique invited me here I thought it sounded like fun."

"You were a nurse? That will come in handy in a spa."

"I hope not," she laughed. "Not planning on hurting people, are you?" she asked Dominique. "God help anyone who asks for my help."

They strolled once more into the living room and the Chief Inspector stopped by the floor-to-ceiling windows, then turned into the room.

"Thank you for the tour. And the tea. But I do have some questions for you."

"About the murder in the bistro," said Marc, and stepped slightly closer to his wife. "It seems so out of character for this village, to have a murder."

"You'd think so, wouldn't you?" said Gamache, and wondered if anyone had told them the history of their own home. Probably wasn't in the real estate agent's description.

"Well, to begin with, have you seen any strangers around?"

"Everyone's a stranger," said Carole. "We know most of the villagers by now, at least to nod to, but this weekend the place is filled with people we've never seen."

"This man would be hard to miss; he'd have looked like a tramp, a vagrant."

"No, I haven't seen anyone like that," said Marc. "Mama, have you?"

"Nobody."

"Where were you all on Saturday night and early Sunday morning?"

"Marc, I think you went to bed first. He usually does. Dominique and I watched the *Téléjournal on Radio-Canada* then went up."

"About eleven, wouldn't you think?" Dominique asked.

"Did any of you get up in the night?"

"I did," said Carole. "Briefly. To use the washroom."

"Why're you asking us this?" Dominique asked. "The murder happened down in the bistro. It has nothing to do with us."

Gamache turned around and pointed out the window. "That's why I'm asking."

They looked. Down in the village a few cars were being packed up. People were hugging, reluctant children were being called off the village green. A young woman was walking briskly up rue du Moulin, in their direction.

"You're the only place in Three Pines with a view over the whole village, and the only place with a direct view into the bistro. If the murderer turned on the lights, you'd have seen."

"Our bedrooms are at the back," Dominique pointed out. Gamache had already noted this in the tour.

"True. But I was hoping one of you might suffer from insomnia."

"Sorry, Chief Inspector. We sleep like the dead here."

Gamache didn't mention that the dead in the old Hadley house had never rested well.

The doorbell rang just then and the Gilberts started slightly, not expecting anyone. But Gamache was. He'd noted Agent Lacoste's progress round the village green and up rue du Moulin.

Something had happened.

"May I see you in private?" Isabelle Lacoste asked the Chief after she'd been introduced. The Gilberts took the cue. After watching them disappear Agent Lacoste turned to Gamache.

"The coroner called. The victim wasn't killed in the bistro."

ELEVEN

Myrna knocked softly on the bistro door, then opened it.

"You okay?" she asked softly into the dim light. It was the first time since she'd lived in Three Pines she'd seen the bistro dark during the day. Even at Christmas Olivier opened.

Olivier was sitting in an armchair, staring. He looked over at her and smiled.

"I'm fine."

"Ruth's FINE? Fucked up, Insecure, Neurotic and Egotistical?"

"That's about right."

Myrna sat across from him and offered a mug of tea she'd brought from her bookshop. Strong, hot, with milk and sugar. Red Rose. Nothing fancy.

"Like to talk?"

She sat quietly, watching her friend. She knew his face, had seen the tiny changes over the years. The crow's-feet appear at his eyes, the fine blond hair thin. What hadn't changed, from what she could tell, was what was invisible, but even more obvious. His kind heart, his thoughtfulness. He was the first to bring soup to anyone ill. To visit in the hospital. To read out loud to someone too weak and tired and near the end to do it for themselves. Gabri, Myrna, Clara, they all organized villagers to help, and when they arrived they'd find Olivier already there.

And now it was their turn to help him.

"I don't know if I want to open again."

Myrna sipped her tea and nodded. "That's understandable. You've been hurt. It must've been a terrible shock to see him here. I know it was for me, and it's not my place."

You have no idea, thought Olivier. He didn't say anything, but stared out the window. He saw Chief Inspector Gamache and Agent Lacoste walking down rue du Moulin from the old Hadley house. He prayed they kept going. Didn't come in here. With their keen eyes and sharp questions.

"I wonder if I should just sell. Move on."

This surprised Myrna, but she didn't show it. "Why?" she asked, softly.

He shook his head and dropped his eyes to his hands, resting in his lap.

"Everything's changing. Everything's changed. Why can't it be like it always was? They took my fireplace pokers, you know. I think Gamache thinks I did it."

"I'm sure he doesn't. Olivier, look at me." She spoke forcefully to him. "It doesn't matter what he thinks. We know the truth about you. And you need to know something about us. We love you. Do you think we come here every day for the food?"

He nodded and smiled slightly. "You mean it wasn't for the croissants? The red wine? Not even the chocolate torte?"

"Well, yes, okay. Maybe the torte. Listen, we come here because of you. You're the attraction. We love you, Olivier."

Olivier raised his eyes to hers. He hadn't realized, until that moment, that he'd always been afraid their affection was conditional. He was the owner of the bistro, the only one in town. They liked him for the atmosphere and welcome. The food and drink. That was the boundary of their feelings for him. They liked him for what he gave to them. Sold to them.

Without the bistro, he was nothing to them.

How'd Myrna know something he hadn't even admitted to himself? As he looked at her she smiled. She was wearing her usual flamboyant caftan. For her birthday coming up Gabri had made her a winter caftan, out of flannel. Olivier imagined her in it in her store. A big, warm ball of flannel.

The world, which had been closing in on him for days, released a bit of its grip.

"We're going to the Brume County Fair. Last day. What do you say? Can we interest you in cotton candy, cream soda, and a bison burger? I hear Wayne's showing his litter of suckling pigs this afternoon. I know how you love a good piglet."

Once, just once, at the annual county fair he'd hurried them over to the pig stalls to look at the babies. And now he was the piglet guy. Still, he quite liked being thought of as that. And it was true, he loved pigs. He had a lot in common with them, he suspected. But he shook his head.

"Not up to it, I'm afraid. But you go along. Bring me back a stuffed animal."

"Would you like company here? I can stay."

And he knew she meant it. But he needed to be alone.

"Thanks, but I really am Fucked up, Insecure, Neurotic and Egotistical."

"Well, as long as you're fine," said Myrna, getting up. After years as a psychologist she knew how to listen to people. And how to leave them alone.

He watched through the window as Myrna, Peter, Clara, Ruth and the duck Rosa got in the Morrows' car. They waved at him and he waved merrily back. Myrna didn't wave. She just nodded. He dropped his hand, caught her eye, and nodded.

He believed her when she'd said they loved him. But he also knew they loved a man who didn't exist. He was a fiction. If they knew the real Olivier they'd kick him out, of their lives and probably the village.

As their car chugged up the hill toward the Brume County Fair he heard the words again. From the cabin hidden in the woods. He could smell the wood smoke, the dried herbs. And he could see the Hermit. Whole. Alive. Afraid.

And he heard again the story. That wasn't, Olivier knew, just a story.

Once upon a time a Mountain King watched over a treasure. He buried it deep and it kept him company for millennia. The other gods were jealous and angry, and warned him if he didn't share his treasure with them they'd do something terrible.

But the Mountain King was the mightiest of the gods, so he simply laughed knowing there was nothing they could do to him. No attack he couldn't repulse, and redouble onto them. He was invincible. He prepared for their attack. Waited for it. But it never came.

Nothing came. Ever.

Not a missile, not a spear, not a war horse, or rider, or dog, or bird. Not a seed in the wind. Not even the wind.

Nothing. Ever. Again.

It was the silence that got to him first, and then the touch. Nothing touched him. No breeze brushed his rocky surface. No ant crawled over him, no bird touched down. No worm tunneled.

He felt nothing.

Until one day a young man came.

Olivier brought himself back to the bistro, his body tense, his muscles strained. His fingernails biting into his palms.

Why, he asked himself for the millionth time. Why had he done it?

Before leaving to see the coroner, the Chief Inspector walked over to the large piece of paper tacked to the wall of their Incident Room. In bold red letters Inspector Beauvoir had written:

WHO WAS THE VICTIM?
WHY WAS HE KILLED?
WHO KILLED HIM?
WHAT WAS THE MURDER WEAPON?

With a sigh the Chief Inspector added two more lines.

WHERE WAS HE MURDERED?
WHY WAS HE MOVED?

So far in their investigation they'd found more questions than clues. But that's where answers came from. Questions. Gamache was perplexed, but not dissatisfid.

Jean Guy Beauvoir was already waiting for him when he arrived at the Cowansville hospital, and they went in together, down the stairs and into the basement, where files and dead people were kept.

"I called as soon as I realized what I was seeing," said Dr. Harris after greeting them. She led them into the sterile room, brightly lit by fluorescents. The dead man was naked on a steel gurney. Gamache wished they'd put a blanket over him. He seemed cold. And, indeed, he was.

"There was some internal bleeding but not enough. This wound," she indicated the collaped back of the victim's head, "would have bled onto whatever surface he fell on."

"There was almost no blood on the floor of the bistro," said Beauvoir.

"He was killed somewhere else," said the coroner, with certainty.

"Where?" asked Gamache.

"Would you like an address?"

"If you wouldn't mind," said the Chief Inspector, with a smile.

Dr. Harris smiled back. "Clearly I don't know, but I've found some things that might be suggestive."

She walked over to her lab table where a few vials sat, labeled. She handed one to the Chief Inspector.

"Remember that bit of white I said was in the wound? I thought it might be ash. Or bone, or perhaps even dandruff. Well, it wasn't any of those things."

Gamache needed his glasses to see the tiny white flake inside the vial, then he read the label.

Paraffin, found in the wound.

"Paraffin? Like wax?"

"Yes, it's commonly called paraffin wax. It's an old-fashioned material, as you probably know. Used to be used for candles, then it was replaced by other sorts of more stable wax."

"My mother uses it for pickling," said Beauvoir. "She melts it on the top of the jar to create a seal, right?"

"That's right," said Dr. Harris.

Gamache turned to Beauvoir. "And where was your mother on Saturday night?"

Beauvoir laughed. "The only one she ever threatens to brain is me. She's no threat to society at large."

Gamache handed the vial back to the coroner. "Do you have any theories?"

"It was buried deep enough in the wound to have been either on the man's head before he was killed or on the murder weapon."

"A jar of pickles?" asked Beauvoir.

"Stranger things have been used," said Gamache, though he couldn't quite think of any.

Beauvoir shook his head. Had to be an Anglo. Who else could turn a dill pickle into a weapon?

"So it wasn't a fireplace poker?" asked Gamache.

"Unless it was a very clean one. There was no evidence of ash. Just that." She nodded to the vial. "There's something else." Dr. Harris pulled a lab chair up to the bench. "On the back of his clothes we found this. Very faint, but there."

She handed Gamache the lab report and pointed to a line. Gamache read.

"Acrylic polyurethane and aluminum oxide. What is that?"

"Varathane," said Beauvoir. "We've just redone our floors. It's used to seal them after they've been sanded."

"Not just floors," said Dr. Harris, taking back the vial. "It's used in a lot of woodworking. It's a finish. Other than the wound to the head the dead man was in good condition. Could've expected to live for twenty-five or thirty years."

"I see he had a meal a few hours before he was killed," said Gamache, reading the autopsy report

"Vegetarian. Organic I think. I'm having it tested," said the coroner. "A healthy vegetarian meal. Not your usual vagrant dinner."

"Someone might've had him in for dinner then killed him," said Beauvoir.

Dr. Harris hesitated. "I considered that, and it's a possibility."

"But?" said Gamache.

"But he looks like a man who ate like that all the time. Not just the once."

"So either he cooked for himself and chose a healthy diet," said Gamache, "or he had someone cook for him and they were vegetarian."

"That's about it," said the coroner.

"I see no alcohol or drugs," said Beauvoir, scanning the report.

Dr. Harris nodded. "I don't think he was homeless. I'm not sure if anyone cared for this man, but I do know he cared for himself."

What a wonderful epitaph, thought Gamache. He cared for himself.

"Maybe he was a survivalist," said Beauvoir. "You know, one of those kooks who take off from the city and hide in the woods thinking the world's coming to an end."

Gamache turned to look at Beauvoir. That was an interesting thought.

"I'm frankly puzzled," said the coroner. "You can see he was hit with a single, catastrophic blow to the back of his head. That in itself is unusual. To find just one blow . . ." Dr. Harris's voice trailed off and she shook her head. "Normally when someone gets up the nerve to bludgeon someone to death they're in the grip of great emotion. It's like a brainstorm. They're hysterical and can't stop. You get multiple blows. A single one like this . . ."

"What does it tell you?" Gamache asked, as he stared at the collapsed skull.

"This wasn't just a crime of passion." She turned to him. "There was passion, yes, but there was also planning. Whoever did this was in a rage. But he was in command of that rage."

Gamache lifted his brows. That was rare, extremely rare. And disconcerting. It would be like trying to master a herd of wild stallions, thundering and rearing, nostrils flared and hooves churning.

Who could control that?

Their murderer could.

Beauvoir looked at the Chief and the Chief looked at Beauvoir. This wasn't good.

Gamache turned back to the cold body on the cold gurney. If he was a survivalist, it hadn't worked. If this man had feared the end of the world he hadn't run far enough, hadn't buried himself deep enough in the Canadian wilderness.

The end of the world had found him.

TWELVE

⁓

Dominique Gilbert stood beside her mother-in-law and looked down the dirt road. Every now and then they had to step aside as a carful of people headed out of Three Pines, to the last day of the fair or into the city early to beat the rush.

It wasn't toward Three Pines they gazed, but away from it. Toward the road that led to Cowansville. And the horses.

It still surprised Dominique that she should have so completely forgotten her childhood dream. Perhaps, though, it wasn't surprising since she'd also dreamed of marrying Keith from the Partridge Family and being discovered as one of the little lost Romanov girls. Her fantasy of having horses disappeared along with all the other unlikely dreams, replaced by board meetings and clients, by gym memberships and increasingly expensive clothing. Until finally her cup, overflowing, had upended and all the lovely promotions and vacations and spa treatments became insubstantial. But at the bottom of that cup filled with goals, objectives, targets, one last drop remained.

Her dream. A horse of her own.

As a girl she'd ridden. With the wind in her hair and the leather reins light in her hands she'd felt free. And safe. The staggering worries of an earnest little girl forgotten.

Years later, when dissatisfaction had turned to despair, when her spirit had grown weary, when she could barely get out of bed in the morning, the dream had reappeared. Like the cavalry, like the Royal Canadian Mounted Police, riding to her rescue.

Horses would save her. Those magnificent creatures who so loved their riders they charged into battle with them, through explosions, through terror, through shrieking men and shrieking weapons. If their rider urged them forward, they went.

Who could not love that?

Dominique had awoken one morning knowing what had to be done. For their sanity. For their souls. They had to quit their jobs, buy a home in the country. And have horses.

As soon as they'd bought the old Hadley house and Roar was working on the barn Dominique had gone to find her horses. She'd spent months researching the perfect breed, the perfect temperaments. The height, weight, color even. Palomino, dapple? All the words from childhood came back. All the pictures torn from calendars and taped to her wall next to Keith Partridge. The black horse with the white socks, the mighty, rearing gray stallion, the Arabian, noble, dignified, strong.

Finally Dominique settled on four magnificent hunters. Tall, shining, two chestnut, a black and one that was all white.

"I hear a truck," said Carole, taking her daughter-in-law's hand and holding it lightly. Like reins.

A truck hove into view. Dominique waved. The truck slowed, then followed her directions into the yard and stopped next to the brand new barn.

Four horses were led from the van, their hooves clunking on the wooden ramp. When they were all standing in the yard the driver walked over to the women, tossing a cigarette onto the dirt and grinding it underfoot.

"You need to sign, madame." He held the clipboard out between them. Dominique reached for it and barely taking her eyes off the horses she signed her name then gave the driver a tip.

He took it then looked from the two bewildered women to the horses.

"You sure you want to keep 'em?"

"I'm sure, thank you," said Dominique with more confidence than she felt. Now that they were actually there, and the dream was a reality, she realized she had no real idea what to do with a horse. Never mind four of them. The driver seemed to sympathize.

"Want me to put them in their stalls?"

"No, that's fine. We can do it. *Merci.*" She wanted him to leave, quickly. To not witness her uncertainty, her bumbling, her ineptness. Dominique Gilbert wasn't used to blundering, but she suspected she was about to become very familiar with it.

The driver reversed the empty van and drove away. Carole turned to Dominique and said, "Well, *ma belle*, I suspect we can't do any worse than their last owners."

As the van headed back to Cowansville they caught a glimpse of the word stenciled on the back door. In bold, black letters, so there could be no doubt. *Abattoir.* Then the two women turned back to the four sorry animals in front of them. Matted, walleyed, swaybacked. Hooves overgrown and coats covered in mud and sores.

"*'Twould ring the bells of Heaven,*" whispered Carole.

Dominique didn't know about the bells of Heaven, but her head was ringing. What had she done? She moved forward with a carrot and offered it to the first horse. A broken-down old mare named Buttercup. The horse hesitated, not used to kindness. Then she took a step toward Dominique and with large, eloquent lips she picked the sweet carrot from the hand.

Dominique had canceled her purchase of the magnificent hunters and had decided to buy horses destined for slaughter. If she was expecting them to save her, the very least she could do was save them first.

An hour and a half later Dominique, Carole and the four horses were still standing in front of the barn. But now they'd been joined by a vet.

"Once they're bathed you'll need to rub this into their sores." He handed Dominique a bucket of ointment. "Twice a day, in the morning and at night."

"Can they be ridden?" Carole asked, holding the halter of the largest horse. Privately she suspected it wasn't a horse at all, but a moose. Its name was Macaroni.

"*Mais, oui.* I'd encourage it." He was walking round them again, his large, sure hands going over the sorry beasts. "*Pauvre cheval,*" he whispered into the ear of the old mare, Buttercup, her mane almost all fallen out, her tail wispy and her coat bedraggled. "They need exercise, they need good food and water. But mostly they need attention."

The vet was shaking his head as he finished his examinations.

"The good news is there's nothing terminally wrong with them. Left to rot in muddy fields and bitter cold barns. Never groomed. Neglected. But this one." He approached the tall, walleyed dark horse, who shied away. The vet waited and approached again quietly, making soothing sounds until the horse settled. "This one was abused. You can see it." He pointed to the scars on the horse's flanks. "He's afraid. What's his name?"

Dominique consulted the bill from the abattoir, then looked at Carole.

"What is it?" the older woman asked, walking over to read the bill as well. "Oh," she said, then looked at the vet. "Can a horse's name be changed?"

"Normally I'd say yes, but not this one. He needs some continuity. They get used to their names. Why?"

"His name's Marc."

"I've heard worse," said the vet, packing up.

The two women exchanged glances. So far Marc, her husband, not the horse, had no idea Dominique had canceled the hunters in favor of these misfits. He almost certainly wouldn't be happy. She'd been hoping he wouldn't notice, and if she gave them mighty, masculine names like Thunder and Trooper he might not care. But he'd certainly notice a half-blind, scarred and scared old wreck named Marc.

"Ride them as soon as you can," said the vet from his car. "Just walk at first until they get their strength back." He gave the two women a warm smile. "You'll be fine. Don't worry. These are four lucky horses."

And he drove off.

"*Oui*," said Carole, "until we saddle the wrong end."

"I think the saddle goes in the middle," said Dominique.

"*Merde*," said Carole.

The Sûreté was out for blood. If the victim hadn't been murdered in the bistro he was killed somewhere else, and they needed to find the crime scene. Blood, and quite a bit of it, had been spilled. And while the murderer had had two days to clean up, blood stained. Blood stuck. It would be almost impossible to completely erase the evidence of this brutal murder. Every home, every business, every shed, every barn, garage, kennel in and around Three Pines was scoured. Jean Guy Beauvoir coordinated it, sending teams of Sûreté officers throughout the village and into the countryside. He stayed in the Incident Room and received their reports, guiding them, occasionally chastising them, his patience eroding as the negative reports flowed in.

Nothing.

No sign of a murder scene or a murder weapon. Not even at the old Hadley house, whose new floors proved bloodless. The lab tests had come back on Olivier's pokers, confirming neither was the weapon. It was still out there, somewhere.

They did find Guylaine's missing boots, and a root cellar under Monsieur Béliveau's house, long overgrown and abandoned, but still housing pickled beets and cider. There was a squirrel's nest in Ruth's attic, not perhaps surprisingly, and suspicious seeds in Myrna's mudroom that turned out to be hollyhock.

Nothing.

"I'll widen the search area," said Beauvoir to the Chief, over the phone.

"Probably a good idea." But Gamache didn't sound convinced.

Through the receiver Beauvoir could hear bells and music and laughter.

Armand Gamache was at the fair.

The Brume County Fair was more than a century old, bringing people in from all over the townships. Like most fairs it had started as a meeting place for farmers, to show their livestock, to sell their autumn produce, to make deals and see friends. There was judging in one barn and displays of handicraft in another. Baking was for sale in the long aisles of open sheds and children lined up for licorice and maple syrup candy, popcorn and freshly made doughnuts.

It was the last celebration of summer, the bridge into autumn.

Armand Gamache walked past the rides and hawkers, then consulted his watch. It was time. He made for a field to the side of the barns, where a crowd had gathered. For the Wellington Boot Toss.

Standing on the edge of the field he watched as kids and adults lined up. The young man in charge settled them down, gave them each an old rubber boot, and standing well back he raised his arm. And held it there.

The tension was almost unbearable.

Then like an ax he dropped it.

The line of people raised their arms in unison and shot them forward, and to whoops of encouragement from onlookers a storm of Wellington boots was released.

Gamache knew in that instant why he'd gotten such an unexpectedly good spot at the side of the field. At least three boots shot his way.

He turned and hunched his back, instinctively bringing his arm up to protect his head. With a series of thuds the boots landed around him, but not on him.

The young man in charge ran over.

"You okay?"

He had curly brown hair that shone auburn in the sun. His face was tanned and his eyes a deep blue. He was stunningly handsome, and pissed off.

"You shouldn't be standing there. I thought for sure you'd move."

Gamache was treated to the look of someone recognizing they were in the presence of immeasurable stupidity.

"*C'était ma faute*," admitted Gamache. "Sorry. I'm looking for Old Mundin."

"That's me."

Gamache stared at the flushed and handsome young man.

"And you're Chief Inspector Gamache." He stuck out his hand, large and calloused. "I've seen you around Three Pines. Didn't your wife take part in the clog dancing on Canada Day?"

Gamache could barely look away from this young man, so full of vigor and light. He nodded.

"Thought so. I was one of the fiddlers. You're looking for me?"

Behind Old Mundin more people were forming up and looking in his direction. He glanced at them, but seemed relaxed.

"I'd like to talk, when you have a moment."

"Sure. We have a couple more heats, then I can leave. Want to try?"

He offered Gamache one of the boots that had almost brained him.

"What do I do?" asked Gamache as he took the boot and followed Mundin to the line.

"It's a Wellington Boot Toss," said Old Mundin, with a laugh. "I think you can figure it out."

Gamache smiled. This perhaps wasn't his brightest day. He took his place beside Clara and noticed Old Mundin jog down the line to a beautiful young woman and a child who'd be about six. He knelt down and handed the boy a small boot.

"Charles," said Clara. "His son."

Gamache looked again. Charles Mundin was also beautiful. He laughed and turned the wrong way, and with patience his parents got him sorted out. Old Mundin kissed his son and jogged back to the line.

Charles Mundin, Gamache saw, had Down syndrome.

"Ready?" called Mundin, raising his arm. "Set."

Gamache gripped his boot and glanced down the line at Peter and Clara, staring intently ahead of them.

"Toss!"

Gamache swung up his arm and felt his boot whack his back. Then he sliced forward, losing his grip on the muddy boot. It headed sideways to land about two feet ahead of him and to the side.

Clara's grip, while stronger, didn't last much longer, and her boot went almost straight up into the air.

"Fore!" everyone yelled and as one they reeled back, straining to see as it plunged toward them out of the blinding sun.

It hit Peter. Fortunately it was a tiny, pink child's boot and bounced off him without effect. Behind Gamache, Gabri and Myrna were taking bets how long it would take Clara to come up with an excuse and what it would be.

"Ten dollars on 'The boot was wet,'" said Myrna.

"Nah, she used that last year. How about 'Peter walked into it'?"

"You're on."

Clara and Peter joined them. "Can you believe they gave me a wet boot again?"

Gabri and Myrna hooted with laughter and Clara, smiling broadly, caught Gamache's eye. Money changed hands. She leaned into Gamache and whispered, "Next year I'm saying Peter leaned into it. Put some money down."

"Suppose you don't hit him?"

"But I always do," she said earnestly. "He leans into it, you know."

"I had heard."

Myrna waved across the field to Ruth, limping along with Rosa beside her. Ruth gave her the finger. Charles Mundin, seeing this, waved, giving everyone the finger.

"Ruth doesn't do the Wellington Boot Toss?" asked Gamache.

"Too much like fun," said Peter. "She came to find children's clothing in the craft barn."

"Why?"

"Who knows why Ruth does anything," said Myrna. "Any headway with the investigation?"

"Well, there was one important finding," said Gamache, and everyone crowded even closer around him. Even Ruth limped over. "The coroner says the dead man wasn't killed in the bistro. He was killed somewhere else and taken there."

He could hear the midway clearly now, and hawkers promising huge stuffed toys if you shot a tin duck. Bells jingled to call attention to games and the ring announcer warned people the horse show was about to start. But from his audience there was silence. Until finally Clara spoke.

"That's great news for Olivier, isn't it?"

"You mean it makes him less of a suspect?" said Gamache. "I suppose. But it raises a lot more questions."

"Like how'd the body get into the bistro," said Myrna.

"And where he was killed," said Peter.

"We're searching the village. House by house."

"You're what?" asked Peter. "Without our permission?"

"We have warrants," said Gamache, surprised by Peter's vehement reaction.

"It's still a violation of our privacy. You knew we'd be back, you could've waited."

"I could have, but chose not to. These weren't social calls, and frankly your feelings are secondary."

"Apparently our rights are too."

"That's not accurate." The Chief Inspector spoke firmly. The more heated Peter became the calmer Gamache grew. "We have warrants. Your right to privacy I'm afraid ended when someone took a life in your village. We're not the ones who've violated your rights, the murderer is. Don't forget that. You need to help us, and that means stepping aside and letting us do our work."

"Letting you search our homes," said Peter. "How would you feel?"

"I wouldn't feel good about it either," admitted Gamache. "Who would? But I hope I'd understand. This has just begun, you know. It's going to get worse. And before it's over we'll know where everything is hidden."

He looked sternly at Peter.

Peter saw the closed door into his studio. He imagined Sûreté officers opening it. Flicking on the light switch. Going into his most private space. The place he kept his art. The place he kept his heart. His latest work was in there, under a sheet. Hiding. Away from critical eyes.

But now strangers would have opened that door, lifted that veil and seen it. What would they think?

"So far we haven't found anything, except, I understand, Guylaine's missing boots."

"So you found them," said Ruth. "The old bitch accused me of stealing them."

"They were found in the hedge between her place and yours," said Gamache.

"Imagine that," said Ruth.

Gamache noticed the Mundins standing on the edge of the field, waiting for him. "Excuse me."

He walked briskly to the young couple and their son and joined them as they walked to the stall Old Mundin had set up. It was full of furniture, hand made. A person's choices were always revealing, Gamache found. Mundin chose to make furniture, fine furniture. Gamache's educated eye skimmed the tables, cabinets and chairs. This was painstaking, meticulous work. All the joints dovetailed together without nails; the details were beautifully inlaid, the finishes smooth. Faultless. Work like this took time and patience. And the young carpenter could never, ever be paid what these tables, chairs, dressers were worth.

And yet Old Mundin chose to do it anyway. Unusual for a young man these days.

"How can we help?" The Wife asked, smiling warmly. She had very dark hair, cut short to her head, and large, thoughtful, eyes. Her clothing was layered and looked both comfortable and bohemian. An earth mother, thought Gamache, married to a carpenter.

"I have a few questions, but tell me about your furniture. It's beautiful."

"*Merci*," said Mundin. "I spend most of the year making pieces to sell at the fair."

Gamache ran his large hand over the smooth surface of a chest of drawers. "Lovely polish. Paraffin?"

"Not unless we want them to burst into flames," laughed Old. "Paraffin's highly flammable."

"Varathane?"

Old Mundin's beautiful face crinkled in a smile. "You are perhaps mistaking us for Ikea. Easy to do," he joked. "No, we use beeswax."

We, thought Gamache. He'd watched this young couple for just a few minutes but it seemed clear they were a team.

"Do you sell much at the fair?" he asked.

"This's all we have left," The Wife said, indicating the few exquisite pieces around them.

"They'll be gone by the end of the fair tonight," said Old Mundin. "Then I need to get going again. Fall's a great time of year to get into the forests and find wood. I do most of my woodwork through the winter."

"I'd like to see your workshop."

"Any time."

"How about now?"

Old Mundin stared at his visitor and Gamache stared back.

"Now?"

"Is that a problem?"

"Well . . ."

"It's okay, Old," said The Wife. "I'll watch the booth. You go."

"Is it okay if we take Charles?" Old asked Gamache. "It's hard for The Wife to watch him and look after customers."

"I insist he comes along," said Gamache, holding out his hand to the boy, who took it without hesitation. A small shard stabbed Gamache's heart as he realized how precious this boy was, and would always be. A child who lived in a perpetual state of trust.

And how hard it would be for his parents to protect him.

"He'll be fine," Gamache assured The Wife.

"Oh, I know he'll be. It's you I worry about," she said.

"I'm sorry," said Gamache, reaching out to shake her hand. "I don't know your name."

"My actual name is Michelle, but everyone calls me The Wife."

Her hand was rough and calloused, like her husband's, but her voice was cultured, full of warmth. It reminded him a little of Reine-Marie's.

"Why?" he asked.

"It started out as a joke between us and then it took. Old and The Wife. It somehow fits."

And Gamache agreed. It did fit this couple, who seemed to live in their own world, with their own beautiful creations.

"Bye." Charles gave his mother the new one-fingered wave.

"Old," she scolded.

"Wasn't me," he protested. But he didn't rat on Ruth, Gamache noticed.

Old strapped his son into the van and they drove out of the fair parking lot.

"Is 'Old' your real name?"

"I've been called 'Old' all my life, but my real name is Patrick."

"How long have you lived here?"

"In Three Pines? A few years." He thought for a moment. "My God, it's been eleven years. Can hardly believe it. Olivier was the first person I met."

"How do people feel about him?"

"Don't know about 'people,' but I know how I feel. I like Olivier. He's always fair with me."

"But not with everyone?" Gamache had noticed the inflection.

"Some people don't know the value of what they've got." Old Mundin was concentrating on the road, driving carefully. "And lots of people just want to stir up trouble. They don't like being told their antique chest is really just old. Not valuable at all. Pisses them off. But Olivier knows what he's doing. Lots of people set up antique businesses here, but not many really know what they're doing. Olivier does."

After a moment or two of silence as both men watched the countryside go by, Gamache spoke. "I've always wondered where dealers find their antiques."

"Most have pickers. People who specialize in going to auctions or getting to know people in the area. Mostly elderly people who might be interested in selling. Around here if someone knocks on your door on a Sunday morning it's more likely to be an antique picker than a Jehovah's Witness."

"Does Olivier have a picker?"

"No, he does it himself. He works hard for what he gets. And he knows what's worth money and what isn't. He's good. And fair, for the most part."

"For the most part?"

"Well, he has to make a profit, and lots of the stuff needs work. He gives the old furniture to me to restore. That can be a lot of work."

"I bet you don't charge what it's worth."

"Now, worth is a relative concept." Old shot Gamache a glance as they bumped along the road. "I love what I do and if I charged a reasonable amount per hour nobody'd be able to buy my pieces, and Olivier wouldn't hire me to repair the great things he finds. So it's worth it to me to charge less. I have a good life. No complaints here."

"Has anyone been really angry at Olivier?"

Old drove in silence and Gamache wasn't sure he'd heard. But finally he spoke.

"Once, about a year ago. Old Madame Poirier, up the Mountain road, had decided to move into a nursing home in Saint-Rémy. Olivier'd been buzzing around her for a few years. When the time came she sold most of her stuff to him. He found some amazing pieces there."

"Did he pay a fair price?"

"Depends who you talk to. She was happy. Olivier was happy."

"So who was angry?"

Old Mundin said nothing. Gamache waited.

"Her kids. They said Olivier'd insinuated himself, taken advantage of a lonely old woman."

Old Mundin pulled into a small farmhouse. Hollyhocks leaned against the wall and the garden was full of black-eyed Susans and old-fashioned roses. A vegetable garden, well tended and orderly, was planted at the side of the house.

The van rolled to a halt and Mundin pointed to a barn. "That's my workshop."

Gamache unbuckled Charles from the child seat. The boy was asleep and Gamache carried him as the two men walked to the barn.

"You said Olivier made an unexpected find at Madame Poirier's place?"

"He paid her a flat fee for all the stuff she no longer needed. She chose what she wanted to keep and he bought the rest."

Old Mundin stopped at the barn door, turning to Gamache.

"There was a set of six Chippendale chairs. Worth about ten thousand each. I know, because I worked on them, but I don't think he told anyone else."

"Did you?"

"No. You'd be surprised how discreet I need to be in my work."

"Do you know if Olivier gave Madame Poirier any extra money?"

"I don't."

"But her kids were angry."

Mundin nodded curtly and opened the barn door. They stepped into a different world. All the complex aromas of the late summer farm had disappeared. Gone was the slight scent of manure, of cut grass, of hay, of herbs in the sun.

Here there was only one note—wood. Fresh sawn wood. Old barn wood. Wood of every description. Gamache looked at the walls, lined with wood waiting to be turned into furniture. Old Mundin smoothed one fine hand over a rough board.

"You wouldn't know it, but there's burled wood under there. You have to know what to look for. The tiny imperfections. Funny how imperfections on the outside mean something splendid beneath."

He looked into Gamache's eyes. Charles stirred slightly and the Chief Inspector brought a large hand up to the boy's back, to reassure him.

"I'm afraid I don't know much about wood but you seem to have different sorts. Why's that?"

"Different needs. I use maple and cherry and pine for inside work. Cedar for outside. This here's red cedar. My favorite. Doesn't look like much now, but carved and polished . . ." Mundin made an eloquent gesture.

Gamache noticed two chairs on a platform. One was upside down. "From the bistro?" He walked over to them. Sure enough one had a loose arm and the leg of the other was wobbly.

"I picked those up Saturday night."

"Is it all right to talk about what happened at the bistro in front of Charles?"

"I'm sure it is. He'll understand, or not. Either way, it's okay. He knows it's not about him."

Gamache wished more people could make that distinction. "You were there the night of the murder."

"True. I go every Saturday to pick up the damaged furniture and drop off the stuff I've restored. It was the same as always. I got there just after midnight. The last of the customers was leaving and the kids were beginning to clean up."

Kids, thought Gamache. And yet they weren't really that much younger than this man. But somehow Old seemed very, well, old.

"But I didn't see a body."

"Too bad, that would've helped. Did anything strike you as unusual at all?"

Old Mundin thought. Charles woke up and squirmed. Gamache lowered him to the barn floor where he picked up a piece of wood and turned it around and around.

"I'm sorry. I wish I could help, but it seemed like any other Saturday night."

Gamache also picked up a chunk of wood and smoothed the sawdust off it.

"How'd you start repairing Olivier's furniture?"

"Oh, that was years ago. Gave me a chair to work on. It'd been kept in a barn for years and he'd just moved it into the bistro. Now, you must understand . . ."

What followed was a passionate monologue on old Quebec pine furniture. Milk paint, the horrors of stripping, the dangers of ruining a fine piece by restoring it. That difficult line between making a piece usable and making it valueless.

Gamache listened, fascinated. He had a passion for Quebec history, and by extension Quebec antiques, the remarkable furniture made by pioneers in the long winter months hundreds of years ago. They'd made the pine furniture both practical and beautiful, pouring themselves into it. Each time Gamache touched an old table or armoire he imagined the *habitant* shaping and smoothing the wood, going over it and over it with hardened hands. And making something lovely.

Lovely and lasting, thanks to people like Old Mundin.

"What brought you to Three Pines? Why not a larger city? There'd be more work, surely, in Montreal or even Sherbrooke."

"I was born in Quebec City, and you'd think there'd be lots of work there for an antique restorer, but it's hard for a young guy starting out. I moved to Montreal, to an antique shop on Notre Dame, but I'm afraid I wasn't cut out for the big city. So I decided to go to Sherbrooke. Got in the car, headed south, and got lost. I drove into Three Pines to ask directions at the bistro, ordered *café au lait*, sat down and the chair collapsed." He laughed, as did Gamache. "I offered to repair it and that was that."

"You said you'd been here for eleven years. You must've been young when you left Quebec City."

"Sixteen. I left after my father died. Spent three years in Montreal, then down here. Met The Wife, had Charles. Started a small business."

This young man had done a lot with his eleven years, thought Gamache. "How did Olivier seem on Saturday night?"

"As usual. Labor Day's always busy but he seemed relaxed. As relaxed as he ever gets, I suppose." Mundin smiled. It was clear there was affection there. "Did I hear you say the man wasn't murdered at the bistro after all?"

Gamache nodded. "We're trying to find out where he was killed. In fact, while you were at the fair I had my people searching the whole area, including your place."

"Really?" They were at the barn door and Mundin turned to stare into the gloom. "They're either very good, or they didn't actually do anything. You can't tell."

"That's the point." But the Chief noticed that, unlike Peter, Old Mundin didn't seem at all concerned.

"Now, why would you kill someone one place, then move them to another?" asked Mundin, almost to himself. "I can see wanting to get rid of a body, especially if you killed him in your own home, but why take him to Olivier's? Seems a strange thing to do, but I guess the bistro's a fairly central location. Maybe it was just convenient."

Gamache let that statement be. They both knew it wasn't true. Indeed, the bistro was a very inconvenient place to drop a body. And it worried Gamache. The murder wasn't an accident, and the placement of the body wasn't either.

There was someone very dangerous walking among them. Someone who looked happy, thoughtful, gentle even. But it was a deceit. A mask. Gamache knew that when he found the murderer and ripped the mask off, the skin would come too. The mask had become the man. The deceit was total.

THIRTEEN

 "We had a great time at the fair. I got you this." Gabri shut the door and turned on the lights in the bistro. He offered the stuffed lion to Olivier, who took it and held it softly in his lap.

"*Merci*."

"And did you hear the news? Gamache says the dead man wasn't killed here. And we'll be getting our pokers back. I'd like to get my poker back, wouldn't you?" he asked, archly. But Olivier didn't even respond.

Gabri moved through the gloomy room, turning on lamps, then lit a fire in one of the stone hearths. Olivier continued to sit in the armchair, staring out the window. Gabri sighed, poured them each a beer and joined him. Together they sipped, ate cashews and looked out at the village, quiet now in the last of the day, and the end of the summer.

"What do you see?" asked Gabri at last.

"What d'you mean? I see what you see."

"Can't be. What I see makes me happy. And you're not happy."

Gabri was used to his partner's moods. Olivier was the quiet one, the contained one. Gabri might appear the more sensitive, but they both knew Olivier was. He felt things deeply, and kept them there. Gabri was covered in the flesh wounds of life, but Olivier's wounds were in the marrow, deep and hidden and perhaps even mortal.

But he was also the kindest man Gabri had met, and he'd met, it must be said, quite a few. Before Olivier. That had all changed as soon as he'd clapped eyes on the slim, blond, shy man.

Gabri had lost his quite considerable heart.

"What is it?" Gabri leaned forward and took Olivier's slender hands. "Tell me."

"It's just no fun anymore," said Olivier at last. "I mean, why even bother? No one's going to want to come back here. Who wants to eat in a restaurant where there's been a body?"

"As Ruth says, we're all just bodies anyway."

"Great. I'll put that in the ads."

"Well, at least you don't discriminate. Dead, predead. They're all welcome here. That might be a better slogan."

Gabri saw a quiver at the ends of Olivier's lips.

"*Voyons*, it was great news that the police say the man wasn't killed here. That makes a difference."

"You think?" Olivier looked at him hopefully.

"Do you know what I really think?" Now Gabri was dead serious. "I think it wouldn't matter. Peter, Clara, Myrna? Do you think they'd stop coming even if that poor man had been murdered here? The Parras? Monsieur Béliveau? They'd all come if a mountain of bodies was found here. Do you know why?"

"Because they like it?"

"Because they like you. They love you. Listen, Olivier, you have the best bistro, the finest food, the most comfortable place. It's brilliant. You're brilliant. Everyone loves you. And you know what?"

"What?" asked Olivier, grumpily.

"You're the kindest, most handsome man in the world."

"You're just saying that." Olivier felt like a little boy again. While other kids ran around collecting frogs and sticks and grasshoppers, he'd sought reassurance. Affection. He'd gather up the words and actions, even from strangers, and he'd stuff them into the hole that was growing.

It had worked. For a while. Then he'd needed more than just words.

"Did Myrna tell you to say that?"

"Right. It's not true at all, just a big lie cooked up by Myrna and me. What's wrong with you anyway?"

"You wouldn't understand."

Gabri followed Olivier's stare out the window. And up the hill. He sighed. They'd been through this before.

"There's nothing we can do about them. Maybe we should just—"

"Just what?" Olivier snapped.

"Are you looking for an excuse to be miserable? Is that it?"

Even by Olivier's standards that had been an unreasonable reaction.

He'd been reassured about the body, he'd been reassured that everyone still loved him. He'd been reassured that Gabri wasn't running away. So what was the problem?

"Listen, maybe we should give them a chance. Who knows? Their inn and spa might even help us."

This was not what Olivier wanted to hear. He stood abruptly, almost knocking the chair to the floor. He could feel that bloom of anger in his chest. It was like a superpower. It made him invincible. Strong. Courageous. Brutal.

"If you want to be friends with them, fine. Why don't you just fuck off?"

"I didn't mean that. I meant we can't do anything about them so we might as well be friends."

"You make this sound like kindergarten. They're out to ruin us. Do you understand? When they first came I was nice, but then they decided to steal our customers, even our staff. Do you think anyone's going to come to your tacky little B and B when they can stay there?"

Olivier's face was red and blotchy. Gabri could see it spread even under his scalp, through the thinning and struggling blond hair.

"What're you talking about? I don't care if people come, you know that. We don't need the money. I just do it for fun."

Olivier struggled to control himself now. To not take that one step too far. The two men glared so that the space between them throbbed.

"Why?" Olivier finally said.

"Why what?"

"If the dead man wasn't killed here, why was he put here?"

Gabri felt his anger lift, evaporated by the question.

"I heard from the police today," said Olivier, his voice almost monotone. "They're going to speak to my father tomorrow."

Poor Olivier, thought Gabri, he did have something to worry about after all.

Jean Guy Beauvoir got out of the car and stared across the road at the Poirier home.

It was ramshackle and in need of way more than just a coat of paint. The porch was sloping, the steps looked unsound, pieces of boarding were missing from the side of the house.

Beauvoir had been in dozens of places like this in rural Quebec. Lived in by a generation born there too. Clotilde Poirier probably drank coffee from a chipped mug her mother had used. Slept on a mattress she'd been conceived on. The walls would be covered with dried flowers and spoons sent by relatives who'd escaped to exotic places like Rimouski or Chicoutimi or Gaspé. And there'd be a chair, a rocking chair, by the window, near the woodstove. It would have a slightly soiled afghan on it and crumbs. And after clearing up the breakfast dishes Clotilde Poirier would sit there, and watch.

What would she be watching for? A friend? A familiar car? Another spoon?

Was she watching him now?

Armand Gamache's Volvo appeared over the hill and came to a stop behind Beauvoir. The two men stood and stared for a moment at the house.

"I found out about the Varathane," said Beauvoir, thinking this place could use a hundred gallons or so of the stuff. "The Gilberts didn't use it when they did the renovations. I spoke to Dominique Gilbert. She said they want to be as green as possible. After they had the floors sanded they used tung oil."

"So the Varathane on the dead man's clothing didn't come from the old Hadley house," said the Chief, disappointed. It had seemed a promising lead.

"Why're we here?" Beauvoir asked as they turned back to survey the gently subsiding home and the rusting pickup truck in the yard. He'd received a call from the Chief to meet him here, but he didn't know why.

Gamache explained what Old Mundin had said about Olivier, Madame Poirier and her furniture. Specifically the Chippendale chairs.

"So her kids think Olivier screwed her? And by extension, them?" asked Beauvoir.

"Seems so." He knocked on the door. After a moment a querulous voice called through it.

"Who is it?"

"Chief Inspector Gamache, madame. Of the Sûreté du Québec."

"I ain't done nothing wrong."

Gamache and Beauvoir exchanged glances.

"We need to speak to you, Madame Poirier. It's about the body found in the bistro in Three Pines."

"So?"

It was very difficult conducting an interview through an inch of chipping wood.

"May we come in? We'd like to talk to you about Olivier Brulé."

An elderly woman, small and slender, opened the door. She glared at them then turned and walked rapidly back into the house. Gamache and Beauvoir followed.

It was decorated as Beauvoir had imagined. Or, really, not decorated. Things were put up on the walls as they'd arrived, over the generations, so that the walls were a horizontal archaeological dig. The farther into the house they went, the more recent the items. Framed flowers, plasticized place mats, crucifixes, paintings of Jesus and the Virgin Mary, and yes, spoons, all marched across the faded floral wallpaper.

But the place was clean, spotless and smelled of cookies. Photos of grandchildren, perhaps even great-grandchildren, sat on shelves and tabletops. A faded striped tablecloth, clean and ironed, was on the kitchen table. And in the center of that table was a vase containing late summer flowers.

"Tea?" She lifted a pot from the stove. Beauvoir declined but Gamache accepted. She returned with cups of tea for them all. "Well, go on."

"We understand Olivier bought some furniture from you," said Beauvoir.

"Not just some. He bought the lot. Thank God. Gave me more than anyone else would, despite what my kids mighta told you."

"We haven't spoken to them yet," said Beauvoir.

"Neither have I. Not since selling the stuff." But she didn't seem upset. "Greedy, all of them. Waiting for me to die so they can inherit."

"How did you meet Olivier?" Beauvoir asked.

"He knocked on the door one day. Introduced himself. Asked if I had anything I'd like to sell. Sent him running the first few times." She smiled at the memory. "But there was something about him. He kept coming back. So I eventually invited him in, just for tea. He'd come about once a month, have tea, then leave."

"When did you decide to sell to him?" Beauvoir asked.

"I'm coming to that," she snapped, and Beauvoir began to appreciate how hard Olivier must have worked for that furniture.

"One winter was particularly long. Lots of snow. And cold. So I decided to hell with this, I'd sell up and move into Saint-Rémy, to that new seniors' home. So I told Olivier and we walked through the house. I showed him all that crap my parents left me. Old armoires and dressers. Big pine things. And painted all sorts of dull colors. Blues and greens. Tried to scrape it off some of them, but it was no good."

Beside him Beauvoir heard the Chief inhale, but that was the only sign of pain. Having spent years with Gamache he knew his passion for antiques, and knew that you never, ever strip old paint. It was like skinning something alive.

"So you showed it all to Olivier? What did he say?"

"Said he'd take the lot, including what was in the barn and attic without even seeing it. Tables and chairs been there since before my grandparents. Was going to send it to the dump, but my lazy sons never showed up to do it. So serves them right. I sold the lot to Olivier."

"Can you remember how much you got?"

"I remember exactly. It was three thousand two hundred dollars. Enough to pay for all of this. Sears."

Gamache looked at the legs of the table. Prefabricated wood. There was an upholstered rocker facing the new television, and a dark wood-veneer cabinet, with decorative plates.

Madame Poirier was also looking at the contents of the room, with pride.

"He came by a few weeks later and you know what he'd brought? A new bed. Plastic still on the mattress. Set it up for me too. He still comes by sometimes. He's a nice man."

Beauvoir nodded. A nice man who'd paid this elderly woman a fraction of what that furniture was worth.

"But you're not in the seniors' home? Why not?"

"After I got the new furniture the place felt different. More mine. I kinda liked it again."

She showed them to the door and Beauvoir noticed the welcome mat. Worn, but still there. They said good-bye and headed for her eldest son's place a mile down the road. A large man with a gut and stubble opened the door.

"Cops," he called into the house. It, and he, smelled of beer and sweat and tobacco.

"Claude Poirier?" Beauvoir asked. It was a formality. Who else would this man be? He was nearing sixty, and looked every moment of it. Beauvoir had taken the time before leaving the Incident Room to look up the Poirier family. To see what they were walking into.

Petty crimes. Drunk and disorderly. Shoplifting. Benefit fraud.

They were the type who took advantage, found fault, pointed fingers. Still, it didn't mean that sometimes they weren't right. Like about Olivier. He'd screwed them.

After the introductions Poirier launched into his long, sad litany. It was all Beauvoir could do to keep him focused on Olivier, so long was this man's list of people who'd done him wrong. Including his own mother.

Finally the two investigators lurched from the stale house, taking deep breaths of fresh late afternoon air.

"Do you think he did it?" asked Gamache

"He's certainly angry enough," said Beauvoir, "but unless he could transport a body to the bistro using the buttons on his remote, I think he's off the suspect list. Can't see him getting off that stinking sofa long enough."

They walked back to their cars. The Chief paused.

"What're you thinking?" Beauvoir asked.

"I was remembering what Madame Poirier said. She was about to take all those antiques to the dump. Can you imagine?"

Beauvoir could see that the thought gave Gamache actual pain.

"But Olivier saved them," said the Chief. "Strange how that works. He might not have given Madame enough money, but he gave her affection and company. What price do you put on that?"

"So, can I buy your car? I'll give you twenty hours of my company."

"Don't be cynical. One day you might be elderly and alone and you'll see."

As he followed the Chief's car back to Three Pines Beauvoir thought about that, and agreed that Olivier had saved the precious antiques, and spent time with the crabby old woman. But he could have done it and still given the old woman a fair price.

But he hadn't.

Marc Gilbert looked at Marc the horse. Marc the horse looked at Marc Gilbert. Neither seemed pleased.

"Dominique!" Marc called from the door of the barn.

"Yes?" she said, cheerily, walking across the yard from the house. She'd hoped it would take Marc a few days to find the horses. Actually, she'd hoped he never would. But that was in the same league as the Mrs. Keith Partridge dream. Unlikely at best.

And now she found him cross-armed in the dim barn.

"What are these?"

"They're horses," she said. Though, it must be said, she suspected Macaroni might be a moose.

"I can see that, but what kind? These aren't hunters, are they?"

Dominique hesitated. For an instant she wondered what would happen if she said yes. But she guessed that Marc, while not a horse expert, wouldn't buy that.

"No, they're better."

"How better?"

His sentences were getting shorter, never a good sign.

"Well, they're cheaper."

She could see that actually had a slight mollifying effect. Might as well tell him the full story. "I bought them from the slaughterhouse. They were going to be killed today."

Marc hesitated. She could see him struggling with his anger. Not trying to let it go, but trying to hold on to it. "Maybe there was a reason they were going to be . . . you know."

"Killed. No, the vet's been to see them and he says they're fine, or will be."

The barn smelled of disinfectant, soap and medication.

"Maybe physically, but you can't tell me he's okay." Marc waved at Marc the horse, who flared his nostrils and snorted. "He isn't even clean. Why not?"

Why did her husband have to be so observant? "Well, no one could get close to him." Then she had an idea. "The vet says he needs a very special touch. He'll only let someone quite exceptional near him."

"Is that right?" Marc looked at the horse again, and walked toward him. Marc, the horse, backed up. Her husband reached out his hand. The horse put his ears back, and Dominique grabbed her husband away just as Marc the horse snapped.

"It's been a long day and he's disoriented."

"Hmm," said her husband, walking with her out of the barn. "What's his name?"

"Thunder."

"Thunder," said Marc, trying the name out. "Thunder," he repeated as though riding the steed and urging him on.

Carole greeted them at the kitchen door. "So," she said to her son. "How're the horses? How's Marc?"

"I'm fine, thank you." He looked at her quizzically and took the drink she offered. "And how's Carole?"

Behind him Dominique gestured frantically at her mother-in-law who was laughing and just about to say something when she saw her daughter-in-law's motions and stopped. "Just fine. Do you like the horses?"

"Like is a strong word, as is 'horses,' I suspect."

"It'll take a while for us all to get used to each other," said Dominique. She accepted the Scotch from Carole and took a gulp. Then they walked out the French doors and into the garden.

As the two women talked, more friends than mother and daughter-in-law, Marc looked at the flowers, the mature trees, the freshly painted white fences and the rolling fields beyond. Soon the horses, or whatever they were, would be out there. Grazing.

Once again he had that hollow feeling, that slight rip as the chasm widened.

Leaving Montreal had been a wrench for Dominique, and leaving Quebec City had been difficult for his mother. They left behind friends. But while Marc had pretended to be sorry, had gone to the going-away parties, had claimed he would miss everyone, the truth was, he didn't.

They had to be part of his life for him to miss them, and they weren't. He remembered that Kipling poem his father loved, and taught him. And that one line. *If all men count with you, but none too much.*

And they hadn't. Over forty-five years not a single man had counted too much.

He had loads of colleagues, acquaintances, buddies. He was an emotional communist. Everyone counted equally, but none too much.

You'll be a man, my son. That was how the poem ended.

But Marc Gilbert, listening to the quiet conversation and looking over the rich, endless fields, was beginning to wonder if that was enough. Or even true.

The officers gathered round the conference table and Beauvoir uncapped his red Magic Marker. Agent Morin was beginning to appreciate that the small "pop" was like a starter's gun. In the short time he'd been with homicide he'd developed a fondness for the smell of marker, and that distinctive sound.

He settled into his chair, a little nervous as always, in case he should say something particularly stupid. Agent Lacoste had helped. As they'd gathered up their papers for the meeting she'd seen his trembling hands and whispered that maybe he should just listen this time.

He'd looked at her, surprised.

"Won't they think I'm an idiot? That I have nothing to say?"

"Believe me, there's no way you're going to listen yourself out of this job. Or any job. Just relax, let me do the talking today, and we'll see about tomorrow. Okay?"

He'd looked at her then, trying to figure out what her motives might be. Everyone had them, he knew. Some were driven by kindness, some not. And he'd been at the Sûreté long enough to know that most in the famous police force weren't guided by a desire to be nice.

It was brutally competitive, and nowhere more so than the scramble to get into homicide. The most prestigious posting. And the chance to work with Chief Inspector Gamache.

He was barely in, and barely hanging on. One wrong move and he'd slide right out the door, and be forgotten in an instant. He wasn't going to let that happen. And he knew, instinctively, this was a pivotal moment. Was Agent Lacoste sincere?

"All right, what've we got?"

Beauvoir was standing by the paper tacked to the wall next to a map of the village.

"We know the victim wasn't murdered at the bistro," said Lacoste. "But we still don't know where he was killed or who he was."

"Or why he was moved," said Beauvoir. He reported on their visit to the Poiriers, *mère et fils*. Then Lacoste told them what she and Morin had learned about Olivier Brulé.

"He's thirty-eight. Only child. Born and raised in Montreal. Father an executive at the railway, mother a homemaker, now dead. An affluent upbringing. Went to Notre Dame de Sion school."

Gamache raised his brows. It was a leading Catholic private school. Annie had gone there too, years after Olivier, to be taught by the rigorous nuns. His son Daniel had refused, preferring the less rigorous public schools. Annie had learned logic, Latin, problem solving. Daniel had learned to roll a spliff. Both grew into decent, happy adults.

"Olivier got an MBA from the Université de Montréal and took a job at the Banque Laurentienne," Agent Lacoste continued, reading from her notes. "He handled high-end corporate clients. Apparently very successfully too. Then he quit."

"Why?" asked Beauvoir.

"Not sure. I have a meeting at the bank tomorrow, and I've also set up an appointment with Olivier's father."

"What about his personal life?" Gamache asked.

"I talked to Gabri. They started living together fourteen years ago. Gabri's a year younger. Thirty-seven. He was a fitness instructor at the local YMCA."

"Gabri?" asked Beauvoir, remembering the large, soft man.

"Happens to the best of us," said Gamache.

"After Olivier quit the bank they gave up their apartment in Old Montreal and moved down here, took over the bistro and lived above it, but it wasn't a bistro then. It'd been a hardware store."

"Really?" asked Beauvoir. He couldn't imagine the bistro as anything else. He tried to see snow shovels and batteries and lightbulbs hanging from the exposed beams or set up in front of the two stone fireplaces. And failed.

"But listen to this." Lacoste leaned forward. "I got this by digging into the land registry records. Ten years ago Olivier bought not just his bistro, but the B and B. But he didn't stop there. He bought it all. The general store, the bakery, his bistro and Myrna's bookstore."

"Everything?" asked Beauvoir. "He owns the village?"

"Just about. I don't think anyone else knows. I spoke to Sarah at her boulangerie and to Monsieur Béliveau at the general store. They said they rented from some guy in Montreal. Long-term leases, reasonable rates. They send their checks to a numbered company."

"Olivier's a numbered company?" asked Beauvoir.

Gamache was taking all this in, listening closely.

"How much did he pay?" asked Beauvoir.

"Seven hundred and twenty thousand dollars for the lot."

"Good God," said Beauvoir. "That's a lot of bread. Where'd he get the money? A mortgage?"

"No. Paid cash."

"You say his mother's dead, maybe it was his inheritance."

"Doubt it," said Lacoste. "She only died five years ago, but I'll look into it when I'm in Montreal."

"Follow the money," said Beauvoir. It was a truism in crime investigations, particularly murder. And there was suddenly a great deal of money to follow. Beauvoir finished scribbling on his sheets on the wall, then told them about the coroner's findings.

Morin listened, fascinated. So this was how murderers were found. Not by DNA tests and petrie dishes, ultraviolet scans or anything else a lab could produce. They helped, certainly, but this was their real lab. He looked across the table to the other person who was just listening, saying nothing.

Chief Inspector Gamache took his deep brown eyes off Inspector Beauvoir for a moment and looked at the young agent. And smiled.

Agent Lacoste headed for Montreal shortly after the meeting broke up. Agent Morin left for home and Beauvoir and Gamache walked slowly back over the stone bridge and into the village. They strolled past the darkened bistro and met Olivier and Gabri on the wide veranda of the B and B.

"I left a note for you," said Gabri. "Since the bistro's closed we're all going out for dinner and you're invited."

"Peter and Clara's again?" asked Gamache.

"No. Ruth," said Gabri and was rewarded with their stunned looks. He'd have thought someone had drawn a gun on the two large Sûreté officers. Chief Inspector Gamache looked surprised but Beauvoir looked afraid.

"You might want to put on your athletic protector," Gabri whispered to Beauvoir, as they passed on the veranda steps.

"Well, I'm sure as hell not going. You?" asked Beauvoir when they went inside.

"Are you kidding? Pass up a chance to see Ruth in her natural habitat? Wouldn't miss it."

Twenty minutes later the Chief Inspector had showered, called Reine-Marie and changed into slacks, blue shirt and tie and a camel-hair cardigan. He found Beauvoir in the living room with a beer and potato chips.

"Sure you won't change your mind, *patron*?"

It was tempting, Gamache had to admit. But he shook his head.

"I'll keep a candle in the window," said Beauvoir, watching the Chief leave.

Ruth's clapboard home was a couple of houses away and faced the green. It was tiny, with a porch in front and two gables on the second floor. Gamache had been in it before, but always with his notebook out, asking questions. Never as a guest. As he entered all eyes turned and as one they made for him, Myrna reaching him first.

"For pity's sake, did you bring your gun?"

"I don't have one."

"What d'you mean, you don't have one?"

"They're dangerous. Why do you want it?"

"So you can shoot her. She's trying to kill us." Myrna grabbed Gamache's sleeve and pointed to Ruth who was circulating among her guests wearing a frilly apron and carrying a bright orange plastic tray.

"Actually," said Gabri, "she's trying to kidnap us and take us back to 1950."

"Probably the last time she entertained," said Myrna.

"Hors d'oeuvre, old fruit?" Ruth spotted her new guest and bore down upon him.

Gabri and Olivier turned to each other. "She means you."

Incredibly, she actually meant Gamache.

"Lord love a duck," said Ruth, in a very bad British accent. Behind Ruth waddled Rosa.

"She started speaking like that as soon as we arrived," said Myrna, backing away from the tray and knocking over a stack of *Times Literary Supplement*s. Gamache could see saltine crackers sliding around on the orange tray, smeared with brown stuff he hoped was peanut butter. "I remember reading something about this," Myrna continued. "People speaking in accents after a brain injury."

"Is being possessed by the devil considered a brain injury?" asked Gabri. "She's speaking in tongues."

"Cor blimey," said Ruth.

But the most striking feature of the room wasn't the hoop lamps, the teak furniture, genteel British Ruth with her dubious offering, nor was it the sofas covered in books and newspapers and magazines, as was the green shag carpet. It was the duck.

Rosa was wearing a dress.

"Duck and cover," said Gabri. "Literally."

"Our Rosa." Ruth had put down the peanut-buttered crackers and was now offering celery sticks stuffed with Velveeta.

Gamache watched and wondered if he'd have to make a couple of calls. One to the Humane Society, the other to the psych ward. But neither Rosa nor Ruth seemed upset. Unlike their guests.

"Would you like one?" Clara offered him a ball covered with what looked like seeds.

"What is it?" he asked.

"We think it's suet, for the birds," said Peter.

"And you're offering it to me?" Gamache asked.

"Well, someone should eat it so it doesn't hurt her feelings." Clara nodded to Ruth, just disappearing into the kitchen. "And we're too afraid."

"*Non, merci,*" he smiled and went in search of Olivier. As he passed the kitchen he looked in and saw Ruth opening a can. Rosa was standing on the table watching her.

"Now, we'll just open this," she mumbled. "Maybe we should smell it? What do you think?"

The duck didn't seem to be thinking anything. Ruth smelled the open can anyway. "Good enough."

The old poet wiped her hands on a towel then reached out and lifted the edge of Rosa's dress to replace a ruffled feather, smoothing it down.

"May I help?" Gamache asked from the door.

"Well, aren't you a love."

Gamache winced, expecting her to throw a cleaver after that. But she just smiled and handed him a plate of olives, each stuffed with a section of canned mandarin orange. He took it and returned to the party. Not surprisingly he was greeted as though he'd joined the dark side. He was very grateful Beauvoir wasn't there to see Ruth, nuttier and more Anglo than usual, Rosa wearing a dress and himself offering food that would almost certainly kill or cripple anyone foolish enough to eat it.

"Olive?" he asked Olivier.

The two men looked down at the plate.

"Does that make me the mandarin?" asked Gabri.

"You need to get your head out of your own asshole," said Olivier.

Gabri opened his mouth, but the warning looks on everyone's faces made him shut it again.

Peter, standing a little way off from the conversation and nursing the glass of water Ruth had offered him, smiled. It was much the same thing Clara had said when he'd told her he'd felt violated by the police search.

"Why?" she'd asked.

"Didn't you? I mean, all those strangers looking at your art."

"Isn't that what we call a show? There were more people looking this afternoon than I've had most of my career. Bring on more cops. Hope they brought their checkbooks." She laughed, and clearly didn't care. But she could see he did. "What's the matter?"

"The picture isn't ready to be seen."

"Look, Peter, you make it sound as though this is something to do with your art."

"Well, it is."

"They're trying to find a murderer, not an artist."

And there it had sat, like most uncomfortable truths. Between them.

Gamache and Olivier had wandered away from the group, into a quiet corner.

"I understand you bought your building a few years ago."

Olivier colored slightly, surprised by the question. He instinctively and furtively scanned the room, making sure they weren't overheard.

"I thought it was a good investment. I'd saved some money from my job, and business here was good."

"Must have been. You paid almost three-quarters of a million dollars."

"I bet it's worth a million today."

"Could be. But you paid cash. Was business all that good?"

Olivier shot a look around but no one could hear them. Still he lowered his voice.

"The bistro and B and B are doing very well, for now anyway, but it's the antiques end that's been the surprise."

"How so?"

"Lots of interest in Quebec pine, and lots of great finds."

Gamache nodded. "We spoke to the Poiriers this afternoon."

Olivier's face hardened. "Look, what they say just isn't true. I didn't screw their mother. She wanted to sell. Was desperate to sell."

"I know. We spoke to her too. And the Mundins. The furniture must have been in very bad shape."

Olivier relaxed a little.

"It was. Years sitting in damp, freezing barns and the attic. Had to chase the mice out. Some were warped almost beyond repair. Enough to make you weep."

"Madame Poirier says you came by her home later with a new bed. That was kind."

Olivier dropped his eyes. "Yeah, well, I wanted to thank her."

Conscience, thought Gamache. This man had a huge and terrible conscience riding herd on a huge and terrible greed.

"You said the bistro and B and B were doing well, for now. What did you mean?"

Olivier looked out the window for a moment, then back at Gamache.

"Hi ho, dinner everyone," sang Ruth.

"What should we do?" Clara whispered to Myrna. "Can we run for it?"

"Too late. Either Ruth or the duck would get us for sure. The only thing to do is hunker down and pray for daylight. If the worst happens, play dead."

Gamache and Olivier rose, the last in for dinner.

"I suppose you know what they're doing up at the old Hadley house?" When Gamache didn't answer Olivier continued. "They've almost completely gutted the place and are turning it into an inn and spa. Ten massage rooms, meditation and yoga classes. They'll do a day spa and corporate retreats. People'll be crawling all over the place, and us. It'll ruin Three Pines."

"Three Pines?"

"All right," snapped Olivier. "The bistro and the B and B."

They joined the others in the kitchen and sat at Ruth's white plastic garden table.

"Incoming," warned Gabri as Ruth put a bowl in front of each of them.

Gamache looked at the contents of his bowl. He could make out canned peaches, bacon, cheese and Gummi Bears.

"They're all the things I love," said Ruth, smiling. Rosa was sitting next to her on a nest of towels, her beak thrust under the sleeve of her dress.

"Scotch?" Ruth asked.

"Please." Six glasses were thrust forward and Ruth poured each a Scotch, into their dinners.

About three centuries and many lifetimes later they left, staggering into the quiet, cool night.

"Toodle-oo," waved Ruth. But Gamache was heartened to hear, just as the door closed: "Fuckers."

FOURTEEN

 They arrived back at the B and B to find Beauvoir waiting up for them. Sort of. He was fast asleep in his chair. Beside him was a plate with crumbs and a glass of chocolate milk. The fireplace glowed with dying embers.

"Should we wake him?" asked Olivier. "He looks so peaceful."

Beauvoir's face was turned to the side and there was a slight glisten of drool. His breathing was heavy and regular. On his chest lay the small stuffed lion Gabri had won for Olivier at the fair, his hand resting on it.

"Like a little baby cop," said Gabri.

"That reminds me. Ruth asked me to give him this." Olivier handed Gamache a slip of paper. The Chief took it and when he declined their offer of help watched as the two men trudged wearily up the stairs. It was nine o'clock.

"Jean Guy," Gamache whispered. "Wake up."

He knelt and touched the younger man's shoulder. Beauvoir started awake with a snort, the lion slipping off his chest onto the floor.

"What is it?"

"Time for bed."

He watched Beauvoir sit up. "How was it?"

"No one died."

"That's a bit of an achievement in Three Pines."

"Olivier said Ruth wanted you to have this." Gamache handed him the slip of paper. Beauvoir rubbed his eyes, unfolded the paper and read it. Then, shaking his head, he handed it to the Chief.

Maybe there's something in all of this
I missed.

"What does it mean? Is it a threat?"

Gamache frowned. "Haven't a clue. Why would she be writing to you?"

"Jealous? Maybe she's just nuts." But they both knew the "maybe" was being generous. "Speaking of nut, your daughter called."

"Annie?" Gamache was suddenly worried, instinctively reaching for his cell phone, which he knew didn't work in the village in the valley.

"Everything's fine. She wanted to talk to you about some upset at work. Nothing major. She just wanted to quit."

"Damn, that was probably what she wanted to talk about yesterday when we got called down here."

"Well don't worry about it. I handled it."

"I don't think telling her to fuck off can be considered 'handling it.'"

Beauvoir laughed and bending down he picked up the stuffed lion. "There's certainly good reason she's known as 'the lion' in your family. Vicious."

"She's known as the lion because she's loving and passionate."

"And a man-eater?"

"All the qualities you hate in her you admire in men," said Gamache. "She's smart, she stands up for what she believes in. She speaks her mind and won't back down to bullies. Why do you goad her? Every time you come for a meal and she's there it ends in an argument. I for one am growing tired of it."

"All right, I'll try harder. But she's very annoying."

"So are you. You have a lot in common. What was the problem at work?" Gamache took the seat next to Jean Guy.

"Oh, a case she'd wanted was assigned to another lawyer, someone more junior. I talked to her for a while. I'm almost certain she won't kill everyone at work after all."

"That's my girl."

"And she's decided not to quit. I told her she'd regret any hasty decision."

"Oh, you did, did you?" asked Gamache with a smile. This from the king of impulse.

"Well, someone had to give her good advice," laughed Beauvoir. "Her parents are quite mad, you know."

"I'd heard. Thank you."

It was good advice. And he could tell Beauvoir knew it. He seemed pleased. Gamache looked at his watch. Nine thirty. He reached for Gabri's phone.

As Gamache spoke to his daughter Beauvoir absently stroked the lion in his hand.

Maybe there's something in all of this
I missed.

That was the fear in a murder investigation. Missing something. Chief Inspector Gamache had assembled a brilliant department. Almost two hundred of them in all, hand picked, investigating crime all over the province.

But this team, Beauvoir knew, was the best.

He was the bloodhound. The one way out in front, leading.

Agent Lacoste was the hunter. Determined, methodical.

And the Chief Inspector? Armand Gamache was their explorer. The one who went where others refused to go, or couldn't go. Or were too afraid to go. Into the wilderness. Gamache found the chasms, the caves, and the beasts that hid in them.

Beauvoir had long thought Gamache did it because he was afraid of nothing. But he'd come to realize the Chief Inspector had many fears. That was his strength. He recognized it in others. Fear more than anything was the thrust behind the knife, the fist. The blow to the head.

And young Agent Morin? What did he bring to the team? Beauvoir had to admit he'd quite warmed to the young man. But that hadn't blinded him to his inexperience. So far Beauvoir the bloodhound could smell fear quite clearly in this case.

But it came from Morin.

Beauvoir left the Chief in the living room speaking to his daughter and walked upstairs. As he climbed he hummed an old Weavers tune and hoped Gamache didn't notice the stuffed animal clutched in his hand.

When Monsieur Béliveau arrived to open his general store the next morning he had a customer already waiting. Agent Paul Morin stood up from the bench on the veranda and introduced himself to the elderly grocer.

"How can I help you?" Monsieur Béliveau asked as he unlocked the door. It wasn't often people in Three Pines were so pressed for his produce they were actually waiting for him. But then, this young man wasn't a villager.

"Do you have any paraffin?"

Monsieur Béliveau's stern face broke into a smile. "I have everything."

Paul Morin had never been in the store before and now he looked around. The dark wooden shelves were neatly stacked with tins. Sacks of dog food and birdseed leaned against the counter. Above the shelves were old boxes with backgammon games. Checkers, Snakes and Ladders, Monopoly. Paint by numbers and jigsaw puzzles were stacked in neat, orderly rows. Dried goods were displayed along one wall, paint, boots, birdfeeders were down another.

"Over there, by the Mason jars. Are you planning on doing some pickling?" he chuckled.

"Do you sell much?" Morin asked.

"At this time of year? It's all I can do to keep it in stock."

"And how about this?" He held up a tin. "Sell many of these?"

"A few. But most people go into the Canadian Tire in Cowansville for that sort of thing, or the building supply shops. I just keep some around in case."

"When was the last time you sold some?" the young agent asked as he paid for his goods. He didn't expect an answer really, but he felt he had to ask.

"July."

"Really?" Morin suspected he'd have to work on his "interrogation" face. "How'd you remember that?"

"It's what I do. You get to know the habits of people. And when they buy something unusual, like this," he held up the tin just before placing it in the paper bag, "I notice. Actually, two people bought some. Regular run on the market."

Agent Paul Morin left Monsieur Béliveau's shop with his goods, and a whole lot of unexpected information.

A gent Isabelle Lacoste started her day with the more straightforward of the interviews. She pressed the button and the elevator swished shut and took her to the top of the Banque Laurentienne tower in Montreal. As she waited she looked out at the harbor in one direction and Mont Royal with its huge cross in the other. Splendid glass buildings clustered all around downtown, reflecting the sun, reflecting the aspirations and achievements of this remarkable French city.

Isabelle Lacoste was always surprised by the amount of pride she felt when looking at downtown Montreal. The architects had managed to make it both impressive and charming. Montrealers never turned their back on the past. The Québécois were like that, for better or worse.

"*Je vous en prie,*" the receptionist smiled and indicated a now-opened door.

"*Merci.*" Agent Lacoste walked into a quite grand office where a slender, athletic-looking middle-aged man was standing at his desk. He came round, extending his hand, and introduced himself as Yves Charpentier.

"I have some of the information you asked for," he said in cultured French. It delighted Lacoste when she could speak her own language to top executives. Her generation could. But she'd heard her parents and grandparents talk, and knew enough recent history to know had it been thirty years earlier she'd probably be speaking to a unilingual Englishman. Her English was perfect, but that wasn't the point.

She accepted the offer of coffee.

"This is rather delicate," said Monsieur Charpentier, when his secretary had left and the door was closed. "I don't want you to think Olivier Brulé was a criminal, and there was never any question of laying charges."

"But?"

"We were very happy with him for the first few years. I'm afraid we tend to be impressed by profit and he delivered on that. He moved up quickly. People liked him, especially his clients. A lot of people in this business can be glib, but Olivier was genuine. Quiet, respectful. It was a relief to deal with him."

"But?" Lacoste repeated, with a slight smile she hoped took the edge off her insistence. Monsieur Charpentier smiled back.

"Some company money went missing. A couple of million." He watched for her response but she simply listened. "A very discreet investigation was launched. In the meantime more money disappeared. Eventually we tracked it down to two people. One of them was Olivier. I didn't believe it, but after a couple of interviews he admitted it."

"Could he have been covering for the other employee?"

"Doubtful. Frankly, the other employee, while bright, wasn't smart enough to do this."

"Surely it doesn't take brains to embezzle. I'd have thought you'd have to be quite stupid."

Monsieur Charpentier laughed. "I agree, but I haven't made myself clear. The money was gone from the company account, but not stolen. Olivier showed us what he'd done. The trail. Seems he'd been following some activity in Malaysia, saw what he thought were some fantastic investment opportunities and took them to his boss, who didn't agree. So Olivier did it on his own, without authorization. It was all there. He'd documented it, intending to put it back, with the profits. And he'd been right. Those three million dollars turned into twenty."

Now Lacoste reacted, not verbally, but her expression made Charpentier nod.

"Exactly. The kid had a nose for money. Where is he now?"

"You fired him?" asked Lacoste, ignoring the question.

"He quit. We were trying to decide what to do with him. The executives were torn. His boss was apoplectic and wanted him dangled from the top of the building. We explained we don't do that. Anymore."

Lacoste laughed. "Some of you wanted to keep him on?"

"He was just so good at what he did."

"Which was making money. Are you convinced he was going to give it back?"

"Now, you've hit on the problem. Half of us believed him, half didn't. Olivier finally resigned, realizing he'd lost our trust. When you lose that, well . . ."

Well, thought Agent Lacoste. Well, well.

And now Olivier was in Three Pines. But like everyone who moved, he took himself with him.

Well, well.

The three Sûreté officers gathered round the table in the Incident Room.

"So where are we?" asked Beauvoir, standing once again by the sheets of paper tacked to the walls. Instead of answers to the questions he'd written there, two more had been added.

WHERE WAS HE MURDERED?
WHY WAS HE MOVED?

He shook his head. They seemed to be moving in the wrong direction. Even the few things that seemed possible in this case, like the fire irons being the weapons, turned out to be nothing.

They had nothing.

"We actually know a great deal," said Gamache. "We know the man wasn't killed in the bistro."

"That leaves the rest of the world to eliminate," said Beauvoir.

"We know paraffin and Varathane are involved. And we know that somehow Olivier's involved."

"But we don't even know who the victim was." Beauvoir underlined that question on his sheet in frustration. Gamache let that sit for a moment, then spoke.

"No. But we will. We'll know it all, eventually. It's a puzzle, and eventually the whole picture will be clear. We just need to be patient. And persistent. We need more background information on other possible suspects. The Parras for instance."

"I have that information you asked for," said Agent Morin, squaring his slight shoulders. "Hanna and Roar Parra came here in the mid-80s. Refugees. Applied for status and got it. They're now Canadian citizens."

"All legal?" asked Beauvoir, with regret.

"All legal. One child. Havoc. Twenty-one years old. The family's very involved in the Czech community here. Sponsored a few people."

"Right, right," waved Beauvoir. "Anything interesting?"

Morin looked down at his copious notes. What would the Inspector consider interesting?

"Did you find anything from before they came here?" asked Gamache.

"No, sir. I have calls in to Prague but their record keeping from that time isn't good."

"Okay." Beauvoir snapped the top back on the Magic Marker. "Anything else?"

Agent Morin placed a paper bag on the conference table.

"I dropped by the general store this morning, and bought these."

Out of the bag he brought a brick of paraffin wax. "Monsieur Béliveau says everyone's been buying paraffin, especially at this time of year."

"Not much help," said Beauvoir, taking his seat again.

"No, but this might be." And from the bag he pulled a tin. On it was written *Varathane*. "He sold two tins like this to two different people in July. One to Gabri and the other to Marc Gilbert."

"Oh, really?" Beauvoir uncapped the marker.

Agent Lacoste, like every Montrealer, knew about Habitat, the strange and exotic apartment building created for Expo 67, the great World's Fair. The buildings had been considered avant garde then, and still were. They sat on Île des Soeurs, in the St. Lawrence River, a tribute to creativity and vision. Once seen Habitat was never forgotten. Instead of a square or rectangular building to house people the architect had made each room a separate block, an elongated cube. It looked like a jumble of children's building blocks, piled on top of each other. One interconnected with another, some above, some below, some off to the side, so that daylight shone through the building and the rooms were all bathed in sun. And the views from each room were spectacular, either of the grand river or of the magnificent city.

Lacoste had never been in a Habitat condo, but she was about to. Jacques Brulé, Olivier's father, lived there.

"Come in," he said, unsmiling, as he opened the door. "You said this was about my son?"

Monsieur Brulé was very unlike his son. He had a full head of dark hair and was robust. Behind him she could see the gleaming wood floors, the slate fireplace and the huge windows looking onto the river. The condo was tasteful and expensive.

"I wonder if we could sit down?"

"I wonder if you could come to the point?"

He stood at the door, blocking her way. Not allowing her farther into his home.

"As I mentioned on the phone, I'm with homicide. We're investigating a murder in Three Pines."

The man looked blank.

"Where your son lives." He nodded, once. Lacoste continued. "A body was found in the bistro there."

She'd intentionally not identified the bistro. Olivier's father waited, showing absolutely no recognition, no alarm, no concern at all.

"Olivier's Bistro," she finally said.

"And what do you want from me?"

It was far from unusual in a murder case to find fractured families, but she hadn't expected to find one here.

"I'd like to know about Olivier, his upbringing, his background, his interests."

"You've come to the wrong parent. You'd need to ask his mother."

"I'm sorry, but I thought she'd died."

"She has."

"You told me on the phone he went to Notre Dame de Sion. Quite a good school, I hear. But it only goes to grade six. How about after that?"

"I think he went to Loyola. Or was it Brébeuf? I can't remember."

"*Pardon?* Were you and his mother separated?"

"No, I'd never divorce." This was the most animated he'd been. Much more upset by the suggestion of divorce than death and certainly than murder. Lacoste waited. And waited. Eventually Jacques Brulé spoke.

"I was away a lot, building a career."

But Agent Lacoste, who hunted killers and still knew what schools her children attended, knew that wasn't much of an explanation, or excuse.

"Was he ever in trouble? Did he get into fights? Any problems?"

"With Olivier? None at all. He was a regular boy, mind you. He'd get into scrapes, but nothing serious."

It was like interviewing a marshmallow, or a salesman about a dining room set. Monsieur Brulé seemed on the verge of calling his son "it" throughout the conversation.

"When was the last time you spoke to him?" She wasn't sure that was exactly on topic, but she wanted to know.

"I don't know."

She should have guessed. As she left he called after her, "Tell him I said hello."

Lacoste stopped at the elevator, pressed the button, and looked back at the large man standing in the door frame, shutting out all the light that she knew was streaming into his apartment.

"Maybe you can tell him yourself. Visit even. Have you met Gabri?"

"Gabri?"

"Gabriel. His partner."

"Gabrielle? He hasn't told me about her."

The elevator came and she stepped in, wondering if Monsieur Brulé would ever find Three Pines. She also wondered about this man who kept so much hidden.

But then, clearly, so did his son.

It was late morning and Olivier was in his bistro, at the front door. Trying to decide if he should unlock it. Let people in. Maybe the crowd would drown out the voice in his head. The Hermit's voice. And that terrible story that bound them together. Even unto death.

The young man appeared at the base of the now barren mountain. Like everyone else in the region he'd heard the stories. Of bad children brought here as a sacrifice to the dreadful Mountain King.

He looked for tiny bones on the dusty soil, but there was nothing. No life. Not even death.

As he was about to leave he heard a small sigh. A breeze had blown up where nothing had stirred before. He felt it on the back of his neck, and he felt his skin grow cool and the hairs stand up. He looked down at the lush, green valley, the thick forests and the thatched roofs, and he wondered how he could have been so stupid as to have come up here. Alone.

"Don't," he heard on the wind. "Don't."

The young man turned round. "Go," he heard.

"Don't go," said the sigh.

FIFTEEN

The three investigators left the Incident Room together, but parted ways at the village green. Beauvoir left the Chief and Agent Morin to interview Olivier and Gabri once again, while he headed to the old Hadley house.

The Inspector was feeling pretty cocky. They'd caught the Gilberts in a lie. Dominique had told him yesterday they never used Varathane. Was quite pleased to tell him how "green" they were. But now there was proof they'd at least bought a *demi-liter* of the stuff.

But the extra spring in his step was because he was curious, anxious even, to see what the Gilberts had done to the old Hadley house.

Gamache tried the door to the bistro and was surprised to find it open. Earlier that morning, over breakfast of *pain doré*, sliced strawberries and bananas, maple syrup and back bacon, Gabri had admitted he didn't know when Olivier might reopen the bistro.

"Maybe never," he said, "then where would we be? I'd have to start taking in paying guests."

"Good thing then that you're a B and B," said Gamache.

"You'd think that would be an advantage, wouldn't you? But I'm handicapped by extreme laziness."

And yet, when Gamache and Agent Morin walked into the bistro there was Gabri behind the bar, polishing it. And from the kitchen came the aroma of fine cooking.

"Olivier," Gabri called, coming around from behind the bar. "Our first customers since the murder are here," he sang out.

"Oh, for God's sake, Gabri," they heard from the kitchen and a pot clanked down. A moment later Olivier punched through the swinging door. "Oh, it's you."

"Just us, I'm afraid. We have a few questions. Do you have a moment?"

Olivier looked as though he was about to say no, but changed his mind and indicated a seat by the hearth. Once again a fire was burning there. And the pokers had been returned.

Gamache looked at Agent Morin. Morin's eyes widened. Surely the Chief Inspector wasn't expecting him to conduct the interview? But the moments dragged by and no one else said anything. Morin searched his mind. *Don't be too forceful*, though he didn't think that would be a problem. *Get the suspect to drop his guard.* Gabri was smiling at him, wiping his hands on an apron and waiting. *So far so good*, thought Morin. *Seems the idiot agent act is working. Now if only it wasn't an act.*

He smiled back at the two men and racked his brain. Up until now the only questioning he'd done was of speeders along Autoroute 10. It didn't seem necessary to ask Gabri whether he had a driver's license.

"Is it about the murder?" asked Gabri, trying to be helpful.

"Yes, it is," said Morin, finding his voice. "Not really so much about the murder as a small issue that's come up."

"Please," said Olivier, indicating a chair, "have a seat."

"This is really nothing," said Morin, sitting along with everyone else. "Just a loose end. We were wondering why you bought Varathane from Monsieur Béliveau in July."

"Did we?" Olivier looked over at Gabri.

"Well, I did. We needed to redo the bar, remember?"

"Will you stop with that? I like the bar the way it is," said Olivier. "Distressed."

"I'm distressed, it's a disgrace. Remember when we bought it? It was all gleaming?"

They looked over at the long wooden bar with the till and jars of all-sorts, jelly beans and licorice pipes. Behind were liquor bottles on shelves.

"It's about atmosphere," said Olivier. "Everything in here should either be old or look old. Don't say it." He held up his hand to ward off Gabri's response to that, then turned to the officers. "We always disagree about this. When we moved here this place was a hardware store. All the original features had been ripped out or covered over."

"The beams were hidden under that sound insulation stuff for ceilings," said Gabri. "Even the fireplaces were ripped out and turned into storage. We had to find a stone mason to rebuild them."

"Really?" said Gamache, impressed. The fireplace looked original. "But what about the Varathane?"

"Yes, Gabri. What about the Varathane?" Olivier demanded.

"Well, I was going to strip the bar and resand and coat it, but . . ."

"But?"

"I was hoping maybe Old Mundin could do it instead. He knows how. He'd love to do it."

"Forget it. No one's going to touch that bar."

"Where's the tin you bought from Monsieur Béliveau?" Agent Morin asked.

"It's in our basement at home."

"Can I see it?"

"If you'd like." Gabri looked at Morin as though he was mad.

Jean Guy Beauvoir couldn't quite believe his eyes. But more than that he couldn't believe something less tangible. He was enjoying this tour of the old Hadley house. So far Marc and Dominique Gilbert had shown him all the magnificent bedrooms, with fireplaces and flat-screen TVs, with spa baths and steam showers. The gleaming mosaic-glass tiles. The espresso maker in each room.

Waiting for the first guests.

And now they were in the spa area, the lower floor, with its muted lighting and soothing colors and calming aromas, even now. Products were being unpacked and waiting to be displayed on shelves not yet built. This area, while clearly as spectacular as the rest of the place, was less finished.

"A month more, we figure," Marc was saying. "We're hoping to have our first guests on the Thanksgiving long weekend. We're just discussing putting an ad in the papers."

"I think it's too soon, but Marc thinks we can get it done. We've hired most of the staff. Four massage therapists, a yoga instructor, a personal trainer and a receptionist. And that's just for the spa."

The two prattled on excitedly. Enid would love it here, Beauvoir thought.

"How much would you charge for a couple?"

"A night at the inn and one healing spa treatment each would start at three hundred and twenty-five dollars," said Marc. "That's for a standard room midweek, but includes breakfast and dinner."

None of the rooms seemed standard to Beauvoir. But neither did the price. How much could creams really cost? Still, for their anniversary, maybe. Olivier and Gabri would kill him, but maybe they didn't need to know. He and Enid could just stay here. At the inn. Not go into Three Pines. Who'd really want to leave?

"That would be each," said Marc, as he turned off the lights and they walked back up the stairs.

"I'm sorry?"

"Three hundred and twenty-five dollars per person. Before tax," said Marc.

Beauvoir was glad he was behind them and no one saw his face. Seemed only the wealthy got healed.

So far, though, he hadn't seen any signs of Varathane. He'd looked at floors, counters, doors, exclaiming over the craftsmanship, to the Gilberts' delight. But he'd also been looking for the telltale gleam. The unnatural shine.

Nothing.

At the front door he debated asking them outright, but he didn't want to show his hand just yet. He wandered around the yard, noticing the now groomed lawns, the newly planted gardens, the trees staked and sturdy.

It all appealed to his sense of order. This was what the country should be. Civilized.

Roar Parra appeared round the corner of the house pushing a wheelbarrow. He stopped when he saw Beauvoir.

"Can I help you?"

Beauvoir introduced himself and looked at the horse manure in the barrow. "More work for you, I suppose." He fell into step with Parra.

"I like horses. Nice to see them back. Old Mrs. Hadley used to keep them. Barns fallen down now and the trails have grown over."

"I hear the new owners have you cutting them again."

Parra grunted. "Big job. Still, my son helps when he can, and I like it. Quiet in the woods."

"Except for the strangers wandering around." Beauvoir saw the wary look on Parra's face.

"What d'you mean?"

"Well, you told Agent Lacoste you'd seen a stranger disappearing into the woods. But it wasn't the dead man. Who do you think it was?"

"I musta been wrong."

"Now, why would you say that? You don't really believe it, do you?"

For once Beauvoir really looked at the man. He was covered in sweat and dirt, and manure. He was stocky and muscled. But none of that made him stupid. In fact, Beauvoir thought this man was very bright. So why had he just lied?

"I'm tired of people looking at me like I just said I'd been kidnapped by aliens. The guy was there one moment, gone the next. I looked for him, but nothing. And no, I haven't seen him since."

"Maybe he's gone."

"Maybe."

They walked in silence. The air was filled with the musky scents of fresh harvested hay and manure.

"I heard the new owners here are very environmentally aware." Beauvoir managed to make it sound a reproach, something slightly silly. Some new-fangled city-folk nonsense. "Bet they won't let you use pesticides or fertilizers."

"I won't use them. Told them so. Had to teach them to compost and even recycle. Not sure they'd ever heard of it. And they still used plastic bags for their groceries, can you believe it?"

Beauvoir, who did too, shook his head. Parra dumped the manure onto a steaming pile and turned back to Beauvoir, chuckling.

"What?" asked Beauvoir.

"They're now greener than green. Nothing wrong with that, of course. Wish everyone was."

"So that means with all those renovations they didn't use any toxic stuff, like Varathane."

Again the stocky man laughed. "Wanted to, but I stopped them. Told them about tung oil."

Beauvoir felt his optimism fade. Leaving Roar Parra to turn over the compost heap he went back to the house and rang the doorbell. It was time to ask them directly. The door was answered by Madame Gilbert, Marc's mother.

"I'd like to speak to your son again, if you don't mind."

"Of course, Inspector. Would you like to come in?"

She was genteel and gracious. Unlike her son. Beneath his cheerful and friendly manner there peeked every now and then a condescension, an awareness that he had a lot and others had less. And somehow that made them less.

"I'll just wait. It's a small point."

After she'd disappeared Beauvoir stood in the entrance admiring the fresh white paint, the polished furniture, the flowers in the hall beyond. The sense of order and calm and welcome. In the old Hadley house. He could hardly believe it. For all Marc Gilbert's flaws, he'd been able to do all this. Light flooded through the window in the foyer and gleamed off the wooden floors.

Gleamed.

SIXTEEN

By the time Madame Gilbert and Marc returned Inspector Beauvoir had the area rug up and was examining the floor of the small entrance hall.

"What is it?" she asked.

Beauvoir looked up from where he was kneeling and gestured to them to stay where they were. Then he bent back down.

The floor had been Varathaned. It was smooth and hard and clear and glossy. Except for one small smudge. He stood up and brushed off his knees.

"Do you have a cordless phone?"

"I'll get it," said Marc.

"Perhaps your mother wouldn't mind." Beauvoir looked at Carole Gilbert who nodded and left.

"What is it?" Marc asked, leaning in and staring at the floor.

"You know what it is, Monsieur Gilbert. Yesterday your wife said you never used Varathane, that you were trying to be as eco-friendly as possible. But that wasn't true."

Marc laughed. "You're right. We did use Varathane here. But that was before we knew there was something better to use. So we stopped."

Beauvoir stared at Marc Gilbert. He could hear Carole returning with the phone, her heels clicking on the wooden floors.

"I use Varathane," said the Inspector. "I'm not as environmentally aware as you, I guess. I know it takes about a day to set. But it really isn't completely hard for a week or so. This Varathane isn't months old. You didn't start with it, did you? This was just done within the last week."

Gilbert finally looked flustered. "Look, I Varathaned it one night when everyone else was asleep. It was last Friday. That's good wood and it's going to get more wear than any other place in the inn, so I decided to use Varathane. But just there. Nowhere else. I don't think Dominique or Mama even know."

"Don't you use this door all the time? It is the main entrance, after all."

"We park around the side and use the kitchen door. We never use the front. But our guests will."

"Here's the phone." Carole Gilbert had reappeared. Beauvoir thanked her and called the bistro.

"Is Chief Inspector Gamache there, *s'il vous plaît*?" he asked Olivier.

"*Oui?*" He heard the Chief's deep voice.

"I've found something. I think you need to come up. And bring a Scene of Crime kit, please."

"Scene of Crime? What's that supposed to mean?" asked Marc, getting irritated now.

But Beauvoir had stopped answering questions.

Within minutes Gamache and Morin arrived and Beauvoir showed them the polished floor. And the little scuff mark marring the perfect shine.

Morin took photographs, then, gloves on and tweezers ready, he took samples.

"I'll get these to the lab in Sherbrooke right away."

Morin left and Gamache and Beauvoir turned back to the Gilberts. Dominique had arrived home with groceries and had joined them.

"What is it?" she asked.

They were standing in the large hall now, away from the entrance, with its yellow police tape and rolled-up carpet.

Gamache was stern, all semblance of the affable man gone. "Who was the dead man?"

Three stunned people stared back.

"We've told you," said Carole. "We don't know."

Gamache nodded slowly. "You did say that. And you also said you'd never seen anyone fitting his description, but you had. Or at least one of you had. And one of you knows exactly what that lab report will tell us."

They stared at each other now.

"The dead man was here, lying in your entrance, on Varathane not quite hardened. He had it stuck to his sweater. And your floor has part of his sweater stuck to it."

"But this is ridiculous," said Carole, looking from Gamache to Beauvoir. She too could shape-shift, and now the gracious chatelaine became a formidable woman, her eyes angry and hard. "Leave our home immediately."

Gamache bowed slightly and to Beauvoir's amazement he turned to go, catching Beauvoir's eye.

They walked down the dirt road into Three Pines.

"Well done, Jean Guy. Twice we searched that house and twice we missed it."

"So why are we leaving? We should be up there, interviewing them."

"Perhaps. But time is on our side. One of them knows we'll have proof, probably before the day's out. Let him stew. Believe me, it's no favor I've done them."

And Beauvoir, thinking about it, knew that to be true.

Just before lunch Marc Gilbert arrived at the Incident Room.

"May I speak to you?" he asked Gamache.

"You can speak to all of us. There're no secrets anymore, are there, Monsieur Gilbert?"

Marc bristled but sat in the chair indicated. Beauvoir nodded to Morin to join them with his notebook.

"I've come voluntarily, you can see that," said Marc.

"I can," said Gamache.

Marc Gilbert had walked down to the old railway station, slowly. Going over and over what he'd tell them. It had sounded good when he'd talked to the trees and stones and the ducks flying south. Now he wasn't so sure.

"Look, I know this sounds ridiculous." He started with the one thing he'd promised himself not to say. He tried to concentrate on the Chief Inspector, not that ferret of an assistant, or the idiot boy taking notes. "But I found the body just lying there. I couldn't sleep so I got up. I was heading to the kitchen to make myself a sandwich when I saw him. Lying there by the front door."

He stared at Gamache who was watching him with calm, interested brown eyes. Not accusing, not even disbelieving. Just listening.

"It was dark, of course, so I turned on a light and went closer. I thought it might be a drunk who'd staggered up the hill from the bistro, saw our place and just made himself comfortable."

He was right, it did sound ridiculous. Still the Chief said nothing.

"I was going to call for help but I didn't want to upset Dominique or my mother, so I crept closer to the guy. Then I saw his head."

"And you knew he'd been murdered," said Beauvoir, not believing a word of this.

"That's it." Marc turned grateful eyes to the Inspector, until he saw the sneer, then he turned back to Gamache. "I couldn't believe it."

"So a murdered man shows up in your house in the middle of the night. Didn't you lock the door?" asked Beauvoir.

"We do, but we're getting a lot of deliveries and since we never use that door ourselves I guess we forgot."

"What did you do, Monsieur Gilbert?" Gamache asked, his voice soothing, reasonable.

Marc opened his mouth, shut it and looked down at his hands. He'd promised himself when it got to this part he wouldn't look away, or down. Wouldn't flinch. But now he did all three.

"I thought about it for a while, then I picked the guy up and carried him down into the village. To the bistro."

There it was.

"Why?" Gamache asked.

"I was going to call the police, actually had the phone in my hand," he held out his empty hand to them as though that was proof, "but then I got to thinking. About all the work we'd put into the place. And we're so close, so close. We're going to open in just over a month, you know. And I realized it would be all over the papers. Who'd want to relax in an inn and spa where someone had just been killed?"

Beauvoir hated to say it, but he had to agree. Especially at those prices.

"So you dumped him in the bistro?" he asked. "Why?"

Now Gilbert turned to him. "Because I didn't want to put him into someone else's home to be found. And I knew Olivier kept the key under a planter by the front door." He could see their skepticism, but plowed ahead anyway. "I took the dead guy down, left him on the floor of the bistro and came home. I moved a rug up from the spa area to cover where the guy had been. I knew no one would miss it downstairs. Too much else going on."

"This is a dangerous time," said Gamache, staring at Marc. "We could charge you with obstruction, with indignities to a body, with hampering the investigation."

"With murder," said Beauvoir.

"We need the full truth. Why did you take the body to the bistro? You could have left him in the woods."

Marc sighed. He didn't think they'd press this point. "I thought about it, but there were lots of kids in Three Pines for the long weekend and I didn't want any of them finding him."

"Noble," said Gamache, with equilibrium. "But that wasn't likely to happen, was it? How often do kids play in the woods around your place?"

"It happens. Would you run that risk?"

"I would call the police."

The Chief let that sentence do its job. It stripped Marc Gilbert of any pretension to higher ground. And left him exposed before them. For a man who, at best, did something unconscionable. At worst he murdered a man.

"The truth," said Gamache, almost in a whisper.

"I took the body to the bistro so that people would think he'd been killed there. Olivier's treated us like shit since we arrived."

"So you paid him back by putting a body there?" asked Beauvoir. He could think of a few people he'd like to dump bodies on. But never would. This man did. That spoke of his hatred of Olivier. A rare, and surprising, degree of hatred. And his resolve.

Marc Gilbert looked at his hands, looked out the window, moved his gaze around the walls of the old railway station. And finally he rested on the large man across from him.

"That's what I did. I shouldn't have done it, I know." He shook his head in wonderment at his own stupidity. Then he looked up suddenly as the silence grew. His eyes were sharp and bright. "Wait a minute. You don't think I killed the man, do you?"

They said nothing.

Gilbert looked from one to the other. He even looked at the idiot agent with the poised pen.

"Why would I do that? I don't even know who he is."

Still they said nothing.

"Really. I'd never seen him before."

Finally Beauvoir broke the silence. "And yet there he was in your house. Dead. Why would a strange body be in your house?"

"You see?" Gilbert thrust his hand toward Beauvoir. "You see? That's why I didn't call the cops. Because I knew that's what you'd think." He put his head into his hands as though trying to contain his scrambling thoughts. "Dominique's going to kill me. Oh, Jesus. Oh, God." His shoulders sagged and his head hung, heavy from the weight of what he'd done and what was still to come.

Just then the phone rang. Agent Morin reached for it. "Sûreté du Québec."

The voice on the other end spoke hurriedly and was muffled.

"*Désolé*," said Morin, feeling bad because he knew he was interrupting the interrogation. "I don't understand." Everyone was looking at him. He colored and tried to listen closely, but he still couldn't make out what was being said. Then he heard and the color in his face changed. "*Un instant.*"

He covered the mouthpiece. "It's Madame Gilbert. There's a man on their land. She saw him in the woods at the back." Morin listened again at the phone. "She says he's approaching the house. What should she do?"

All three men stood up.

"Oh my God, he must have seen me leave and knows they're alone," said Marc.

Gamache took the phone. "Madame Gilbert, is the back door locked? Can you get to it now?" He waited. "Good. Where is he now?" He listened, then began striding to the door, Inspector Beauvoir and Marc Gilbert running beside him. "We'll be there in two minutes. Take your mother-in-law and lock yourselves in an upstairs bathroom. That one you took me to. Yes, with the balcony. Lock the doors, close the curtains. Stay there until we come to get you."

Beauvoir had started the car and Gamache slammed the door and handed the phone back to Morin. "Stay here. You too."

"I'm coming," said Gilbert, reaching for the passenger door.

"You'll stay here and talk to your wife. Keep her calm. You're delaying us, monsieur."

Gamache's voice was intense, angry.

Gilbert grabbed the phone from Morin as Beauvoir gunned the car and they took off over the stone bridge, around the common and up du Moulin, to stop short of the old Hadley house. They were there in less than a minute. They got quickly and quietly out of the car.

"Do you have a gun?" Beauvoir whispered as they ran, crouched, to the corner of the house. Gamache shook his head. Really, thought Beauvoir. There were times he just felt like shooting the Chief himself.

"They're dangerous," said Gamache.

"Which is why he," Beauvoir jerked his head toward the back of the property, "probably has one."

Gamache brought his hand up and Beauvoir was silent. The Chief motioned in one direction, then disappeared around the side of the house. Beauvoir ran past the front door and around the far side. Both making for the back, where Dominique had seen the man.

Hugging the wall and staying low Gamache edged along. There was a need for speed. The stranger had been here for at least five minutes, uninterrupted. He could be in the house by now. A lot can happen in a minute, never mind five.

He edged around a bush and got to the far end of the large old house. There he saw movement. A man. Large. In a hat and gloves and field coat. He was close to the house, close to the back door. If he got inside their job would be far more difficult. So many places to hide. So much closer to the women.

As the Chief Inspector watched the man looked around then made for the French doors into the kitchen.

Gamache stepped out from the wall.

"Hold it," he commanded. "Sûreté du Québec."

The man stopped. His back was to Gamache and he couldn't see whether Gamache had a gun. But neither could Gamache see if he had one.

"I want to see your hands," said Gamache.

There was no movement. That wasn't good, Gamache knew. He prepared to dive sideways if the man swung around and shot. But both stood their ground. Then the man turned quickly.

Gamache, trained and experienced, felt time slow down and the world collapse, so that all that existed was the turning man in front of him. His body, his arms. His hands. And as the man's body swung Gamache saw something gripped in his right hand.

Gamache ducked.

Then the man was on the ground, and Beauvoir was on top of him. Gamache raced forward, pinning the man's hand to the ground.

"He had something in his hand, do you see it?" demanded Gamache.

"Got it," said Beauvoir and Gamache hauled the man to his feet.

Both of them looked at him. The hat had fallen off and the iron-gray hair was disheveled. He was tall and lanky.

"What the hell are you doing?" the man demanded.

"You're trespassing," said Beauvoir, handing what the man had held to Gamache, who looked at it. It was a bag. Of granola. And on the front was a stamp.

Manoir Bellechasse.

Gamache looked more closely at the man. He looked familiar. The man glared back, angry, imperious.

"How dare you. Do you know who I am?"

"As a matter of fact," said Gamache, "I do."

After a call to Morin, Marc Gilbert was released and showed up at his home minutes later, out of breath from running. He'd been told his wife and mother were safe but was relieved to see it for himself. He kissed and hugged them both then turned to Gamache.

"Where is he? I want to see him."

Clearly "see" was a euphemism.

"Inspector Beauvoir's with him in the barn."

"Good," said Marc and headed toward the door.

"Marc, wait." His mother ran after him. "Maybe we should just leave this to the police." Carole Gilbert looked frightened still. And with good reason, thought Gamache as he thought of the man in the barn.

"Are you kidding? This man's been spying on us, maybe more."

"What do you mean, 'maybe more'?"

Gilbert hesitated.

"What aren't you telling us?" his wife asked.

He shot a look at Gamache. "I think he might have killed that man and left his body in our house. As a threat. Or maybe he meant to kill one of us. Thought the stranger was one of us. I don't know. But first the body shows up, then this guy tries to break in. Someone's trying to hurt us. And I want to find out why."

"Wait. Wait a minute." Dominique had her hands up to stop her husband. "What are you saying? That body really was here?" She looked toward the vestibule. "In our home?" She looked at Gamache. "It's true?" She looked back at her husband. "Marc?"

He opened and shut his mouth. Then took a deep breath. "He was here. The police were right. I found him when I got up in the middle of the night. I got scared and did something stupid."

"You took the body to the bistro?" Dominique looked as though she'd been slapped by someone she loved, so great was her shock. His mother was staring at him as though he'd peed in the Château Frontenac dining room. He knew that look from when he was a boy and peed in the Château Frontenac dining room.

Gilbert's lightning mind zipped all over the place, searching dark corners for someone else to blame. Surely it wasn't his fault. Surely there were factors his wife didn't appreciate. Surely this couldn't be the act of complete idiocy her face accused him of.

But he knew it was.

Dominique turned to Gamache. "You have my permission to shoot him."

"*Merci, madame*, but I'd need more than that to shoot him. A gun for instance."

"Pity," she said, and looked at her husband. "What were you thinking?"

He told them, as he had the cops, the reasoning that had appeared so obvious, so dazzling, at three in the morning.

"You did it for the business?" said Dominique when he'd finished. "Something's very wrong when dumping bodies is part of our business plan."

"Well, it wasn't exactly planned," he tried to defend himself. "And yes, I made a terrible mistake, but isn't there a bigger question?" He'd finally found something curled up in one of those dark corners. Something that would take the heat off him. "Yes, I moved the body. But who put it here in the first place?"

They'd obviously been so stunned by his admission they hadn't even thought of that. But Gamache had. Because he'd noticed something else about the Varathaned floor. The shine, the mar. And the complete lack of blood. So had Beauvoir. Even if Marc Gilbert had scrubbed and scrubbed he'd never have gotten all the blood up. There'd be traces.

But there was nothing. Just some fluff from the dead man's cardigan.

No, Gilbert might have killed the man, but he didn't do it at his own front door. The man had already been dead when he'd been placed there.

Gilbert stood up. "That's one of the reasons I want to see the man who tried to break in. I think he had something to do with it."

His mother stood up and touched her son's arm. "I really think you should leave this to the police. The man's probably unwell."

She looked to Gamache, but the Chief Inspector had no intention of stopping Marc Gilbert from confronting the intruder. Just the opposite. He wanted to see what happened.

"Come with me," he said to Marc, then turned to the women. "You're welcome to join us, if you like."

"Well, I'm going," said Dominique. "Maybe you should stay here," she said to her mother-in-law.

"I'm coming too."

As they approached the barn the horses looked up from the field. Beauvoir, who hadn't seen them before, almost stopped in his tracks. He hadn't seen that many horses in real life. On film, yes. And these didn't look like any film horses. But then, most men didn't look like Sean Connery and most women didn't look like Julia Roberts. But even allowing for natural selection, these horses seemed, well, odd. One didn't even look like a horse. They began to mosey over, one walking sideways.

Paul Morin, who had seen a lot of horses, said, "Nice cows."

Dominique Gilbert ignored him. But she felt drawn to the horses. As their own lives so suddenly unraveled the horses' calm attracted her. As did, she thought, their suffering. No, not their suffering, but their forbearance. If they could endure a lifetime of abuse and pain she could take whatever blow that barn had in store. As the others moved past her Dominique stopped and walked back to the paddock, where she stood on a bucket and leaned over the fence. The other horses, still shy, held back. But Buttercup, big, awkward, ugly and scarred, came forward. Buttercup's broad, flat forehead pushed softly into Dominique's chest, as though it fit there. As though it was the key. And as she walked away to join the others and confront whatever that shadow was they could see standing in the barn, she smelled horse on her hands. And felt the reassuring pressure between her breasts.

It took a moment or two for their eyes to adjust as they stepped into the dim barn. Then the shadow became solid, firm. Human. Before them appeared a tall, slender, graceful older man.

"You've kept me waiting," the darkness said.

Marc, whose vision wasn't quite as good as he pretended, could only just see the outline of the man. But the words, the voice, told him more than enough. He felt light-headed and reached out. His mother, standing next to him, took his hand and held him steady.

"Mother?" he whispered.

"It's all right, Marc," the man said.

But Marc knew it wasn't all right. He'd heard the rumors about the old Hadley house, the ghouls that lived there. He'd loved the stories because it meant no one else had wanted the house, and they could get it dirt cheap.

Dirt to dirt. Something filthy had indeed risen. The old Hadley house had produced one more ghost.

"Dad?"

SEVENTEEN

"Dad?"

Marc stared from the shadow, darker than the shade, to his mother. The voice was unmistakable, indelible. The deep, calm voice that carried censure with a slight smile, so that the child, the boy, the man, had never really known where he stood. But he'd suspected.

"Hello, Marc."

The voice held a hint of humor, as though this was in any way close to funny. As though Marc's staggering shock was reason for mirth.

Dr. Vincent Gilbert walked out of the shed and out of the dead, into the light.

"Mom?" Marc turned to the woman beside him.

"I'm sorry, Marc. Come with me." She tugged her only child out into the sun and sat him on a bale of hay. He felt it pricking into his bottom, uncomfortable.

"Can you get him something to drink?" Carole asked her daughter-in-law, but Dominique, hand to her face, seemed almost as stunned as her husband.

"Marc?" Dominique said.

Beauvoir looked at Gamache. This was going to be a long day if all they said was each other's names.

Dominique recovered and walked quickly, breaking into a run, back to the house.

"I'm sorry, have I surprised you?"

"Of course you surprised him, Vincent," snapped Carole. "How did you think he'd feel?"

"I thought he'd be happier than this."

"You never think."

Marc stared at his father, then he turned to his mother. "You told me he was dead."

"I might have exaggerated."

"Dead? You told him I was dead?"

She turned on her husband again. "We agreed that's what I'd say. Are you senile?"

"Me? Me? Do you have any idea what I've done with my life while you played bridge?"

"Yes, you abandoned your family—"

"Enough," said Gamache, and raised a hand. With an effort the two broke off and looked at him. "Let me be absolutely clear about this," said Gamache. "Is he your father?"

Marc finally took a long hard look at the man standing beside his mother. He was older, thinner. It'd been almost twenty years, after all. Since he'd gone missing in India. Or at least that's what his mother had told him. A few years later she said she'd had him declared dead, and did Marc think they should hold a memorial for him?

Marc had given it absolutely no thought. No. He had better things to do than help plan a memorial for a man missing all his life.

And so that had ended that. The Great Man, for that was what Marc's father was, was forgotten. Marc never spoke of him, never thought of him. When he'd met Dominique and she'd asked if his father had been "that" Vincent Gilbert he'd agreed that, yes, he had. But he was dead. Fallen into some dark hole in Calcutta or Bombay or Madras.

"Isn't he a saint?" Dominique had asked.

"That's right. St. Vincent. Who raised the dead and buried the living."

She hadn't asked any more.

"Here." Dominique had returned with a tray of glasses and bottles, not sure what the occasion called for. Never, in all the board meetings she'd chaired, all the client dinners she'd hosted, all the arbitrations she'd attended, had anything quite like this arisen. A father. Risen. But obviously not revered.

She put the drinks tray on a log and brought her hands to her face, softly inhaling the musky scent of horse, and felt herself relax. She dropped her hands, though not her guard. She had an instinct for trouble, and this was it.

"Yes, he's my father," said Marc, then turned to his mother again. "He isn't dead?"

It was, thought Gamache, an interesting question. Not, *He's alive?* but rather, *He isn't dead?* There seemed a difference.

"I'm afraid not."

"I'm standing right here, you know," said Dr. Gilbert. "I can hear."

But he didn't seem put off by any of this, just amused. Gamache knew Dr. Vincent Gilbert would be a formidable opponent. And he hoped this Great Man, for that was what Gamache knew him to be, wasn't also a wicked man.

Carole handed Marc a glass of water and took one herself, sitting on the hay beside him. "Your father and I agreed our marriage was over a long time ago. He went off to India as you know."

"Why did you say he was dead?" Marc asked. If he hadn't Beauvoir would have. He'd always thought his own family more than a little odd. Never a whisper, never a calm conversation. Everything was charged, kinetic. Voices raised, shouting, yelling. Always in each other's faces, in each other's lives. It was a mess. He'd yearned for calm, for peace, and had found it in Enid. Their lives were relaxed, soothing, never going too far, or getting too close.

He really should call her.

But odd as his family might be, they were nothing compared to this. In fact, that was one of the great comforts of his job. At least his family compared well to people who actually killed each other, rather than just thought about it.

"It seemed easier," Carole said. "I was happier being a widow than a divorcee."

"But what about me?" Marc asked.

"I thought it would be easier for you too. Easier to think your father had died."

"How could you think that?"

"I'm sorry. I was wrong," said his mother. "But you were twenty-five, and never close to your father. I really thought you wouldn't care."

"So you killed him?"

Vincent Gilbert, silent until now, laughed. "Well put."

"Fuck off," said Marc. "I'll get to you in a minute." He shifted on the prickly hay bale. His father really was a pain in the ass.

"He agreed, no matter how he's rewritten it now. I couldn't have done it without his cooperation. In exchange for his freedom he agreed to be dead."

Marc turned to his father. "Is that right?"

Now Vincent Gilbert looked less regal, less certain. "I wasn't myself. I wasn't well. I'd gone to India to find myself and felt the best way to do that was to shed the old life completely. Become a new man."

"So I just didn't exist anymore?" Marc asked. "What a fucking great family. Where have you been?"

"The Manoir Bellechasse."

"For twenty years? You've been at a luxury inn for twenty years?"

"Oh, well, no. I've been there off and on all summer. I brought you that." He gestured to the package sitting on a shelf in the shed. "It's for you," he said to Dominique. She picked it up.

"Granola," she said. "From the Bellechasse. Thank you."

"Granola?" asked Marc. "You come back from the dead and bring breakfast cereal?"

"I didn't know what you needed," said his father. "I'd heard from your mother that you'd bought a place down here so I came and watched every now and then."

"You're the one Roar Parra spotted in the woods," said Dominique.

"Roar Parra? Roar? Are you kidding? Is he the troll? The dark, stocky man?"

"The nice man helping your son turn this place around, you mean?" asked Carole.

"I say what I mean."

"Will you two please stop it." Dominique glared at Marc's parents. "Behave yourselves."

"Why're you here?" Marc finally asked.

Vincent Gilbert hesitated than sat on a nearby hay bale. "I'd kept in touch with your mother. She told me about your marriage. Your job. You seemed to be happy. But then she said you'd quit your job and moved to the middle of nowhere. I wanted to make sure you were all right. I'm not a complete fool, you know," said Vincent Gilbert, his handsome, aristocratic face somber. "I know what a shock this is. I'm sorry. I should never have let your mother do it."

"*Pardon?*" said Carole.

"Still, I wouldn't have contacted you, but then that body was found and the police showed up and I thought you might need my help."

"Yes, what about that body?" Marc asked his father, who just stared. "Well?"

"Well what? Wait a minute." Vincent Gilbert looked from his son to Gamache, watching with interest, then back again. He laughed. "You're kidding? You think I had something to do with it?"

"Did you?" demanded Marc.

"Do you really expect me to answer that?" The genial man in front of them didn't just bristle, he radiated. It happened so quickly even Gamache was taken aback by the transformation. The cultured, urbane, slightly amused man suddenly overflowed with a rage so great it engulfed him then spilled off him and swallowed everyone. Marc had poked the monster, either forgetting he was in there or wanting to see if he still existed. And he had his answer. Marc stood stock still, his only reaction being a slight, telltale widening of his eyes.

And what a tale those eyes told Gamache. In them he saw the infant, the boy, the young man, afraid. Never certain what he would find in his father. Would he be loving and kind and warm today? Or would he sizzle the skin off his son? With a look, a word. Leaving the boy naked and ashamed. Knowing himself to be weak and needy, stupid and selfish. So that the boy grew an outer hull to withstand assault. But while those skins saved tender young souls, Gamache knew, they soon stopped protecting and became the problem. Because while the hard outer shell kept the hurt at bay, it also kept out the light. And inside the frightened little soul became something else entirely, nurtured only in darkness.

Gamache looked at Marc with interest. He'd poked the monster in front of him, and sure enough, it came awake and lashed out. But had he also awakened a monster inside himself? Or had that happened earlier?

Someone had left a body on their doorstep. Was it father? Or son? Or someone else?

"I expect you to answer, monsieur," said Gamache, turning back to Vincent Gilbert and holding his hard eyes.

"Doctor," Gilbert said, his voice cold. "I will not be diminished by you or anyone else." He looked again at his son, then back to the Chief Inspector.

"*Désolé*," said Gamache and bowed slightly, never taking his deep brown eyes off the angry man. The apology seemed to further enrage Gilbert, who realized one of them was strong enough to withstand insult and one of them wasn't.

"Tell us about the body," Gamache repeated, as though he and Gilbert were having a pleasant conversation. Gilbert looked at him with loathing. Out of the corner of his eye Gamache noticed Marc the horse approaching from the fields. He looked like something a demon might ride, bony, covered with muck and sores. One eye mad, the other eye blind. Attracted, Gamache supposed, by something finally familiar. Rage.

The two men stared at each other. Finally Gilbert snorted derision and waved, dismissing Gamache and his question as trivial. The monster retreated into his cave.

But the horse came closer and closer.

"I know nothing about it. But I thought it looked bad for Marc so I wanted to be here in case he needed me."

"Needed you to do what?" demanded Marc. "Scare everyone half to death? Couldn't you just ring the doorbell or write a letter?"

"I didn't realize you'd be so sensitive." The lash, the tiny wound, the monster smiled and retreated. But Marc had had enough. He reached over the fence and bit Vincent Gilbert on the shoulder. Marc the horse, that is.

"What the hell?" Gilbert yelped and jumped out of the way, his hand on his slimy shoulder.

"Are you going to arrest him?" Marc asked Gamache.

"Are you going to press charges?"

Marc stared at his father, then at the wreck of a creature behind him. Black, wretched, probably half mad. And Marc the man smiled.

"No. Go back to being dead, Dad. Mom was right. It is easier."

He turned and strode back to his home.

What a family," said Beauvoir. They were strolling into the village. Agent Morin had gone ahead to the Incident Room, and they'd left the Gilberts to devour each other. "Still, there does seem a sort of equilibrium about this case."

"What do you mean?" asked Gamache. Off to their left he noticed Ruth Zardo leaving her home followed by Rosa wearing a sweater. Gamache had written a thank-you note for the dinner the night before and stuck it in her rusty mailbox during his morning stroll. He watched as she collected it, glanced at it, and stuck it into the pocket of her ratty old cardigan.

"Well, one man's dead and another comes alive."

Gamache smiled and wondered if it was a fair exchange. Ruth spotted them just as Beauvoir spotted her.

"Run," he hissed to the Chief. "I'll cover you."

"Too late, old son. The duck's seen us."

And indeed, while Ruth seemed happy to ignore them, Rosa was waddling forward at an alarming pace.

"She appears to like you," said Ruth to Beauvoir, limping behind the duck. "But then she does have a birdbrain."

"Madame Zardo," Gamache greeted her with a smile while Beauvoir glared.

"I hear that Gilbert fellow put the body in Olivier's Bistro. Why haven't you arrested him?"

"You heard that already?" asked Beauvoir. "Who told you?"

"Who hasn't? It's all over the village. Well? Are you going to arrest Marc Gilbert?"

"For what?" asked Beauvoir.

"Murder for one. Are you nuts?"

"Am I nuts? Who's the one with a duck in a sweater?"

"And what would you have me do? Let her freeze to death when winter comes? What kind of man are you?"

"Me? Speaking of nuts, what was with that note you had Olivier give me? I can't even remember what it said, but it sure didn't make sense."

"You think not?" the wizened old poet snarled.

"Maybe there's something in all of this I missed."

Gamache quoted the lines and Ruth turned cold eyes on him. "That was a private message. Not meant for you."

"What does it mean, madame?"

"You figure it out. And this one too." Her hand dived into her other pocket and came out with another slip of paper, neatly folded. She handed it to Beauvoir and walked toward the bistro.

Beauvoir looked at the perfect white square in his palm, then closed his fingers over it.

The two men watched Ruth and Rosa walk across the village green. At the far end they saw people entering the bistro.

"She's crazy, of course," said Beauvoir as they walked to the Incident Room. "But she did ask a good question. Why didn't we arrest anyone?

Between father and son we could've been filling out arrest sheets all afternoon."

"To what end?"

"Justice."

Gamache laughed. "I'd forgotten about that. Good point."

"No, really sir. There was everything from trespassing to murder we could have charged them with."

"We both know the victim wasn't murdered in that foyer."

"But that doesn't mean Marc Gilbert didn't kill him somewhere else."

"And put him in his own house, then picked him up again and took him to the bistro?"

"The father could have done it."

"Why?"

Beauvoir thought about that. He couldn't believe that family wasn't guilty of something. And murder seemed right up their alley. Though it seemed most likely they'd kill each other.

"Maybe he wanted to hurt his son," said Beauvoir. But that didn't seem right. They paused on the stone bridge over the Rivière Bella Bella and the Inspector stared over the side, thinking. The sun bounced off the water and he was momentarily mesmerized by the movement. "Maybe it's just the opposite," he began, feeling his way forward. "Maybe Gilbert wanted back in his son's life but needed an excuse. For anyone else I would think that was ridiculous but he has an ego and it might not have let him just knock and apologize. He needed an excuse. I could see him killing a vagrant, someone he considered so far beneath him. Someone he could use for his purpose."

"And what would that be?" asked Gamache, also staring into the clear waters beneath them.

Beauvoir turned to the Chief, noticing the reflected light playing on the man's face. "To be reunited with his son. But he'd need to be seen as the savior, not just as some deadbeat dad crawling back to the family."

Gamache turned to him, interested. "Go on."

"So he killed a vagrant, a man no one would miss, put him in his son's vestibule and waited for the fireworks, figuring he could sweep in and take command of the family when it needed help."

"But then Marc moved the body and there was no excuse," said Gamache.

"Until now. The timing is interesting. We discover the body was in the old Hadley house and an hour later dad appears."

Gamache nodded, his eyes narrowing, and once again he looked into the flowing waters of the river. Beauvoir knew the Chief well enough to know he was walking slowly now through the case, picking his way along the slippery rocks, trying to make out a path obscured by deceit and time.

Beauvoir unfolded the paper in his hands.

I just sit where I'm put, composed
of stone, and wishful thinking:

"Who's Vincent Gilbert, sir? You seemed to know him."

"He's a saint."

Beauvoir laughed, but seeing Gamache's serious face he stopped. "What do you mean?"

"There're some people who believe that."

"Seemed like an asshole to me."

"The hardest part of the process. Telling them apart."

"Do you believe he's a saint?" Beauvoir was almost afraid to ask.

Gamache smiled suddenly. "I'll leave you here. What do you say to lunch in the bistro in half an hour?"

Beauvoir looked at his watch. Twelve thirty-five. "Perfect."

He watched the Chief walk slowly back across the bridge and into Three Pines. Then he looked down again, at the rest of what Ruth had written.

that the deity who kills for pleasure
will also heal,

Someone else was watching Gamache. Inside the bistro Olivier was looking out the window while listening to the sweet sounds of laughter and the till. The place was packed. The whole village, the whole countryside, had emptied into his place, for lunch, for news, for gossip. To hear about the latest dramatic developments.

The old Hadley house had produced another body and spewed it into the bistro. Or at least, its owner had. Any suspicion of Olivier was lifted, the taint gone.

All round him Olivier heard people talking, speculating, about Marc Gilbert. His mental state, his motives. Was he the murderer? But one thing wasn't debated, wasn't in doubt.

Gilbert was finished.

"Who's gonna wanna stay in that place?" he heard someone say. "Parra says they dumped a fortune into the Hadley place, and now this."

There was general agreement. It was a shame. It was inevitable. The new inn and spa was ruined before it even opened. Olivier watched through the window as Gamache walked slowly toward the bistro. Ruth appeared at Olivier's elbow. "Imagine being chased," she said, watching the Chief Inspector's steadfast approach, "by that."

Clara and Gabri squeezed through the crowd to join them.

"What're you looking at?" Clara asked.

"Nothing," said Olivier.

"Him." Ruth pointed at Gamache, apparently deep in thought, but making progress. Without haste, but also without hesitation.

"He must be pleased," said Gabri. "I hear Marc Gilbert killed that man and put him here, in the bistro. Case closed."

"Then why didn't Gamache arrest him?" Clara asked, sipping her beer.

"Gamache's an idiot," said Ruth.

"I hear Gilbert says he found the body in his house," said Clara. "Already dead."

"Right, like that just happens," said Olivier. His friends decided not to remind Olivier that was exactly what happened to him.

Clara and Gabri fought their way over to the bar to get more drinks.

The waiters were being run ragged. He'd give them a bonus, Olivier decided. Something to make up for two days of lost wages. Faith. Gabri was always telling him he had to have faith, trust that things would work out.

And they had worked out. Beautifully.

Beside him Ruth was tapping her cane rhythmically on the wooden floor. It was more than annoying. It was somehow threatening. So soft, but so unstoppable. Tap, tap, tap, tap.

"Scotch?"

That would get her to stop. But she stood ramrod straight, her cane lifting and dropping. Tap, tap, tap. Then he realized what she was tapping out.

Chief Inspector Gamache was still approaching, slowly, deliberately. And with each footfall came a beat of Ruth's cane.

"I wonder if the murderer knows just how terrible a thing is pursuing him?" asked Ruth. "I feel almost sorry for him. He must feel trapped."

"Gilbert did it. Gamache'll arrest him soon."

But the thumping of Ruth's cane matched the thudding in Olivier's chest. He watched Gamache approach. Then, miraculously, Gamache passed them by. And Olivier heard the little tinkle of Myrna's bell.

So, there was some excitement up at the old Hadley house."

Myrna poured Gamache a coffee and joined him by the bookshelves.

"There was. Who told you?"

"Who didn't? Everyone knows. Marc Gilbert was the one who put the body in the bistro. But what people can't figure out is whether he killed the man."

"What're some of the theories?"

"Well." Myrna took a sip of coffee and watched as Gamache moved along the rows of books. "Some think he must have done it, and dumped the body in the bistro to get back at Olivier. Everyone knows they dislike each other. But the rest think if he was really going to do that he'd kill the man in the bistro. Why kill him somewhere else, then move him?"

"You tell me. You're the psychologist." Gamache gave up his search of the shelves and turned to Myrna.

"Former."

"But you can't retire your knowledge."

"Can't crawl back into Paradise?" Taking their coffee to the armchairs in the bay window they sat and sipped while Myrna thought. Finally she spoke.

"Seems unlikely." She didn't look pleased with her answer.

"You want the murderer to be Marc Gilbert?" he asked.

"God help me, I do. Hadn't thought about it before, really, but now that the possibility's here it would be, well, convenient."

"Because he's an outsider?"

"Beyond the pale," said Myrna.

"I'm sorry?"

"Do you know the expression, Chief Inspector?"

"I've heard it, yes. It means someone's done something unacceptable. That's one way of looking at murder, I suppose."

"I didn't mean that. Do you know where the expression comes from?" When Gamache shook his head she smiled. "It's the sort of arcane knowledge a bookstore owner collects. It's from medieval times. A fortress was built with thick stone walls in a circle. We've all seen them, right?"

Gamache had visited many old castles and fortresses, almost all in ruins now, but it was the brightly colored illustrations from the books he'd pored over as a child he remembered most vividly. The towers with vigilant archers, the crenellated stone, the massive wooden doors. The moat and drawbridge. And inside the circle of the walls was a courtyard. When attacked the villagers would race inside, the drawbridge would be raised, the massive doors closed. Everyone inside was safe. They hoped.

Myrna was holding out her palm, and circling it with a finger. "All around are walls, for protection." Then her finger stopped its movement and rested on the soft center of her palm. "This is the pale."

"So if you're beyond the pale . . ."

"You're an outsider," said Myrna. "A threat." She slowly closed her hand. As a black woman she knew what it meant to be "beyond the pale." She'd been on the outside all her life, until she'd moved here. Now she was on the inside and it was the Gilberts' turn.

But it wasn't as comfortable as she'd always imagined the "inside" to be.

Gamache sipped his coffee and watched her. It was interesting that everyone seemed to know about Marc Gilbert moving the body, but no one seemed to know about the other Gilbert, risen from the dead.

"What were you looking for just now?" she asked.

"A book called *Being.*"

"*Being*? That's the one about Brother Albert and the community he built?" She got up and walked toward the bookshelves. "We've talked about this before."

She changed direction and walked to the far end of her bookstore.

"We did, years ago." Gamache followed her.

"I remember now. I gave Old Mundin and The Wife a copy when Charles was born. The book's out of print, I think. Shame. It's brilliant."

They were in her used-books section.

"Ah, here it is. I have one left. A little dog-eared, but the best books are."

She handed Gamache the slim volume. "Can I leave you here? I told Clara I'd meet her in the bistro for lunch."

Armand Gamache settled into his armchair and in the sunshine through the window he read. About an asshole. And a saint. And a miracle.

Jean Guy Beauvoir arrived at the crowded bistro and after ordering a beer from a harried Havoc he squeezed through the crowd. He caught snippets of conversation about the fair, about how horrible the judging was this year, really, the worst so far. About the weather. But mostly he heard about the body.

Roar Parra and Old Mundin were sitting in a corner with a couple of other men. They looked up and nodded at Beauvoir, but didn't move from their precious seats.

Beauvoir scanned the room for Gamache, but knew he wasn't there. Knew as soon as he'd walked in. After a few minutes he managed to snag a table. A minute later he was joined by the Chief Inspector.

"Hard at work, sir?" Beauvoir brushed cookie crumbs from the Chief's shirt.

"Always. You?" Gamache ordered a ginger beer and turned his full attention to his Inspector.

"I Googled Vincent Gilbert."

"And?"

"This is what I found out." Beauvoir flipped open his notebook. "Vincent Gilbert. Born in Quebec City in 1934 into a prominent francophone family. Father a member of the National Assembly, mother from the francophone elite. Degree in philosophy from Laval University then medical degree from McGill. Specializing in genetics. Made a name for himself by creating a test for Down syndrome, in utero. So that they could be found early enough and possibly treated."

Gamache nodded. "But he stopped his research, went to India, and when he returned instead of going back into the lab immediately and completing his research he joined Brother Albert at LaPorte."

The Chief Inspector put a book on the table and slid it toward Beauvoir.

Beauvoir turned it over. There on the back was a scowling, imperious face. Exactly the same look Beauvoir had seen while kneeling on the man's chest just an hour earlier.

"*Being*," he read, then put it down.

"It's about his time at LaPorte," said Gamache.

"I read about it," said Beauvoir. "For people with Down syndrome. Gilbert volunteered there, as medical director, when he got back from India. After that he refused to continue his research. I'd have thought working there he'd want to cure it even more."

Gamache tapped the book. "You should read it."

Beauvoir smirked. "You should tell me about it."

Gamache hesitated, gathering his thoughts. "*Being* isn't really about LaPorte. It's not even about Vincent Gilbert. It's about arrogance, humility and what it means to be human. It's a beautiful book, written by a beautiful man."

"How can you say that about the man we just met? He was a shit."

Gamache laughed. "I don't disagree. Most of the saints were. St. Ignatius had a police record, St. Jerome was a horrible, mean-spirited man, St. Augustine slept around. He once prayed, 'Lord, give me chastity, but not just yet.'"

Beauvoir snorted. "Sounds like lots of people. So why's one a saint and someone else just an asshole?"

"Can't tell you that. It's one of the mysteries."

"Bullshit. You don't even go to church. What do you really think?"

Gamache leaned forward. "I think to be holy is to be human, and Vincent Gilbert is certainly that."

"You think more than that, though, don't you? I can see it. You admire him."

Gamache picked up the worn copy of *Being*. He looked over and saw Old Mundin drinking a Coke and eating cheese and pâté on a baguette. Gamache remembered Charles Mundin's tiny hand grasping his finger. Full of trust, full of grace.

And he tried to imagine a world without that. Dr. Vincent Gilbert, the Great Man, would almost certainly have earned a Nobel Prize, had he continued his research. But he'd stopped his research and earned the scorn of his colleagues and much of the world instead.

And yet *Being* wasn't an apology. It wasn't even an explanation. It just was. Like Charles Mundin.

"Ready?" Gabri appeared. They ordered and just as Gabri was about to leave Agent Morin showed up.

"Hope you don't mind."

"Not at all," said Gamache. Gabri took his order, and just as he was about to leave again Agent Lacoste arrived. Gabri ran his hand through his hair.

"Jeez," said Beauvoir. "They'll be coming out of the closet next."

"You'd be surprised," said Gabri, and took Lacoste's order. "Is that it? Are you expecting the Musical Ride?"

"*C'est tout, patron*," Gamache assured him. "*Merci.* I wasn't expecting you," he said to Lacoste when Gabri was out of earshot.

"I didn't expect to come, but I wanted to talk in person. I spoke to both Olivier's boss at the bank and his father."

She lowered her voice and told them what the executive at the Banque Laurentienne had said. When she finished her salad had arrived. Shrimp, mango and cilantro, on baby spinach. But she looked with envy at the steaming plate of Portobello mushrooms, garlic, basil and Parmesan on top of homemade pasta in front of the Chief.

"So it wasn't clear whether Olivier was going to steal the money or give it back," said Beauvoir, eyeing his charcoal steak and biting into his seasoned thin fries.

"The man I talked to believed Olivier was making the money for the bank. Still, he'd probably have been fired, if he hadn't quit."

"Are they sure all the money he made in the Malaysian deal was given to the bank?" Gamache asked.

"They think it was, and so far we can't find any other account for Olivier."

"So we still don't know where the money came from to buy all that property," said Beauvoir. "What did Olivier's father have to say?"

She told them about her visit to Habitat. By the time she finished their plates had been cleared away and dessert menus were placed in front of them.

"Not for me." Lacoste smiled at Havoc Parra. He smiled back, motioned to another waiter to clear and set a nearby table.

"Who'll share a profiterole with me?" asked Beauvoir. They'd have to solve this case soon or he'd need a whole new wardrobe.

"I will," said Lacoste.

The choux pastries filled with ice cream and covered in warm chocolate sauce arrived. Gamache regretted not ordering some himself. He watched, mesmerized, as Beauvoir and Lacoste took spoonfuls of the now melting ice cream mixed with pastry and the warm, dark chocolate.

"So Olivier's father's never been here," said Beauvoir, wiping his face with his napkin. "He has no idea where Olivier lives or what he's doing. He doesn't even know his son's gay?"

"Can't be the only son afraid to tell his father," said Lacoste.

"Secrets," said Beauvoir. "More secrets."

Gamache noticed Morin's face change as he looked out the window. Then the murmur of conversation in the bistro died away. The Chief followed his agent's gaze.

A moose was galumphing down rue du Moulin, into the village. As it got closer Gamache rose. Someone was on its back, clinging to the massive neck.

"You, stay here. Guard the door," he said to Agent Morin. "You come with me," he said to the others. Before anyone else could react Gamache and his team were out the door. By the time anyone else wanted to follow Agent Morin was standing at the door. Short, weedy, but determined. No one was getting by him.

Through the glass panes they watched as the creature bore down, its long legs pumping, awkward and frantic. Gamache walked foward but it didn't slow, its rider no longer in control. The Chief spread his arms to corral him and as it got closer they recognized it as one of the Gilbert animals. A horse, supposedly. Its eyes wild and white, and its hooves spastic and plunging. Beauvoir and Lacoste stood on either side of the Chief, their arms also out.

At his station by the door young Agent Morin couldn't see what was happening outside. All he could see were the faces of the patrons as they watched. He'd been at enough accident scenes to know that at really bad ones people screamed. At the worst, there was silence.

The bistro was silent.

The three officers stood their ground and the horse came straight for them, then veered, shrieking like a creature possessed. The rider fell off onto the grass of the green and Agent Lacoste managed to grab the reins as the horse skidded and twisted. Beside her Gamache also grabbed the reins and between them they fought the horse to a halt.

Inspector Beauvoir was on his knees on the grass, bending over the fallen rider.

"Are you all right? Don't move, just lie still."

But like most people given that advice, the rider sat up and yanked off her riding helmet. It was Dominique Gilbert. Like the horse's, her eyes were wild and wide. Leaving Lacoste to calm the skittish animal Gamache quickly joined Beauvoir, kneeling beside him.

"What's happened?" asked Gamache.

"In the woods," Dominique Gilbert gasped. "A cabin. I looked inside. There was blood. Lots of it."

EIGHTEEN

⌒

The young man, not much more than a boy, heard the wind. Heard the moan, and heeded it. He stayed. After a day his family, afraid of what they might find, came looking and found him on the side of the terrible mountain. Alive. Alone. They pleaded with him to leave, but, unbelievably, he refused.

"He's been drugged," said his mother.

"He's been cursed," said his sister.

"He's been mesmerized," said his father, backing away.

But they were wrong. He had, in fact, been seduced. By the desolate mountain. And his loneliness. And by the tiny green shoots under his feet.

He'd done this. He'd brought the great mountain alive again. He was needed.

And so the boy stayed, and slowly warmth returned to the mountain. Grass and trees and fragrant flowers returned. Foxes and rabbits and bees came back. Where the boy walked fresh springs appeared and where he sat ponds were created.

The boy was life for the mountain. And the mountain loved him for it. And the boy loved the mountain for it too.

Over the years the terrible mountain became beautiful and word spread. That something dreadful had become something peaceful. And kind. And safe. Slowly the people returned, including the boy's family.

A village sprang up and the Mountain King, so lonely for so long, protected them all. And every night, while the others rested, the boy, now a young man, walked to the very top of the mountain, and lying down on the soft green moss he listened to the voice deep inside.

*Then one night while he lay there the young man heard something un-
expected. The Mountain King told him a secret.*

Olivier watched the wild horse and the fallen rider along with the rest
of the bistro crowd. His skin crawled and he longed to break out, to
scream and push his way out of the crowd. And to run away. Run, run,
run. Until he dropped.

Because, unlike them, he knew what it meant.

Instead he stood and watched as though he was still one of them. But
Olivier knew now he never would be again.

Armand Gamache walked into the bistro and scanned the faces.

"Is Roar Parra still here?"

"I am," said a voice at the back of the bistro. The bodies parted and
the stocky man appeared.

"Madame Gilbert's found a cabin deep in the forest. Does that sound
familiar?"

Parra, along with everyone else, thought. Then he, and everyone
else, shook their heads. "Never knew there was one there."

Gamache thought for a moment then looked outside where Domin-
ique was just catching her breath. "A glass of water, please," he said, and
Gabri appeared with one. "Come with me," the Chief Inspector said to
Parra.

"How far was the cabin?" he asked Dominique after she'd swallowed
the water. "Can we get there on ATVs?"

Dominique shook her head. "No, the forest's too thick."

"How'd you get there?" asked Beauvoir.

"Macaroni took me." She stroked the sweating horse's neck. "After
what happened this morning I needed time alone, so I saddled up and
decided to try to find the old bridle paths."

"That wasn't very smart," said Parra. "You could've been lost."

"I did get lost. That's how I found the cabin. I was on one of the trails
you cut, then it ended, but I could just make out the old path so I kept
on. And that's when I saw it."

Dominique's mind was filled with images. Of the dark cabin, of the
dark stains on the floor. Of jumping on the horse and trying to find the
path back, and holding down the panic. The warnings every Canadian
hears since childhood. Never, ever go into the woods alone.

"Can you find your way back there?" asked Gamache.

Could she? She thought about it, then nodded. "Yes."

"Good. Would you like to rest?"

"I'd like to get this over with."

Gamache nodded, then turned to Roar Parra. "Come with us, please."

As they walked up the hill, Dominique leading Macaroni with Parra beside her and the Sûreté officers behind, Beauvoir whispered to the Chief.

"If we can't get in with ATVs, how're we going to go?"

"Can you say giddyup?"

"I can say whoa." Beauvoir looked as though Gamache had suggested something obscene.

"Well, I suggest you practice."

Within half an hour Roar had saddled Buttercup and Chester. Marc the horse was nowhere to be seen but Marc the husband emerged from the barn, a riding helmet on his head.

"I'm coming with you."

"I'm afraid not, Monsieur Gilbert," said Gamache. "It's simple math. There are three horses. Your wife needs to be on one, and Inspector Beauvoir and I need to be with her."

Beauvoir eyed Chester, who shuffled from one hoof to another as though listening to a Dixieland band in his head. The Inspector had never ridden a horse before and was pretty certain he wasn't about to now.

They set out, Dominique leading, Gamache behind her with a roll of bright pink ribbon to mark their path and Beauvoir bringing up the rear, though Gamache chose not to describe it as that to him. The Chief had ridden many times before. When he'd started dating Reine-Marie they'd go on the bridle paths on Mont Royal. They'd pack a picnic and take the trails through the forest right in the center of Montreal, stopping at a clearing where they could tie up the horses and look over the city, sipping chilled wine and eating sandwiches. The stables on Mont Royal were now closed, but every now and then he and Reine-Marie would head out on a Sunday afternoon and find a place to go trail riding.

Riding Buttercup, however, was a whole other experience. More like being in a small boat on the high seas. He felt slightly nauseous as Buttercup swayed back and forth. Every ten paces or so he reached out and tied another pink ribbon to a tree. Ahead Dominique was way off the ground on Macaroni, and Gamache didn't dare look behind him, but he knew Beauvoir was still there by the constant stream of swear words.

"*Merde. Tabarnac.* Duck."

Branches snapped back so that it felt as though they were being spanked by nature.

Beauvoir, instructed to keep his heels down and his hands steady, quickly lost both stirrups and clung to the gray mane. Regaining the stirrups he straightened up in time to catch another branch in the face. After that it was an inelegant, inglorious exercise in holding on.

"*Tabarnac, Merde.* Duck."

The path narrowed and the forest darkened, and their pace slowed. Gamache was far from convinced they were still on the path, but there was nothing he could do about it now. Agents Lacoste and Morin were gathering the Crime Scene kit and would join them on ATVs as soon as Parra had opened the path. But that would take a while.

How long would it take Lacoste to realize they were lost? An hour? Three? When would night fall? How lost could they get? The forest grew darker and cooler. It felt as though they'd been riding for hours. Gamache checked his watch but couldn't see the dial in the dimness.

Dominique stopped and the following horses crowded together.

"Whoa," said Beauvoir.

Gamache reached out and took the reins, settling the Inspector's horse.

"There it is," Dominique whispered.

Gamache swayed this way and that, trying to see around the trees. Finally he dismounted and tying his horse to a tree walked in front of Dominique. And still he couldn't see it.

"Where?"

"There," Dominique whispered. "Right beside that patch of sunlight."

One thick column of sun beamed through the trees. Gamache looked beside it, and there it was. A cabin.

"Stay here," he said to her, then motioned to Beauvoir who looked around, trying to figure out how to get off. Eventually he leaned over, hugged a tree and hauled himself sideways. Any other horse might have been upset but Chester had seen worse. He seemed quite fond of Beauvoir by the time the Inspector slid off his back. Not once had Beauvoir kicked him, whipped him, or punched him. In Chester's lifetime, Beauvoir was by far the gentlest and kindest of riders.

The two men stared at the cabin. It was made of logs. A single rocking chair with a large cushion sat on the front porch. There were windows on either side of the closed door, each with boxes in full bloom. A stone chimney rose at the side of the cabin, but no smoke came out.

Behind them they could hear the soft rumble of the horses, and the swish of their tails. They could hear small creatures scurrying for cover. The forest smelt of moss and sweet pine needles and decaying leaves.

They crept forward. Onto the porch. Gamache scanned the floorboards. A few dry leaves but no blood. He nodded to Beauvoir and indicated one of the windows. Beauvoir quietly positioned himself beside it, his back against the wall. Gamache took the other window then gave a small signal. Together they looked in.

They saw a table, chairs, a bed at the far end. No lights, no movement.

"Nothing," said Beauvoir. Gamache nodded agreement. He reached out for the door handle. The door swung open an inch with a slight creak. The Chief put his foot forward and pushed it open all the way. Then looked in.

The cabin was a single room and Gamache saw at once there was no one there. He walked in. But Beauvoir kept his hand on his gun. In case. Beauvoir was a cautious man. Being raised in chaos had made him so.

Dust swirled in the little light that struggled through the window. Beauvoir, by habit, felt for a light switch then realized he wouldn't find one. But he did find some lamps and lit those. What came to light was a bed, a dresser, some bookcases, a couple of chairs and a table.

The room was empty. Except for what the dead man had left behind. His belongings and his blood. There was a large, dark stain on the wooden floor.

There was no doubt they'd finally found the crime scene.

An hour later Roar Parra had followed the Chief's pink ribbons and used his chainsaw to widen the path. The ATVs arrived and with them the Crime Scene investigators. Inspector Beauvoir took photographs while Agents Lacoste, Morin and the others combed the room for evidence.

Roar Parra and Dominique Gilbert had mounted the horses and gone home, leading Chester behind them. Chester looked back, hoping to catch a peek at the funny man who had forgotten to beat him.

As the clip-clop of the hooves receded the quiet closed in.

With his team inside working, and the space cramped, Gamache decided to explore outside the cabin. Finely carved window boxes bloomed with cheery nasturtiums and greenery. He rubbed his fingers first on one plant then the others. They smelled of cilantro, rosemary, basil and tarragon. He walked over to the column of sunlight breaking through the trees beside the cabin.

A fence, made of twisted branches, formed a large rectangle about twenty feet wide by forty feet long. Vines grew through the fence, and as he got closer Gamache noticed they were heavy with peas. He opened the wooden gate and walked into the garden. Neat rows of vegetables had been planted and tended, intended for a harvest that would not now come. Up and down the long, protected garden the victim had planted tomatoes and potatoes, peas and beans, and broccoli and carrots. Gamache broke off a bean and ate it. A wheelbarrow with some dirt and a shovel stood halfway along the path and at the far end there sat a chair of bent branches, with comfortable and faded cushions. It was inviting and Gamache had an image of the man working in the garden, then resting. Sitting quietly in the chair.

The Chief Inspector looked down and saw the impression of the man in the cushions. He'd sat there. Perhaps for hours. In the column of light.

Alone.

Not many people, Gamache knew, could do that. Even if they wanted to, even if they chose to, most people couldn't take the quiet. They grew fidgety and bored. But not this man, Gamache suspected. He imagined him there, staring at his garden. Thinking.

What did he think about?

"Chief?"

Turning around Gamache saw Beauvoir walking toward him.

"We've done the preliminary search."

"Weapon?"

Beauvoir shook his head. "But we did find Mason jars of preserves and paraffin. Quite a bit of it. I guess we know why." The Inspector looked around the garden, and seemed impressed. Order always impressed him.

Gamache nodded. "Who was he?"

"I don't know."

Now the Chief Inspector turned fully to his second in command. "What do you mean? Did this cabin belong to our victim?"

"We think so. It's almost certainly where he died. But we haven't found any ID. Nothing. No photographs, no birth certificate, passport, driver's license."

"Letters?"

Beauvoir shook his head. "There're clothes in the dressers. Old clothing, worn. But mended and clean. In fact, the whole place is clean and tidy. A lot of books, we're just going through them now. Some have names in them, but all different names. He must have picked them up at used-book stores. We found woodworking tools and sawdust by one of the chairs. And an old violin. Guess we know what he did at night."

Gamache had a vision of the dead man, alive. Healthy even. Coming in after working the garden. Making a simple dinner, sitting by the fire and whittling. Then, as the night drew in, he'd pick up the violin and play. Just for himself.

Who was this man who loved solitude so much?

"The place is pretty primitive," Beauvoir continued. "He had to pump water into the sink in his kitchen. Haven't seen that in years. And there's no toilet or shower."

Gamache and Beauvoir looked around. Down a winding well-worn path they found an outhouse. The thought almost made Beauvoir gag. The Chief opened the door and looked in. He scanned the tiny one-holer, then closed the door. It too was clean, though spider's webs were beginning to form and soon, Gamache knew, more and more creatures and plants would invade until the outhouse disappeared, eaten by the forest.

"How did he wash?" asked Beauvoir as they walked back to the cabin. They knew he had, and regularly, according to the coroner.

"There's a river," said Gamache, pausing. Ahead sat the cabin, a tiny perfect gem in the middle of the forest. "You can hear it. Probably the Bella Bella, as it heads into the village."

Sure enough Beauvoir heard what sounded strangely like traffic. It was comforting. There was also a cistern beside the cabin, designed to catch rainfall.

"We've found fingerprints." Beauvoir held the door open for the

Chief as they entered the cabin. "We think they belong to two different people."

Gamache's brows rose. The place looked and felt as though only one person lived here. But judging by events, someone else had found the cabin, and the man.

Could this be their break? Could the murderer have left his prints?

The cabin was growing dimmer. Morin found a couple more lamps and some candles. Gamache watched the team at work. There was a grace to it, one perhaps only appreciated by another homicide officer. The fluid motions, stepping aside, leaning in and out and down, bowing and lifting and kneeling. It was almost beautiful.

He stood in the middle of the cabin and took it in. The walls were made of large, round logs. Strangely enough there were curtains at the windows. And in the kitchen a panel of amber glass leaned against the window.

A hand pump at the sink was attached to the wooden kitchen counter, and dishes and glasses were neatly placed on the exposed shelves. Gamache noticed food on the kitchen counter. He walked over and looked, without picking anything up. Bread, butter, cheese. Nibbled, and not by anything human. Some Orange Pekoe tea in an open box. A jar of honey. A quart of milk sat opened. He sniffed. Rancid.

He motioned Beauvoir over.

"What do you think?"

"The man did his shopping."

"How? He sure didn't walk into Monsieur Béliveau's general store, and I'm pretty sure he didn't walk to Saint-Rémy. Someone brought this food to him."

"And killed him? Had a cup of tea then bashed his head in?"

"Maybe, maybe," murmured the Chief Inspector as he looked around. The oil lamps threw light very unlike anything an electric bulb produced. This light was gentle. The edges of the world seemed softer.

A woodstove separated the rustic kitchen and the living area. A small table, covered in cloth, seemed to be his dining table. A riverstone fireplace was on the opposite wall with a wing chair on either side. At the far end of the cabin was a large brass bed and a chest of drawers.

The bed was made, the pillows fluffed and ready. Fabric hung on the walls, presumably to keep out the cold drafts, as you'd find in medieval castles. There were rugs scattered about the floor, a floor marred only, but deeply, by a dark stain of blood.

A bookcase lining an entire wall was filled with old volumes. Approaching it Gamache noticed something protruding from between the logs. He picked at it and looked at what he held.

A dollar bill.

It'd been years, decades, since Canada used dollar bills. Examining the wall more closely he noticed other paper protruding. More dollar bills. Some two-dollar bills. In a couple of cases there were twenties.

Was this the man's banking system? Like an old miser, instead of stuffing his mattress had he stuffed his walls? After a tour of the walls Gamache concluded the money was there to keep the cold out. The cabin was made of wood and Canadian currency. It was insulation.

Next he walked over to the riverstone fireplace, pausing at one of the wing chairs. The one with the deepest impressions in the seat and back. He touched the worn fabric. Looking down at the table beside the chair he saw the whittling tools Beauvoir had mentioned, and leaning against the table was a fiddle and bow. A book, closed but with a bookmark, sat beside the tools. Had the man been reading when he was interrupted?

He picked it up and smiled.

"*I had three chairs in my house,*" Gamache read quietly. "*One for solitude, two for friendship, three for society.*"

"*Pardon?*" said Lacoste, from where she was crouching, looking under the table.

"Thoreau. From *Walden.*" Gamache held up the book. "He lived in a cabin, you know. Not unlike this, perhaps."

"But he had three chairs," smiled Lacoste. "Our man had only two."

Only two, thought Gamache. But that was enough, and that was significant. *Two for friendship.* Did he have a friend?

"I think he might have been Russian," she said, straightening up.

"Why?"

"There're a few icons on the shelf here, by the books." Lacoste waved behind her, and sure enough, in front of the leather-bound volumes were Russian icons.

The Chief frowned and gazed around the small cabin. After a minute he grew very quiet, very still. Except for his eyes, which darted here and there.

Beauvoir approached. "What is it?"

The Chief didn't answer. The room grew hushed. He moved his eyes around the cabin again, not really believing what he saw. So great was his surprise he closed his eyes then opened them again.

"What is it?" Beauvoir repeated.

"Be very careful with that," he said to Agent Morin, who was holding a glass from the kitchen.

"I will," he said, wondering why the Chief would suddenly say that.

"May I have it, please?"

Morin gave it to Gamache who took it to an oil lamp. There, in the soft light, he saw what he expected to see, but never expected to hold in his own hands. Leaded glass, expertly cut. Hand cut. He couldn't make out the mark on the bottom of the glass, and even if he could it would be meaningless to him. He was no expert. But he was knowledgeable enough to know what he held was priceless.

It was an extremely old, even ancient, piece of glass. Made in a method not seen in hundreds of years. Gamache gently put the glass down and looked into the kitchen. On the open rustic shelves there stood at least ten glasses, all different sizes. All equally ancient. As his team watched, Armand Gamache moved along the shelves, picking up plates and cups and cutlery, then over to the walls to examine the hangings. He looked at the rugs, picking up the corners, and finally, like a man almost afraid of what he'd find, he approached the bookcases.

"What is it, *patron*?" asked Beauvoir, joining him.

"This isn't just any cabin, Jean Guy. This is a museum. Each piece is an antiquity, priceless."

"You're kidding," said Morin, putting down the horse figurine jug.

Who was this man? Gamache wondered. Who chose to live this far from other people? *Three for society.*

This man wanted no part of society. What was he afraid of? Only fear could propel a man so far from company. Was he a survivalist, as they'd theorized? Gamache thought not. The contents of the cabin argued against that. No guns, no weapons at all. No how-to magazines, no publications warning of dire plots.

Instead, this man had brought delicate leaded crystal with him into the woods.

Gamache scanned the books, not daring to touch them. "Have these been dusted?"

"They have," said Morin. "And I looked inside for a name, but they're no help. Different names written in most of them. Obviously secondhand."

"Obviously," whispered Gamache to himself. He looked at the one still in his hand. Opening it to the bookmark he read, *I went to the woods because I wished to live deliberately, to front only the essential facts of life, and to see if I could not learn what it had to teach, and not, when I came to die, discover that I had not lived.*

Gamache turned to the front page and inhaled softly.

It was a first edition.

NINETEEN

 "Peter?" Clara knocked lightly on the door to his studio.

He opened it, trying not to look secretive but giving up. Clara knew him too well, and knew he was always secretive about his art.

"How's it going?"

"Not bad," he said, longing to close the door and get back to it. All day he'd been picking up his brush, approaching his painting then lowering the brush again. Surely the painting wasn't finished? It was so embarrassing. What would Clara think? What would his gallery think? The critics? It was unlike anything else he'd ever done. Well, not ever. But certainly since childhood.

He could never let anyone see this.

It was ridiculous.

What it needed, clearly, was more definition, more detail. More depth. The sorts of things his clients and supporters had come to expect. And buy.

He'd picked up and lowered his brush a dozen times that day. This had never happened to him before. He'd watched, mystified, as Clara had been racked by self-doubt, had struggled and had finally produced some marginal piece of work. Her *March of the Happy Ears*, her series inspired by dragonfly wings, and, of course, her masterpiece, the *Warrior Uteruses*.

That's what came of inspiration.

No, Peter was much more clear. More disciplined. He planned each piece, drew and drafted each work, knew months in advance what he'd be working on. He didn't rely on airy-fairy inspiration.

Until now. This time he'd come into the studio with a fireplace log, cut cleanly so that the rings of age were visible. He'd taken his magnifying glass and approached it, with a view to enlarging a tiny part of it beyond recognition. It was, he liked to tell art critics at his many sold-out *vernissages*, an allegory for life. How we blow things out of all proportion, until a simple truth was no longer recognizable.

They ate it up. But this time it hadn't worked. He'd been unable to see the simple truth. Instead, he'd painted this.

When Clara left Peter plopped down in his chair and stared at the bewildering piece of work on his easel and repeated silently to himself, *I'm brilliant, I'm brilliant*. Then he whispered, so quietly he barely heard it himself, "I'm better than Clara."

Olivier stood on the *terrasse* outside the bistro and looked into the dark forest on the hill. In fact, Three Pines was surrounded by forest, something he'd never noticed, until now.

The cabin had been found. He'd prayed this wouldn't happen, but it had. And for the first time since he'd arrived in Three Pines he felt the dark forest closing in.

But if all these things," Beauvoir nodded to the interior of the single room, "are priceless why didn't the murderer take them?"

"I've been wondering that myself," said Gamache from the comfort of the large wing chair by the empty fireplace. "What was the murder about, Jean Guy? Why kill this man who seems to have lived a quiet, secret life in the woods for years, maybe decades?"

"And then once he's dead, why take the body but leave the valuables?" Beauvoir sat in the chair opposite the Chief.

"Unless the body was more valuable than the rest?"

"Then why leave it at the old Hadley house?"

"If the murderer had just left the body here we'd never have found it," reasoned Gamache, perplexed. "Never known there'd been a murder."

"Why kill the man, if not for his treasure?" asked Beauvoir.

"Treasure?"

"What else is it? Priceless stuff in the middle of nowhere? It's buried treasure, only instead of being buried in the ground it's buried in the forest."

But the murderer had left it there. And instead, had taken the only thing he wanted from that cabin. He'd taken a life.

"Did you notice this?" Beauvoir got up and walked to the door. Opening it he pointed upward, with a look of amusement.

There on the lintel above the door was a number.

16

"Now, you can't tell me he got mail," said Beauvoir as Gamache stared, puzzled. The numbers were brass and tarnished green. Almost invisible against the dark wooden door frame. Gamache shook his head then looked at his watch. It was almost six.

After a bit of discussion it was decided Agent Morin would stay at the cabin overnight, to guard the possessions.

"Come with me," Gamache said to Morin. "I'll drive you in while the others finish the job. You can pack an overnight bag and arrange for a satellite phone."

Morin got on the ATV behind the Chief Inspector and searched for something to grip, settling on the bottom of the seat. Gamache started up the machine. His investigations had taken him into tiny fishing outports and remote settlements. He'd driven snowmobiles, power boats, motorcycles and ATVs. While appreciating their convenience, and necessity, he disliked them all. They shattered the calm with their banshee screams, polluting the wilderness with noise and fumes.

If anything could wake the dead, these could.

As they bounced along Morin realized he was in trouble, and letting go of the seat he flung his small arms around the large man in front of him and held on tight, feeling the Chief's wax coat against his cheek and the strong body underneath. And he smelled sandalwood and rosewater.

The young man sat up, one hand on the Mountain, the other to his face. He couldn't quite believe what the Mountain had told him. Then he started to giggle.

Hearing this, the Mountain was puzzled. It wasn't the shriek of terror he normally heard from creatures who came near him.

As he listened the Mountain King realized this was a happy sound. An infectious sound. He too started to rumble and only stopped when the people in the village grew frightened. And he didn't want that. Never again did he want to scare anything away.

He slept well that night.

The boy, however, did not. He tossed and turned and finally left his cabin to stare up at the peak.

Every night from then on the boy was burdened by the Mountain's secret. He grew weary and weak. His parents and friends commented on this. Even the Mountain noticed.

Finally, one night well before the sun rose the boy nudged his parents awake.

"We need to leave."

"What?" his bleary mother asked.

"Why?" his father and sister asked.

"The Mountain King has told me of a wonderful land where people never die, never grow sick or old. It's a place only he knows about. But he says we need to leave now. Tonight. While it's still dark. And we need to go quickly."

They woke up the rest of the village and well before dawn they'd packed up. The boy was the last to leave. He took a few steps into the forest and kneeling down he touched the surface of the sleeping Mountain King.

"Good-bye," he whispered.

Then he tucked the package under his arm, and disappeared into the night.

Jean Guy Beauvoir stood outside the cabin. It was almost dark and he was starving. They'd finished their work and he was just waiting for Agent Lacoste to pack up.

"I have to pee," she said, joining him on the porch. "Any ideas?"

"There's an outhouse over there." He pointed away from the cabin.

"Great," she said and grabbed a flashlight. "Isn't this how horror movies start?"

"Oh no, we're well into the second reel by now," said Beauvoir with a smirk. He watched Lacoste pick her way along the path to the outhouse.

His stomach growled. At least, he hoped it was his stomach. The sooner they got back to civilization, the better. How could anyone live out here? He didn't envy Morin spending the night.

A bobbing flashlight told him Lacoste was returning.

"Have you been into the outhouse?" she asked.

"Are you kidding? The Chief looked in, but I didn't." Even thinking about it made him gag.

"So you didn't see what was in there."

"Don't tell me, the toilet paper was money too."

"Actually it was. One- and two-dollar bills."

"You're joking."

"I'm not. And I found this." She held a book in her hand. "A first edition. Signed by E. B. White. It's *Charlotte's Web*."

Beauvoir stared at it. He had no idea what she was talking about.

"It was my favorite book as a child. Charlotte the spider?" she asked. "Wilbur the pig?"

"If they didn't get blown up I didn't read it."

"Who leaves a signed first edition in an outhouse?"

"Who leaves money there?" Beauvoir suddenly felt an urge to go.

Salut, patron," waved Gabri from the living room. He was folding tiny outfits and putting them into a box. "So, the cabin in the woods. Was it where the guy lived? The dead man?"

"We think so." Gamache joined him. He watched Gabri fold the small sweaters.

"For Rosa. We're collecting them from everyone to give to Ruth. Is this too big for Rosa?" He held up a boy's blazer. "It's Olivier's. He says he made it himself but I can't believe that, though he's very good with his hands." Gamache ignored that.

"It's a little big. And masculine, for Rosa, don't you think?" he said.

"True." Gabri put it in the reject pile. "In a few years it might fit Ruth though."

"Did no one ever mention a cabin before? Not old Mrs. Hadley?"

Gabri shook his head but continued working. "No one." Then he stopped folding and put his hands in his lap. "I wonder how he survived? Did he walk all the way to Cowansville or Saint-Rémy for food?"

One more thing we don't know, thought Gamache as he went up the stairs. He showered and shaved and called his wife. It was getting dark and in the distance he could hear the shriek from the forest. The ATVs returning. To the village and to the cabin.

In the living room of the B and B, Gabri had been replaced by someone else. Sitting in the comfortable chair by the fire was Vincent Gilbert.

"I've been over to the bistro but people kept bothering me, so I came here to bother you. I've been trying to get out of my son's way. Funny how coming back from the dead isn't as popular as it once was."

"Did you expect him to be happy?"

"You know, I actually did. Amazing, isn't it, our capacity for self-deceit."

Gamache looked at him quizzically.

"All right, my capacity for it," snapped Gilbert. He studied Gamache. Tall, powerfully built. Probably ten pounds overweight, maybe more. Go to fat if he's not careful. Die of a heart attack.

He imagined Gamache suddenly clutching his chest, his eyes widening then closing in pain. Staggering against the wall and gasping. And Dr. Vincent Gilbert, the celebrated physician, folding his arms, doing nothing, as this head of homicide slipped to the ground. It comforted him to know he had that power, of life and death.

Gamache looked at this rigid man. In front of him was the face he'd seen staring, glaring, from the back of that lovely book, *Being*. Arrogant, challenging, confident.

But Gamache had read the book, and knew what lay behind that face.

"Are you staying here?" They'd told Gilbert not to leave the area and the B and B was the only guesthouse.

"Actually, no. I'm the first guest at Marc's inn and spa. Don't think I'll ask for a treatment, though." He had the grace to smile. Like most stern people, he looked very different when he smiled.

Gamache's surprise was obvious.

"I know," agreed Gilbert. "It was actually Dominique who invited me to stay, though she did suggest I might want to be . . ."

"Discreet?"

"Invisible. So I came into town."

Gamache sat in an armchair. "Why did you come looking for your son now?"

It had escaped no one that both Gilbert and the body had shown up at the same time. Again Gamache saw the cabin, with its two comfortable chairs by the fire. Had two older men sat there on a summer's night? Talking, discussing? Arguing? Murdering?

Vincent Gilbert looked down at his hands. Hands that had been inside people. Hands that had held hearts. Repaired hearts. Got them beating again, and restored life. They trembled, unsteady. And he felt a pain in his chest.

Was he having a heart attack?

He looked up and saw this large, steady man watching him. And he thought if he was having a heart attack this man would probably help.

How to explain his time at LaPorte, living with men and women with Down syndrome? At first he'd thought his job was to simply look after their bodies.

Help others.

That's what the guru had told him to do. Years he'd been at the ashram in India and the guru had finally acknowleged his presence. Almost a decade he'd spent there, in exchange for two words.

Help others.

So that's what he did. He returned to Quebec and joined Brother Albert at LaPorte. To help others. It never, ever occurred to him that they'd help him. After all, how could people that damaged have anything to offer the great healer and philosopher?

It had taken years, but he'd woken up one morning in his cottage in the grounds of LaPorte and something had changed. He'd gone down to breakfast and realized he knew everyone's name. And everyone spoke to him, or smiled. Or came up and showed him something they'd found. A snail, a stick, a blade of grass.

Mundane. Nothing. And yet the whole world had changed, as he slept. He'd gone to bed helping others, and woken up healed himself.

That afternoon, in the shade of a maple tree, he'd started writing *Being.*

"I'd kept an eye on Marc. Watched his successes in Montreal. When they sold their home and bought down here I knew the signs."

"Signs of what?" Gamache asked.

"Burnout. I wanted to help."

Help others.

He was just beginning to appreciate the power of those two simple words. And that help came in different forms.

"By doing what?" asked Gamache.

"By making sure he was all right," Gilbert snapped. "Look, they're all upset up there about the body. Marc did a stupid thing moving it, but I know him. He's not a murderer."

"How do you know?"

Gilbert glared at him. His rage back in full force. But Armand Gamache knew what was behind that rage. What was behind all rage.

Fear.

What was Vincent Gilbert so afraid of?

The answer was easy. He was afraid his son would be arrested for murder. Either because he knew his son had done it, or because he knew he hadn't.

A few minutes later a voice cut across the crowded bistro, aimed at the Chief Inspector, who'd arrived seeking a glass of red wine and quiet to read his book.

"You bugger."

More than one person looked up. Myrna sailed across the room and stood next to Gamache's table, glaring down at him. He got up and bowed slightly, indicating a chair.

Myrna sat so suddenly the chair gave a little crack.

"Wine?"

"Why didn't you tell me why you wanted that?" She gestured toward *Being* in his hand. Gamache grinned.

"Secrets."

"And how long did you think it'd remain a secret?"

"Long enough. I hear he was over here having a drink. Did you meet him?"

"Vincent Gilbert? If you can call ogling and sputtering and fawning 'meeting,' then yes. I met him."

"I'm sure he'll have forgotten it was you."

"Because I'm so easily mistaken for someone else? Is he really Marc's father?"

"He is."

"Do you know, he ignored me when I tried to introduce myself? Looked at me like I was a crumb." The wine and a fresh bowl of cashews had arrived. "Thank God I told him I was Clara Morrow."

"So did I," said Gamache. "He might be growing suspicious."

Myrna laughed and felt her annoyance slip away. "Old Mundin says it was Vincent Gilbert in the forest, spying on his own son. Was it?"

Gamache wondered how much to say, but it was clear this was not much of a secret anymore. He nodded.

"Why spy on his own son?"

"They were estranged."

"First good thing I've heard about Marc Gilbert," said Myrna. "Still, it's ironic. The famous Dr. Gilbert helps so many kids, but is estranged from his own."

Gamache thought again about Annie. Was he doing the same thing to her? Was he listening to the troubles of others, but deaf to his own daughter? He'd spoken to her the night before and reassured himself she was fine. But fine and flourishing were two different things. It had clearly gotten bad when she was willing to listen to Beauvoir.

"*Patron*," said Olivier, handing Gamache and Myrna menus.

"I'm not staying," said Myrna.

Olivier hovered. "I hear you found out where the dead man lived. He was in the forest all along?"

Lacoste and Beauvoir arrived just then and ordered drinks. With one last gulp of wine, and taking a large handful of cashews, Myrna got up to leave.

"I'm going to be paying a lot more attention to the books you buy," she said.

"Do you happen to have *Walden*?" Gamache asked.

"Don't tell me you found Thoreau back there too? Anyone else hiding in our woods? Jimmy Hoffa perhaps? Amelia Earhart? Come by after dinner and I'll give you my copy of *Walden*."

She left and Olivier took their orders then brought warm rolls smothered in melting monarda butter and spread with pâté. Beauvoir produced a sheaf of photographs of the cabin from his satchel and handed them to the Chief.

"Printed these out as soon as we got back." Beauvoir took a bite of his warm roll. He was starving. Agent Lacoste took one as well and sipping on her wine she looked out the window. But all she could see was the reflection of the bistro. Villagers eating dinner, some sitting at the bar with beer or whiskey. Some relaxing by the fire. No one paying attention to them. But then she met a pair of eyes in the reflection. More specter than person. She turned just as Olivier disappeared into the kitchen.

A few minutes later a plate of *escargots* bathed in garlic butter was placed in front of Beauvoir with a bowl of minted sweetpea soup for Lacoste and cauliflower and stilton soup with pear and date relish for Gamache.

"Hmm," said Lacoste, taking a spoonful. "Fresh from the garden. Yours too, probably." She nodded to Beauvoir's snails. He smirked but ate them anyway, dipping the crusty bread into the liquid garlic butter.

Gamache was looking at the photographs. Slowly he lowered the pictures. It was like stumbling across King Tut's tomb.

"I have a call in to Superintendent Brunel," he said.

"The head of property crime?" asked Lacoste. "That's a good idea."

Thérèse Brunel was an expert in art theft and a personal friend of Gamache.

"She's going to die when she sees that cabin," Beauvoir laughed. Olivier removed their dishes.

"How could the dead man have collected all these things?" Gamache wondered. "And gotten them in there?"

"And why?" said Beauvoir.

"But there were no personal items," said Lacoste. "Not a single photograph, no letters, bank books. ID. Nothing."

"And no obvious murder weapon," said Beauvoir. "We sent the fireplace poker and a couple of garden tools to be tested, but it doesn't look promising."

"But I did find something after you left." Lacoste put a bag onto the table and opened it. "It was way under the bed, against the wall. I missed it the first time I looked," she explained. "I fingerprinted it and took samples. They're on the way to the lab."

On the table was a carved piece of wood, stained with what looked like blood.

Someone had whittled a word in the wood.

Woe.

TWENTY

Agent Morin wandered round inside the cabin, humming. In one hand he gripped the satellite phone, in the other he gripped a piece of firewood. Not for the woodstove, which was lit and throwing good heat. Nor the fireplace, also lit and light. But in case anything came at him out of the shadows, out of the corners.

He'd lit all the oil lamps and all the candles. The dead man seemed to have made them himself, from paraffin left over after the preserves had been sealed.

Morin missed his television. His cell phone. His girlfriend. His mother. He brought the phone up to his mouth again, then lowered it for what felt like the hundredth time.

You can't call the Chief Inspector. What'll you say? You're scared? To be alone in a cabin in the woods? Where a man was murdered?

And he sure couldn't call his mother. She'd find a way to reach the cabin, and the team would find him next morning, with his mother. Ironing his shirts and frying bacon and eggs.

No, he'd rather die.

He wandered around some more, poking things here and there, but being very, very careful. Elmer Fudd–like he crept round, picking up glass and peering at odds and ends. A pane of amber at the kitchen window, an engraved silver candlestick. Eventually he took a sandwich from the brown paper bag and unfolded the waxed paper. Ham and Brie on baguette. Not bad. He took the Coca-Cola, snapped it open, then he sat by the fire. The chair was exceptionally comfortable. As he ate he relaxed and by the time he got to the pastry he was feeling himself again.

He reached for the fiddle by his side, but thought better of it. Instead he took a book at random from the shelves and opened it.

It was by an author he'd never heard of. Some guy named Currer Bell. He started to read about a girl named Jane growing up in England. After a while his eyes, strained from reading by the weak light, grew tired. He thought it was probably time for bed. It must be after midnight.

He looked at his watch. Eight thirty.

Reaching over, he hesitated, then picked up the violin. Its wood was deep and seemed warm to the touch. He smoothed his young hand over it, softly, caressing and turning it round in practiced hands. He put it down quickly. He shouldn't be touching it. He went back to the book, but after a minute or so he found the fiddle in his hands again. Knowing he shouldn't, begging himself not to, he reached for the horse-hair bow. Knowing there was no going back now, he stood up.

Agent Morin tucked the violin under his chin and drew the bow across the strings. The sound was deep and rich and seductive. It was more than the young agent could resist. Soon the comforting strains of "Colm Quigley" filled the cabin. Almost to the corners.

Their main courses had arrived. A fruit-stuffed Rock Cornish game hen, done on the spit, for Gamache; melted Brie, fresh tomato and basil fettuccine for Lacoste; and a lamb and prune tagine for Beauvoir. A platter of freshly harvested grilled vegetables was also brought to the table.

Gamache's chicken was tender and tasty, delicately flavored with Pommery-style mustard and vermouth.

"What does that piece of wood mean?" Gamache asked his team as they ate.

"Well, it was just about the only thing in the cabin that wasn't an antique," said Lacoste. "And what with the whittling tools I'm guessing he made it himself."

Gamache nodded. It was his guess as well. "But why woe?"

"Could that be his name?" Beauvoir asked, but without enthusiasm.

"Monsieur Woe?" asked Lacoste. "That might also explain why he lived alone in a cabin."

"Why would someone carve that for himself?" Gamache put down his knife and fork. "And you found nothing else in the cabin that looked as though it had been whittled?"

"Nothing," said Beauvoir. "We found axes and hammers and saws. All well used. I think he must have made that cabin himself. But he sure didn't whittle it."

Woe, thought Gamache, picking up his knife and fork again. Was the Hermit that sad?

"Did you notice our photographs of the stream, sir?" Lacoste asked.

"I did. At least now we know how the dead man kept his groceries cool."

Agent Lacoste, on investigating the stream, had found a bag anchored there. And in it were jars of perishable foods. Dangling in the cold water.

"But he obviously didn't make his own milk and cheese, and no one remembers seeing him in the local shops," said Beauvoir. "So that leaves us with one conclusion."

"Someone was taking him supplies," said Lacoste.

"Everything all right?" asked Olivier.

"Fine, *patron, merci*," said Gamache with a smile.

"Do you need more mayonnaise or butter?" Olivier smiled back, trying not to look like a maniac. Trying to tell himself that no matter how many condiments or warm buns or glasses of wine he brought it would make no difference. He could never ingratiate himself.

"*Non, merci*," said Lacoste, and reluctantly Olivier left.

"We at least have prints from the cabin. We should find out something tomorrow," said Beauvoir.

"*I think we know why he was killed just now*," said Gamache.

"The paths," said Lacoste. "Roar Parra was cutting riding paths for Dominique. One path was almost at the cabin. Close enough to see it."

"Which Madame Gilbert did," said Beauvoir. "But we have only her word that she didn't find the cabin on an earlier ride."

"Except that they didn't have the horses then," said Lacoste. "They didn't arrive until the day after the murder."

"But she might have walked the old paths," suggested Gamache, "in preparation for the horses, and to tell Roar which ones he should open."

"Roar might have walked them too," said Beauvoir. "Or that son of his. Havoc. Parra said he was going to help him."

The other two thought. Still, there seemed no very good reason why either Parra would walk the old riding paths before clearing them.

"But why kill the recluse?" Lacoste said. "Even supposing one of the Parras or Dominique Gilbert found him. It makes no sense. Killing for the treasure, maybe. But why leave it all there?"

"Maybe it wasn't," said Beauvoir. "We know what we found. But maybe there was more."

It struck Gamache like a ton of bricks. Why hadn't he thought of that? He'd been so overwhelmed by what was there, he'd never even considered what might be missing.

Agent Morin lay in the bed and tried to get comfortable. It felt strange to be sleeping in a bed made by a dead man.

He closed his eyes. Turned over. Turned back. Opening his eyes he stared at the firelight flickering in the hearth. The cabin was less frightening. In fact, it was almost cozy.

He punched the pillow a few times to fluff it up, but something resisted.

Sitting up he took the pillow and scrunched it around. Sure enough, there was something besides feathers inside. He got up and lighting an oil lamp he took the pillow out of its case. A deep pocket had been sewn inside. Carefully, feeling like a vet with a pregnant horse, he slipped his arm in up to the elbow. His hand closed over something hard and knobby.

Withdrawing it he held an object to the oil lamp. It was an intricate carving. Of men and women on a ship. They were all facing the bow. Morin marveled at the workmanship. Whoever carved this had captured the excitement of a journey. The same excitement Morin and his sister had felt as kids when they took family car trips to the Abitibi or the Gaspé.

He recognized the happy anticipation on the shipboard faces. Looking closer he saw most had bags and sacks and there was a variety of ages, from newborns to the very old and infirm. Some were ecstatic, some expectant, some calm and content.

All were happy. It was a ship full of hope.

The sails of the ship were, incredibly, carved of wood shaved thin. He turned it over. Something was scratched into the bottom. He took it right up to the lamp.

OWSVI

Was it Russian? Agent Lacoste thought the dead man might be Russian because of the icons. Was this his name? Written in that strange alphabet they use?

Then he had an idea. He went back to the bed and tried the other pillow, which had been below the first. There was something hard in there too. Pulling it out he held another sculpture, also of wood, equally detailed. This one showed men and women gathered at a body of water, looking out at it. Some seemed perplexed, but most appeared content to just be there. He found letters scratched on the bottom of that one too.

MRKBVYDDO

Righting it again he placed it on the table beside the other one. There was a sense of joy, of hope, about these works. He stared at them with more fascination than he ever got from TV.

But the more he looked the more uneasy he became until it felt as though something was watching him. He looked into the kitchen then quickly scanned the room. Turning back to the carvings he was surprised to find the sense of foreboding was coming from them.

He felt a creeping up and down his back and turned quickly into the dark room, instantly regretting not putting on more lamps. A glittering caught his attention. Up high. In the farthest corner of the cabin. Was it eyes?

Picking up his piece of wood he crept closer, crouching down. As he approached the corner the glitter began to form a pattern. It was a spider's web, just catching the soft glow of the lamp. But there was something different about it. As his eyes adjusted the hair on the back of his neck rose.

A word had been woven into the web.

Woe.

TWENTY-ONE

Everyone was already around the table next morning when Morin arrived, more than a little disheveled. They glanced at him, and Agent Lacoste indicated the seat next to her, where, miraculously for the hungry young agent, there waited a bowl of strong *café au lait* along with a plate of scrambled eggs, bacon and thick-cut toast with jams.

Morin wolfed down the food and listened to the reports, and then it was his turn.

He placed the two carvings on the table and moved them slowly to the center. So lively were the sculptures it looked as though the ship had taken sail and was moving on its own. And it looked as though the people on the shore were eagerly awaiting the arrival of the ship.

"What are those?" asked Gamache, rising from his chair and moving round the table for a closer look.

"I found them last night. They were hidden in the pillows on the bed."

The three officers looked stunned.

"You're kidding," said Lacoste. "In the pillows?"

"Sewn into the pillows on the bed. Well hidden, though I'm not sure whether he was hiding them or protecting them."

"Why didn't you call?" demanded Beauvoir, tearing his eyes from the carvings to look at Morin.

"Should I have?" He looked stricken, his eyes bouncing among the officers. "I just thought there was nothing we could do until now anyway."

He'd longed to call; only a mighty effort had stopped him from dialing the B and B and waking them all up. But he didn't want to give in to his fear. But he could see by their faces he'd made a mistake.

All his life he'd been afraid, and all his life it had marred his judgment. He'd hoped that had stopped, but apparently not.

"Next time," the Chief said, looking at him sternly, "call. We're a team, we need to know everything."

"*Oui, patron.*"

"Have these been dusted?" Beauvoir asked.

Morin nodded and held up an envelope. "The prints."

Beauvoir grabbed it out of his hand and took it to his computer to scan in. But even from there his eyes kept going back to the two carvings.

Gamache was leaning over the table, peering at them through his half-moon glasses

"They're remarkable."

The joy of the little wooden travelers was palpable. Gamache knelt down so that he was at eye level with the carvings, and they were sailing toward him. It seemed the carvings were two halves of a whole. A ship full of people sailing toward a shore. And more happy people waiting.

So why did he feel uneasy? Why did he want to warn the ship to go back?

"There's something written on the bottom of each," Morin offered. He picked one up and showed it to the Chief who looked then handed it to Lacoste. Beauvoir picked up the other and saw a series of letters. It was nonsense, but of course it wasn't really. It meant something. They just had to figure it out.

"Is it Russian?" Morin asked.

"No. The Russian alphabet is Cyrillic. This is the Roman alphabet," said Gamache.

"What does it mean?"

The three more seasoned officers looked at each other.

"I have no idea," admitted the Chief Inspector. "Most artisans mark their works, sign them in some way. Perhaps this is how the carver signed his works."

"Then wouldn't the lettering under each carving be the same?" asked Morin.

"That's true. I'm at a loss. Perhaps Superintendent Brunel can tell us. She'll be here this morning."

"I found something else last night," said Morin. "I took a picture of it. It's still in my camera. You can't see it too well, but . . ."

He turned on his digital camera and handed it to Beauvoir, who looked briefly at the image.

"Too small. I can't make it out. I'll throw it up onto the computer."

They continued to discuss the case while Beauvoir sat at his computer, downloading the image.

"*Tabarnac*," they heard him whisper.

"What is it?" Gamache walked to the desk. Lacoste joined him and they huddled round the flat screen.

There was the web, and the word.

Woe.

"What does it mean?" Beauvoir asked, almost to himself.

Gamache shook his head. How could a spider have woven a word? And why that one? The same word they'd found carved in wood and tossed under the bed.

"Some pig."

They looked at Lacoste.

"*Pardon?*" Gamache asked.

"When I was in the outhouse yesterday I found a signed first edition."

"About a girl named Jane?" Morin asked, then wished he hadn't. They all looked at him as though he'd said "some pig." "I found a book in the cabin," he explained. "By a guy named Currer Bell."

Lacoste looked blank, Gamache looked perplexed, and Morin didn't even want to think what look Beauvoir was giving him.

"Never mind. Go on."

"It was *Charlotte's Web*, by E. B. White," said Agent Lacoste. "One of my favorites as a child."

"My daughter's too," said Gamache. He remembered reading the book over and over to the little girl who pretended she wasn't afraid of the dark. Afraid of the closed closet, afraid of the creaks and groans of the house. He'd read to her every night until finally she'd fall asleep.

The book that gave her the most comfort, and that he'd practically memorized, was *Charlotte's Web*.

"Some pig," he repeated, and gave a low, rumbling laugh. "The book's about a lonely piglet destined for the slaughterhouse. A spider named Charlotte befriends him and tries to save his life."

"By weaving things about him into her web," explained Lacoste.

"Things like 'Some pig' so the farmer would think Wilbur was special. The book in the outhouse is signed by the author."

Gamache shook his head. Incredible.

"Did it work?" asked Morin. "Was the pig saved?"

Beauvoir looked at him with disdain. And yet, he had to admit, he wanted to know as well.

"He was," said Gamache. Then his brows drew together. Obviously in real life spiders don't weave messages into their webs. So who had put it there? And why? And why "woe?"

He was itching to get back up there.

"There's something else."

All eyes once again turned to the simple-looking agent.

"It's about the outhouse." He turned to Lacoste. "Did you notice anything?"

"You mean besides the signed first edition and the stacks of money as toilet paper?"

"Not inside. Outside."

She thought then shook her head.

"It was probably too dark," said Agent Morin. "I used it last night and didn't notice then either. It wasn't until this morning."

"What, for God's sake?" Beauvoir snapped.

"There's a trail. It runs to the outhouse, but doesn't stop there. It goes on. I followed it this morning and it came out here."

"At the Incident Room?" asked Beauvoir.

"Well, not exactly. It wound through the woods and came out up there."

He waved toward the hill overlooking the village.

"I marked the place it comes out. I think I can find it again."

"That was foolish of you," said Gamache. He looked stern and his voice was without warmth. Morin instantly reddened. "Never, ever wander on your own into the woods, do you understand? You might have been lost."

"But you'd find me, wouldn't you?"

They all knew he would. Gamache had found them once, he'd find them again.

"It was an unnecessary risk. Don't ever let your guard down." Gamache's deep brown eyes were intense. "A mistake could cost you your life. Or the life of someone else. Never relax. There are threats all around, from the woods, and from the killer we're hunting. Neither will forgive a mistake."

"Yes sir."

"Right," said Gamache. He got up and the rest jumped to their feet. "You need to show us where the path comes out."

Down in the village, Olivier stood at the window of the bistro, oblivious of the conversation and laughter of breakfasters behind him. He saw Gamache and the others walk along the ridge of the hill. They paused, then walked back and forth a bit. Even from there he could see Beauvoir gesture angrily at the young agent who always looked so clueless.

It'll be fine, he repeated to himself. *It'll be fine. Just smile.*

Their pacing stopped. They stared at the forest, as he stared at them.

And a wave crashed over Olivier, knocking the breath he'd been holding for so long out of him. Knocking the fixed smile off his face.

It was almost a relief. Almost.

There it is," said Morin.

He'd tied his belt around a branch. It had seemed a clever solution when he'd done it, but now searching for a thin brown belt on the edge of a forest didn't seem such a brilliant idea.

But they found it.

Gamache looked at the path. Once you knew it was there it was obvious. It almost screamed. Like those optical illusions deliberately placed in paintings that once found you couldn't stop seeing. The tiger in the crockery, the spaceship in the garden.

"I'll join you at the cabin when I can," said Gamache and watched with Lacoste as Beauvoir and Morin headed into the woods. Like nuns, he felt they were safe if not alone. It was, he supposed, a conceit. But it comforted him. He watched until he couldn't see them anymore. But still he waited, until he could no longer hear them. And only then did he descend into Three Pines.

Peter and Clara Morrow were both in their studios when the doorbell rang. It was an odd, almost startling sound. No one they knew ever rang the bell, they just came in and made themselves at home. How often had Clara and Peter found Ruth in their living room? Feet up on the sofa reading a book and drinking a martini at ten in the morning, Rosa nestled on the worn carpet beside her. They thought they'd have to call a priest to get rid of them.

More than once they'd found Gabri in their bath.

"Anybody home?" sang a man's deep voice.

"I'll get it," Clara called.

Peter didn't bother to answer. He was wandering around his studio, circling the work on the easel, getting close, then heading away. His mind might be on his art, as it always was, but his heart was elsewhere. Since word of Marc Gilbert's treachery had hit the village Peter had thought of little else.

He'd genuinely liked Marc. Was drawn to him in a way he felt drawn to cadmium yellow and marian blue, and Clara. He'd felt excited, almost giddy, at the thought of visiting Marc. Having a quiet drink together. Talking. Going for walks.

Marc Gilbert had ruined that as well. Trying to ruin Olivier was one thing, a terrible thing. But secretly Peter couldn't help but feel this was just as bad. Like taking a rusty nail to something lovely. And rare. At least for Peter.

He hated Marc Gilbert now.

Outside his studio he heard Clara talking, and a familiar voice replying.

Armand Gamache.

Peter decided to join them.

"Coffee?" Clara offered the Chief Inspector, after he and Peter had greeted each other.

"*Non, merci.* I can't stay long. I've come on business."

Clara thought that was a funny way of putting it. Murder business.

"You had a busy day yesterday," said Clara, as the three of them sat at the kitchen table. "It's all Three Pines can talk about. It's hard to know what's the most shocking. That Marc Gilbert was the one who moved the body, that Vincent Gilbert's here or that the dead man seemed to be living in the forest all along. Did he really live there?"

"We think so, but we're just waiting for confirmation. We still don't know who he was."

Gamache watched them closely. They seemed as puzzled as he was.

"I can't believe no one knew he was there," said Clara.

"We think someone knew. Someone was taking him food. We found it on the counter."

They looked at each other in amazement.

"One of us? Who?"

One of us, thought Gamache. Three short words, but potent. They more than anything had launched a thousand ships, a thousand attacks. One of us. A circle drawn. And closed. A boundary marked. Those inside and those not.

Families, clubs, gangs, cities, states, countries. A village.

What had Myrna called it? Beyond the pale.

But it went beyond simple belonging. The reason "belonging" was so potent, so attractive, so much a part of the human yearning, was that it also meant safety, and loyalty. If you were "one of us" you were protected.

Was that what he was up against, Gamache wondered. Not just the struggle to find the killer, but the efforts of those on the inside to protect him? Was the drawbridge up? The pale closed? Was Three Pines protecting a killer? One of them?

"Why would someone take him food then kill him?" asked Clara.

"Doesn't make sense," agreed Peter.

"Unless the murderer didn't show up intending to kill," said Gamache. "Maybe something happened to provoke him."

"Okay, but then if he lashed out and murdered the man, wouldn't he have just run away? Why take the body all the way through the woods to the Gilbert place?" asked Clara.

"Why indeed," asked Gamache. "Any theories?"

"Because he wanted the body found," said Peter. "And the Gilberts' is the nearest place."

The murderer wanted the body found. Why? Most murderers went to huge lengths to hide the crime. Why had this man advertised it?

"Either the body found," Peter continued, "or the cabin."

"We think it would have been found in a few days anyway," Gamache said. "Roar Parra was cutting riding paths in that area."

"We're not being much help," said Clara.

Gamache reached into his satchel. "I actually came by to show you something we found in the cabin. I'd like your opinions."

He brought out two towels and placed them carefully on the table.

They looked like newborns, protected against a chilly world. He slowly unwrapped them.

Clara leaned in.

"Look at their faces." She looked up directly into Gamache's. "So beautiful."

He nodded. They were. Not just their features. It was their joy, their vitality, that made them beautiful.

"May I?" Peter reached out and Gamache nodded. He picked up one of the sculptures and turned it over.

"There's writing, but I can't make it out. A signature?"

"Of sorts, perhaps," said Gamache. "We haven't figured out what the letters mean."

Peter studied the two works, the ship and the shore. "Did the dead man carve them?"

"We think so."

Though, given what else was in the cabin, it wouldn't have surprised Gamache to discover they were carved by Michelangelo. The difference was every other piece was in plain sight, but the dead man had kept these hidden. Somehow these were different.

As he watched he saw first Clara's then Peter's smile fade until they both looked almost unhappy. Certainly uncomfortable. Clara fidgeted in her chair. It had taken the Morrows less time than it took the Sûreté officers that morning to sense something wrong. Not surprising, thought Gamache. The Morrows were artists and presumably more in tune with their feelings.

The carvings emanated delight, joy. But beneath that was something else. A minor key, a dark note.

"What is it?" Gamache asked.

"There's something wrong with them," said Clara. "Something's off."

"Can you tell me what?"

Peter and Clara continued to stare at the pieces, then looked at each other. Finally they looked at Gamache.

"Sorry," said Peter. "Sometimes with art it can be subliminal, unintended by the artist even. A proportion slightly off. A color that jars."

"I can tell you though," said Clara, "they're great works of art."

"How can you tell?" asked Gamache.

"Because they provoke a strong emotion. All great art does."

Clara considered the carvings again. Was there too much joy? Was that the problem? Was too much beauty and delight and hope disquieting?

She thought not, hoped not. No, it was something else about these works.

"That reminds me," said Peter. "Don't you have a meeting with Denis Fortin in a few minutes?"

"Oh, damn, damn, damn," said Clara, springing up from the table.

"I won't keep you," said Gamache, rewrapping the sculptures.

"I have a thought," she said, joining Gamache at the door. "Monsieur Fortin might know more about sculpture than us. Hard to know less, really. Can I show one to him?"

"It's a good idea," said Gamache. "A very good idea. Where're you meeting him?"

"In the bistro in five minutes."

Gamache took one of the towels out of his satchel and handed it to Clara.

"This is great," she said as they walked down the path to the road. "I'll just tell him I made it."

"Would you have liked to?"

Clara remembered the blossoming horror in her chest as she'd looked at the carvings.

"No," she said.

TWENTY-TWO

Gamache arrived back at the Incident Room to find Superintendent Thérèse Brunel sitting at the conference table, surrounded by photographs. As he entered she rose, smiling.

"Chief Inspector." She advanced, her hand out. "Agent Lacoste has made me so comfortable I feel I could move right in."

Thérèse Brunel was of retirement age, though no one in the Sûreté would ever point that out. Not out of fear of the charming woman, or delicacy. But because she, more than any of them, was irreplaceable.

She'd presented herself at the Sûreté recruitment office two decades earlier. The young officer on duty thought it was a joke. Here was a sophisticated woman in her mid-forties, dressed in Chanel and wanting an application form. He'd given it to her, thinking it was almost certainly a threat for a disappointing son or daughter, then watched with increasing bafflement as she'd sat, legs crossed at the ankles, delicate perfume just a hint in the air, and filled it out herself.

Thérèse Brunel had been the chief of acquisitions at the world famous Musée des Beaux Arts in Montreal, but had nursed a secret passion for puzzles. Puzzles of all sorts. And once her children had gone off to college she'd marched right over to the Sûreté and signed up. What greater puzzle could there be than unravelling a crime? Then, taking classes at the police college from Chief Inspector Armand Gamache, she'd discovered another puzzle and passion. The human mind.

She now out-ranked her mentor and was the head of the property crime division. She was in her mid-sixties and as vibrant as ever.

Gamache shook her hand warmly. "Superintendent Brunel."

Thérèse Brunel and her husband Jérôme had often been to the

Gamaches' for dinner, and had them back to their own apartment on rue Laurier. But at work they were "Chief Inspector" and "Superintendent."

He then walked over to Agent Lacoste, who'd also stood as he entered.

"Anything yet?"

She shook her head. "But I just called and they expect the lab results any moment."

"*Bon. Merci*." He nodded to Agent Lacoste and she sat once more at her computer. Then he turned his attention to Superintendent Brunel.

"We're expecting fingerprint results. I really am most grateful to you for coming at such short notice."

"*C'est un plaisir*. Besides, what could be more exciting?" She led him back to the conference table and leaning close she whispered, "*Voyons*, Armand, is this for real?"

She pointed to the photographs scattered across the table.

"It is," he whispered back. "And we might need Jérôme's help as well."

Jérôme Brunel, now retired from medicine, had long shared his wife's love of puzzles, but while hers veered toward the human mind, his settled firmly on ciphers. Codes. From his comfortable and disheveled study in their Montreal home he entertained desperate diplomats and security people. Sometimes cracking cryptic codes and sometimes creating them.

He was a jolly and cultured man.

Gamache took the carving from his bag, unwrapped it and placed it on the table. Once again the blissful passengers were sailing across the conference table.

"Very nice," she said, putting on her glasses and leaning closer. "Very nice indeed," she mumbled to herself as she studied the piece, not touching it. "Beautifully made. Whoever the artist is, he knows wood, feels it. And knows art."

She stepped back now and stared. Gamache waited for it, and sure enough her smile faded and she even leaned a little away from the work.

This was the third time he'd seen it that morning. And he had felt it himself. The carvings seemed to burrow to the core, to the part most deeply hidden and the part most commonly shared. They found people's humanity. Then, like a dentist, they began to drill. Until that joy turned to dread.

After a moment her face cleared, and the professional mask descended. The problem-solver replaced the person. She leaned in to the work, moving herself round the table, not touching the carving. Finally, when she'd seen it from all angles, she picked it up, and like everyone else looked underneath.

"OWSVI," she read. "Upper case. Scratched into the wood, not painted." She sounded like a coroner, dissecting and dictating. "It's a heavy wood, a hardwood. Cherry?" She looked closer and even sniffed. "No, the grain isn't right. Cedar? No, the color is off, unless . . ." She took it to the window and placed it in a stream of sunshine. Then lowering it she smiled at Gamache over her glasses. "Cedar. Redwood. From British Columbia almost certainly. It's a good choice of wood, you know. Cedar lasts forever, especially the redwood. It's a very hard wood too. And yet it's surprisingly easy to sculpt. The Haida on the west coast used it for centuries to make totem poles."

"And they're still standing."

"They would be, if most of them hadn't been destroyed in the late 1800s by the government or the church. But you can still see a fine one in the Museum of Civilization in Ottawa."

The irony wasn't lost on either of them.

"So what are you doing here?" she said to the sculpture. "And what are you so afraid of?"

"Why do you say that?"

Over at her desk Agent Lacoste looked up, wanting to know the answer too.

"Surely you felt it too, Armand?" She'd used his first name, a sign that while she appeared composed she was in fact nonplussed. "There's something cold about this work. I hesitate to say evil . . ."

Gamache cocked his head in surprise. Evil wasn't a word he heard often outside a sermon. Brutal, malevolent, cruel, yes. Horror, even; investigators sometimes talked about the horror of a crime.

But never evil. But that was what made Thérèse Brunel a brilliant investigator, a solver of puzzles and crimes. And his friend. She placed conviction above convention.

"Evil?" asked Lacoste from her desk.

Superintendent Brunel looked at Agent Lacoste. "I said I hesitated to call it that."

"And do you still hesitate?" Gamache asked.

Brunel picked up the work once again and bringing it up to eye level she peered at the Lilliputian passengers. All dressed for a long voyage, the babies in blankets, the women with bags of bread and cheese, the men strong and resolute. And all looking ahead, looking forward to something wonderful. The detail was exquisite.

She turned it round then jerked it away from her as though it had bitten her nose.

"What is it?" Gamache asked.

"I've found the worm," she said.

Neither Carole Gilbert nor her son had slept well the night before, and she suspected Dominique hadn't either. To Vincent, sleeping in the small room off the landing, she gave no thought. Or rather every time he emerged into her conscious mind she shoved him back into his little room, and tried to lock the door.

It had been a lovely, soft dawn. She'd shuffled around the kitchen making a pot of strong French Pressé coffee, then putting a mohair throw round her shoulders she'd picked up the tray and taken it outside, installing herself on the quiet patio overlooking the garden and the mist-covered fields.

The day before had felt like one endless emergency, with claxtons sounding in her head for hours on end. They'd pulled together as a family and presented a united front through revelation after revelation.

That Marc's father was still alive.

That Vincent was in fact standing right there.

That the murdered man had been found in their new home.

And that Marc had moved him. To the bistro. In a deliberate attempt to hurt, perhaps even ruin, Olivier.

By the time Chief Inspector Gamache had left they all felt punchdrunk. Too dazed and tired to go at each other. Marc had made his feelings clear, then gone into the spa area to plaster and paint and hammer. Vincent had had the sense to leave, only returning late that night. And Dominique had found the cabin while out riding on the least damaged of the horses.

'Twould ring the bells of Heaven, Carole thought to herself as she stared at the horses, now in the misty field. Grazing. Leery of one another. Even from there she could see their sores.

The wildest peal for years,
If Parson lost his senses
And people came to theirs,
And he and they together
knelt down with fervent prayers
For tamed and shabby tigers,
And dancing dogs and bears.

"Mother."

Carole jumped, lost in her own thoughts and now found by her son. She got to her feet. He looked bleary, but showered and shaved. His voice was cold, distant. They stared at each other. Would they blink, sit down, pour coffee and talk about the weather? The headlines? The horses. Would they try to pretend the storm wasn't all around them? And wasn't of their own making.

Who had done worse? Carole by lying to her son for years, and telling him his father was dead? Or Marc by moving a dead man down to the bistro, and in one gesture ruining their chances of being accepted in the small community.

She'd marred his past, and he'd marred their future.

They were quite a team.

"I'm sorry," said Carole, and opened her arms. Silently Marc moved across the stones and almost fell into them. He was tall and she wasn't, but still she held him and rubbed his back and whispered, "There, there."

Then they sat, the tray with croissants and fresh strawberry jam between them. The world looked very green that morning, very fresh, from the tall maples and oaks to the meadow. Marc poured coffee while Carole pulled the mohair throw round her shoulders and watched as the horses ate grass in the field and occasionally looked up into a day they should not have seen, into a world they should have left two days ago. Even now, standing in the mist, they seemed to straddle the two worlds.

"They almost look like horses," said Marc, "if you squint."

Carole looked over at her son and laughed. He was making a face, trying to morph the creatures in the field into the magnificent hunters he'd been expecting.

"Seriously, is that really a horse?" He pointed to Chester, who in the uncertain light looked like a camel.

Carole was suddenly very sad that they might have to leave this house, cast out by their own actions. The garden had never looked lovelier, and with time it would only get better as it matured and the various plants mingled and grew together.

"I'm worried about that one." Marc pointed to the darkest horse, off on his own. "Thunder."

"Yes, well." Carole shifted uncomfortably to look at him. "About him . . ."

"Suppose he decides to bite one of the guests? Not that I don't appreciate what he did to Dad."

Carole suppressed a smile. Seeing the Great Man with horse slime on his shoulder was the only good thing about a very bad day.

"What do you suggest?" she asked.

"I don't know."

Carole was silent. They both knew what Marc was suggesting. If the horse didn't learn manners in a month, by Thanksgiving he'd have to be put down.

"*For wretched, blind pit ponies,*" she murmured. "*And little hunted hares.*"

"*Pardon?*" asked Marc.

"His, ah, his name isn't really Thunder. It's Marc."

"You're kidding." But neither was laughing. Marc looked out into the field at the malevolent, mad animal keeping his distance from the others. A black blotch in the misty meadow. Like a mistake. A mar.

A Marc.

Later, when Marc headed off with Dominique to get groceries and building supplies, Carole found four carrots in the kitchen and fed them to the horses, who at first were reluctant to trust. But first Buttercup, then Macaroni and finally Chester tiptoed forward and seemed to kiss the carrot off her palm.

But one remained.

She whispered to Marc the horse, cooing at him. Enticing him. Begging him. Standing at the fence she leaned forward, quietly holding the carrot out as far as she could. "Please," she coaxed. "I won't hurt you."

But he didn't believe her.

She went inside, climbed the stairs and knocked on the door to the small bedroom.

Armand Gamache took the carving and stared into the crowd on deck.

It was easy to miss, but still he could have kicked himself. It now appeared so obvious. The small figure at the very back of the boat, crouching just in front of the matronly woman and her large sack.

He felt his skin crawl as he examined the face of the tiny wooden man, barely more than a boy, looking over his shoulder. Past the matronly woman. Looking behind the boat. While everyone else was gazing ahead, he was slumped down and staring back. To where they'd been.

And the look on his face turned Gamache's blood cold. Cold to the bone, cold to the marrow. Cold to the core.

This was what terror looked like. Felt like. The small, wooden face was a transmitter. And its message was horrific. Gamache suddenly had the nearly uncontrollable urge to look behind himself, see what might be lurking there. Instead, he put his glasses on and leaned closer.

In his arms the young man was gripping a package.

Finally Gamache put it down and removed his glasses. "I see what you mean."

Superintendent Brunel sighed. "Evil. There's evil on that voyage."

Gamache didn't disagree. "Does it look familiar? Could the carving be on your active list of stolen art?"

"There're thousands of items on that list," she smiled. "Everything from Rembrands to engraved toothpicks."

"And I bet you have them all memorized."

Her smile broadened and she inclined her head slightly. He knew her well.

"But nothing like this. It would stand out."

"Is it art?"

"If you mean is it valuable, I'd say it's almost priceless. If one of these had come on the market while I was at the Musée des Beaux Arts I'd have jumped at it. And paid a small fortune."

"Why?"

She looked at the large, calm man in front of her. So like an academic. She could see him in cap and gown moving like a ship of state through the halls of an ancient university, eager students in his wake. When she'd first met him, lecturing at the police college, he'd been twenty years younger but still a commanding figure. Now he carried that authority with even greater ease. His wavy dark hair was receding, his temples were graying as was his trim mustache, his body was expanding. As was, she knew, his influence.

He'd taught her many things. But one of the most valuable was not to just see, but to listen. As he listened to her now.

"What makes a work of art unique isn't its color or composition or subject. It has nothing whatsoever to do with what we see. Why are some paintings masterpieces while others, perhaps even more competent, are forgotten? Why are some symphonies still beloved hundreds of years after the composer has died?"

Gamache thought about it. And what came to mind was the painting placed so causally on an easel after dinner a few nights ago. Badly lit, unframed.

And yet he could have stared at it forever.

It was the painting of the elderly woman, her body headed forward, but her face turned back.

He'd known her longing. That same root which spasmed when gazing at the carving had ached when he'd looked at that woman. Clara hadn't simply painted a woman, hadn't even painted a feeling. She'd created a world. In that one image.

That was a masterpiece.

He suddenly felt very badly for Peter, and hoped deeply that Peter was no longer trying to compete with his wife. She was nowhere to be found on that battlefield.

"That," Superintendent Brunel pointed with one manicured finger at the carving, "will be remembered long after you and I are dead. Long after this charming village has fallen to dust."

"There's another one, you know," he said and had the rare pleasure of seeing Thérèse Brunel surprised. "But before we see it I think we should head to the cabin."

He looked at her feet. She wore elegant new shoes.

"I've brought boots with me, Chief Inspector," she said, her voice holding a faint and mocking reproach as she walked briskly ahead of him to the door. "When have you ever taken me anywhere that didn't have mud?"

"I believe they hosed down Place des Arts before the last symphony we were at," he said, smiling over his shoulder at Agent Lacoste as they left.

"Professionally, I meant. Always mud and always a body."

"Well this time there is certainly mud, but no body."

"Sir." Lacoste jogged over to the car, holding a printout. "I thought you'd like to see this."

She handed the paper to him and pointed. It was a lab report. The results were beginning to come in, and would continue all day. And this one brought a satisfied smile to his face. He turned to Thérèse Brunel.

"They found woodchips, sawdust really, beside a chair in the cabin. They also found traces on his clothes. The lab says it was red cedar. From British Columbia."

"I guess we found the artist," she said. "Now if we only knew why he carved so much terror."

Why indeed, thought Gamache as he got into the car and drove up du Moulin. ATVs were waiting for them and they headed deep into the Quebec forest. A professor and an elegant expert on art. Neither was as they appeared, and they were heading for a rustic cabin that certainly wasn't.

Gamache stopped the ATV just before the final turn in the path. He and Superintendent Brunel dismounted and walked the rest of the way. It was another world inside the forest, and he wanted to give her a feeling for where the victim had chosen to live. A world of cool shadows and diffuse light, of rich dark scents of things decaying. Of creatures unseen but heard, scampering and scurrying.

Gamache and Brunel were very aware of being the outsiders here.

And yet it wasn't threatening. Not now. In twelve hours, when the sun was down, it would feel different again.

"I see what you mean." Brunel looked around. "A man could easily live here without being found. It's very peaceful, isn't it?" She sounded almost wistful.

"Could you live here?" Gamache asked.

"I think I could, you know. Does that surprise you?"

Gamache was silent but smiled as he walked.

"I don't need much," she continued. "I used to. When I was younger. Trips to Paris, a nice apartment, good clothes. I have all that now. And I'm happy."

"But not because you have those thing," suggested Gamache.

"As I get older I need less and less. I really believe I could live here. Between us, Armand? Part of me yearns for it. Could you?"

He nodded and saw again the simple little cabin. One room.

"One chair for solitude, two for friendship and three for society," he said.

"*Walden*. And how many chairs would you need?"

Gamache thought about it. "Two. I don't mind society, but I need one other person."

"Reine-Marie," said Thérèse. "And I only need Jérôme."

"There's a first edition of *Walden* in the cabin, you know."

Thérèse sighed. "*Incroyable*. Who was this man, Armand? Do you have any idea?"

"None."

He stopped and beside him she stopped too, following his gaze.

At first it was difficult to see, but then, slowly, she made out the simple log cabin, as though it had materialized just for them. And was inviting them in.

Come in," he said.

Carole Gilbert breathed deeply then stepped forward, past the solid ground she'd cultivated for decades. Past the quiet lunches with lifelong friends, past the bridge nights and volunteer shifts, past the enjoyable rainy afternoons reading by the window watching the container ships move slowly up and down the St. Lawrence river. She plunged past this gentle widow's life within the fortified old walls of Quebec City, constructed to keep anything unpleasant out.

"Hello, Carole."

The tall, slender man stood in the center of the room, contained. Looking as though he'd been expecting her. Her heart pounded and her hands and feet had gone cold, numb. She was a little afraid she'd fall down. Not faint, but lose all ability to stand up for herself.

"Vincent." Her voice was firm.

His body had changed. That body she knew better than most. It had shrunk, shriveled. His hair, once thick and shiny, had thinned and grown almost white. His eyes were still brown, but where they'd been sharp and sure now they were questioning.

He held out one hand. It all seemed to happen excruciatingly slowly.

The hand had spots on it she didn't recognize. How often had she held that hand in the first years, then later longed for it to hold her? How often had she stared at it as it held *Le Devoir* up to his face? Her only contact with the man she'd given her heart to, those long, sensitive fingers holding the daily news that was clearly more important than her news. Those fingers were evidence of another human in the room, but barely. Barely there and barely human.

And then one day he'd lowered the paper, stared at her with laser eyes and said he wasn't happy.

She'd laughed.

It was, she remembered, a genuinely mirthful laugh. Not that she thought it was a joke. It was because he was serious. This brilliant man actually seemed to think if he wasn't happy it was a catastrophe.

It was, in many ways, perfect. Like so many men his age he was having an affair. She'd known it for years. But this affair he was having was with himself. He adored himself. In fact, that was just about the only thing they had in common. They both loved Vincent Gilbert.

But suddenly that wasn't enough. He needed more. And like the great man he knew he was, the answer could never be found close to home. It would have to be hiding in some mountain cave in India.

Because he was so extraordinary, his salvation would have to be too.

They'd spent the rest of the breakfast plotting his death. It appealed to Vincent's sense of drama, and her sense of relief. It was, ironically, the best talk they'd had in years.

Of course, they'd made one very big mistake. They should have told Marc. But who'd have thought he'd care?

Too late she'd realized—was it less than a day ago?—that Marc had been deeply damaged by his father's death. Not the actual death, mind. That he'd accepted easily. No, it was his father's resurrection that had created the scars, as though Vincent, in rising, had clawed his way past Marc's heart.

And now the man stood, shriveled, dotted and maybe even dotty, with one unwavering hand out. Inviting her in.

"We need to talk," she said.

He lowered his hand and nodded. She waited for him to point out her faults and flaws, all the mistakes she'd made, the immeasurable hurt she'd caused him.

"I'm sorry," said Vincent. She nodded.

"I know you are. So am I." She sat on the side of the bed and patted it. He sat next to her. This close she could see worry lines crawling over his face. It struck her as interesting that worry lines only appeared on the head.

"You look well. Are you?" he asked.

"I wish none of this had happened."

"Including my coming back?" He smiled and took her hand.

But instead of setting her heart racing, it turned her heart to stone. And she realized she didn't trust this man, who'd blown in from the past and was suddenly eating their food and sleeping in their bed.

He was like Pinocchio. A man made of wood, mimicking humanity. Shiny and smiling and fake. And if you cut into him you'd see rings. Circles of deceit and scheming and justification. It's what he was made of. That hadn't changed.

Lies within lies within lies lay within this man. And now he was here, inside their home. And suddenly their lives were unravelling.

TWENTY-THREE

"Bon Dieu."

It was all Superintendent Brunel could say, and she said it over and over as she walked round the log cabin. Every now and then she stopped and picked up an object. Her eyes widened as she stared at it, then replaced it. Carefully. And went on to the next.

"Mais, ce n'est pas possible. This's from the Amber Room, I'm sure of it." She approached the glowing orange panel leaning against the kitchen window. *"Bon Dieu,* it is," she whispered and all but crossed herself.

The Chief Inspector watched for a while. He knew she hadn't really been prepared for what she'd find. He'd tried to warn her, though he knew the photographs didn't do the place justice. He'd told her about the fine china.

The leaded crystal.

The signed first editions.

The tapestries.

The icons.

"Is that a violin?" She pointed to the instrument by the easy chair, its wood deep and warm.

"It's moved," said Beauvoir, then stared at the young agent. "Did you touch it last night?"

Morin blushed and looked frightened. "A little. I just picked it up. And . . ."

Superintendent Brunel held it now up to the light at the window, tipping it this way and that. "Chief Inspector, can you read this?" She handed him the violin and pointed to a label. As Gamache tried to read she picked up the bow and examined it.

"A Tourte bow," she almost snorted and looked at their blank faces. "Worth a couple of hundred thousand." She batted it in their direction then turned to Gamache. "Does it say Stradivari?"

"I don't think so. It seems to say Anno 1738," he strained, "Carlos something. *Fece in Cremona*." He took off his glasses and looked at Thérèse Brunel. "Mean anything to you?"

She was smiling and still holding the bow. "Carlos Bergonzi. He was a luthier. Stradivari's best pupil."

"So it's not the finest violin?" asked Beauvoir, who'd at least heard of Stradivarius violins, but never this other guy.

"Perhaps not quite as fine as his master, but a Bergonzi is still worth a million."

"A Bergonzi?" said Morin.

"Yes. Do you know about them?"

"Not really, but we found some original sheet music for violin with a note attached. It mentions a Bergonzi." Morin went over to the bookcase and rummaged for a moment, emerging with a sheaf of music and a card. He handed it to the Superintendent who glanced at it and passed it on to Gamache.

"Any idea what language it's in?" she asked. "Not Russian, not Greek."

Gamache read. It seemed addressed to a B, it mentioned a Bergonzi and was signed C. The rest was unintelligible, though it seemed to include terms of endearment. It was dated December 8, 1950.

"Could B be the victim?" Brunel asked.

Gamache shook his head. "The dates don't match. He wouldn't have been born yet. And I presume B couldn't be Bergonzi?"

"No, too late. He was long dead. So who were B and C and why did our man collect the music and the card?" Brunel asked herself. She glanced at the sheet music and smiled. Handing the sheaf to Gamache she pointed to the top line. The music was composed by a BM.

"So," said Gamache, lowering the pages. "This original score was composed by a BM. The note attached was addressed to a B and mentions a Bergonzi violin. Seems logical to assume B played the violin and composed and someone, C, gave him this gift." He nodded to the violin. "So who was BM and why did our victim have his music and his violin?"

"Is it any good?" Brunel asked Morin. Gamache handed him the score. The young agent, mouth slightly open, thick lips glistening, was looking particularly stupid. He stared at the music and hummed. Then looked up.

"Seems okay."

"Play it." Gamache handed him the million-dollar violin. Morin took it, reluctantly. "You played it last night, didn't you?" the Chief asked.

"You what?" demanded Beauvoir.

Morin turned to him. "It'd been dusted and photographed and I didn't think it'd matter."

"Did you also juggle the china or have batting practice with the glasses? You don't mess around with evidence."

"Sorry."

"Play the music, please," said Gamache. Superintendent Brunel gave him the near-priceless bow.

"I didn't play this last night. I only really know fiddle music."

"Just do your best," said the Chief.

Agent Morin hesitated then placed the violin under his chin and curving his body he brought the bow up. And down. Across the gut strings.

The slow, full notes of a tune left the instrument. So rich was the sound the notes were almost visible as they filled the air. The tune they heard was slower than intended by BM, Gamache suspected, since Agent Morin was stuggling to follow the music. But it was still beautiful, complex and accomplished. Obviously BM knew what he was doing. Gamache closed his eyes and imagined the dead man there, alone. On a winter's night. Snow piling up outside. A simple vegetable soup on the stove, the fireplace lit and throwing heat. And the small cabin filled with music. This music.

Why this music and no other?

"Do you know it?" Gamache looked at Superintendent Brunel, who was listening with her eyes closed. She shook her head and opened her eyes.

"*Non*, but it's lovely. I wonder who BM was."

Morin lowered the violin, relieved to stop.

"Was the violin in tune when you played yesterday or did you have to adjust it?" she asked.

"It was in tune. He must have played it recently." He went to put it down but the Chief Inspector stopped him.

"What did you play last night, if not that?" He pointed to the sheet music.

"Just some fiddle music my father taught me. Nothing much. I know I shouldn't have—"

Gamache put up his hand to silence the apologies. "It's all right. Just play for us now what you played last night."

When Morin looked surprised Gamache explained, "What you just did wasn't really a fair test for the violin, was it? You were picking out the tune. I'd like to hear the violin as the victim heard it. As it was meant to be played."

"But, sir, I only play fiddle, not violin."

"What's the difference?" Gamache asked.

Morin hesitated. "No real difference, at least not in the instrument. But the sound of course is different. My dad always said a violin sings and a fiddle dances."

"Dance, then."

Morin, blushing in the most unbecoming way, put the fiddle, né violin, up to his chin once again. Paused. Then drew the bow across the strings.

What came out surprised them all. A Celtic lament left the bow, left the violin, left the agent. It filled the cabin, filled the rafters. Almost into the corners. The simple tune swirled around them like colors and delicious meals and conversation. And it lodged in their chests. Not their ears, not their heads. But their hearts. Slow, dignified, but buoyant. It was played with confidence. With poise.

Agent Morin had changed. His loose-limbed awkward body contorted perfectly for the violin, as though created and designed for this purpose. To play. To produce this music. His eyes were closed and he looked the way Gamache felt. Filled with joy. Rapture even. Such was the power of this music. This instrument.

And watching his agent the Chief Inspector suddenly realized what Morin reminded him of.

A musical note. The large head and the thin body. He was a walking note, awaiting an instrument. And this was it. The violin might be a masterpiece, but Agent Paul Morin certainly was.

After a minute he stopped and the music faded, absorbed by the logs, the books, the tapestries. The people.

"That was beautiful," said Superintendent Brunel.

He handed the violin to her. "It's called 'Colm Quigley.' My favorite."

As soon as the violin left his hand he went back to being the gangly, awkward young man. Though never again totally that for the people who had heard him play.

"*Merci*," said Gamache.

Superintendent Brunel put the violin down.

"Let me know what you find out about these." Gamache handed Morin the note and sheet music.

"Yes sir."

Thérèse Brunel returned to the rest of the room, walking up to the treasures, mumbling "*Bon Dieu*" every now and then. Each seemed more astonishing than the last.

But nothing was more surprising than what awaited Chief Inspector Gamache. In the farthest corner of the cabin, near the rafters. If the search team the day before had seen it they'd have dismissed it as the only normal thing in the whole place. What could be more natural than a spider's web in a cabin?

But it turned out to be the least normal, the least natural.

"*Bon Dieu*," they heard from the Superintendent as she held up a plate with frogs on it. "From the collection of Catherine the Great. Lost hundreds of years ago. Unbelievable."

But if she wanted "unbelievable," thought Gamache, she needed to look over here. Beauvoir had turned on his flashlight.

Until he'd seen it Gamache hadn't quite believed it. But there it was, twinkling almost merrily in the harsh artificial light, as though mocking them.

Woe, said the web.

"Woe," whispered Gamache.

Superintendent Brunel found Armand Gamache an hour later in the bent branch chair in the corner of the vegetable garden.

"I've finished looking round."

Gamache stood and she sat wearily in the chair, exhaling deeply.

"I've never seen anything like it, Armand. We've broken art theft rings and found the most amazing collections. Remember the Charbonneau case last year in Lévis?"

"The van Eycks."

She nodded, then shook her head as though trying to clear it. "Fantastic finds. All sorts of original sketches and even an oil no one knew existed."

"Wasn't there a Titian too?"

"*Oui.*"

"And you're saying this place is even more amazing?"

"I don't mean to lecture, but I'm not sure you or your people appreciate the scope of the find."

"Lecture away," Gamache reassured her. "That's why I invited you."

He smiled and not for the first time she thought the rarest thing she'd ever found was Chief Inspector Gamache.

"You might want to grab a seat," she said. He found a sawn log and turned it on its end and sat on it. "The Charbonneau case was spectacular," Superintendent Brunel went on. "But in many ways mundane. Most art theft rings, and most black market collectors, have one maybe two specialties. Because the market's so specialized and there's so much money involved, the thieves become experts, but only in one or two tiny areas. Italian sculpture from the 1600s. Dutch masters. Greek antiquities. But never all of those fields. They specialize. How else would they know they weren't stealing forgeries, or replicas? That's why with Charbonneau we found some astonishing things, but all in the same 'family.' *Vous comprenez?*"

"*Oui.* They were all Renaissance paintings, mostly by the same artist."

"*C'est ça.* That's how specialized most thieves are. But here," she waved at the cabin, "there're handmade silk tapestries, ancient leaded glass. Under that embroidered tablecloth do you know what we found? Our victim ate off the most exquisite inlaid table I've ever seen. It must be five hundred years old and made by a master. Even the table cloth was a masterpiece. Most museums would keep it under glass. The Victoria and Albert in London would pay a fortune for it."

"Maybe they did."

"You mean it might have been stolen from there? Could be. I have a lot of work to do."

She looked as though she could hardly wait. And yet, she also looked as though she was in no hurry to leave this cabin, this garden.

"I wonder who he was." She reached out and pulled a couple of runner beans from a vine, handing one to her companion. "*Most unhappiness comes from not being able to sit quietly in a room.*"

"Pascal," said Gamache, recognizing the quote, and the appropriateness of it. "This man could. But he surrounded himself with objects that had a lot to say. That had stories."

"That's an interesting way of putting it."

"What's the Amber Room?"

"How do you know about that?" She turned a searching eye on him.

"When you were looking around you mentioned it."

"Did I? You can see it from here. That orange thing in the kitchen window." He looked and sure enough, there it was, glowing warm in what little light it caught. It looked like a large, thick piece of stained glass. She continued to stare, mesmerized, then finally came out of it. "Sorry. I just never expected to be the one to find it."

"What do you mean?"

"The Amber Room was created in the early 1700s in Prussia by Friedrich the First. It was a huge room made of amber and gold. Took artists and artisans years to construct and when it was completed it was one of the wonders of the world." He could tell she was imagining what it looked like, her eyes taking on a faraway look. "He had it made for his wife, Sophia Charlotte. But a few years later it was given to the Russian Emperor and stayed in St. Petersburg until the war."

"Which war?"

She smiled. "Good point. The Second World War. The Soviets apparently dismantled it once they realized the Nazis would take the city, but they didn't manage to hide it. The Germans found it."

She stopped.

"Go on," said Gamache.

"That's it. That's all we know. The Amber Room disappeared. Historians, treasure hunters, antiquarians have been searching for it ever since. We know the Germans, under Albert Speer, took the Amber Room away. Hid it. Presumably for safe keeping. But it was never seen again."

"What're the theories?" the Chief Inspector asked.

"Well, the most accepted is that it was destroyed in the Allied bombing. But there's another theory. Albert Speer was very bright, and many argue he wasn't a true Nazi. He was loyal to Hitler, but not to most of his ideals. Speer was an internationalist, a cultured man whose priority became saving the world's treasures from destruction, by either side."

"Albert Speer may have been cultured," said Gamache, "but he was a Nazi. He knew of the death camps, knew of the slaughter, approved it. He simply looked good while doing it."

The Chief Inspector's voice was cold and his eyes hard.

"I don't disagree with you, Armand. Just the opposite. I'm simply telling you what the theories are. The one involving Speer had him hiding the Amber Room far from both the German and the Allied armies. In the Ore Mountains."

"Where?"

"A mountain range between Germany and what's now the Czech Republic."

They both thought about that, and finally Gamache spoke. "So how did a piece of the Amber Room get here?"

"And where's the rest of it?"

Denis Fortin sat across from Clara Morrow. He was younger than he had any right to be. Early forties probably. A failed artist who'd discovered another, greater, talent. He recognized talent in others.

It was enlightened self-interest. The best kind, as far as Clara could see. No one was the martyr, no one was owed or owing. She was under no illusion that the reason Denis Fortin held a St. Amboise beer in Olivier's Bistro in Three Pines was not because he thought there was something in it for him.

And the only reason Clara was there, besides unbridled ego, was to get something from Fortin. Namely fame and fortune.

At the very least a free beer.

But there was something she needed to do before she got caught up in the unparalleled glory that was Clara Morrow. Reaching into her bag she brought out the balled-up towel. "I was asked to show you this. A man was found dead here a couple of days ago. Murdered."

"Really? That's unusual, isn't it?"

"Not as unusual as you might think. What was unusual is that no one knew him. But the police just found a cabin in the woods, and this was inside it. The head of the investigation asked me to show it to you, in case you could tell us anything about it."

"A clue?" He looked keen and watched closely as she unwrapped the bundle. Soon the little men and women were standing on the shore, looking across the expanse of wood to the micro-brew in front of Fortin.

Clara watched him. His eyes narrowed and he leaned closer to the work, pursing his lips in concentration.

"Very nice. Good technique, I'd say. Detailed, each face quite different, with character. Yes, all in all I'd say a competent piece of carving. Slightly primitive, but what you'd expect from a backwoods whittler."

"Really?" said Clara. "I thought it was very good. Excellent even."

He leaned back and smiled at her. Not patronizing, but as one friend smiles at another, a kinder, friend.

"Perhaps I'm being too harsh, but I've seen so many of these in my career."

"These? Exactly the same?"

"No, but close enough. Carved images of people fishing or smoking a pipe or riding a horse. They're the most valuable. You can always find a buyer for a good horse or dog. Or pig. Pigs are popular."

"Good to know. There's something written underneath." Clara turned it over and handed it to Fortin.

He squinted then putting on his glasses he read, frowned and handed it back. "I wonder what it means."

"Any guesses?" Clara wasn't about to give up. She wanted to take something back to Gamache.

"Almost certainly a signature, or a lot number. Something to identify it. Was this the only one?"

"There're two. How much would this be worth?"

"Hard to say." He picked it up again. "It's quite good, for what it is. It's no pig, though."

"Pity."

"Hmm." Fortin considered for a moment. "I'd say two hundred, maybe two hundred and fifty dollars."

"Is that all?"

"I might be wrong."

Clara could tell he was being polite, but getting bored. She rewrapped the carving and put it in her bag.

"Now." Denis Fortin leaned forward, an eager look on his handsome face. "Let's talk about really great art. How would you like your work to be hung?"

"I've done a few sketches." Clara handed him her notebook and after a few minutes Fortin lifted his head, his eyes intelligent and bright.

"This is wonderful. I like the way you've clustered the paintings then left a space. It's like a breath, isn't it?"

Clara nodded. It was such a relief talking to someone who didn't need everything explained.

"I particularly like that you haven't placed the three old women together. That would be the obvious choice, but you've spread them around, each anchoring her own wall."

"I wanted to surround them with other works," said Clara excitedly.

"Like acolytes, or friends, or critics," said Fortin, excited himself. "It's not clear what their intentions are."

"And how they might change," said Clara, leaning forward. She'd shown Peter her ideas, and he'd been polite and encouraging, but she could tell he really didn't understand what she was getting at. At first glance her design for the exhibition might seem unbalanced. And it was. Intentionally. Clara wanted people to walk in, see the works that appeared quite traditional and slowly appreciate that they weren't.

There was a depth, a meaning, a challenge to them.

For an hour or more Clara and Fortin talked, exchanging ideas about the show, about the direction of contemporary art, about exciting new artists, of which, Fortin was quick to assure Clara, she was in the forefront.

"I wasn't going to tell you because it might not happen, but I sent your portfolio to FitzPatrick at MoMA. He's an old friend and says he'll come to the *vernissage*—"

Clara exclaimed and almost knocked her beer over. Fortin laughed and held up his hand.

"But wait, that wasn't what I wanted to tell you. I suggested he spread the word and it looks as though Allyne from the *New York Times* will be there . . ."

He hesitated because it looked as though Clara was having a stroke. When she closed her mouth he continued. "And, as luck would have it, Destin Browne will be in New York that month setting up a show with MoMA and she's shown interest."

"Destin Browne? Vanessa Destin Browne? The chief curator at the Tate Modern in London?"

Fortin nodded and held tightly to his beer. But now, far from being in danger of knocking anything over, Clara appeared to have ground to a complete halt. She sat in the cheery little bistro, late summer light teeming through the mullioned windows. Beyond Fortin she saw the old homes, warming in the sun. The perennial beds with roses and clematis and hollyhocks. She saw the villagers, whose names she knew and whose habits she was familiar with. And she saw the three tall pines, like beacons. Impossible to miss, even surrounded by forest. If you knew what to look for, and needed a beacon.

Life was about to take her away from here. From the place where she'd become herself. This solid little village that never changed but helped its inhabitants to change. She'd arrived straight from art college full of avant-garde ideas, wearing shades of gray and seeing the world in black and white. So sure of herself. But here, in the middle of nowhere, she'd discovered color. And nuance. She'd learned this from the villagers, who'd been generous enough to lend her their souls to paint. Not as perfect human beings, but as flawed, struggling men and women. Filled with fear and uncertainty and, in at least one case, martinis.

But who remained standing. In the wilderness. Her graces, her stand of pines.

She was suddenly overcome with gratitude to her neighbors, and to whatever inspiration had allowed her to do them justice.

She closed her eyes and tilted her face into the sun.

"You all right?" he asked.

Clara opened her eyes. He seemed bathed in light, his blond hair glowing and a warm, patient smile on his face.

"You know, I probably shouldn't tell you this, but a few years ago no one wanted my works. Everyone just laughed. It was brutal. I almost gave up."

"Most great artists have the same story," he said, gently.

"I almost flunked out of art school, you know. I don't tell many people that."

"Another drink?" asked Gabri, taking Fortin's empty glass.

"Not for me, *merci*," he said, then turned back to Clara. "Between us? Most of the best people did flunk out. How can you test an artist?"

"I was always good at tests," said Gabri, picking up Clara's glass. "No, wait. That was testes."

He gave Clara an arch look and swept away.

"Fucking queers," said Fortin, taking a handful of cashews. "Doesn't it make you want to vomit?"

Clara froze. She looked at Fortin to see if he was kidding. He wasn't. But what he said was true. She suddenly wanted to throw up.

TWENTY-FOUR

⁓

Chief Inspector Gamache and Superintendent Brunel walked back to the cabin, each lost in thought.

"I told you what I found," said the Superintendent, once back on the porch. "Now it's your turn. What were you and Inspector Beauvoir whispering about in the corner, like naughty schoolboys?"

Not many people would consider calling Chief Inspector Gamache a naughty schoolboy. He smiled. Then he remembered the thing that had gleamed and mocked and clung to the corner of the cabin.

"Would you like to see?"

"No, I think I'll go back to the garden and pick turnips. Of course I'd like to see," she laughed and he took her over to the corner of the room, her eyes darting here and there, stealing glances at the masterpieces she was passing. Until they stopped in the darkest corner.

"I don't see anything."

Beauvoir joined them and switched on his flashlight. She followed it. Up the wall to the rafters.

"I still don't see."

"But you do," said Gamache. As they waited Beauvoir thought about other words, left up to be found. Tacked to the door of his bedroom at the B and B that morning.

He'd asked Gabri if he knew anything about the piece of paper stuck into the wood with a thumbtack, but Gabri had looked perplexed and shaken his head.

Beauvoir had stuffed it into his pocket and only after the first *café au lait* of the day did he have the guts to read.

and the soft body of a woman
and lick you clean of fever,

What upset Beauvoir most wasn't the thought that the mad old poet had invaded the B and B and put that on his door. Nor was it that he didn't understand a word of it. What upset him the most was the comma.

It meant there was more.

"I'm sorry, I really don't see anything." Superintendent Brunel's voice brought Beauvoir back to the cabin.

"Do you see a spider's web?" Gamache asked.

"Yes."

"Then you see it. Look more closely."

It took a moment but finally her face changed. Her eyes widened and her brows lifted. She tilted her head slightly as though she wasn't seeing quite straight.

"But there's a word up there, written in the web. What does it say? Woe? How is that possible? What kind of spider does that?" she asked, clearly not expecting an answer, and not getting one.

Just then the satellite phone rang and after answering it Agent Morin handed it to the Chief Inspector. "Agent Lacoste for you, sir."

"*Oui, allô?*" he said, and listened for a few moments. "Really?" He listened some more, glancing around the room then up again at the web. "*D'accord. Merci.*"

Gamache hung up, thought a moment, then reached for the nearby stepladder.

"Would you like me . . ." Beauvoir gestured to it.

"*Ce n'est pas necessaire.*" Taking a breath Gamache started up the Annapurna ladder. Two steps up he put out an unsteady hand and Beauvoir moved forward until the large trembling fingers found his shoulder. Steadied, Gamache reached up and poked the web with a pen. Slowly, unseen by the people craning their necks below, he moved a single strand of the web.

"*C'est ça,*" he murmured.

Backing down the ladder and onto terra firma he nodded toward the corner. Beauvoir's light shone on the web.

"How did you do that?" asked Beauvoir.

The web had changed its message. It no longer said Woe. Now it said Woo.

"A strand had come loose."

"But how did you know it had?" Beauvoir persisted. They'd all taken a close look at the web. Clearly a spider hadn't spun it. It appeared to be made from thread, perhaps nylon fishing line, made to look like a spider's web. They'd take it down soon and have it properly analyzed. It had a great deal to tell them, though changing the word from Woe to Woo didn't seem a move toward clarity.

"More results are coming into the Incident Room. Fingerprint results, which I'll tell you about in a minute, but remember that piece of wood that was found under the bed?"

"The one that also said Woe?" asked Morin, who had joined them.

Gamache nodded. "It had blood on it. The victim's blood, according to the lab. But when they removed it they discovered something else. The block of wood wasn't carved to say Woe. The smear of blood made a mess of the lettering. When the blood was lifted it said—"

"Woo," said Beauvoir. "So you thought if one said it maybe the other did too."

"Worth a try."

"I think I prefer Woe." Beauvoir looked at the web again. "At least it's a word. What does Woo mean?"

They thought. Had someone been wandering by the cabin and chanced to look in they would have seen a group of adults standing quite still, staring into space and muttering "Woo" every now and then.

"Woo," Brunel said. "Don't people pitch woo?"

"Woohoo? No, that's boo," said Beauvoir. "Boohoo, not woo."

"Isn't it what they call kangaroos?" asked Morin.

"Kangawoos? That's roo," snapped Beauvoir.

"*Chalice*," swore Brunel.

"Woo, woo," said Morin under his breath, begging himself to come up with something that didn't sound like a choo-choo train. But the more he said it the more it sounded like nonsense. "Woo," he whispered.

Only Gamache said nothing. He listened to them but his mind kept going to the other piece of news. His face grew stern as he thought about what else had been revealed when the bloody fingerprints were lifted from the carving.

He can't stay here."

Marc swished his arms under the tap at the kitchen sink.

"I don't want him here either, but at least here we can watch him," his mother said.

All three looked out the kitchen window to the old man sitting cross-legged on the grass, meditating.

"What do you mean, 'watch him'?" asked Dominique. She was fascinated by her father-in-law. He had a sort of broken-down magnetism about him. She could see he once had had a powerful personality, and a powerful hold over people. And he behaved as though that was still true. There was a shabby dignity about him, but also a cunning.

Marc grabbed the bar of soap and rubbed it over his forearms, looking like a surgeon scrubbing up. In fact, he was scrubbing away dust and plaster after dry-walling.

It was hard work, and work he was almost certainly doing for someone else. The next owner of the inn and spa. Which was just as well, since he was doing it very badly.

"I mean that things happen around Vincent," said Carole. "Always have. He's sailed through life, this glorious ship of state. Oblivious of the wreckage in his wake."

It might not have sounded like it, but she was being charitable. For the sake of Marc. The truth was, she wasn't at all convinced Vincent had been oblivious of the damage he caused. She'd come to believe he actually deliberately sailed right over people. Destroyed them. Gone out of his way to do it.

She'd been his nurse, his assistant, his dogsbody. His witness and, finally, his conscience. Which was probably why he'd grown to hate her. And her him.

Once again they looked at the cross-legged man, sitting calmly in their garden.

"I can't cope with him right now," said Marc, drying his hands.

"We have to let him stay," said Dominique. "He's your father."

Marc looked at her with a mixture of amusement and sadness. "He's done it to you, now, hasn't he? Charmed you."

"I'm not some naïve schoolgirl, you know."

And this brought Marc up short. He realized she'd faced down some of the wealthiest, most manipulative bullies in Canadian finance. But Dr. Vincent Gilbert was different. There was something bewitching about him. "I'm sorry. So much is happening."

He'd thought moving to the country would be a breeze compared to the greed and fear and manipulation of the financial district. But so far here he'd found a dead body, moved it, ruined their reputation in the village, and been accused of murder; now he was about to kick a saint out of their home, and had almost certainly messed up the dry-walling.

And the leaves hadn't even changed yet.

But by then they'd be gone. To find another home somewhere else and hope they did better. He longed for the relative ease of the business world, where cut-throats lurked in every cubicle. Here everything looked so pleasant and peaceful, but wasn't.

He looked out the window again. In the foreground was his father, sitting cross-legged in the garden, and behind him in the field two broken-down old horses, what might or might not be a moose, and in the distance a muck-encrusted horse that by all rights should have been dog food by now. This wasn't what he had in mind when he'd moved to the country.

"Marc's right, you know," said Carole to her daughter-in-law. "Vincent either bullies, charms, or guilts his way in. But he always gets what he wants."

"And what does he want?" Dominique asked. It seemed a sensible question. Then why was it so difficult to answer?

The doorbell rang. They looked at each other. They'd come, in the last twenty-four hours, to dread that sound.

"I'll get it," said Dominique and walked briskly out of the kitchen, reappearing a minute later followed by a little boy and Old Mundin.

"I think you know my son," said Old, after greeting everyone with a smile. "Now, Charlie, what did The Mother tell you to say to these nice people?"

They waited while Charlie considered, then he gave them the finger.

"He learned that from Ruth, actually," Old explained.

"Quite a role model. Would he like a Scotch?" asked Carole. Old Mundin's handsome tanned face broke into a smile.

"No, Ruth just gave him a martini and we're trying not to mix drinks." Now the young man looked uncomfortable and putting his hands down on his son's shoulders he hugged Charlie to him. "I've heard he's here. Would you mind?"

Marc, Dominique, and Carole looked confused.

"Mind?" Dominique asked.

"Dr. Gilbert. I'd seen him in the forest, you know. I knew who he was but didn't know he was your father."

"Why didn't you say something?" Dominique asked.

"It wasn't my business. He didn't seem to want to be seen."

And Marc thought maybe it was simpler here after all, and he was the one who complicated things. The business world had somehow made him think everything was his business, when it wasn't.

"I don't want to disturb him," Mundin continued, "but I just wondered if maybe we could see him. Maybe introduce Charlie to him." The dignified young father looked as though this effort was hurting him. "I've read and reread his book, *Being*. Your father's a great man. I envy you."

And Marc envied him. His touching his son, holding him. Protecting him and loving him. Being willing to humble himself, for his son.

"He's in the garden," said Marc.

"Thanks." At the door Old Mundin stopped. "I have tools. Maybe I can come back tomorrow and help. A man can always use help."

You'll be a man, my son. Why hadn't his own father told him a man could always use help?

Marc nodded, not unaware of the significance of what had just happened. Old Mundin was offering to help the Gilberts build their home, not leave it. Because his father was Vincent Gilbert. His fucking father had saved them.

Mundin turned to Dominique. "The Wife says hello, by the way."

"Please say hello back," said Dominique, then hesitated a breath. "To The Wife."

"I will." He and Charlie went into the garden leaving the other three to watch.

Dr. Vincent Gilbert, late of the forest, had somehow become the center of attention.

As the young man and his son approached, Vincent Gilbert opened one eye and through the slit in his long lashes he watched. Not the two walking quietly toward him, but the three in the window.

Help others, he'd been told. And he intended to. But first he had to help himself.

It was quiet in the bistro. A few villagers sat at tables outside in the sunshine, relishing their *café* and Camparis and calm. Inside Olivier stood at the window.

"Good God, man, you'd think you'd never seen the village before," Gabri said from behind the bar where he was polishing the wood and replenishing the candy jars, most of which he'd helped empty.

For the last few days, every time Gabri looked for Olivier he'd find him standing in the same spot, in the bay window, looking out.

"Pipe?" Gabri walked over to his partner and offered him a licorice pipe, but Olivier seemed under a spell. Gabri bit into the licorice himself, eating the candied end first, as per the rules.

"What's bothering you?" Gabri followed the other man's gaze and saw only what he'd expect to see. Certainly nothing riveting. Just the customers on the *terrasse*, then the village green with Ruth and Rosa. The duck was now wearing a knitted sweater.

Olivier's eyes narrowed as he too focused on the duck. Then he turned to Gabri.

"Does that sweater look familiar to you?"

"Which?"

"The duck's, of course." Olivier studied Gabri closely. The large man never could lie. Now he ate the rest of the pipe and put on his most perplexed face.

"I have no idea what you're talking about."

"That's my sweater, isn't it?"

"Come off it, Olivier. Do you really think you and the duck wear the same size?"

"Not now, but when I was a kid. Where're my baby clothes?"

Now Gabri was silent, damning Ruth for parading Rosa in her new wardrobe. Well, maybe not so new.

"I thought it was time to get rid of them," said Gabri. "Ruth needed sweaters and things for Rosa to keep her warm in the fall and winter and I thought of your baby clothes. What were you saving them for anyway? They were just taking up space in the basement."

"How much space could they take up?" Olivier demanded, feeling himself breaking apart inside, his reserve crumbling. "How could you?" he snarled at Gabri, who leaned away, shocked.

"But you'd talked about getting rid of them yourself."

"Me, me. Me getting rid of them. Not you. You had no right."

"I'm sorry, I had no idea they meant that much to you."

"Well they do. Now what am I going to do?"

Olivier watched as Rosa waddled behind Ruth, who muttered away to the duck, saying God knew what. And Olivier felt tears sting his eyes, and a swell of emotion erupt from his throat. He couldn't very well take the clothes back. Not now. They were gone. Gone forever.

"Do you want me to get them back?" asked Gabri, taking Olivier's hand.

Olivier shook his head. Not even sure why he felt so strongly. He had so much else to worry about. And it was true, he'd thought about getting rid of the box of old baby clothes. The only reasons he hadn't were laziness, and not being sure who to give them to.

Why not Rosa? A distant honking was heard in the sky and both Rosa and Ruth lifted their heads. Overhead a formation of ducks headed south.

Sadness washed over Olivier. Gone. It was all gone. Everything.

For weeks and weeks the villagers journeyed through the forests. At first the young man hurried them along looking behind him now and then. He regretted telling his family and friends to leave with him. He could have been much farther away without the old men and women, and the children. But as the weeks went by and peaceful day followed peaceful day, he began to worry less and was even grateful for the company.

He'd almost forgotten to look over his shoulder when the first sign appeared.

It was twilight, only the twilight never died. Night never fell completely. He wasn't sure if any of the others noticed. It was, after all, just a small glow in the distance. At the horizon. The next day the sun rose, but not completely. There was a darkness to the sky. But again, just at the horizon. As though a shadow had spilled over from the other side.

The young man knew then.

He clutched his parcel tighter and hurried everyone along, rushing forward. Driving them onward. They were willing to hurry. After all, immortality, youth, happiness awaited. They were almost giddy with joy. And in that joy he hid.

At night the light grew in the sky. And during the day the shadow stretched toward them.

"Is that it?" his elderly aunt asked eagerly, as they crested a hill. "Are we there?"

In front of them was water. Nothing but water.

And behind them the shadow lengthened.

TWENTY-FIVE

〜

"Olivier?"

The blond head was bowed, studying the receipts of the day so far. It was getting on for lunch and the bistro was filled with the aroma of garlic and herbs and roast chicken.

Olivier had seen them coming, had heard them even. That shriek as though the forest itself was crying out. They'd emerged from the woods on their ATVs and parked at the old Hadley house. Much of the village stopped what it was doing to watch as Chief Inspector Gamache and Inspector Beauvoir walked into the village. They were deep in conversation and no one disturbed them. Olivier had turned away then, walking further into his bistro and behind the bar. Around him the young waiters set tables while Havoc Parra wrote specials on the board.

The door opened and Olivier turned his back. Claiming every last moment.

"Olivier?" said the Chief Inspector. "We need to talk. In private, please."

Olivier turned and smiled, as though if he ingratiated himself enough they might not do this thing. The Chief Inspector smiled back, but it never reached his thoughtful eyes. Leading them into the back room that overlooked the Rivière Bella Bella Olivier indicated the chairs at the dining table and sat himself.

"How can I help?"

His heart thudded in his chest and his hands were cold and numb. He could no longer feel his extremities, and dots danced before his eyes. He struggled for breath and felt light-headed.

"Tell us about the man who lived in the cabin," Chief Inspector

Gamache said, matter-of-factly. "The dead man." He folded his hands, settling in. A good dinner companion who wanted to hear your stories.

There was no escape, Olivier knew. He'd known it from the instant he'd seen the Hermit dead on the bistro floor. He'd seen this avalanche sliding toward him, gaining momentum. Olivier couldn't run. Could never outrun what was coming.

"He was one of my first customers when Gabri and I moved to Three Pines."

The words, kept inside for so long, crawled out. Rotting. Olivier was surprised his breath didn't stink.

Gamache gave him a small nod of encouragement.

"We just had an antique shop then. I hadn't turned this into a bistro, yet. We rented the space above to live in. It was awful. Crammed full of junk, and filthy. Someone had plastered over all the original features. But we worked day and night to restore it. I think we'd only been here a few weeks when he walked in. He wasn't the man you saw on the floor. Not then. This was years ago."

Olivier saw it all again. Gabri was upstairs in their new home, stripping the beams and taking the drywall off, exposing the magnificent original brick walls. Each discovery more exciting than the last. But none could rival the growing awareness that they'd found a home. A place they could finally settle. At first they'd been so intent on unpacking they didn't really take in the details of the village. But slowly, over the first few weeks and months, the village revealed itself.

"I was still setting up the business and didn't have much stuff, just odds and ends collected over the years. I'd always dreamed of opening an antique store, since I was a kid. Then the chance came."

"It didn't just come," said Gamache quietly. "It was helped along."

Olivier sighed. He should have known Gamache would find out.

"I'd quit my job in the city. I'd been quite successful, as you might have heard."

Gamache nodded again.

Olivier smiled, remembering those heady days. Of silk suits and gym memberships, of visiting the Mercedes dealership when the only issue was the color of the car.

And of taking that one step too far.

It'd been humiliating. He'd been so depressed he was afraid of what he might do to himself, so he'd sought help. And there, in the waiting room of the therapist, was Gabri. Large, voluble, vain and full of life.

At first Olivier had been repulsed. Gabri was everything he'd come to despise. Olivier thought of himself and his friends as gay men. Discreet, elegant, cynical.

Gabri was just queer. Common. And fat. There was nothing discreet about him.

But neither was there anything mean. And over time Olivier grew to appreciate how very beautiful kindness was.

And he fell in love with Gabri. Deeply, totally, indiscreetly in love.

Gabri had agreed to leave his job at the Y in Westmount and move out of the city. It didn't matter where. They got in their car and drove south. And there, over a rise in the road, they'd stopped the car. Finally admitting they were lost. Though since they had no destination they couldn't be lost, Gabri happily told Olivier, who was busy in the driver's side wrestling with a Carte Routière du Québec. Eventually he realized Gabri was standing outside and softly tapping on his window. He lowered it and Gabri gestured.

Annoyed, Olivier shoved the map into the backseat and got out.

"What?" he snapped at Gabri, who was looking ahead. Olivier followed his gaze. And found home.

He knew it immediately.

It was the place in all the fairy tales he'd read as a kid, under the bedding, when his father thought, hoped, he was reading about naval battles. Or naked girls. Instead he'd been reading about villages, and cottages, and gardens. And little wisps of smoke, and dry stone walls older than anyone in the village.

He'd forgotten all that, until that very moment. And in that instant he remembered his other childhood dream. Of opening an antique shop. A modest little affair where he could put his finds.

"Shall we, *ma belle*?" Gabri took Olivier's hand and leaving the car where it stood they walked down the dirt road and into Three Pines.

"I was disappointed at first when the Hermit came in—"

"The Hermit?" Gamache asked.

"That's what I called him."

"But didn't you know his name?"

"He never told me and I never asked."

Gamache caught Beauvoir's eye. The Inspector was looking both disappointed and disbelieving.

"Go on," said Gamache.

"His hair was a little long and he looked a bit scruffy. Not the sort to do a lot of buying. But it was quiet and I talked to him. He came back a week later, and then about once a week for a few months. Finally he took me aside and said he had something he wanted to sell. That was pretty disappointing too. I'd been nice to the guy but now he was asking me to buy some piece of junk and it pissed me off. I almost asked him to leave, but by then he had the piece in his hand."

Olivier remembered looking down. They were at the back and the lighting wasn't good, but it didn't gleam or glitter. In fact it looked very dull. Olivier reached out for it but the Hermit drew his hand back. And then it caught the light.

It was a miniature portrait. The two men walked to the window and Olivier got a good view.

It was in a tarnished old frame and must have been painted with a single horse hair, so fine was the detail. It showed a man in profile, powdered wig, blowsy clothing.

Even the memory made Olivier's heart quicken.

"How much do you want?"

"Maybe some food?" the Hermit had asked, and the deal was sealed.

Olivier looked at Gamache, whose thoughtful brown eyes never wavered.

"And that's how it started. I agreed to take the painting in exchange for a few bags of groceries."

"And what was it worth?"

"Not much." Olivier remembered carefully taking the miniature from its frame, and seeing the old lettering on the back. It was some Polish count. With a date. 1745. "I sold it for a few dollars."

He held Gamache's eyes.

"Where?"

"Some antique place along rue Notre Dame in Montreal."

Gamache nodded. "Go on."

"After that the Hermit brought stuff to the shop every now and then and I'd give him food. But he became more and more paranoid. Didn't want to come into the village anymore. So he invited me to his cabin."

"Why did you agree to go? It was quite an inconvenience."

Olivier had been afraid of that question.

"Because the things he was giving me turned out to be quite good. Nothing spectacular, but decent quality and I was curious. When I first visited the cabin it took me a few minutes to realize what he had. It all just looked like it belonged, in a strange sort of way. Then I looked closer. He was eating off plates worth tens of thousands, hundreds of thousands of dollars. Did you see the glasses?" Olivier's eyes were gleaming with excitement. "*Fantastique.*"

"Did he ever explain how he came to have items that were priceless?"

"Never, and I never asked. I was afraid to scare him off."

"Did he know the value of what he had?"

That was an interesting question, and one Olivier had debated himself. The Hermit treated the finest engraved silver the way Gabri treated Ikea flatware. There was no attempt to coddle anything. But neither was the Hermit cavalier. He was a cautious man, that much was certain.

"I'm not sure," said Olivier.

"So you gave him groceries and he gave you near-priceless antiques?"

Gamache's voice was neutral, curious. It held none of the censure Olivier knew it could, and should.

"He didn't give me the best stuff, at least not at first. And I did more than take him groceries. I helped dig his vegetable garden, and brought the seeds to plant."

"How often did you visit?"

"Every two weeks."

Gamache considered, then spoke. "Why was he living in the cabin away from everyone else?"

"Hiding, I guess."

"But from what?"

Olivier shook his head. "Don't know. I tried to ask but he was having none of it."

"What can you tell us?" Gamache's voice wasn't quite as patient as it had been. Beauvior looked up from his notebook, and Olivier shifted in his seat.

"I know the Hermit built the cabin over several months. Then he carried all the stuff in himself." Olivier was studying Gamache, eager for his approval, eager for the thaw. The large man leaned forward slightly and Olivier rushed on. "He told me all about it. Most of his things weren't big.

Just the armchairs, really, and the bed. The rest anybody could've carried. And he was strong."

Still, Gamache was silent. Olivier squirmed.

"I'm telling the truth. He never explained how he got all those things, and I was afraid to ask, but it's kind of obvious, isn't it? He must have stolen them. Otherwise, why hide?"

"So you thought they were stolen and you didn't say anything?" asked Gamache, his voice still without criticism. "Didn't call the police."

"No. I know I should have, but I didn't."

For once Beauvoir didn't sneer. This he found completely natural and understandable. How many people would, after all? It always amazed Beauvoir when he heard about people finding suitcases full of money, and turning it in. He had to wonder about the sanity of such people.

For his part Gamache was thinking about the other end of the deal. The people who'd owned the things. The fabulous violin, the priceless glassware, the china and silver and inlaid wood. If the Hermit was hiding in the woods someone had chased him there. "Did he say where he was from?" Gamache asked.

"No. I asked once but he didn't answer."

Gamache considered. "What did he sound like?"

"I'm sorry?"

"His voice."

"It was normal. We spoke in French."

"Quebec French, or France French?"

Olivier hesitated. Gamache waited.

"Quebec, but . . ."

Gamache was still, as though he could wait all day. All week. A lifetime.

". . . but he had a slight accent. Czech, I think," said Olivier in a rush.

"Are you sure?"

"Yes. He was Czech," said Olivier in a mumble. "I'm sure."

Gamache saw Beauvoir make a note. It was the first clue to the man's identity.

"Why didn't you tell us you knew the Hermit when the body was found?"

"I should have, but I thought you might not find the cabin."

"And why would you hope that?"

Olivier tried to take a breath, but the oxygen didn't seem to reach his lungs. Or his brain. His compressed lips felt cold and his eyes burned. Hadn't he told them enough? But still Gamache sat across from him, waiting. And Olivier could see it in his eyes. He knew. Gamache knew the answer, and still he demanded Olivier say it himself.

"Because there were things in the cabin I wanted. For myself."

Olivier looked exhausted, as though he'd coughed up his insides. But Gamache knew there was more.

"Tell us about the carvings."

Clara walked along the road from the Incident Room, over the bridge into Three Pines, and stood looking first one way then the other.

What should she do?

She'd just been to the Incident Room to return the carving.

Fucking queers.

Two words.

Surely she could ignore them. Pretend Fortin hadn't said it. Or, better still, maybe she could find someone who'd assure her what she'd done was quite right.

She'd done nothing. Said nothing. She'd simply thanked Denis Fortin for his time, agreed this was exciting, agreed to keep in touch as the show approached. They'd shaken hands and kissed on both cheeks.

And now she stood, lost, looking this way and that. Clara had considered talking to Gamache about it, then dismissed the idea. He was a friend, but he was also a cop, investigating a crime worse than nasty words.

And yet, Clara wondered. Was that where most murders began? Did they start as words? Something said that lodged and festered. That curdled. And killed.

Fucking queers.

And she'd done nothing.

Clara turned right and made for the shops.

What carvings?"

"This carving for one." Gamache placed the sailing ship, with its miserable passenger hiding among the smiles, on the table.

Olivier stared at it.

They camped at the very edge of the world, crowded together, looking out to the ocean. Except the young man, who stared back. To where they'd come from.

It was impossible to miss the lights in the dark sky now. And the sky was almost perpetually dark. There was no longer a distinction between night and day. And yet, such was the villagers' joy and anticipation, they didn't seem to notice, or care.

The light sliced like a saber through the darkness, through the shadow thrown toward them. Almost upon them.

The Mountain King had arisen. Had assembled an army made of Bile and Rage and led by Chaos. Their wrath carved the sky ahead of them, searching for one man, one young man. Barely more than a boy. And the package he held.

They marched on, closer and closer. And the villagers waited on shore, to be taken to the world they'd been promised. Where nothing bad happened, and no one sickened or grew old.

The young man ran here and there, trying to find a hiding place. A cave perhaps, somewhere he could curl up and hide, and be very, very small. And quiet.

"Oh," said Olivier.
"What can you tell me about this?" asked Gamache.

One small hill separated the dreadful army from the villagers. An hour, maybe less.

Olivier heard the voice again, the story filling the cabin, even the dark corners.

"Look," one of the villagers shouted, pointing to the water. The young man turned, wondering what horror was coming from the sea. But instead he saw a ship. In full sail. Hurrying toward them.

"Sent by the gods," said his old aunt as she stepped on board. And he knew that was true. One of the gods had taken pity on them and sent a strong ship and a stronger wind. They hurried aboard and the ship left immediately. Out at sea the young man looked back in time to see, rising behind the final hill, a dark shape. It rose higher and higher and around its

*peak flew the Furies, and on its now naked flank there marched Sorrow
and Grief and Madness. And at the head of the army was Chaos.*

*As the Mountain spied the tiny vessel on the ocean it shrieked, and the
howl filled the sails of the vessel so that it streaked across the ocean. In
the bow the happy villagers searched for land, for their new world. But the
young man, huddling among them, looked back. At the Mountain of Bitterness he'd created. And the rage that filled their sails.*

"Where did you find that?" Olivier asked.

"In the cabin." Gamache was watching him closely. Olivier seemed
stunned by the carving. Almost frightened. "Have you seen it before?"

"Never."

"Or others like it?"

"No."

Gamache handed it to Olivier. "It's a strange subject matter, don't
you think?"

"How so?"

"Well, everyone's so happy, joyful even. Except him." Gamache
placed his forefinger on the head of the crouching figure. Olivier looked
closer and frowned.

"I know nothing about art. You'll have to ask someone else."

"What did the Hermit whittle?"

"Nothing much. Just pieces of wood. Tried to teach me once but I
kept cutting myself. Not good with my hands."

"That's not what Gabri says. He tells me you used to make your own
clothes."

"As a kid." Olivier reddened. "And they were crap."

Gamache took the carving from Olivier. "We found whittling tools
in the cabin. The lab's working on them and we'll know soon enough if
they were used to make this. But we both know the answer to that, don't
we?"

The two men stared at each other.

"You're right," said Olivier with a laugh. "I'd forgotten. He used to
whittle these strange carvings, but he never showed me that one."

"What did he show you?"

"I can't remember."

Gamache rarely showed impatience, but Inspector Beauvoir did. He slammed his notebook shut. It made a not very satisfactory sound. Certainly not nearly enough to convey his frustration at a witness who was behaving like his six-year-old nephew accused of stealing cookies. Denying everything. Lying about everything however trivial, as though he couldn't help himself.

"Try," said Gamache.

Olivier sighed. "I feel badly about this. He loved carving, and he asked me to get him the wood. He was very specific. Red cedar, from British Columbia. I got it from Old Mundin. But when the Hermit started handing me these I was pretty disappointed. Especially since he wasn't giving me as many antiques from his cabin. Just those." He flicked his hand at the carving.

"What did you do with them?"

"I threw them away."

"Where?"

"Into the woods. When I walked home I tossed them into the forest. Didn't want them."

"But he didn't give you this one, or even show it to you?"

Olivier shook his head.

Gamache paused. Why did the Hermit hide this one, and the other? What was different about them? Maybe he suspected Olivier had thrown the others away. Maybe he realized his visitor couldn't be trusted with his creations.

"What does this mean?" The Chief Inspector pointed to the letters carved under the ship.

OWSVI

"I don't know." Olivier seemed perplexed. "The others didn't have that."

"Tell me about woo," said Gamache so quietly Olivier thought he'd misheard.

Clara sat in the deep, comfortable armchair and watched Myrna serve Monsieur Béliveau. The old grocer had come in for something to read, but he wasn't sure what. He and Myrna talked about it and she made some suggestions. Myrna knew everyone's tastes, both the ones they declared and their actual ones.

Finally Monsieur Béliveau left with his biographies of Sartre and

Wayne Gretzky. He bowed slightly to Clara, who bowed back from her chair, never sure what to do when the courtly old man did that.

Myrna handed Clara a cool lemonade and sat in the chair opposite. The afternoon sun poured through the bookshop window. Here and there they saw a dog chase a ball for a villager, or vice versa.

"Didn't you have your meeting this morning with Monsieur Fortin?" Clara nodded.

"How'd it go?"

"Not bad."

"Do you smell smoke?" asked Myrna, sniffing. Clara, alarmed, looked around. "Oh, there it is," Myrna pointed to her companion. "Your pants are on fire."

"Very funny." But that was all the encouragement Clara needed. She tried to keep her voice light as she described the meeting. When Clara listed the people who would almost certainly be at the opening night at Fortin's gallery Myrna exclaimed and hugged her friend.

"Can you believe it?"

"Fucking queer."

"Stupid whore. Is this a new game?" laughed Myrna.

"You're not offended by what I said?"

"Calling me a fucking queer? No."

"Why not?"

"Well, I know you don't mean it. Did you?"

"Suppose I did?"

"Then I'd be worried for you," smiled Myrna. "What's this about?"

"When we were sitting in the bistro Gabri served us and as he left Fortin called him a fucking queer."

Myna took a deep breath. "And what did you say?"

"Nothing."

Myna nodded. Now it was her turn to say nothing.

What?"

"Woo," repeated the Chief Inspector.

"Woo?" Olivier seemed baffled, but he'd feigned that at every turn in this interview. Beauvoir had long stopped believing anything the man said.

"Did the Hermit ever mention it?" Gamache asked.

"Mention woo?" Olivier asked. "I don't even know what you're asking."

"Did you notice a spider's web, in a corner of the cabin?"

"A spider's web? What? No, I never noticed one. But I'll tell you something, I'd be surprised if there was one. The Hermit kept that cabin spotless."

"*Propre*," said Gamache.

"*Propre*," Olivier repeated.

"Woo, Olivier. What does it mean to you?"

"Nothing."

"And yet it was the word on the piece of wood you took from the hand of the Hermit. After he'd been murdered."

It was worse than Olivier had imagined, and he'd imagined pretty bad. It seemed Gamache knew everything. Or at least almost everything.

Pray God he doesn't know it all, thought Olivier.

"I picked it up," Olivier admitted. "But I didn't look at it. It was lying on the floor by his hand. When I saw there was blood on it I dropped it. It said Woo?"

Gamache nodded and leaned forward, his powerful hands lightly holding each other as his elbows rested on his knees.

"Did you kill him?"

TWENTY-SIX

Finally Myrna spoke. She leaned forward and took Clara's hand.

"What you did was natural."

"Really? Because it feels like shit."

"Well, most of your life is shit," said Myrna, nodding her head sagely. "So it would feel natural."

"Har, har."

"Listen, Fortin is offering you everything you ever dreamed of, everything you ever wanted."

"And he seemed so nice."

"He probably is. Are you sure he wasn't kidding?"

Clara shook her head.

"Maybe he's gay himself," suggested Myrna.

Clara shook her head again. "I thought of that, but he has a wife and a couple of kids and he just doesn't seem gay."

Both Clara and Myrna had a finely honed gay-dar. It was, they both knew, imperfect, but it probably would have picked up the Fortin blip. But nothing. Only the immense, unmistakable object that was Gabri, sailing away.

"What should I do?" Clara asked.

Myrna remained silent.

"I need to speak to Gabri, don't I?"

"It might help."

"Maybe tomorrow."

As she left she thought about what Myrna had said. Fortin was offering her everything she'd ever wanted, the only dream she'd had since childhood. Success, recognition as an artist. All the sweeter after years in the wilderness. Mocked and marginalized.

And all she had to do was say nothing.

She could do that.

No, I didn't kill him."

But even as Olivier said it he realized the disaster of what he'd done. In lying at every turn he'd made the truth unrecognizable.

"He was already dead when I arrived."

God, even to his own ears it sounded like a lie. I didn't take the last cookie, I didn't break the fine bone china cup, I didn't steal the money from your purse. I'm not gay.

All lies. All his life. All the time. Until he'd come to Three Pines. For an instant, for a glorious few days he'd lived a genuine life. With Gabri. In their little rented wreck of an apartment above the shop.

But then the Hermit had arrived. And with him a trail of lies.

"Listen, it's the truth. It was Saturday night and the place was hopping. The Labor Day long weekend's always a madhouse. But by midnight or so there were only a few stragglers. Then Old Mundin arrived with the chairs and a table. By the time he left the place was empty and Havoc was doing the final cleanup. So I decided to visit the Hermit."

"After midnight?" Gamache asked.

"That's normally when I went. So no one could see."

Across from Olivier the Chief Inspector slowly leaned back, distancing himself. The gesture was eloquent. It whispered that Gamache didn't believe him. Olivier stared at this man he'd considered a friend and he felt a tightening, a constriction.

"Weren't you afraid of the dark?"

Gamache asked it so simply, and in that instant Olivier knew the genius of the man. He was able to crawl into other people's skins, and burrow beyond the flesh and blood and bone. And ask questions of deceptive simplicity.

"It's not the dark I'm afraid of," said Olivier. And he remembered the freedom that came only after the sun set. In city parks, in darkened theaters, in bedrooms. The bliss that came with being able to shed the outer shell and be himself. Protected by the night.

It wasn't the dark that scared him, but what might come to light.

"I knew the way and it only took about twenty minutes to walk it."

"What did you see when you arrived?"

"Everything looked normal. There was a light in the window and the lantern on the porch was lit."

"He was expecting company."

"He was expecting me. He always lit the lantern for me. I didn't realize there was anything wrong until I was in the door and saw him there. I knew he was dead, but I thought he'd just fallen, maybe had a stroke or a heart attack and hit his head."

"There was no weapon?"

"No, nothing."

Gamache leaned forward again.

Were they beginning to believe him, Olivier wondered.

"Did you take him food?"

Olivier's mind revved, raced. He nodded.

"What did you take?"

"The usual. Cheese, milk, butter. Some bread. And as a treat I took some honey and tea."

"What did you do with it?"

"The groceries? I don't know. I was in shock. I can't remember."

"We found them in the kitchen. Open."

The two men stared at each other. Then Gamache's eyes narrowed in a look that Olivier found harrowing.

Gamache was angry.

"I was there twice that night," he mumbled into the table.

"Louder, please," said the Chief.

"I returned to the cabin, okay?"

"It's time now, Olivier. Tell me the truth."

Olivier's breath came in short gasps, like something hooked and landed and about to be filleted.

"The first time I was there that night the Hermit was alive. We had a cup of tea and talked."

"What did you talk about?"

Chaos is coming, old son, and there's no stopping it. It's taken a long time, but it's finally here.

"He always asked about people who'd come to the village. He peppered me with questions about the outside world."

"The outside world?"

"You know, out here. He hadn't been more than fifty feet from his cabin in years."

"Go on," said Gamache. "What happened then?"

"It was getting late so I left. He offered to give me something for the groceries. At first I refused, but he insisted. When I got out of the woods I realized I'd left it behind, so I went back." No need to tell them about the thing in the canvas bag. "When I got there he was dead."

"How long were you gone?"

"About half an hour. I didn't dawdle."

He saw again the tree limbs snapping back and felt them slapping him, smelled the pine needles, and heard the crashing through the woods, like an army, running. Racing. He'd thought it was just his own noise, magnified by fear and the night. But maybe not.

"You saw and heard nothing?"

"Nothing."

"What time was that?" Gamache asked.

"About two I guess, maybe two thirty."

Gamache laced his fingers together. "What did you do once you realized what had happened?"

The rest of the story came out quickly, in a rush. Once he'd realized the Hermit was dead, another idea had come to Olivier. A way the Hermit might help. He'd put the body in the wheelbarrow and taken him through the woods to the old Hadley house.

"It took a while, but I finally got him there. I'd planned to leave him on the porch, but when I tried the door it was unlocked, so I laid him in the front hall."

He made it sound gentle, but he knew it wasn't. It was a brutal, ugly, vindictive act. A violation of a body, a violation of a friendship, a violation of the Gilberts. And finally, it was a betrayal of Gabri and their lives in Three Pines.

It was so quiet in the room he could almost believe himself alone. He looked up and there was Gamache, watching him.

"I'm sorry," said Olivier. He scolded himself, desperate not to be the gay guy who cried. But he knew his actions had taken him far beyond cliché, or caricature.

And then Armand Gamache did the most extraordinary thing. He leaned forward so that his large, certain hands were almost touching

Olivier's, as though it was all right to be that close to someone so vile, and he spoke in a calm, deep voice.

"If you didn't kill the man, who else could have? I need your help."

In that one sentence Gamache had placed himself next to Olivier. He might still be on the outer reaches of the world, but at least he wasn't alone.

Gamache believed him.

Clara stood outside Peter's closed studio door. She almost never knocked, almost never disturbed him. Unless it was an emergency. Those were hard to come by in Three Pines and were generally Ruth-shaped and difficult to avoid.

Clara had walked around the garden a few times, then come inside and walked around the living room, and then the kitchen in ever decreasing circles until finally she found herself here. She loved Myrna, she trusted Gamache, she adored Gabri and Olivier and many other friends. But it was Peter she needed.

She knocked. There was a pause, then the door opened.

"I need to talk."

"What is it?" He came out immediately and closed the door behind him. "What's wrong?"

"I met Fortin, as you know, and he said something."

Peter's heart missed a beat. And in that missed beat lived something petty. Something that hoped Fortin would change his mind. Would cancel Clara's solo show. Would say they'd made a mistake and Peter was really the one they wanted.

His heart beat for Clara every hour of every day. But every now and then it stumbled.

He took her hands. "What'd he say?"

"He called Gabri a fucking queer."

Peter waited for the rest. The part about Peter being the better artist. But Clara just stared at him.

"Tell me about it." He led her to a chair and they sat.

"Everything was going so well. He loved my ideas for hanging the show, he said FitzPatrick would be there from MoMA, and so would Allyne from the *Times*. And he thinks even Vanessa Destin Browne, you know, from the Tate Modern. Can you believe it?"

Peter couldn't. "Tell me more."

It was like throwing himself over and over at a wall of spikes.

"And then he called Gabri a fucking queer, behind his back. And said it made him want to vomit."

The spiked wall turned smooth, and soft.

"What did you say?"

"Nothing."

Peter dropped his eyes, then looked up. "I probably wouldn't have either."

"Really?" asked Clara, searching his face.

"Really." He smiled and squeezed her hands. "You weren't expecting it."

"It was a shock," said Clara, eager to explain. "What should I do?"

"What d'you mean?"

"Should I just forget about it, or say something to Fortin?"

And Peter saw the equation immediately. If she confronted the gallery owner she was running the risk of angering him. In fact, it almost certainly would. At the very least it would mar their relationship. He might even cancel her show.

If she said nothing, she'd be safe. Except that he knew her. It would eat away at Clara's conscience. A conscience, once aroused, could be a terrible thing.

Gabri poked his head into the back room.

"*Salut*. Why so serious?"

Olivier, Gamache and Beauvoir all looked at him. None was smiling.

"Wait a minute, are you telling Olivier about your visit to his father?" Gabri sat down beside his partner. "I wanna hear too. What'd he say about me?"

"We weren't talking about Olivier's father," said Gamache. Across from him Olivier's eyes were pleading for a favor Gamache couldn't grant. "We were talking about Olivier's relationship with the dead man."

Gabri looked from Gamache to Olivier, then over to Beauvoir. Then back to Olivier. "What?"

Gamache and Olivier exchanged looks and finally Olivier spoke. He told Gabri about the Hermit, his visits to the cabin, and the body. Gabri listened, silent. It was the first time Beauvoir had ever seen him go more than a minute without talking. And even when Olivier stopped, Gabri didn't start. He sat there as though he might never speak again.

But then, he did. "How could you be so stupid?"

"I'm sorry. It was dumb."

"It was more than dumb. I can't believe you didn't tell me about the cabin."

"I should've told you, I know. But he was so afraid, so secretive. You didn't know him—"

"I guess not."

"—but if he'd known I'd told anyone he'd have stopped seeing me."

"Why did you want to see him anyway? He was a hermit, in a cabin for God's sake. Wait a minute." There was silence while Gabri put it all together. "Why'd you go there?"

Olivier looked at Gamache, who nodded. It would all come out anyway.

"His place was full of treasure, Gabri. You wouldn't believe it. Cash stuffed between the logs for insulation. There was leaded crystal and tapestries. It was fantastic. Everything he had was priceless."

"You're making that up."

"I'm not. We ate off Catherine the Great's china. The toilet paper was dollar bills."

"*Sacré.* It's like your wet dream. Now I know you're kidding."

"No, no. It was unbelievable. And sometimes when I visited he'd give me a little something."

"And you took it?" Gabri's voice rose.

"Of course I took it," Olivier snapped. "I didn't steal it, and those things are no use to him."

"But he was probably nuts. It's the same as stealing."

"That's a horrible thing to say. You think I'd steal stuff from an old man?"

"Why not? You dumped his body at the old Hadley house. Who knows what you're capable of."

"Really? And you're innocent in all this?" Olivier's voice had grown cold and cruel. "How do you think we could afford to buy the bistro? Or the B and B? Eh? Didn't you ever wonder how we went from living in that dump of an apartment—"

"I fixed it up. It wasn't a dump anymore."

"—to opening the bistro and a B and B? How did you think we could afford it suddenly?"

"I thought the antique business was going well." There was silence. "You should've told me," said Gabri, finally, and wondered, as did Gamache and Beauvoir, what else Olivier wasn't saying.

It was late afternoon and Armand Gamache walked through the woods. Beauvoir had volunteered to go with him, but he preferred to be alone with his thoughts.

After they left Olivier and Gabri they'd returned to the Incident Room where Agent Morin had been waiting.

"I know who BM is," he said, eagerly following them, barely allowing them to take off their coats. "Look."

He took them over to his computer. Gamache sat and Beauvoir leaned over his shoulder. There was a black-and-white, formal, photo of a man smoking a cigarette.

"His name is Bohuslav Martinù," said Morin. "He wrote that violin piece we found. His birthday was December the eighth, so the violin must have been a birthday present from his wife. C. Charlotte was her name."

Gamache, while listening, was staring at one line in the biography his agent had found. Martinù had been born December 8, 1890. In Bohemia. What was now the Czech Republic.

"Did they have any children?" Beauvoir asked. He too had noticed the reference.

"None."

"Are you sure?" Gamache twisted in his chair to look at Morin, but the agent shook his head.

"I double- and triple-checked. It's almost midnight there but I have a call in to the Martinù Conservatory in Prague to get more information and I'll ask them, but it doesn't seem so."

"Ask about the violin, would you?" said Gamache, rising and putting his coat back on. He'd headed to the cabin, walking slowly through the woods, thinking.

A Sûreté officer guarding the cabin greeted him on the porch.

"Come with me, please," said Gamache and led the agent to the wheelbarrow sitting by the vegetable patch. He explained it had been used to carry a body and asked the officer to take samples. While she did that, Gamache went into the cabin.

It would be emptied the next morning, everything taken away for cataloguing, safe keeping. Put away in a dark vault. Away from human hands and eyes.

But before that happened Gamache wanted to see it all one last time.

Closing the door behind him he waited for his eyes to adjust to the dim interior. As always, it was the smell that first impressed him. Wood, and woodsmoke. Then the musky undertone of coffee and finally the sweeter scent of coriander and tarragon, from the window boxes.

The place was peaceful, restful. Cheerful even. While everything in it was a masterpiece, it all seemed at home in the rustic cabin. The Hermit might have known their worth, but he certainly knew their use, and used everything as it was intended. Glasses, dishes, silverware, vases. All put to purpose.

Gamache picked up the Bergonzi violin and cradling it he sat in the Hermit's chair by the fireplace. *One for solitude, two for friendship.*

The dead man had no need, or desire, for society. But he did have company.

They now knew who had sat in that other comfortable chair. Gamache had thought it was Dr. Vincent Gilbert, but he'd been wrong. It was Olivier Brulé. He'd come to keep the Hermit company, to bring him seeds and staples, and companionship. And in return the Hermit had given him what Olivier wanted. Treasure.

It was a fair trade.

But had someone else found him? If not, or if Gamache couldn't prove it, then Olivier Brulé would be arrested for murder. Arrested, tried and probably convicted.

Gamache couldn't shake the thought that it was too convenient that Dr. Vincent Gilbert had arrived just as the Hermit had been killed. Hadn't Olivier said the dead man was worried about strangers? Maybe Gilbert was that stanger.

Gamache tipped his head back and thought some more. Suppose Vincent Gilbert wasn't the one the Hermit was hiding from. Suppose it was another Gilbert. After all, it was Marc who'd bought the old Hadley house. He'd quit a successful job in the city to come here. He and Dominique had plenty of money; they could have bought any place in the

Townships. So why buy a broken-down old wreck? Unless it wasn't the house they wanted, but the forest.

And what about the Parras? Olivier had said the Hermit spoke with a slight accent. A Czech accent. And Roar was clearing the trail. Heading straight here.

Maybe he'd found the cabin. And the treasure.

Maybe they knew he was here somewhere and had been looking. When Gilbert bought the place maybe Roar took the job so that he could explore the woods. Searching for the Hermit.

And Havoc. What was the case against him? He seemed, by all reports, like a regular young man. But a young man who chose to stay here, in this backwater, while most of his friends had moved away. To university. To careers. Waiting table couldn't be considered a career. What was such a personable, bright young man doing here?

Gamache sat forward. Seeing the last night of the Hermit's life. The crowd at the bistro. Old Mundin arriving with the furniture then leaving. Olivier leaving. Havoc locking up. Then noticing his employer do something unexpected. Something bizarre even.

Had Havoc seen Olivier turn toward the woods instead of going home?

Curious, Havoc would have followed Olivier. Straight to the cabin. And the treasures.

It played out before Gamache's eyes. Olivier leaving and Havoc confronting the frightened man. Demanding some of the things. The Hermit refusing. Maybe he shoved Havoc away. Maybe Havoc struck out, picking up a weapon and smashing the Hermit. Frightened, he'd fled. Just before Olivier returned.

But that didn't explain everything.

Gamache put down the violin and looked up at the web in the corner. No, this wasn't a murder that had happened out of the blue. There was cunning here. And cruelty. The Hermit was tortured first, then killed. Tortured by a tiny word.

Woo.

After a few minutes Gamache got up and slowly wandered the room, picking up pieces here and there, touching things he never thought he'd see never mind hold. The panel from the Amber Room that threw pumpkin light into the kitchen. Ancient pottery used by the Hermit for herbs. Stunning enameled spoons and silk tapestries. And first editions. One was on the bedside table. Gamache picked it up idly, and looked at it.

Currer Bell was the author. Agent Morin had mentioned this book. He flipped it open. Another first edition. Then he noticed the title of the book.

Jane Eyre: An Autobiography. Currer Bell. That was the pseudonym used by—

He opened the book again. Charlotte Brontë. He was holding a first edition of *Jane Eyre*.

Armand Gamache stood very quietly in the cabin. But there wasn't complete silence. One word whispered to him, and had from the first moment they'd found the cabin. Repeated over and over. In the children's book found in the outhouse, in the Amber panel, in the violin, and now in the book he held in his hand. One word. A name.

Charlotte.

TWENTY-SEVEN

———

"We're getting more results from the lab," said Lacoste.

Upon his return the Chief had gathered his team at the conference table and now Agent Lacoste was handing around the printouts. "The web was made of nylon fishing line. Readily available. No prints, of course, and no trace of DNA. Whoever made it probably used surgical gloves. All they found was a little dust and a cobweb." She smiled.

"Dust?" asked Gamache. "Do they have any idea how long it was up?"

"No more than a few days, they guess. Either that or the Hermit dusted it daily, which seems unlikely."

Gamache nodded.

"So who put it there?" asked Beauvoir. "The victim? The murderer?"

"There's something else," said Lacoste. "The lab's been looking at the wooden Woo. They say it was carved years ago."

"Was it made by the Hermit?" Gamache asked.

"They're working on it."

"Any progress on what woo might mean?"

"There's a film director named John Woo. He's from China. Did *Mission Impossible II*," said Morin seriously, as though giving them vital information.

"Woo can stand for World of Outlaws. It's a car-racing organization." Lacoste looked at the Chief, who stared back blankly. She looked down hurriedly at her notes for something more helpful to say. "Or there's a video game called Woo."

"Oh, no. I can't believe I forgot that," said Morin, turning to Gamache.

"Woo isn't the name of the game, it's the name of a character in a game. The game is called King of the Monsters."

"King of the Monsters?" Gamache thought it unlikely the Hermit or his tormentor had a video game in mind. "Anything else?"

"Well, there's the woo cocktail," suggested Lacoste. "Made from peach schnapps and vodka."

"Then there's woo-woo," said Beauvoir. "It's English slang."

"*Vraiment?*" said Gamache. "What does it mean?"

"It means crazy." Beauvoir smiled.

"And there's wooing a person. Seducing them," said Lacoste, then shook her head. They weren't any closer.

Gamache dismissed the meeting, then walking back to his computer he typed in a word.

Charlotte.

Gabri chopped the tomatoes and peppers and onions. He chopped and he chopped and he chopped. He'd already chopped the golden plums and strawberries, the beets and pickles. He'd sharpened his knife and chopped some more.

All afternoon and into the evening.

"Can we talk now?" asked Olivier, standing in the doorway to the kitchen. It smelled so comforting, but felt so foreign.

Gabri, his back to the door, didn't pause. He reached for a cauliflower and chopped that.

"Mustard pickles," said Olivier, venturing into the kitchen. "My favorite."

Clunk, clunk, clunk, and the cauliflower was tossed into the boiling pot to blanch.

"I'm sorry," said Olivier.

At the sink Gabri scrubbed lemons, then cutting them into quarters he shoved them into a jar and sprinkled coarse salt on top. Finally he squeezed the leftover lemons and poured the juice over the salt.

"Can I help?" asked Olivier, reaching for the top of a jar. But Gabri put his body between Olivier and the jars and silently sealed them.

Every surface of the kitchen was packed with colorful jars filled with jams and jellies, pickles and chutneys. And it looked as though

Gabri would keep this up forever. Silently preserving everything he could.

Clara chopped the ends off the fresh carrots and watched Peter toss the tiny new potatoes into boiling water. They'd have a simple dinner tonight of vegetables from the garden with herbs and sweet butter. It was one of their favorite meals in late summer.

"I don't know who to feel worse for, Olivier or Gabri," she said.

"I do," said Peter, shelling some peas. "Gabri didn't do anything. Can you believe Olivier's been visiting that guy in the woods for years and didn't tell anyone? I mean, what else isn't he telling us?"

"Did you know he's gay?"

"He's probably straight and isn't telling us."

Clara smirked. "Now that would really piss Gabri off, though I know a couple of women who'd be happy." She paused, knife in mid-air. "I think Olivier feels pretty horrible."

"Come on. He'd still be doing it if the old man hadn't been murdered."

"He didn't do anything wrong, you know," said Clara. "The Hermit gave him everything."

"So he says."

"What do you mean?"

"Well, the Hermit's dead. Isn't that convenient?"

Clara stopped chopping. "What're you saying?"

"Nothing. I'm just angry."

"Why? Because he didn't tell us?"

"Aren't you pissed off?"

"A little. But I think I'm more amazed. Listen, we all know Olivier likes the finer things."

"You mean he's greedy and tight."

"What amazes me is what Olivier did with the body. I just can't imagine him lugging it through the woods and dumping it in the old Hadley house," said Clara. "I didn't think he had the strength."

"I didn't think he had the anger," said Peter.

Clara nodded. Neither did she. And she also wondered what else their friend hadn't told them. All this, though, had also meant that

Clara couldn't possibly ask Gabri about being called a "fucking queer." Over dinner she explained this to Peter.

"So," she concluded, her plate almost untouched, "I don't know what to do about Fortin. Should I go into Montreal and speak to him directly about this, or just let it go?"

Peter took another slice of baguette, soft on the inside with a crispy crust. He smeared the butter to the edges, covering every millimeter, evenly. Methodically.

Watching him Clara felt she'd surely scream or explode, or at the very least grab the fucking baguette and toss it until it was a grease stain on the wall.

Still Peter smoothed the knife over the bread. Making sure the butter was perfect.

What should he tell her? To forget it? That what Fortin said wasn't that bad? Certainly not worth risking her career. Just let it go. Besides, saying something almost certainly wouldn't change Fortin's mind about gays, and might just turn him against Clara. And this wasn't some tiny show Fortin was giving her. This was everything Clara had dreamed of. Every artist dreamed of. Everyone from the art world would be there. Clara's career would be made.

Should he tell her to let it go, or tell Clara she had to speak to Fortin? For Gabri and Olivier and all their gay friends. But mostly for herself.

But if she did that Fortin might get angry, might very well cancel her show.

Peter dug the tip of the knife into a hole in the bread to get the butter out.

He knew what he wanted to say, but he didn't know if he'd be saying it for his sake, or for Clara's.

"Well?" she asked, and heard the impatience in her voice. "Well?" she asked more softly. "What do you think?"

"What do you think?"

Clara searched his face. "I think I should just let it go. If he says it again maybe then I'll say something. It's a stressful time for all of us."

"I'm sure you're right."

Clara looked down at her uneaten plate. She'd heard the hesitation in Peter's voice. Still, he wasn't the one risking everything.

Rosa quacked a little in her sleep. Ruth eased the little flannel night-shirt off the duck and Rosa fluttered her wings then went back to sleep, tucking her beak under her wing.

Olivier had come to visit, flushed and upset. She'd cleared old *New Yorkers* off a chair and he'd sat in her front room like a fugitive. Ruth had brought him a glass of cooking sherry and a celery stick smeared with Velveeta and sat with him. For almost an hour they sat, not speaking, until Rosa entered the room. She waddled in wearing a gray flannel blazer. Ruth saw Olivier's lips press together and his chin pucker. Not a sound escaped. But what did escape were tears, wearing warm lines down his handsome face.

And then he told her what had happened. About Gamache, about the cabin, about the Hermit and his belongings. About moving the body and owning the bistro, and the boulangerie and almost everything else in Three Pines.

Ruth didn't care. All she could think of was what she'd give in exchange for words. To say something. The right thing. To tell Olivier that she loved him. That Gabri loved him and would never, ever leave. That love could never leave.

She imagined herself getting up and sitting beside him, and taking his trembling hand and saying, "There, there."

There, there. And softly rubbing his heaving back until he caught his breath.

Instead she'd poured herself more cooking sherry and glared.

Now, with the sun set and Olivier gone, Ruth sat in her kitchen in the white plastic garden chair at the plastic table she'd found at the dump. Sufficiently drunk, she pulled the notebook close and with Rosa quietly quacking in the background, a small knit blanket over her, Ruth wrote:

> *She rose up into the air and the jilted earth let out a sigh.*
> *She rose up past telephone poles and rooftops of houses where the*
> *earthbound hid.*
> *She rose up but remembered to politely wave good-bye . . .*

And then kissing Rosa on the head she limped up the stairs to bed.

TWENTY-EIGHT

 When Clara came down the next morning she was surprised to find Peter in the garden, staring into space. He'd put on the coffee, and now she poured a couple of cups and joined him.

"Sleep well?" she asked, handing him a mug.

"Not really. You?"

"Not bad. Why didn't you?"

It was an overcast morning with a chill in the air. The first morning that really felt as though summer was over, and autumn on the way. She loved the fall. The brilliant leaves, the lit fireplaces, the smell of woodsmoke through the village. She loved huddling at a table outside the bistro, wrapped in sweaters and sipping *café au lait*.

Peter pursed his lips and looked down at his feet, in rubber boots to protect against the heavy dew.

"I was thinking about your question. What to do about Fortin."

Clara grew still. "Go on."

Peter had thought about it most of the night. Had got up and gone downstairs, pacing around the kitchen and finally ending up in his studio. His refuge. It smelled of him. Of body odor, and oil paint and canvas. It smelled faintly of lemon meringue pie, which he couldn't explain. It smelled like no other place on earth.

And it comforted him.

He'd gone into his studio last night to think, and finally to stop thinking. To clear his mind of the howl that had grown, like something massive approaching. And finally, just before sunrise, he knew what he had to say to Clara.

"I think you should talk to him."

There. He'd said it. Beside him Clara was silent, her hands grasping the warm cup of coffee.

"Really?"

Peter nodded. "I'm sorry. Do you want me to come with you?"

"I'm not even sure I'm going yet," she snapped and walked a couple of paces away.

Peter wanted to run to her, to take it back, to say he was wrong. She should stay there with him, should say nothing. Should just do the show.

What had he been thinking?

"You're right." She turned back to him, miserable. "He won't mind, will he?"

"Fortin? No. You don't have to be angry, just tell him how you feel, that's all. I'm sure he'll understand."

"I can just say that maybe I misheard. And that Gabri is one of our best friends."

"That's it. Fortin probably doesn't even remember saying it."

"I'm sure he won't mind." Clara walked slowly inside to call Fortin.

"Denis? It's Clara Morrow. Yes, that was fun. Really, is that a good price? Sure, I'll tell the Chief Inspector. Listen, I'm going to be in Montreal today and thought maybe we could get together again. I have . . . well, a few thoughts." She paused. "Uh-huh. Uh-huh. That sounds great. Twelve thirty at the Santropole on Duluth. Perfect."

What have I done? Peter asked himself.

Breakfast at the B and B was a somber affair of burned toast, rubber eggs and black bacon. The coffee was weak and the milk seemed curdled, as did Gabri. By mutual, unspoken consent they didn't discuss the case, but waited until they were back at the Incident Room.

"Oh, thank God," said Agent Lacoste, as she fell on the Tim Hortons double double coffees Agent Morin had brought. And the chocolate-glazed doughnuts. "I never thought I'd prefer this to Gabri's breakfasts." She took a huge bite of soft, sweet doughnut. "If this keeps up we might have to solve the case and leave."

"There's a thought," said Gamache, putting on his half-moon reading glasses.

Beauvoir went over to his computer to check messages. There, taped to the monitor, was a scrap of paper with familiar writing. He ripped it off, scrunched it up and tossed it to the floor.

Chief Inspector Gamache also looked at his screen. The results of his Google search of "Charlotte."

Sipping his coffee he read about Good Charlotte, the band, and Charlotte Brontë, and Charlotte Church and *Charlotte's Web*, the city of Charlotte in North Carolina and Charlottetown on Prince Edward Island and the Queen Charlotte Islands on the other side of the continent, off British Columbia. Most of the places were named after Queen Charlotte, he discovered.

"Does the name Charlotte mean anything to you?" he asked his team.

After thinking for a moment, they shook their heads.

"How about Queen Charlotte? She was married to King George."

"George the Third? The crazy one?" Morin asked. The others looked at him in amazement. Agent Morin smiled. "I was good at history in school."

It helped, thought Gamache, that school for him wasn't all that long ago. The phone rang and Agent Morin took it. It was the Martinù Conservatory, in Prague. Gamache listened to Morin's side of the conversation until his own phone rang.

It was Superintendent Brunel.

"I arrived to find my office looking like Hannibal's tent. I can barely move for your Hermit's items, Armand." She didn't sound displeased. "But I'm not calling about that. I have an invitation. Would you like to join Jérôme and me for lunch at our apartment? He has something he'd like to show you. And I have news as well."

It was confirmed he'd meet them at one o'clock at the Brunel apartment on rue Laurier. As he hung up the phone rang again.

"Clara Morrow for you, sir," said Agent Morin.

"*Bonjour*, Clara."

"*Bonjour*. I just wanted to let you know I spoke to Denis Fortin this morning. In fact, we're having lunch today. He told me he'd found a buyer for the carvings."

"Is that right? Who?"

"I didn't ask, but he says they're willing to pay a thousand dollars for the two. He seemed to think that was a good price."

"That is interesting. Would you like a lift into town? I'm meeting someone myself."

"Sure, thank you."

"I'll be by in about half an hour."

When he hung up Agent Morin was off his call.

"They said Martinù had no children. They were aware of the violin, but it disappeared after his death in," Morin consulted his notes, "1959. I told them we'd found the violin and an original copy of the score. They were very excited and said it would be worth a lot of money. In fact, it would be considered a Czech national treasure."

There was that word again. Treasure.

"Did you ask about his wife, Charlotte?"

"I did. They were together a long time, but only actually married on his deathbed. She died a few years ago. No family."

Gamache nodded, thinking. Then he spoke to Agent Morin again. "I need you to look into the Czech community here, especially the Parras. And find out about their lives in the Czech Republic. How they got out, who they knew there, their family. Everything."

He went over to Beauvoir. "I'm heading into Montreal for the day to talk to Superintendent Brunel and follow some leads."

"*D'accord*. As soon as Morin gets the information on the Parras I'll go up there."

"Don't go alone."

"I won't."

Gamache stooped and picked up the scrap of paper on the floor by Beauvoir's desk. He opened it and read, *In the midst of your nightmare,*

"*In the midst of your nightmare,*" he repeated, handing it to Beauvoir. "What do you think it means?"

Beauvoir shrugged and opened the drawer to his desk. A nest of balled-up words lay there. "I find them everywhere. In my coat pocket, pinned to my door in the morning. This one was taped to my computer."

Gamache reached into the desk and chose a scrap at random.

> *that the deity who kills for pleasure*
> *will also heal,*

"They're all like this?"

Beauvoir nodded. "Each crazier than the last. What'm I supposed to do with them? She's just pissed off because we took over her fire hall. Do you think I can get a restraining order?"

"Against an eighty-year-old winner of the Governor General's award, to stop her sending you verse?"

When put that way it didn't sound likely.

Gamache looked again at the balls of paper, like hail. "Well, I'm off."

"Thanks for your help," Beauvoir called after him.

"*De rien*," waved Gamache and was gone.

In the hour or so drive into Montreal Gamache and Clara talked about the people of Three Pines, about the summer visitors, about the Gilberts, who Clara thought might stay now.

"Old Mundin and Charles were in the village the other day. Old is very taken with Vincent Gilbert. He apparently knew it was him in the woods, but didn't want to say anything."

"How would he have recognized him?"

"*Being*," said Clara.

"Of course," said Gamache, merging onto the autoroute into Montreal. "Charles has Down syndrome."

"After he was born Myrna gave them a copy of *Being*. Reading it changed their lives. Changed lots of lives. Myrna says Dr. Gilbert's a great man."

"I'm sure he wouldn't disagree."

Clara laughed. "Still, I don't think I'd like to be raised by a saint."

Gamache had to agree. Most saints were martyrs. And they took a lot of people down with them. In companionable silence they drove past signs for Saint-Hilaire, Saint-Jean and a village named Ange Gardien.

"If I said 'woo,' what would you think?" Gamache asked.

"Beyond the obvious?" She gave him a mock-worried look.

"Does the word mean anything to you?"

The fact he'd come back to it alerted Clara. "Woo," she repeated. "There's pitching woo, an old-fashioned way of saying courting."

"Old-fashioned for courting?" He laughed. "But I know what you mean. I don't think that's what I'm looking for."

"Sorry, can't help."

"Oh, it probably doesn't matter." They were over the Champlain Bridge. Gamache drove up Boulevard Saint-Laurent, turned left then left again and dropped her at the Santropole restaurant for lunch.

Climbing the steps she turned and walked back. Leaning into the car window she asked, "If a person insulted someone you cared about, would you say something?"

Gamache thought about that. "I hope I would."

She nodded and left. But she knew Gamache, and knew there was no "hope" about it.

TWENTY-NINE

After a luncheon of herbed cucumber soup, grilled shrimp and fennel salad and peach tarte Gamache and the Brunels settled into the bright living room of the second-floor apartment. It was lined with bookcases. *Objets trouvés* lay here and there. Pieces of aged and broken pottery, chipped mugs. It was a room that was lived in, where people read, and talked and thought and laughed.

"I've been researching the items in the cabin," said Thérèse Brunel.

"And?" Gamache leaned forward on the sofa, holding his *demi-tasse* of espresso.

"So far nothing. Amazing as it sounds, none of the items has been reported stolen, though I haven't finished yet. It'll take weeks to properly trace them."

Gamache slowly leaned back and crossed his long legs. If not stolen, then what? "What's the other option?" he asked.

"Well, that the dead man actually owned the pieces. Or that they were looted from dead people, who couldn't report it. In a war, for instance. Like the Amber Room."

"Or maybe they were given to him," suggested her husband, Jérôme.

"But they're priceless," objected Thérèse. "Why would someone give them to him?"

"Services rendered?" he said.

All three were silent then, imagining what service could exact such a payment.

"*Bon*, Armand, I have something to show you." Jérôme rose to his full height of just five and a half feet. He was an almost perfect square but carried his bulk with ease as though his body was filled with the thoughts overflowing from his head.

He wedged himself onto the sofa beside Gamache. He had in his hands the two carvings.

"First of all, these are remarkable. They almost speak, don't you find? My job, Thérèse told me, was to figure out what they're saying. Or, more specifically, what these mean."

He turned the carvings over to reveal the letters carved there.

MRKBVYDDO was etched under the people on the shore.

OWSVI was under the sailing ship.

"This's a code of some sort," explained Jérôme, putting his glasses on and peering closely at the letters again. "I started with the easiest one. Qwerty. It's the one an amateur's most likely to use. Do you know it?"

"It's a typewriter's keyboard. Also a computer's," said Gamache. "Qwerty is the first few letters on the top line."

"What the person using Qwerty generally does is go to the keyboard and type the letter next to the one you really mean. Very easy to decode. This isn't it, by the way. No." Jérôme hauled himself up and Gamache almost tumbled into the void left by his body. "I went through a whole lot of ciphers and frankly I haven't found anything. I'm sorry."

Gamache had been hopeful this master of codes would be able to crack the Hermit's. But like so much else with this case, it wouldn't reveal itself easily.

"But I think I know what sort of code it is. I think it's a Caesar's Shift."

"Go on."

"*Bon*," said Jérôme, relishing the challenge and the audience. "Julius Caesar was a genius. He's really the cipher fanatic's emperor. Brilliant. He used the Greek alphabet to send secret messages to his troops in France. But later he refined his codes. He switched to the Roman alphabet, the one we use now, but he shifted the letters by three. So if the word you want to send is kill, the code in Caesar's Shift becomes . . ." He grabbed a piece of paper and wrote the alphabet.

A B C D E F G H I J K L M N O P Q R S T U V W X Y Z

Then he circled four letters.

NLOO

"See?"

Gamache and Thérèse leaned over his messy desk.

"So he just shifted the letters," said Gamache. "If the code under the carvings is a Caesar's Shift, can't you just decode it that way? Move the letters back by three?"

He looked at the letters under the sailing ship.

"That would make this . . . L, T, P. Okay, I don't have to go further. It makes no sense."

"No, Caesar was smart and I think this Hermit was too. Or at least, he knew his codes. The brilliance of the Caesar's Shift is that it's almost impossible to break because the shift can be whatever length you want. Or, better still, you can use a key word. One you and your contact aren't likely to forget. You write it at the beginning of the alphabet, then start the cipher. Let's say it's Montreal."

He went back to his alphabet and wrote Montreal under the first eight letters, then filled in the rest of the twenty-six beginning with A.

A B C D E F G H I J K L M N O P Q R S T U V W X Y S
M O N T R E A L A B C D E F G H I J K L M N O P Q R

"So, now if the message we want to send is kill, what's the code?" Jérôme asked Gamache.

The Chief Inspector took the pencil and circled four letters.

CADD

"Exactly," beamed Dr. Brunel. Gamache stared, fascinated. Thérèse, who'd seen all this before, stood back and smiled, proud of her clever husband.

"We need the key word." Gamache straightened up.

"That's all," laughed Jérôme.

"Well, I think I have it."

Jérôme nodded, pulled up a chair and sat down. In a clear hand he wrote the alphabet once again.

A B C D E F G H I J K L M N O P Q R S T U V W X Y Z

His pencil hovered over the next line down.

"Charlotte," said Gamache.

Clara and Denis Fortin lingered over their coffee. The back garden of the Santropole restaurant was almost empty. The rush of the lunch crowd, mostly bohemian young people from the Plateau Mont Royal *quartier*, had disappeared.

The bill had just arrived and Clara knew it was now or never.

"There is one other thing I wanted to talk to you about."

"The carvings? Did you bring them?" Fortin leaned forward.

"No, the Chief Inspector still has them, but I told him about your offer. I think part of the problem is they're evidence in the murder case."

"Of course. There's no rush, though I suspect this buyer might not be interested for long. It really is most extraordinary that anyone would want them."

Clara nodded and thought maybe they could just leave. She could go back to Three Pines, make up a guest list for the *vernissage* and forget about it. Already Fortin's comment about Gabri was fading. Surely it wasn't that serious.

"So, what did you want to talk about? Whether you should buy a home in Provence or Tuscany? How about a yacht?"

Clara wasn't sure if he was kidding, but she did know he wasn't making this easy.

"It's just a tiny thing, really. I must have heard wrong, but it seemed to me when you came down to Three Pines yesterday you said something about Gabri."

Fortin looked interested, concerned, puzzled.

"He was our waiter," Clara explained. "He brought us our drinks."

Fortin was still staring. She could feel her brain evaporate. Suddenly, after practicing most of the morning what she'd say, she couldn't even remember her own name. "Well, I just thought, you know . . ."

Her voice trailed off. She couldn't do it. This must be a sign, she thought, a sign from God that she wasn't supposed to say anything. That she was making something out of nothing.

"Doesn't matter," she smiled. "I just thought I'd tell you his name."

Fortunately she figured Fortin was used to dealing with artists who were drunk, deranged, stoned. Clara appeared to be all three. She must, in his eyes, be a brilliant artist to be so unhinged.

Fortin signed for the bill and left, Clara noticed, a very large tip.

"I remember him." Fortin led her back through the restaurant with its dark wood and scent of tisane. "He was the fag."

Vdtk?? mmf/x

They stared at the letters. The more they stared the less sense they made, which was saying something.

"Any other suggestions?" Jérôme looked up from his desk.

Gamache was flabbergasted. He was sure they had it, that "Charlotte" was the key to break the cipher. He thought for a moment, scanning the case.

"Woo," he said. They tried that.

Nothing.

"Walden." But he knew he was grasping. And sure enough, nothing.

Nothing, nothing, nothing. What had he missed?

"Well, I'll keep trying," said Jérôme. "It might not be a Caesar's Shift. There're plenty of other codes."

He smiled reassuringly and the Chief Inspector had a sense of what Dr. Brunel's patients must have felt. The news was bad, but they had a man who wouldn't give up.

"What can you tell me about one of your colleagues, Vincent Gilbert?" Gamache asked.

"He was no colleague of mine," said Jérôme, testily. "Not of anyone's from what I remember. He didn't suffer fools easily. Do you notice most people who feel like that consider everyone a fool?"

"That bad?"

"Jérôme's only annoyed because Dr. Gilbert thought himself God," said Thérèse, perching on the arm of her husband's chair.

"Difficult to work with," said Gamache, who'd worked with a few gods himself.

"Oh no, it wasn't that," smiled Thérèse. "It annoyed Jérôme because he knows he's the one true God and Gilbert refused to worship."

They laughed but Jérôme's smile faded first. "Very dangerous man, Vincent Gilbert. I think he really does have a God complex. Megalomaniac. Very clever. That book he wrote . . ."

"*Being*," said Gamache.

"Yes. It was designed, every word calculated for effect. And I've got to hand it to him, it worked. Most people who've read it agree with him. He is at the very least a great man, and perhaps even a saint."

"You don't believe it?"

Dr. Brunel snorted. "The only miracle he's performed is convincing everyone of his saintliness. No mean feat, given what an asshole he is. Do I believe it? No."

"Well, it's time for my news." Thérèse Brunel stood up. "Come with me."

Gamache followed her, leaving Jérôme to fiddle with the cipher. The study was filled with more papers and magazines. Thérèse sat at her computer and after a few quick taps a photograph appeared. It showed a carving of a shipwreck.

Gamache pulled up a chair and stared. "Is it . . ."

"Another carving? *Oui.*" She smiled, like a magician who'd produced a particularly spectacular rabbit.

"The Hermit made this?" Gamache twisted in his chair and looked at her. She nodded. He looked back at the screen. The carving was complex. On one side was the shipwreck, then some forest, and on the other side a tiny village being built. "Even in a photograph it seems alive. I can see the little people. Are they the same ones from the other carvings?"

"I think so. But I can't find the frightened boy."

Gamache searched the village, the ship on the shore, the forest. Nothing. What happened to him? "We need to have the carving," he said.

"This's in a private collection in Zurich. I've contacted a gallery owner I know there. Very influential man. He said he'd help."

Gamache knew enough not to press Superintendent Brunel about her connections.

"It's not just the boy," he said. "We need to know what's written underneath it."

Like the others this one was, on the surface, pastoral, peaceful. But something lurked on the fringes. A disquiet.

And yet, once again, the tiny wooden people seemed happy.

"There's another one. In a collection in Cape Town." The screen flickered and another carving appeared. A boy was lying, either asleep or dead, on the side of a mountain. Gamache put on his glasses and leaned closer, squinting.

"Hard to tell, but I think it's the same young man."

"So do I," said the Superintendent.

"Is he dead?"

"I wondered that myself, but I don't think so. Do you notice something about this carving, Armand?"

Gamache leaned back and took a deep breath, releasing some of the tension he felt. He closed his eyes, then opened them again. But this time not to look at the image on the screen. This time he wanted to sense it.

After a moment he knew Thérèse Brunel was right. This carving was different. It was clearly the same artist, there was no mistaking that, but one significant element had changed.

"There's no fear."

Thérèse nodded. "Only peace. Contentment."

"Even love," said the Chief Inspector. He longed to hold this carving, to own it even, though he knew he never would. And he felt, not for the first time, that soft tug of desire. Of greed. He knew he'd never act on it. But he knew others might. This was a carving worth owning. All of them were, he suspected.

"What do you know about them?" he asked.

"They were sold through a company in Geneva. I know it well. Very discreet, very high end."

"What did he get for them?"

"They sold seven of them. The first was six years ago. It went for fifteen thousand. The prices went up until they reached three hundred thousand for the last one. It sold this past winter. He says he figures he could get at least half a million for the next one."

Gamache exhaled in astonishment. "Whoever sold them must have made hundreds of thousands."

"The auction house in Geneva takes a hefty commission, but I did a quick calculation. The seller would have made about one point five million."

Gamache's mind was racing. And then it ran into a fact. Or rather into a statement.

I threw the carvings away, into the woods, when I walked home.

Olivier had said it. And once again, Olivier had lied.

Foolish, foolish man, thought Gamache. Then he looked back at the computer screen and the boy lying supine on the mountain, almost caressing it. Was it possible, he asked himself.

Could Olivier have actually done it? Killed the Hermit?

A million dollars was a powerful motive. But why kill the man who supplied the art?

No, there was more Olivier wasn't telling, and if Gamache had any hope of finding the real killer it was time for the truth.

Why does Gabri have to be such a fucking queer, thought Clara. And a fag. And why do I have to be such a fucking coward?

"Yes, that's the one," she heard herself say, in an out-of-body moment. The day had warmed up but she pulled her coat closer as they stood on the sidewalk.

"Where can I drive you?" Denis Fortin asked.

Where? Clara didn't know where Gamache would be but she had his cell-phone number. "I'll find my own way, thanks."

They shook hands.

"This show's going to be huge, for both of us. I'm very happy for you," he said, warmly.

"There is one other thing. Gabri. He's a friend of mine."

She felt his hand release hers. But still, he smiled at her.

"I just need to say that he's not queer and he's not a fag."

"He isn't? He sure seems gay."

"Well, yes, he's gay." She could feel herself growing confused.

"What're you saying, Clara?"

"You called him queer, and a fag."

"Yes?"

"It just didn't seem very nice."

Now she felt like a schoolgirl. Words like "nice" weren't used very often in the art world. Unless it was as an insult.

"You're not trying to censor me, are you?"

His voice had become like treacle. Clara could feel his words sticking to her. And his eyes, once thoughtful, were now hard. With warning.

"No, I'm just saying that I was surprised and I didn't like hearing my friend called names."

"But he is queer and a fag. You admitted it yourself."

"I said he's gay." She could feel her cheeks sizzling and knew she must be beet red.

"Oh," he sighed and shook his head. "I understand." He looked at her with sadness now, as one might look at a sick pet. "It's the small-town girl after all. You've been in that tiny village too long, Clara. It's made you small-minded. You censor yourself and now you're trying to stifle my voice. That's very dangerous. Political correctness, Clara. An artist needs to break down boundaries, push, challenge, shock. You're not willing to do that, are you?"

She stood staring, unable to grasp what he was saying.

"No, I didn't think so," he said. "I tell the truth, and I say it in a way that might shock, but is at least real. You'd prefer something just pretty. And nice."

"You insulted a lovely man, behind his back," she said. But she could feel the tears now. Of rage, but she knew how it must look. It must look like weakness.

"I'm going to have to reconsider the show," he said. "I'm very disappointed. I thought you were the real deal, but obviously you were just pretending. Superficial. Trite. I can't risk my gallery's reputation on someone not willing to take artistic risks."

There was a rare break in traffic and Denis Fortin darted across Saint-Urbain. On the other side he looked back and shook his head again. Then he walked briskly to his car.

Inspector Jean Guy Beauvoir and Agent Morin approached the Parra home. Beauvoir had expected something traditional. Something a Czech woodsman might live in. A Swiss chalet perhaps. To Beauvoir there was Québécois and then "other." Foreign. The Chinese were all alike, as were Africans. The South Americans, if he thought of them at all, looked the same, ate the same foods and lived in exactly the same homes. A place somewhat less attractive than his own. The English he knew to be all the same. Nuts.

Swiss, Czech, German, Norwegian, Swedish all blended nicely together. They were tall, blond, good athletes if slightly thick and lived in A-frame homes with lots of paneling and milk.

He slowed the car and it meandered to a stop in front of the Parra place. All he saw was glass, some gleaming in the sun, some reflecting the sky and clouds and birds and woods, the mountains beyond and a small white steeple. The church at Three Pines, in the distance, brought forward by this beautiful house that was a reflection of all life around it.

"You just caught me. I was heading back to work," said Roar, opening the door.

He led Beauvoir and Morin into the house. It was filled with light. The floors were polished concrete. Firm, solid. It made the house feel very secure while allowing it to soar. And soar it did.

"*Merde*," Beauvoir whispered, walking into the great room. The combination kitchen, dining area and living room. With walls of glass on three sides it felt as though there was no division between this world and the next. Between in and out. Between forest and home.

Where else would a Czech woodsman live but in the woods. In a home made of light.

Hanna Parra was at the sink, drying her hands, and Havoc was just putting away the lunch dishes. The place smelled of soup.

"Not working at the bistro?" Beauvoir asked Havoc.

"Split shift today. Olivier asked if I'd mind."

"And do you?"

"Mind?" They walked over to the long dining table and sat. "No. I think he's pretty stressed."

"What's he like to work for?" Beauvoir noticed Morin take out his notebook and a pen. He'd told the young agent to do that when they arrived. It rattled suspects and Beauvoir liked them rattled.

"He's great, but I only have my dad to compare him to."

"And what's that supposed to mean?" asked Roar. Beauvoir studied the small, powerful man for signs of aggression, but it seemed a running joke in the family.

"At least Olivier doesn't make me work with saws and axes and machetes."

"Olivier's chocolate torte and ice cream are far more dangerous. At least you know to be careful with an axe."

Beauvoir realized he'd cut to the quick of the case. What appeared threatening wasn't. And what appeared wonderful, wasn't.

"I'd like to show you a picture of the dead man."

"We've already seen it. Agent Lacoste showed it to us," said Hanna.

"I'd like you to look again."

"What's this about, Inspector?" asked Hanna.

"You're Czech."

"What of it?"

"Been here for a while, I know," Beauvoir continued, ignoring her. "Lots came after the Russian invasion."

"There's a healthy Czech community here," Hanna agreed.

"In fact, it's so big there's even a Czech Association. You meet once a month and have pot-luck dinners."

All this and more he'd learned from Agent Morin's research.

"That's right," said Roar, watching Beauvoir carefully, wondering where this was leading.

"And you've been the president of the association a few times," Beauvoir said to Roar, then turned to Hanna. "You both have."

"That's not much of an honor, Inspector," smiled Hanna. "We take turns. It's on a rotation basis."

"Is it fair to say you know everyone in the local Czech community?"

They looked at each other, guarded now, and nodded.

"So you should know our victim. He was Czech." Beauvoir took the photograph out of his pocket and placed it on the table. But they didn't look. All three were staring at him. Surprised. That he knew? Or that the man was Czech?

Beauvoir had to admit it could have been either.

Then Roar picked up the photo and stared at it. Shaking his head he handed it to his wife. "We've already seen it, and told Agent Lacoste the same thing. We don't know him. If he was Czech he didn't come to any dinners. He made no contact with us at all. You'll have to ask the others, of course."

"We are." Beauvoir tucked the picture into his pocket. "Agents are talking to other members of your community right now."

"Is that profiling?" asked Hanna Parra. She wasn't smiling.

"No, it's investigating. If the victim was Czech it's reasonable to ask around that community, don't you think?"

The phone rang. Hanna went to it and looked down. "It's Eva." She picked it up and spoke in French, saying a Sûreté officer was with her now, and no she didn't recognize the photograph either. And yes, she was also surprised the man had been Czech.

Clever, thought Beauvoir. Hanna put down the receiver and it immediately rang again.

"It's Yanna," she said, this time leaving it. The phone, they realized, would ring all afternoon. As the agents arrived, interviewed and left. And the Czech community called each other.

It seemed vaguely sinister, until Beauvoir reluctantly admitted to himself he'd do the same thing.

"Do you know Bohuslav Martinù?"

"Who?"

Beauvoir repeated it, then showed them the printout.

"Oh, Bohuslav Martinù," Roar said, pronouncing it in a way that was unintelligible to Beauvoir. "He's a Czech composer. Don't tell me you suspect him?"

Roar laughed, but Hanna didn't and neither did Havoc.

"Does anyone here have ties to him?"

"No, no one," said Hanna, with certainty.

Morin's research of the Parras had turned up very little. Their relations in the Czech Republic seemed limited to an aunt and a few cousins. They'd escaped in their early twenties and claimed refugee status in Canada, which had been granted. They were now citizens.

Nothing remarkable. No ties to Martinù. No ties to anyone famous or infamous. No woo, no Charlotte, no treasure. Nothing.

And yet Beauvoir was convinced they knew more than they were telling. More than Morin had managed to find.

As they drove away, their retreating reflection in the glass house, Beauvoir wondered if the Parras were quite as transparent as their home.

I have a question for you," said Gamache as they wandered back into the Brunel living room. Jerome looked up briefly then went back to trying to tease some sense from the cryptic letters.

"Ask away."

"Denis Fortin—"

"Of the Galerie Fortin?" the Superintendent interrupted.

Gamache nodded. "He was visiting Three Pines yesterday and saw one of the carvings. He said it wasn't worth anything."

Thérèse Brunel paused. "I'm not surprised. He's a respected art dealer. Quite remarkable at spotting new talent. But his specialty isn't sculpture, though he handles some very prominent sculptors."

"But even I could see the carvings are remarkable. Why couldn't he?"

"What're you suggesting, Armand? That he lied?"

"Is it possible?"

Thérèse considered. "I suppose. I always find it slightly amusing, and sometimes useful, the general perception of the art world. People on the outside seem to think it's made up of arrogant, crazed artists, numbskull buyers and gallery owners who bring the two together. In fact it's a business, and anyone who doesn't understand that and appreciate it gets buried. In some cases hundreds of millions of dollars are at stake. But even bigger than the piles of cash are the egos. Put immense wealth and even larger egos together and you have a volatile mix. It's a brutal, often ugly, often violent world."

Gamache thought about Clara and wondered if she realized that. Wondered if she knew what was waiting for her, beyond the pale.

"But not everyone's like that, surely," he said.

"No. But at that level," she nodded to the carvings on the table by her husband, "they are. One man's dead. It's possible as we look closer others have been killed."

"Over these carvings?" Gamache picked up the ship.

"Over the money."

Gamache peered at the sculpture. He knew that not everyone was motivated solely by money. There were other currencies. Jealousy, rage, revenge. He looked not at the passengers sailing into a happy future, but at the one looking back. To where they'd been. With terror.

"I do have some good news for you, Armand."

Gamache lowered the ship and looked at the Superintendent.

"I've found your 'woo.'"

THIRTY

"There it is." Thérèse Brunel pointed.

They'd driven into downtown Montreal and now the Superintendent was pointing at a building. Gamache slowed the car and immediately provoked honking. In Quebec it was almost a capital crime to slow down. He didn't speed up, ignored the honking, and tried to see what she was pointing at. It was an art gallery. Heffel's. And outside was a bronze sculpture. But the car had drifted past before he got a good look. He spent the next twenty minutes trying to find a parking spot.

"Can't you just double-park?" asked Superintendent Brunel.

"If we want to be slaughtered, yes."

She harrumphed, but didn't disagree. Finally they parked and walked back along Sherbrooke Street until they were in front of Heffel's Art Gallery, staring at a bronze sculpture Gamache had seen before but never stopped to look at.

His cell phone vibrated. "*Pardon,*" he said to the Superintendent, and answered it.

"It's Clara. I'm wondering when you might be ready."

"In just a few minutes. Are you all right?" She'd sounded shaky, upset.

"I'm just fine. Where can I meet you?"

"I'm on Sherbrooke, just outside Heffel's Gallery."

"I know it. I can be there in a few minutes. Is that okay?" She sounded keen, even anxious, to leave.

"Perfect. I'll be here."

He put the phone away and went back to the sculpture. Silently he walked around it while Thérèse Brunel watched, a look of some amusement on her face.

What he saw was an almost life-sized bronze of a frumpy middle-aged woman standing beside a horse, a dog at her side and a monkey on the horse's back. When he arrived back at Superintendent Brunel he stopped.

"This is 'woo'?"

"No, this is Emily Carr. It's by Joe Fafard and is called *Emily and Friends*."

Gamache smiled then and shook his head. Of course it was. Now he could see it. The woman, matronly, squat, ugly, had been one of Canada's most remarkable artists. Gifted and visionary, she'd painted mostly in the early 1900s and was now long dead. But her art only grew in significance and influence.

He looked more closely at the bronze woman. She was younger here than the images he'd seen of her in grainy old black-and-white photos. They almost always showed a masculine woman, alone. In a forest. And not smiling, not happy.

This woman was happy. Perhaps it was the conceit of the sculptor.

"It's wonderful, isn't it?" Superintendent Brunel said. "Normally Emily Carr looks gruesome. I think it's brilliant to show her happy, as she apparently only was around her animals. It was people she hated."

"You said you'd found 'woo.' Where?"

He was disappointed and far from convinced Superintendent Brunel was right. How could a long dead painter from across the continent have anything to do with the case?

Thérèse Brunel walked up to the sculpture and placed one manicured hand on the monkey.

"This is Woo. Emily Carr's constant companion."

"Woo's a monkey?"

"She adored all animals, but Woo above all."

Gamache crossed his arms over his chest and stared. "It's an interesting theory, but the 'woo' in the Hermit's cabin could mean anything. What makes you think it's Emily Carr's monkey?"

"Because of this."

She opened her handbag and handed him a glossy brochure. It was for a retrospective of the works of Emily Carr, at the Vancouver Art Gallery. Gamache looked at the photographs of Carr's unmistakable paintings of the West Coast wilderness almost a century ago.

Her work was extraordinary. Rich greens and browns swirled together so that the forest seemed both frenzied and tranquil. It was a forest long gone. Logged, clear-cut, ruined. But still alive, thanks to the brush and brilliance of Emily Carr.

But that wasn't what had made her famous.

Gamache flipped through the brochure until he found them. Her signature series. Depicting what haunted any Canadian soul who saw them.

The totem poles.

Sitting on the shores of a remote Haida fishing village in northern British Columbia. She'd painted them where the Haida had put them.

And then a single perfect finger pointed to three small words.

Queen Charlotte Islands.

That's where they were.

Charlotte.

Gamache felt a thrill. Could they really have found Woo?

"The Hermit's sculptures were carved from red cedar," said Thérèse Brunel. "So was the word Woo. Red cedar grows in a few places, but not here. Not Quebec. One of the places it grows is in British Columbia."

"On the Queen Charlotte Islands," whispered Gamache, mesmerized by the paintings of the totem poles. Straight, tall, magnificent. Not yet felled as heathen, not yet yanked down by missionaries and the government.

Emily Carr's paintings were the only images of the totems as the Haida meant them to be. She never painted people, but she painted what they created. Long houses. And towering totem poles.

Gamache stared, losing himself in the wild beauty, and the approaching disaster.

Then he looked again at the inscription. Haida village. Queen Charlottes.

And he knew Thérèse was right. Woo pointed to Emily Carr, and Carr pointed to the Queen Charlotte Islands. This must be why there were so many references to Charlotte in the Hermit's cabin. *Charlotte's Web*, Charlotte Brontë. Charlotte Martinù, who'd given her husband the violin. The Amber Room had been made for a Charlotte. All leading him here. To the Queen Charlotte Islands.

"You can keep that." Superintendent Brunel pointed to the brochure. "It has a lot of biographical information on Emily Carr. It might be helpful."

"*Merci*." Gamache closed the catalog and stared at the sculpture of Carr, the woman who had captured Canada's shame, not by painting the displaced, broken people, but by painting their glory.

Clara stared at the gray waters of the St. Lawrence as they drove over the Champlain Bridge.

"How was your lunch?" Gamache asked when they were on the autoroute heading to Three Pines.

"Well, it could have been better."

Clara's mood was swinging wildly from fury to guilt to regret. One moment she felt she should have told Denis Fortin more clearly what a piece of *merde* he was, the next she was dying to get home so she could call and apologize.

Clara was a fault-magnet. Criticisms, critiques, blame flew through the air and clung to her. She seemed to attract the negative, perhaps because she was so positive.

Well, she'd had enough. She sat up straighter in her seat. Fuck him. But, then again, maybe she should apologize and stand up for herself after the solo show.

What an idiot she'd been. Why in the world had she thought it was a good idea to piss off the gallery owner who was offering her fame and fortune? Recognition. Approval. Attention.

Damn, what had she done? And was it reversible? Surely she could have waited until the day after the opening, when the reviews were in the *New York Times*, the London *Times*. When his fury couldn't ruin her, as it could now.

As it would now.

She'd heard his words. But more important, she'd seen it in Fortin's face. He would ruin her. Though to ruin implied there was something built up to tear down. No, what he'd do was worse. He'd make sure the world never heard of Clara Morrow. Never saw her paintings.

She looked at the time on Gamache's dashboard.

Ten to four. The heavy traffic out of the city was thinning. They'd be home in an hour. If they got back before five she could call his gallery and prostrate herself.

Or maybe she should call and tell him what an asshole he was.

It was a very long drive back.

"Do you want to talk about it?" Gamache asked after half an hour of silence. They'd turned off the highway and were heading toward Cowansville.

"I'm not really sure what to say. Denis Fortin called Gabri a fucking queer yesterday in the bistro. Gabri didn't hear it, but I did, and I didn't say anything. I talked to Peter and Myrna about it, and they listened, but they pretty much left it up to me. Until this morning when Peter kinda said I should talk to Fortin."

Gamache turned off the main road. The businesses and homes receded and the forest closed in.

"How did Fortin react?" he asked.

"He said he'd cancel the show."

Gamache sighed. "I'm sorry about that, Clara."

He glanced over at her unhappy face staring out the window. She reminded him of his daughter Annie the other night. A weary lion.

"How was your day?" she asked. They were on the dirt road now, bumping along. It was a road not used by many. Mostly just by people who knew where they were going, or had completely lost their way.

"Productive, I think. I have a question for you."

"Ask away." She seemed relieved to have something else to do besides watching the clock click closer to five.

"What do you know about Emily Carr?"

"Now, I'd never have bet that was the question," she smiled, then gathered her thoughts. "We studied her in art school. She was a huge inspiration to lots of Canadian artists, certainly the women. She inspired me."

"How?"

"She went into the wilderness where no one else dared to go, with just her easel."

"And her monkey."

"Is that a euphemism, Chief Inspector?"

Gamache laughed. "No. Go on."

"Well, she was just very independent. And her work evolved. At first it was representational. A tree was a tree, a house a house. It was almost a documentary. She wanted to capture the Haida, you know, in their villages, before they were destroyed."

"Most of her work was on the Queen Charlotte Islands, I understand."

"Many of her most famous works are, yes. At some point she realized that painting exactly what could be seen wasn't enough. So she really let go, dropped all the conventions, and painted not just what she saw, but what she felt. She was ridiculed for it. Ironically those are now her most famous works."

Gamache nodded, remembering the totem poles in front of the swirling, vibrant forest. "Remarkable woman."

"I think it all started with the brutal telling," said Clara.

"The what?"

"The brutal telling. It's become quite well known in artistic circles. She was the youngest of five daughters and very close to her father. It was apparently a wonderful relationship. Nothing to suggest it wasn't simply loving and supportive."

"Nothing sexual, you mean."

"No, just a close father-daughter bond. And then in her late teens something happened and she left home. She never spoke to him or saw him again."

"What happened?" Gamache was slowing the car. Clara noticed this, and watched the clock approaching five to five.

"No one knew. She never told anyone, and her family said nothing. But she went from being a happy, carefree child to an embittered woman. Very solitary, not very likeable apparently. Then, near the end of her life, she wrote to a friend. In the letter she said that her father had said something to her. Something horrible and unforgivable."

"The brutal telling."

"That's how she described it."

They'd arrived. He stopped in front of her home and they sat there quietly for a moment. It was five past five. Too late. She could try, but knew Fortin wouldn't answer.

"Thank you," he said. "You've been very helpful."

"And so have you."

"I wish that was true." He smiled at her. But, remarkably, she seemed to be feeling better. Clara got out of the car, and instead of going inside she paused on the road then slowly started to walk. Around the village green. Round and round she strolled, until the end met the beginning and she was back where she started. And as she walked she thought about Emily Carr. And the ridicule she'd endured at the hands of gallery owners, critics, a public too afraid to go where she wanted to take them.

Deeper. Deeper into the wilderness.

Then Clara went home.

It was late at night in Zurich when an art collector picked up the odd little carving he'd paid so much for. The one he'd been assured was a great work of art, but more important, a great investment.

At first he'd displayed it in his home, until his wife had asked him to move it. Away. So he'd put in into his private gallery. Once a day he'd sit in there with a cognac, and look at the masterpieces. The Picassos, the Rodins and Henry Moores.

But his eyes kept going back to the jolly little carving, of the forest, and the happy people building a village. At first it had given him pleasure, but now he found it spooky. He was considering putting it somewhere else again. A closet perhaps.

When the broker had called earlier in the day and asked if he'd consider sending it back to Canada for a police investigation he'd refused. It was an investment, after all. And there was no way he could be forced. He'd done nothing wrong and they had no jurisdiction.

The broker, though, had passed on two requests from the police. He knew the answer to the first, but still he picked up the carving and looked at its smooth base. No letters, no signature. Nothing. But the other question just sounded ridiculous. Still, he'd tried. He was just about to replace the carving and e-mail that he'd found nothing when his eyes caught something light among the dark pines.

He peered closer. There, deep in the forest, away from the village, he found what the police were looking for.

A tiny wooden figure. A young man, not much more than a boy, hiding in the woods.

THIRTY-ONE

It was getting late. Agent Lacoste had left and Inspector Beauvoir and Agent Morin were reporting on their day.

"We checked into the Parras, the Kmeniks, the Mackus. All the Czech community," said Beauvoir. "Nothing. No one knew the Hermit, no one saw him. They'd all heard of that violinist guy—"

"Martinů," said Morin.

"—because he's some famous Czech composer, but no one actually knew him."

"I spoke to the Martinů Institute and did background checks on the Czech families," said Morin. "They're what they claim to be. Refugees from the communists. Nothing more. In fact, they seem more law-abiding than most. No connection at all with Martinů."

Beauvoir shook his head. If lies annoyed the Inspector the truth seemed to piss him off even more. Especially when it was inconvenient.

"Your impression?" Gamache asked Agent Morin, who glanced at Inspector Beauvoir before answering.

"I think the violin and the music have nothing to do with the people here."

"You may be right," conceded Gamache, who knew they'd have to look into many empty caves before they found their killer. Perhaps this was one. "And the Parras?" he asked, though he knew the answer. If there'd been anything there Beauvoir would have told him already.

"Nothing in their background," Beauvoir confirmed. "But . . ."

Gamache waited.

"They seemed defensive, guarded. They were surprised that the dead man was Czech. Everyone was."

"What do you think?" asked the Chief.

Beauvoir wiped a weary hand across his face. "I can't put it all together, but I think it fits somehow."

"You think there is a connection?" pressed Gamache.

"How can there not be? The dead man was Czech, the sheet music, the priceless violin, and there's a big Czech community here including two people who could have found the cabin. Unless . . ."

"Yes?"

Beauvoir leaned forward, his nervous hands clasped together on the table. "Suppose we've got it wrong. Suppose the dead man wasn't Czech."

"You mean, that Olivier was lying?" said Gamache.

Beauvoir nodded. "He's lied about everything else. Maybe he said it to take us off the trail, so that we'd suspect others."

"But what about the violin and the music?"

"What about it?" Beauvoir was gaining momentum. "There're lots of other things in that cabin. Maybe Morin's right." Though he said it in the same tone he'd use to say maybe a chimp was right. With a mixture of awe at witnessing a miracle, and doubt. "Maybe the music and violin have nothing to do with it. After all, there were plates from Russia, glass from other places. The stuff tells us nothing. He could've been from anywhere. We only have Olivier's word for it. And maybe Olivier wasn't exactly lying. Maybe the guy did speak with an accent, but it wasn't Czech. Maybe it was Russian or Polish or one of those other countries."

Gamache leaned back, thinking, then he nodded and sat forward. "It's possible. But is it likely?"

This was the part of investigating he liked the most, and that most frightened him. Not the cornered and murderous suspect. But the possibility of turning left when he should have gone right. Of dismissing a lead, of giving up on a promising trail. Or not seeing one in his rush to a conclusion.

No, he needed to step carefully now. Like any explorer he knew the danger wasn't in walking off a cliff, but in getting hopelessly lost. Muddled. Disoriented by too much information.

In the end the answer to a murder investigation was always devastatingly simple. It was always right there, obvious. Hiding in facts and evidence and lies, and the misperceptions of the investigators.

"Let's leave if for now," he said, "and keep an open mind. The Hermit might have been Czech, or not. Either way there's no denying the contents of his cabin."

"What did Superintendent Brunel have to say? Any of it stolen?" asked Beauvoir.

"She hasn't found anything, but she's still looking. But Jérôme Brunel's been studying those letters under the carving and he thinks they're a Caesar's Shift. It's a type of code."

He explained how a Caesar's Shift worked.

"So we just need to find the key word?" asked Beauvoir. "Should be simple enough. It's Woo."

"Nope. Tried that one."

Beauvoir went to the sheet of foolscap on the wall and uncapped the magic marker. He wrote the alphabet. Then the marker hovered.

"How about violin?" asked Morin. Beauvoir looked at him again as at an unexpectedly bright chimp. He wrote *violin* on a separate sheet of paper. Then he wrote *Martinù, Bohuslav*.

"Bohemia," suggested Morin.

"Good idea," said Beauvoir. Within a minute they had a dozen possibilities, and within ten minutes they'd tried them all and found nothing.

Beauvoir tapped his Magic Marker with some annoyance and stared at the alphabet, as though it was to blame.

"Well, keep trying," said Gamache. "Superintendent Brunel is trying to track down the rest of the carvings."

"Do you think that's why he was killed?" asked Morin. "For the carvings?"

"Perhaps," said Gamache. "There's not much some people wouldn't do for things that valuable."

"But when we found the cabin it hadn't been searched," said Beauvoir. "If you find the guy, find the cabin, go there and kill him, wouldn't you tear the place apart to find the carvings? And it's not like the murderer had to worry about disturbing the neighbors."

"Maybe he meant to but heard Olivier returning and had to leave," said Gamache.

Beauvoir nodded. He'd forgotten about Olivier coming back. That made sense.

"That reminds me," he said, sitting down. "The lab report came in on the whittling tools and the wood. They say the tools were used to do the sculptures but not to carve Woo. The grooves didn't match, but apparently the technique didn't either. Definitely different people."

It was a relief to have something definite about this case.

"But red cedar was used for all of them?" Gamache wanted to hear the confirmation.

Beauvoir nodded. "And they're able to be more specific than that, at least with the Woo carving. They can tell by looking at water content, insects, growth rings, all sorts of things, where the wood actually came from."

Gamache leaned forward and wrote three words on a sheet of paper. He slid it across the table and Beauvoir read and snorted. "You talked to the lab?"

"I talked to Superintendent Brunel."

He told them then about Woo, and Emily Carr. About the Haida totem poles, carved from red cedar.

Beauvoir looked down at the Chief's note.

Queen Charlotte Islands, he'd written.

And that's what the lab had said. The wood that became Woo had started life as a sapling hundreds of years earlier, on the Queen Charlotte Islands.

Gabri walked, almost marched, up rue du Moulin. He'd made up his mind and wanted to get there before he changed it, as he had every five minutes all afternoon.

He'd barely exchanged five words with Olivier since the Chief Inspector's interrogation had revealed just how much his partner had kept from him. Finally he arrived and looked at the gleaming exterior of what had been the old Hadley house. Now a carved wooden sign hung out front, swinging slightly in the breeze.

Auberge et Spa.

The lettering was tasteful, clear, elegant. It was the sort of sign he'd been meaning to have Old Mundin make for the B and B, but hadn't gotten around to. Above the lettering three pine trees were carved in a row. Iconic, memorable, classic.

He'd thought of doing that for the B and B as well. And at least his place was actually in Three Pines. This place hovered above it. Not really part of the village.

Still, it was too late now. And he wasn't here to find fault. Just the opposite.

He stepped onto the porch and realized Olivier had stood there as well, with the body. He tried to shove the image away. Of his gentle, kind and quiet Olivier. Doing something so hideous.

Gabri rang the bell and waited, noting the shining brass of the handle, the bevelled glass and fresh red paint on the door. Cheerful and welcoming.

"*Bonjour*?" Dominique Gilbert opened the door, her face the image of polite suspicion.

"Madame Gilbert? We met in the village when you first arrived. I'm Gabriel Dubeau."

He put out his large hand and she took it. "I know who you are. You run that marvelous B and B."

Gabri knew when he was being softened up, having specialized in that himself. Still, it was nice to be on the receiving end of a compliment, and Gabri never refused one.

"That's right," he smiled. "But it's nothing compared to what you've done here. It's stunning."

"Would you like to come in?" Dominique stood aside and Gabri found himself in the large foyer. The last time he'd been there it'd been a wreck and so had he. But it was clear the old Hadley house no longer existed. The tragedy, the sigh on the hill, had become a smile. A warm, elegant, gracious *auberge*. A place he himself would book into, for pampering. For an escape.

He thought about his slightly worn B and B. What moments ago had seemed comfortable, charming, welcoming, now seemed just tired. Like a grande dame past her prime. Who would want to visit Auntie's place when you could come to the cool kids' inn and spa?

Olivier had been right. This was the end.

And looking at Dominique, warm, confident, he knew she couldn't fail. She seemed born to success, to succeed.

"We're just in the living room having drinks. Would you like to join us?"

He was about to decline. He'd come to say one thing to the Gilberts and leave, quickly. This wasn't a social call. But she'd already turned, assuming his consent, and was walking through a large archway.

But for all the easy elegance, of the place and the woman, something didn't fit.

He examined his hostess as she walked away. Light silk blouse, Aquascutum slacks, loose scarf. And a certain fragrance. What was it?

Then he had it. He smiled. Instead of wearing Chanel this chatelaine was wearing Cheval. And not just horse, but a haughty undercurrent of horse shit.

Gabri's spirits lifted. At least his place smelled of muffins.

"It's Gabriel Dubeau," Dominique announced to the room. The fire was lit and an older man was standing staring into it. Carole Gilbert sat in an armchair and Marc was by the drinks tray. They all looked up.

Chief Inspector Gamache had never seen the bistro so empty. He sat in an armchair by the fire and Havoc Parra brought him a drink.

"Quiet night?" he asked as the young man put down the Scotch and a plate of Quebec cheese.

"Dead," Havoc said and reddened a little. "But it'll probably pick up."

They both knew that wasn't true. It was six thirty. The height of what should be the cocktail and predinner rush. Two other customers sat in the large room while a small squadron of waiters waited. For a rush that would never come. Not that night. Perhaps not ever again.

Three Pines had forgiven Olivier a lot. The body had been dismissed as bad luck. Even Olivier knowing about the Hermit and the cabin had been shrugged off. Not easily, granted. But Olivier was loved and with love there was leeway. They'd even managed to forgive Olivier's moving the body. It was seen as a kind of *grand mal* on his part.

But that had ended when they'd found out that Olivier had secretly made millions of dollars off a recluse who was probably demented. Over the course of years. And then had quietly bought up most of Three Pines. He was Myrna's, Sarah's and Monsieur Béliveau's landlord.

This was Olivierville, and the natives were restless. The man they had thought they knew was a stranger after all.

"Is Olivier here?"

"In the kitchen. He let the chef off and decided to do the cooking himself tonight. He's a terrific cook, you know."

Gamache did know, having enjoyed his private meals a number of times. But he also knew this decision to cook allowed Olivier to hide. In the kitchen. Where he didn't have to see the accusing, unhappy faces of people who were his friends. Or worse still, see the empty chairs where friends once sat.

"I wonder if you could ask him to join me?"

"I'll do my best."

"Please."

In that one word Chief Inspector Gamache conveyed that while it might sound like a polite request, it wasn't. A couple of minutes later Olivier lowered himself into the chair across from Gamache. They needn't worry about keeping their voices down. The bistro was now empty.

Gamache leaned forward, took a sip of Scotch, and watched Olivier closely.

"What does the name Charlotte mean to you?"

Olivier's brows went up in surprise. "Charlotte?" He thought for a few moments. "I've never known a Charlotte. I knew a girl named Charlie once."

"Did the Hermit ever mention the name?"

"He never mentioned any name."

"What did you talk about?"

Olivier heard again the dead man's voice, not deep but somehow calming. "We talked about vegetable gardens and building and plumbing. He learned from the Romans, the Greeks, the early settlers. It was fascinating."

Not for the first time Gamache wished there'd been a third chair in that cabin, for him. "Did he ever mention Caesar's Shift?"

Once again Olivier looked perplexed, then shook his head.

"How about the Queen Charlotte Islands?" Gamache asked.

"In British Columbia? Why would he talk about them?"

"Is anyone in Three Pines from BC that you know?"

"People're from all over, but I can't remember anyone from British Columbia. Why?"

Gamache brought out the sculptures and placed them on the table so that the ship looked to be running from the cheese, and the cheese, runny, seemed to be chasing it.

"Because these are. Or at least, the wood is. It's red cedar from the

Queen Charlottes. Let's start again," Gamache said quietly. "Tell me what you know about these sculptures."

Olivier's face was impassive. Gamache knew that look. It was the look of a liar, caught. Trying to find the last way out, the back door, the crack. Gamache waited. He sipped his Scotch and smoothed a bit of cheese on the very excellent nut bread. He placed a slice in front of Olivier then prepared one for himself. He ate and waited.

"The Hermit carved them," said Olivier, his voice even, flat.

"You've told us that already. You also told us he gave you some and you threw them into the forest."

Gamache waited, knowing the rest would come out now. He looked through the window and noticed Ruth walking Rosa. The duck, for some reason, was wearing a tiny, red raincoat.

"I didn't throw them away. I kept them," Olivier whispered, and the world beyond the circle of light from the fireplace seemed to disappear. It felt as though the two men were in their own little cabin. "I'd been visiting the Hermit for about a year when he gave me the first."

"Can you remember what it was?"

"A hill, with trees. More like a mountain really. And a boy lying on it."

"This one?" Gamache brought out the photo Thérèse Brunel had given him.

Olivier nodded. "I remember it clearly because I didn't know the Hermit did stuff like this. His cabin was packed with wonderful things, but things other people made."

"What did you do with it?"

"I kept it for a while, but had to hide it so Gabri wouldn't start asking questions. Then I figured it was just easier to sell it. So I put it up on eBay. It went for a thousand dollars. Then a dealer got in touch. Said he had buyers, if there were any more. I thought he was joking, but when the Hermit gave me another one eight months later I remembered the guy and contacted him."

"Was it Denis Fortin?"

"Clara's gallery owner? No. It was someone in Europe. I can give you his coordinates."

"That would be helpful. What did the second carving look like?"

"Plain. Simple. On the surface. I was kind of disappointed. It was a forest, but if you looked closely beneath the canopy of trees you could see people walking in a line."

"Was the boy one of them?"

"Which boy?"

"The one from the mountain."

"Well, no. This was a different piece."

"I realize that," said Gamache, wondering if he was making himself clear. "But it seems possible the Hermit carved the same figures into each of his sculptures."

"The boy?"

"And the people. Anything else?"

Olivier thought. There was something else. The shadow over the trees. Something loomed just behind them. Something was rising up. And Olivier knew what it was.

"No, nothing. Just a forest and the people inside. The dealer was pretty excited."

"What did it sell for?"

"Fifteen thousand." He watched for the shock on Gamache's face.

But Gamache's gaze didn't waver, and Olivier congratulated himself on telling the truth. It was clear the Chief Inspector already knew the answer to that question. Telling the truth was always a crapshoot. As was the telling of lies. It was best, Olivier had found, to mingle the two.

"How many carvings did he make?"

"I thought eight, but now that you've found those, I guess he did ten."

"And you sold all the ones he gave you?"

Olivier nodded.

"You'd told us he started out giving you other things from his cabin, as payment for food. Where did those go?"

"I took them to the antique stores on rue Notre Dame in Montreal. But then once I realized the stuff was valuable I found private dealers."

"Who?"

"I haven't used them in years. I'll have to look it up. People in Toronto and New York." He leaned back and looked around the empty room. "I suppose I should let Havoc and the others off for the night."

Gamache remained quiet.

"Do you think people'll come back?"

The Chief Inspector nodded. "They're hurt by what you did."

"Me? Marc Gilbert's way worse. Be careful with him. He's not what he seems."

"And neither are you, Olivier. You've lied all along. You may be lying now. I'm going to ask you a question and I need you to think carefully about the answer."

Olivier nodded and straightened up.

"Was the Hermit Czech?"

Olivier immediately opened his mouth but Gamache quickly brought up a hand to stop him. "I asked you to think about your answer. Consider it. Could you have been wrong? Maybe there was no accent," Gamache watched his companion closely. "Maybe he spoke with an accent but it wasn't necessarily Czech. Maybe you just assumed. Be careful what you say."

Olivier stared at Gamache's large, steady hand and as it lowered he switched his gaze to the large, steady man.

"There was no mistake. I've heard enough Czech over the years from friends and neighbors. He was Czech."

It was said with more certainty than anything Olivier had said to Gamache since the investigation began. Still, Gamache stared at the slight man across from him. He examined his mouth, his eyes, the lines on his forehead, his coloring. Then the Chief Inspector nodded.

"Chilly night," said Ruth, plopping onto the seat beside Gamache and managing to knock his knee quite hard with her muddy cane. "Sorry," she said, then did it again.

She was completely oblivious of the conversation she was interrupting and the tension between the two men. She looked from Olivier to Gamache.

"Well, enough of this gay banter. Can you believe what Olivier did with that body? His idiocy eclipses even your own. Gives me a sense of the infinite. It's almost a spiritual experience. Cheese?"

She took the last bite of Gamache's Saint-André and reached for his Scotch, but he got there first. Myrna arrived, then Clara and Peter dropped by and told everyone about Denis Fortin. There was general commiserating and all agreed Clara had done the right thing. Then they agreed she should call in the morning and beg his forgiveness. Then they agreed she shouldn't.

"I saw Rosa outside," said Clara, anxious to change the subject. "She's looking very smart in her rain jacket." It had occurred to her to wonder why a duck might need a raincoat, but she supposed Ruth was just training Rosa to get used to wearing coats.

Eventually the conversation came back to Olivier, and the Hermit, dead, and the Hermit alive. Ruth leaned over and took Olivier's hand. "It's all right, dear, we all know you're greedy." Then she looked at Clara. "And we all know you're needy, and Peter's petty and Clouseau here," she turned to Gamache, "is arrogant. And you're . . ." She looked at Myrna, then turned back to Olivier, whispering loudly, "Who is that anyway? She's always hanging around."

"You're a nasty, demented, drunken old fart," said Myrna.

"I'm not drunk, yet."

They finished their drinks and left, but not before Ruth handed Gamache a piece of paper, carefully, precisely folded, the edges sharpened. "Give this to that little fellow who follows you around."

Olivier kept looking out into the village where Rosa was sitting quietly on the village green, waiting for Ruth. There was no sign of the one not there, the one Olivier longed to see.

Gabri was mostly curious to meet the saint. Vincent Gilbert. Myrna was in awe of him, and she wasn't in awe of many people. Old Mundin and The Wife said he'd changed their lives with his book *Being*, and his work at LaPorte. And by extension, he'd changed little Charlie's life.

"*Bonsoir*," said Gabri, nervously. He looked over to Vincent Gilbert. Growing up in the Catholic Church he'd spent endless hours staring at the gleaming windows showing the wretched lives and glorious deaths of the saints. When Gabri had wandered from the Church he'd taken one thing with him. The certainty that saints were good.

"What do you want?" Marc Gilbert asked. He stood with his wife and mother by the sofa. Forming a semicircle. His father a satellite off to the side. Gabri waited for Vincent Gilbert to calm his son, to tell him to greet their guest nicely. To invite Marc to be reasonable.

Gilbert said nothing.

"Well?" said Marc.

"I'm sorry I haven't been up sooner to welcome you."

Marc snorted. "The Welcome Wagon's already left us our package."

"Marc, please," said Dominique. "He's our neighbor."

"Not by choice. If he had his way we'd be long gone."

And Gabri didn't deny it. It was true. Their troubles arrived with the Gilberts. But here they were and something had to be said.

"I came to apologize," he said, standing to his full six foot one. "I'm sorry I haven't made you feel more welcome. And I'm very sorry about the body."

Yes, that definitely sounded as lame as he'd feared. But he hoped it at least sounded genuine.

"Why isn't Olivier here?" Marc demanded. "You didn't do it. It's not up to you to apologize."

"Marc, really," said Dominique. "Can't you see how difficult this is for him?"

"No, I can't. Olivier probably sent him hoping we won't sue. Or won't tell everyone what a psycho he is."

"Olivier's not a psycho," said Gabri, feeling a kind of trill inside as his patience unraveled. "He's a wonderful man. You don't know him."

"You're the one who doesn't know him if you think he's wonderful. Does a wonderful man dump a body at a neighbor's home?"

"You tell me."

The two men advanced on each other.

"I didn't take the body into a private home to scare the occupants half to death. That was a terrible thing to do."

"Olivier was pushed to it. He tried to make friends when you first arrived but then you tried to steal our staff and open this huge hotel and spa."

"Ten guest rooms isn't huge," said Dominique.

"Not in Montreal, but out here it is. This's a small village. We've been here for a long time living quietly. You come here and change all that. Made no effort to fit in."

"By 'fit in' you mean tug our forelocks and be grateful you've allowed us to live here?" Marc demanded.

"No, I mean being respectful of what's here already. What people've worked hard to establish."

"You want to raise the drawbridge, don't you?" said Marc in disgust. "You're in and you want to keep everyone else out."

"That's not true. Most of the people in Three Pines have come from somewhere else."

"But you only accept people who follow your rules. Who do as you say. We came here to live our dream and you won't let us. Why? Because it clashes with yours. You're threatened by us and so you need to run us out of town. You're nothing but bullies, with big smiles."

Marc was almost spitting.

Gabri stared at him, amazed. "But you didn't really expect us to be happy about it, did you? Why would you come here and deliberately upset people who were going to be your neighbors? Didn't you want us as friends? You must've known how Olivier would react."

"What? That he'd put a body in our home?"

"That was wrong. I've already said that. But you provoked him. All of us. We wanted to be your friends but you made it too difficult."

"So, you'll be friends with us as long as what? We're just a modest success? Have a few guests, a couple of treatments a day? Maybe a small dining room, if we're lucky? But nothing to compete with you and Olivier?"

"That's right," said Gabri.

That shut Marc up.

"Listen, why do you think we don't make croissants?" Gabri continued. "Or pies? Or any baking? We could. It's what I love to do. But Sarah's Boulangerie was already here. She'd lived in the village all her life. The bakery belonged to her grandmother. So we opened a bistro instead. All our croissants, and pies, and breads are baked by Sarah. We adjusted our dreams to fit the dreams already here. It'd be cheaper and more fun to bake ourselves but that's not the point."

"What is the point?" asked Vincent Gilbert, speaking for the first time.

"The point isn't to make a fortune," said Gabri, turning to him gratefully. "The point is to know what's enough. To be happy."

There was a pause and Gabri silently thanked the saint for creating that space for reason to return.

"Maybe you should remind your partner of that," said Vincent Gilbert. "You talk a good line but you don't live it. It suits you to blame my son. You dress up your behavior as moral and kindly and loving, but you know what it is?"

Vincent Gilbert was advancing, closing in on Gabri. As he neared he seemed to grow and Gabri felt himself shrink.

"It's selfish," Gilbert hissed. "My son has been patient. He's hired local workers, created jobs. This is a place of healing, and you not only try to ruin it, you try to make him out to be at fault."

Vincent stepped next to his son, having finally found the price of belonging.

There was nothing more to say, so Gabri left.

Lights glowed at windows as he made his way back into the village. Overhead ducks flew south in their V formation, away from the killing cold that was gathering and preparing to descend. Gabri sat on a tree stump by the side of the road and watched the sun set over Three Pines and thought about *les temps perdus* and felt very alone, without even the certainty of saints for comfort.

A beer was placed on the table for Beauvoir and Gamache nursed his Scotch. They settled into their comfortable chairs and examined the dinner menu. The bistro was deserted. Peter, Clara, Myrna and Ruth had all gone and Olivier had retreated to his kitchen. Havoc, the last of the waiters, took their order then left them to talk.

Gamache broke up a small baguette and told his second in command about his conversation with Olivier.

"So, he still says the Hermit was Czech. Do you believe him?"

"I do," said Gamache. "At least, I believe Olivier is convinced of it. Any luck with the Caesar's Shift?"

"None." They'd given up when they started putting their own names in. Both slightly relieved it didn't work.

"What's wrong?" Gamache asked. Beauvoir had leaned back in his seat and tossed his linen napkin onto the table.

"I'm just frustrated. It seems every time we make progress it gets all muddied. We still don't even know who the dead man was."

Gamache smiled. It was their regular predicament. The further into a case they went the more clues they gathered. There came a time when it seemed a howl, as though they had hold of something wild that screamed clues at them. It was, Gamache knew, the shriek of something cornered and frightened. They were entering the last stages of this investigation. Soon the clues, the pieces, would stop fighting, and start betraying the murderer. They were close.

"By the way, I'm going away tomorrow," said the Chief Inspector after Havoc brought their appetizers and left.

"Back to Montreal?" Beauvoir took a forkful of chargrilled calamari while Gamache ate his pear and prosciutto.

"A little further than that. The Queen Charlotte Islands."

"Are you kidding? In British Columbia? Up by Alaska? Because of a monkey named Woo?"

"Well, when you put it like that . . ."

Beauvoir speared a blackened piece of calamari and dipped it in garlic sauce. "*Voyons*, doesn't it strike you as, well, extreme?"

"No, it doesn't. The name Charlotte keeps repeating." Gamache ticked the points off on his fingers. "The Charlotte Brontë first edition, *Charlotte's Web* first edition, the Amber Room panel? Made for a princess named Charlotte. The note the Hermit kept about the violin was written by a Charlotte. I've been trying to figure out what they could all mean, this repetition of the name Charlotte, then this afternoon Superintendent Brunel gave me the answer. The Queen Charlotte Islands. Where Emily Carr painted. Where the wood for the carvings came from. It might be a dead end, but I'd be a fool not to follow this lead."

"But who's doing the leading? You or the murderer? I think they're leading you away. I think the murderer is here, in Three Pines."

"So do I, but I think the murder began on the Queen Charlotte Islands."

Beauvoir huffed, exasperated. "You're taking a bunch of clues and putting them together to suit your purpose."

"What are you suggesting?"

Beauvoir needed to watch himself now. Chief Inspector Gamache was more than his superior. They had a relationship that went deeper than any other Beauvoir had. And he knew Gamache's patience had its limits.

"I think you see what you want to see. You see things that aren't really there."

"You mean just aren't visible."

"No, I mean aren't there. To leap to one conclusion isn't the end of the world, but you're leaping all over the place and where does it take you? The end of the fucking world. Sir."

Beauvoir glanced out the window, trying to cool down. Havoc removed their plates and Beauvoir waited for him to leave before continuing. "I know you love history and literature and art and that the Hermit's cabin must seem like a candy shop, but I think you're seeing a whole lot more in this case than exists. I think you're complicating it. You know I'd follow you anywhere, we all would. You just point, and I'm there. I trust you that much. But even you can make mistakes. You always say that murder is, at its core, very simple. It's about an emotion. That emotion is here, and so's the murderer. We have plenty of clues to follow without thinking about a monkey, a hunk of wood and some godforsaken island to hell and gone across the country."

"Finished?" Gamache asked.

Beauvoir sat upright and took a deep breath. "There may be more."

Gamache smiled. "I agree with you, Jean Guy, the murderer is here. Someone here knew the Hermit, and someone here killed him. You're right. When you strip away all the shiny baubles it's simple. A man ends up with antiquities worth a fortune. Perhaps he stole them. He wants to hide so he comes to this village no one knows about. But even that isn't enough. He takes it a step further and builds a cabin deep in the woods. Is he hiding from the police? Maybe. From something or someone worse? I think so. But he can't do it on his own. If nothing else he needs news. He needs eyes and ears on the outside. So he recruits Olivier."

"Why him?"

"Ruth said it tonight."

"More Scotch, asshole?"

"Well, that too. But she said Olivier was greedy. And he is. So was the Hermit. He probably recognized himself in Olivier. That greed. That need to own. And he knew he could have a hold over Olivier. Promising him more and better antiques. But over the years something happened."

"He went nuts?"

"Maybe. But maybe just the opposite. Maybe he went sane. The place he built to hide became a home, a haven. You felt it. There was something peaceful, comforting even, about the Hermit's life. It was simple. Who doesn't long for that these days?"

Their dinners arrived and Beauvoir's gloom lifted as the fragrant boeuf bourguignon landed in front of him. He looked across at the Chief Inspector smiling down at his lobster Thermidor.

"Yes, the simple life in the country." Beauvoir lifted his red wine in a small toast.

Gamache tipped his glass of white toward his Inspector, then took a succulent forkful. As he ate he thought of those first few minutes in the Hermit's cabin. And that moment when he realized what he was looking at. Treasures. And yet everything was put to purpose. There was a reason for everything in there, whether practical or pleasure, like the books and violin.

But there was one thing. One thing that didn't seem to have a purpose.

Gamache slowly laid his fork down and stared beyond Beauvoir. After a moment the Inspector also put his fork down and looked behind him. There was nothing there. Just the empty room.

"What is it?"

Gamache put up a finger, a subtle and gentle request for quiet. Then he reached into his breast pocket and bringing out a pen and notebook he wrote something down, quickly, as though afraid it would get away. Beauvoir strained to read it. Then, with a thrill, saw what it was.

The alphabet.

Silently he watched his Chief write the line beneath. His face opened in wonder. Wonder that he could have been so stupid. Could have missed what now seemed obvious.

Beneath the alphabet, Chief Inspector Gamache had written: SIXTEEN.

"The number above the door," whispered Beauvoir, as though he too was afraid he might scare this vital clue away.

"What were the code letters?" asked Gamache, in a hurry now. Anxious to get there.

Beauvoir scrambled in his pocket and brought out his notebook.

"MRKBVYDDO under the people on the shore. And OWSVI under the ship."

He watched as Gamache worked to decode the Hermit's messages.

A B C D E F G H I J K L M N O P Q R S T U V W X Y Z

S I X T E E N A B C D E F G H I J K L M N O P Q R S

Gamache read the letters out as he found them. "T, Y, R, I, something . . ."

"Tyri," Beauvoir mumbled. "Tyri . . ."

"Something, K, K, V." He looked up at Beauvoir.

"What does it mean? Is it a name? Maybe a Czech name?"

"Maybe it's an anagram," said Gamache. "We have to rearrange the letters."

They tried that for a few minutes, taking bites of their dinner as they worked. Finally Gamache put his pen down and shook his head. "I thought I had it."

"Maybe it's right," said Beauvoir, not ready to let go yet. He jotted more letters, tried the other code. Rearranged letters and finally staggered to the same conclusion.

The key wasn't "sixteen."

"Still," said Beauvoir, dipping a crusty baguette into his gravy, "I wonder why that number's up there."

"Maybe some things don't need a purpose," said Gamache. "Maybe that's their purpose."

But that was too esoteric for Beauvoir. As was the Chief Inspector's reasoning about the Queen Charlotte Islands. In fact, Beauvoir wouldn't call it reasoning at all. At best it was intuition on the Chief's part, at worst it was a wild guess, maybe even manipulated by the murderer.

The only image Beauvoir had of the moody archipelago at the very end of the country was of thick forests and mountains and endless gray water. But mostly it was mist.

And into that mist Armand Gamache was going, alone.

"I almost forgot, Ruth Zardo gave me this." Gamache handed him the slip of paper. Beauvoir unfolded it and read out loud.

> *"and pick your soul up gently by the nape of the neck*
> *and caress you into darkness and paradise."*

There was, at least, a full stop after "paradise." Was this, finally, the end?

THIRTY-TWO

~

Armand Gamache arrived in the late afternoon on the brooding islands after taking increasingly smaller planes until it seemed the last was nothing more than fuselage wrapped round his body and thrust off the end of the Prince Rupert runway.

As the tiny float plane flew over the archipelago off the coast of northern British Columbia Gamache looked down on a landscape of mountains and thick ancient forests. It had been hidden for millennia behind mists almost as impenetrable as the trees. It had remained isolated. But not alone. It was a cauldron of life that had produced both the largest black bears in the world and the smallest owls. It was teeming with life. Indeed, the first men were discovered in a giant clam shell by a raven off the tip of one of the islands. That, according to their creation stories, was how the Haida came to live there. More recently loggers had also been found on the islands. That wasn't part of creation. They'd looked beyond the thick mists and seen money. They'd arrived on the Charlottes a century ago, blind to the crucible they'd stumbled upon and seeing only treasure. The ancient forests of red cedar. Trees prized for their durability, having been tall and straight long before Queen Charlotte was born and married her mad monarch. But now they fell to the saw, to be made into shingles and decks and siding. And ten small carvings.

After landing smoothly on the water the young bush pilot helped extricate the large man from her small plane.

"Welcome to Haida Gwaii," she said.

When Gamache had woken early that morning in Three Pines and found a groggy Gabri in the kitchen making a small picnic for the drive to the Montreal airport, he knew nothing about these islands half a world away. But on the long flights from Montreal to Vancouver, to Prince Rupert and into the village of Queen Charlotte, he'd read about the islands and he knew that phrase.

"Thank you for bringing me to your homeland."

The pilot's deep brown eyes were suspicious, as well they would be, thought Gamache. The arrival of yet another middle-aged white man in a suit was never a good sign. You didn't have to be Haida to know that.

"You must be Chief Inspector Gamache."

A burly man with black hair and skin the color of cedar was walking across the dock, his hand out. They shook.

"I'm Sergeant Minshall, of the RCMP. We've been corresponding."

His voice was deep and had a slight sing-song quality. He was Haida.

"*Ah, oui, merci.* Thank you for meeting the plane."

The Mountie took the overnight bag from the pilot and slung it over his shoulder. Thanking the pilot, who ignored them, the two men walked to the end of the dock, up a ramp and along the road. There was a bite to the air and Gamache had to remember they were closer to Alaska than Vancouver.

"I see you're not staying long."

Gamache looked out into the ocean and knew the mainland had disappeared. No, it was not that it had vanished, but that it didn't exist at all here. This was the mainland.

"I wish I could stay longer, it's beautiful. But I have to get back."

"Right. I've arranged a room for you at the lodge. I think you'll enjoy it. There aren't many people on the Queen Charlottes, as you probably know. Maybe five thousand, with half being Haida and half," he hesitated slightly, "not. We get quite a few tourists, but the season's ending."

The two men had slowed and now they stopped. They'd walked by a hardware store, a coffee shop, a little building with a mermaid out front. But it was the harbor that drew Gamache's attention. He'd never seen such scenery in all his life, and he'd seen some spectacularly beautiful places in Quebec. But none, he had to admit, came close to this.

It was wilderness. As far as he could see there were mountains rising from the water, covered in dark forest. He could see an island and fishing boats. Overhead, eagles soared. The men walked onto the beach, which was covered in pebbles and shells, and stood silent for a few minutes, listening to the birds and the lapping water and smelling the air with that combination of seaweed and fish and forest.

"There're more eagle nests here than anywhere else in Canada, you know. It's a sign of good luck."

It wasn't often an RCMP officer spoke of signs, unless it was traffic signs. Gamache didn't turn to look at the man, he was too taken by the view, but he listened.

"The Haida have two clans. The Eagle and the Raven. I've arranged for you to meet with elders from both clans. They've invited you for dinner."

"Thank you. Will you be there?"

Sergeant Minshall smiled. "No. I thought it'd be more comfortable without me. The Haida are very warm people, you know. They've lived here for thousands of years, undisturbed. Until recently."

It was interesting, Gamache thought, that he referred to the Haida as "they" not "we." Perhaps it was for Gamache's benefit, so he didn't appear biased.

"I'll try not to disturb them tonight."

"It's too late."

Armand Gamache showered, shaved and wiped the vapor from the mirror. It was as though the mist that hung over the ancient forests had crept into his room. Perhaps to watch him. To divine his intentions.

He made a small hole in the moisture and saw a very tired Sûreté officer, far from home.

Changing into a fresh shirt and dark slacks he picked out a tie and sat on the side of the double bed, which was covered in what looked like a hand-stitched quilt.

The room was simple and clean and comfortable. But it could be filled with turnips and it wouldn't matter. All anyone would notice was the view. It looked directly over the bay. The sunset filled the sky with gold and purples and reds, undulating and shifting. Alive. Everything seemed alive here.

He gravitated to the window and stared while his hands tied his green silk tie. There was a knock on the door. He opened it, expecting the landlady or Sergeant Minshall, and was surprised to see the young bush pilot.

"Noni, my great-grandmother, asked me to bring you to dinner."

She still didn't smile. In fact, she seemed singularly unhappy about the fact. He put on a gray jacket and his coat and they walked into the darkening night. Lights were on in the homes that hugged the harbor. The air was cold and damp, but fresh, and it woke him up so that he felt more alert than he had all afternoon. They climbed into an old pickup truck and headed out of town.

"So you're from the Charlottes?"

"I'm from Haida Gwaii," she said.

"Of course, I'm sorry. Are you with the Eagle clan?"

"Raven."

"Ah," said Gamache, and realized he sounded slightly ridiculous, but the young woman beside him didn't seem to care. She seemed more interested in ignoring him completely.

"Your family must be very pleased you're a pilot."

"Why?"

"Well, flying."

"Because I'm a Raven? Everyone here flies, Chief Inspector. I just need more help."

"Have you been a pilot long?"

There was silence then. Evidently his question wasn't worth answering. And he had to agree. Silence was better. His eyes adjusted to the night and he was able to make out the line of mountains across the bay as they drove. After a few minutes they arrived at another village. The young pilot stopped the pickup in front of a nondescript white building that had a sign out front. *Skidegate Community Hall.* She got out and walked to the door, never looking back to see if he was following. She either trusted he was there or, more likely, didn't care.

He left the twilit harbor and followed her through the door into the Community Hall. And into an opera house. Gamache turned round to make sure there was a door there and he hadn't, magically, emerged into another world. They were surrounded by ornate balconies on three sides. Gamache did a slow 360, his feet squeaking a little on the polished wood floor. Only then did he realize his mouth was slightly open. He closed it and looked at the young woman beside him.

"*Mais, c'est extraordinaire.*"

"*Haw'aa.*"

Wide, gracious staircases led up to the balconies and at the far end of the room was a stage. Behind it a mural had been painted on the wall.

"That's a Haida village," she said, nodding toward it.

"*Incroyable*," whispered Gamache. The Chief Inspector was often surprised, astonished, by life. But he was rarely dumbfounded. He was now.

"Do you like it?"

Gamache looked down and realized they'd been joined by another woman, much older than his companion or himself. And unlike his companion this woman smiled. It looked, by the ease of it, as though she found a lot of humor in life.

"Very much." He put out his hand, and she took it.

"This is my noni," said the pilot.

"Esther," she said.

"Armand Gamache," said the Chief, bowing slightly. "It's an honor."

"The honor is mine, Chief Inspector. Please." She motioned into the center of the room where a long table had been set. There was a rich aroma of cooked food, and the room was filled with people talking, greeting, calling to each other. And laughing.

He'd expected the gathering of Haida elders to be in traditional garb. He was embarrassed now by that cliché. Instead the men and women were dressed as they'd come from work, some in T-shirts and heavy sweaters, some in suits. Some worked in the bank, the school, the clinic; some worked on the cold waters. Some were artists. Painters, but mostly carvers.

"This is a matrilineal society, Chief Inspector," Esther explained. "But most of the chiefs are men. Though that doesn't mean women are powerless. Quite the opposite."

She looked at him, her eyes clear. It was a simple statement. Not a boast.

She then introduced him to everyone, one by one. He repeated their names and tried to keep them straight, though he was frankly lost after half a dozen. Finally Esther took him over to the buffet table, where food had been put out.

"This is Skaay," she said, introducing a tiny old man who looked up from his plate. His eyes were milky, blind. "Of the Eagle clan."

"Robert, if you prefer," Skaay said, his voice strong and his grip stronger. He smiled. "The women of both clans have done a traditional Haida feast for you, Chief Inspector." The blind man led Gamache down the long table, naming each dish. "This is *k'aaw*. It's herring roe on kelp. This over here is pepper-smoked salmon, or if you prefer there's wood-smoked salmon over there. Caught this morning by Reg. He spent the day smoking it. For you."

They walked slowly the length of the buffet. Octopus balls, crab cakes, halibut. Potato salad; fresh bread, still warm. Juices and water. No alcohol.

"We have dances here. This is where most people have their wedding parties. And funerals. So many dinners. When the Eagle clan is hosting the Raven clan serves. And vice versa, of course. But tonight we're all hosting. And you're our honored guest."

Gamache, who'd been to state dinners in grand palaces, banquets given for him, awards presentations, had rarely felt so honored.

He took a helping of everything and sat down. To his surprise, the young pilot joined him. Over dinner they all talked, but he noticed the Haida elders asked more questions than they answered. They were interested in his work, his life, his family. They asked about Quebec. They were informed and thoughtful. Kind, and guarded.

Over cake, fresh bumbleberries and Cool Whip, Gamache told them about the murder. The Hermit in the cabin buried deep in the forest. The elders, always attentive, grew even more still as he told them about the man, surrounded by treasure, but alone. A man whose life had been taken, his goods left behind. A man with no name, surrounded by history, but with none himself.

"Was he happy, do you think?" Esther asked. It was almost impossible to figure out if there was a leader of this group, by election or mutual consent. But Gamache guessed if there was one, it would be her.

He hesitated. He hadn't actually asked himself that question.

Was the Hermit happy?

"I think he was content. He led a small, peaceful life. One that appeals to me."

The young pilot turned to look at him. Up until that moment she'd been looking straight ahead.

"He was surrounded by beauty," continued Gamache. "And he had company every now and then. Someone who'd bring him what he couldn't provide for himself. But he was afraid."

"Hard to be both happy and afraid," said Esther. "But fear can lead to courage."

"And courage can lead to peace," said a young man in a suit.

It reminded Gamache of what the fisherman had written on the wall of the diner in Mutton Bay a few years earlier. He'd looked at Gamache across the room and smiled so fully it had taken the Chief Inspector's breath away. Then the fisherman had scribbled something on the wall and left. Gamache had gone to the wall, and read:

> *Where there is love there is courage,*
> *where there is courage there is peace,*
> *where there is peace there is God.*
> *And when you have God, you have everything.*

Gamache spoke the words, and then there was silence in the hall. The Haida were good at silence. And so was Gamache.

"Is that a prayer?" Esther finally asked.

"A fisherman wrote it on a wall in a place called Mutton Bay, a long way off."

"Perhaps not so far," said Esther.

"A fisherman?" asked the man in the suit, with a smile. "Figures. They're all crazy."

An older man beside him, dressed in a thick sweater, gave him a swat and they laughed.

"We're all fishermen," said Esther, and Gamache had the feeling she was including him. She thought for a moment then asked, "What did your Hermit love?"

Gamache thought about that. "I don't know."

"Perhaps when you do, you'll find his killer. How can we help?"

"There were a couple of references to Woo and Charlotte in the Hermit's cabin. They led me to Emily Carr, and she led me here."

"Well, you're far from the first," an elderly man said with a laugh. It wasn't a smug or derisive laugh. "Her paintings have been bringing people to Haida Gwaii for years."

It was hard to tell if that was considered a good thing.

"I think the Hermit was on the Queen Charlotte Islands, maybe fifteen or more years ago. We think he was Czech. He'd have spoken with an accent."

Gamache brought out the photographs, taken at the morgue. He'd warned them what they'd see but he wasn't worried. These were people who lived comfortably with life and death in a place where the line was blurred, and people, animals, and spirits walked together. Where blind men saw and everyone had the gift of flight.

Over strong tea they looked at the dead man. They looked long and hard. Even the young pilot gave the photographs her attention.

And as they looked at the photos, Gamache looked at them. To see a flicker of recognition. A twitch, a change in breathing. He became hyperaware of every one of them. But all he saw were people trying to help.

"We've disappointed you, I'm afraid," said Esther as Gamache put the pictures back in his satchel. "Why didn't you just e-mail them to us?"

"Well, I e-mailed them to Sergeant Minshall and he circulated them among the police, but I wanted to be here myself. And there's something I couldn't e-mail. Something I brought with me."

He put the two balls of towel on the table and carefully unwrapped the first.

Not a spoon clinked against a mug, not a creamer was popped, peeled and opened, not a breath. It was as though something else had joined them then. As though silence had taken a seat.

He gently unwrapped the next one. And it sailed across the table to join its sibling.

"There're others. Eight we think."

If they heard him they gave no indication. Then one man, middle-aged and stocky, reached out. Stopping, he looked at Gamache.

"May I?"

"Please."

He picked it up and in large, worn hands he held the sailing ship. He lifted it to his face so that he was staring into the eyes of the tiny men and women who were looking ahead with such pleasure, such joy.

"That's Haawasti," whispered the bush pilot. "Will Sommes."

"That's Will Sommes?" Gamache asked. He'd read about this man. He was one of Canada's greatest living artists. His Haida carvings were bursting with life and snapped up by private collectors and museums worldwide. He'd assumed Sommes was a recluse, having grown so famous surely he'd be in hiding. But the Chief Inspector was beginning to appreciate that on Haida Gwaii legends came alive, walked among them, and sometimes sipped black tea and ate Cool Whip.

Sommes picked up the other piece and turned it round and round. "Red cedar."

"From here," confirmed Gamache.

Sommes looked under the sailing ship. "Is that a signature?"

"Perhaps you could tell me."

"Just letters. But it must mean something."

"It seems to be in code. We haven't figured it out yet."

"The dead man made these?" Sommes held up the carving.

"He did."

Sommes looked down at what he held in his hand. "I can't tell you who he was, but I can tell you this much. Your Hermit wasn't just afraid, he was terrified."

THIRTY-THREE

———

Next morning Gamache awoke to a fresh, cold breeze bringing sea air and the shriek of feeding birds through his open window. He turned over in bed and, drawing the warm quilt around him, he stared out the window. The day before had seemed a dream. To wake up in Three Pines and go to sleep in this Haida village beside the ocean.

The sky was brilliant blue and he could see eagles and seagulls gliding. Getting out of bed he quickly put on his warmest clothing and cursed himself for forgetting his long underwear.

Downstairs he found a full breakfast of bacon, eggs, toast and strong coffee.

"Lavina called and said to be at the dock by nine or she was leaving without you."

Gamache looked round to see who the landlady was talking to.

He was alone in the room. "*Moi?*"

"Yes you. Lavina said don't be late."

Gamache looked at his watch. It was half past eight and he had no idea who Lavina was, where the dock was, or why he should go. He had one more cup of coffee, went to his room to use the washroom and get his coat and hat, then came back down to speak to the landlady.

"Did Lavina say which dock?"

"I suppose it's the one she always uses. Can't miss it."

How often had Gamache heard that, just before missing it? Still, he stood on the porch and taking a deep breath of bracing air he surveyed the coastline. There were several docks.

But at only one was there a seaplane. And the young bush pilot looking at her watch. Was her name Lavina? To his embarrassment he realized he'd never asked her.

He walked over and as his feet hit the wooden boards of the dock he saw she wasn't alone. Will Sommes was with her.

"Thought you'd like to see where those pieces of wood came from," the carver said, inviting Gamache into the small pontoon plane. "My granddaughter's agreed to fly us. The plane you came in on yesterday's a commercial flight. This is her own."

"I have a granddaughter too," said Gamache, looking he hoped not too frantically for the seat belt as the plane pushed off from the wharf and headed into the sound. "And another on the way. My granddaughter makes me finger paintings."

He almost added that at least a finger painting wasn't likely to kill you, but he thought that would be ungracious.

The plane gathered speed and began bouncing off the small waves. It was then Gamache noticed the torn canvas straps inside the plane, the rusting seats, the ripped cushions. He looked out the window and wished he hadn't had that full breakfast.

Then they were airborne and banking to the left they climbed into the sky and headed down the coastline. For forty minutes they flew. It was too noisy inside the tiny cabin to do anything other than yell at each other. Every now and then Sommes would lean over and point something out. He'd gesture down to a small bay and say things like, "That's where man first appeared, in the clam shell. It's our Garden of Eden." Or a little later, "Look down. Those are the last virgin red cedars in existence, the last ancient forest."

Gamache had an eagle's-eye view of this world. He looked down on rivers and inlets and forest and mountains carved by glaciers. Eventually they descended into a bay whose peaks were shrouded in mist even on this clear day. As they got lower and skimmed over the water toward the dark shoreline Will Sommes leaned in to Gamache again and shouted, "Welcome to Gwaii Haanas. The place of wonders."

And it was.

Lavina got them as close as she could then a man appeared on the shore and shoved a boat out, leaping into it at the last moment. At the door to the seaplane he held out his hand to help the Chief Inspector into the tippy boat and introduced himself.

"My name's John. I'm the Watchman."

Gamache noticed he was barefooted, and saw Lavina and her grand-father taking their shoes and socks off and rolling up their cuffs as John rowed. Gamache soon saw why. The boat could only get so close. They'd have to walk the last ten feet. He removed his shoes and socks, rolled up his pants and climbed over the side. Almost. As soon as his big toe touched the water it, and he, recoiled. Ahead of him he saw Lavina and Sommes smile.

"It is cold," admitted the Watchman.

"Oh, come on, princess, suck it up," said Lavina. Gamache wondered if she was channeling Ruth Zardo. Was there one in every pack?

Gamache sucked it up and joined them on the beach, his feet purple from just a minute in the water. He nimbly walked over the stones to a stump and, sitting down, he rubbed the dirt and shards of shell from his soles and put his socks and shoes back on. He couldn't remember the last time he felt such relief. Actually, when the pontoon plane landed was probably the last time.

He'd been so struck by the surroundings, by the Watchman, by the frigid water, he'd failed to see what was actually there. Now he saw. Standing on the very edge of the forest was a solemn semicircle of totem poles.

Gamache felt all his blood rush to his core, his center.

"This is Ninstints," whispered Will Sommes.

Gamache didn't answer. He couldn't. He stared at the tall poles into which was carved the Mythtime, that marriage of animals and spirits. Killer whales, sharks, wolves, bears, eagles and crows were all staring back at him. And something else. Things with long tongues and huge eyes, and teeth. Creatures unknown outside the Mythtime, but very real here.

Gamache had the feeling he was standing at the very edge of memory.

Some totem poles were straight and tall, but most had tumbled over or were lurching sideways.

"We are all fishermen," said Will. "Esther was right. The sea feeds our bodies, but that feeds our souls." He opened his hands in a simple, small gesture toward the forest.

John the Watchman spoke softly as they picked their way among the totem poles.

"This is the largest collection of standing totem poles in the world.

The site's now protected, but it wasn't always. Some poles commemorate a special event, some are mortuary poles. Each tells a story. The images build on each other and are in a specific and intentional order."

"This is where Emily Carr did much of her painting," said Gamache.

"I thought you'd like to see it," said Sommes.

"*Merci.* I'm very grateful to you."

"This settlement was the last to fall. It was the most isolated, and perhaps the most ornery," said John. "But eventually it collapsed too. A tidal wave of disease, alcohol and missionaries finally washed over this place, as it had all the others. The totems were torn down, the longhouses destroyed. That's what's left." He pointed to a bump in the forest, covered by moss. "That was a longhouse."

For an hour Armand Gamache wandered the site. He was allowed to touch the totems and he found himself reaching high and placing his large, certain hand on the magnificent faces, trying to feel whoever had carved such a creature.

Eventually he walked over to John, who'd spent that hour standing in one spot, watching.

"I'm here investigating a murder. May I show you a couple of things?"

John nodded.

"The first is a photograph of the dead man. I think he might have spent time on Haida Gwaii, though I think he'd have called them the Charlottes."

"Then he wasn't Haida."

"No, I don't think he was." Gamache showed John the picture.

He took it and studied it carefully. "I'm sorry, I don't know him."

"It would have been a while ago. Fifteen, maybe twenty years."

"That was a difficult time. There were a lot of people here. It was when the Haida finally stopped the logging companies, by blocking the roads. He might have been a logger."

"He might have been. He certainly seemed comfortable in a forest. And he built himself a log cabin. Who here could teach him that?"

"Are you kidding?"

"No."

"Just about anyone. Most Haida live in villages now, but almost all of us have cabins in the woods. Ones we built ourselves, or our parents built."

"Do you live in a cabin?"

Did John hesitate? "No, I have a room at the Holiday Inn Ninstints," he laughed. "Yes. I built my own cabin a few years ago. Want to see it?"

"If you don't mind."

While Will Sommes and his granddaughter wandered around, John the Watchman took Gamache deeper into the forest. "Some of these trees are more than a thousand years old, you know."

"Worth saving," said Gamache.

"Not all would agree." He stopped and pointed. To a small cabin, in the forest, with a porch, and one rocking chair.

The image of the Hermit's.

"Did you know him, John?" asked Gamache, suddenly very aware he was alone in the woods with a powerful man.

"The dead man?"

Gamache nodded.

John smiled again. "No." But he'd come very close to Gamache.

"Did you teach him to build a log cabin?"

"No."

"Did you teach him to carve?"

"No."

"Would you tell me if you had?"

"I have nothing to fear from you. Nothing to hide."

"Then why are you here, all alone?"

"Why are you?" John's voice was barely a whisper, a hiss.

Gamache unwrapped a carving. John stared at the men and women in the boat and backed away.

"It's made from red cedar. From Haida Gwaii," said Gamache. "Perhaps even from these trees in this forest. The murdered man made it."

"That means nothing to me," said John and with a last glance at the carving he walked away.

Gamache followed him out and found Will Sommes on the beach, smiling.

"Have a nice talk with John?"

"He hadn't much to say."

"He's a Watchman, not a Chatter."

Gamache smiled and started rewrapping the carving, but Sommes touched his hand to stop him and took the carving once again.

"You say it's from here. Is it old growth?"

"We don't know. The scientists can't say. They'd have to destroy the carving to get a big enough sample and I wouldn't let them."

"This is worth more than a man's life?" Sommes held the carving up.

"Few things are worth more than a man's life, monsieur. But that life has already been lost. I'm hoping to find who did it without destroying his creation as well."

This seemed to satisfy Sommes, who handed the carving back, but reluctantly.

"I'd like to have met the man who did that. He was gifted."

"He might have been a logger. Might have helped cut down your forests."

"Many in my family were loggers. It happens. Doesn't make them bad men or lifelong enemies."

"Do you teach other artists?" Gamache asked, casually.

"You think maybe he came here to talk to me?" asked Sommes.

"I think he came here. And he's a carver."

"First he was a logger, now he's a carver. Which is it, Chief Inspector?"

It was said with humor, but the criticism wasn't lost on Gamache. He was fishing, and he knew it. So did Sommes. So did Esther. We're all fishermen, she'd said.

Had he found anything on this visit? Gamache was beginning to doubt it.

"Do you teach carving?" he persisted.

Sommes shook his head. "Only to other Haida."

"The Hermit used wood from here. Does that surprise you?"

"Not at all. Some stands are now protected, but we've agreed on areas that can be logged. And replanted. It's a good industry, if managed properly. And young trees are great for the ecosystem. I advise all wood carvers to use red cedar."

"We should be going. The weather's changing," said Lavina.

As the float plane took off and banked away from the sheltered bay Gamache looked down. It appeared as though one of the totem poles had come alive, and waved. But then he recognized it as John, who guarded the haunting place but had been afraid of the small piece of wood in Gamache's hand. John, who'd placed himself beyond the pale.

"He was involved in the logging dispute, you know," Sommes shouted over the old engine.

"Seems a good person to have on your side."

"And he was. On your side, I mean. John was a Mountie. He was forced to arrest his own grandmother. I can still see him as he led her away."

"John's my uncle," Lavina shouted from the cockpit. It took Gamache a moment to put it all together. The quiet, somber, solitary man he'd met, the man who watched their plane fly away, had arrested Esther.

"And now he's a Watchman, guarding the last of the totem poles," said Gamache.

"We all guard something," said Sommes.

Sergeant Minshall had left a message for him at the guesthouse, and an envelope. Over a lunch of fresh fish and canned corn, he opened it and drew out more photographs, printed from the sergeant's computer. And there was an e-mail.

Armand,

We've tracked down four of the remaining carvings. There are two we still can't find, the one Olivier sold on eBay and one of the ones auctioned in Geneva. None of the collectors has agreed to send us the actual work of art, but they did send photos (see attached). No other carving has printing underneath.

Jérôme continues to work on your code. No luck yet.

What do you make of these pictures? Quite shocking, don't you think?

I've been working on the items from the cabin. So far none has been reported stolen and I can't seem to find a connection among them. I thought a gold bracelet might be Czech, but turns out to be Dacian. An astonishing find. Predates the current Romanians.

But it's very odd. The items don't seem to be related. Unless that's the key? Will have to think about it some more. I'm trying to keep the lid on these finds, but already I'm getting calls from around the world. News agencies, museums. Can't imagine how the word spread, but it has. Mostly about the Amber Room. Wait until they find out about the rest.

I hear you're on the Queen Charlotte Islands. Lucky man. If you meet Will Sommes tell him I adore his work. He's a recluse, so I doubt you'll see him.

Thérèse Brunel

He pulled out the photographs and looked at them as he ate. By the time the coconut cream pie arrived he'd been over them all. He'd laid them out on the table in a fan in front of him. And now he stared.

The tone of them had shifted. In one the figures seemed to be loading up carts, packing their homes. They seemed excited. Except the young man, who was gesturing anxiously to them to hurry. But in the next there seemed a growing unease among the people. And the last two were very different. In one the people were no longer walking. They were in huts, homes. But a few figures looked out the windows. Wary. Not afraid. Not yet. That was saved for the very last one Superintendent Brunel sent. It was the largest carving and the figures were standing and staring. Up. At Gamache, it seemed.

It was the oddest perspective. It made the viewer feel like part of the work. And not a pleasant part. He felt as though he was the reason they were so afraid.

Because they were, now. What had Will Sommes said the night before, when he'd spotted the boy huddled inside the ship?

Not just afraid, but terrified.

Something terrible had found the people in his carvings. And something terrible had found their creator.

What was odd was that Gamache couldn't see the boy in the last two carvings. He asked the landlady for a magnifying glass and feeling like Sherlock Holmes he leaned over and minutely examined the photographs. But nothing.

Leaning back in his chair he sipped his tea. The coconut cream pie remained untouched. Whatever terror had taken the happiness from the carvings had also stolen his appetite.

Sergeant Minshall joined him a few minutes later and they walked once more through town, stopping at Greeley's Construction.

"What can I do for you?" An older man, beard and hair and eyes all gray, but his body green and powerful.

"We wanted to talk to you about some of the workers you might've had back in the eighties and early nineties," said Sergeant Minshall.

"You're kidding. You know loggers. They come and go. Especially then."

"Why especially then, monsieur?" asked Gamache.

"This is Chief Inspector Gamache, of the Sûreté du Québec." Minshall introduced the men and they shook hands. Gamache had the definite impression that Greeley wasn't a man to be crossed.

"Long way from home," said Greeley.

"I am. But I'm being made to feel most welcome. What was so special about that time?"

"The late eighties and early nineties? Are you kidding? Ever heard of Lyall Island? The roadblocks, the protests? There're thousands of acres of forest and the Haida suddenly get all upset about the logging. You didn't hear about it?"

"I did, but I wasn't here. Maybe you can tell me what happened."

"It wasn't the Haida's fault. They were wound up by the shit-disturbers. Those über-environmentalists. Terrorists, nothing more. They recruited a bunch of thugs and kids who just wanted attention. It had nothing to do with the forests. Listen, it wasn't like we were killing people, or even killing animals. We were taking down trees. Which grow back. And we were the biggest employer around. But the environmentalists got the Haida all worked up. Fed the kids a bunch of bullshit."

Beside Gamache, Sergeant Minshall shifted his feet. But said nothing.

"And yet the average age of the arrested Haida was seventy-six," said Gamache. "The elders placed themselves between the young protesters and you."

"A stunt. Means nothing," Greeley snapped. "I thought you said you didn't know anything about it."

"I said I wasn't here. I've read the reports, but it's not the same thing."

"Fucking right. Media swallowed it whole. We looked like the bad guys and all we were trying to do was log a few hundred acres that we had a right to."

Greeley's voice was rising. The wound, the rage, wasn't far beneath the surface.

"There was violence?" asked Gamache.

"Some. Bound to be. But we never started it. We just wanted to do our jobs."

"A lot of people came and went at that time? Loggers and protesters, I suppose."

"People crawling all over the place. And you want help finding one?" Greeley snorted. "What was his name?"

"I don't know." Gamache ignored the derisive laugh from Greeley and his people. Instead he showed the photo of the dead man. "He might have spoken with a Czech accent." Greeley looked at it and handed it back.

"Please look more closely," said the Chief Inspector.

The two men stared at each other for a moment.

"Perhaps if you stared at the picture instead of me, monsieur." His voice, while reasonable, was also hard.

Greeley took it back and looked longer. "Don't know him. He might've been here but who can tell? He'd have been a lot younger too, of course. Frankly he doesn't look like a logger or any forester. Too small."

It was the first helpful thing Greeley had said. Gamache glanced again at the dead recluse. Three sorts of visitors were on the Queen Charlottes in that time. Loggers, environmentalists, and artists. It seemed most likely this man was the latter. He thanked Greeley and left.

Once on the street he looked at his watch. If he could get Lavina to fly him to Prince Rupert he could still catch the red-eye to Montreal. But Gamache took a moment to make one more call.

"Monsieur Sommes?"

"Yes, Chief Inspector. Do you suspect your man might have been an eco-terrorist now?"

"*Voyons*, how did you know?"

Will Sommes laughed. "How can I help you?"

"John the Watchman showed me his cabin in the woods. Have you seen it?"

"I have."

"It's exactly the same as our dead man's home, across the country, in the woods of Quebec."

There was a pause on the line. "Monsieur Sommes?" Gamache wasn't sure if he'd lost the connection.

"I'm afraid that can't mean much. My cabin is also the same. All of them are, with very few exceptions. Sorry to disappoint you."

Gamache hung up, anything but disappointed. He knew one thing now without question. The Hermit had been on the Queen Charlotte Islands.

Chief Inspector Gamache only just managed to make the red-eye flight out of Vancouver. He squeezed into his middle seat and as soon as the plane took off the man in front put his seat all the way back until he was almost on Gamache's lap. The two people on either side each claimed an arm rest, and that left the Chief Inspector seven hours to listen to the little boy across the aisle play GI Joe.

He put on his half-moon glasses and read more about Emily Carr, her art, her travels, her "brutal telling." He stared at her paintings of the Queen Charlotte Islands, and appreciated even more the powerful, poetic images. He stared longest at her paintings of Ninstints. She'd captured it just before the fall, when the totems were tall and straight and the longhouses weren't yet covered by moss.

Flying over Winnipeg he pulled out the photographs of the Hermit's sculptures.

He looked at them, letting his mind drift. In the background the boy had developed an entire intricate story of war and attack and heroics. Gamache thought about Beauvoir back in Three Pines, hounded by an onslaught of facts, and Ruth Zardo's words. He closed his eyes and rested his head, thinking of the couplets Ruth kept sending, as though poetry was a weapon, which of course, it was. For her.

> *and pick your soul up gently by the nape of the neck*
> *and caress you into darkness and paradise.*

How beautiful was that, thought Gamache, drifting off to an uneasy sleep as Air Canada flew him home. And just as he nodded off another couplet floated up.

> *that the deity who kills for pleasure*
> *will also heal,*

By the time they were flying over Toronto Gamache knew what the carvings meant, and what he had to do next.

THIRTY-FOUR

 While Gamache had been in the mist of the Queen Charlotte Islands Clara had been in her own sort of fog. She'd spent the day circling the telephone, getting closer and closer then shooting away.

Peter watched all this from his studio. He no longer knew what he hoped would happen. That Clara would call Fortin, or not. He no longer knew what would be best. For her, for himself.

Peter stared at the picture on his easel. Picking up his brush, he dipped it in paint and approached. Determined to give it the detail people expected from his works. The complexity. The layers.

He added a single dot, then stepped back.

"Oh, God," he sighed and stared at the fresh dot on the white canvas.

Clara was once again approaching the telephone, via the refrigerator. Chocolate milk in one hand and Oreo cookies in the other she stared at the phone.

Was she being willful? Obstinate? Or was she standing up for what she believed in? Was she a hero or a bitch? Strange how often it was hard to tell.

She went into the garden and weeded without enthusiasm for a few minutes, then showered, changed, kissed Peter good-bye, got in her car and drove to Montreal. To the Galerie Fortin, to pick up her portfolio.

On the way home she made a last-minute detour, to visit Miss Emily Carr. Clara stared at the sculpture of the frumpy, eccentric woman with the horse and the dog and the monkey. And conviction in the face of a brutal telling.

Inspector Beauvoir met Gamache at Trudeau Airport.

"Any word from Superintendent Brunel?" the Chief Inspector asked as Beauvoir tossed his case into the backseat.

"She found one more carving. Some guy in Moscow has it. Won't let it out of his hands but he sent some pictures." Beauvoir handed an envelope to the Chief Inspector. "You? What did you find out?"

"Did you realize the lines Ruth's given you are all part of a single poem?"

"You found that out on the Queen Charlotte Islands?"

"Indirectly. Have you kept them?"

"The scraps of paper? Of course not. Why? Are they important to the case?"

Gamache sighed. He was weary. He had a distance to go that day and he couldn't afford a stumble. Not now.

"No. I suppose not. But it's a shame to lose them."

"Yeah, you say that. Just wait until she turns her pen on you."

" . . . *and pick your soul up gently by the nape of the neck and caress you into darkness and paradise*," Gamache whispered.

"Where to?" Beauvoir asked as they bumped along the road toward Three Pines.

"The bistro. We need to speak to Olivier again. You looked into his finances?"

"He's worth about four million. One and a half from the sales of the carvings, a little over a million from the antiques the Hermit gave him and his property's worth about a million. We're not much further along," said Beauvoir, grimly.

But Gamache knew they were very close indeed. And he knew this was when the ground either became solid, or fell out from beneath them.

The car glided to a stop in front of the bistro. The Chief Inspector had been so quiet in the passenger seat Beauvoir thought maybe he was catching a nap. He looked tired, and who wouldn't after the long flight on Air Canada? The carrier that charged for everything. Beauvoir was convinced there'd soon be a credit card slot next to the emergency oxygen.

The Inspector looked over and sure enough Gamache's head was down and his eyes closed. Beauvoir hated to disturb him, he looked so peaceful. Then he noticed the Chief's thumb softly rubbing the picture he held loosely in his hand. Beauvoir looked more closely. The Chief's eyes weren't closed, not altogether.

They were narrow and staring intently at the image in his hand.

On it was the carving of a mountain. Barren, desolate. As though it had been clear-cut. Just a few scraggly pines at its base. There was a sadness about it, Gamache felt, an emptiness. And yet there was something about this work that was very different from the others. There was also a kind of levity. He narrowed his eyes and peering closer he saw it. What he'd mistaken for another pine at the foot of the mountain wasn't.

It was a young man. A boy, stepping hesitantly onto the base of the carving.

And where he stepped, some seedlings sprouted.

It reminded him of Clara's painting of Ruth. Capturing that moment when despair turned to hope. This remarkable carving was forlorn, but also strangely hopeful. And without needing to look any closer Gamache knew this boy was the one in the other works. But the fear was gone. Or had it not yet arrived?

Rosa quacked on the village green. Today she wore a pale pink sweater set. And pearls?

"*Voyons*," said Beauvoir, jerking his head toward the duck as they got out of the car. "Can you imagine listening to that all day long?"

"Wait till you have kids," said Gamache, pausing outside the bistro to watch Rosa and Ruth.

"They quack?"

"No, but they sure make noise. And other things. Are you planning on kids?"

"Maybe one day. Enid isn't keen." He stood next to the Chief and they both stared at the peaceful village. Peaceful except for the quacking. "Any word from Daniel?"

"Madame Gamache spoke to them yesterday. All's well. Baby should be along in a couple of weeks. We'll be going to Paris as soon as it happens."

Beauvoir nodded. "That's two for Daniel. How about Annie? Any plans?"

"None. I think David would like a family but Annie's not good with kids."

"I saw her with Florence," said Beauvoir, remembering when Daniel had visited with the Chief Inspector's granddaughter. He'd watched Annie holding her niece, singing to her. "She adores Florence."

"She claims not to want any. Frankly we don't want to push her."

"Best not to interfere."

"It's not that. We saw what a balls-up she made of every babysitting job she had as a kid. As soon as the child cried Annie called us and we'd have to go over. We made more money babysitting than she did. And Jean Guy." Gamache leaned toward his Inspector and lowered his voice. "Without going into details, whatever happens never let Annie diaper me."

"She asked the same thing of me," Beauvoir said and saw Gamache smile. Then the smile dimmed.

"Shall we?" The Chief gestured to the door to the bistro.

The four men chose to sit away from the windows. In the cool and quiet interior. A small fire muttered in both open fireplaces, at either end of the room. Gamache remembered the first time he'd walked into the bistro years before and seen the mismatched furniture, the armchairs and wing chairs and Windsor chairs. The round and square and rectangular tables. The stone fireplaces and wooden beams. And the price tags hanging from everything.

Everything was for sale. And everyone? Gamache didn't think so, but sometimes he wondered.

"*Bon Dieu*, are you saying you haven't told your father about me?" Gabri asked.

"I did. I told him I was with a Gabriel."

"Your father thinks it's a Gabrielle you're with," said Beauvoir.

"*Quoi?*" said Gabri, glaring at Olivier. "He thinks I'm a woman? That means . . ." Gabri looked at his partner, incredulous. "He doesn't know you're gay?"

"I never told him."

"Maybe not in so many words, but you sure told him," said Gabri, then turned to Beauvoir. "Almost forty, not married, an antiques dealer. Good God, he told me when the other kids would dig for China he dug for Royal Doulton. How gay is that?" He turned back to Olivier. "You had an Easy Bake oven and you sewed your own Halloween costumes."

"I haven't told him and don't plan to," Olivier snapped. "It's none of his business."

"What a family," sighed Gabri. "It's actually a perfect fit. One doesn't want to know and the other doesn't want to tell."

But Gamache knew it was more than simply not wanting to tell. It was about a little boy with secrets. Who became a big boy with secrets. Who became a man. He brought an envelope out of his satchel and placed seven photographs on the table in front of Olivier. Then he unwrapped the carvings and put them on the table too.

"What order do they go in?"

"I can't remember which he gave me when," said Olivier. Gamache stared at him then spoke softly.

"I didn't ask you that. I asked what order they go in. You know, don't you?"

"I don't know what you mean." Olivier looked confused.

Then Armand Gamache did something Beauvoir had rarely seen. He brought his large hand down so hard on the table the little wooden figures jumped. As did the men.

"Enough. I've had enough."

And he looked it. His face was hard, carved and sharp and burnished by lies and secrets. "Do you have any idea what trouble you're in?" His voice was low, strained, forced through a throat that threatened to close. "The lies must stop now. If you have any hope, any hope at all, you must tell us the truth. Now."

Gamache moved his splayed hand over the photographs and shoved them toward Olivier, who stared as though petrified.

"I don't know," he stumbled.

"For God's sake, Olivier, please," Gabri begged.

Gamache radiated anger now. Anger, frustration and fear that the real murderer would slip away, hiding in another man's lies. Olivier and the Chief Inspector stared at each other. One man who spent his life burying secrets and the other who spent his life unearthing them.

Their partners stared, aware of the battle but unable to help.

"The truth, Olivier," Gamache rasped.

"How did you know?"

"The place of wonders. Ninstints on the Queen Charlotte Islands. The totem poles told me."

"They told you?"

"In their way. Each image built on the last. Each told its own story and was a wonder unto itself. But when taken as a whole they told a larger story."

Beauvoir, listening to this, thought about Ruth's couplets. The Chief had told him they did the same thing. If put together, in the right order, they too would tell a story. His hand slipped into his pocket and touched the scrap of paper shoved under his door that morning.

"What story do these tell, Olivier?" Gamache repeated. It had actually come to him on the plane as he'd listened to the little boy and the intricate GI Joe world he created. He'd thought about the case, thought about the Haida, the Watchman. Who, driven by his conscience, had finally found peace. In the wilderness.

The Chief Inspector suspected the same thing had happened to the Hermit. He'd gone into the forest a greedy man, to hide. But he'd been found. Years ago. By himself. And so he used his money as insulation and toilet paper. He used his first editions for knowledge and companionship. He used his antiquities as everyday dishes.

And in that wilderness he found freedom and happiness. And peace.

But something still eluded him. Or, perhaps more to the point, something still clung to him. He'd unburdened himself of the "things" of his life, but one more burden remained. The truth.

And so he decided to tell it to someone. Olivier. But he couldn't go quite that far. Instead, he hid the truth in a fable, an allegory.

"He made me promise never to tell." Olivier had dropped his head and spoke into his lap.

"And you didn't. Not while he was alive. But you need to tell now."

Without another word Olivier reached out and moved the photographs about, hesitating briefly over a couple, switching the order at least once. Until finally, spread in front of them, was the Hermit's story.

And then Olivier told them, placing his hand over each image as he spoke. And as Olivier's soft, almost hypnotic voice filled the space between them Gamache could see the dead man, alive again. In his cabin late at night. His one visitor sitting across the flickering fireplace. Listening, to this tale of hubris, of punishment and love. And betrayal.

Gamache watched as the villagers, happy in their ignorance, left their homes. And the young man raced ahead, clutching his small package, encouraging them to hurry. Toward paradise, they thought. But the boy knew differently. He'd stolen the Mountain's treasure.

And worse.

He'd stolen the Mountain's trust.

Now each figure the Hermit had carved took on a significance. The men and women waiting by the shore, having run out of land. And the boy, cowering, having run out of hope.

Then the ship arrived, sent by gods jealous of the Mountain.

But behind was the ever-present shadow. And the threat of something unseen but very real. The ghastly army, assembled by the Mountain. Made up of Fury and Vengeance, promising catastrophe. Fueled by Rage. And behind them the Mountain itself. That couldn't be stopped and wouldn't be denied.

It would find all the villagers and it would find the young man. And it would find the treasure he'd stolen.

As this army pressed forward it provoked wars and famine, floods and plagues. It laid waste to the world. Chaos led the army and chaos was left behind.

Beauvoir listened to this. His hand in his pocket scrunched Ruth's latest couplet and he could feel it damp with sweat. He looked down at the photos of the carvings and saw the happy, ignorant villagers slowly transformed as they too first sensed something approaching, then knew it.

And he shared their horror.

Finally the wars and famine arrived on the shores of the New World. For years the wars raged around their new home, not quite touching it. But then . . .

They all looked at the final image. Of the villagers bunched together. Emaciated, their clothing in tatters. Looking up. In terror.

At them.

Olivier's voice stopped. The story stopped.

"Go on," whispered Gamache.

"That's it."

"What about the boy?" asked Gabri. "He's not in the carvings anymore. Where'd he go?"

"He buried himself in the forest, knowing the Mountain would find the villagers."

"He betrayed them too? His own family? His friends?" asked Beauvoir.

Olivier nodded. "But there was something else."

"What?"

"Something was behind the Mountain. Something driving it on. Something that terrified even the Mountain."

"Worse than Chaos? Worse than death?" asked Gabri.

"Worse than anything."

"What was it?" Gamache asked.

"I don't know. The Hermit died before we got that far. But I think he carved it."

"What do you mean?" asked Beauvoir.

"There was something in a canvas sack that he never showed me. But he saw me looking at it. I couldn't help myself. He'd laugh and say one day he'd show it to me."

"And when you found the Hermit dead?" asked Gamache.

"It was gone."

"Why didn't you tell us this before?" snapped Beauvoir.

"Because then I'd have to admit everything. That I knew him, that I'd taken the carvings and sold them. It was his way of ensuring I'd come back, you know. Parceling out bits of his treasure."

"A pusher to an addict," said Gabri, with no rancor, but with no surprise either.

"Like Sheherazade."

Everyone turned to Gamache.

"Who?" Gabri asked.

"It's an opera, by Rimsky-Korsakov. It tells the story of the Thousand and One Nights."

They looked blank.

"The king would take a wife at night and kill her in the morning," said the Chief Inspector. "One night he chose Sheherazade. She knew his habits and knew she was in trouble so she came up with a plan."

"Kill the king?" asked Gabri.

"Better. Every night she told him a story, but left it unfinished. If he wanted to know the ending he had to keep her alive."

"Was the Hermit doing it to save his life?" asked Beauvoir, confused.

"In a way, I suppose," said the Chief. "Like the Mountain, he longed for company, and perhaps he knew Olivier well enough to realize the only way to get him to keep coming back was to promise more."

"That's not fair. You make me sound like a whore. I did more than take his things. I helped him garden and brought supplies. He got a lot out of it."

"He did. But so did you." Gamache folded his large hands together and looked at Olivier. "Who was the dead man?"

"He made me promise."

"And secrets are important to you. I understand that. You've been a good friend to the Hermit. But you have to tell us now."

"He was from Czechoslovakia," said Olivier at last. "His name was Jakob. I never knew his last name. He came here just as the Berlin wall was falling. I don't think we understood how chaotic it was. I remember thinking how exciting it must have been for the people. To finally have freedom. But he described something else. Every system they knew collapsed. It was lawless. Nothing worked. The phones, the rail service. Planes fell out of the air. He said it was horrible. But it was also a perfect time to run. To get out."

"He brought everything in that cabin with him?"

Olivier nodded. "For American money, hard currency he called it, you could arrange anything. He had contacts with antiques dealers here so he sold them some of his stuff and used the money to bribe officials in Czechoslovakia. To get his things out. He put them on a container ship and got them to the Port of Montreal. Then he put them all in storage and waited."

"For what?"

"To find a home."

"He first went to the Queen Charlotte Islands, didn't he?" said Gamache. After a pause Olivier nodded. "But he didn't stay there," Gamache continued. "He wanted peace and quiet, but the protests began and people came from all over the world. So he left. Came back here. Close to his treasures. And he decided to find a place in Quebec. In the woods here."

Again Olivier nodded.

"Why Three Pines?" Beauvoir asked.

Olivier shook his head, "I don't know. I asked, but he wouldn't tell me."

"Then what happened?" Gamache asked.

"As I said before, he came down here and started to build his cabin. When it was ready he got the things out of storage and put them there. It took a while, but he had the time."

"The treasures that he got out of Czechoslovakia, were they his?" Gamache asked.

"I never asked, and he never told me, but I don't think they were. He was just too afraid. I know he was hiding from something. Someone. But I don't know who."

"Do you have any idea how much time you've wasted? My God, what were you thinking?" demanded Beauvoir.

"I just kept thinking you'd find who'd killed him and none of this other stuff needed to come out."

"Other stuff?" said Beauvoir. "Is that how you think of it? As though it was all just details? How'd you think we'd find the murderer with you lying and letting us hare off all over the place?"

Gamache raised his hand slightly and with an effort Beauvoir pulled back, taking a deep breath.

"Tell us about Woo," Gamache asked.

Olivier lifted his head, his eyes strained. He was pale and gaunt and had aged twenty years in a week. "I thought you'd said it was that monkey that belonged to Emily Carr."

"I thought so too, but I've been thinking about it. I think it meant something else to the dead man. Something more personal. Frightening. I think it was left in the web, and carved, as a threat. Something maybe only he and his murderer understood."

"Then why ask me?"

"Because Jakob might have told you. Did he, Olivier?"

Gamache's eyes bored into Olivier's, insisting on the truth.

"He told me nothing," said Olivier at last.

Disbelief met this remark.

Gamache stared at him, trying with his considerable might to look beyond the mist of lies. Was Olivier finally telling the truth?

Gamache got up. At the door he turned and looked back at the two men. Olivier drained, empty. Nothing left. At least, Gamache hoped there was nothing left. Each lie was like ripping off a piece of Olivier's skin, until finally he sat in the bistro, torn to pieces.

"What happened to the young man?" asked Gamache. "The one in the story. Did the Mountain find him?"

"It must have. He's dead, isn't he?" said Olivier.

THIRTY-FIVE

At the B and B Gamache showered and shaved and changed his clothing. He glanced briefly at his bed, with its clean, crisp sheets and the duvet turned back. Waiting for him. But he avoided that siren song and before long he and Beauvoir were back across the village green and at the Incident Room, where Agents Lacoste and Morin waited.

They sat round the conference table, mugs of strong coffee and the Hermit's carvings in front of them. Succinctly the Chief Inspector told them about his trip to the Queen Charlottes and their interview with Olivier.

"So the dead man was telling a story all along. With his carvings," said Lacoste.

"Let's walk through this," said Beauvoir, going over to the sheets of paper on the wall. "The Hermit gets out of Czechoslovakia with the treasures just as the Soviet Union's crumbling. It's chaos there so he bribes port officials to get the goods shipped to the Port of Montreal. Once there he puts them into storage."

"If he was a refugee or an immigrant his fingerprints would've shown up on record," said Agent Morin.

Agent Lacoste turned to him. He was young, she knew, and inexperienced. "There're illegal immigrants all over Canada. Some hiding, some with false papers that pass for real. A little money to the right people."

"So he snuck in," said Morin. "But what about the antiques? Were they stolen? Where'd he get them? Like the violin, and that Amber Room thing?"

"Superintendent Brunel says the Amber Room disappeared in the

Second World War," said Gamache. "There're a lot of theories about what happened to it, including that it was hidden by Albert Speer in a mountain range. Between Germany and Czechoslovakia."

"Really?" said Lacoste, her mind working rapidly. "Suppose this Jakob found it?"

"If he found it he'd have the whole thing," said Beauvoir. "Suppose someone else found it, or part of it, and sold it to the Hermit."

"Suppose," said Morin, "he stole it."

"Suppose," said Gamache, "you're all right. Suppose someone found it, maybe decades ago. And split it up. And all that was left to one family was the one pane. Suppose that pane was entrusted to the Hermit, to smuggle out of the country."

"Why?" asked Lacoste, leaning forward.

"So they could start a new life," Beauvoir jumped in. "They wouldn't be the first who smuggled a family treasure out and sold it to start a business or buy a home in Canada."

"So they gave it to the Hermit to get out of the country," said Morin.

"Did it all come from different people?" wondered Lacoste. "A book here, a piece of priceless furniture or glass or silver there? Suppose all his things came from different people, all hoping to start a new life here? And he smuggled it all out."

"It would answer Superintendent Brunel's question about why there's such a range of items," said Gamache. "It's not from one collection, but many."

"No one would trust anyone with things that valuable," said Beauvoir.

"Maybe they had no choice," said the Chief. "They needed to get them out of the country. If he was a stranger they might not have trusted him. But if he was a friend . . ."

"Like the boy in the story," said Beauvoir. "Betraying everyone who trusted him."

They stared ahead. Silent. Morin had never realized murderers were caught in silence. But they were.

What would have happened? Families waited in Prague, in smaller cities and towns and villages. Waiting for word. From their trusted friend. At what stage did hope turn to despair? And finally to rage? And revenge?

Had one of them made it out, come across to the New World, and found the Hermit?

"But why did he come here?" asked Agent Morin.

"Why not?" asked Beauvoir.

"Well, there's a big Czech population here. If he was bringing all sorts of stolen goods, stuff he'd taken from people in Czechoslovakia, wouldn't he stay as far away from them as possible?"

They appealed to Gamache, who was listening, and thinking. Then he sat forward and drew the photographs of the carvings to him. Particularly the one of the happy people building a new village, in their new home. Without the young man.

"Maybe Olivier isn't the only one who lies," he said, getting up. "Maybe the Hermit wasn't alone when he came here. Maybe he had accomplices."

"Who are still in Three Pines," said Beauvoir.

Hanna Parra was clearing up lunch. She'd made a hearty soup and the place smelled of her mother's home in her Czech village. Of broth and parsley and bay leaves, and garden vegetables.

Her own gleaming metal and glass home couldn't be more different from the wooden chalet she'd grown up in. Full of wonderful aromas, and a hint of fear. Fear of attracting attention. Of standing out. Her parents, her aunts, her neighbors, had all lived comfortable lives of conformity. The fear of being found different, though, created a thin film between people.

But here everything really was transparent. She'd felt light as soon as they'd arrived in Canada. Where people minded their own business.

Or so she thought. Her hand hovered over the marble counter as some glint in the sun caught her eye. A car rolling up the drive.

Armand Gamache stared at the glass and metal cube in front of him. He'd read reports of the interviews with the Parras, including descriptions of their home, but still it took him aback.

The house gleamed in the sun. Not blinding, but it seemed to glow as though it lived in a world slightly different from theirs. A world of light.

"It's beautiful," said Gamache, almost under his breath.

"You should see inside."

"I think I should," Gamache nodded and the two men strolled across the yard.

Hanna Parra let them in and took their coats. "Chief Inspector, this is a pleasure."

Her voice was slightly accented but her French was perfect. Someone who'd not just learned the language but loved it. And it showed with every syllable. Gamache knew it was impossible to split language from culture. That without one the other withered. To love the language was to respect the culture.

That was why he'd learned English so well.

"We'd like to speak to your husband and son as well, if possible."

He spoke gently but somehow the very civility of the man lent his words weight.

"Havoc's out in the woods, but Roar's here."

"Where in the woods, madame?" Beauvoir asked.

Hanna seemed slightly flustered. "Out back. Cutting deadwood for the winter."

"Can you get him in, please?" said Beauvoir. His attempts at politeness simply made him seem sinister.

"We don't know where he is."

The voice came from behind them and both men turned to see Roar standing in the doorway to the mudroom. He was four-square, stocky and powerful. His hands were on his hips and his elbows out, like a threatened animal trying to make itself appear larger.

"Then perhaps we can speak to you," said Gamache.

Roar didn't budge.

"Please, come into the kitchen," said Hanna. "It's warmer there."

She led them deeper into the house and shot Roar a warning look as she passed.

The kitchen was filled with natural warmth from the sun that spilled in.

"*Mais, c'est formidable*," Gamache said. Out of the floor-to-ceiling windows he could see field then forest and in the distance St. Thomas's steeple, in Three Pines. It felt as though they were living in nature, that the house was no intrusion at all. It was unexpected, certainly unusual. But it wasn't foreign. Just the opposite. This home belonged here. It was perfect.

"*Félicitations*." He turned to the Parras. "This is a magnificent achievement. It must've been something you'd dreamed of for a long time."

Roar dropped his arms and indicated a seat at the glass table. Gamache accepted.

"We talked about it for a while. It wasn't my first choice. I wanted something more traditional."

Gamache looked at Hanna, who'd taken the chair at the head of the table. "Must've taken some convincing," he smiled.

"He did," she said, returning his smile. Hers was polite, without warmth or humor. "Took years. There'd been a cabin on the property and we lived there until Havoc was about six, but he was growing and I wanted a place that felt like ours."

"*Je comprends*, but why this?"

"You don't like it?" She didn't sound defensive, only interested.

"Just the reverse. I think it really is magnificent. It feels as though it belongs here. But you must admit, it's unusual. No one else has a place quite like it."

"We wanted something completely different from where we grew up. We wanted a change."

"We?" asked Gamache.

"I came around," said Roar, his voice hard, his eyes wary. "What's all this about?"

Gamache nodded and sat forward, splaying his large hands on the cool surface of the table. "Why did your son work for Olivier?"

"He needs the money," said Hanna. Gamache nodded.

"I understand. But wouldn't he make more money working in the woods? Or working construction? Surely a waiter is paid very little, even with the tips."

"Why're you asking us?" Hanna asked.

"Well, I would ask him, if he were here."

Roar and Hanna exchanged glances.

"Havoc takes after his mother," said Roar finally. "He looks like me, but has his mother's temperament. He likes people. He enjoys working in the woods but prefers working with people. The bistro suits him perfectly. He's happy there."

Gamache nodded slowly.

"Havoc worked late at the bistro every night," said Beauvoir. "What time did he get home?"

"About one, rarely later."

"But sometimes later?" Beauvoir asked.

"Sometimes, I guess," said Roar. "I didn't wait up."

"I imagine you did." Beauvoir turned to Hanna.

"I did," she admitted. "But I can't remember him ever coming home after one thirty. If customers were late, especially if there was a party, he'd have to clean up, so he'd be a little later than usual, but never much."

"Be careful, madame," said Gamache quietly.

"Careful?"

"We need the truth."

"You're getting the truth, Chief Inspector," said Roar.

"I hope so. Who was the dead man?"

"Why do you people keep asking us that?" asked Hanna. "We didn't know him."

"His name was Jakob," said Beauvoir. "He was Czech."

"I see," said Roar, his face twisting in anger. "And all Czech people know each other? Do you have any idea how insulting that is?"

Armand Gamache leaned toward him. "It's not insulting. It's human nature. If I lived in Prague I'd gravitate to the Québécois there, especially at first. He came here more than a decade ago and built a cabin in the woods. He filled it with treasures. Do you know where they might have come from?"

"How would we know?"

"We think he might have stolen them from people back in Czechoslovakia."

"And because they came from Czechoslovakia we'd know about it?"

"If he'd stolen the things do you really think the first thing he'd do is come to a potluck dinner with the Czech Association?" Hanna demanded. "We don't know this Jakob."

"What did you do before you came here?" Gamache asked them.

"We were both students. We met at Charles University in Prague," said Hanna. "I was studying political science and Roar was studying engineering."

"You're a councilor for the area," said Gamache to Hanna, then turned to Roar. "But you don't seem to have pursued your interests here. Why not?"

Parra paused, then looked down at his large, rough hands, picking at a callus. "I was fed up with people. Wanted nothing to do with them. Why do you think there's a huge Czech community out here, away from cities? It's because we're sickened by what people can do. People goaded by others, emboldened. Infected by cynicism and fear and suspicion. By jealousy and greed. They turn on each other. I want nothing to do with them. Let me work quietly in a garden, in the woods. People are horrible creatures. You must know that, Chief Inspector. You've seen what they can do to each other."

"I have," Gamache admitted. He stopped talking for a moment, and in that moment lived all the terrible things the head of homicide might see. "I know what people are capable of." He smiled then, and spoke quietly. "The bad, but also the good. I've seen sacrifice, and I've seen forgiveness where none seemed possible. Goodness exists, Monsieur Parra. Believe me."

And for a moment it seemed Roar Parra might. He stared wide-eyed at Gamache as though the large, calm man was inviting him into a home he longed to enter. But then he stepped back.

"You're a fool, Chief Inspector," he laughed derisively.

"But a happy one," smiled Gamache. "Now, what were we talking about? Ah, yes. Murder."

"Whose car's in the driveway?" The young voice floated to them from the mudroom and a moment later a door slammed shut.

Beauvoir stood up. Hanna and Roar also rose and stared at each other. Gamache went to the door of the kitchen.

"It's my car, Havoc. Can we have a word?"

"Sure."

The young man walked into the kitchen, taking off his cap. His face was sweaty and dirty and he smiled disarmingly. "Why so serious?" Then his expression changed. "There hasn't been another murder, has there?"

"Why'd you say that?" asked Gamache, watching him.

"Well, you all look so glum. I feel like it's report card day."

"In a way it is, I guess. Time to take stock." Gamache pointed to a chair next to Havoc's father and the young man sat. Gamache also sat.

"You and Olivier were the last people in the bistro last Saturday night?"

"That's right. Olivier left and I locked up."

"And where did Olivier go?"

"Home, I guess." Havoc looked amused by the question.

"We know now that Olivier visited the Hermit late at night. Saturday nights."

"Is that right?"

"That's right." The young man's composure was a little too perfect. A little too practiced, Gamache thought. "But someone else knew about the Hermit. Not just Olivier. There are a couple of ways Jakob could have been found. One was to follow the overgrown horse trails. The other was to follow Olivier. To the cabin."

Havoc's smile faltered. "Are you saying I followed Olivier?" The young man looked from Gamache to his parents, searching their faces, and back again.

"Where were you just now?"

"In the woods."

Gamache nodded slowly. "Doing what?"

"Cutting wood."

"And yet we heard no saw."

"I'd already cut it and was just stacking it." Now the boy's eyes moved more quickly from Gamache to his father and back.

Gamache got up, walked a couple of steps to the door to the kitchen, bent down and picked something up. He sat back down and placed it on the polished table. It was a wood chip. No. A shaving. It curled back on itself.

"How did you afford this house?" Gamache asked Roar.

"What do you mean?" Roar asked.

"It would cost hundreds of thousands of dollars. The materials alone are worth that. Add in designs and specifications for such an unusual house, then labor? You say you built it about fifteen years ago. What happened then that allowed you to do it? Where'd you get the money?"

"What do you think happened?" Roar leaned in to the Chief Inspector. "You Québécois, so insular. What happened all those years ago? Let's see. There was a sovereignty referendum in Quebec, there was a huge forest fire in Abitibi, there was an election in the province. Nothing much else to report."

The shaving on the table trembled as his words brushed past on their way to Gamache.

"I've had it," Roar said. "God, how can you not know what happened back then?"

"Czechoslovakia broke up," said Gamache. "And became Slovakia and the Czech Republic. That actually happened twenty years ago, but the impact can take time. Those walls came down, and these ones," he glanced at the bank of glass, "went up."

"We could see our families again," said Hanna. "So many of the things we left behind we could have again. Family, friends."

"Art, silver, heirlooms," said Beauvoir.

"Do you think those things mattered?" asked Hanna. "We'd lived without them for so long. It was the people we missed, not the things. We barely dared hope it was real. We'd been fooled before. The summer of '68. And certainly the reports we were seeing in the West were different from the stories we heard from people back home. Here we only heard how wonderful it was. We saw people waving flags and singing. But my cousins and aunts told a different story. The old system was horrible. Corrupt, brutal. But it was at least a system. When it went they were left with nothing. A vacuum. Chaos."

Gamache tilted his head slightly at the word. Chaos. Again.

"It was terrifying. People were being beaten, murdered, robbed, and there were no cops, no courts."

"A good time to smuggle things out," said Beauvoir.

"We wanted to sponsor our cousins but they decided to stay," said Roar.

"And my aunt wanted to stay with them, of course."

"Of course," said Gamache. "If not people, what about things?"

After a moment Hanna nodded. "We managed to get some family heirlooms out. My mother and father hid them after the war and told us they were to be kept for barter, for bargaining, if things got bad."

"Things got bad," said Gamache.

"We smuggled them out and sold them. So that we could build the home of our dreams," said Hanna. "We struggled with that decision a long time, but finally I realized both my parents would understand and approve. They were only things. Home is what matters."

"What did you have?" asked Beauvoir.

"Some paintings, some good furniture, some icons. We needed a house more than we needed an icon," said Hanna.

"Who did you sell them to?"

"A dealer in New York. A friend of a friend. I can give you his name. He took a small commission but got a fair price," said Parra.

"Please. I'd like to speak to him. You certainly made good use of the money." The Chief Inspector turned to Roar. "Are you a carpenter too?"

"I do some."

"And you?" Gamache asked Havoc, who shrugged. "I'll need more than that."

"I do some."

Gamache reached out and slowly pushed the wood shaving along the glass table until it sat in front of Havoc. He waited.

"I was in the woods whittling," admitted Havoc. "When I finish my work I like to sit quietly and shave down a piece of wood. It's relaxing. A chance to think. To cool off. I make little toys and things for Charles Mundin. Old gives me chunks of old wood and showed me how. Most of the stuff I make is crap and I just throw it away or burn it. But sometimes it's not too bad, and I give it to Charles. Why do you care if I whittle?"

"A piece of wood was found near the dead man. It was carved into the word Woo. Jakob didn't do it. We think the murderer did."

"You think Havoc—" Roar couldn't finish the sentence.

"I have a search warrant and a team on the way."

"What're you looking for?" asked Hanna, blanching. "Just the whittling tools? We can give them to you."

"It's more than that, madame. Two things are missing from Jakob's cabin. The murder weapon and a small canvas sack. We're looking for them too."

"We've never seen them," said Hanna. "Havoc, get your tools."

Havoc led Beauvoir to the shed while Gamache waited for the search team, who showed up a few minutes later. Beauvoir returned with the tools, and something else.

Chunks of wood. Red cedar. Whittled.

It was agreed that Beauvoir would direct the search while Gamache returned to the Incident Room. At the car the two men talked.

"Which of them did it, do you think?" Beauvoir asked, handing the keys to Gamache. "Havoc could've followed Olivier and found the cabin. But it might've been Roar. He might've found the cabin when he was clearing the trail. Could've been the mother, of course. The murder didn't take a lot of strength. Anger, yes, adrenaline, but not strength. Suppose Jakob stole from the Parra family back in Czechoslovakia then when he came here they recognized him. And he recognized them. So he took off into the woods and hid there."

"Or perhaps Jakob and the Parras were in it together," said Gamache. "Maybe all three convinced friends and neighbors in Czechoslovakia to give them their precious things, then disappeared with them."

"And once here Jakob screwed his partners, taking off into the woods. But Roar found the cabin as he cut the trails."

Gamache watched the search teams start their methodical work. Before long there wouldn't be anything they didn't know about the Parras.

He needed to gather his thoughts. He handed the car keys to Beauvoir. "I'll walk."

"Are you kidding?" asked Beauvoir, for whom walking was a punishment. "It's miles."

"It'll do me good, clear my mind. I'll see you back in Three Pines." He set off down the dirt road, giving Beauvoir a final wave. A few wasps buzzed in the ripe autumn air but were no threat. They were fat and lazy, almost drunk on the nectar from apples and pears and grapes.

It felt a little as though the world was on the verge of rotting.

As Gamache strolled, the familiar scents and sounds receded and he was joined by John the Watchman, and Lavina who could fly, and the little boy across the aisle on Air Canada. Who also flew, and told stories.

This murder seemed to be about treasure. But Gamache knew it wasn't. That was just the outward appearance. It was actually about something unseen. Murder always was.

This murder was about fear. And the lies it produced. But, more subtly, it was about stories. The tales people told the world, and told themselves. The Mythtime and the totems, that uneasy frontier between fable and fact. And the people who fell into the chasm. This murder was about the stories told by Jakob's carvings. Of Chaos and the Furies, of a Mountain of Despair and Rage. Of betrayal. And something else. Something that horrified even the Mountain.

And at its heart there was, Gamache now knew, a brutal telling.

THIRTY-SIX

———

The search parties had already been over the structure a couple of times, but they looked again. Even more closely this time. Beneath floorboards, beneath eaves, behind paintings. They looked and they looked and they looked.

And finally, they found.

It was behind the bricks in the huge stone fireplace. Behind what seemed a perpetual fire. The fire had had to be extinguished and the smoldering logs removed. But there the Sûreté team found first one, then two, then four loose bricks. Removed, they revealed a small compartment.

Inspector Beauvoir reached a gloved hand in carefully, but not before smearing soot on his arm and shoulder.

"I have something," he said. All eyes were on him. Everyone stared as his arm slowly came out of the cavity. On the table in front of the Chief Inspector he placed a silver candelabra. A menorah. Even Beauvoir, who knew nothing about silver, recognized it as something remarkable. It was simple and refined and old.

This menorah had survived sieges, pogroms, slaughters, the holocaust. People had cherished it, hidden it, guarded it, prayed before it. Until one night in a forest in Quebec, someone had ruined it.

The menorah had killed a man.

"Paraffin?" Inspector Beauvoir pointed to bits of translucent material stuck to it. Mixed with dried blood. "He made his own candles. That's what the paraffin in the cabin was for, not just preserves but candles." The Chief nodded.

Beauvoir returned to the hearth and put his arm back down the black hole. They watched his face and finally saw that slight change, the surprise. As his hand hit something else.

He placed a small burlap bag beside the menorah. No one spoke, until finally Chief Inspector Gamache asked a question of the man sitting opposite him.

"Have you looked inside?"

"No."

"Why not?"

There was another long pause, but Gamache didn't hurry him. There was no rush now.

"I didn't have time. I just grabbed it out of the Hermit's cabin and hid it along with the candlestick, thinking I could take a closer look in the morning. But then the body was discovered and there was too much attention."

"Is that why you lit the fires, Olivier? Before the police arrived?"

Olivier hung his head. It was over. Finally.

"How'd you know where to look?" he asked.

"I didn't, at first. But sitting here watching the search I remembered you'd said the bistro used to be a hardware store. And that the fireplaces had to be rebuilt. They were the only new thing in the room, though they looked old. And I remembered the fires, lit on a damp but not cold morning. The first thing you did when the body was discovered. Why?" He nodded toward the things on the table. "To make sure we wouldn't find those."

Armand Gamache leaned forward, toward Olivier on the other side of the menorah and the burlap bag. Beyond the pale. "Tell us what happened. The truth this time."

Gabri sat beside Olivier, still in shock. He'd been amused at first when the Sûreté search party had shown up, moved from the Parra place back to the bistro. He had made a few feeble jokes. But as the search became more and more invasive Gabri's amusement had faded, replaced by annoyance, then anger. And now shock.

But he'd never left Olivier's side, and he didn't now.

"He was dead when I found him. I admit, I took those." Olivier gestured to the items on the table. "But I didn't kill him."

"Be careful, Olivier. I'm begging you to be careful." Gamache's voice held an edge that chilled even the Sûreté officers.

"It's the truth." Olivier shut his eyes, almost believing if he couldn't see them they weren't there. The silver menorah and squalid little sack wouldn't be sitting on a table in his bistro. The police wouldn't be there. Just he and Gabri. Left in peace.

Finally he opened his eyes, to see the Chief Inspector looking directly at him.

"I didn't do it, I swear to God, I didn't do it."

He turned to Gabri who stared back, then took his hand and turned to the Chief Inspector. "Look, you know Olivier. I know Olivier. He didn't do this."

Olivier's eyes darted from one to the other. Surely there was a way out? Some crack, even the tiniest one, he could squeeze through.

"Tell me what happened," Gamache repeated.

"I already did."

"Again," said Gamache.

Olivier took a deep breath. "I left Havoc to close up and went to the cabin. I stayed for about forty-five minutes, had a cup of tea, and when I left he wanted to give me a little creamer. But I forgot it. When I got back to the village I realized what I'd done and was angry. Pissed off that he kept promising me that," he jabbed his finger at the sack, "but never gave it to me. Only small stuff."

"That creamer was valued at fifty thousand dollars. It belonged to Catherine the Great."

"But it wasn't that." Again Olivier shot a look at the bag. "When I returned the Hermit was dead."

"You told us the sack was gone."

"I lied. It was there."

"Had you seen the menorah before?"

Olivier nodded. "He used it all the time."

"For worship?"

"For light."

"It's also almost certainly priceless. You knew that, I suppose."

"You mean that's why I took it? No, I took it because it had my fingerprints all over it. I'd touched it hundreds of times, lighting candles, putting new ones in."

"Walk us through it," said Gamache, his voice calm and reasonable.

And as Olivier spoke the scene unfolded before them. Of Olivier arriving back at the cabin. Seeing the door partly open, the sliver of light spilling onto the porch. Olivier pushing the door open and seeing the

Hermit there. And blood. Olivier'd approached, stunned, and picked up the object by the Hermit's hand. And seeing the blood, too late, he'd dropped it. It had bounced under the bed to be found by Agent Lacoste. Woo.

Olivier had also seen the menorah, toppled over on the floor. Coated with blood.

He'd backed out of the room, onto the porch, preparing to run. Then he stopped. In front of him was the horrible scene. A man he knew and had come to care about, violently dead. And behind him the dark forest, and the trail running through it.

And caught between the two?

Olivier.

He'd collapsed into the rocking chair on the porch to think. His back to the terrible scene in the cabin behind him. His thoughts stretching forward.

What to do?

The problem, Olivier knew, was the horse trail. He'd known it for weeks. Since the Gilberts unexpectedly bought the old Hadley house, and even more unexpectedly decided to reopen the bridle paths.

"Now I understand why you hated them so much," said Gabri softly. "It seemed such an overreaction. It wasn't just the competition with the bistro and B and B, was it?"

"It was the trails. I was afraid, angry at them for getting Roar to open them. I knew he'd find the cabin and it'd all be over."

"What did you do?" asked Gamache.

And Olivier told them.

He'd sat on the porch for what seemed ages, thinking. Going round and round the situation. And finally he'd arrived at his *coup de grâce*. He decided the Hermit could do him one more favor. He could ruin Marc Gilbert and stop the trails, all at once.

"So I put him in the wheelbarrow and took him to the old Hadley house. I knew if another body was found there it would kill the business. No inn and spa, then no horse trails. Roar would stop work. The Gilberts would leave. The paths would grow over."

"And then what?" asked Gamache, again. Olivier hesitated.

"I could take what I wanted from the cabin. It would all work out."

Three people stared at him. None with admiration.

"Oh, Olivier," said Gabri.

"What else could I do?" he pleaded with his partner. "I couldn't let them find the place." How to explain how reasonable, brilliant even, this all seemed at two thirty in the morning. In the dark. With a body ten feet away.

"Do you know how this looks?" rasped Gabri.

Olivier nodded and hung his head.

Gabri turned to Chief Inspector Gamache. "He'd never have done it if he'd actually killed the man. You wouldn't, would you? You'd want to hide the murder, not advertise it."

"Then what happened?" Gamache asked. Not ignoring Gabri but not wanting to be sidetracked either.

"I took the wheelbarrow back, picked up those two things and left."

They looked at the table. The most damning items. And the most precious. The murder weapon and the sack.

"I brought them back here and hid them in the space behind the fireplace."

"You didn't look in the bag?" Gamache asked again.

"I thought I'd have plenty of time, when all the attention was on the Gilbert place. But then when Myrna found the body here the next morning I almost died. I couldn't very well dig the things out. So I lit the fires, to make sure you wouldn't look in there. For days after there was too much attention on the bistro. And by then I just wanted to pretend they didn't exist. That none of this had happened."

Silence met the story.

Gamache leaned back and watched Olivier for a moment. "Tell me the rest of the story, the one the Hermit told in his carvings."

"I don't know the rest. I won't know until we open that." Olivier's eyes were barely able to look away from the sack.

"I don't think we need to just yet." Gamache sat forward. "Tell me the story."

Olivier looked at Gamache, flabbergasted. "I've told you all I know. He told me up to the part where the army found the villagers."

"And the Horror was approaching, I remember. Now I want to hear the end."

"But I don't know how it ends."

"Olivier?" Gabri looked closely at his partner.

Olivier held Gabri's gaze then looked over at Gamache. "You know?"

"I know," said Gamache.

"What do you know?" asked Gabri, his eyes moving from the Chief Inspector to Olivier. "Tell me."

"The Hermit wasn't the one telling the story," said Gamache.

Gabri stared at Gamache, uncomprehending, then over at Olivier. Who nodded.

"You?" Gabri whispered.

Olivier closed his eyes and the bistro faded. He heard the mumbling of the Hermit's fire. Smelled the wood of the log cabin, the sweet maple wood from the smoke. He felt the warm tea mug in his hands, as he had hundreds of times. Saw the violin, gleaming in the firelight. Across from him sat the shabby man, in clean and mended old clothing surrounded by treasure. The Hermit was leaning forward, his eyes glowing and filled with fear. As he listened. And Olivier spoke.

Olivier opened his eyes and was back in the bistro. "The Hermit was afraid of something, I knew that the first time I met him in this very room. He became more and more reclusive as the years passed until he'd hardly leave his cabin to go into town. He'd ask me for news of the outside world. So I'd tell him about the politics and the wars, and some of the things happening locally. Once I told him about a concert at the church here. You were singing," he looked at Gabri, "and he wanted to go."

There he was, at the point of no return. Once spoken, these words could never be taken back.

"I couldn't let that happen. I didn't want anyone else to meet him, to maybe make friends with him. So I told the Hermit the concert had been canceled. He wanted to know why. I don't know what came over me, but I started making up this story about the Mountain and the villagers and the boy stealing from it, and running away and hiding."

Olivier stared down at the edge of the table, focusing on it. He could see the grain of the wood where it had been worn smooth. By hands touching it, rubbing it, resting on it, for generations. As his did now.

"The Hermit was scared of something, and the stories made him more afraid. He'd become unhinged, impressionable. I knew if I told him about terrible things happening outside the forest he'd believe me."

Gabri leaned away, to get the full picture of his partner. "You did that on purpose? You made him so afraid of the outside world he wouldn't leave? Olivier."

The last word was exhaled, as though it stank.

"But there was more to it than that," said Gamache, quietly. "Your stories not only kept the Hermit prisoner, and his treasure safe from anyone else, but they also inspired the carvings. I wonder what you thought when you saw the first."

"I did almost throw it away, when he gave it to me. But then I convinced myself it was a good thing. The stories were inspiring him. Helping him create."

"Carvings with walking mountains, and monsters and armies marching his way? You must have given the poor man nightmares," said Gabri.

"What did Woo mean?" Gamache asked.

"I don't know, not really. But sometimes when I told the story he'd whisper it. At first I thought it was just an exhale, but then I realized he was saying a word. Woo."

Olivier imitated the Hermit saying the word, under his breath. Woo.

"So you made the spider's web with the word in it, to mimic *Charlotte's Web*, a book he'd asked you to find."

"No. How could I do that? I wouldn't even know how to start."

"And yet Gabri told us you'd made your own clothes as a kid. If you wanted to, you could figure it out."

"No," Olivier insisted.

"And you admitted the Hermit taught you how to whittle, how to carve."

"But I wasn't any good at it," said Olivier, pleading. He could see the disbelief in their faces.

"It wasn't very well made. You carved Woo." Gamache forged forward. "Years ago. You didn't have to know what it meant, only that it meant something to the Hermit. Something horrible. And you kept that word, to be used one day. As countries warehouse the worst of weapons, against the day it might be needed. That word carved in wood was your final weapon. Your Nagasaki. The last bomb to drop on a weary and frightened and demented man.

"You played on his sense of guilt, magnified by isolation. You guessed he'd stolen those things so you made up the story of the boy and the Mountain. And it worked. It kept him there. But it also inspired him to produce those carvings, which ironically turned out to be his greatest treasure."

"I didn't kill him."

"You just kept him prisoner. How could you?" said Gabri.

"I didn't say anything he wasn't willing to believe."

"You don't really think that?" said Gabri.

Gamache glanced at the items on the table. The menorah, used to murder. And the small sack. The reason for murder. He couldn't put it off any longer. It was time for his own brutal telling. He stood.

"Olivier Brulé," said Chief Inspector Gamache, his voice weary and his face grim, "I'm arresting you on a charge of murder."

THIRTY-SEVEN

The frost was thick on the ground when Armand Gamache next appeared in Three Pines. He parked his car by the old Hadley house and took the path deeper and deeper into the woods. The leaves had fallen from the trees and lay crisp and crackling beneath his feet. Picking one up he marveled, not for the first time, at the perfection of nature where leaves were most beautiful at the very end of their lives.

He paused now and then, not to get his bearings because he knew where he was going and how to get there, but to appreciate his surroundings. The quiet. The soft light now allowed through the trees and hitting ground that rarely saw the sun. The woods smelled musky and rich and sweet. He walked slowly, in no rush, and after half an hour came to the cabin. He paused on the porch, noticing again with a smile the brass number above the door.

Then he entered.

He hadn't seen the cabin since all the treasures had been photographed, fingerprinted, catalogued and taken away.

He paused at the deep burgundy stain on the plank floor.

Then he walked round the simple room. He could call this place home, he knew, if it had only one precious thing. Reine-Marie.

Two chairs for friendship.

As he stood quietly, the cabin slowly filled with glittering antiques and antiquities and first editions. And with a haunting Celtic melody. The Chief Inspector again saw young Morin turn the violin into a fiddle, his loose limbs taut, made for this purpose.

Then he saw the Hermit Jakob, alone, whittling by the fire. Thoreau on the inlaid table. The violin leaning against the river rock of the hearth. This man who was his own age, but appeared so much older. Worn down by dread. And something else. The thing that even the Mountain feared.

He remembered the two carvings hidden by the Hermit. Somehow different from the rest. Distinguished by the mysterious code beneath. He'd really thought the key to breaking the Caesar's Shift had been Charlotte. Then he'd been sure the key was sixteen. That would explain those odd numbers over the door.

But the Caesar's Shift remained unbroken. A mystery.

Gamache paused in his thinking. Caesar's Shift. How had Jérôme Brunel explained it? What had Julius Caesar done with his very first code? He hadn't used a key word, but a number. He'd shifted the alphabet over by three letters.

Gamache walked to the mantelpiece and reaching into his breast pocket he withdrew a notebook and pen. Then he wrote. First the alphabet, then beneath it he counted spaces. That was the key. Not the word sixteen but the number. 16.

A B C D E F G H I J K L M N O P Q R S T U V W X Y Z
K L M N O P Q R S T U V W X Y Z A B C D E F G H I J

Carefully, not wanting to make a mistake in haste, he checked the letters. The Hermit had printed MRKBVYDDO under the carving of the people on the shore. C, H, A, R . . . Gamache concentrated even harder, forcing himself to slow down. L, O, T, T, E.

A long sigh escaped, and with it the word. Charlotte.

He then worked on the code written under the hopeful people on the boat. OWSVI.

Within moments he had that too.

Emily.

Smiling he remembered flying over the mountains covered in mist and legend. Spirits and ghosts. He remembered the place forgotten by time, and John the Watchman, who could never forget. And the totems, captured forever by a frumpy painter.

What message was Jakob the Hermit sending? Did he know he was in danger and wanted to pass on this message, this clue? Or was it, as Gamache suspected, something much more personal? Something comforting, even?

This man had kept these two carvings for a reason. He'd written under them for a reason. He'd written Charlotte and Emily. And he'd made them out of red cedar, from the Queen Charlotte Islands, for a reason.

What does a man alone need? He had everything else. Food, water, books, music. His hobbies and art. A lovely garden. But what was missing?

Company. Community. To be within the pale. Two chairs for friendship. These carvings kept him company.

He might never be able to prove it, but Gamache knew without doubt the Hermit had been on the Queen Charlotte Islands, almost certainly when he'd first arrived in Canada. And there he'd learned to carve, and learned to build log cabins. And there he'd found his first taste of peace, before having it disrupted by the protests. Like a first love, the place where peace is first found is never, ever forgotten.

He'd come into these woods to re-create that. He'd built a cabin exactly like the ones he'd seen on the Charlottes. He'd whittled red cedar, to be comforted by the familiar smell and feel. And he'd carved people for company. Happy people.

Except for one.

These creations became his family. His friends. He kept them, protected them. Named them. Slept with them under his head. And they in turn kept him company on the long, cold, dark nights as he listened for the snap of a branch, and the approach of something worse than slaughter.

Then Gamache heard a twig crack and tensed.

"May I join you?"

Standing on the porch was Vincent Gilbert.

"*S'il vous plaît.*"

Gilbert walked in and the two men shook hands.

"I was at Marc's place and saw your car. Hope you don't mind. I followed you."

"Not at all."

"You looked deep in thought just now."

"A great deal to think about," said Gamache, with a small smile, tucking his notebook back into his breast pocket.

"What you did was very difficult. I'm sorry it was necessary."

Gamache said nothing and the two men stood quietly in the cabin.

"I'll leave you alone," said Gilbert eventually, making for the door.

Gamache hesitated then followed. "No need. I'm finished here." He closed the door without a backward glance and joined Vincent Gilbert on the porch.

"I signed this for you." Gilbert handed him a hardcover book. "They've reissued it after all the publicity surrounding the murder and the trial. Seems it's a bestseller."

"*Merci*." Gamache turned over the gleaming copy of *Being* and looked at the author photo. No more sneer. No more scowl. Instead a handsome, distinguished man looked back. Patient, understanding. "*Félicitations*," said Gamache.

Gilbert smiled, then unfolded a couple of aluminum garden chairs. "I brought these with me just now. The first of a few things. Marc says I can live in the cabin. Make it my home."

Gamache sat. "I can see you here."

"Away from polite society," smiled Gilbert. "We saints do enjoy our solitude."

"And yet, you brought two chairs."

"Oh, you know that quote too?" said Gilbert. "*I had three chairs in my house: one for solitude, two for friendship, three for society.*"

"My favorite quote from Thoreau is also from *Walden*," said Gamache. "*A man is rich in proportion to the number of things he can afford to let alone.*"

"In your job you can't let many things alone, can you?"

"No, but I can let them go, once they're done."

"Then why are you here?"

Gamache sat quietly for a moment then spoke. "Because some things are harder to let go than others."

Vincent Gilbert nodded but said nothing. While the Chief Inspector stared into space the doctor pulled out a small Thermos from a knapsack and poured them each a cup of coffee.

"How are Marc and Dominique?" Gamache asked, sipping the strong black coffee.

"Very well. The first guests have arrived. They seem to be enjoying it. And Dominique's in her element."

"How's Marc the horse?" He was almost afraid to ask. And the slow shaking of Vincent's head confirmed his fears. "Some horse," murmured Gamache.

"Marc had no choice but to get rid of him."

Gamache saw again the wild, half-blind, half-mad, wounded creature. And he knew the choice had been made years ago.

"Dominique and Marc are settling in, and have you to thank for that," Gilbert continued. "If you hadn't solved the case they'd have been ruined. I take it from the trial that was Olivier's intention in moving the body. He wanted to close the inn and spa."

Gamache didn't say anything.

"But it was more than that, of course," said Gilbert, not letting it go. "He was greedy, I suppose."

And still Gamache said nothing, not wanting to further condemn a man he still considered a friend. Let the lawyers and judges and jury say those things.

"The Hungry Ghost," said Gilbert.

That roused Gamache, who twisted in his garden chair to look at the dignified man next to him.

"*Pardon?*"

"It's a Buddhist belief. One of the states of man from the Wheel of Life. The more you eat the hungrier you get. It's considered the very worst of the lives. Trying to fill a hole that only gets deeper. Fill it with food or money or power. With the admiration of others. Whatever."

"The Hungry Ghost," said Gamache. "How horrible."

"You have no idea," said Gilbert.

"You do?"

After a moment Gilbert nodded. He no longer looked quite so magnificent. But considerably more human. "I had to give it all up to get what I really wanted."

"And what was that?"

Gilbert considered for a long time. "Company."

"You came to a cabin in the woods to find company?" smiled Gamache.

"To learn to be good company for myself."

They sat quietly until Gilbert finally spoke. "So Olivier killed the Hermit for the treasure?"

Gamache nodded. "He was afraid it'd be found. He knew it was only a matter of time, once your son moved here and Parra started opening the trails."

"Speaking of the Parras, did you consider them?"

Gamache looked at the steaming mug of coffee warming his large hands. He'd never tell this man the full story. It wouldn't do to admit that Havoc Parra in particular had been their main suspect. Havoc worked late. He could have followed Olivier to the cabin after closing the bistro. And while Havoc's whittling tools had tested negative maybe he used others. And wasn't the Hermit Czech?

Or if not Havoc then his father Roar, who cut the trails and was almost certainly heading straight for the cabin. Maybe he found it.

Maybe, maybe, maybe.

A wide trail of "maybe's" led directly to the Parras.

But Gamache also chose not to tell Gilbert that he had also been a suspect, as had his son and daughter-in-law. The cabin was on their land. Why had they bought the ruined old house when they could have had any place? Why had they ordered the trails reopened so quickly? It was almost the first thing they did.

And why had the saintly Dr. Gilbert and the body both appeared at the same time?

Why, why, why.

A wide trail of "why's" led directly to the front door of the old Hadley house.

They all made good suspects. But all the actual evidence pointed to Olivier. The fingerprints, the murder weapon, the canvas sack, the carvings. They'd found no whittling tools in Olivier's possession, but that meant nothing. He would have gotten rid of them years ago. But they had found nylon line in the B and B. The same weight and strength used for the web. Olivier's defense argued it was the standard ply and proved nothing. Gabri testified that he'd used it for gardening, to tie up honeysuckle.

It proved nothing.

"But why put that word up in the web, and carve it in wood?" asked Vincent.

"To frighten the Hermit into giving him the treasure in the sack."

It had been a shockingly simple solution. The trail was getting closer every day. Olivier knew time was running out. He had to convince the Hermit to hand it over, before the cabin was found. Because once that happened the Hermit would realize the truth: Olivier had been lying. There was no Mountain. No army of Dread and Despair. No Chaos. Just a greedy little antique dealer, who could never get enough.

No approaching horror, just another Hungry Ghost.

Olivier's last hope of getting the burlap bag from the Hermit was to convince him the danger was imminent. To save his life Jakob had to get rid of the treasure. So that when the Mountain arrived he'd find the Hermit, but no sack.

But when the story failed to terrify enough, when the trail had come too close, Olivier had brought out his napalm, his mustard gas, his buzz bomb. His *Enola Gay*.

He'd put the web up in the corner. And placed the whittled word somewhere in the cabin, for Jakob to find. Knowing that when the Hermit saw it he would—what? Die? Perhaps. But he would certainly panic. Knowing he'd been found. The thing he'd hidden from, the thing he'd fled from. The thing he most feared. Had found him. And left its calling card.

What had gone wrong? Had the Hermit not seen the web? Had the Hermit's greed exceeded even Olivier's? Whatever happened one thing Gamache knew for certain. Olivier, his patience at an end, his nerves frazzled, his rage in full flood, had reached out, clasped the menorah. And struck.

His lawyer had opted for a jury trial. A good strategy, thought Gamache. A jury could be convinced it was temporary insanity. Gamache himself had argued that Olivier should be tried for manslaughter, not murder, and the prosecution had agreed. The Chief Inspector knew Olivier had done many terrible things to the Hermit, on purpose. But killing him wasn't one. Imprisoning Jakob, yes. Manipulating and taking advantage of him, yes. Unbalancing an already fragile mind, yes. But not murder. That, Gamache believed, had surprised and appalled even Olivier.

Such an appropriate word. Manslaughter.

That's what Olivier had done. He'd slaughtered a man. Not with that one terrible blow, but over time. Wearing him down, so that the Hermit's face was scored with worry lines and his soul cringed with every scrape of a twig.

But it turned into a murder/suicide. Olivier had killed himself in the process. Whittling away what was kind and good about himself, until loathing replaced self-respect. The man he could have been was dead. Consumed by the Hungry Ghost.

What finally damned Olivier wasn't speculation but facts. Evidence.

Only Olivier could be placed at the cabin. His prints were found here, and on the murder weapon. He knew the Hermit. He sold some of his treasures. He sold the carvings. He stole the burlap bag. And finally, the murder weapon was found hidden in the bistro, along with the bag. His lawyer would try to come up with all sorts of arguments, but this case would hold. Gamache had no doubt.

But while facts might be enough for a prosecutor, a judge, a jury, they weren't enough for Gamache. He needed more. He needed motive. That thing that could never be proved because it can't be seen.

What drove a man to slaughter?

And that's what had sealed it for Gamache. As he'd been walking back to Three Pines, having ordered the Parra place searched yet again, he'd thought about the case. The evidence. But also the malevolent spirit behind it.

He realized that all the things that pointed to the Parras' possibly doing it also applied to Olivier. Fear and greed. But what tipped it toward Olivier was that while the Parras had shown little inclination toward greed, Olivier had wallowed in it.

Olivier was afraid of two things, Gamache knew. Being exposed, and being without.

Both were approaching, both threatening.

Gamache sipped his coffee and thought again about those totem poles in Ninstints, rotting, falling, fallen. But they still had a story to tell.

It was there the idea had been planted. That this murder was about tales told. And the Hermit's carvings were the key. They weren't random, individual carvings. They were a community of carvings. Each could stand on its own, but taken together they told an even bigger story. Like the totem poles.

Olivier had told tales to control and imprison the Hermit. The Hermit had used them to create his remarkable carvings. And Olivier had used those carvings to get wealthier even than he had dreamed.

But what Olivier hadn't appreciated was that his stories were actually true. An allegory, yes. But no less real for that. A mountain of misery was approaching. And growing with each new lie, each new tale.

A Hungry Ghost.

The wealthier Olivier grew the more he wanted. And what he wanted more than anything was the one thing denied him. The contents of the little canvas sack.

Jakob had come to Three Pines with his treasures, almost certainly stolen from friends and neighbors in Czechoslovakia. People who had trusted him. Once the Iron Curtain had collapsed and those people could leave, they started asking for their money. Demanding it. Threatening to show up. Perhaps even showing up.

So he'd taken his treasure, their treasures, and hidden it and himself in the woods. Waiting for it to blow over, for the people to give up. To go home. To leave him in peace.

Then he could sell it all. Buy private jets and luxury yachts. A townhouse in Chelsea, a vineyard in Burgundy.

Would he have been happy then? Would it have finally been enough?

Find out what he loved, and maybe then you'll find his murderer, Gamache had been told by Esther, the Haida elder. Had the Hermit loved money?

Perhaps at first.

But then hadn't he used money in the outhouse? As toilet paper. Hadn't they found twenty-dollar bills stuffed into the walls of the log cabin, as insulation?

Had the Hermit loved his treasure? Perhaps at first.

But then he'd given it away. In exchange for milk and cheese and coffee.

And company.

When Olivier had been taken away Gamache had sat back down and stared at the sack. What could be worse than Chaos, Despair, War? What would even the Mountain flee from? Gamache had given it a lot of thought. What haunted people even, perhaps especially, on their deathbed? What chased them, tortured them and brought some to their knees? And Gamache thought he had the answer.

Regret.

Regret for things said, for things done, and not done. Regret for the people they might have been. And failed to be.

Finally, when he was alone, the Chief Inspector had opened the sack and looking inside had realized he'd been wrong. The worst thing of all wasn't regret.

Clara Morrow knocked on Peter's door.

"Ready?"

"Ready," he said, and came out wiping the oil paint from his hand. He'd taken to sprinkling his hands with paint so that Clara would think he'd been hard at work when in fact he'd finished his painting weeks earlier.

He'd finally admitted that to himself. He just hadn't admitted it to anyone else.

"How do I look?"

"Great." Peter took a piece of toast from Clara's hair.

"I was saving that for lunch."

"I'll take you out for lunch," he said, following her out the door. "To celebrate."

They got in the car and headed into Montreal. That terrible day when she'd gone to pick up her portfolio from Fortin, she'd stopped at the sculpture of Emily Carr. Someone else was there eating her lunch and Clara had sat at the far end of the bench and stared at the little bronze woman. And the horse, the dog and the monkey. Woo.

Emily Carr didn't look like one of the greatest visionary artists ever. She looked like someone you'd meet across the aisle on the Number 24 bus. She was short. A little dumpy. A little frumpy.

"She looks a bit like you," came the voice beside Clara.

"You think so?" said Clara, far from convinced it was a compliment.

The woman was in her sixties. Beautifully dressed. Poised and composed. Elegant.

"I'm Thérèse Brunel." The woman reached out her hand. When Clara continued to look perplexed she added, "Superintendent Brunel. Of the Sûreté du Québec."

"Of course. Forgive me. You were in Three Pines with Armand Gamache."

"Is that your work?" She nodded toward the portfolio.

"Photographs of it, yes."

"May I see?"

Clara opened the portfolio and the Sûreté officer looked through, smiling, commenting, drawing in breath occasionally. But she stopped at one picture. It was of a joyous woman facing forward but looking back.

"She's beautiful," said Thérèse. "Someone I'd like to know."

Clara hadn't said anything. Just waited. And after a minute her companion blinked then smiled and looked at Clara.

"It's quite startling. She's full of Grace, but something's just happened, hasn't it?"

Still Clara remained silent, staring at the reproduction of her own work.

Thérèse Brunel went back to looking at it too. Then she inhaled sharply and looked at Clara. "The Fall. My God, you've painted the Fall. That moment. She's not even aware of it, is she? Not really, but she sees something, a hint of the horror to come. The Fall from Grace." Thérèse grew very quiet, looking at this lovely, blissful woman. And that tiny, nearly invisible awareness.

Clara nodded. "Yes."

Thérèse looked at her more closely. "But there's something else. I know what it is. It's you, isn't it? She's you."

Clara nodded.

After a moment Thérèse whispered so that Clara wasn't even sure the words had been spoken aloud. Maybe it was the wind. "What are you afraid of?"

Clara waited a long time to speak, not because she didn't know the answer, but because she'd never said it out loud. "I'm afraid of not recognizing Paradise."

There was a pause. "So am I," said Superintendent Brunel.

She wrote a number and handed it to Clara. "I'm going to make a call when I get back to my office. Here's my number. Call me this afternoon."

Clara had, and to her amazement the elegant woman, the police officer, had arranged for the Chief Curator at the Musée d'art contemporain in Montreal to see the portfolio.

That had been weeks ago. A lot had happened since. Chief Inspector Gamache had arrested Olivier for murder. Everyone knew that had been a mistake. But as the evidence grew so did their doubts. As all of this was happening Clara had taken her work into the MAC. And now they'd asked for a meeting.

"They won't say no," said Peter, speeding along the autoroute. "I've never known a gallery to invite an artist to a meeting to turn him down. It's good news, Clara. Great news. Way better than anything Fortin could have done for you."

And Clara dared to think that was true.

As he drove Peter thought about the painting on his own easel. The one he now knew was finished. As was his career. On the white canvas

Peter had painted a large black circle, almost, but not quite, closed. And where it might have closed he'd put dots.

Three dots. For infinity. For society.

Jean Guy Beauvoir was in the basement of his home looking down at the ragged strips of paper. Upstairs he could hear Enid preparing lunch.

He'd gone to the basement every chance he got in the last few weeks. He'd flip the game on the television then sit with his back to the TV. At his desk. Mesmerized by the scraps of paper. He'd hoped the mad old poet had written the whole thing on a single sheet of paper and simply torn it into strips so he could fit them together like a jigsaw puzzle. But, no, the pieces of paper wouldn't fit together. He had to find the meaning in the words.

Beauvoir had lied to the Chief. He didn't do it often, and he had no idea why he'd done it this time. He'd told the Chief he'd thrown them all out, all the stupid words Ruth had tacked onto his door, shoved into his pocket. Given others to give to him.

He'd wanted to throw them out, but even more than that he'd wanted to know what they meant. It was almost hopeless. Perhaps the Chief could decipher it, but poetry had always been a big fat pile of crap to Beauvoir. Even when presented with it whole. How could he ever assemble a poem?

But he'd tried. For weeks.

He slipped one scrap between two and moved another to the top.

> *I just sit where I'm put, composed*
> *of stone and wishful thinking:*
> *that the deity who kills for pleasure*
> *will also heal,*

He took a swig of beer.

"Jean Guy," his wife sang to him. "Luh-hunch."

"Coming."

> *that in the midst of your nightmare,*
> *the final one, a kind lion*

will come with bandages in her mouth
and the soft body of a woman,

Enid called again and he didn't answer but instead stared at the poem. Then his eyes moved to the furry little feet dangling over the shelf above his desk. At eye level, where he could see it. The stuffed lion he'd quietly taken from the B and B. First to his room, for company. He'd sat it in the chair where he could see it from his bed. And he imagined her there. Maddening, passionate, full of life. Filling the empty, quiet corners of his life. With life.

And when the case was over he'd slipped the lion into his bag and brought it down here. Where Enid never came.

The kind lion. With its soft skin and smile. "Wimoweh, a-wimoweh," he sang under his breath as he read the final stanza.

and lick you clean of fever,
and pick your soul up gently by the nape of the neck
and caress you into darkness and paradise.

An hour later Armand Gamache walked out of the woods and down the slope into Three Pines. On the porch of the bistro he took a deep breath, composed himself, and entered.

It took a moment for his eyes to adjust. When they did he saw Gabri behind the bar, where Olivier had always stood. The large man had diminished, lost weight. He looked careworn. Tired.

"Gabri," said Gamache, and the two old friends stared at each other.

"Monsieur," said Gabri. He shifted a jar of allsorts and another of jelly beans on the polished wood counter, then came around. And offered Gamache a licorice pipe.

Myrna walked in a few minutes later to find Gabri and Gamache sitting quietly by the fire. Talking. Their heads together. Their knees almost touching. An uneaten licorice pipe between them.

They looked up as she entered.

"I'm sorry." She stopped. "I can come back. I just wanted to show you this." She held a piece of paper out to Gabri.

"I got one too," he said. "Ruth's latest poem. What do you think it means?"

"I don't know." She couldn't get used to coming into the bistro and seeing only Gabri. With Olivier in jail it felt as though something vital was missing, as though one of the pines had been cut down.

It was excruciating, what was happening. The village felt torn and ragged. Wanting to support Olivier and Gabri. Appalled at the arrest. Not believing it. And yet knowing that Chief Inspector Gamache would never have done it unless he was certain.

It was also clear how much it had cost Gamache to arrest his friend. It seemed impossible to support one without betraying the other.

Gabri rose, as did Gamache. "We were just catching up. Did you know the Chief Inspector has another granddaughter? Zora."

"Congratulations." Myrna embraced the grandfather.

"I need fresh air," said Gabri, suddenly restless. At the door he turned to Gamache. "Well?"

The Chief Inspector and Myrna joined him and together they walked slowly round the village green. Where all could see. Gamache and Gabri, together. The wound not healed, but neither was it getting deeper.

"Olivier didn't do it, you know," said Gabri, stopping to look at Gamache directly.

"I admire you for standing by him."

"I know there's a lot about him that sucks. Not surprisingly, those are some of my favorite parts." Gamache gave a small guffaw. "But there's one question I need answered."

"*Oui?*"

"If Olivier killed the Hermit, why move the body? Why take it to the Hadley house to be found? Why not leave it in the cabin? Or stick it in the woods?"

Gamache noticed the "he" had become an "it." Gabri couldn't accept that Olivier had killed, and he certainly couldn't accept that Olivier had killed a "he" not an "it."

"That was answered in the trial," said Gamache, patiently. "The cabin was about to be found. Roar was cutting a path straight for it."

Gabri nodded, reluctantly. Myrna watched and willed her friend to be able to accept the now undeniable truth.

"I know," said Gabri. "But why move it to the Hadley house? Why not just take it deeper into the woods and let the animals do the rest?"

"Because Olivier realized the body wasn't the most damning evidence against him. The cabin was. Years of evidence, of fingerprints, of hairs, of food. He couldn't hope to clean it all up, at least not right away. But if our investigation focused on Marc Gilbert and the Hadley house he might stop the progress of the paths. If the Gilberts were ruined there was no need of horse trails."

Gamache's voice was calm. No sign of the impatience Myrna knew it could hold. This was at least the tenth time she'd heard the Chief Inspector explain it to Gabri, and still Gabri didn't believe it. And even now Gabri was shaking his head.

"I'm sorry," said Gamache, and clearly meant it. "There was no other conclusion."

"Olivier isn't a murderer."

"I agree. But he did kill. It was manslaughter. Unintentional. Can you really tell me you believe he's not capable of killing out of rage? He'd worked years to get the Hermit to give him the treasure, and feared he might lose it. Are you sure Olivier wouldn't be driven to violence?"

Gabri hesitated. Neither Gamache nor Myrna dared breathe, for fear of chasing away timid reason fluttering around their friend.

"Olivier didn't do it." Gabri sighed heavily, exasperated. "Why would he move the body?"

The Chief Inspector stared at Gabri. Words failed him. If there was any way to convince this tormented man, he would. He'd tried. He hated the thought that Gabri would carry this unnecessary burden, the horror of believing his partner falsely imprisoned. Better to accept the wretched truth than struggle, twisting, to make a wish a reality.

Gabri turned his back on the Chief Inspector and walked onto the green, to the very center of the village, and sat on the bench.

"What a magnificent man," said Gamache, as he and Myrna resumed their walk.

"He is that. He'll wait forever, you know. For Olivier to come back."

Gamache said nothing and the two strolled in silence. "I ran into Vincent Gilbert," he finally said. "He says Marc and Dominique are settling in."

"Yes. Turns out when he's not moving bodies around the village Marc's quite nice."

"Too bad about Marc the horse."

"Still, he's probably happier."

This surprised Gamache and he turned to look at Myrna. "Dead?"

"Dead? Vincent Gilbert had him sent to LaPorte."

Gamache snorted and shook his head. The asshole saint indeed.

As they passed the bistro he thought about the canvas bag. The thing that had, more than anything else, condemned Olivier when found hidden behind the fireplace.

Ruth's door opened and the old poet, wrapped in her worn cloth coat, hobbled out, followed by Rosa. But today the duck was without clothing. Just feathers.

Gamache had grown so used to seeing Rosa in her outfits it seemed almost unnatural that she should be without one now. The two walked across the road to the green where Ruth opened a small paper bag and tossed bread for Rosa, who waddled after the crumbs, flapping her wings. A quacking could be heard overhead, getting closer. Gamache and Myrna turned to the sound. But Ruth's eyes remained fixed, on Rosa. Overhead, ducks approached in V formation flying south for the winter.

And then, with a cry that sounded almost human Rosa rose up and flew into the air. She circled and for an instant everyone thought she would return. Ruth raised her hand, offering bread crumbs from her palm. Or a wave. Good-bye.

And Rosa was gone.

"Oh, my God," breathed Myrna.

Ruth stared, her back to them, her face and hand to the sky. Bread crumbs tumbling to the grass.

Myrna took out the crumpled paper from her pocket and gave it to Gamache.

> *She rose up into the air and the jilted earth let out a sigh.*
> *She rose up past telephone poles and rooftops of houses where the*
>   *earthbound hid.*
> *She rose up sleeker than the sparrows that swirled around her like a*
>   *jubilant cyclone*
> *She rose up, past satellites and every cell phone down on earth*
>   *rang at once.*

"Rosa," whispered Myrna. "Ruth."

Gamache watched the old poet. He knew what was looming behind the Mountain. What crushed all before it. The thing the Hermit most feared. The Mountain most feared.

Conscience.

Gamache remembered opening the coarse sack, his hand sliding over the smooth wood inside. It was a simple carving. A young man in a chair, listening.

Olivier. He'd turned it over and found three letters etched into the wood. GYY.

He'd decoded them in the cabin just minutes before and had stared at the word.

Woo.

Hidden in the rude rough sack it was far finer, even, than the more detailed carvings. This was simplicity itself. Its message was elegant and horrific. The carving was beautiful and yet the young man seemed utterly empty. His imperfections worn away. The wood hard and smooth so that the world slid right off it. There would be no touch and therefore no feeling.

It was the Mountain King, as a man. Unassailable, but unapproachable. Gamache felt like throwing it deep into the forest. To lie where the Hermit had put himself. Hiding from a monster of his own making.

But there was no hiding from Conscience.

Not in new homes and new cars. In travel. In meditation or frantic activity. In children, in good works. On tiptoes or bended knee. In a big career. Or a small cabin.

It would find you. The past always did.

Which was why, Gamache knew, it was vital to be aware of actions in the present. Because the present became the past, and the past grew. And got up, and followed you.

And found you. As it had the Hermit. As it had Olivier. Gamache stared at the cold, hard, lifeless treasure in his hand.

Who wouldn't be afraid of this?

Ruth limped across the green to the bench and sat. With a veined hand she clutched her blue cloth coat to her throat while Gabri reached out and taking her other hand in his and rubbing it softly and murmured, "there, there."

She rose up but remembered to politely wave good-bye . . .

BURY YOUR DEAD

This book is dedicated to second chances—
Those who give them
And those who take them

ACKNOWLEDGMENTS

Michael and I spent a magical month in Quebec City researching *Bury Your Dead*. Québec is a glorious place, and the old walled city is even more beautiful. I hope I've managed to capture how it felt to walk those streets every day and see not just the lovely old stone buildings, but see my history. Canadian history. Alive. It was very moving for both of us. But Quebec City isn't a museum. It's a vibrant, modern, thriving capital. I hope I've captured that too. But mostly I hope *Bury Your Dead* contains the great love I feel for this society I have chosen as home. A place where the French and English languages and cultures live together. Not always in agreement, both have suffered and lost too much to be completely at peace, but there is deep respect and affection.

Much of the action in *Bury Your Dead* takes place in the Literary and Historical Society library, in old Quebec City. It is a stunning library, and a stunning achievement to have created and kept this English institution alive for generations. I was helped in my researches by the members, volunteers and staff of the Lit and His (as it is affectionately known). Because this is a work of fiction I have taken liberties with some of the history of Québec, and the Literary and Historical Society. Especially as it concerns one of its most distinguished members, Dr. James Douglas. I realize some will not be pleased with my extrapolating, but I hope you understand.

I also need to make clear that I have met the Chief Archeologist of Québec many times and he is charming, helpful and gracious. Not at all like my fictional Chief Archeologist.

The majority of the history in the book concerns Samuel de Champlain. I have to admit, to my shame, I wasn't all that familiar with him before starting my researches. I knew the name, I knew he was one of the founders of Québec and therefore Canada. I knew his burial place is a mystery. No one has found it. And this has confounded archeologists and historians for decades. This mystery is at the center of my mystery. But it demanded I learn about Champlain. To do that I read a fair amount and spoke with local historians, chief among them Louisa Blair and David Mendel. I was also helped by a wonderful book called *Champlain's Dream*, by Professor David Hackett Fischer, of Brandeis University. Professor Fischer actually came to Quebec City during our stay and when we heard this Michael and I decided to hear him lecture. It struck us (belatedly) as odd that the venue would be a government conference room. When we arrived we sat at the far end of the large table. A very nice young woman approached and asked, in perfect French, who we might be. We, in not so perfect French, explained that I was an English Canadian writer doing research on Champlain and had come to hear the professor speak. She thanked me and a few minutes later a man came by, shook our hands and escorted us to the head of the table. Then everyone stood and the Minister of Culture arrived along with other high government officials. Finally Professor Fischer came in and was seated right in front of us.

Way too late Michael and I figured out this was a private briefing of high Québec government officials—and us. When they realized who we were, instead of showing us the door, the government officials gave us the best seats and much of the conference was held in English.

This is Québec. Where there is great kindness and accommodation. But there can also be, in some quarters, great suspicions—on both sides.

That is part of what makes Québec so fascinating.

I'd like to thank Jacquie Czernin and Peter Black, of the local CBC Radio, for their help with contacts. And Scott Carnie for his help on some tactical issues.

For those of you who love, as I do, the poetry of the Great War, you'll recognize that I paraphrase a stunning poem by Wilfred Owen called "Dulce et Decorum Est."

Bury Your Dead owes a great deal to my wonderful agent Teresa

Chris and editors, Hope Dellon, Sherise Hobbs and Dan Mallory. Their kind words and critical eyes bring out the best in the book and in me as a writer.

Finally, I'd like to mention that the Literary and Historical Society is a gem, but like most libraries it now functions on little money and the good will of volunteers both Francophone and Anglophone. If you'd like to join, or visit, please contact them at: www.morrin.org.

This is a very special book for me, on so many levels, as I hope you'll see. Like the rest of the Chief Inspector Gamache books, *Bury Your Dead* is not about death, but about life. And the need to both respect the past and let it go.

ONE

~

Up the stairs they raced, taking them two at a time, trying to be as quiet as possible. Gamache struggled to keep his breathing steady, as though he was sitting at home, as though he had not a care in the world.

"Sir?" came the young voice over Gamache's headphones.

"You must believe me, son. Nothing bad will happen to you."

He hoped the young agent couldn't hear the strain in his voice, the flattening as the Chief Inspector fought to keep his voice authoritative, certain.

"I believe you."

They reached the landing. Inspector Beauvoir stopped, staring at his Chief. Gamache looked at his watch.

47 seconds.

Still time.

In his headphones the agent was telling him about the sunshine and how good it felt on his face.

The rest of the team made the landing, tactical vests in place, automatic weapons drawn, eyes sharp. Trained on the Chief. Beside him Inspector Beauvoir was also waiting for a decision. Which way? They were close. Within feet of their quarry.

Gamache stared down one dark, dingy corridor in the abandoned factory then down the other.

They looked identical. Light scraped through the broken, grubby windows lining the halls and with it came the December day.

43 seconds.

He pointed decisively to the left and they ran, silently, toward the door at the end. As he ran Gamache gripped his rifle and spoke calmly into the headset.

"There's no need to worry."

"There's forty seconds left, sir." Each word was exhaled as though the man on the other end was having difficulty breathing.

"Just listen to me," said Gamache, thrusting his hand toward a door. The team surged ahead.

36 seconds.

"I won't let anything happen to you," said Gamache, his voice convincing, commanding, daring the young agent to contradict. "You'll be having dinner with your family tonight."

"Yes sir."

The tactical team surrounded the closed door with its frosted, filthy window. Darkened.

Gamache paused, staring at it, his hand hanging in the air ready to give the signal to break it down. To rescue his agent.

29 seconds.

Beside him Beauvoir strained, waiting to be loosed.

Too late, Chief Inspector Gamache realized he'd made a mistake.

Give it time, Armand."

"Avec le temps?" Gamache returned the older man's smile and made a fist of his right hand. To stop the trembling. A tremble so slight he was certain the waitress in the Quebec City café hadn't noticed. The two students across the way tapping on their laptops wouldn't notice. No one would notice.

Except someone very close to him.

He looked at Émile Comeau, crumbling a flaky croissant with sure hands. He was nearing eighty now, Gamache's mentor and former chief. His hair was white and groomed, his eyes through his glasses a sharp blue. He was slender and energetic, even now. Though with each visit Armand Gamache noticed a slight softening about the face, a slight slowing of the movements.

Avec le temps.

Widowed five years, Émile Comeau knew the power, and length, of time.

Gamache's own wife, Reine-Marie, had left at dawn that morning after spending a week with them at Émile's stone home within the old walled city of Québec. They'd had quiet dinners together in front of the fire, they'd walked the narrow snow-covered streets. Talked. Were silent. Read the papers, discussed events. The three of them. Four, if you counted their German shepherd, Henri.

And most days Gamache had gone off on his own to a local library, to read.

Émile and Reine-Marie had given him that, recognizing that right now he needed society but he also needed solitude.

And then it was time for her to leave. After saying good-bye to Émile she turned to her husband. Tall, solid, a man who preferred good books and long walks to any other activity, he looked more like a distinguished professor in his mid-fifties than the head of the most prestigious homicide unit in Canada. The Sûreté du Québec. He walked her to her car, scraping the morning ice from the windshield.

"You don't have to go, you know," he said, smiling down at her as they stood in the brittle, new day. Henri sat in a snow bank nearby and watched.

"I know. But you and Émile need time together. I could see how you were looking at each other."

"The longing?" laughed the Chief Inspector. "I'd hoped we'd been more discreet."

"A wife always knows." She smiled, looking into his deep brown eyes. He wore a hat, but still she could see his graying hair, and the slight curl where it came out from under the fabric. And his beard. She'd slowly become used to the beard. For years he'd had a moustache, but just lately, since it happened, he'd grown the trim beard.

She paused. Should she say it? It was never far from her mind now, from her mouth. The words she knew were useless, if any words could be described as that. Certainly she knew they could not make the thing happen. If they could she would surround him with them, encase him with her words.

"Come home when you can," she said instead, her voice light.

He kissed her. "I will. In a few days, a week at the most. Call me when you get there."

"*D'accord.*" She got into the car.

"*Je t'aime*," he said, putting his gloved hand into the window to touch her shoulder.

Watch out, her mind screamed. *Be safe. Come home with me. Be careful, be careful, be careful.*

She put her own gloved hand over his. "*Je t'aime.*"

And then she was gone, back to Montreal, glancing in the rear-view mirror to see him standing on the deserted early morning street, Henri naturally at his side. Both watching her, until she disappeared.

The Chief Inspector continued to stare even after she'd turned the corner. Then he picked up a shovel and slowly cleared the night's fluffy snowfall from the front steps. Resting for a moment, his arms crossed over the handle of the shovel, he marveled at the beauty as the first light hit the new snow. It looked more pale blue than white, and here and there it sparkled like tiny prisms where the flakes had drifted and collected, then caught, remade, and returned the light. Like something alive and giddy.

Life in the old walled city was like that. Both gentle and dynamic, ancient and vibrant.

Picking up a handful of snow, the Chief Inspector mashed it into a ball in his fist. Henri immediately stood, his tail going so hard his entire rear swayed. His eyes burning into the ball.

Gamache tossed it into the air and the dog leapt, his mouth closing over the snowball, and chomping down. Landing on all fours Henri was once again surprised that the thing that had been so solid had suddenly disappeared.

Gone, so quickly.

But next time would be different.

Gamache chuckled. He might be right.

Just then Émile stepped out from his doorway, bundled in an immense winter coat against the biting February cold.

"Ready?" The elderly man clamped a tuque onto his head, pulling it down so that it covered his ears and forehead, and put on thick mitts, like boxing gloves.

"For what? A siege?"

"For breakfast, *mon vieux*. Come along, before someone gets the last croissant."

He knew how to motivate his former subordinate. Hardly pausing for Gamache to replace the shovel, Émile headed off up the snowy street. Around them the other residents of Quebec City were waking up. Coming out into the tender morning light to shovel, to scrape the snow from their cars, to walk to the boulangerie for their morning baguette and *café*.

The two men and Henri set out along rue St-Jean, past the restaurants and tourist shops, to a tiny side street called rue Couillard, and there they found Chez Temporel.

They'd been coming to this café for fifteen years, ever since Superintendent Émile Comeau had retired to old Quebec City, and Gamache had come to visit, to spend time with his mentor, and to help with the little chores that piled up. Shoveling, stacking wood for the fireplace, sealing windows against drafts. But this visit was different. Like no other in all the winters Chief Inspector Gamache had been coming to Quebec City.

This time it was Gamache who needed help.

"So," Émile leaned back, cupping his bowl of *café au lait* in slender hands. "How's the research going?"

"I can't yet find any references to Captain Cook actually meeting Bougainville before the Battle of Québec, but it was 250 years ago. Records are scattered and weren't well kept. But I know they're in there," said Gamache. "It's an amazing library, Émile. The volumes go back centuries."

Comeau watched his companion talk about sifting through arcane books in a local library and the tidbits he was unearthing about a battle long ago fought, and lost. At least, from his point of view lost. Was there a spark in those beloved eyes at last? Those eyes he'd stared into so often at the scenes of dreadful crimes as they'd hunted murderers. As they'd raced through woods and villages and fields, through clues and evidence and suspicions. *Adown Titanic glooms of chasmed fears*, Émile remembered the quote as he remembered those days. Yes, he thought, that described it. *Chasmed fears*. Both their own, and the murderers. Across tables across the province he and Gamache had sat. Just like this.

But now it was time to rest from murder. No more killing, no more deaths. Armand had seen too much of that lately. No, better to bury himself in history, in lives long past. An intellectual pursuit, nothing more.

Beside them Henri stirred and Gamache instinctively lowered his hand to stroke the shepherd's head and reassure him. And once again Émile noted the slight tremble. Barely there now. Stronger at times. Sometimes it disappeared completely. It was a tell-tale tremble, and Émile knew the terrible tale it had to tell.

He wished he could take that hand and hold it steady and tell him it would be all right. Because it would, he knew.

With time.

Watching Armand Gamache he noticed again the jagged scar on his left temple and the trim beard he'd grown. So that people would stop staring. So that people would not recognize the most recognizable police officer in Québec.

But, of course, it didn't matter. It wasn't them Armand Gamache was hiding from.

The waitress at Chez Temporel arrived with more coffee.

"*Merci*, Danielle," the two men said at once and she left, smiling at the two men who looked so different but seemed so similar.

They drank their coffees and ate *pain au chocolat* and *croissants aux amandes* and talked about the Carnaval de Québec, starting that night. Occasionally they'd lapse into silence, watching the men and women hurrying along the icy cold street outside to their jobs. Someone had scratched a three-leaf clover into a slight indent in the center of their wooden table. Émile rubbed it with his finger.

And wondered when Armand would want to talk about what happened.

It was ten thirty and the monthly board meeting of the Literary and Historical Society was about to start. For many years the meetings had been held in the evening, when the library was closed, but then it was noticed that fewer and fewer members were showing up.

So the Chairman, Porter Wilson, had changed the time. At least, he thought he'd changed the time. At least, it had been reported in the board minutes that it had been his motion, though he privately seemed to remember arguing against it.

And yet, here they were meeting in the morning, and had been for some years. Still, the other members had adjusted, as had Porter. He had to, since it had apparently been his idea.

The fact the board had adjusted at all was a miracle. The last time they'd been asked to change anything it had been the worn leather on the Lit and His chairs, and that had been sixty-three years ago. Members still remembered fathers and mothers, grandparents, ranged on either side of the upholstered Mason-Dixon Line. Remembered vitriolic comments made behind closed doors, behind backs, but before children. Who didn't forget, sixty-three years later, that devious alteration from old black leather to new black leather.

Pulling out his chair at the head of the table Porter noticed it was looking worn. He sat quickly so that no one, least of all himself, could see it.

Small stacks of paper were neatly arranged in front of his and every other place, marching down the wooden table. Elizabeth MacWhirter's doing. He examined Elizabeth. Plain, tall and slim. At least, she had been that when the world was young. Now she just looked freeze-dried. Like those ancient cadavers pulled from glaciers. Still obviously human, but withered and gray. Her dress was blue and practical and a very good cut and material, he suspected. After all, she was one of those MacWhirters. A venerable and moneyed family. One not given to displays of wealth, or brains. Her brother had sold the shipping empire about a decade too late. But there was still money there. She was a little dull, he thought, but responsible. Not a leader, not a visionary. Not the sort to hold a community in peril together. Like him. And his father before him. And his grandfather.

For the tiny English community within the walls of old Quebec City had been in peril for many generations. It was a kind of perpetual peril that sometimes got better and sometimes got worse, but never disappeared completely. Just like the English.

Porter Wilson had never fought a war, being just that much too young, and then too old. Not, anyway, an official war. But he and the other members of his board knew themselves to be in a battle nevertheless. And one, he secretly suspected, they were losing.

At the door Elizabeth MacWhirter greeted the other board members as they arrived and looked over at Porter Wilson already seated at the head of the table, reading over his notes.

He'd accomplished many things in his life, Elizabeth knew. The choir he'd organized, the amateur theater, the wing for the nursing home. All built by force of will and personality. And all less than they might have been had he sought and accepted advice.

The very force of his personality both created and crippled. How much more could he have accomplished had he been kinder? But then, dynamism and kindness often didn't go together, though when they did they were unstoppable.

Porter was stoppable. Indeed, he stopped himself. And now the only board that could stand him was the Lit and His. Elizabeth had known Porter for seventy years, since she'd seen him eating lunch alone, every day, at school and gone to keep him company. Porter decided she was sucking up to one of the great Wilson clan, and treated her with disdain.

Still, she kept him company. Not because she liked him but because she knew even then something it would take Porter Wilson decades to realize. The English of Quebec City were no longer the juggernauts, no longer the steamships, no longer the gracious passenger liners of the society and economy.

They were a life raft. Adrift. And you don't make war on others in the raft.

Elizabeth MacWhirter had figured that out. And when Porter rocked the boat, she righted it.

She looked at Porter Wilson and saw a small, energetic, toupéed man. His hair, where not imported, was dyed a shade of black the chairs would envy. His eyes were brown and darted about nervously.

Mr. Blake arrived first. The oldest board member, he practically lived at the Lit and His. He took off his coat, revealing his uniform of gray flannel suit, laundered white shirt, blue silk tie. He was always perfectly turned out. A gentleman, who managed to make Elizabeth feel young and beautiful. She'd had a crush on him when she'd been an awkward teen and he in his dashing twenties.

He'd been attractive then and sixty years later he was still attractive, though his hair was thin and white and his once fine body had rounded and softened. But his eyes were smart and lively, and his heart was large and strong.

"Elizabeth," Mr. Blake smiled and took her hand, holding it for a moment. Never too long, never too familiar. Just enough, so that she knew she'd been held.

He took his seat. A seat, Elizabeth thought, that should be replaced. But then, honestly, so should Mr. Blake. So should they all.

What would happen when they died out and all that was left of the board of the Literary and Historical Society were worn, empty chairs?

"Right, we need to make this fast. We have a practice in an hour."

Tom Hancock arrived, followed by Ken Haslam. The two were never far apart these days, being unlikely team members in the ridiculous upcoming race.

Tom was Elizabeth's triumph. Her hope. And not simply because he was the minister of St. Andrew's Presbyterian Church next door.

He was young and new to the community, having moved to Quebec City three years earlier. At thirty-three he was about half the age of the next youngest board member. Not yet cynical, not yet burned out. He still believed his church would find new parishioners, the English community would suddenly produce babies with the desire to stay in Quebec City. He believed the Québec government when it promised job equality for Anglophones. And health care in their own language. And education. And nursing homes so that when all hope was lost, they might die with their mother tongue on caregivers' lips.

He'd managed to inspire the board to believe maybe all wasn't lost. And even, maybe, this wasn't really a war. Wasn't some dreadful extension of the Battle of the Plains of Abraham, one which the English lost this time. Elizabeth glanced up at the oddly petite statue of General James Wolfe. The martyred hero of the battle 250 years ago hovered over the library of the Literary and Historical Society, like a wooden accusation. To witness their petty battles and to remind them, in perpetuity, of the great battle he'd fought, for them. Where he'd died, but not before triumphing on that blood-soaked farmers field. Ending the war, and securing Québec for the English. On paper.

And now from his corner of the lovely old library General Wolfe looked down on them. In every way, Elizabeth suspected.

"So, Ken," Tom said, taking his place beside the older man. "You in shape? Ready for the race?"

Elizabeth didn't hear Ken Haslam's response. But then she didn't expect to. Ken's thin lips moved, words were formed, but never actually heard.

They all paused, thinking perhaps this was the day he would produce a word above a whisper. But they were wrong. Still, Tom Hancock continued to talk to Ken, as though they were actually having a conversation.

Elizabeth loved Tom for that as well. For not giving in to the notion that because Ken was quiet he was stupid. Elizabeth knew him to be anything but. In his mid-sixties he was the most successful of all of them, building a business of his own. And now, having achieved that Ken Haslam had done something else remarkable.

He'd signed up for the treacherous ice canoe race. Signed on to Tom Hancock's team. He would be the oldest member of the team, the oldest member of any team. Perhaps the oldest racer ever.

Watching Ken, quiet and calm and Tom, young, vital, handsome, Elizabeth wondered if maybe they understood each other very well after all. Perhaps both had things they weren't saying.

Not for the first time Elizabeth wondered about Tom Hancock. Why he'd chosen to minister to them, and why he stayed within the walls of old Quebec City. It took a certain personality, Elizabeth knew, to choose to live in what amounted to a fortress.

"Right, let's start," said Porter, sitting up even straighter.

"Winnie isn't here yet," said Elizabeth.

"We can't wait."

"Why not?" Tom asked, his voice relaxed. But still Porter heard a challenge.

"Because it's already past ten thirty and you're the one who wanted to make this quick," Porter said, pleased at having scored a point.

Once again, thought Elizabeth, Porter managed to look at a friend and see a foe.

"Quite right. Still, I'm happy to wait," smiled Tom, unwilling to take to the field.

"Well, I'm not. First order of business?"

They discussed the purchase of new books for a while before Winnie arrived. Small and energetic, she was fierce in her loyalty. To the English community, to the Lit and His, but mostly to her friend.

She marched in, gave Porter a withering look, and sat next to Elizabeth.

"I see you started without me," she said to him. "I told you I'd be late."

"You did, but that doesn't mean we had to wait. We're discussing new books to buy."

"And it didn't occur to you this might be an issue best discussed with the librarian?"

"Well, you're here now."

The rest of the board watched this as though at Wimbledon, though with considerably less interest. It was pretty clear who had the balls, and who would win.

Fifty minutes later they'd almost reached the end of the agenda. There was one oatmeal cookie left, the members staring but too polite to take it. They'd discussed the heating bills, the membership drive, the ratty old volumes left to them in wills, instead of money. The books were generally sermons, or lurid Victorian poetry, or the dreary daily diary of a trip up the Amazon or into Africa to shoot and stuff some poor wild creature.

They discussed having another sale of books, but after the last debacle that was a short discussion.

Elizabeth took notes and had to force herself not to lip-synch to each board member's comments. It was a liturgy. Familiar, soothing in a strange way. The same words repeated over and over every meeting. For ever and ever. Amen.

A sound suddenly interrupted that comforting liturgy, a sound so unique and startling Porter almost jumped out of his chair.

"What was that?" whispered Ken Haslam. For him it was almost a shout.

"It's the doorbell, I think," said Winnie.

"The doorbell?" asked Porter. "I didn't know we had one."

"Put in in 1897 after the Lieutenant Governor visited and couldn't get in," said Mr. Blake, as though he'd been there. "Never heard it myself."

But he heard it again. A long, shrill bell. Elizabeth had locked the front door to the Literary and Historical Society as soon as everyone had arrived. A precaution against being interrupted. Though since hardly anyone ever visited it was more habit than necessity. She'd also hung a sign on the thick wooden door. *Board Meeting in Progress. Library will reopen at noon. Thank you.* Merci.

The bell sounded again. Someone was leaning on it, finger jammed into the button.

Still they stared at each other.

"I'll go," said Elizabeth.

Porter looked down at his papers, the better part of valor.

"No," Winnie stood. "I'll go. You all stay here."

They watched Winnie disappear down the corridor and heard her feet on the wooden stairs. There was silence. Then a minute later her feet on the stairs again.

They listened to the footsteps clicking and clacking closer. She arrived but stopped at the door, her face pale and serious.

"There's someone there. Someone who wants to speak to the board."

"Well," demanded Porter, remembering he was their leader, now that the elderly woman had gone to the door. "Who is it?"

"Augustin Renaud," she said and saw the looks on their faces. Had she said "Dracula" they could not have been more startled. Though, for the English, startled meant raised eyebrows.

Every eyebrow in the room was raised, and if General Wolfe could have managed it, he would have.

"I left him outside," she said into the silence.

As if to underscore that the doorbell shrieked again.

"What should we do?" Winnie asked, but instead of turning to Porter she looked at Elizabeth. They all did.

"We need to take a vote," Elizabeth said at last. "Should we see him?"

"He's not on the agenda," Mr. Blake pointed out.

"That's right," said Porter, trying to wrestle back control. But even he looked at Elizabeth.

"Who's in favor of letting Augustin Renaud speak to the board?" Elizabeth asked.

Not a hand was raised.

Elizabeth lowered her pen, not taking note of the vote. Giving one curt nod she stood. "I'll tell him."

"I'll go with you," said Winnie.

"No, dear, you stay here. I'll be right back. I mean, really?" She paused at the door, taking in the board and General Wolfe above. "How bad could it be?"

But they all knew the answer to that. When Augustin Renaud came calling it was never good.

TWO

⌒

Armand Gamache settled into the worn leather sofa beneath the statue of General Wolfe. Nodding to the elderly man across from him he pulled the letters out of his satchel. After a walk through the city with Émile and Henri, Gamache had returned home, picked up his mail, collected his notes, stuffed it all into his satchel, then he and Henri had walked up the hill.

To the hushed library of the Literary and Historical Society.

Now he looked at the bulging manila envelope on the sofa beside him. Daily correspondence from his office in Montreal sent on to Émile's home. Agent Isabelle Lacoste had sorted his mail and sent it with a note.

> *Cher Patron,*
> *It was good to speak to you the other day. I envy you a few weeks in Québec. I keep telling my husband we must take the children to Carnaval but he insists they're too young yet. He's probably right. The truth is, I'd just like to go.*
> *The interrogation of the suspect (so hard to call him that when we all know there are no suspicions, only certainties) continues. I haven't heard what he's said, if anything. As you know, a Royal Commission has been formed. Have you testified yet? I received my summons today. I'm not sure what to tell them.*

Gamache lowered the note for a moment. Agent Lacoste would, of course, tell them the truth. As she knew it. She had no choice, by temperament and training. Before he left he'd ordered all of his department to cooperate.

As he had.

He went back to the note.

> No one yet knows where it will lead, or end. But there are
> suspicions. The atmosphere is tense.
> I will keep you informed.
> Isabelle Lacoste

Too heavy to hold, the letter slowly lowered to his lap. He stared ahead and saw Agent Isabelle Lacoste in flashes. Images moved, uninvited, in and out of his mind. Of her staring down at him, seeming to shout though he couldn't make out her words. He felt her small, strong hands gripping either side of his head, saw her leaning close, her mouth moving, her eyes intense, trying to communicate something to him. Felt hands ripping away the tactical vest from his chest. He saw blood on her hands and the look on her face.

Then he saw her again.

At the funeral. The funerals. Lined up in uniform with the rest of the famous homicide division of the Sûreté du Québec as he took his place at the head of the terrible column. One bitter cold day. To bury those who died under his command that day in the abandoned factory.

Closing his eyes he breathed deeply, smelling the musky scents of the library. Of age, of stability, of calm and peace. Of old-fashioned polish, of wood, of words bound in worn leather. He smelled his own slight fragrance of rosewater and sandalwood.

And he thought of something good, something nice, some kind harbor. And he found it in Reine-Marie, as he remembered her voice on his cell phone earlier in the day. Cheerful. Home. Safe. Their daughter Annie coming over for dinner with her husband. Groceries to buy, plants to water, correspondence to catch up on.

He could see her on the phone in their Outremont apartment standing by the bookcase, the sunny room filled with books and periodicals and comfortable furniture, orderly and peaceful.

There was a calm about it, as there was about Reine-Marie.

And he felt his racing heart settle and his breathing deepen. Taking one last long breath, he opened his eyes.

"Would your dog like some water?"

"I beg your pardon?" Gamache refocused and saw the elderly man sitting across from him motioning to Henri.

"I used to bring Seamus here. He'd lie at my feet while I read. Like your dog. What's his name?"

"Henri."

At the sound of his name the young shepherd sat up, alert, his huge ears swinging this way and that, like satellite dishes searching for a signal.

"I beg you, *monsieur*," smiled Gamache, "don't say B-A-L-L or we'll all be lost."

The man laughed. "Seamus used to get excited whenever I'd say B-O-O-K. He'd know we were coming here. I think he loved it even more than I do."

Gamache had been coming to this library every day for almost a week and except for whispered conversations with the elderly female librarian as he searched for obscure volumes on the Battle of the Plains of Abraham, he hadn't spoken to anyone.

It was a relief to not talk, to not explain, or feel an explanation was desired if not demanded. That would come soon enough. But for now he'd yearned for and found peace in this obscure library.

Though he'd been visiting his mentor for years, and had come to believe he knew old Québec intimately, he'd never actually been in this building. Never even noticed it among the other lovely homes and churches, convents, schools, hotels and restaurants.

But here, just up rue St-Stanislas where Émile had his old stone home, Gamache had found sanctuary in an English library, among books. Where else?

"Would he like water?" the elderly man asked again. He seemed to want to help and though Gamache doubted Henri needed anything he said yes, please. Together they walked out of the library and down the wooden hall, past portraits of former heads of the Literary and Historical Society. It was as though the place was encrusted with its own history.

It gave it a feeling of calm and certainty. Though much of old Quebec City was like that within the thick walls. The only fortress city in North America, protected from attack.

It was, these days, more symbolic than practical but Gamache knew symbols were at least as powerful as any bomb. Indeed, while men and women perished, and cities fell, symbols endured, grew.

Symbols were immortal.

The elderly man poured water into a bowl and Gamache carried it back to the library, putting it on a towel so as not to get water on the wide, dark floorboards. Henri, of course, ignored it.

The two men settled back into their seats. Gamache noticed the man was reading a heavy horticultural reference book. He himself went back to the correspondence. A selection of letters Isabelle Lacoste had thought he might like to see. Most from sympathetic colleagues around the world, others from citizens who also wanted to let him know how they felt. He read them all, responded to them all, grateful Agent Lacoste sent only a sampling.

At the very end he read the letter he knew was there. Was always there. Every day. It was in a now familiar hand, dashed off, almost illegible but Gamache had grown used to it and could now decode the scrawl.

> *Cher Armand,*
> *This brings my thoughts, and prayers that you're feeling better. We speak of you often and hope you'll visit. Ruth says to bring Reine-Marie, since she doesn't actually like you. But she did ask me to say hello, and fuck off.*

Gamache smiled. It was one of the kinder things Ruth Zardo said to people. Almost an endearment. Almost.

> *I do, however, have one question. Why would Olivier move the body? It doesn't make sense. He didn't do it, you know.*
> *Love,*
> *Gabri*

Inside, as always, Gabri had put a licorice pipe. Gamache took it out, hesitated, then offered the treat to the man across the way.

"Licorice?"

The man looked up at Gamache then down at the offering.

"Are you offering candy to a stranger? Hope I won't have to call the police."

Gamache felt himself tense. Had the man recognized him? Was this a veiled message? But the man's faded blue eyes were without artifice, and he was smiling. Reaching out the elderly man broke the pipe in half and handed the larger portion back to his companion. The part with the candy flame, the biggest and the best part.

"Merci, vous êtes très gentil." Thank you, you're very kind, the man said.

"C'est moi qui vous remercie." It is I who thank you, Gamache responded. It was a well-known, but no less sincere, exchange among gracious people. The man had spoken in perfect, educated, cultured French. Perhaps slightly accented, but Gamache knew that might just be his preconception, since he knew the man to be English, while he himself was Francophone.

They ate their candy and read their books. Henri settled in and by three thirty the librarian, Winnie, was turning on the lamps. The sun was already setting on the walled city and the old library within the walls.

Gamache was reminded of a nesting doll. The most public face was North America and huddled inside that was Canada and huddled inside Canada was Québec. And inside Québec? An even smaller presence, the tiny English community. And within that?

This place. The Literary and Historical Society. That held them and all their records, their thoughts, their memories, their symbols. Gamache didn't have to look at the statue above him to know who it was. This place held their leaders, their language, their culture and achievements. Long forgotten or never known by the Francophone majority outside these walls but kept alive here.

It was a remarkable place almost no Francophone even knew existed. When he'd told Émile about it his old friend had thought Gamache was joking, making it up, and yet the building was just two blocks from his own home.

Yes, it was like a nesting doll. Each held within the other until finally at the very core was this little gem. But was it nesting or hiding?

Gamache watched Winnie make her way around the library with its floor-to-ceiling books, Indian carpets scattered on the hardwood floors, a long wooden table and beside that the sitting area. Two leather wing chairs and the worn leather sofa where Gamache sat, his correspondence and books on the coffee table. Arched windows broke up the bookcases and flooded the room with light, when there was light to catch. But the most striking part of the library was the balcony that curved above it. A wrought iron spiral staircase took patrons to the second story of bookshelves that rose to the plaster ceiling.

The room was filled with volume and volumes. With light. With peace.

Gamache couldn't believe he'd never known it was here, had stumbled over it quite by accident one day while on a walk trying to clear his mind of the images. But more than the flashes that came unbidden, were the sounds. The gunshots, the exploding wood and walls as bullets hit. The shouts, then the screams.

But louder than all of that was the quiet, trusting, young voice in his head.

"I believe you, sir."

Armand and Henri left the library and did their rounds of the shops, picking up a selection of raw milk cheeses, pâté and lamb from J.A. Moisan, fruit and vegetables from the grocery store across the way, and a fresh, warm baguette from the Paillard bakery on rue St-Jean. Arriving home before Émile he put another log on the fire to warm up the chilly home. It had been built in 1752 and while the stone walls were three feet thick and would easily repel a cannonball, it was defenseless against the winter wind.

As Armand cooked the home warmed up and by the time Émile arrived the place was toasty warm and smelled of rosemary and garlic and lamb.

"*Salut*," Émile called from the front door, then a moment later arrived in the kitchen carrying a bottle of red wine and reaching for the corkscrew. "Smells terrific."

Gamache carried the evening tray of baguette, cheeses and pâté into the living room, placing it on the table before the fire while Émile brought in their wine.

"*Santé.*"

The two men sat facing the fireplace and toasted. When they each had something to eat they discussed their days, Émile describing lunching with friends at the bar in the Château Frontenac and research he was doing for the Société Champlain. Gamache described his quiet hours in the library.

"Did you find what you were looking for?" Émile took a bite of wild boar pâté.

Gamache shook his head. "It's in there somewhere. Otherwise it doesn't make sense. We know the French troops were not more than half a mile from here in 1759, waiting for the English."

It was the battle every Québec school child learned about, dreamed about, fought again with wooden muskets and imaginary horses. The dreadful battle that would decide the fate of the city, the territory, the country and the continent. The Battle of Québec that in 1759 would effectively end the Seven Years' War. Ironic that after so many years of fighting between the French and the English over New France, the final battle should be so short. But brutal.

As Gamache spoke the two men imagined the scene. A chilly September day, the forces under Général Montcalm a mix of elite French troops and the Québécois, more used to guerrilla tactics than formal warfare. The French were desperate to lift the siege of Québec, a vicious and cruel starvation. More than fifteen thousand cannonballs had bombarded the tiny community and now, with winter almost upon them, it had to end or they'd all die. Men, women, children. Nurses, nuns, carpenters, teachers. All would perish.

Général Montcalm and his army would engage the mighty English force in one magnificent battle. Winner take all.

Montcalm, a brave, experienced soldier, a frontline commander who led by example. A hero to his men.

And against him? An equally brilliant and brave soldier, General Wolfe.

Québec was built on a cliff where the river narrowed. It was a huge strategic advantage. No enemy could ever attack it directly, they'd have to scale the cliff and that was impossible.

But they could attack just upriver, and that's where Montcalm waited. There was, however, another possibility, an area just slightly further away. Being a cunning commander, Montcalm sent one of his best men there, his own *aide-de-camp*, Colonel Bougainville.

And so, in mid-September 1759 he waited.

But Montcalm had made a mistake. A terrible mistake. Indeed, he'd made several, as Armand Gamache, a student of Québec history, was determined to prove.

"It's a fascinating theory, Armand," said Émile. "And you really think this little library holds the key? An English library?"

"Where else would it be?"

Émile Comeau nodded. It was a relief to see his friend so interested. When Armand and Reine-Marie had arrived a week before it took Émile a day to adjust to the changes in Gamache. And not just the beard, and the scars, but he seemed weighed down, leaden and laden by the recent past. Now, Gamache was still thinking of the past, but at least it was someone else's, not his own. "Did you get to the letters?"

"I did, and have some to send back," Gamache retrieved the parcel of correspondence. Hesitating for a moment, he made up his mind and took one out. "I'd like you to read this."

Émile sipped his wine and read, then began laughing. He handed the letter back to Gamache.

"That Ruth clearly has a crush on you."

"If I had pigtails she'd be pulling them," smiled Gamache. "But I think you might know her.

> *"Who hurt you, once,*
> *so far beyond repair*
> *that you would meet each overture*
> *with curling lip?"*

Gamache quoted.

"That Ruth?" asked Émile. "Ruth Zardo? The poet?" And then he finished the astonishing poem, the work now taught in schools across Québec.

"While we, who knew you well,
your friends, (the focus of your scorn)
could see your courage in the face of fear,
your wit, and thoughtfulness,
and will remember you
with something close to love."

The two men were quiet for a moment, staring into the mumbling fire, lost in their own thoughts of love and loss, of damage done beyond repair.

"I thought she was dead," said Émile at last, spreading pâté on the chewy bread.

Gamache laughed. "Gabri introduced her to Reine-Marie as something they found when they dug up the basement."

Émile reached for the letter again. "Who's this Gabri? A friend?"

Gamache hesitated. "Yes. He lives in that little village I told you about. Three Pines."

"You've been there a few times, I remember. Investigating some murders. I tried to find the village on a map once. Just south of Montreal you said, by the border with Vermont?"

"That's right."

"Well," Émile continued. "I must have been blind, because I couldn't see it."

Gamache nodded. "Somehow the mapmakers missed Three Pines."

"Then how do people find it?"

"I don't know. Perhaps it suddenly appears."

"I was blind but now I see?" quoted Émile. "Only visible to a wretch like you?"

Gamache laughed. "The best *café au lait* and croissants in Québec. I'm a happy wretch." He got up again and put a stack of letters on the coffee table. "I also wanted to show you these."

Émile read through them while Gamache sipped his wine and ate cheese and baguette, relaxing in the room as familiar and comfortable as his own.

"All from that Gabri man," said Émile at last, patting the small pile of letters beside him. "How often does he write?"

"Every day."

"Every day? Is he obsessed with you? A threat?" Émile leaned forward, his eyes suddenly keen, all humor gone.

"No, not at all. He's a friend."

"*Why would Olivier move the body?*" Émile read from one of the letters. "*It doesn't make sense. He didn't do it, you know.* He says the same thing in each letter." Émile picked up a few and scanned them. "What does he mean?"

"It was a case I investigated last autumn, over the Labor Day weekend. A body was found in Olivier's bistro in Three Pines. The victim had been hit once on the back of the head, killed."

"Once?"

His mentor had immediately picked up on the significance of that. A single, catastrophic blow. It was extremely rare. A person, if hit once, was almost certainly hit often, the murderer in a rage. He'd rain blow after blow on his victim. Almost never did they find just one blow, hard enough to kill. It meant someone was filled with enough rage to power a terrible blow, but enough control to stop there. It was a frightening combination.

"The victim had no identification, but we finally found a cabin hidden in the woods, where he lived and where he'd been murdered. Émile, you should have seen what was in there."

Émile Comeau had a vivid imagination, fed by decades of grisly discoveries. He waited for Gamache to describe the terrible cabin.

"It was filled with treasure."

"Treasure?"

"I know," smiled Gamache, seeing Émile's face. "We weren't expecting it either. It was unbelievable. Antiques and artifacts. Priceless."

He had his mentor's full attention. Émile sat forward, his lean hands holding each other, relaxed and alert. Once a hunter of killers, always that, and he could smell blood. Everything Gamache knew about homicide he'd learned from this man. And more besides.

"Go on," said Comeau.

"There were signed first editions, ancient pottery, leaded glass thousands of years old. There was a panel from the Amber Room and dinnerware once belonging to Catherine the Great."

And a violin. In a breath Gamache was back in that cabin watching Agent Paul Morin. Gangly, awkward, young, picking up the priceless violin, tucking it under his chin and leaning into it. His body suddenly making sense, as though bred to play this instrument. And filling the rustic, log cabin with the most beautiful, haunting Celtic lament.

"Armand?"

"Sorry," Gamache came back to the stone home in Quebec City. "I was just remembering something."

His mentor examined him. "All right?"

Gamache gave a nod and smiled. "A tune."

"You found out who killed this recluse though?"

"We did. The evidence was overwhelming. We found the murder weapon and other things from the cabin in the bistro."

"Olivier was the murderer?" Émile lifted the letters and Gamache nodded.

"It was hard for everyone to believe, hard for me to believe, but it was the truth."

Émile watched his companion. He knew Armand well. "You liked him, this Olivier?"

"He was a friend. Is a friend."

Gamache remembered again sitting in the cheery bistro, holding the evidence that damned his friend. The terrible realization that Olivier was indeed the murderer. He'd taken the man's treasure from his cabin. But more than that. He'd taken the man's life.

"You said the body was found in the bistro, but he was murdered in his own cabin? Is that what Gabri means? Why would Olivier move the body from the cabin to the bistro?"

Gamache didn't say anything for a long time, and Émile gave him that time, sipping his wine, thinking his own thoughts, staring into the soft flames and waiting.

Finally Gamache looked at Émile. "Gabri asks a good question."

"Are they partners?"

Gamache nodded.

"Well, he just doesn't want to believe Olivier did it. That's all."

"That's true, he doesn't. But the question is still good. If Olivier murdered the Hermit in a remote cabin, why move the body to a place it would be found?"

"And his own place at that."

"Well, no, that's where it gets complicated. He actually moved it to a nearby inn and spa. He admits to moving the body, to try to ruin the spa. He saw it as a threat."

"So you have your answer."

"But that's just it," said Gamache, turning so that his whole body faced Émile. "Olivier says he found the Hermit already dead and decided to use the body as a kind of weapon, to hurt the competition. But he says if he'd actually murdered the man he'd never have moved the body. He'd have left it there, or taken it into the woods to be eaten by coyotes. Why would a murderer kill someone then make sure the body was found?"

"But wait a second," said Émile, trying to piece it together. "You said the body was found in Olivier's own bistro. How did that happen?"

"A bit awkward for Olivier that," said Gamache. "The owner of the inn and spa had the same idea. When he found the body, he moved it to the bistro, to try to ruin Olivier."

"Nice neighborhood. Quite a Merchants' Association."

Gamache nodded. "It took a while but we eventually found the cabin and the contents and the evidence the Hermit had been killed there. All the forensics confirmed only two people had spent time in the cabin. The Hermit, and Olivier. And then we found items from the cabin hidden in Olivier's bistro, including the murder weapon. Olivier admitted to stealing them—"

"Foolish man."

"Greedy man."

"You arrested him?"

Gamache nodded, remembering that terrible day when he knew the truth and had to act on it. Seeing Olivier's face, but worse, seeing Gabri's.

And then the trial, the evidence, the testimony.

The conviction.

Gamache looked down at the pile of letters on the sofa. One every day since Olivier had been sentenced. All cordial, all with the same question.

Why would Olivier move the body?

"You keep calling this man 'the Hermit.' Who was he?"

"A Czech immigrant named Jakob, but that's all we know."

Émile stared at him, then nodded. It was unusual not to identify a murder victim but not unheard of, particularly one who so clearly didn't want to be identified.

The two men moved into the dining room with its wall of exposed stone, open plan kitchen and aroma of roasting lamb and vegetables. After dinner they bundled up, put Henri on a leash and headed into the bitterly cold night. Their feet crunching on the hard snow, they joined the crowds heading out the great stone archway through the wall, to Place d'Youville and the ceremony opening the Carnaval de Québec.

In the midst of the festivities, as fiddlers sawed away and kids skated and the fireworks lit the sky over the old city Émile turned to Gamache.

"Why did Olivier move the body, Armand?"

Gamache steeled himself against the thrashing explosions, the bursts of light, the people crowding all around, shoving and shrieking.

Across the abandoned factory he saw Jean-Guy Beauvoir fall, hit. He saw the gunmen above them, shooting, in a place that was supposed to be almost undefended.

He'd made a mistake. A terrible, terrible mistake.

THREE

———

The next morning, Saturday, Gamache took Henri and walked through gently falling snow up rue Ste-Ursule for breakfast at Le Petit Coin Latin. Waiting for his *omelette*, a bowl of *café au lait* in front of him, he read the weekend papers and watched the revelers head to the *creperies* along rue St-Jean. It was fun to be both a part of it and apart from it, warm and toasty in the bistro just off the beaten track with Henri at his side.

After reading *Le Soleil* and *Le Devoir* he folded the newspapers and once again took out his correspondence from Three Pines. Gamache could just imagine Gabri, large, voluble, quite magnificent sitting in the bistro he now ran, leaning on the long, polished wooden counter, writing. The fieldstone fireplaces at either end of the beamed room would be lit, roaring, filling the place with light and warmth and welcome.

And even in Gabri's private censure of the Chief Inspector there was always kindness, concern.

Gamache stroked the envelopes with one finger and almost felt the gentleness. But he felt something else, he felt the man's conviction.

Olivier didn't do it. Gabri repeated it over and over in each letter, as though with repetition it would be true.

Why would he move the body?

Gamache's finger stopped caressing the paper, and he stared out the window, then he picked up his cell phone and made a call.

After breakfast he climbed the steep, slippery street. Turning left, Gamache made his way to the Literary and Historical Society. Every now and then he stepped into a snow bank to let families glide by. Kids were wrapped and bound, mummified, preserved against a bitterly cold Québec winter and heading for Bonhomme's Ice Palace, or the ice slide, or the *cabane à sucre* with its warm maple syrup hardening to taffy on snow. The evenings of Carnaval were for university students, drunk and partying but the bright days were for children.

Once again Gamache marveled at the beauty of this old city with its narrow winding streets, the stone buildings, the metal roofs piled with snow and ice. It was like falling into an ancient European town. But Quebec City was more than an attractive anachronism, a pretty theme park. It was a living, vibrant haven, a gracious city that had changed hands many times, but kept its heart. The flurries were falling more heavily now, but without much wind. The city, always lovely, looked even more magical in the winter, with the snow, and the lights, the horse-drawn *calèches*, the people wrapped brightly against the cold.

At the top of the street he paused to catch his breath. A breath that was easier and easier to catch with each passing day as his health returned thanks to long, quiet walks with Reine-Marie, Émile, or Henri, or sometimes alone.

Though these days he was never alone. He longed for it, for blessed solitude.

Avec le temps, Émile had said. With time. And maybe he was right. His strength was coming back, why not his sanity?

Resuming his walk Gamache noticed activity ahead. Police cars. No doubt trouble with some hung-over university students, come to Québec to discover the official drink of the Winter Carnival, Caribou, a near lethal blend of port and alcohol. Gamache could never prove it, but he was pretty sure Caribou was the reason he'd started losing his hair in his twenties.

As he neared the Literary and Historical Society he noticed more Quebec City police cars and a cordon.

He stopped. Beside him Henri also stopped and sat alert, watching.

This side street was quieter, less traveled, than the main streets. He could see people streaming by twenty feet away, oblivious to the events happening right here.

Officers were standing at the foot of the steps up to the front door of the old library. Others were milling about. A telephone repair truck was parked at the curb and an ambulance had arrived. But there were no flashing lights, no urgency.

That meant one of two things. It had been a false alarm or it hadn't, but there was no longer any need to rush.

Gamache knew which it was. A few of the cops leaning against the ambulance laughed and poked each other. Across the street Gamache bristled at the hilarity, something he never allowed at crime scenes. There was a place for laughter in life but not in recent, violent, death. And this was a death, he knew that. It wasn't just instinct, it was all the clues. The number of police, the lack of urgency, the ambulance.

And this was violent death. The cordon told him that.

"Move along, *monsieur*," one of the officers, young and officious, came up to him. "No need to stare."

"I wanted to go in there," said Gamache. "Do you know what happened?"

The young officer turned his back and walked away but it didn't upset Gamache. Instead he watched the officers talk among themselves inside the cordon. While he and Henri stood outside.

A man walked down the stone steps, spoke a few words to one of the officers on guard then went to an unmarked car. Pausing there he looked round, then stooped to get into the car. But he didn't. Instead he stopped and slowly straightening he looked right at Gamache. He stared for ten seconds or more, which, when eating a chocolate cake isn't much, but when staring, is. Softly, he closed the car door and walking to the police tape he stepped over it. Seeing this, the young officer broke away from his companions and trotted over, falling into step with the plainclothes officer.

"I already told him to leave."

"Did you now."

"*Oui*. Do you want me to insist?"

"No. I want you to come with me."

Watched by the others, the two men crossed the snowy street and walked right up to Gamache. There was a pause, as the three men stared at each other.

Then the plainclothes officer stepped back and saluted. Astonished, the young cop beside him stared at the large man in the parka and scarf and tuque, with the German shepherd dog. He looked more closely. At the trim, graying beard, the thoughtful brown eyes, and the scar.

Blanching, he stepped back and saluted as well.

"*Chef*," he said.

Chief Inspector Gamache saluted back and waved them to drop the formalities. These men weren't even members of his force. He was with the Sûreté du Québec and they were with the local Quebec City police. Indeed, he recognized the plainclothes officer from crime conferences they'd both attended.

"I didn't know you were visiting Québec, sir," said the senior officer, obviously perplexed. Why was the head of homicide for the Sûreté du Québec standing just outside a crime scene?

"It's Inspector Langlois, isn't it? I'm on leave, as you might know."

Both men gave curt nods. Everyone knew.

"I'm just here visiting a friend and doing some personal research in the library. What's happened?"

"A body was found this morning by a telephone repairman. In the basement."

"Homicide?"

"Definitely. An effort had been made to bury him, but when the repairman dug for a broken cable he found the body."

Gamache looked at the building. It had been the original courthouse and jail, hundreds of years before. Prisoners had been executed, hanged from the window above the front door. It was a place that knew violent death and the people who committed it, on either side of the law. Now there'd been another.

As he watched the door opened and a figure appeared on the top step. It was hard to tell with the distance and the winter clothing, but he thought he recognized her as one of the library volunteers. An older woman, she glanced in their direction and hesitated.

"The coroner's just arrived but it doesn't look as though the victim's been there long. Hours perhaps, but not days."

"He hasn't begun smelling yet," said the young officer. "Those make me want to puke."

Gamache took a breath and exhaled, his breath freezing as soon as it hit the air. But he said nothing. This officer wasn't his to train in the etiquette of the recently dead, in the respect necessary when in their presence. In the empathy necessary to see the victim as a person, and the murderer as a person. It wasn't with cynicism and sarcasm, with dark humor and crass comments a killer was caught. He was caught by seeing and thinking and feeling. Crude comments didn't make the path clearer or the interpretation of evidence easier. Indeed, they obscured the truth, with fear.

But this wasn't the Chief Inspector's trainee, nor was it his case.

Shifting his eyes from the young man he noticed the elderly woman had disappeared. Since she hadn't had time to walk out of sight he presumed she'd gone back inside.

It was an odd thing to do. To get all dressed for the cold, then not to actually leave.

But, he reminded himself again, this wasn't his case, wasn't his business.

"Would you like to come in, sir?" Inspector Langlois asked.

Gamache smiled. "I was just reminding myself this wasn't my case, Inspector. Thank you for your courtesy, but I'm fine out here."

Langlois shot a glance at the officer beside him then took Gamache's elbow and steered him out of hearing range.

"I wasn't asking just to be kind. My English isn't very good. It's OK, but you should hear the head librarian speak French. At least, I think she's speaking French. She clearly thinks she is. But I can't understand a word. In the entire interview she spoke French and I spoke English. It was like something out of a cartoon. She must think I'm a moron. So far all I've done is grinned and nodded and I think I might have asked whether she's descended from the lower orders."

"Why did you ask that?"

"I didn't mean to. I wanted to ask if she had access to the basement, but something went wrong," he smiled ruefully. "I think clarity might be important in a murder case."

"I think you might be right. What did she say to your question?"

"She got quite upset and said that the night is a strawberry."

"Oh dear."

Langlois sighed a puff of frustration. "Will you come in? I know you speak English, I've heard you at conferences."

"But how do you know I wasn't mangling the language too? Maybe the night is a strawberry."

"We have other officers whose English is better than mine, and I was just about to call to the station to get them, but then I saw you. We could use your help."

Gamache hesitated. And felt a tremble in his hand, blessedly hidden by his thick mitts. "Thank you for the invitation." He met the Inspector's searching eyes. "But I can't."

There was silence. The Inspector, far from being upset, nodded. "I should not have asked. My apologies."

"Not at all. I'm most grateful you did. *Merci.*"

Unseen by either man, they were being watched from the second-floor window. The window put in a century ago to replace the door. That led to the platform. That led to execution.

Elizabeth MacWhirter, her scarf still on but her coat now in the closet downstairs, stared at the two men. Earlier she'd looked out the window, anxious to turn her back on the alien activity behind her. She sought solace, peace, in the unchanging view outside the window. From there she could see St. Andrew's Presbyterian Church, the presbytery, the sloping, familiar roofs of her city. And the snow drifting gently down to land on them, as though there wasn't a care in the world.

From that window she'd noticed the man and the dog, standing just outside the cordon, staring. He was, she knew, the same man who'd visited the library every day for a week now sitting quietly with his German shepherd. Reading, sometimes writing, sometimes consulting Winnie on volumes unread in a hundred years or more.

"He's researching the Battle of the Plains of Abraham," Winnie had reported one afternoon as they stood on the gallery above the library. "Particularly interested in the correspondence of both James Cook and Louis-Antoine de Bougainville."

"Why?" Porter had whispered.

"How would I know?" said Winnie. "Those books are so old I don't think anyone's ever cataloged them. In fact, they were earmarked for the next sale, before it was canceled."

Porter had glanced at the large, quiet man on the leather sofa below.

Elizabeth was pretty sure Porter hadn't recognized him. She was certain Winnie hadn't. But she had.

And now, as she watched the local police inspector shake hands and walk away she again examined the large man with the dog and remembered the last time she'd seen him on a street.

She'd been watching the CBC along with the rest of the province, indeed the rest of the country. It was even, she'd learned later, broadcast on CNN around the world.

She'd seen him then. In uniform, without the beard, his face bruised, his Sûreté du Québec officer's hat not quite hiding the ugly scar. His dress coat warm but surely not warm enough to keep out the bitter day. He'd walked slowly, limping slightly, at the head of the long, long solemn column of men and women in uniform. A near endless cortege of officers from Québec, from Canada, from the States and England and France. And at the head, their commander. The man who'd led them, but didn't follow them all the way. Not into death. Not quite.

And that image that appeared on front pages of newspapers, on covers of magazines from *Paris Match* to *Maclean's* to *Newsweek* and *People*.

Of the Chief Inspector, his eyes momentarily closed, his face tipped slightly upward, a grimace, a moment of private agony made public. It was almost too much to bear.

She'd told no one who the quiet man reading in their library was, but that was about to change. Putting her coat on again she walked carefully down the icy steps and along the street to catch him up. He was moving along rue Ste-Anne, the dog on a leash beside him.

"*Pardon*," she called. "*Excusez-moi*." He was some distance ahead, weaving in and out of the happy tourists and weekend revelers. He turned left onto rue Ste-Ursule. She picked up her pace. At the corner she saw him half a block ahead. "*Bonjour*." She raised her voice and waved but his back was to her, and if he heard he would very probably think she was calling to someone else.

He was nearing rue St-Louis and the throng heading to the Ice Palace. She'd almost certainly lose him among the thousands of people.

"Chief Inspector."

It wasn't said as loudly as all her other cries but it stopped the large man dead in his tracks. His back was to her, and she noticed some people giving him nasty looks as they suddenly had to swing around to avoid him on the narrow sidewalk.

He turned back. She was afraid he would look annoyed, but instead his face was mild, inquisitive. He quickly scanned the faces and came to rest on her standing stock-still half a block away. He smiled and together they closed the gap.

"*Désolé*," she said, reaching out to him. "I'm sorry to disturb you."

"Not at all."

There was an awkward silence. He didn't comment on the fact she knew who he was. That much was obvious and like her, he clearly felt no need to waste time with the obvious.

"I know you from the library, don't I?" he said. "What can I do for you?"

They were at the busy corner of St-Louis and Ste-Ursule. Families were trying to squeeze by. It didn't take much to clog the narrow artery.

She hesitated. Gamache looked round and motioned down the street, against the river of people.

"Would you like a coffee? I suspect you could use something."

She smiled for the first time that day, and sighed. "*Oui, s'il vous plaît*."

They fought their way a block down, finally stopping in front of the smallest building on the street. It was whitewashed, with a brilliant red metal roof and above it a sign. *Aux Anciens Canadienes*.

"It's a bit of a tourist trap but at this time of day it might be quiet," he said in English, opening the door. They found themselves in the not unusual situation in Québec where, to be polite, the French person was speaking English and, to be polite, the English spoke French. They stepped into the dark, intimate restaurant, the oldest in the province with its low ceiling and stone walls and original beams.

"Perhaps," Gamache suggested when they were seated and the waiter had taken their orders, "we should also choose a language."

Elizabeth laughed and nodded.

"How's English?" he asked. She hadn't been this close to him before. He was in his mid-fifties, she knew from the reports. He was solid, comfortably built, but it was his eyes that caught her. They were deep brown, and calm.

She hadn't expected that. She thought they'd be sharp, cold, analytical, eyes that had seen so many dreadful things their soft centers had hardened. But this man's eyes were thoughtful, kind.

The waiter brought her a cappuccino and him an espresso. The late breakfast crowd was thinning and they'd been placed in a quiet corner.

"You know, of course, what happened this morning?" Elizabeth asked. The coffee was fragrant and delicious. She didn't often splurge on good coffees, and this was a treat.

"Inspector Langlois told me a body has been found in the basement of the Literary and Historical Society." Gamache watched her as he spoke. "It wasn't a natural death."

She was grateful he hadn't said murder. It was too shocking a word. She'd been testing it out in the safety of her own head, but wasn't yet ready to take it out in public.

"When we arrived this morning the phones didn't work, so Porter called Bell Canada for repairs."

"The repairman came quickly," said Gamache.

"We're known to them. It's an old building and in need of repairs. The phones are often out, either through some sort of short, or a mouse has eaten through the line. This surprised us, though, since we'd only just redone all the wiring."

"What time did you arrive?"

"Nine o'clock. Gives us an hour to sort books and do other work before the library opens. We unlock the door at ten every morning, as you know."

He smiled. "I do. It's a wonderful library."

"We're very proud of it."

"So you arrived at nine and called Bell right away?"

"He came within twenty minutes. Took him about half an hour to track down the problem. He figured it was a broken wire in the basement. We all thought it was just another mouse."

She paused.

"When did you realize it wasn't that?" Gamache asked, recognizing she now needed help telling her story.

"We heard him, actually. The repairman. His feet on the stairs. He's not a small man and it sounded like a stampede in our direction. He arrived at the office and just stared for a moment. Then he told us. There was a dead man in the basement. He'd dug him up. Poor man. It'll take him a while to recover, I suspect."

Gamache agreed. Some got over an experience like that quite quickly, others never did.

"You say he dug the man up. Your basement isn't concrete?"

"It's dirt. Used to be a root cellar centuries ago."

"I thought it was a prison. Were there cells there at one point?"

"No, the cells were in the level above, this was the lowest. Hundreds of years old, of course, used for keeping food cool. When the repair-man said he'd found a body I thought he meant a skeleton. They're dug up in Quebec City all the time. Perhaps this was an executed prisoner. Winnie and I went to look. I didn't go all the way in, didn't have to. We could see from the doorway that it wasn't a skeleton. The man was recently dead."

"It must have been a shock."

"It was. I've seen bodies before, in a hospital or funeral home. Once a friend died in her sleep and I found her when I went by to take her to bridge. But that's different."

Gamache nodded. He understood. There were places dead people should be, and places they shouldn't. Half buried under a library was where they should not be.

"What did the Inspector tell you?" Elizabeth asked. There was no use being coy with this man, she realized. Might as well come right out with it.

"I'm afraid I didn't ask much, but he confirmed it was a violent death."

She looked down at her now empty cup, drunk without even notic-ing. This rare treat wasted, just a rim of foam left. She was tempted to stick her finger in and scoop it up, but resisted.

The bill had arrived and was sitting on the table. It was time to leave. The Chief Inspector slid it toward him, but made no other move. In-stead he continued to watch her. Waiting.

"I came after you to ask a favor."

"*Oui, madame?*"

"We need your help. You know the library. I think you like it." He inclined his head. "You certainly know English, and not just the lan-guage. I'm afraid of what this might do to us. We're a small community and the Literary and Historical Society is precious to us."

"I understand. But you're in good hands with Inspector Langlois. He'll treat you with respect."

She watched him then plunged ahead. "Can you just come and take a look, maybe ask some questions? You have no idea what a disaster this is. For the victim, of course, but also for us." She hurried on before he could refuse. "I know what an imposition this is. I really do."

Gamache knew she was sincere but doubted she did know. He looked down at his hands, loose fists on the table. He was silent, and into that silence, as always, crept the young voice. More familiar now than those of his own children.

"And then at Christmas, we visit both Suzanne's family and my own. We go to hers for *réveillon* and mine for Mass on Christmas morning." The voice went on and on about trivial, minute, mundane events. The things that made up an average life. A voice that was no longer tinny in his ears, but living now in his brain, his mind. Always there, talking. Ad infinitum.

"I'm sorry, *madame*, I can't help you."

He watched the older woman across the table. Mid-seventies, he guessed. Slim, with beautiful bone structure. She wore little makeup, just some around the eyes, and lipstick. If less was more, she had a great deal. She was the image of cultured restraint. Her suit wasn't the latest fashion, but it was classic and would never be out of style.

She'd introduced herself as Elizabeth MacWhirter and even Gamache, not a native of Quebec City, knew that name. The MacWhirter Shipyards. MacWhirter paper mills in the north of the province.

"Please. We need your help."

He could tell this plea had cost her, because she knew what a position it put him in. And still, she'd done it. He hadn't quite appreciated how desperate she must be. Her keen blue eyes never left his.

"*Désolé*," he said, softly but firmly. "It gives me no pleasure to say that. And if I could help, I would. But . . ." He didn't finish. He didn't even know what would come after the "but."

She smiled. "I'm so sorry, Chief Inspector. I should never have asked. Forgive me. I'm afraid my own needs blinded me. I'm sure you're right and Inspector Langlois will be just fine."

"I understand that the night is a strawberry," said Gamache, smiling slightly.

"Oh, you heard about that, did you?" Elizabeth smiled. "Poor Winnie. No ear for languages. Reads French perfectly, you know. Always the highest marks in school, but can't seem to speak it. Her accent would stop a train."

"Inspector Langlois might have thrown her off by asking about her birth."

"That didn't help," Elizabeth admitted. Her mirth disappeared, to be replaced by worry once again.

"You have no need for concern," he reassured her.

"But you don't know everything, I think. You don't know who the dead man is."

She'd lowered her voice and was whispering now. She sounded as Reine-Marie did when reading their infant granddaughters a fairy tale. It was the voice she used not for the fairy godmother, but the wicked witch.

"Who is it?" he asked, lowering his own voice.

"Augustin Renaud," she whispered.

Gamache sat back and stared. Augustin Renaud. Dead. Murdered in the Literary and Historical Society. Now he knew why Elizabeth Mac-Whirter was so desperate.

And he knew she had reason to be.

FOUR

~

Gabri sat in the worn armchair by the roaring fire. Around him in the bistro he now ran he heard the familiar hubbub of the lunch crowd. People laughing, chatting. At some tables people were quietly reading the Saturday paper or a book, some had come in for breakfast and stayed through lunch, and might very well be there for dinner.

It was a lazy Saturday in February, the dead of winter, and the bistro was mumbling along with conversation and the clinking of silverware on china. His friends Peter and Clara Morrow were with him, as was Myrna, who ran the new and used bookstore next door. Ruth had promised to join them, which generally meant she wouldn't be there.

Through the window he could see the village of Three Pines covered in snow, and more falling. It wouldn't be a blizzard, not enough driving wind for that, but he'd be surprised if they got less than a foot by the time it was finished. That was the thing with a Québec winter, he knew. It might look gentle, beautiful even, but it could take you by surprise.

The roofs of the homes surrounding the village were white and smoke curled from the chimneys. Snow was lying thick on the evergreens and on the three magnificent pines clustered together at the far end of the village green like guardians. The cars parked outside homes had become white lumps, like ancient burial mounds.

"I tell you, I'm going to do it," Myrna was saying, sipping her hot chocolate.

"No you're not," laughed Clara. "Every winter you say you will and you never do. Besides, it's too late now."

"Have you seen the last-minute deals? Look." Myrna handed her friend the Travel section from the weekend Montreal *Gazette*, pointing to a box.

Clara read, raising her brows. "Actually, it's not bad. Cuba?"

Myrna nodded. "I could be there in time for dinner tonight. Four star resort. All inclusive."

"Let me see that," said Gabri, leaning toward Clara. Somehow Clara had managed to get a bit of jam on the newspaper, though there was no jam around. It was, they all knew, Clara's particular miracle. She seemed to produce condiments and great works of art. Interestingly, they never found dabs of jam or croissant flakes on her portraits.

Gabri scanned the page then leaned back in his seat. "Nope, not interested. *Condé Nast* has better ads."

"*Condé Nast* has near naked men smothered in olive oil lying on beaches," said Myrna.

"Now that I would pay for," said Gabri. "All inclusive."

Every Saturday they had the same conversation. Comparing travel deals to beaches, choosing Caribbean cruises, debating the Bahamas versus Barbados, San Miguel de Allende versus Cabo San Lucas. Exotic locales far from the falling snow, the endless snow. Deep and crisp and even.

And yet, they never went, no matter how tempting the deals. And Gabri knew why. Myrna, Clara, Peter knew why. And it wasn't Ruth's theory.

"You're all too fucking lazy to move."

Well, not entirely.

Gabri sipped his *café au lait* and looked into the leaping flames, listening to the familiar babble of familiar voices. He looked across the bistro with its original beams, wide plank floor, mullioned windows, its mismatched, comfortable antique furniture. And the quiet, gentle village beyond.

No place could ever be warmer than Three Pines.

Out the window he saw a car descend rue du Moulin, past the new inn and spa on the hill, past St. Thomas's Anglican Church, around the village green. Its progress was slow, and left tire marks in the fresh, fallen snow. As he watched it drew up beside Jane Neal's old brick home. And stopped.

It was an unfamiliar vehicle. If Gabri had been a mutt he'd have barked. Not a warning, not out of fear, but excitement.

Wasn't often Three Pines had visitors unless it was people stumbling across the tiny village in the valley by accident, having gone too far astray. Become confused. Lost.

That was how Gabri and his partner Olivier had found Three Pines. Not intending to. They had other, grander, plans for their lives but once they'd laid eyes on the village, with its fieldstone cottages, and clapboard homes, and United Empire Loyalist houses, its perennial beds of roses and delphiniums and sweet peas, its bakery, and general store, well, they'd never left. Instead of taking New York, or Boston or even Toronto by storm they'd settled into this backwater. And never wanted to leave.

Olivier had set up the bistro, furnishing it with finds from the neighborhood, all for sale. Then they'd bought the former stagecoach inn across the way and made it a bed and breakfast. That had been Gabri's baby.

But now, with Olivier gone, Gabri also ran the bistro. Keeping it open for his friends. And for Olivier.

As Gabri watched a man got out of the car. He was too far away to recognize, and dressed against the snow with a heavy parka, tuque, scarves. Indeed, it could have been a woman, could have been anyone. But Gabri rose and his heart leapt ahead of him.

"What is it?" Peter asked. His long legs uncrossing and his tall, slim body leaning forward on the sofa. His handsome face was curious, happy for relief from the vacation conversation. Peter, while an artist himself, wasn't great at the "what if" conversations. He took them too literally and found himself stressed when Clara pointed out that for only fifteen thousand dollars they could upgrade to a Princess Suite on the *Queen Mary 2*. It was his cardio exercise for the day. Having had it, he now focused on Gabri, who was focused on the stranger walking very slowly through the snow.

"Nothing," said Gabri. He would never admit what he was now thinking, what he thought every time the phone rang, every time there was a knock on the door or an unfamiliar car arrived.

Gabri looked down at the coffee table, with their drinks and a plate of chocolate chip cookies and the thick Diane de Poitiers writing paper with its partly finished message. The same one he wrote every day and mailed, along with a licorice pipe.

Why would Olivier move the body? he'd written. Then added, *Olivier didn't do it.* He would mail it that afternoon, and tomorrow he'd write another one to Chief Inspector Gamache.

But now a man was walking, almost creeping, toward the bistro out of the thickly falling snow. In just the twenty yards from his car snow had already gathered on his hat, his scarf, his slender shoulders. Olivier had slender shoulders.

The snowman arrived at the bistro and opened the door. The outside world blew in and people looked over, then went back to their meals, their conversations, their lives. Slowly the man unveiled himself. His scarf, his boots, then he shook his coat, the snow falling to the wooden floor and melting. He put on a pair of slippers, kept in a basket by the door for people to grab.

Gabri's heart thudded. Behind him Myrna and Clara were continuing to discuss whether, for a few thousand more, it might be worth upgrading all the way, to the Queen Suites.

He knew it couldn't be Olivier. Not really. But, well, maybe Gamache had been convinced by all the letters, maybe he'd let him out. Maybe it had been last-minute, like the travel deals, a last-minute escape that instead of taking him away had brought Olivier home.

Gabri stepped forward, unable to help himself now.

"Gabri?" Peter asked, standing up.

Gabri got halfway across the bistro.

The man had taken off his hat and turned into the room. Slowly, as recognition dawned, the conversation died out.

It wasn't Olivier. It was one of the men who'd taken him away, arrested Olivier, put him in prison for murder.

Inspector Jean-Guy Beauvoir surveyed the room and smiled, uncertainly.

When the phone call had come that morning from the Chief Inspector, Beauvoir had been in his basement making a bookcase. He didn't read but his wife Enid did, and so he was making it for her. She was upstairs, singing. Not loudly and not well. He could hear her cleaning up the breakfast dishes.

"You okay down there?" she'd called.

He wanted to tell her he wasn't. He was bored stupid. He hated woodwork, hated the damned crossword puzzles she shoved on him. Hated the books she'd piled up next to the sofa, hated the pillows and blankets that followed him around, in her arms as though he was an invalid. Hated how much he owed her. Hated how much she loved him.

"I'm fine," he called up.

"If you need anything, just call."

"I will."

He walked over to the workbench, pausing for breath at the counter. He'd done his exercises for the day, his physio. He hadn't been very disciplined until the doctor had pointed out that the more he did them the sooner he could get out from under Enid's crushing concern.

The doctor didn't exactly put it that way, but that's what Beauvoir heard and it had been motivation enough. Morning, noon and night he did his exercises to regain his strength. Not too much. He could tell when he did too much. But sometimes he felt it was worth it. He'd rather die trying to escape than be trapped much longer.

"Cookie?" she sang down.

"Yes, Cupcake?" he replied. It was their little joke. He heard her laugh and wondered how much it would hurt to cut his hand off with the jigsaw. But not his gun hand, he might need that later.

"No, do you want a cookie? I thought I'd do a batch."

"Sounds great. *Merci.*"

Beauvoir had never particularly wanted children, but now he was desperate for them. Maybe then Enid would transfer her love to them. The kids would save him. He felt momentarily bad for them, being dragged under by her unconditional, undying, unrelenting love, but, well, *sauve qui peut.*

Then the phone rang.

And his heart stopped. He'd thought, hoped, with time it would stop doing that. It was inconvenient having a heart that halted every time there was a call. Especially annoying when it was a wrong number. But instead of going away it seemed to be getting worse. He heard Enid hurrying to answer it and he knew she was running because she knew how much the sound upset him.

And he hated himself, for hating her.

"*Oui, allô?*" he heard her say and immediately Beauvoir was back there, to that day.

"Homicide." The Chief's secretary had answered the phone in the office. It was a large, open space taking an entire floor of the Sûreté du Québec headquarters in Montreal. There were, however, a few enclosed spaces. There was a private conference room with Beauvoir's beloved Magic Markers, and long sheets of paper on the walls, and blackboards and corkboards. All neatly organized.

He had his own office, being the second in command.

And the Chief had a large office in the corner, with windows looking out over Montreal. From there Armand Gamache ran the province-wide operation, looking into murders in a territory that stretched from the Ontario border to the Atlantic Ocean, from the frontier with Vermont and New York to the Arctic Circle. They had hundreds of agents and investigators in stations across the province and special teams that went into areas without a homicide squad.

All coordinated by Chief Inspector Gamache.

Beauvoir had been in Gamache's office discussing a singularly gnarly case in Gaspé when the phone had rung. Gamache's secretary had answered it. Inspector Beauvoir glanced at the clock on the Chief"s wall just as the phone rang. 11:18 A.M.

"Homicide," he'd heard her say.

And nothing had been the same since.

A small tapping on the door brought Elizabeth MacWhirter out of her reverie. She'd been staring down at the list of members, putting off the time she'd have to phone them. But she knew that time had already come and gone. She should have made the calls an hour ago. Already messages were coming in from members of the English community, including CBC Radio and the weekly English newspaper, the *Chronicle-Telegraph*. She, Winnie and Porter had tried to be coy, but had only succeeded in sounding secretive.

Reporters were on their way.

And still Elizabeth put off phoning, clinging, she knew to the last moments of anything that resembled normalcy. Of their quiet, uneventful lives, volunteering to be custodians of a dusty and all but irrelevant past, but a past precious to them.

The knocking sounded again. No louder, but not going away either. Were the reporters here already? But they, she suspected, would pound at the door as would the police. This tapping was a request, not a demand.

"I'll get it," said Winnie, walking across the large room and up the two steps to the door. At their desks in front of the large Palladian windows Elizabeth and Porter watched. Winnie was speaking with someone they couldn't see, nor could they hear her conversation but she seemed to be trying to explain something. Then she seemed to be trying to close the door. Then she stopped, and opening it wide she turned into the room.

"Chief Inspector Gamache wants to speak to you," she said to Elizabeth, almost in a daze.

"Who?" asked Porter, popping up at his desk, taking charge, now that the elderly woman had answered the door.

Winnie swung the door wide and there stood Armand Gamache. He looked at the people, but took in his surroundings. The office had a cathedral ceiling, huge arched windows and was sunken a few steps from the door. It was paneled in wood, with wood floors and bookcases and looked like an old-fashioned, miniature, gymnasium where the activity was intellectual not physical.

"I'm sorry to disturb you," he said, coming further into the room. His coat was off and he was wearing a camel hair cardigan, a shirt and tie, and deep blue corduroy slacks. Henri, his German shepherd, was at his side.

Porter stared. Winnie backed down the stairway. Elizabeth got up from her desk and walked over.

"You came," she said, smiling, her hand out. He took it in his large hand and held it.

"What do you mean?" asked Porter. "I don't understand."

"I asked if he could come and watch over the investigation for us. This is Chief Inspector Gamache," Elizabeth waited for recognition. "Of the Sûreté du Québec."

"I know who it is," lied Porter. "Knew all along."

"Chief Inspector Gamache, let me introduce the head of our Board of Directors," said Elizabeth. "Porter Wilson."

The two men shook hands.

"We don't need help, you know. We're fine on our own," said Porter.

"I know, I just wanted to make sure. You've been so kind allowing me to use your library, I thought I'd offer some of my own expertise in return."

"This isn't even your jurisdiction," Porter grumbled, turning his back on the Chief Inspector. "The separatists are going to have a field day. How do we know you're not one of them?"

Elizabeth MacWhirter could have died. "For God's sake, Porter, he's here to help. I invited him."

"We'll talk about that later."

"Not all separatists wish you harm, *monsieur*," said Gamache, his voice friendly but firm. "But you're right, this isn't my jurisdiction. I'm impressed you know that." Elizabeth watched with some amusement as Porter began to melt. "You clearly follow politics." Porter nodded and relaxed further. Much more, thought Elizabeth, and he'd curl up in Gamache's lap.

"The Sûreté has no jurisdiction in cities," Gamache continued. "The death of Monsieur Renaud is a case for the local Quebec City homicide force. I happen to know Inspector Langlois and he was kind enough to also ask me to join them. After some thought," he looked over at Elizabeth, "I decided I would just have a look." He turned back to Porter. "With your permission of course, sir."

Porter Wilson all but swooned. Winnie and Elizabeth exchanged glances. If they'd only realized it was so easy. But then Porter's face clouded again as the reality sunk in.

This might not be an improvement. They'd gone from no police to now two forces occupying their building.

Not to mention the body.

"I wonder if I could leave Henri with you while I go into the basement?"

"Absolutely," said Winnie, taking the leash. Gamache also gave her some biscuits for Henri, patted him, told him to be a gentleman, then left.

46

"I don't like this," he heard Porter say just as the door closed. He suspected he was meant to hear it. But, then, he didn't much like it either.

A uniformed officer was waiting for him in the corridor and together they made their way through the warren of hallways and staircases. Gamache had to admit he was completely lost, and suspected the officer was too. Boxes full of books and papers lined the linoleum floors, elaborate stairways led to grotty washrooms and deserted offices. They came to two huge wooden doors and opening them they walked into a spectacular double-height ballroom that led into an equally spectacular twin. Both empty except for a few ladders and the ubiquitous boxes of books. He opened one of them. More leather-bound volumes. He knew if he picked one up he would be well and truly lost, so he ignored it and instead followed the increasingly frustrated officer down another corridor.

"Never seen anything like it," said the officer. "All this beautiful space, gone to waste. Doesn't seem right. What're they doing with this great building? Shouldn't it be used for something worthwhile?"

"Like what?"

"I don't know. But there must be something someone could use it for."

"Someone is using it."

"*Les Anglais.*"

Gamache stopped. "*Excusez-moi?*"

"*Les têtes carré,*" the young officer explained.

The square heads.

"You will treat these people with respect," said Gamache. "They're no more *tête carré* than you and I are frogs." His voice was hard, sharp. The officer stiffened.

"I meant no harm."

"Is that really true?" Gamache stared at the young officer, who stared back. Finally Gamache smiled a little. "You won't solve this crime by insulting these people, or mocking them. Don't be blinded."

"Yes sir."

They walked on, down endless hallways, past some magnificent rooms and past some dreary rooms, all empty. As though the Literary and Historical Society was in full retreat, regrouping into that one splendid library where General Wolfe watched over them.

"Over here, sir. I think I've found it."

They went down some steps and found a uniformed officer standing bored guard over a trap door. On seeing the Chief Inspector he stood straighter. Gamache nodded and watched his young guide leap down the metal ladder.

Gamache hadn't been prepared for this.

At the bottom the officer stared up, waiting, his face going from eager to questioning. What could be keeping this man? Then he remembered. He walked a few rungs up the ladder and extended his hand.

"It's all right, sir," he said quietly. "I won't let you fall."

Gamache looked at the hand. "I believe you." He carefully descended and took the strong young hand in his.

Jean-Guy Beauvoir sat by the fire, a beer and a steak sandwich in front of him. Peter and Clara had joined him and Myrna and Gabri sat on the sofa facing the fireplace.

It was Beauvoir's first time back in Three Pines since they'd arrested Olivier Brulé for the murder of the Hermit, Jakob. He looked into the huge, open fire and remembered loosening the bricks at the back and sticking his arm all the way in, right up to his shoulder and rummaging around. Afraid of what he might feel, or what might feel him. Was there a rat's nest back there? Mice? Spiders? Maybe snakes.

As much as he declared himself to be rationality itself, the truth was, he had an active and untamed imagination. His hand brushed something soft and rough. He'd stiffened and stopped. His heart pounding and his imagination in overdrive, he forced his hand back. It closed around the thing, and he'd brought it out.

Around him the Sûreté team had clustered, watching. Chief Inspector Gamache, Agent Isabelle Lacoste and the trainee, Agent Paul Morin.

Slowly he dragged the thing out from its hiding place behind the fire. It was a small, coarse burlap sack, tied with twine. He'd placed it on the very table where his beer and sandwich now sat. And he'd gone in again, finding something else hidden back there. A simple, elegant, beautiful candelabra. A menorah, actually. Centuries old, perhaps thousands of years, the experts later said.

But the experts had told them something else, something more precise.

This ancient menorah that had brought light to so many homes, so many solemn ceremonies, that had been worshiped, hidden, prayed around, treasured, had also been used to kill.

The Hermit's blood and hair and tissue were found on it as were his fingerprints. As were the fingerprints of only one other.

Olivier.

And inside the sack? A carving the Hermit had done. His finest work. An exquisite study of a young man, sitting, listening. It was simple and powerful, and telling. It told of aching loneliness, of desire, of need. It was clearly a carving of Olivier, listening. And that carving told them something else.

Jakob's sculptures had been worth hundreds of thousands, finally millions of dollars. He'd given them to Olivier in exchange for food and company and Olivier had sold them. Making millions for himself.

But that hadn't been enough, Olivier had wanted more. He wanted the one thing the Hermit had refused to give him. The thing in the sack.

Jakob's last treasure, his most precious possession.

And Olivier wanted it.

In a fit of rage and greed he'd taken the Hermit's life, then he'd taken the beautiful and priceless murder weapon and the sack, and hidden them.

Behind the fireplace Beauvoir now stared at.

And once found, the sack with its carving started to speak. It had only one thing to say and it said it eloquently, over and over. Olivier had killed its creator.

Between finding the carving and the murder weapon hidden in the bistro, as well as all the other evidence, there was no question what had to happen next. The Chief Inspector had arrested Olivier Brulé for murder. He'd been found guilty of manslaughter and sentenced to ten years. Painfully, Three Pines had come to accept this terrible truth.

Except Gabri, who every day wrote the Chief Inspector to ask that question. *Why would Olivier move the body?*

"How's the Chief Inspector?" Myrna asked, leaning her considerable body forward. She was large and black. A retired psychologist, now the owner of the bookstore.

"He's all right. We speak every day."

He wouldn't tell them the full truth, of course. That Chief Inspector Gamache was far from "all right." As was he.

"We've been in touch a few times," said Clara.

In her late forties Clara Morrow was on the cusp, everyone knew, of making it huge in the art world. She had a solo show coming up in a few months at the Musée d'art Contemporain, or MAC, in Montreal. Her unruly dark hair was growing lighter with gray and she always looked as though she'd just emerged from a wind tunnel.

Her husband, Peter, was another matter. Where she was short and getting a little dumpy, he was tall and slender. Every gray hair in place, his clothing simple and immaculate.

"We spoke to him a few times," said Peter. "And I know you're in touch." He turned to Gabri.

"If you can call stalking him, 'in touch.'" Gabri laughed and gestured to the half-finished letter on the table then looked at Beauvoir. "Did Gamache send you? Are you reopening Olivier's case?"

Beauvoir shook his head. "I'm afraid not. I've just come for a vacation. To relax."

He'd looked them square in the face, and lied.

"Do you mind, Jean-Guy?" Chief Inspector Gamache had asked that morning. "I'd do it myself, but I don't think that would be much use. If a mistake was made it was mine. You might be able to see where it is."

"We all investigated the case, not just you, sir. We all agreed with the findings. There was no doubt. What makes you think now there was a mistake?" Beauvoir had asked. He'd been in the basement with the dreaded phone. And if he hated the phone, Beauvoir thought, how must the Chief feel about them?

He didn't think they'd made a mistake. In fact, he knew the case against Olivier to be complete, thorough and without fault.

"Why did he move the body?" Gamache had said.

It was, Beauvoir had to admit, a good question. The only slight chink in a perfect case. "So, what do you want me to do?"

"I want you to go to Three Pines and ask some more questions."

"Like what? We asked all the questions, got all the answers. Olivier murdered the Hermit. *Point final.* End of discussion. The jury agreed. Besides, the murder happened five months ago, how'm I supposed to find new evidence now?"

"I don't think you do," the Chief had said. "I think if a mistake was made it was in interpretation."

Beauvoir had paused. He knew he'd go to Three Pines, would do as the Chief asked. He always would. If the Chief asked him to conduct the interviews naked, he would. But of course he would never ask that, which was why he trusted the Chief. With his life.

For a moment, unbidden, he felt again the shove, the pressure, and then the horror as his legs had collapsed and he knew what had happened. He'd crumpled to the filthy floor of the abandoned factory. And he'd heard, from far off, the familiar voice, shouting.

"Jean-Guy!" So rarely raised, but raised then.

The Chief was speaking to him again, but now his voice was calm, thoughtful, trying to work out the best strategy. "You'll be there as a private citizen, not a homicide investigator. Not trying to prove him guilty. Maybe the thing to do is look at it from the other direction."

"What do you mean?"

"Go to Three Pines and try to prove Olivier didn't murder the Hermit Jakob."

So there Jean-Guy Beauvoir sat, trying to pretend he liked these people.

But he didn't.

Jean-Guy Beauvoir didn't like many people and these ones in Three Pines had given him little reason to change. They were cunning, deceitful, arrogant, and nearly incomprehensible, especially the Anglos. They were dangerous, because they hid their thoughts, hid their feelings, behind a smiling face. Who could tell what was really going on in their heads? They said one thing and thought another. Who knew what rancid thing lived, curled up, in that space between words and thoughts?

Yes. These people might look kind and concerned. But they were dangerous.

The sooner this was over, thought Beauvoir smiling at them over the rim of his beer, the better.

FIVE

〰

Once at the bottom of the ladder Gamache looked round. Industrial lamps had been brought down and he could see light flooding from one of the chambers. Like anyone else he was drawn to it, but resisted and instead looked into the gloom, allowing his eyes to adjust.

After a moment he saw what men and women stretching back hundreds of years had seen. A low, vaulted, stone basement, a *sous-sol* in French. No sun had ever reached here, only darkness, interrupted over the centuries by candlelight, by whale oil lamps, by gaslight and now, finally, by blinding, brilliant electric lights. Brighter than the sun, brought down so they could see the darkest of deeds.

The taking of a life.

And not just any life, but Augustin Renaud.

Porter Wilson, for all his paranoia was right, thought Gamache. The people who wanted Québec to separate from Canada will have a field day. Anything that cast suspicion on the English population was fodder for the separatist cause. Or at least, the more radical factions. The vast majority of separatists, Gamache knew, were thoughtful, reasonable, decent people. But a few were quite crazy.

Gamache and his young guide were in an antechamber. The ceilings were low, though perhaps not for the people who'd built it. Poor diet and grinding conditions had made them many inches shorter. But still, Gamache suspected, most would have ducked, as he did now. The floors were dirt, and it was cool but not cold down there. They were well below the frost line, beneath the sun but also beneath the frozen earth. Into a sort of dim purgatory, a place never hot, nor cold.

The Chief Inspector touched the rough stone wall, wondering how many men and women, long dead, had touched it too as they'd come down to get root vegetables from the cellars. To keep starving prisoners alive long enough to kill them.

Off the antechamber there was a room. The room with the light.

"After you," he gestured to the officer, and followed him.

Inside his eyes had to adjust again though this didn't take so long. Large industrial lamps were positioned to bounce off the vaulted stone ceiling and walls but most were beamed into one corner of the room. And in that corner a handful of men and women worked. Some taking photographs, some collecting samples, some huddled over something Gamache couldn't quite see but could imagine.

A body.

Inspector Langlois stood and brushing dirt from his knees he approached. "I'm glad you changed your mind."

They shook hands.

"I needed to think about it. Madame MacWhirter also asked me to come, to act as a sort of honest-broker between them and you."

Langlois smiled. "She thinks they need one?"

"Well, it's more or less what you asked, wasn't it?"

The Inspector nodded. "It's true. And I'm grateful you're here, but I wonder if we might keep this on an informal basis. Perhaps we could consider you a consultant?" Langlois looked behind him. "Would you like to see?"

"*S'il vous plaît.*"

It was a scene familiar to the Chief Inspector. A homicide team in the early stages of collecting evidence that would one day convict a man of murder, or a woman. The coroner was still there, just rising, a young doctor sent over from Hôtel-Dieu hospital where the Chief Coroner of Québec kept an office. This man wasn't the Chief. Gamache knew him, but he was a doctor and judging by his composure he was experienced.

"He was hit from behind with that shovel there." The doctor pointed to a partly buried tool beside the body. He was speaking to Inspector Langlois but shooting glances at Gamache. "Fairly straightforward. He was hit a few times. I've taken samples and need to get him onto my table, but there doesn't seem to be any other trauma."

"How long?" Langlois asked.

"Twelve hours, give or take an hour or so. We're lucky with the environment. It's consistent. No rain or snow, no fluctuation in temperature. I'll tell you more precisely later." He turned, collected his kit then nodded to Langlois and Gamache. But instead of leaving the coroner hesitated, looking round the cellar.

He seemed reluctant to leave. When Langlois peered at him the young doctor lost some of his composure but rallied.

"Would you like me to stay?"

"Why?" asked Langlois, his voice uninviting.

But still the doctor persevered. "You know."

Now Inspector Langlois turned to him completely, challenging him to go further.

"Tell me."

"Well," the doctor stumbled. "In case you find anything else."

Beside him Gamache felt the Inspector tense, but Gamache leaned in and whispered, "Perhaps he should stay."

Langlois nodded once, his face hard, and the coroner stepped away from the pool of light, across the sharp border into darkness. And there he waited.

In case.

Everyone in that room knew "in case" of what.

Chief Inspector Gamache approached the body. The harsh light left nothing to the imagination. It bounced off the man's dirty clothing, off his stringy, long, white hair, off his face, twisted. Off his hands, clasped closed, over dirt. Off the horrible wounds on his head.

Gamache knelt.

Yes, he was unmistakable. The extravagant black moustache, at odds with the white hair. The long, bushy eyebrows political cartoonists were so fond of caricaturing. The bulbous nose and fierce, almost mad, blue eyes. Intense even in death.

"Augustin Renaud," said Langlois. "No doubt."

"And Samuel de Champlain?"

Gamache had said out loud what everyone in that room, everyone in that *sous-sol*, everyone in that building had been thinking. But none had voiced. This was the "in case."

"Any sign of him?"

"Not yet," said Langlois, unhappily.

For where Augustin Renaud was there was always someone else.

Samuel de Champlain. Dead for almost four hundred years, but clinging to Augustin Renaud.

Champlain, who in 1608 had founded Québec, was long dead and buried.

But where?

That was the great mystery that hounded the Québécois. Somehow, over the centuries, they'd lost the founder.

They knew where minor functionaries from the early 1600s were buried, lieutenants and captains in Champlain's brigade. They'd un-earthed, and reburied, countless missionaries. The pioneers, the farmers, the nuns, the first *habitants* were all accounted for. With solemn graves and headstones, visited by school children, by priests on celebration days, by tourists and tour guides. Names like Hébert and Frontenac and Marie de l'Incarnation resonated with the Québécois, and stories were told of their selflessness, their bravery.

But one remained missing. One's remains were missing.

The father of Québec, the most revered, the most renowned, the most courageous. The first Québécois.

Samuel de Champlain.

And one man had spent his entire adult life trying to find him. Au-gustin Renaud had dug and tunneled and hacked away under much of old Quebec City, following any whimsical clue that surfaced.

And now here he was, beneath the Literary and Historical Society, that bastion of Anglo Quebéc. With a shovel.

Dead himself. Murdered.

Why was he here? There seemed only one answer to that.

"Should I tell the *premier ministre*?" Langlois asked Gamache.

"*Oui*. The *premier ministre*, the Minister for Public Security. The Chief Archeologist. The Voice of English-speaking Québec. The Saint-Jean-Baptiste Society. The Parti Québécois." Gamache looked at Lan-glois sternly. "Then you need to call a news conference and tell the population. Equally. At the same time."

Langlois was clearly amazed by the suggestion. "Don't you think it's better to downplay this? I mean, really, it's only Augustin Renaud, not the *premier ministre*. The man was a bit of a buffoon. No one took him seriously."

"But they took his search seriously."

Inspector Langlois stared at Gamache but said nothing.

"You'll do as you want, of course," said the Chief Inspector, sympathizing with the man. "But as your consultant that's my counsel. Tell all and tell it quickly before the militant elements start spreading rumors."

Gamache looked past the circle of intense light to the dark caverns beyond the main room.

Was Samuel de Champlain here right now? Armand Gamache, a student of Québec history, felt a *frisson*, an involuntary thrill.

And if he felt that, he thought, what will others feel?

Elizabeth MacWhirter was feeling ill. She turned her back to the window, a window and view that had always given her pleasure, until now. Out of it she still saw the metal roofs, the chimneys, the solid fieldstone buildings, the snow falling thicker now, but she also saw the television trucks and cars with radio station logos stenciled to the sides. She saw men and women she recognized from television, and photos in *Le Soleil* and *La Presse*. Journalists. And not the gutter press. Not just *Allô Police*, though they were there too. But respected news anchors.

They stood in front of the building, artificial lights on them, cameras pointed, they lined up like some game of Red Rover, and told their stories to the province. Elizabeth wondered what they were saying.

But it couldn't be good, just degrees of bad.

She'd called the members of the library to give them what little information was available. It didn't take long.

Augustin Renaud was found murdered in the basement. Pass it on.

She glanced out the window again at the quickly gathering reporters and snow, a storm of each, a blizzard, and moaned.

"What is it?" asked Winnie, joining her friend by the window. "Oh."

Together they watched Porter descend the stairs, approach the swarming reporters and give what amounted to a news conference.

"Jesus," sighed Winnie. "Do you think I can reach him with this?" She hefted the first volume of the *Shorter Dictionary*.

"You going to throw the book at him?" smiled Elizabeth.

"Shame no one donated a crossbow to the library."

Inspector Langlois sat at the head of the polished table in the library of the Literary and Historical Society. It was a room at once intimate and grand. It smelled of the past, of a time before computers, before information was "Googled" and "blogged." Before laptops and BlackBerries and all the other tools that mistook information for knowledge. It was an old library, filled with old books and dusty old thoughts.

It was calm and comforting.

It had been a long while since Inspector Langlois had been in a library. Not since his school days. A time filled with new experiences and the aromas that would be forever associated with them. Gym socks. Rotting bananas in lockers. Sweat. Old Spice cologne. Herbal Essence shampoo on the hair of girls he kissed, and more. A scent so sweet, so filled with longing his reaction was still physical whenever he smelt it.

And libraries. Quiet. Calm. A harbor from the turmoil of teenage life. When the Herbal Essence girls had pulled away, and mocked, when the gym sock boys had shoved and he'd shoved back, laughing. Roughhousing. Keeping the terror behind savage eyes.

He remembered how it felt to find himself in the library, away from possible attack but surrounded by things far more dangerous than what roamed the school corridors.

For here thoughts were housed.

Young Langlois had sat down and gathered that power to him. The power that came from having information, knowledge, thoughts, and a calm place to collect them.

Inspector Langlois, of the Quebec City homicide squad, looked round the double-height library with its carved wood and old volumes and wondered at the people he was about to interview. People who had access to all these books, all this calm, all this power.

English people.

To his right sat his assistant, taking notes. On his left sat a man he'd only seen at a distance before today. Heard lecture. Seen on television.

At trials, at public hearings, on talk shows. And at the funerals, six weeks ago. Close up, Chief Inspector Gamache looked different. Langlois had only ever seen him in a suit, with his trim moustache. Now the man was not only wearing a cardigan, and corduroys, but also a beard. Shot with gray. And a scar above his left temple.

"*Alors,*" Langlois started. "Before the first one comes in I want to go over what we know so far."

"The victim," his assistant read from his notebook, "is identified as Augustin Renaud. Seventy-two years of age. His next of kin has been notified, an ex-wife. No children. She'll formally identify him later, but there's no doubt. His driver's license and health card both identify him. Also in his wallet was forty-five dollars and there was a further three dollars and twenty-two cents change in his pockets. When the body was removed we found another twenty-eight cents beneath him, fallen from his pocket we think. They're modern coins. All Canadian."

"Good," said Langlois. "Go on."

Beside him Chief Inspector Gamache listened, one hand holding the other on the table.

"We found a satchel underneath the body. Inside was a map of Québec, hand-drawn by him."

It was on the table in front of them. The map showed areas of the city he'd excavated for Champlain, and the dates, going back decades.

"Any ideas?" Langlois asked Gamache as all three men examined the paper.

"I find this significant." The Chief's finger hovered over a blank spot on the map. A map that only acknowledged buildings and streets significant to Renaud's search. Places Samuel de Champlain might have been buried. It showed the Basilica, it showed the Café Buade, it showed assorted restaurants and homes unfortunate enough to be targeted by Renaud.

It was as though the rest of the magnificent old city didn't exist for Augustin Renaud.

And where Gamache's finger pointed was the Literary and Historical Society. Missing. Not plotted. Not in existence in Renaud's Champlain-centric world.

Langlois nodded. "I'd seen that too. Maybe he just didn't have time to put it in."

"It's possible," said Gamache.

"What're you thinking?"

"I'm thinking it would be a mistake to be blinded by Renaud's passion. This murder may have nothing to do with Champlain."

"Then why was he digging?" the young assistant asked.

"Good question," smiled Gamache, ruefully. "It would seem a clue."

"Right." Langlois gathered up the map and returned it to the satchel. As he watched Gamache wondered why Renaud had needed the large leather bag to carry just that one slim piece of paper.

"Nothing else was in there?" Gamache nodded to the satchel in Langlois's hand. "Just the map?"

"That's all. Why?"

"He could have carried the map in his pocket. Why the satchel?"

"Habit," said the assistant. "He probably carried it everywhere in case he found something."

Gamache nodded. It was probably right.

"The coroner says Renaud was killed by the shovel sometime around eleven last night," said Langlois. "He fell face forward into the dirt and an attempt was made to bury him."

"Not deeply," said the assistant. "Not well. Do you think he was meant to be found?"

"I wonder how often that cellar is used," mused Langlois. "We'll have to ask. Send in the first person, the head of the board. A," the Inspector consulted his notes, "Porter Wilson."

Porter entered. He tried not to show it, but he was deeply shocked to see this library, his library, occupied by the police force.

He had no rancor toward the French. It was impossible to live in Quebec City and feel like that. It would be a torturous life and an unnecessary torment. No, Porter knew the Francophones to be gracious and inclusive, thoughtful and stable. Most of them. There were radicals on either side.

And that was his problem. Tom Hancock, the minister, kept telling him so. He saw it as "sides," no matter how many years went by, no matter how many French friends he had. No matter his daughter had married a Francophone and his grandchildren went to French schools and he himself spoke perfect French.

He still saw it as "sides," with himself on the out-side. Because he was English. Still, he knew himself to be as much a Québécois as anyone else in that elegant room. Indeed, his family had been there for hundreds of years. He'd lived in Québec longer than that young officer, or the man at the head of the table, or Chief Inspector Gamache.

He'd been born there, lived a full life there, would be buried there. And yet, for all their friendliness, he would never be considered a Québécois, would never totally belong.

Except here. In the Literary and Historical Society, in the very center of the old city. Here he was at home, in an English world created by English words, surrounded by the busts of great Anglos before him.

But today, on his watch, the French force had moved in and were occupying the Lit and His.

"Please," said Inspector Langlois, swiftly standing and indicating a seat. He spoke in his best, highly accented, English. "Join us."

As though Mr. Wilson had a choice. They were the hosts and he was the guest. With an effort he swallowed a retort, and sat, though not in the seat indicated.

"We have some questions," said Inspector Langlois, getting down to business.

Over the course of the next hour they interviewed everyone there. They learned from Porter Wilson that the library was locked every evening at six, and had been locked that morning when he'd arrived. Nothing was out of place. But Langlois's people had examined the large, old lock on the front door and while it showed no signs of tampering a clever six-year-old could have unlocked it without a key.

There was no alarm system.

"Why would we bother with an alarm?" Porter had asked. "No one comes when we're open, why would anyone come when we're closed?"

They learned this was the only place in old Quebec City English books could be found.

"And you seem to have a lot of them," said Gamache. "I couldn't help but notice as I walked through the back corridors and rooms that you have quite a few books not displayed."

That was an understatement, he thought, remembering the boxes of books piled everywhere.

"What's that supposed to mean?"

"Just an observation."

"It's true," said Porter, reluctantly. "And more coming every day. Every time someone dies they leave us their books. That's how we find out someone's dead. A box of worthless books appears. More accurate than the *Chronicle-Telegraph* obits."

"Are they always worthless?" asked Langlois.

"Well, we found a nice book of drawings once."

"When was that?"

"1926."

"Can you not sell some?" Gamache asked.

Porter stared at the Chief Inspector. Gamache stared back, not certain what had caused this sudden vitriolic look.

"Are you kidding?"

"*Non, monsieur.*"

"Well, we can't. Tried once, members didn't like it."

"In 1926?" Langlois asked.

Wilson didn't answer.

Winnie Manning came in next and confirmed that the night was indeed a strawberry, but added that the English were good pumpkins and that the library had a particularly impressive section on mattresses and mattress warfare.

"In fact," she turned to Gamache. "I think that's an area you're interested in."

"It is," he admitted, to the surprise of both Langlois and his assistant. After Winnie left, saying she had to launch a new line of doorknobs, Gamache explained.

"She meant 'naval', not 'mattress'."

"Really?" asked the assistant, who'd made notes but had decided to burn them in case anyone thought he was stoned when he'd taken them down.

Mr. Blake took Winnie's place.

"Stuart Blake," the elderly man said, sitting in the chair offered and looking at them with polite interest. He was immaculately dressed, shaved, his face smooth and pink and soft. His eyes bright. He looked at Gamache and smiled.

"*Monsieur l'inspecteur,*" he inclined his head. "*Désolé.* I had no idea who you were."

"You knew what mattered," said Gamache. "That I was a man in need of this magnificent library. That was enough to know."

Mr. Blake smiled, folded his hands, and waited. At ease.

"You spend a lot of time in the library, I believe," said Inspector Langlois.

"I do. For many years, since my retirement."

"And what was your profession?"

"I was a lawyer."

"So it's *Maître* Blake," said Langlois.

"No, please, I've been retired for years. Plain 'Mister' will do."

"How long have you been involved with the Literary and Historical Society?"

"Oh, all my life in one way or another, and my parents and grandparents before that. It was the first historical society in the country, you know. Pre-dates the national archives. Been around since 1824, though not in this building."

"This building," said Gamache, picking up on the opening. "It has an interesting history?"

"Very." Mr. Blake turned to face the Chief Inspector. "It didn't become the Literary and Historical Society until 1868. This was originally the Redoubt Royale, a military barracks. It also housed prisoners of war, mostly American. Then it became a regular prison. There were public hangings, you know."

Gamache said nothing, though he was interested that this refined, cultured, civilized man seemed to get pleasure telling them of such barbarity.

"Hung right out there." He waved toward the front door. "If you believe in ghosts, this is the place for you."

"Have you seen any?" Gamache asked, surprising both Langlois and the young officer.

Blake hesitated, then shook his head. "No. But I can feel them sometimes, when no one else is here."

"Are you often here, when no one else is?" Gamache asked, pleasantly.

"Sometimes. I find it peaceful. I think you do too."

"*C'est la vérité*," agreed the Chief Inspector. "But I don't have a key to get in after hours. You do. And, I presume, you use it."

Again, Mr. Blake hesitated. "I do. But not often. Only when I can't sleep and a question troubles me."

"Like what?" Gamache asked.

"Like what grasses grow on Rum Island, and when the last coelacanth was caught."

"And were you troubled by such questions last night?"

The two men looked at each other. Finally Mr. Blake smiled and shook his head.

"I was not. Slept like a child last night. As Shakespeare said, the best way to peace is to have a still and quiet conscience."

Or none at all, thought Gamache, watching Mr. Blake with interest.

"Can anyone confirm that?" Inspector Langlois asked.

"I'm a widower. Lost my wife eight years ago, so no, I have no witnesses."

"*Désolé,*" said Langlois. "Tell me, Mr. Blake, why do you think Augustin Renaud was here last night?"

"Isn't it obvious? He must have thought Champlain is buried here."

And there it was. The obvious answer, out in the open.

"And is he?"

Blake smiled. "No, I'm afraid not."

"Why would he think Champlain was here?" Langlois asked.

"Why did Augustin Renaud think anything? Has anyone ever figured out his logic? Perhaps his digs were more alphabetical than archeological and he'd come to the 'Ls'. That makes as much sense as any of his reasoning. Poor man," Blake added. "I imagine you'll be digging?"

"Right now it's still a crime scene."

"Incredible," said Mr. Blake, almost to himself. "Why would Augustin Renaud be here in the Lit and His?"

"And why would someone murder him?" said Langlois.

"Here," added Gamache.

Finally Elizabeth MacWhirter entered and sat.

"What is your job, exactly?" Langlois asked.

"Well, 'job' is a loose term. We're all volunteer. Used to be paid, but the government's cut back on library funding, so now any money we get goes in to upkeep. Heating alone is ruinous and we just had the wiring redone. In fact, if it hadn't been done we might never have found Mr. Renaud."

"What do you mean?" Langlois asked.

"When we rewired the place we decided to do the phone lines too. Bury them in the basement. If the line hadn't been cut we'd never have found the body, and he'd have been concreted over."

"*Pardon?*" asked Langlois.

"Next week. The concrete people are supposed to come on Monday to put down the forms."

The men looked at each other.

"You mean, if either Renaud or his murderer hadn't cut the telephone line while digging last night, the whole floor would have been concreted? Sealed?" asked the Inspector.

Elizabeth nodded.

"Who knew this was going to happen?" Langlois asked.

"Everyone." She walked over to a table and returned with three pamphlets which she handed out. There, on the front page, was the announcement.

The wiring, telephones and basement were to be redone.

Refolding the pamphlet and leaving it on the table in front of him Chief Inspector Gamache looked at the slim elderly woman.

"It says the work is to be done, but not the timing. The timing seems to me significant."

"You may be right, Chief Inspector, but we didn't keep the timing a secret. Many people knew. The board, the volunteers, the construction workers."

"Where'd you get the money for all this? It must have cost a fortune."

"It was expensive," she admitted. "We got grants and donations and sold some books."

"So the sale of books was fairly recent," said Langlois. "But we heard from Monsieur Wilson that it wasn't very successful."

"Now there's an understatement," said Elizabeth. "It was a disaster. We sold a few boxes, books that had been sitting for decades gathering dust. A shame. They should be in someone's collection, appreciated, not piling up here. And God knows, we need the money. It was a perfect solution. Turn unwanted books into wiring."

"So what went wrong?" asked Gamache.

"The community went wrong. They decided we were as much a

museum as a library and every item ever donated was a treasure. The books became symbolic, I'm afraid."

"Symbolic of what?" Gamache asked.

"Of the value of the English language. Of the English culture. There was a fear that if even the Lit and His didn't value the English language, the written word, then there was no hope. They stopped being books and became symbols of the English community. They had to be preserved. Once that happened there was no fighting, no arguing. And certainly, no selling."

Gamache nodded. She was quite right. The battle was lost at that moment. Best to quit the field.

"And so you stopped the sale?"

"We did. Which is why you see boxes piled in the corridors. If one more elderly Anglo dies, the Literary and Historical Society will explode." She laughed, but without humor.

"Why do you think Augustin Renaud was here?" Langlois asked.

"For the same reason you do. He must have thought Champlain was here."

"Why would he think that?"

Elizabeth shrugged, making even that look refined. "Why did he think Champlain was buried under that Chinese restaurant? Or that primary school? Why did Augustin Renaud think anything?"

"Did he ever come here?"

"Well, he did last night."

"I mean, did you ever see him here before that?"

Elizabeth MacWhirter hesitated.

"Never inside, as far as I know. But I saw him at the front door. Yesterday morning."

The young assistant, so shocked something worthwhile had actually been said, almost forgot to write this down. But then his pen whirled into action.

"Go on," said Langlois.

"He asked to see the Board of Directors."

"When was this?"

"Around eleven thirty. We'd locked the door as we always do during a board meeting."

"He just showed up?"

"That's right."

"How'd he even know you were meeting?"

"We put the announcement in the paper."

"*Le Soleil*?"

"The Québec *Chronicle-Telegraph*."

"The what?"

"The *Chronicle-Telegraph*." Elizabeth spelled it for the assistant. "It's the oldest newspaper in North America," she said by rote.

"Go on. You say he showed up. What happened?" asked the Inspector.

"He rang the bell and Winnie answered it, then came up here with his request. She left him downstairs, outside."

"And what did you say?"

"We took a vote and decided not to see him. It was unanimous."

"Why not?"

Elizabeth thought about this. "We don't react well to anything different, I'm afraid. Myself included. We've created a quiet, uneventful, but very happy life. One based on tradition. We know that every Tuesday there'll be a bridge club, they'll serve ginger snaps and orange pekoe tea. We know the cleaner comes on Thursdays, and we know where the paper towels are kept. In the same place my grandmother kept them, when she was secretary to the Lit and His. It's not an exciting life but it's deeply meaningful to us."

She stopped then appealed to Chief Inspector Gamache.

"Augustin Renaud's visit upset all that," he said.

She nodded.

"How'd he react when told you wouldn't see him?" Gamache asked.

"I went down to tell him. He wasn't pleased but he accepted it, said he'd be back. I didn't think he meant quite so soon."

She remembered standing at the thick wooden door, opened a sliver as though she was cloistered and Renaud a sinner. His white hair sticking out from under his fur hat, frost and icicles and angry breath dripping from his black moustache. His blue eyes not just mad, but livid.

"You cannot stop me, *madame*," he'd said.

"I have no desire to stop you, Monsieur Renaud," she'd said in a voice that she hoped sounded reasonable. Friendly even.

But they both knew she was lying. She wanted to stop him almost as badly as he wanted in.

When all the interviews had been completed Gamache returned to the office. There he found them sitting over a pot of tea.

"Welcome to our little lifeboat," said Elizabeth, getting to her feet and inviting him to join Winnie, Porter and herself. "And this is our fuel." She indicated the teapot and smiled.

Henri rushed over to greet him.

"I hope he wasn't too much trouble." Gamache patted Henri's flank and taking a seat he accepted a cup of strong tea.

"Never," said Winnie. "What happens next?"

"In the investigation? They'll get the coroner's report and start looking into Augustin Renaud's movements, friends, family. Who'd want him dead."

They sat together around the table. Not exactly a huddled mass, but reminiscent of it.

"You said Monsieur Renaud asked to speak to the board," Gamache turned to Elizabeth.

"You told them that?" Porter asked, his voice more clipped than usual. "Now you've done it."

"She had no choice," said Gamache. "You all should have told us. You must have known it was important." He looked at them sternly. "You refused to see him, but would you have listened to him eventually?"

He spoke now to Porter Wilson but noticed everyone looked at Elizabeth, who remained silent.

"Eventually, maybe. But there was no advantage for us, and a whole lot of—" Porter searched for a word. "Inconvenience."

"Monsieur Renaud could be very persuasive," said Gamache, remembering the vitriolic campaigns the amateur archeologist had waged against anyone who denied him permission to dig.

"True," admitted Porter. He seemed tired now, as the full import of what had happened weighed more and more heavily. As horrible as it would have been to have Augustin Renaud dig for Champlain beneath their Lit and His Society, the only thing worse was what had happened.

"May I see your minutes for the meeting?"

"I haven't done them up yet," said Elizabeth.

"Your notebook will do."

He waited. Eventually she handed him her notebook and putting on his half-moon reading glasses he scanned the minutes, noting who was there for the meeting.

"I see Tom Hancock and Ken Haslam were there, but left early. Were they there when Augustin Renaud showed up?"

"Yes," said Porter. "They left shortly after that. We were all there."

Gamache continued to scan the minutes then over his glasses he looked at Elizabeth.

"There's no mention of Monsieur Renaud's visit."

Elizabeth MacWhirter stared back. It seemed clear that when she'd asked for his help she hadn't expected him to ask them quite so many questions, and uncomfortable ones at that.

"I decided not to mention it. He didn't speak to us, after all. Nothing happened."

"A great deal happened, *madame*," said Gamache. But he'd also noticed that she'd said "I," not "we." Was she letting them off the hook? Taking the burden of responsibility herself? Or was it really a unilateral decision?

They might be in a lifeboat, but Gamache now had a clear idea who was captain.

SIX

It was early afternoon and Jean-Guy Beauvoir realized he'd already made a mistake. Not a big one, more an annoyance.

He had to return to Montreal and interview Olivier Brulé. He should have done that first, before coming down to Three Pines. Instead, he'd spent the last hour quietly in the bistro. Everyone had left, but not before making sure he was in the best chair, the big, worn, leather armchair beside the fireplace. He dipped an orange biscotti into his *café au lait* and looking through the frosty window he could see the snow, falling gently but steadily. Billy Williams had been by once with the plow, but the snow had already filled in behind him.

Beauvoir dropped his gaze to the dossier in his hand and continued reading, snug and warm inside. Half an hour later he glanced at the mariner's clock on the mantelpiece. One twenty.

Time to go.

But not to Montreal. Not in this weather.

Returning to his room in the B and B, Beauvoir changed into his silk long underwear then layered his clothing strategically, putting on his snowsuit last. He rarely wore it, since he preferred being runway-ready and this suit made him look like the robot from *Lost in Space*. Indeed, in the winter, Québec looked like the staging area for an alien invasion.

Fortunately the chances of running into the editor of *Vogue Hommes* in the woods was pretty small.

He walked up the hill, hearing his thighs zinging together and barely able to put his arms flat to his sides. Now he felt a bit like a zombie, clump, clump, clumping up the hill to the inn and spa.

"*Oui?*"

Carole Gilbert answered the door and looked at the snow-covered zombie. But the older woman showed absolutely no fright, not even surprise. Gracious as ever she took two steps back and let the alien into the inn, run by her son and daughter-in-law.

"May I help you?"

Beauvoir unwrapped himself, now feeling like The Mummy. He was an entire B-grade film festival. Finally he removed his hat and Carole Gilbert smiled warmly.

"It's Inspector Beauvoir, *non?*"

"*Oui, madame, comment allez-vous?*"

"I'm well, thank you. Have you come to stay? I didn't see your name on the register."

She looked behind her into the large, open entrance hall, with its black and white tile floor, gleaming wood desk and fresh flowers, even in the middle of winter. It was inviting and for a moment Beauvoir wished he had booked in. But then he remembered the prices, and remembered why he was there.

Not for massages and gourmet meals, but to find out whether Olivier had actually killed the Hermit.

Why did Olivier move the body?

And the very spot he was standing was where Olivier had dumped the Hermit. Olivier had admitted as much. He'd hauled the dead man through the woods that Labor Day weekend, in the middle of the night. Finding the door unlocked he simply dropped the sad bundle here. Right here.

Beauvoir looked down. He was melting, like the Wicked Witch of the West, his snow-covered boots puddling on the tile floor. But Carole Gilbert didn't seem to care. She was more concerned for his comfort.

"No, I'm staying at the B and B," he said.

"Of course." He searched her face for any sign of professional jealousy, but saw none. And why would he? It seemed inconceivable the owners of this magnificent inn and spa would be jealous of any establishment, especially Gabri's somewhat weary B and B.

"And what brings you back to us?" she asked, her voice light, conversational. "Is the Chief Inspector with you?"

"No, I'm on vacation. Leave, actually."

"Of course, I'm sorry." And she looked it, her face suddenly concerned. "How stupid of me. How are you?"

"I'm well. Better."

"And Monsieur Gamache?"

"Better also." He was, it must be admitted, a little tired of answering these kind questions.

"I'm so glad to hear it." She motioned him into the inn but he held his ground. He was in a hurry and it was his temperament to show it. He consciously tried to slow himself down. He was supposed to be there for a vacation, after all.

"How can I help you?" she asked. "I don't suppose you've come for the hot mud treatment? The Tai Chi class perhaps?"

He noticed her bemused look. Laughing at him? He thought not. More likely poking gentle fun at herself and the services of the spa. Her son Marc and his wife Dominique had bought the run-down place a year or so ago and turned it into this magnificent inn and spa. And had invited his mother, Carole Gilbert, to move from Quebec City to Three Pines, to help them run it.

"I can see how you might think so, since I've worn my Tai Chi outfit." He opened his arms so she could see the full splendor of his ski suit. She laughed. "I've actually come to ask a favor. May I borrow one of your snowmobiles? I understand you have some for your guests."

"That's true, we do. I'll get Roar Parra to help you."

"*Merci.* I thought I'd go into the woods, to the cabin."

He watched her as he spoke, hoping for a reaction, and got one. The gracious woman became glacial. Interesting how a moment before she'd seemed calm, content, relaxed. And now, while hardly anything had physically changed she suddenly seemed to be made of ice. A chill radiated from her.

"Is that so? Why?"

"Just to see it again. Something to do."

She examined him closely, her eyes reptilian. Then the mask descended and she once again became the *gentille grande dame* of the manor house.

"In this weather?" She glanced outside to the falling snow.

"If snow kept me from doing things I'd get nothing done in winter," he said.

"That's true," she admitted. Reluctantly? he wondered. "I don't suppose you've heard, but my husband is living there now."

"Is that so?" He hadn't heard. But he did hear her say "husband," not "former husband." They'd been separated for years, until Vincent Gilbert had suddenly shown up, uninvited, at the inn and spa at almost exactly the same time the Hermit's body had appeared.

"Are you sure you wouldn't prefer a mud wrap?" she asked. "It's quite similar to an hour with Vincent, I find."

He laughed. "*Non, madame, merci.* Will he mind if I drop in?"

"Vincent? I'm afraid I've given up trying to figure out how his mind works." But she relented a little and smiled at the melting man. "I'm sure he'll be delighted for the company. But you'd better hurry, before it gets too late."

It was already two in the afternoon. It would be dark by four.

And when the winter sun set on a Québec forest, monsters crawled out of the shadows. Not the B-grade movie monsters, not zombies or mummies or space aliens. But older, subtler wraiths. Invisible creatures that rode in on plunging temperatures. Death by freezing, death by exposure, death by going even a foot off the path, and getting lost. Death, ancient and patient, waited in Québec forests for the sun to set.

"Come with me."

Carole Gilbert, petite and refined, put on her bulbous coat and joined the alien army. They walked around the side of the inn and spa, through large soft flakes of snow. In the middle distance Inspector Beauvoir could see cross-country skiers striding across the field on well-marked paths. In a few minutes they'd be inside, sipping buttery rum toddies or hot chocolate by the fire, their cheeks rosy, their noses running, rubbing their feet to get the circulation back.

If they were staying at the inn they'd be healthy and wealthy and warm.

And he'd be heading deep into the forest, racing the setting sun, to a cabin where a murder had happened and an asshole now lived.

"Roar," Carole Gilbert called and the short, squat man in the shed straightened up. His hair and eyes were almost black and he was powerfully built.

"Madame Gilbert," he said, nodding to her. Not in an obsequious manner, but with respect. And Inspector Beauvoir realized this woman would naturally receive respect because she treated others with it. As she did now with this woodsman.

"You remember Inspector Beauvoir, I believe."

There was an awkward hesitation before Roar Parra put out his hand. Beauvoir wasn't surprised. He and the rest of the homicide team had made this man's life miserable. He, his wife Hanna and son Havoc had been the chief suspects in the murder of the Hermit.

The Inspector looked at their former suspect. A man familiar with the forest, a man who'd been cutting a trail, straight for the recluse's cabin. He was Czech. The dead man was Czech. His son Havoc worked for Olivier and could have followed him one night through the woods and found the cabin, and found the treasure.

The Hermit had amassed his treasures almost certainly by stealing them from people in the Eastern Bloc when the walls were crumbling. When communism was crumbling, when people were desperate to get out, to the West.

They'd entrusted their family treasures, guarded and hidden for generations of communist rule, to the wrong man. To the Hermit, before he was a hermit, when he was a man with a plan. To steal from them. But he'd stolen more than antiquities and works of art. He'd stolen hope, he'd stolen trust.

Had he stolen from Roar and Hanna Parra? Had they found him? Had they killed him?

Carole Gilbert had left and the two men were alone in the shed.

"Why're you heading back to the cabin?"

There was nothing subtle about this brick of a man.

"Just curious. You have a problem with that?"

They stared at each other.

"Are you here to cause trouble?"

"I'm here to relax. A nice trip through the woods, that's all. If you don't hurry it'll get too late."

Was that Parra's goal, Beauvoir wondered as he put the helmet over his tuque and straddled the machine, revving the motors. Was he deliberately going slow in the hopes Beauvoir would get stuck in the woods, after nightfall?

No, he decided. Too refined. This was a man who whacked his enemies on the head. As the Hermit had died.

With a wave Beauvoir was away, feeling the powerful machine vibrating beneath him. He'd been on dozens of Ski-Doos in the past decade, since joining homicide. He loved them. The noise, the power, the freedom. The bracing cold and snow on his face. His body, insulated by the suit, was toasty and warm, almost too warm. He could feel the perspiration.

Beauvoir gripped the handles and leaned into a corner, the heavy machine following him. But something was different.

Something was wrong.

Not with the machine, but with him. He felt a familiar ache in his abdomen.

Surely not. He was just sitting on the machine, it wasn't like he was doing any real work.

Deeper along the narrow path he went, into the woods. Without leaves the forest looked cold and bare. The shadows were sharp and long as was the pain now, in his stomach, in his side, shooting down into his groin.

Beauvoir breathed deeply but the pain grew worse.

Finally he had to stop.

Clutching his middle he slowly fell forward, his arm folding over the handles of the idling Ski-Doo. His head dropped and rested on his arm. He tried to concentrate on the vibration, on the calming, deep, predictable, civilized sound. But his world had collapsed to a single sensation.

Pain.

An agonizing, familiar pain. One he'd thought was gone forever, but it had found him again in the darkening woods in winter.

Closing his eyes he concentrated on his breath, hearing it, feeling it. Long, relaxed breath in. Long, relaxed breath out.

How big a mistake was this? An hour, perhaps slightly more, until the woods were in darkness. Would anyone sound an alarm? Would he be missed? Would Roar Parra simply go home? Would Carole Gilbert lock the door and toss another log on the fire?

Then he felt a hand on his face and jerked his head up. But the hand restrained him. Not violently, but certainly. Beauvoir's eyes flew open and he looked into very blue ones.

"Don't move, just lie still."

The man was old. His face worn, but his eyes sharp. His bare hand, which had started on Beauvoir's face now slipped quickly beneath the scarf and collar and turtleneck to Beauvoir's pulse.

"Shh," the man said. And Beauvoir shushed.

He knew who this man was. Vincent Gilbert. Dr. Gilbert.

The asshole.

But Gamache, and Myrna, Old Mundin and others claimed he was also a saint.

Beauvoir hadn't seen it. The man had seemed all asshole to him when they'd investigated the murder of the Hermit.

"Come with me." Gilbert reached across Beauvoir and turned the Ski-Doo off, then he put his long arms around Beauvoir and gradually helped him up. The two men walked, slowly, along the path, Beauvoir pausing for breath now and then. He threw up once. Gilbert took his own scarf and cleaned Beauvoir's face and waited. And waited. In the snow and cold, until Beauvoir could go on. Then carefully, wordlessly, they limped deeper into the woods, Beauvoir leaning heavily on the tall, elderly asshole.

His eyes closed, Beauvoir concentrated on putting one plodding foot in front of the other. He felt the pain radiating from his side but he also felt the kiss of the snowflakes on his face and tried to concentrate on that. Then the sensations changed. The snow stopped touching his face, and he heard his footsteps echo on wood.

They were at the log cabin. He almost wept, with exhaustion and relief.

Opening his eyes as they entered he saw, a million miles across the single room, a large bed. It was covered with a warm duvet and soft pillows.

And all Beauvoir wanted to do was make it across the room, so much larger than he remembered, to the bed at the very far end.

"Almost there," whispered Dr. Gilbert.

Beauvoir stared at the bed, willing it to come to him, as he and Gilbert inched their way across the wooden floorboards. Until, finally, finally. There.

Dr. Gilbert sat him on the side and while Beauvoir sagged, his head lolling for the pillow, the doctor held him upright and undressed him.

Only then did he let Beauvoir slowly subside, until his weary head hit the pillow and the soft flannel sheets were pulled snug around him and finally, finally, the duvet.

And Beauvoir drifted off to sleep, smelling sweet maple smoke from the hearth, and homemade soup and feeling the warmth close in around him as out the window he saw the snow piling up and the darkness arriving.

Beauvoir awoke a few hours later, coming back to consciousness slowly. His side ached, as though he'd been kicked hard, but the nausea had passed. A hot water bottle had been placed in the bed and he found himself hugging it, curled around it.

Sleepily, lazily, he lay in the bed and slowly the room came into focus.

Vincent Gilbert was sitting in a large easy chair by the fireplace. He was reading a book, a glass of red wine on the table beside him, his slippered feet resting on a hassock.

The cabin seemed at once familiar but different.

The walls were still log, the windows and hearth unchanged. Rugs were scattered around the floorboards, but no longer the fine, hand-stitched Oriental rugs the Hermit had. These were rag rugs, also homemade, but much closer to home.

A few paintings hung on the walls, but not the masterpieces the Hermit had collected, and hidden here. Now they were modest examples of Québécois artists. Fine but not, perhaps, spectacular.

The glass Dr. Gilbert used looked like any other glass, not the cut leaded crystal they'd found here after the murder.

But the biggest change was where the Hermit had had silver and gold and fine bone china candelabras to provide light, Dr. Gilbert had a lamp. An electric lamp. And on the table next to Gilbert, Beauvoir noticed a phone.

Electricity had been brought deep into the forest to power this rustic little cabin.

Then Beauvoir remembered why he'd made the trek into the woods.

It was to see once again where the murder had been committed. He looked over to the door and noticed a rug there, right where the bloodstain had been. Might still be.

Death had come to this peaceful little cabin, but in what form? Olivier or someone else. And driven by what? As Chief Inspector

Gamache impressed upon them, murder was never about a gun or a knife or a blow to the head, it was what powered that thrust.

What had taken the Hermit's life? Greed, as the Crown prosecution and Gamache contended? Or was it something else? Fear? Rage? Revenge? Jealousy?

The treasures discovered here had been remarkable, but not the most amazing part of the case. The cabin had produced something else, something far more disquieting.

A word, woven into a spider's web. Up in the corner of the cabin, where the shadows were the deepest.

Woo.

The word had also been found carved, not well, into a piece of bloodstained wood. It had tumbled from the dead man's hand and ended up under the bed as though cowering there. A little wooden word. Woo.

But what did it mean?

Had the Hermit made the word?

It didn't seem likely, since he was a master carver and the wooden Woo was rustic, child-like.

The prosecution had concluded Olivier had put Woo into the web and carved it in wood as part of his campaign to terrify the Hermit, keep him hiding in the cabin. And Olivier had admitted, finally, that had been his goal, to convince the mad old man that the outside world was dangerous. Filled with demons and Furies and terrible, terrible beings.

Chaos is coming, old son, the Hermit had whispered to Olivier the last night of his life. Olivier had done his job well. The Hermit was well and truly terrified.

But while admitting to everything else, Olivier denied two things.

Killing the Hermit.

And making the word, Woo.

The court hadn't believed him. Olivier had been found guilty and sentenced to prison. It was a case Chief Inspector Gamache had painstakingly, painfully, built against his friend. A case Inspector Jean-Guy Beauvoir had collaborated on and believed in.

And one the Chief now asked him to dismantle and put together again. Only this time seeing if the same evidence could exonerate Olivier and point to someone else.

Like the man in the cabin with him.

Gilbert looked up and smiled.

"Hello," he said, closing the book and getting up slowly. Beauvoir had to remember this tall, slender man, with the white hair and searching eyes was in his late seventies.

Gilbert sat on the side of the bed and smiled reassuringly. "May I?" he asked Beauvoir before touching him. Beauvoir nodded. "I've spoken to Carole and told her you'd be spending the night," Dr. Gilbert said, pulling down the duvet. "She said she'd call the B and B and let Gabri know. No need to worry."

"*Merci.*"

Gilbert's warm, sure hands were pressing against Beauvoir's abdomen.

Beauvoir had been prodded countless times in the past two months, especially those first days. It seemed his new alarm clock. Every few hours he awoke, dazed from medication, to someone else shoving their cold hands against his stomach.

None felt like Gilbert. Beauvoir winced a few times, despite his pledge not to. The pain took him by surprise. As soon as he showed signs of discomfort Gilbert's hands stopped, pausing to let Beauvoir catch his breath, then they moved on.

"You probably shouldn't have taken the Ski-Doo out," Gilbert smiled, replacing the bed sheets and duvet, "but I imagine you know that already. The bullet itself did some damage, but the longer-term effect is from a sort of shock wave the impact creates. Did your doctors explain that?"

Beauvoir shook his head.

"Perhaps they were too busy. The bullet went straight through your side. You probably lost quite a bit of blood."

Beauvoir nodded, trying to keep the images at bay.

"It didn't hit your internal organs," Dr. Gilbert continued. "But the waves from the impact bruised the tissue. That's what you'll feel if you push yourself too hard, like this afternoon. But you're healing well."

"*Merci,*" said Beauvoir. It helped to understand.

And Beauvoir knew then the man was a saint. He'd been touched by any number of medical men and women. All healers, all well intentioned, some kind, some rough. All made it clear they wanted him to live, but none had made him feel that his life was precious, was worth saving, was worth something.

Vincent Gilbert did. His healing went beyond the flesh, beyond the blood. Beyond the bones.

Gilbert patted the covers and made to get up, but hesitated. He picked up a small bottle of pills on the bedside table. "I found these in your pocket."

Beauvoir reached out but Gilbert closed them in his hand and searched Beauvoir's face. There was a long pause. Finally Gilbert relented and opened his fist. "Be careful with these."

Beauvoir took the bottle and shook out a pill.

"Perhaps half," said Dr. Gilbert, reaching for it.

Beauvoir watched Dr. Gilbert skillfully snap a small OxyContin in two.

"I keep them just in case," Beauvoir said, swallowing the tiny half pill as Gilbert handed him clean pajamas.

"In case you do something foolish?" asked Gilbert with a smile. "You might need another bottle."

"Har har," said Beauvoir. But already he could feel the warmth spreading and the pain dulling and any sting there might have been in Gilbert's comment drifted away.

As he dressed, Beauvoir watched the doctor in the kitchen spooning soup into two bowls and cutting fresh baked bread.

"Les Canadiens are playing tonight, aren't they?" Gilbert returned with the food and made Beauvoir comfortable sitting up in bed. "Want to watch?"

"Please."

Within moments they were eating soup, baguette and watching Les Canadiens slaughter New York.

"Too salty," snapped Gilbert. "I told Carole not to put so much salt in the food."

"Tastes fine to me."

"Then you have no taste. Raised on poutine and burgers."

Beauvoir looked at Dr. Gilbert expecting to see a smile. Instead his handsome face was sour, angry. Entitled, petulant, petty.

The asshole was back. Or, more likely, had been there all along in deceptively easy company with the saint.

SEVEN

—

Armand Gamache rose quietly in the night, putting on his bedside lamp and dressing warmly. Henri watched all this with his tail swishing and the tennis ball in his mouth. They tiptoed down the narrow, winding wood stairs that seemed carved into the center of the old home. Émile had put him on the top floor, in what had been the master bedroom. It was a magnificent loft space with wood beams and dormer windows out each side of the roof. Émile had explained that he no longer felt comfortable on the steep, narrow stairs, worn by hundreds of years of feet, and did Armand mind?

Gamache didn't, except that it proved what he already knew. His mentor was slowing down.

Now he and Henri descended two floors to the living room where the woodstove still burned and radiated heat. There he put on a single light, slipped into his warmest coat, hat, scarf and mitts and went out, not forgetting to take the most crucial item. The Chuck-it for Henri. Henri was in love with the Chuck-it. As was Gamache.

They walked through the deserted streets of old Québec, up St-Stanislas, past the Literary and Historical Society where they paused. Twenty-four hours ago Augustin Renaud lay hidden in the basement. Murdered. Had the telephone cable not been severed while digging the shallow grave the basement would have been cemented over and Augustin Renaud would have joined the countless other corpses hidden in and around Québec. It wasn't all that long ago archeologists discovered skeletons actually inside the stone walls surrounding the city. The bodies of American soldiers captured after a raid in 1803.

The authorities had quickly said the men were already dead when walled up, but privately Gamache wondered. After all, why put bodies into a wall unless it was a grotesque punishment, or to conceal a crime? Since Québec was built on bones and irony, the invading soldiers had become part of the city defenses.

Augustin Renaud had almost gone the way of the soldiers and become a permanent part of Québec, encased in concrete beneath the Literary and Historical Society, helping prop up the venerable Anglophone institution. Indeed, Renaud's life was a mother lode of irony. Like the time he'd dug for Champlain on live television only to break through into the basement of a Chinese restaurant. Since Champlain had spent much of his life trying to find China it seemed, well, ironic. Or the time Renaud had opened a sealed coffin, once again convinced it was Champlain, only to have the pressurized contents explode into the atmosphere in a plumb of missionary fervor. The Jesuit inside, turned to dust, was sent to the heavens, immortal. Though not the sort of immortality he'd prayed for or expected. The priest tumbled back to earth in raindrops, to join the food chain and end up in the breast milk of the native women he'd tried to wipe out.

Renaud himself had narrowly escaped a similar fate, coming within hours of forming the foundation of the Literary and Historical Society.

Armand Gamache had hoped that after the initial interviews his obligation to Elizabeth MacWhirter and the rest of the Lit and His would be over. But he now knew that wasn't true. Renaud had demanded to meet the board, the board had refused, then they'd purged the incident from the minutes. When word got out there'd be hell to pay. And it would be the Anglos who had to pay it.

No, Gamache thought as he and Henri trudged out the gates, he couldn't leave them. Not yet.

The snow had almost stopped and the temperature was dropping. There was no traffic, not a sound except Gamache's feet squeaking on the snow.

It was three twenty in the morning.

Every day Gamache woke at about that time. At first he'd tried to get back to sleep, had stayed in bed, had fought it. But now, after weeks and weeks, he'd decided this was it, for now. Instead of fighting, he and

Henri would get up quietly and go for a walk, first around their Montreal neighborhood and now here in Quebec City.

Gamache knew that in order to get through the day he needed this quiet time with his thoughts at night.

He needed this quiet time with the voice in his head.

"My father taught me to play the fiddle," Agent Paul Morin said, in answer to Gamache's question. "I was about four. We have some home video of it somewhere. My father and grandfather playing the fiddle behind me, and me in front wearing these great big sagging shorts, they look like diapers." Morin laughed. "I had my little fiddle. My grandmother was on piano and my sister pretended to conduct. She was about three. She's married now, you know, and expecting."

Gamache turned left and walked through the darkened Carnaval site at the foot of the Plains of Abraham. A couple of guards watched but didn't approach. Too cold for confrontation. Gamache and Henri wound along the pedestrian walk, past attractions that would be filled with excited kids and freezing parents in just a few hours. Then the stalls and temporary buildings and rides trailed off and they were walking through thin forest toward the infamous open field and the monument erected where the English General Wolfe fell, and died, on September 13, 1759.

Gamache scooped up a handful of snow and crushed it into a ball. Henri immediately dropped the tennis ball and danced around. The Chief cocked his arm, smiling at Henri, who suddenly crouched. Muscles tense. Waiting.

Then Gamache threw the snowball and Henri raced after it, catching it in mid-air. He was ecstatic for a moment then his jaws closed, the snow disintegrated and Henri landed, perplexed as always.

Gamache took the tennis ball encrusted with frozen saliva, put it in the Chuck-it and tossed. The brilliant yellow ball sailed into the darkness with the shepherd sailing after it.

The Chief Inspector knew every inch of the Champs-de-Bataille, in every season. He knew the changing face of the battlefield. Had stood there in spring and seen the daffodils, had stood there in summer and seen the picnickers, had stood there in winter and watched families cross-country ski and snowshoe, and he'd stood there in early autumn.

On September 13. The exact day of the battle, when more than one thousand men had died or been wounded in an hour. He'd stood there and believed he heard the shouts, heard the shots, smelled the gunpowder, seen the men charging. He'd stood where he believed Général Montcalm had been when he realized the full nature of his mistake.

Montcalm had underestimated the English. Their courage and their cunning.

At what point did he know the battle was lost?

A runner had appeared in Montcalm's camp, upriver from Québec, the night before. Exhausted, almost incoherent, he'd reported the English were scaling the 150-foot cliffs from the river and were on the field belonging to the farmer Abraham just outside the city.

Montcalm's camp hadn't believed him. Thought the man mad. No commander would issue such an order, no army would obey it. They'd have to have wings, Montcalm had laughingly told his generals and gone back to bed.

By dawn the English were on the Plains of Abraham, prepared for battle.

Was that when Montcalm knew all was lost? When the English, armed with wings, had done the impossible? The Général rushed there and had stood on the very spot Gamache now stood. From there he'd looked over the fields and seen the enemy.

Did Montcalm know then?

But still the battle needn't have been lost. He could have prevailed. But Montcalm, the brilliant strategist, had more mistakes to make.

And Gamache thought about that moment when he'd realized his own final and fatal mistake. The enormity of it. Though it had taken him a few moments to grasp as everything unraveled, fell apart. With such speed, and yet it seemed now, so slowly.

"Homicide," his secretary had said, answering the phone.

Beauvoir had been in his office when the call came through, discussing a case in Gaspé. She'd stuck her head in the door.

"It's Inspector Norman, in Ste-Agathe."

Gamache looked up. She rarely interrupted him. They'd worked together for years and she knew when to handle it herself, and when not to.

"Put him through," said the Chief. "*Oui*, Inspector. What can I do for you?"

And so the battle had begun.

Je me souviens, thought Gamache. The motto of Québec. The motto of the Québécois. I remember.

"I was at Carnaval once," Agent Morin said. "It was great. My dad took us and we even played fiddle at the skating rink. Mom tried to stop him. She was embarrassed, and my sister could have died, but Dad and I took out our fiddles and started playing and everyone seemed to really like it."

"That piece you played for us? 'Colm Quigley'?"

"No, that's a lament. It gets faster, but the beginning's too slow for skaters. They wanted something peppier, so we did some jigs and reels."

"How old were you?" Gamache asked.

"Thirteen, maybe fourteen. It was about ten years ago. Never went back."

"Maybe this year."

"*Oui*. I'll take Suzanne. She'd love it. Might even take the fiddle again."

Je me souviens, thought Gamache. That was the problem. Always the problem. I remember. Everything.

In the cabin in the woods Beauvoir lay awake. Normally he slept soundly, even after what happened. But now he found himself staring into the dark rafters, then at the glow of the fireplace. He could see Dr. Gilbert asleep on the two chairs he'd pulled together. The asshole saint had given Beauvoir the bed. Beauvoir felt horrible, having an elderly man who'd been so kind, sleep on a couple chairs. And he wondered, briefly, if that was the point. Why be a saint unless you could also be a martyr?

Perhaps it was the peaceful cabin, perhaps it was exhaustion after pushing himself too far, or the little half pill, but Beauvoir's defenses were down.

And over the wall swarmed the memories.

"Homicide," the Chief's secretary had said. Gamache had taken the call.

11:18 the clock had said. Beauvoir had looked around the room, letting his mind wander, as the Chief spoke on the phone with the Ste-Agathe detachment.

"Agent Morin's on the phone." Gamache's secretary appeared again at the doorway a moment later. The Chief covered the mouthpiece and said, "Ask him to call back in a few minutes."

Gamache's voice was hard and Beauvoir immediately looked at him. He was taking notes as Inspector Norman spoke.

"When was this?" Gamache's sentences were clipped. Something had happened.

"He says he can't." The Chief's secretary hovered, uncomfortable, but insistent.

Gamache nodded to Beauvoir to take the Morin call, but Gamache's secretary stood her ground.

"He says he needs to speak to you, sir," she said. "Now."

Both Chief Inspector Gamache and Inspector Beauvoir stared at her, amazed she would contradict the boss. Then Gamache made up his mind.

"*Désolé*," he said into the receiver to Inspector Norman. "I have to give you to Inspector Beauvoir. Wait, I have a question. Was your agent alone?"

Beauvoir saw Gamache's face change. He waved for Beauvoir to take the other phone in his office. Beauvoir picked up the receiver and saw the Chief take Agent Morin's call on the other line.

"*Oui*, Norman, what's happened?" Beauvoir remembered asking. For something had, something serious. The worst, in fact.

"One of our agents has been shot," Norman said, obviously on a cell phone. He sounded far away, though Beauvoir knew he was only about an hour north of Montreal, in the Laurentian Mountains. "He was checking out a car stopped on the side of a secondary road."

"Is he—?"

"He's unconscious, on his way to the Ste-Agathe hospital. But reports I'm getting aren't hopeful. I'm on my way to the scene."

"We'll be right there, give me the location." Beauvoir knew not only was time crucial, but so was coordination. In a case like this every cop and every department was in danger of descending and then they'd have chaos.

Across the room he could see Gamache standing at his desk, the phone to his ear, his hand gesturing for calm. Not to anyone in the room, but to whoever he was speaking with, presumably Agent Morin.

"He wasn't alone," Norman was saying, the transmission cutting in and out as he raced through the mountains to the scene. "We're looking for the other agent."

It didn't take a homicide detective to know what that meant. One agent shot, the other missing? Lying dead or gravely wounded in some culvert. That's what Inspector Norman was thinking, that's what Beauvoir was thinking.

"Who's the other agent?"

"Morin. One of yours. He's on loan to us for the week. I'm sorry."

"Paul Morin?"

"*Oui.*"

"He's still alive," said Beauvoir, and felt the relief. "He's on the phone with the Chief Inspector."

"Oh, thank God for that. Where is he?"

"I don't know."

Gamache took Morin's call, his mind racing in response to what he'd heard from Inspector Norman. An agent gravely wounded, another missing.

"Agent Morin? What is it?"

"Chief?" The voice sounded hollow, tentative. "I'm sorry. Did you find—"

"Is this Chief Inspector Gamache?" The phone had clearly changed hands.

"Who is this?" the Chief demanded. He gestured to his secretary to get a trace and make sure it was being recorded.

"I can't tell you." The voice sounded middle-aged, perhaps late middle-aged, with a thick country accent. A backwoods voice. Gamache had to strain to understand the words.

"I didn't mean to do it. I just got scared." And the man sounded scared, his voice rising to near hysterics.

"Easy, softly. Calm down. Tell me what this is about."

But in the pit of his stomach he knew what this was about.

An agent injured. An agent missing.

Paul Morin had been seconded to the Ste-Agathe detachment the day before, to fill in for a week. Morin was the missing agent.

At least he was alive.

"I didn't mean to shoot him, but he surprised me. Stopped behind my truck." The man seemed to be losing it. Gamache forced himself to speak slowly, reasonably.

"Is Agent Morin hurt?"

"No. I just didn't know what to do. So I took him."

"You need to let him go now. You need to turn yourself in."

"Are you nuts?" The last word was shrieked. "Turn myself in? You'll kill me. And if you didn't I'd spend the rest of my life in jail. No way."

Gamache's secretary appeared at the door, giving him the "stretch it out" sign.

"I understand. You want to get away, is that right?"

"Yes," the man sounded uncertain, surprised at Gamache's response. "Can I?"

"Well, let's just talk about it. Tell me what happened."

"I was parked. My truck had broken down. Blown tire. I'd just replaced it when the police car pulled up behind."

"Why would that be upsetting?" Gamache kept his voice conversational and he could hear the stress, the panic, on the other end subside a bit. He also stared at his secretary who was looking into the large outer room where there was sudden, frantic, activity.

Still no trace.

"Never you mind. It just was."

"I understand," said Gamache. And he did. There were two big crops in the backwoods of Québec. Maple syrup and marijuana. Chances were the truck wasn't loaded with syrup. "Go on."

"My gun was sitting on the seat and I just knew what would happen. He'd see the gun, arrest me and you'd find . . . what I had in the truck."

The man, thought Gamache, had just shot, perhaps killed a Sûreté officer, kidnapped another, and yet his main concern still seemed to be concealing that he either had or worked for a marijuana plantation. But it was so instinctive, this need to hide, to be secretive. To lie. Hundreds of thousands of dollars could be at stake.

Liberty was at stake.

For a woodsman, the idea of years behind bars must seem like murder.

"What happened?"

Still no trace? It was inconceivable it should take this long.

"I didn't mean to," the man's voice rose again, almost to a squeal. He was pleading now. "It was a mistake. But then it happened and I saw there was another one, so I pointed my gun at him. By then I didn't know what to do. I couldn't just shoot him. Not in cold blood like that. But I couldn't let him go either. So I brought him here."

"You must let him go, you know," said the Chief Inspector. "Just untie him and leave him there. You can take your truck and go, disappear. Just don't hurt Paul Morin."

Vaguely, in the back of Gamache's mind, he wondered why the hostage-taker hadn't asked about the condition of the officer he'd shot. He'd seemed so upset, and yet never asked. Perhaps, thought the Chief, he didn't want to know. He seemed a man best suited to hiding from the truth.

There was a pause and Gamache thought maybe the man would do as he'd asked. If he could just get Agent Morin safely away they would find this man. Gamache had no doubt of that.

But Armand Gamache had already made his first mistake.

Beauvoir drifted back to sleep and in his sleep he replaced the receiver, got in the car with the Chief and raced up to Ste-Agathe. They found where Morin was being held and rescued him. Safe and sound. No one hurt, no one killed.

That was Beauvoir's dream. That was always his dream.

Armand Gamache picked up the ball and chucked it for Henri. He knew the dog would happily do this all day and all night, and it held its attractions for Gamache. A simple, repetitive activity.

His feet crunched on the pathway and his breath puffed in the crisp, dark air. He could just see Henri ahead and hear the slight wind knocking the bare branches together, like the fingers of skeletons. And he could hear the young voice talking, always talking.

Paul Morin told him about his first swimming lesson in the cold Rivière Yamaska and losing his trunks to some bullies. He heard about the summer the family went whale watching in Tadoussac and how much Morin loved fishing, about the death of Morin's grandmother, about the new apartment in Granby he and Suzanne had rented and the paint colors she'd chosen. He heard about the minutiae of the young agent's life.

And as Morin talked Gamache saw again what had happened. All the images he kept locked away during the day he let out at night. He had to. He'd tried to keep them in, behind the groaning door but they'd pounded and pressed, hammering away until he had no choice.

And so every night he and Henri and Agent Morin went for a walk. Henri chasing his ball, Gamache being chased. At the end of the hour Gamache, Henri, the Chuck-it and Agent Morin walked back along Grande Allée, the bars and restaurants closed. Even the drunk college students gone. All gone. All quiet.

And Gamache invited, asked, begged Agent Morin to be quiet too. Now. Please. But while he became a whisper, the young voice was never totally hushed.

EIGHT

$\sim$

Gamache awoke to the welcome smell of strong coffee. After show-ering he joined Émile for breakfast.

The elderly man poured Gamache a cup as they sat at the long wooden table. In the center was a plate of flaky croissants, honey and jams and some sliced fruit.

"Did you see this?" Émile put the morning copy of *Le Soleil* in front of Gamache. The Chief sipped and read the headline.

AUGUSTIN RENAUD MURDERED WHILE DIGGING FOR CHAMPLAIN

He skimmed the story. He knew enough not to be dismissive of media reports. They often got hold of people and information the po-lice themselves might not have found. But there was nothing new there. Mostly a recap of Renaud's startling hobby of looking for Cham-plain and the ancillary benefits of pissing people off. There were quotes from the Chief Archeologist of Québec, Serge Croix, speaking glowingly of Renaud's achievements which, everyone knew, amounted to putting holes in the old city and perhaps spoiling some legitimate digs. There was no respect lost between Croix and Renaud, though you'd never know it by the tribute in today's paper.

Except the reporter had been smart enough to also gather Croix's previous comments about Renaud. And not just Croix but a host of other Champlain experts, historians and archeologists. All dismissive of Ren-aud, all derisive, all mocking his amateur status, while he was alive.

Without a doubt, Augustin Renaud alive had become a bit of a buffoon. And yet, reading the papers, there emerged today another

Augustin Renaud. Not just dead, but something else. There seemed an affection for him as for a beloved, but nutty, uncle. Renaud was misguided, perhaps, but passionate. A man who loved his home, loved his city, loved his country. Québec. Loved and lived history, to the exclusion of all else, including it seemed, his sanity.

He was a harmless eccentric, one of many in Québec, and the province was the poorer for having lost him.

That was the dead Augustin Renaud. Finally respected.

The paper, Gamache was relieved to see, had been careful to simply report on where the body was found. While they mentioned it was a respected Anglophone institution they left it at that. There was no suggestion of Anglo involvement, of conspiracy, of political or linguistic motivation behind the crime.

But Gamache suspected the tabloids would be less reticent.

"That's that library, isn't it? The place you've been working?" Émile broke open a croissant and the flakes tumbled to the table. Émile had had dinner with friends the night before so he and Gamache hadn't seen each other since the murder.

"The Lit and His, yes," said Gamache.

Émile looked at him with mock seriousness. "You can tell me Armand. You didn't—"

"Kill him? I could never kill a stranger. Now, a friend . . ."

Émile Comeau laughed then grew quiet. "Poor man."

"Poor man. I was there you know. Inspector Langlois was good enough to let me sit in on the initial questioning."

As they ate Gamache told Émile about his day, his mentor peppering him with succinct questions.

Finally Émile Comeau leaned back in his chair, his breakfast finished but another appetite piqued. "So what do you think, Armand? Are the English hiding something? Why ask for your help if they aren't afraid?"

"You're quite right, they are afraid, but not of the truth. I think they're afraid of how this looks."

"With good reason," said Émile. "What was Renaud doing there?"

That was the big question, Gamache thought. Almost as big as who killed the man. Why was he at the Literary and Historical Society?

"Émile?" Gamache leaned forward, cupping his large hands round his mug. "You're a member of the Champlain Society. You know a lot more about this than I do. Could Renaud have had something? Could Champlain possibly be buried there?"

"Come for lunch at the St-Laurent Bar." Émile stood. "I'll have some people there who can better answer that."

Gamache left Henri at home, something he rarely did but the place he was going didn't welcome dogs, though privately he thought they should. Dogs, cats, hamsters, horses, chipmunks. Birds.

And yet there were only people at St. Andrew's Presbyterian Church for Sunday service, and quite a few. The benches were filling quickly. He recognized some as reporters, the rest were probably more interested in gossip than God. Most of the day's congregants, he suspected, had never been inside this church, perhaps never even realized it was there. It had been discovered, along with the body.

English Quebec was on parade.

All the pews were built in a semi-circle facing the pulpit and Gamache found a seat on a curving bench near the side of the church. He sat quietly for a few minutes, marveling at his surroundings.

The church seemed filled with light. It streamed through the bright and cheerful stained glass windows. The thick walls were plastered and painted a cream color, but it was the ceiling he couldn't help staring at. It was painted a fresh robin's egg blue and rose above the sweeping, graceful semi-circular balcony.

Something else struck the Chief Inspector. There wasn't a crucifix in sight.

"Lovely, isn't it?"

Gamache turned and noticed Elizabeth MacWhirter had slipped in beside him.

"It is," he whispered. "Has the church been here long?"

"Two hundred and fifty years. We just celebrated the anniversary. Of course, Holy Trinity Anglican is the big church. Most of the English community goes there, but we struggle along."

"Is it affiliated with the Literary and Historical Society? It seems to be on the same grounds."

"Only informally. The minister sits on the board, but that's just coincidence. The Anglican archbishop used to be on the board but he moved a few years ago so we decided to ask the Presbyterian to join us."

"Do you always get this sort of turnout?" Gamache nodded to the people now needing to stand at the back.

Elizabeth shook her head and smiled. "Normally we could stretch out and sleep in the pews, and don't think a few of us haven't done it."

"It'll be a good collection today."

"Better be. The church needs a new roof. But I suspect this lot is only here to gawk. Did you see the article in *Le Journaliste* this morning?"

The local rag, Gamache knew. He shook his head. "Only *Le Soleil*. Why? What did it say?"

"It didn't actually say anything, but it did suggest that the English had murdered Renaud to keep our dark secret."

"And that would be?"

"That Champlain is buried under the Lit and His, of course."

"And is he?"

It was his impression Elizabeth MacWhirter had been startled by his question. But the organ had begun and the congregation rose and she was spared the need to answer. He knew what she would say.

Of course he isn't.

He sang "Lord of All Hopefulness" from the hymnal and watched the congregants. Most seemed lost, not even trying to sing, some moved their mouths but he'd be surprised if any sound came out. And about a dozen, he guessed, raised their voices in song.

A young man climbed into the pulpit and the service began.

Gamache turned his attention to the minister. Thomas Hancock. He looked about twenty. His hair was dark blond, his face handsome though not classically so, more the handsome that went with robust health. Vitality. It was impossible, Gamache had noticed, to be both vital and unattractive. He looked a bit, Gamache thought, like Matt Damon. Intelligent and charming.

They prayed for Augustin Renaud.

Then Thomas Hancock did something Gamache would never have thought possible. While acknowledging that Renaud had been murdered only yards away he didn't dwell on it, or on the curiosity of God's Will.

Instead the Reverend Mr. Hancock, in his long blue cassock and his baby face, spoke of passion and purpose. Of Renaud's obvious delight in life. He connected it to God. As a great gift of God.

The rest of the sermon was about joy.

It was an extremely risky strategy, Gamache knew. The pews were filled with Francophones curious about this subculture unearthed in the very center of their city. English. Most Québécois probably never even knew they were there, never mind so firmly ensconced.

They were an oddity, and most of the people in the church had come to stare, and come to judge. Including a number of reporters, notebooks out, ready and eager to report on the official reaction of the English community. By concentrating on joy instead of tragedy, the church, the Anglos, might be perceived as uncaring, as trivializing the tragedy of a life stolen. A man murdered a stone's throw away.

And yet, instead of playing to the crowd, instead of offering a muted apology, of finding appropriately contrite biblical passages, this minister spoke of joy.

Armand Gamache didn't know how it would sound when written up in tomorrow's *Le Journaliste*, but he couldn't help but admire the man for not pandering. Indeed, for offering another, a more positive, perspective. Gamache thought if his church spoke more about joy and less about sin and guilt, he might be tempted to return himself.

The service ended with a hymn and the collection followed by a silent prayer, in which Agent Morin told Gamache about his late grandmother, who smoked incessantly without ever removing the cigarette from her mouth.

"Her right eye was always winking because of the smoke," Morin explained. "And the cigarette just burned down. She never tapped off the ash. It hung there, this long tube of gray. We could watch her for hours. My sister thought she was disgusting but I kinda liked her. She drank too. She could eat and drink without once taking the cigarette out."

He sounded impressed.

"Once when she was preparing breakfast the whole line of ash fell into the porridge. She just kept stirring. God knows how much ash and crap we ate."

"Did the smoking kill her?" Gamache asked.

"No. She choked on a brussels sprout."

There was a pause and despite himself, Gamache chuckled.

Elizabeth looked at him. "Thinking of joy?" she whispered.

"In a way, I suppose," said Gamache and felt his chest constrict so fiercely he almost gasped.

After the service the congregation was invited back to the church hall for coffee and cookies, but Gamache hung back. Having shaken everyone's hand the Reverend Hancock noticed the large man sitting in the pew and approached.

"Can I help you?"

His eyes were a soft blue. Close up Gamache noticed he was older than he appeared. Closer to thirty-five than twenty-five.

"I don't want to take you away from your congregation, Reverend, but I wondered if we might have a talk sometime today?"

"Why not now?" He sat down. "And please don't call me Reverend. Tom will do."

"I'm afraid I can't do that."

Hancock examined him. "Then you may call me Your Excellency."

Gamache stared at the earnest young man, then broke into a smile. "Perhaps I could call you Tom."

Hancock laughed. "Actually, in very formal circumstances I'm called The Reverend Mr. Hancock, but just plain Mr. Hancock would do, if that makes you feel better."

"It does. *Merci.*" Gamache extended his hand. "My name is Armand Gamache."

The minister's hand paused for a moment. "Chief Inspector," he said finally. "I thought it might be you. Elizabeth said you'd helped yesterday. I'm afraid I was practicing for the canoe race. We haven't a hope, but we're having fun."

Gamache could believe they didn't have a hope. He'd seen the famous canoe race across the St. Lawrence River every Carnaval for decades, and every year he wondered what could possess a person to do such a thing. It took huge athleticism and more than a little insanity. And while the young minister looked fit enough Gamache knew from his notes that his teammate, Ken Haslam was in his sixties. It would be, not to put too fine a point on it, like dragging an anvil across the river. Haslam on the team certainly handicapped them.

One day he might ask this man why he, or anyone, would enter such a race. But not today. Today belonged to a different subject.

"I'm glad I was able to help a little," said Gamache. "But I'm afraid it's far from over, despite your sermon today."

"Oh, my sermon wasn't meant to dismiss what happened, but to accept and celebrate the man's life. There are enough people out there," he waved toward the beautiful stained glass windows and the genteel city beyond, "who'll condemn us, I thought I might as well try to be uplifting. Do you not approve?"

"Would it matter?"

"It always matters. I'm not preaching at you, you know."

"As a matter of fact I thought your sermon was inspired. Beautiful."

The Reverend Mr. Hancock looked at Gamache. "*Merci*. It's a risk. I just hope I haven't done harm. We'll see."

"Are you a Quebecker by birth?"

"No, I was born in New Brunswick. Shediac. Lobster Capital of the World. It's a regulation that when you say Shediac you must also say—"

"Lobster Capital of the World."

"Thank you," Hancock smiled and Gamache could see he spoke of joy for a reason. He knew it. "This is my first assignment. I came three years ago."

"How long have you sat on the board of the Lit and His?"

"About eighteen months I guess. It's not very onerous. My biggest job is to remember not to actually suggest anything. It takes a lot of effort to halt time, and for the most part they've done it."

Gamache smiled. "Living history?"

"Sort of. They can be old and cranky, but they love Québec and they love the Literary and Historical Society. They've spent years trying to keep a low profile. They just want to be left alone, really. And now this."

"The murder of Augustin Renaud," said Gamache.

Hancock was shaking his head. "He came to speak to us, you know. Friday morning. But the board refused to see him. Quite right too. He can go through regular channels, like everyone else. He seemed unpleasant."

"You saw him?"

Hancock hesitated. "No."

"Why wasn't Renaud's visit mentioned in the minutes?"

Hancock looked nonplussed. "We just decided it didn't matter."

But Gamache had the impression this had been news to Hancock.

"I understand you and Monsieur Haslam left early?"

"We had a practice at noon so yes, we left."

"Was Augustin Renaud still outside?"

"Not that I saw."

"Who had access to the basement?"

Hancock thought for a moment. "Winnie would know better. She's the head librarian, you know. I don't think the basement doors were ever locked. It's really more a question of who could find them. Did you go down?"

Gamache nodded.

"Then you know you have to go through a trap door and down a ladder. Not exactly the grand staircase. A casual visitor would never find that basement."

"But renovations were being done and they included the sub-basement, where he was found. In fact, I understand it's scheduled to be concreted over in the next couple of days."

"That soon? I knew the work was being done but didn't know when. Won't happen now, I suppose?"

"Not for a while, I'm afraid."

The Chief Inspector wondered if the Reverend Mr. Hancock realized he'd all but admitted only a member of the Literary and Historical Society could have killed Renaud. And not a casual user of the fine library, but someone intimately familiar with the old building. The Chief remembered wandering the labyrinthine corridors. It was a warren of hallways, staircases, back rooms.

Would Augustin Renaud have been able to find that trap door on his own?

Almost certainly not.

Someone guided him down there then killed him.

Someone who knew all about the Lit and His.

Someone who knew the sub-basement was about to be concreted over.

Beside him, the Reverend Mr. Hancock had risen. "I'm sorry, I really need to get in to coffee. I'm expected to make an appearance." He paused and looked closely at the bearded man in front of him.

Like every other Quebecker, he was familiar with Chief Inspector Gamache. The head of homicide appeared on weekly talk shows and news reports trying to explain the decisions the Sûreté was making. Often giving information about a case.

He was always patient, thoughtful, clear in the face of questions shouted and not always civil. He never lost his temper, though Hancock had seen him mightily provoked.

But the man he saw now differed from the man he'd watched for the past three years, and it wasn't just the beard or the scar. He was still thoughtful, civil, gentle almost.

But he seemed tired.

"The coffee will keep." Hancock sat back down. The church was tranquil, cool and quiet. "Would you like to talk?"

Armand Gamache knew this young man didn't mean about the case, and he was tempted. Tempted to tell him everything. But Thomas Hancock was a suspect in a murder case and as much as he longed to confide his sins to this young minister, he resisted.

"Go, please. We can talk another time."

"I hope so," said Hancock, rising. "Joy doesn't ever leave, you know. It's always with you. And one day you'll find it again."

"*Merci,*" said Gamache, and sat quietly in the church until the ringing of the man's feet on the floor was silenced, and he was alone with the whispering in his head.

Over at the Literary and Historical Society the library was open again, as were the offices. A yellow police tape, though, was across one door, that led to the trap door that led to the ladder that led to the sub-basement.

And there Inspector Langlois stood.

His team had collected all the evidence, every inch had been gone over, every hair collected, every masticated rat, every bit of cloth. Soil samples had been put in vials. Photos taken, infrared, ultraviolet, black light. Everything.

They'd found, besides the body, a bloody shovel, a satchel with the map, and footprints. All sorts of footprints. Too many, he suspected, to be able to narrow it down.

He had investigators interviewing Renaud's former wife, his friends, of which there were precious few, his neighbors. They were scouring his home, but it was so packed with books and papers and all sorts of crap it could take weeks.

They were all over this case. Because, like Gamache, Langlois knew a frenzy was just beginning. Whipped by the tabloids, and eventually picked up by the legitimate press. The case was being hijacked. It was no longer just about Renaud's body, it had become about another, an older mystery, an older body.

Champlain.

Was he here?

Which was why instead of being at Renaud's apartment sifting through clues, he was in the dim basement, staring at a bucket of potatoes. At least, he hoped that's what they were.

Beside him Québec's Chief Archeologist, Serge Croix, stooped.

Neither man was happy to be there. Both knew it to be a waste of time.

"Well, Inspector, I can tell you for certain, that is not Champlain."

The two men continued to stare at the potatoes.

A trained excavator, brought by the Chief Archeologist, leaned against his shovel. Another held a device and was walking slowly over the dirt floor. Already they'd dug three holes, and in each they found a metal box or bucket with root vegetables. Probably hundreds of years old. Turnips, potatoes, parsnips. But no Samuel de Champlain.

"*Bon*," said Croix. "That's enough. We all know he isn't here. In fact, if Augustin Renaud believed he was that's just about a guarantee Champlain is somewhere else."

"Wait, I have something over here," said the woman with the device.

Croix sighed but they all trooped to the dark corner. The excavator repositioned the bright industrial lights.

Inspector Langlois felt his heart speed up and around him he could see the others looking expectant, hopeful. Even Croix.

Despite the fact he knew Champlain could not possibly be buried there, Croix could still get his hopes up. Like homicide inspectors, thought Langlois, archeologists dug and dug, and always believed it wasn't in vain. Something important might lie just below the surface.

The excavator put his shovel into the hard earth and loosened it, nudging it deeper and deeper, an inch at a time so as not to destroy whatever was beneath.

And then they heard the tap and the slight scraping. They'd found something.

Once again, the Chief Archeologist for Québec stooped. Bringing out his tools, finer than the rest, he carefully, painstakingly, cleared away the dirt to reveal a box.

Opening it he shone a light inside.

Turnips. Though one did look a little like the *premier ministre*.

NINE

⁓

Armand Gamache walked briskly up the slippery sidewalk and into the park known as Place d'Armes, the bitter wind full in his face. Foot paths were worn through the deep snow criss-crossing the park. Horse-drawn carriages, the *calèches*, waited at the top of the park to take visitors around the old city. Behind Gamache was a row of small, picturesque stone buildings, all turned into restaurants. To his right rose the magnificent Anglican Cathedral of the Holy Trinity. Gamache knew this, from experience. But he didn't look at it. Like everyone else, he kept his head down against the wind, only glancing up now and then to make sure he wasn't about to hit a person or a pole. His eyes watered and the tears froze. Everyone else looked just like him, their faces round and red and glowing. Like mobile stoplights.

Losing his footing on some ice hidden under a dusting of snow he righted himself just in time, then turned his back to the wind and caught his breath. At the top of the hill, beyond the park and *calèches*, was the most photographed building in Canada.

The Château Frontenac hotel.

It was huge and gray, turreted and imposing, and rose as though expelled from the cliff face. Inspired by castles it was named for the first governor of Québec, Frontenac. It was both magnificent and forbidding.

Gamache walked toward the Château, past the large statue in the middle of the small park. The Monument de la Foi. A monument to Faith. For Québec had been built on Faith. And fur. But the city fathers preferred to raise a statue to martyrs than to a beaver.

Just ahead, the Château promised warmth, a glass of wine, a crusty bowl of French onion soup. Émile. But the Chief Inspector stopped just short of the shelter, and stared. Not at the Château, not at the gothic statue to Faith, but to another monument off to the left, much larger, even, than the one to Faith.

It was of a man looking out over the city he'd founded four hundred years earlier.

Samuel de Champlain.

Bare-headed, bold, stepping forward as though wanting to join them, to be a part of this city that existed only because he had. And at the base of the statue another, smaller, image. An angel, sounding a trumpet to the glory of the founder. And even Gamache, who was no great fan of nationalism, felt wonder, awe, at the unshakable vision and courage of this man to do what many had tried and failed.

To not just come to these shores to harvest furs and fish and timber, but live here. Create a colony, a community. A New World. A home.

Gamache stared until he could no longer feel his face and his fingers in his warm mitts were numb. But still he stared at the father of Québec and wondered.

Where are you? Where did they bury you? And why don't we know?

Émile rose and waved him to their table by the window.

The two men with him also got up.

"Chief Inspector," they said and introduced themselves.

"René Dallaire," the tall, rotund man said, shaking Gamache's hand.

"Jean Hamel," the small, slim one said. Had René sported a cropped moustache the two men could have passed for Laurel and Hardy.

Gamache handed his coat to a waiter, shoving his hat, scarf and mitts into a sleeve. He sat and put his hands to his face, feeling the burning. Extreme cold left its ironic mark. It was indistinguishable from a sunburn. But within minutes it had subsided, and the circulation had returned to his hands, helped along by sitting on them.

They ordered drinks and lunch and chatted about Carnaval, about the weather, about politics. It was clear the three men knew each other well. And Gamache knew they'd all belonged to the same club for decades.

The Champlain Society.

Their drinks and a basket of rolls arrived. They sipped their Scotches and Gamache resisted the urge to take a warm roll in each hand. The men talked casually among themselves, Gamache sometimes contributing, sometimes just listening, sometimes glancing out the window.

The St-Laurent Bar was at the far end of the Château, down the gracious, wide, endless corridor, through the double doors and into another world. Unlike the rest of the mammoth hotel, this bar was modest in size and circular, being built into one of the turrets of the Château. Its curved walls were paneled in dark wood and fireplaces stood on either side. A round bar took up the center, with tables surrounding it.

That, for any normal place, would have been impressive enough but Quebec City was far from normal, and within it, the Château was unique.

For curving along the far wall of the bar were windows. Tall, framed in mahogany, wide and mullioned. Out of them opened the most splendid vista Gamache had ever seen. True, as a Québécois, no other view could ever match up. This was their Grand Canyon, Niagara Falls, Everest. This was Machu Picchu, Kilimanjaro, Stonehenge. It was their wonder.

From the bar he could see up and down the great river, the view so distant it broke into the past. From there, Gamache could see four hundred years in the past. The ships, surprisingly small and fragile, sailing down from the Atlantic, dropping anchor at the narrowest spot.

Kebek. An Algonquin word. Where the river narrows.

Gamache could almost see the sails being furled, men pulling ropes, securing lines, crawling up and down the masts. He could almost see the boats lowered into the water, and the men rowing ashore.

Did they know what they were in for? What the New World held?

Almost certainly not, or they'd never have come. Most never left, but were buried right below them, on the shores. Dying of scurvy, of exposure.

Unlike Gamache they had no Château to duck into. No warm soup and amber Scotch. He'd barely survived ten minutes in the biting, bitter wind, how had they survived days, weeks, months, with no warm clothing and barely any shelter?

Of course, the answer was obvious. They hadn't. Most had died, slow, agonizing, dreadful deaths those first winters. What Gamache saw as he glanced out the window to the river with its gray water and ice floes, was history. His history, flowing by.

He also saw a dot in the distance. An ice canoe. Shaking his head Gamache turned his attention back to his companions.

"Why're you looking so puzzled?" Émile asked.

The Chief Inspector nodded out the window. "An ice canoe team. The settlers had to do it. Why would someone choose to?"

"I agree," said René, breaking up a roll and smearing butter on it. "I can barely watch them, and yet, I can't seem to look away either." He laughed. "I sometimes think we're a rowboat society."

"A what?" asked Jean.

"A rowboat. It's why we do things like that." He jerked his head toward the window and the dot on the river. "It's why Québec is so perfectly preserved. It's why we're all so fascinated with history. We're in a rowboat. We move forward, but we're always looking back."

Jean laughed and leaned away as the waiter placed a huge burger and *frites* in front of him. A bubbling French onion soup sat in front of Émile and Gamache was given a hot bowl of pea soup.

"I met a fellow this morning who's training for the race," said Gamache.

"Bet he's in good shape," said Émile, lifting his spoon almost over his head, trying to get the stringy, melted cheese to break.

"He is. He's also the minister at the Presbyterian church. St. Andrews."

"Muscular Christianity," René chuckled.

"There's a Presbyterian church?" asked Jean.

"And a congregation to go with it," said Gamache. "He was saying he has a teammate for the race who's over sixty."

"Sixty what?" asked René. "Pounds?"

"Must be IQ," said Émile.

"I'm hoping to meet him this afternoon. Name's Ken Haslam. Do you know him?"

They looked at each other, but the answer was clear. No.

After lunch, over espressos, Gamache turned the conversation to the reason they were together.

"As you know, Augustin Renaud was murdered on Friday night, or early yesterday morning."

They nodded, their good cheer subsiding. Three shrewd faces stared back at him. They were of an age, late seventies, all successful in their fields, all retired. But none had lost their edge. He could see that clearly.

"What I want to know from you is this. Could Champlain be buried beneath the Literary and Historical Society?"

They looked at each other, and finally, silently, it was decided that René Dallaire, the large, Hardy-esque man, would take the lead. The table had been cleared of all but their *demi-tasses*.

"I brought this along when Émile told us what you wanted to talk about." He spread out a map, pinning it down with their cups. "I'm embarrassed to say I had no idea there was a Literary and Historical Society."

"That's not quite true," said Jean to his friend. "We're familiar with the building. It's quite historic you know. Originally a redoubt, a military barracks in the 1700s. Then in the latter part of the century it housed prisoners of war. Then another prison was built somewhere else and the building must have fallen into private hands."

"And now you say it's called the Literary and Historical Society?" René spoke the English words with a heavy accent.

"Quite magnificent," said Gamache.

René placed his substantial finger on the site of the building, by rue St-Stanislas. "That's it, right?"

Gamache bent over the map, as did they all, narrowly avoiding knocking heads. He nodded agreement.

"Then there can be no doubt. You agree?" René Dallaire looked at Jean and Émile.

They agreed.

"I can guarantee you," René looked Gamache in the eye. "Samuel de Champlain is not buried there."

"How can you be so certain?"

"When you arrived at the Château, did you happen to notice the statue of Champlain out front?"

"I did. Hard to miss."

"*C'est vrai.* That's not simply a monument to the man, but it marks the exact spot he died."

"As exact as we can get, anyway," said Jean. René shot him a small, annoyed look.

"How do you know that's where he died?" Gamache asked. Now it was Émile's turn to answer.

"There're reports written by his lieutenants and the priests. He died after a short illness on Christmas Day, 1635, during a storm. It's one of the few things we know about Champlain without a doubt. The fortress was right there, where the statue is."

"But he wouldn't have been buried right where he died, would he?" asked Gamache.

René unfolded another map or, at least, a reproduction and placed it on top of the modern city map. It was little more than an illustration.

"This was drawn in 1639, four years after Champlain died. It's not much different than the Québec he would have known." The map showed a stylized fort, a parade grounds in front, and a scattering of buildings around. "This is where he died." His finger landed on the fort. "It's where the statue now stands. And this is where they buried Champlain."

René Dallaire's thick finger pointed to a small building a few hundred yards from the fort.

"The chapel. The only one in Québec at the time. There're no official records but it seems obvious Champlain would have been buried there, either right in the chapel or in a cemetery beside it."

Gamache was perplexed. "So, if we know where he was buried, what's the mystery? Where is he? And why aren't there any official records of the burial of the most important man in the colony?"

"Ahh, but nothing is ever straightforward is it?" said Jean. "The chapel burned a few years later, destroying all the records."

Gamache thought about that. "A fire would burn the records, yes, but not a buried body. We should still have found him by now, no?"

René shrugged. "Yes, we should have. There're a number of theories, but the most likely is that they buried him in the cemetery, not the chapel, so the fire wouldn't have disturbed him at all. Over time the colony grew—"

René paused but his hands were expressive. He opened them wide. The other two men were also silent, eyes down.

"Are you saying they put a building on top of Champlain?" Gamache asked.

The three men looked unhappy but none contradicted him until Jean spoke.

"There is another theory."

Émile sighed. "Not that again. There's no proof."

"There's no proof of any of this," Jean pointed out. "I agree it's a guess. You just don't want to believe it."

Émile was silent. It seemed Jean had made a direct hit. The little man turned to Gamache. "The other theory is that as Quebec City grew there was a huge amount of building work, as René says. But along with it was excavation, digging down beneath the frost line before they put up the new buildings. The city was booming, and things went up in a hurry. They didn't have time to worry about the dead."

Gamache was beginning to see where this was going. "So the theory is that they didn't build on top of Champlain."

Jean shook his head slowly. "No. They dug him up along with hundreds of others and dumped him in a landfill somewhere. They didn't mean to, they just didn't know."

Gamache was silent, stunned. Would the Americans have done that to Washington? Or the British to Henry the Eighth?

"Could that have happened?" He turned, naturally, to Émile Comeau who shrugged, then finally nodded.

"It is possible, but Jean's right. None of us wants to admit it."

"To be fair," said Jean. "It is the least likely of the theories."

"The point is," said René, looking at the map again. "This is the limit of the original settlement in 1635." He twirled his finger over the old map, then swept it aside and found the same place on the modern map. "Pretty much from where we're sitting now, in the Château, to a radius of a few hundred yards. They'd keep it small. Easier to defend."

"And what would the rest have been?" asked Gamache, beginning to understand what they were saying.

"Nothing," said Jean. "Forest. Rock."

"And where the Literary and Historical Society is now?"

"Woods." René brought the old map out and placed his finger on a big blank space, far from any habitation.

Nothing.

There was no way they'd have buried Champlain that far from civilization.

There was no way the father of Québec could be in the basement of the Lit and His.

"So," Gamache leaned back. "Why was Augustin Renaud there?"

"Because he was mad?" asked Jean.

"He was you know," said Émile. "Champlain loved Québec, to the exclusion of everything else in his life. It was all he knew, all he lived for. And Renaud loved Champlain with the same devotion. A devotion bordering on madness."

"Bordering?" asked René. "He was the capital of the state of madness. Augustin Renaud was the Emperor of it. Bordering," he muttered.

"Maybe," said Émile, staring down at the old map again. "Maybe he wasn't looking for Champlain. Maybe there was another reason he was there."

"Like what?"

"Well," his mentor looked at him. "It is a literary society. Maybe he was looking for a book."

Gamache smiled. Maybe. He got up and paused as the waiter fetched his coat. Looking down at the modern map he noticed something.

"The old chapel, the one that burned. Where would it have been on this map?"

René put out his finger one more time and pointed.

It landed on the Notre-Dame Basilica, the mighty church where the great and good used to pray. As the waiter helped Gamache into his parka René leaned over and whispered, "Speak to Père Sébastien."

Jean-Guy Beauvoir waited.

He wasn't very good at it. First he looked as though he didn't care, then he looked as though he had all the time in the world. That lasted about twenty seconds. Then he looked annoyed. That was more successful and lasted until Olivier Brulé arrived a quarter hour later.

It had been a few months since he'd last seen Olivier. Prison changed some men. Well, it changed all men. But externally some showed it more than others. Some actually seemed to flourish. They lifted weights, bulked up, exercised for the first time in years, ate three square meals. They even thrived, though few would admit it, on the regimen, the structure. Many had never had that in their lives, and so they'd wandered off course.

Here their course was clearer.

Though most, Beauvoir knew, withered in confinement.

Olivier walked through the doors, wearing his prison blues. He was in his late thirties and of medium build. His hair was cut far shorter than Beauvoir had ever seen, but it disguised the fact he was balding. He looked pale but healthy. Beauvoir felt a revulsion, as he did in the presence of all murderers. For that's what he knew in his heart Olivier was.

No, he sharply reminded himself. I need to think of this man as innocent. Or at least, as not guilty.

But try as he might he saw a convict.

"Inspector," said Olivier, standing at the far end of the visitors' room, unsure what to do.

"Olivier," said Beauvoir and smiled, though judging by the look on Olivier's face it was probably more of a sneer. "Please. Call me Jean-Guy. I'm here privately."

"Just a social call?" Olivier sat at a table across from Beauvoir. "How's the Chief Inspector?"

"He's in Quebec City for Carnaval. I'm expecting to have to bail him out any minute."

Olivier laughed. "There's more than one fellow in here who arrived via Carnaval. Apparently the 'I was drunk on Caribou' defense isn't all that effective."

"I'll alert the Chief."

They both laughed, a little longer than necessary, then fell into an uneasy silence. Now that he was there Beauvoir wasn't sure what to say.

Olivier stared at him, waiting.

"I wasn't totally honest with you just now," Beauvoir began. He'd never done anything like this before and felt as though he'd wandered into a wilderness and hated Olivier all the more for making him do that. "I'm on leave as you know, so this really isn't an official call but . . ."

Olivier waited, better at it than Beauvoir. Finally he raised his brows in a silent, "go on."

"The Chief asked me to look into a few aspects of your case. I don't want you to get your hopes up—" But he could see it was already too late for that. Olivier was smiling. Life seemed to have returned to him. "Really, Olivier, you can't expect anything to come from this."

"Why not?"

"Because I still think you did it."

That shut him up, Beauvoir was happy to see. Still, there swirled around Olivier a residue of hope. Was this just cruel? Beauvoir hoped so. The Inspector leaned on the metal table. "Listen, there're just a few questions. The Chief asked me to be absolutely certain, that's all."

"You might think I did it, but he doesn't, does he?" said Olivier, triumphant.

"He isn't so sure, and he wants to be sure. Wants to make certain he—we—didn't make a mistake. Look, if you tell anyone about this, anyone at all, it's off. You understand?" Beauvoir's eyes were hard.

"I understand."

"I mean it, Olivier. Especially Gabri. You can't tell him anything."

Olivier hesitated.

"If you tell him he'll tell others. He couldn't help but. Or at the very least his mood will change and people'll notice. If I'm going to ask questions, dig some more, it has to be subtle. If someone else killed the Hermit I don't want them on their guard."

This made sense to Olivier, who nodded. "I promise."

"*Bon.* You need to tell me again what happened that night. And I need the truth."

The air crackled between the two men.

"I told you the truth."

"When?" Beauvoir demanded. "Was it the second or third version of the story? If you're in here you did it to yourself. You lied at every turn."

It was true, Olivier knew. He'd lied all his life about everything, until the habit became who he was. It didn't even occur to him to tell the truth. So when all this happened of course he'd lie.

Too late he'd realized what that did. It made the truth unrecognizable. And while he was very good, very glib, at lying, all his truths sounded like falsehoods. He blushed, stumbled for words, got confused when telling the truth.

"All right," he said to Beauvoir. "I'll tell you what happened."

"The truth."

Olivier gave a single, curt, nod.

"I met the Hermit ten years ago, when Gabri and I first arrived in Three Pines and were living above the shop. He wasn't a hermit yet. He'd still leave his cabin and get his own supplies, but he looked pretty ragged. We were renovating the shop. I hadn't turned it into a bistro, it was just an antique store back then. One day he showed up and said he wanted to sell something. I wasn't very happy. It seemed he wanted a favor from me. Looking at the guy I figured it was some piece of junk he found on the side of the road but when he showed it to me I knew it was special."

"What was it?"

"A miniature, a tiny portrait, in profile. Some Polish aristocrat, I think. Must have been painted with a single hair. It was beautiful. Even the frame it was in was beautiful. I agreed to buy it from him in exchange for a bag of groceries."

He'd told the story so often Olivier was almost immune to the disgust in people's faces. Almost.

"Go on," said Beauvoir. "What did you do with the portrait?"

"Took it to Montreal and sold it on rue Notre-Dame, the antique district."

"Can you remember which shop?" Beauvoir pulled out his notebook and a pen.

"Not sure if it's still there. They change a lot. It was called Le Temps perdu."

Beauvoir made a note. "How much did you get for it?"

"Fifteen hundred dollars."

"And the Hermit kept coming back?"

"Kept offering me things. Some fantastic, some not so great but still better than I'm likely to find in most attics or barns. At first I sold them through that antiques shop but then realized I could get more on eBay. Then one day the Hermit arrived looking really bad. Skinny, and stressed. He said, 'I'm not coming back, old son. I can't.' This was a disaster for me. I'd come to pretty much rely on his stuff. He said he didn't want to be seen anymore, then he invited me to his cabin."

"You went?"

Olivier nodded. "I had no idea he lived in the woods. He was way the hell and gone. Well, you know it."

Beauvoir did. He'd spent the night there with the asshole saint.

"When we finally got there I couldn't believe it." For a moment Olivier was transported to that magical moment when he'd first stepped into the scruffy old man's log cabin. And into a world where ancient glass was used for milk, a Queen's china was used for peanut butter sandwiches and priceless silk tapestries hung on walls to keep the drafts out.

"I visited him every two weeks. By then I'd turned the antique shop into a bistro. Every second Saturday night after the bistro closed I'd sneak up to the cabin. We'd talk and he'd give me something for the groceries I'd bring."

"What did Charlotte mean?" Beauvoir asked. It was Chief Inspector Gamache who'd noticed the strange repetition of "Charlotte." There were references to the name all over the Hermit's cabin, from the book *Charlotte's Web*, to a first-edition Charlotte Brontë, to the rare violin. Everyone else had missed it, except the Chief.

Olivier was shaking his head. "Nothing, it meant nothing. Or, at least, not anything I know about. He never mentioned the name."

Beauvoir stared at him. "Careful, Olivier. I need the truth."

"I have no reason to lie anymore."

For any rational person that would be true, but Olivier had behaved so irrationally Beauvoir wondered if he was capable of anything else.

"The Hermit had scratched the name Charlotte in code under one of those wooden sculptures he'd made," Beauvoir pointed out. He could see the carvings, deeply disturbing works showing people fleeing some terror. And under three of his works the Hermit had carved words in code.

Charlotte. Emily. And under the last one? The one that showed Olivier in a chair, listening, he'd carved that one, short, damning word.

Woo.

"And 'Woo'?" Beauvoir asked. "What did that mean?"

"I don't know."

"Well it meant something," snapped Beauvoir. "He put it under the carving of you."

"That wasn't me. It doesn't look like me."

"It's a carving not a photograph. It's you and you know it. Why did he write 'Woo' under it?"

But it wasn't just under the carving. Woo had appeared in the web and in that piece of wood, covered in the Hermit's blood, that had bounced under the bed. Into a dark corner. A piece of red cedar carved, according to the forensic experts, years before.

"I'm asking you again, Olivier, what did 'Woo' mean?"

"I don't know." Now Olivier was exasperated but he took a breath and regained himself. "Look, I told you. He said it a couple of times, but under his breath. At first I thought it was just a sigh. It sounded like a sigh. Then I realized he was saying 'Woo.' He only said it when he was afraid."

Beauvoir stared at him. "I'm going to need more than that."

Olivier shook his head. "There is no more than that. That's all I know. I'd tell you more, if I could. Honestly. It meant something to him, but he never explained, and I never asked."

"Why not?"

"It didn't seem important."

"It was clearly important to him."

"Yes, but not to me. I'd have asked if it meant he'd give me more of his treasures, but that didn't seem to be the case."

And Beauvoir heard the truth in that, the humiliating, shameful truth. He shifted imperceptibly in his seat, and as he did his perception shifted just a little.

Maybe, maybe, this man really was telling the truth. Finally.

"You visited him for years, but near the end something changed. What happened?"

"That Marc Gilbert bought the old Hadley house and decided to turn it into an inn and spa. That would've been bad enough, but his wife Dominique decided they needed horses and asked Roar Parra to reopen the trails. One of the trails led right past the Hermit's cabin. Eventually Parra would find the cabin and everyone would know about the Hermit and his treasure."

"What did you do?"

"What could I do? I'd spent years trying to convince the Hermit to give me that thing he kept in the canvas sack. He promised it to me, kept teasing me with it. I wanted it. I'd earned it."

A whiny tone had crept into Olivier's voice and made itself at home. A tone not often let out in public, preferring privacy.

"Tell me again about the thing in the sack."

"You know it, you've seen it," said Olivier, then took a deep breath and regrouped. "The Hermit had everything on display, all his antiquities, all those beautiful things but one thing he kept hidden. In the sack."

"And you wanted it."

"Wouldn't you?"

Beauvoir considered. It was true. It was human nature to want the one thing denied you.

The Hermit had teased Olivier with it but he hadn't appreciated who he was dealing with. The depth of Olivier's greed.

"So you killed him and stole it."

That was the Crown's case. Olivier had killed the demented old man for his treasure, the one he kept hidden, the one found in Olivier's bistro along with the murder weapon.

"No." Olivier leaned forward suddenly, as though charging Beauvoir. "I went back for it, I admit that, but he was already dead."

"And what did you see?" Beauvoir asked the question quickly, hoping to trip him up in the rush.

"The cabin door was open and I saw him lying on the floor. There was blood. I thought he'd just hit his head, but when I got closer I could see he was dead. There was a piece of wood I'd never seen before by his hand. I picked it up."

"Why?" The word was snapped out.

"Because I wanted to see."

"See what?"

"What it was."

"Why?"

"In case it was important."

"Important. Explain."

Now it was Beauvoir who was leaning forward, almost crawling across the metal table. Olivier didn't lean back. The two men were in each other's faces, almost shouting.

"In case it was valuable."

"Explain."

"In case it was another one of his carvings, okay?" Olivier almost screamed, then threw himself back into his chair. "Okay? There. I thought it might be one of his carvings and I could sell it."

This hadn't come out in court. Olivier had admitted he'd picked up the wood carving, but said he'd dropped it as soon as he'd seen blood on it.

"Why'd you drop it?"

"Because it was a worthless piece of junk. Something a kid would do. I only noticed the blood later."

"Why did you move the body?"

It was the question that hounded Gamache. The question that had brought Beauvoir back to this case. Why, if he'd killed the man, would Olivier put him into a wheelbarrow and take him like so much compost through the woods? And dump him in the front hall of the new inn and spa.

"Because I wanted to screw Marc Gilbert. Not literally."

"Seems pretty literal to me," said Beauvoir.

"I wanted to ruin his fancy inn. Who'd pay a fortune to stay in a place where someone had just been murdered?"

Beauvoir leaned back, examining Olivier for a long moment.

"The Chief Inspector believes you."

Olivier closed his eyes and exhaled.

Beauvoir held up his hand. "He thinks you did do it to ruin Gilbert. But in ruining Gilbert you'd also have stopped the horse trails and if you stopped Parra from opening the paths, no one would find the cabin."

"All that's true. But if I killed him, why would I let everyone know there'd been a murder?"

"Because the paths were close. The cabin, and the murder, would have been discovered within days anyway. Your only hope was to stop the trails. Stop the discovery of the cabin."

"By putting the dead man on display? There was nothing left to hide then."

"There was the treasure."

They stared at each other.

Jean-Guy Beauvoir sat in his car mulling over the interview. Nothing really new had come out of it but Gamache had advised him to believe Olivier this time, take him at his word.

Beauvoir couldn't bring himself to do it. He could pretend to, could go through the motions. He could even try to convince himself that Olivier was indeed telling the truth, but he'd be lying to himself.

He pulled the car out of the parking lot and headed toward rue Notre-Dame and Le Temps perdu. Lost time. Perfect. Because that's what this is, he thought as he negotiated the light Sunday afternoon traffic in Montreal. A waste of time.

As he drove he went back over the case. Only Olivier's fingerprints were found in the cabin. No one else even knew the Hermit existed.

The Hermit. It was what Olivier called him, always called him.

Beauvoir parked across the street from the antique shop. It was still there, cheek by jowl with other antique shops up and down rue Notre-Dame, some high end, some little more than junk shops.

Le Temps perdu looked pretty high end.

Beauvoir reached for the car door handle, then paused, staring into space for a moment, whipping through the interview. Looking for a word, a single, short, word. Then he flipped through his notes.

Not there either. He closed his notebook and getting out of the car he crossed the street and entered the shop. There was only one window, at the front. As he made his way further back, past the pine and oak furniture, past the chipped and cracked paintings on the walls, past the ornaments, the blue and white plates, past the vases and umbrella stands, it got darker. Like going into a well-furnished cave.

"May I help you?"

An elderly man sat at the very back, at a desk. He wore glasses and peered at Beauvoir, assessing him. The Inspector knew the look, but he was normally the one giving it.

The two men assessed each other. Beauvoir saw a slim man, well but comfortably dressed. Like his merchandise, he seemed old and refined and he smelled a little of polish.

The antique dealer saw a man in his mid to late thirties. Pale, perhaps a little stressed. Not out for a lazy Sunday stroll through the antique district. Not a buyer.

A man, perhaps, in need of something. Probably a toilet.

"This shop," Beauvoir began. He didn't want to sound like an investigator, but suddenly realized he didn't know how to sound like anything else. It was like a tattoo. Indelible. He smiled and softened his tone. "I have a friend who used to come here, but that was years ago. Ten years or more. It's still called Le Temps perdu, but has it changed hands?"

"No. Nothing's changed."

And Beauvoir could believe it.

"Were you here then?"

"I'm always here. It's my shop." The elderly man stood and put out his hand. "Fréderic Grenier."

"Jean-Guy Beauvoir. You might remember my friend. He sold you a few things."

"Is that right? What were they?"

The man, Beauvoir noticed, didn't ask Olivier's name, just what he sold. Is that how shopkeepers saw people? He's the pine table? She's the chandelier? Why not? That's how he saw suspects. She's the knifing. He's the shotgun.

"I think he said he sold you a miniature painting."

Beauvoir watched the man closely. The man was watching him closely.

"He might have. You say it was ten years ago. That's a long time. Why're you asking?"

Normally Beauvoir would have whipped out his Sûreté homicide ID, but he wasn't on official business. And he didn't have a ready answer.

"My friend just died and his widow wonders if you sold it. If not she'd buy it back. It'd been in the family for a long time. My friend sold it when he needed money, but that's no longer a problem."

Beauvoir was quite pleased with himself, though not altogether surprised. He lived with lies all the time, had heard thousands. Why shouldn't he be good at it himself?

The antique dealer watched him, then nodded. "That sometimes happens. Can you describe the painting?"

"It was European and very fine. Apparently you paid him fifteen hundred dollars for it."

Monsieur Grenier smiled. "Now I remember. It was a lot of money, but worth it. I didn't often pay that much for such a small piece. Exquisite. Polish, I believe. Unfortunately I sold it on. He came in with a few other things after that, if I remember. A carved cane that needed work. It was a little cracked. I gave it to my restorer then sold it too. Went quickly. Those sorts of things do. I'm sorry. I remember him now. Young, blond. You say his wife wanted the things back?"

Beauvoir nodded.

The man frowned. "That must have come as a surprise to his partner. The man, as I remember, was gay."

"Yes. I was trying to be delicate. In fact, I'm his partner."

"I'm sorry to hear of your loss. But at least you had a chance to get married."

The man pointed to Beauvoir's wedding band.

Time to leave.

That had certainly, thought Beauvoir once back in the car and driving over the Champlain Bridge, been *le temps perdu*. Except for announcing that his husband, Olivier, had died nothing of significance had happened.

He was almost back in Three Pines when he remembered what had been bothering him after the interview with Olivier. The word that had been missing.

Pulling off to the side of the road he dialed the prison and was eventually connected to Olivier.

"People will begin to talk, Inspector."

"You have no idea," said Beauvoir. "Listen, during the trial and investigation you said the Hermit didn't tell you anything about himself, except that he was Czech and his name was Jakob."

"Yes."

"There's a large Czech community around Three Pines, including the Parras."

"Yes."

"And quite a few of his pieces came from former Eastern Bloc countries. Czechoslovakia, Poland, Russia. You testified that your impression was he'd stolen their family treasures, then skipped to Canada in the confusion when communism was collapsing. You thought he was hiding from his countrymen, the people he stole from."

"Yes."

"And yet, through our whole interview today you never once called him Jakob. Why was that?"

There was a long pause now.

"You won't believe me."

"Chief Inspector Gamache ordered me to believe you."

"That's a comfort."

"Listen, Olivier, this is your only hope. Your last hope. The truth, now."

"His name wasn't Jakob."

Now it was Beauvoir's turn to fall silent.

"What was it?" he finally asked.

"I don't know."

"Are we back there?"

"You didn't seem to believe me the first time when I said I didn't know his name, so I made one up. One that sounded Czech."

Beauvoir was almost afraid to ask the next question. But he did.

"Was he even Czech?"

"No."

TEN

—

"I beg your pardon?"

It was, by Gamache's rough count, the millionth time he'd said that, or words to that effect, in the past ten minutes. He leaned even closer, risking toppling headlong off his chair. It didn't help that Ken Haslam had a very, very large oak desk.

"*Excusez?*" Gamache felt his chair tip as he strained forward. He leaned back just in time. Across the chasm of the desk Mr. Haslam continued to talk or at least move his lips.

Murmur, murmur, murder, murmur, board. Haslam looked sharply at Chief Inspector Gamache.

"Pardon?"

Normally Gamache concentrated on people's eyes, but was aware of their entire body. Clues came coded, and how people communicated was one of them. Their words were often the least informative. The vilest, bitterest, nastiest people often said nice things. But there was the sugar the words rode in on, or the little wink, or the insincere smile. Or the tense arm wrapped round the tense chest or legs, or the fingers intertwined tightly, white knuckled.

It was vital for him to be able to pick up on all the signals, and normally he could.

But this man confounded him because the only thing Gamache could see was Haslam's mouth. He stared at it, desperately trying to lip-read.

Ken Haslam didn't whisper. A whisper would have been, at this point, a welcome shout. He seemed, instead, to be simply mouthing his words. It was possible, thought Gamache, the man had had an operation. Perhaps his larynx had been removed.

But Gamache didn't think so. Every now and then a word was intelligible, like "murder." That word had popped out clearly.

Gamache was straining, physically and intellectually. Reaching to understand. It was exhausting. If only suspects realized, he thought, that screaming and shouting and throwing furniture wouldn't wear their interrogators down, but whispering would.

"I'm sorry, sir." Gamache was speaking English with the slight British accent he'd picked up at Cambridge.

Haslam's office was in the Basse-Ville, the Lower Town. The fastest way to get to the Lower Town was the glass-enclosed elevator called the Funicular that swept up and down the cliff-face from the upper to the lower city. Gamache had paid his two dollars and walked into the Funicular. It dropped over the side and descended. It was a short, very beautiful trip, though the Chief Inspector stayed at the back of the elevator, away from the glass and the sheer drop beyond.

Once there he stepped out into Petit-Champlain, a narrow, charming street closed to traffic and filled with snow and bustling people. Pedestrians ambled along, bundled against the cold, stopping now and then to look into the festive windows at the handmade lace, the art, the blown glass, the pastries.

Gamache continued down to Place Royale, where the first settlement had been built beside the river.

There he found Ken Haslam's office. *Royale Tourists*, the sign said. It was well placed, in a graystone building right on the open square. He walked in, spoke to the bright and helpful receptionist, explaining that no, he wasn't interested in a tour but in speaking to the owner of the company.

"Do you have an appointment?" she asked.

"I'm afraid not." Just at the very moment Beauvoir in Montreal was tempted to reach for his Sûreté ID, the Chief felt his hand move toward his breast pocket then stop. "I'd hoped he might be available."

He smiled at her. Finally she smiled back.

"As a matter of fact, he is in. Let me go in and just see if he has a minute."

And so, a few minutes later, he found himself in a quite magnificent office overlooking Place Royale and the Église Notre-Dame-des-Victoires. The church built to commemorate two great victories over the English.

It had taken Gamache about ten seconds to appreciate the difficulty of the situation. It's not that he didn't understand what Ken Haslam was saying, it was just that he couldn't hear it. Finally, when even lip-reading failed, the Chief interrupted.

"*Désolé*," Gamache put up a hand. Haslam's lips stopped moving. "Can we perhaps move closer together. I'm afraid I'm having some trouble hearing you."

Haslam looked perplexed but got up and moved to the chair beside the Chief.

"I really just need to know what happened at the board meeting of the Lit and His, the one where Augustin Renaud appeared."

Mumble, mumble, arrogant, murmur, couldn't possibly mumble. Haslam looked quite stern. He was a handsome man with steel gray hair, clean shaven, ruddy complexion that looked like it came from the sun and not the bottle. And now that they were closer together Gamache was better able to understand him. While he still spoke below a whisper it was now almost intelligible and the other signals were clearer.

Haslam was annoyed.

Not at Gamache, he thought, but at what had happened. Someone familiar with the Literary and Historical Society had murdered Augustin Renaud. And the fact the lunatic archeologist had asked to see the board on the very day he died, and been refused, cannot be seen as a coincidence.

But Haslam was mouthing again.

Murmur, mumble, Champlain, mumble idiocy, mumble, canoe race.

"Yes, I understand from Mr. Hancock that you and he left early for a practice. You're entered in the ice canoe race this coming Sunday."

Haslam smiled and nodded. "It's a lifelong dream."

The words were spoken low, but clear. In a gravelly whisper. It was a warm voice and Gamache wondered why he didn't use it more, especially in his job. Surely this was a financially fatal flaw, being a tour guide who didn't speak.

"Why enter the race?" Gamache couldn't help himself. He was dying to know why anyone, never mind someone closing in on seventy, would do this to themselves.

Haslam's answer surprised him. He'd expected the Everest answer, or something about history, which the man clearly loved, since the canoe races re-created the old mail-runs before ice breaking ships appeared.

Mumble, like, murmur, people.

"You like the people?" Gamache asked.

Mumble, Haslam nodded and smiled.

"Can't you just join a choir?"

Haslam smiled. "Not quite the same, is it Chief Inspector?" And Haslam's eyes were warm, searching, intelligent.

He knows, thought Gamache. Somehow this man knows the value of not only friendship but camaraderie. What happens to people thrown together in extreme situations.

Gamache's right hand began to tremble and he very slowly curled it into a fist but not before those thoughtful eyes across from him dropped to them. Saw the tremor.

And said nothing.

Armand Gamache walked slowly back up the small hill, to Petit-Champlain and the Funicular. As he walked he thought about his conversations with Haslam and the receptionist, who had been equally, perhaps even more, informative.

No, Mr. Haslam doesn't do tours himself, he arranges them through emails. Mostly high-end, private tours of Québec for visiting dignitaries and celebrities. He was a little, she said, like a concierge. He'd done it so long people had come to ask for very strange things, and he almost always could accommodate them. Never, she rushed to assure him, illegal, or even immoral. Mr. Haslam was a very upstanding man. But unusual, yes.

Her French was excellent, and Haslam's, when audible was even better. Had his name been anything other than Ken Haslam, Gamache would have thought him Francophone. According to the receptionist, Mr. Haslam lost his only child to leukemia when she was eleven, and his wife had died six years ago. Both buried in the Anglican cemetery in the old city.

His roots went deep into Québec.

Once up the Funicular, forcing himself to appreciate the magnificent view but gripping the wall behind him, Gamache leaned into the biting wind. His next stop was clear, but first he needed to gather his thoughts. He walked through the little alley called rue du Trésor which even in the bitter cold February day had artists selling their gaudy images of Québec. Bars carved out of blocks of ice had been set up off the alley and were selling Caribou to tourists who would soon regret this lapse in judgment. Once out of the alley he found the Café Buade and went in to both warm up and think.

Sitting in a banquette with a bowl of *chocolat chaud* he pulled out a notebook and pen. Occasionally sipping, sometimes staring into space, sometimes jotting thoughts, eventually he was ready for the next visit.

From the café he hadn't far to go. Just across the street to the great monolith that was Notre-Dame Basilica, the magnificent gilded church that wed, christened, chastised, guided and buried the highest officials and the lowest beggars.

While Québec never lacked for churches they were the satellites and Notre-Dame the sun.

As he walked through the gates and up the steps he stopped at the board listing the Sunday services. One had just ended and the next wasn't until 6 P.M. Opening the heavy doors he walked in and felt the warmth and smelled the years and years of sacred ritual. Of candles and incense, and heard the echoing of feet on the slate floors.

The church was dim, the chandeliers and wall sconces sending a feeble light into the vast space. But at the far end, past near empty pews, there was a glow. The entire altar appeared dipped in gold. It shone and beckoned, angels pranced, stern saints stood and stared, a model of St. Peter's in Rome, like a spoiled child's doll house sat in the very center.

It was both glorious and vaguely repulsive. Gamache crossed himself, a habit unbroken and sat quietly for a few moments.

"My family wanted me to become a priest, you know," said the young voice.

"Having built up a tolerance for ash and smoke, I suppose," said Gamache.

"Exactly. And I think they figured anyone who could tolerate my grandmother was either a saint or demented. Either way, good material for a life with the Jesuits."

"But you decided against it."

"I never seriously considered it," Agent Morin spoke in Gamache's ear. "I'd fallen in love with Suzanne when she was six and I was seven. I figured that was God's plan."

"You've known each other that long?"

"All my life, it seems. We met in confirmation class."

Gamache could see the young man and tried to imagine him at seven. It wasn't hard. He looked far younger than his twenty-five years. He had a curious knack for looking like an imbecile. It wasn't something Morin tried to do, but he succeeded. He often had his mouth slightly open and his thick lips moistened as though he was about to drool. It could be either disconcerting or disarming. One thing it never was was attractive.

But it had grown on Gamache and his team as they realized what his face was doing had nothing to do with his brain or his heart.

"I like to just sit in our village church after everyone's left. Sometimes I go in in the evening."

"Do you talk to your priest?"

"Father Michel? Sometimes. Mostly I just sit. These days I imagine my wedding next June. I see the decorations and picture all my friends and family there. Some of the people I work with." He hesitated. "Would you come?"

"If I'm asked, I'd definitely be there."

"Really?"

"Absolutely."

"Wait 'til I tell Suzanne. When I sit in the church mostly I see her coming down the aisle to me. Like a miracle."

"*Now there is no more loneliness.*"

"*Pardon?*"

"It's a blessing Madame Gamache and I had at our wedding. It was read at the end of the ceremony. *Now you will feel no rain, for each of you will be shelter for the other,*" Gamache quoted.

Now you will feel no cold
For each of you will be warmth for the other
Now there is no loneliness for you
Now there is no more loneliness
Now there is no more loneliness.

Gamache stopped. "Are you cold?"

"No."

But Gamache thought the young agent was lying. It was early December, cold and damp and he was immobile.

"Can we use that blessing at our wedding?"

"If you'd like. I can send it to you and you can decide."

"Great. How does it end? Can you remember?"

Gamache gathered his thoughts, remembering his own wedding. Remembering looking out and seeing all their friends and Reine-Marie's huge family. And Zora, his grandmother, the only one of his family left, but she was enough. There was no bride's side and no groom's side. Instead they all mixed in together.

And then the music had changed and Reine-Marie appeared and Armand knew then he'd been alone all his life, until this moment.

Now there is no more loneliness.

And at the end of the ceremony, the final blessing.

"*Go now to your dwelling place,*" he said to Morin. "*To enter into the days of your togetherness. And may your days be good and long upon the earth.*"

There was a pause. But not too long. Gamache was about to speak when Agent Morin broke the silence.

"That's how I feel, that I'm not really alone. Not since I met Suzanne. You know?"

"I do."

"The only thing wrong with my image of our wedding is that Suzanne always faints or throws up in church."

"Really? How extraordinary. Why do you think that is?"

"The incense, I think. I hope. Either that or she's the antichrist."

"That would mess up the wedding," said Gamache.

"Not to mention the marriage. I've asked and she assures me she isn't."

"Well, good enough. Have you considered a pre-nup?"

Paul Morin laughed.

May your days be good and long upon this earth, thought Gamache.

"You asked to speak with me?"

Gamache's eyes flew open, jolted. A middle-aged man in a cassock was staring down at him.

"Père Sébastien?"

"That's right." The voice was clipped, efficient, officious.

"My name is Armand Gamache. I was hoping for some of your time."

The man's beady eyes were hard, wary. "It's a busy day." He looked closely at Gamache. "Do I know you?"

Since the priest showed no interest in sitting Gamache stood. "Not personally, no, but you might have heard of me. I'm the head of homicide for the Sûreté du Québec."

The man's face cleared of annoyance and he smiled. "Of course, Chief Inspector." Now he put out a slender hand and greeted him. "I'm sorry. It's dark in here, and, do you normally wear a beard?"

"No, I'm incognito," smiled Gamache.

"Then you might not want to be telling people you're the head of homicide."

"Good suggestion." Gamache looked around. "It's been a while since I was in the basilica. Not since the *premier*'s funeral a few years ago."

"I was one of the celebrants," said Père Sébastien. "Beautiful service."

Gamache remembered it as formal, stilted, and very, very long.

"Now," Father Sébastien sat and patted the wood next to him. "Tell me what you'd like to know. Unless it's the confessional you need?"

"I'm sorry, I'm so sorry," the young voice repeated, over and over. Gamache had reassured him it wasn't his fault, and assured Morin he'd find him before it was too late.

"You'll be having dinner with your parents and Suzanne tonight." There'd been a pause and Gamache thought he heard a sob. "I'll find you."

Another pause.

"I believe you."

"No," Gamache said to the priest, "just information."

"How can I help?"

"It's about the murder of Augustin Renaud."

The priest didn't look surprised. "Terrible. But I don't think I can be of much help. I hardly knew the man."

"But you did know him?"

Père Sébastien looked at Gamache with some suspicion now. "Of course I knew him. Isn't that why you're here?"

"Frankly I don't know why I'm here, except someone suggested I speak with you. Can you think why?"

The priest became prickly, offended. "Well, maybe because I'm the leading scholar on the early settlement of Québec and the role of the church. But maybe that's not important."

Dear God, thought Gamache, save me from a huffy priest. "Forgive me, but I'm not from Quebec City so I'm unfamiliar with your work."

"My articles are published worldwide."

This wasn't getting better.

"*Désolé*. It's not an area of expertise for me, but it's clearly of immense importance and I desperately need your help."

The priest relaxed a bit, his hackles slowly lying flat. "How can I help?" he asked, coldly.

"What can you tell me about Augustin Renaud?"

"Well, he wasn't crazy, I can tell you that." He was the first person to say that and Gamache leaned forward. The priest continued, "He was passionate and obstinate and he was certainly offensive, but he wasn't crazy. People called him that in order to dismiss the man, take away his credibility. It was a cruel thing to do."

"You liked him?"

Père Sébastien shifted a little on the hard pew. "I wouldn't say that. He was a difficult man to like, not very socially adept. Maladroit, in fact. He had only one goal in life and everything else was trivial to him, including people's feelings. I can see how he'd make a lot of enemies."

"Could someone have hated him enough to kill?" asked Gamache.

"There're a lot of reasons for murder, Chief Inspector, as you know."

"Actually, *mon Père*, I've found there's only one. Beneath all the justifications, all the psychology, all the motives given, like revenge or greed or jealousy, there lies the real reason."

"And what's that?"

"Fear. Fear of losing what you have or not getting what you want."

"And yet, fear of eternal damnation doesn't stop them."

"No. Neither does fear of getting caught. Because they don't believe in either."

"You think it's not possible to believe in God and commit murder?"

The priest was staring at Gamache now, his face relaxed, amused even. His eyes calm, his voice light. Then why was he clutching his cassock in his fist?

"Depends on the God you believe in," said Gamache.

"There is only one God, Chief Inspector."

"Perhaps, but all sorts of humans who see imperfectly. Even God. Especially God."

The priest smiled and nodded but his hand tensed even more.

"I'm afraid we've wandered off topic," said Gamache. "My fault. It was foolish of me to debate faith with such a celebrated priest. I am sorry, *mon Père*. We were talking about Augustin Renaud and you were saying he was dismissed as crazy, but in your view he was quite sane. How did you know him?"

"I found him in the basement of the chapel to St. Joseph. He was digging."

"He'd just started digging?"

"I told you he was monomaniacal. He lost all judgment when it came to Champlain. But he actually found something."

"What?"

"Some old coins from the 1620s and two coffins. One was very plain and semi-collapsed, but the other was lead-lined. Our theory is that Champlain, like other dignitaries, would have been buried in a lead-lined coffin."

"And this was where the original chapel stood, before the fire."

"You're not quite as ignorant as you pretend, Chief Inspector."

"Oh, my ignorance knows no bounds, Father."

"The dig was immediately shut down by the city. It was unauthorized and considered akin to grave robbing. But then Renaud went to the media and made a huge stink. Champlain finally found, the tabloids declared, but uptight, regulation-bound bureaucrats had stopped the excavation. The media decided to portray it as a David and Goliath fight. Little old Augustin Renaud, valiantly struggling to find the man symbolic of French Québec, and the official archeologists and politicians stopping him."

"Serge Croix must have loved that," said Gamache.

Père Sébastien chuckled. "The Chief Archeologist was livid. I had him in here dozens of times over that period, ranting and raving. It wasn't clear how much of his anger was directed at Renaud personally and how much was fear that Renaud might be right, and maybe this little amateur archeologist would make the biggest discovery of anyone's career."

"Champlain."

"The Father of Québec."

"But why is it important? Why're so many people so passionate about where Champlain might be buried?"

"Aren't you?"

"I'm curious, absolutely. And if he was found I'd visit the site and read everything I could about the discovery, but I don't take it personally."

"You think not? I wonder if that's true. I see a lot of people who don't realize they have a belief, a faith, until they're dying, and then they discover it buried deep inside them. There all along."

"But Champlain was a man, not a faith."

"Perhaps at first, but he's become more than that, to some. Come with me."

Père Sébastien stood, bobbed briefly toward the gold crucifix at the altar and hurried out of the vast church. Gamache followed. Up wooden stairs, through back halls and finally into a cramped office, piled high with books and papers. And on the wall two reproductions. One of Christ, crucified, the other of Champlain.

The priest cleared magazines off two chairs and they sat.

"Champlain was a remarkable man, you know, and yet we know almost nothing about him. Even his birthday is a mystery. We don't even know what he looked like. This painting? Does it look familiar?"

He motioned to the one on the wall. It was the image of Champlain every Quebecker knew, every Canadian knew. It showed a man about thirty wearing a green doublet, a lace collar, white gloves and a sword and hilt. His hair was in the style of the 1600s, long, dark and slightly curled. He had a trim beard and moustache. It was a handsome, intelligent face, a lean, athletic face with large, thoughtful eyes.

Samuel de Champlain. Gamache would pick him out of any lineup. He nodded.

"That's not him," said Père Sébastien.

"It isn't?"

"Look at this." Sébastien pulled a book from the burdened bookcase. Flipping it open he handed it to the Chief Inspector. "Look familiar?"

There was the painting of a man, slightly pudgy, standing in front of a window with a verdant scene behind him. He was about thirty, wearing a green doublet, a lace collar, white gloves and a sword and hilt. His hair was in the style of the 1600s, long, dark and slightly curled. He had a trim beard and moustache. It was a handsome, intelligent face, with large, thoughtful eyes.

"That's Michel Particelli d'Emery, an accountant for Louis XIII."

"But it's Champlain," said Gamache. "Slightly heavier, and turned in the other direction, but essentially the same man, even down to the clothing."

He handed the book back to the priest, stunned. Father Sébastien was smiling and nodding. "Someone lifted this image, tweaked it to make him look more courageous, more our image of a brave explorer, and called it Champlain."

"But why would anyone have to? If there're paintings of minor aristocrats and tradesmen, isn't there a portrait of Champlain?"

The priest leaned forward, animated. "There's not a single portrait of the man done during his life. We have no idea what he looked like. That's not all. Why wasn't Champlain ever given a title, or land here? He wasn't even officially the Governor of Québec."

"Have we exaggerated his significance?" asked Gamache and immediately regretted it. Again the priest bristled as though the Chief Inspector had thrown dirt on his idol.

"No. Every document we do have confirms he was the father of Québec. The records were written at the time by the Récollets. They founded the mission and the chapel. Champlain left half his money to them. He had the church built to celebrate the return of Québec from the English. He hated the English you know."

"Hard not to hate an enemy. I suspect the English felt the same about him."

"Perhaps. But it wasn't just because they were enemies. He considered the English the real savages. Considered them cruel, especially to the natives. Reading Champlain's diaries it became clear he'd developed a special relationship with the Huron and Algonquins. They taught him how to live in this country, and gave him detailed information on the waterways.

"He hated the English because they were more interested in slaughtering the Indians than working with them. Don't get me wrong, Champlain saw the Indians as savages too. But he knew he could learn from them and he worried about their immortal souls."

"And their furs?"

"Well, he was a businessman," admitted Père Sébastien.

Gamache looked again at the painting on the wall next to the crucified Christ. "So we don't know what Champlain looked like, when he was born, or where he's buried. What do his diaries tell us about him?"

"That's interesting too. They tell us next to nothing. They're basically agendas about his travels and daily life here, but not his internal life, not his thoughts and feelings. He kept his private life private."

"Even in his own diaries? Why?"

Sébastien put his palms to the ceiling in a stupefied manner. "There're some theories. One is that he was a spy for the King of France, another is even more compelling. Some think he was actually the son of the King. Illegitimate, of course. But that might explain the mystery of his birth and the secrecy surrounding a man who should have been celebrated. It might also explain why he was sent here, to the middle of nowhere."

"You said Augustin Renaud found a lead-lined coffin beneath one of the sanctuaries along with some coins but that the dig was stopped. Could he have been right? Might it be Champlain?"

"Would you like to see?"

Gamache stood. "Please."

They walked back the way they came, each pausing to cross himself, and across the nave to a small grotto area with a tiny altar lit by votives.

"It's through here." Sébastien squeezed behind the altar and through a tiny archway. A flashlight balanced on a rough rock ledge and the priest turned it on, flooding the cramped area. The center of the beam played over the stones and came to rest on a coffin.

Gamache felt a thrill. Could this be him?

"Has it been opened?" Gamache dropped his voice.

"No," whispered the priest. "After all that publicity the city finally agreed to let Renaud continue the dig, under their supervision. Privately the official archeologists were furious, publicly they sounded happy with the compromise. But after more imaging was done and records pored over it was decided this wasn't Champlain but a much more recent coffin of a mid-level curate."

"Are they sure?" Gamache turned to Father Sébastien, barely visible in the gloom. "Are you sure?"

"I was the one who convinced the city to continue the dig. I actually respected Renaud. He didn't have a degree and he wasn't trained, but he wasn't a fool. And he'd found something no one else had, including me."

"But had he found Champlain?"

"Not here. I wanted to believe it was. It would've been a coup for the church, brought in more people, and yes, more money. But when we looked closer and added it all up, it just wasn't going to be Champlain."

"But the coins?"

"They were from the 1600s and confirmed this was once the site of the original chapel and the cemetery, but nothing more."

The two men emerged into the light of the little sanctuary.

"What do you think happened to Champlain, Father?"

The priest paused. "I think after the fire he was reburied. There's a reference to a reburial taking place, but they don't say where, and no official documents exist. This church has burned down a few times, taking valuable records with it each time."

"You've studied Champlain most of your life, what do you think?"

"You asked me earlier why he mattered, why any of this mattered, and certainly why finding his body matters. It does. Champlain wasn't simply the founder of a colony, there was something different about him, something that separated him from every explorer who'd gone before. And that I think explains how he managed to succeed where others failed. And why he's remembered today, and revered."

"What made him different?"

"He never referred to Québec as New France, you know. In France they did. Later regimes did. But never Champlain. Do you know what he called this place?"

Gamache thought about that. They were in the body of the church again and he stared, almost unseeing, down the long empty path that ended in the golden altar and the saints and martyrs, angels and crucifixes.

"The New World," said Gamache at last.

"The New World," agreed Père Sébastien. "That is why he's loved. He's a symbol of all that is great, all that is brave, all that Québec could have been and might be again. He's a symbol of freedom and sacrifice and vision. He didn't just create a colony, he created a New World. And he's adored for it."

"By the separatists."

"By everyone," the priest eyed Gamache closely. "By yourself included, I think."

"It's true," admitted Gamache and thought of that painting of Samuel de Champlain, and realized it reminded him of someone. Not just the plump and prosperous accountant, but someone else.

Christ. Jesus Christ.

They'd made Champlain look like the savior. And now the man who would raise him was dead. Killed, if you believed the tabloids, by the English, who may very well be also hiding the body of Champlain.

"Could Champlain be buried in the Literary and Historical Society?"

"Not a chance," said Père Sébastien without hesitation. "That was wilderness in his day. They'd not have reburied him there."

Unless, thought Gamache, the founder wasn't quite the saint he'd become.

"Where do you think he is?" Gamache asked, again.

They were standing at the door, on the icy steps of the Basilica.

"Not far."

Before ducking back into the church the priest nodded. Across the street. To the Café Buade.

ELEVEN

~

It wasn't quite five in the afternoon and the sun was down. Elizabeth MacWhirter looked out the window. A small crowd had been milling outside the Literary and Historical Society all day. A bold few had come inside, almost daring the members to toss them out. Instead Winnie had greeted them, given them the bilingual brochures and invited them to join.

She'd even given some of the more brazen a brief tour of the library, pointing out the fine pillows on the walls, the collection of figs on the shelves and asking if any of them would like to become umlauts.

Not surprisingly few did. But three people actually paid twenty dollars and joined, shamed into it by Winnie's obvious kindness and handicap.

"Did you mention that the night is a strawberry?" Elizabeth asked when Winnie returned with a membership payment.

"I did. They didn't disagree. Ready?"

Before turning out the lights and locking up they checked the main library. More than once they'd locked poor Mr. Blake in, but his chair was empty. He'd already gone across to the rectory.

The crowd had disappeared, the dark and cold having killed curiosity. The two women walked cautiously over the path of hardened snow, planting their feet firmly and carefully. Watching their own steps, watching each other's.

In winter the very ground seemed to reach up and grab the elderly, yanking them to earth as though hungry for them. Shattering a hip or wrist, or neck. Best to take it slow.

Their destination wasn't far. They could see the lights through the windows of the rectory. It was a lovely stone building, gracious in proportions with tall windows to catch every ray of a miserly winter sun. Walking slowly, side by side, Elizabeth could feel her cheeks freeze in just this short stroll. Their feet squeaked on the snow, making a sound she'd heard for almost eighty years. A sound she'd never trade for waves lapping on a Florida shore.

Lights were appearing in homes and restaurants, reflecting off the white snow. It was a city that lent itself to winter, and to darkness. It became even cozier, more inviting, more magical, like a fairy-tale kingdom. And we're the peasants, thought Elizabeth with a wry smile.

As they crept up the walk they could see through the window the fire in the hearth and Tom handing around drinks. Mr. Blake and Porter were already there and Ken Haslam was sitting in an armchair, reading a newspaper.

He missed nothing, Elizabeth knew. It was a mistake to underestimate Ken, as people had all his life. People always dismissed the quiet ones, which was ironic in Ken's case, Elizabeth knew. She also knew why he was quiet. But she'd never tell a soul.

Elizabeth MacWhirter knew everything, and forgot nothing.

The two women entered the rectory without knocking, took off their coats and boots and before long they too were in front of the roaring fire in the large living room. Porter handed a Scotch to Winnie and a sherry to Elizabeth and the two women sat beside each other on the sofa.

It was a room they knew well from the intimate chamber music concerts, from the tea parties and cocktail parties. From the lunches and bridge parties and dinners. Larger community events were held in the church hall just across the way, but this home had become the center of their more intimate gatherings.

Elizabeth noticed Ken's lips were moving. He smiled and she smiled.

Being with Ken was like being with a permanently foreign friend. It was impossible to understand them, but all you really needed to do was reflect back their own expressions. When Ken looked sad, they looked sad. When he looked happy, they smiled. It was actually very relaxing to be around him. Not much was expected.

"Well, I've had quite a day," said Porter, rocking on his feet in front of the fire. "Spent most of it giving interviews. Taped Jacquie Czernin's show for CBC Radio. It'll be on any minute. Want to hear it?"

He walked over to the stereo and turned on the CBC.

"I must've done ten interviews today," Porter said, guarding the radio.

"I did the crossword puzzle," said Mr. Blake. "Very satisfying. What's a six-letter word for 'idiot'?"

"Do proper names count?" asked Tom with a smile.

"Oh, here it comes." Porter turned up the volume.

"As we heard in the news," a melodious woman's voice said, "the amateur archeologist Augustin Renaud was found dead yesterday morning at the Literary and Historical Society. Police confirm he was murdered though they haven't made any arrests yet.

"Porter Wilson is the President of the Lit and His and he joins me now. Hello, Mr. Wilson."

"Hello Jacquie."

Porter looked around the rectory living room, expecting applause for his brilliance so far.

"What can you tell us about the death of Mr. Renaud?"

"I can tell you that I didn't do it."

Porter on the radio laughed. Porter in the rectory laughed. No one else did.

"But why was he there?"

"Frankly, we don't know. We're shocked, as you can imagine. It's tragic. Such a respected member of the community."

Porter, in the rectory, was nodding in agreement with himself.

"For God's sake, Porter, turn it off," said Mr. Blake, struggling out of his chair. "Don't be a horse's ass."

"No, wait," Porter stood before the stereo, blocking it. "It gets better. Listen."

"Can you describe what happened?"

"Well, Jacquie, I was in the office of the Lit and His when the telephone repairman arrived. I'd called him because the telephones weren't working. They should have been because, as you know, we're in the middle of a huge restoration of the library. In fact, you've helped us with the fundraisers."

What followed were five excruciating minutes of Porter plugging the fundraising and the interviewer desperately trying to get him to talk about anything other than himself.

Finally she cut off the interview and went to music.

"Is it over?" Tom asked. "Can I stop praying now?"

"What were you thinking?" Winnie asked Porter.

"What d'you mean? I was thinking this was a great chance to get more donations for the library."

"A man was murdered," snapped Winnie. "Honestly, Porter, this wasn't a marketing opportunity."

As they argued Elizabeth went back to reading the press. The papers were full of the Renaud murder. There were photographs of the astonishing-looking man, there were tributes, eulogies, editorials. He was barely cold and already he'd risen, a new man. Respected, beloved, brilliant and on the verge of finding Champlain.

In the Literary and Historical Society, apparently.

One paper, *La Presse*, had discovered that Renaud had approached the board shortly before his death and been turned down. Something that had seemed so reasonable, just following procedure, now seemed ominous, suspicious.

But the most disconcerting of all was the astonishment in all the French papers. Just as shocking as the discovery of Augustin Renaud's dead body was the discovery of so many live bodies, so many Anglo bodies, among them all this time.

Quebec City seemed to only now be awakening to the fact that the English were still there.

"How could they not know we're here?" said Winnie, reading over Elizabeth's shoulder.

Elizabeth had felt the sting too. It was one thing to be vilified, to be seen as suspects, as threats. Even to be seen as the enemy, she was prepared for all that. What she was unprepared for was not being seen at all.

When had that happened? When had they disappeared, become ghosts in their home town? Elizabeth looked over at Mr. Blake who'd also lowered his newspaper and was staring ahead.

"What're you thinking?"

"That it must be dinner time," he said.

Yes, thought Elizabeth, going back to reading, best not to underestimate the English.

"I was also remembering 1966."

Elizabeth lowered her paper.

"What do you mean?"

"But you remember, Elizabeth. You were there. I was telling Tom about it just a week or so ago."

Elizabeth looked over at their minister, so young and vibrant. Laughing with Porter, charming the prickly old man. He hadn't even been born in 1966 but she remembered it as though it was yesterday.

The thugs arriving. The Québec flag waving. The insults. *Maudits Anglais. Têtes Carré* and worse. The singing outside the Literary and Historical Society. *Gens du Pays.* The separatist anthem, with such achingly beautiful words, hurled as an insult at the building and to the frightened Anglos inside.

Then the attack, the separatists racing through the doors and up the sweeping staircase, into the library itself. Into the very heart of the Lit and His. Then the smoke, the books on fire. She'd run, trying to stop them, trying to put out the fires, pleading with them to stop. In her perfect French, appealing to them. Porter and Mr. Blake and Winnie and others, trying to stop it. The smoke, the shouting, the breaking glass.

She'd looked over and seen Porter breaking the fine leaded glass windows, windows that had been in place for centuries, now shattered. And she saw him tossing books out, at random. Handfuls, armfuls. And Mr. Blake joining him. While the separatists burned the books, the Anglos threw them out the windows, their covers splaying as though trying to take flight.

Winnie, Porter, Ken, Mr. Blake and others, saving their history before saving themselves.

Yes. She did remember.

Armand Gamache got home just in time for Henri's dinner then they went for a walk. The streets of Québec were dark, but they were also clogged with revelers celebrating Carnaval. Rue St-Jean had been closed and filled with entertainment. Choirs, jugglers, fiddlers.

Man and dog wove in and out of the crowds, stopping now and then to appreciate the music, or to people watch. It was one of Henri's favorite things, after the Chuck-it. And bananas. And dinner time. Lots of people stopped and made a fuss of the young shepherd with the unnaturally large ears. Gamache, beside him, might as well have been a lamppost.

Henri lapped up the attention, then they went home where the Chief Inspector glanced at the clock. Past five. He made a call.

"*Oui allô?*"

"Inspector Langlois?"

"Ah, Chief Inspector, I was just about to call you with an update."

"Any news?"

"Not much, I'm afraid. You know what these things are like. If we don't find someone immediately then it becomes a slog. This is a slog. I'm just over at Augustin Renaud's home." He hesitated. "You wouldn't want to come, would you? It's not far from where you are."

"I'd love to see it."

"Bring your reading glasses and a sandwich. And a couple of beers."

"That bad?"

"Unbelievable. I don't know how people live like this."

Gamache got the address, played with Henri for a few minutes, wrote a note for Émile, then left. On the way he stopped at Paillard, the marvelous bakery on rue St-Jean, and at a *dépanneur* for beer then headed up rue Ste-Ursule, pausing to check the address he'd been given, unconvinced he had it right.

But no. There it was. 9¾ rue Ste-Ursule. He shook his head. 9¾.

It would figure that Augustin Renaud would live there. He lived a marginal life, why not in a fractional home? Gamache walked down the short tunnel and into a small courtyard. Knocking, he waited a moment then entered.

He'd been in homes of every description in his thirty years of investigating crime. Hovels, glass and marble trophy homes, caves even. He'd seen hideous conditions, and uncovered hideous things and yet he was constantly surprised by how people lived.

But Augustin Renaud's home was exactly as Armand Gamache had imagined it would be. Small, cluttered, papers, journals, books piled everywhere. It was certainly a fire hazard, and yet the Chief had to admit he felt more at home here than in the glass and marble wonders.

"Anybody here?" he called.

"Through here. In the living room. Or maybe it's the dining room. Hard to say."

Gamache followed the trail cleared, like snow, through the paper and found Inspector Langlois bent over a desk reading. He looked up and smiled.

"Champlain. Every single scrap of paper's about Champlain. I didn't think this much had been written about the man."

Gamache picked up a magazine from the top of a stack, an old *National Geographic* detailing the first explorations of what is now New England. There was a reference to Champlain, whose name was on Lake Champlain in Vermont.

"My people are going through it all slowly," said Langlois. "But I estimate it will take forever."

"Would you like some help?"

Langlois looked relieved. "Yes, please. Could you?"

Gamache smiled and placing two bags on the desk he brought out an assortment of sandwiches and a couple of beers.

"Perfect. I haven't even had lunch yet."

"Busy day," said Gamache.

Langlois nodded, taking a huge bite from a roast beef, hot mustard and tomato sandwich on a baguette then took a swig of beer.

"We've only really had a chance to fingerprint and get DNA samples here. Even that's taken two days. The forensics people have been through and now the work begins." He glanced round.

Gamache pulled up a chair, grabbed a baguette filled with thick sliced maple-cured ham, brie and arugula and took a beer. For the next few hours the two men went through Augustin Renaud's home, organizing it, separating his original papers from photocopies of other people's works.

Gamache found reproductions of Champlain's diaries and scanned them. They were as Père Sébastien had said, little more than "to do" lists. It was a fascinating insight into everyday life in Québec in the early 1600s, but it could have been written by anyone. There was certainly no personal information. Gamache came away with no feeling for the man.

"Found anything?" Langlois wiped a weary hand across his face and looked up.

"Copies of Champlain's diary, but nothing else."

"Don't you think Renaud must have kept a journal or a diary himself?"

Gamache looked round the room and into the next, seeing stack after stack of papers. Bookcases stuffed to bursting, closets filled with magazines. "We might find some yet. Have you found any personal papers at all?" Gamache took off his reading glasses and looked across the desk at Langlois.

"Some letters from people replying to Renaud. I've made a file, but most seem to just be telling him with varying degrees of civility that he was wrong."

"About what?"

"Oh, different theories he had about Champlain. That he was a spy, or the son of the King, or even that he was Protestant. As one said, if he was a Huguenot why give most of his money to the Catholic Church in his will? It was like all of Renaud's theories. Close, but just a little wacky."

Gamache thought Langlois was being charitable by calling Renaud "a little" wacky. He glanced at his watch. Ten to eight.

"Are you still hungry?"

"Starving."

"Great. Let me take you to dinner. There's a place just down the street I've been dying to try."

On their way they stopped at a shop so Langlois could pick up a nice bottle of red wine then they carefully made their way just a few steps down the slide that was rue Ste-Ursule, to a hole-in-the-wall restaurant in the basement.

As soon as they entered they were met by warmth, by rich Moroccan spices and by the owner who introduced himself, took their coats and wine and led them to a quiet corner table by a wall of exposed stone.

He returned a moment later with the wine uncorked, two glasses and menus. After ordering they compared notes. Gamache told the Inspector about his day and his conversations with the members of the Champlain Society and Père Sébastien.

"Well, that dovetails nicely with my day. Among other things I spent much of it in the basement of the Literary and Historical Society with one very annoyed archeologist."

"Serge Croix?"

"Exactly. Not pleased to be called out on a Sunday, though he did admit it often happens. They're like doctors, I suppose. On call all the time in case someone suddenly digs up bones or an old wall or piece of pottery. Apparently it's quite common in Québec."

Their dinners arrived, steaming, fragrant plates of lamb tagine with couscous and stewed vegetables.

"Croix brought a couple of technicians and a metal-detector thing. But more sophisticated than anything I'd seen before."

Gamache tore a piece of baguette off the loaf and dipped it in the tagine juices. "Did he think Renaud might have been right? That Champlain was there?"

"Not for a moment, but he felt they at least had to look, if only to tell reporters that Renaud was wrong, yet again."

"And never again," said Gamache.

"Hmm." Langlois was enjoying his dinner, as was Gamache.

"So you didn't find anything?"

"Potatoes and some turnips."

"It was a root cellar, I suppose that makes sense." Still, while Gamache was relieved for the English, he was a little disappointed. Part of him hoped Renaud had finally, perhaps fatally, gotten it right.

So why had he been killed? And why had he been at the Lit and His?

What did he want to talk to the board about?

But really, thought Gamache, whether Champlain was buried there or not was irrelevant. All that mattered was what Renaud believed. And what he could make others believe, which seemed was just about anything.

After dinner Langlois and Gamache parted ways, the Inspector to go home to his wife and family and the Chief Inspector to return to Renaud's home and sort through more papers.

An hour later he found them, hidden behind books two rows deep on the bookcase. The diaries of Augustin Renaud.

TWELVE

⌒

Jean-Guy Beauvoir got back to Three Pines by mid-afternoon after his visits to Olivier in prison and the antique shop in Montreal. He'd stopped at the Tim Hortons at exit 55 for a sandwich, a chocolate glazed doughnut and a double double coffee.

And now he was tired.

This was way more activity than he'd had since it had all happened, and he knew he needed to rest. At the B and B he had a long, luxurious bath and thought about what to do next.

Olivier had dropped a bombshell. Now he was saying the Hermit's name wasn't Jakob, and he wasn't even Czech. He'd only said that to spread round the guilt, put attention onto the Parras and the other Czech families in the areas.

Not only was that not very neighborly, it wasn't very effective. They'd still decided Olivier was the murderer and the courts had agreed.

OK. So. Beauvoir slipped deeper into the tub. Soaping himself he barely even noticed the ragged scar on his abdomen anymore. What he did notice was that his muscles were no longer toned. He wasn't fat, but he was flabby from inactivity. Still, he could feel his strength slowly returning, more slowly than he would have imagined.

He cleared his mind of those thoughts and instead concentrated on what the Chief had asked him to do. Quietly reopen Olivier's case.

Where do the day's findings leave us? he wondered.

But nothing came to mind except his large, inviting bed which he could see through the bathroom door, with its crisp white sheets and down duvet and soft pillows.

Ten minutes later the bath was drained, the *Do Not Disturb* sign was outside his door and Jean-Guy was fast asleep, warm and safe under the covers.

He awoke to darkness and rolling over contentedly he looked at the bedside clock. 5:30. He sat up. 5:30? A.M. or P.M.?

Had he been asleep for two hours or fourteen? He felt rested but it could be either.

Putting on the light he got dressed then stood on the landing outside his door. The B and B was quiet. A couple of lights were on, but they often were. Feeling disoriented, disconcerted, he went downstairs and looking out the bay window of the B and B he had his answer.

Lights were on at the homes around the village green and they glowed bright and cheery at the bistro. Happy that he was in for dinner and not breakfast Jean-Guy threw on his coat and boots and crunched across the green to be greeted inside by Gabri who was, unexpectedly, in his pajamas.

Beauvoir was back to his original question. Was it A.M. or P.M.? He was damned if he was going to ask.

"Welcome back. I hear you spent last night in the woods with the saint. Was it as much fun as it sounds? You don't look converted."

Beauvoir looked at the large man in pajamas and slippers and decided not to tell him what he looked like.

"What can I get you, *patron*?" asked Gabri when Beauvoir didn't respond.

What did he want? Scrambled eggs or a beer?

"A beer would be great, *merci*." He took the micro-brewery ale and found a comfortable wing chair by the window. A paper lay on the table and picking it up, he read about the murder of Augustin Renaud in Quebec City. The mad archeologist.

"May I join you?"

He looked at Clara Morrow. She was also in pajamas and a dressing gown and, he glanced down, slippers. Could this be a new, and nightmarish, fashion trend? How long had he slept? While he knew flannel was an aphrodisiac to Anglos, it did nothing for Beauvoir. He'd never, ever worn it and didn't plan to start.

Glancing around he noticed every third or fourth person was in a dressing gown. He'd always secretly suspected this was not a village but an out-patient clinic from an asylum, now he had his proof.

"Here for your meds?" he asked as she sat.

Clara laughed and held up her beer. "Always." She nodded at his Maudite beer. "You too?"

Leaning forward he whispered, "What time is it?"

"Six." When he still stared she added, "In the evening."

"Then why . . ." He indicated her get-up.

"After Olivier was arrested it took Gabri a while to really function, so some of us helped out. He didn't want to open on Sundays, but Myrna and I convinced him to and he finally agreed, on one condition."

"Pajamas?"

"You are clever," she smiled. "He didn't want to have to get dressed. After a while most of us started doing the same thing, showing up in our pajamas. It's very relaxing. I stay in them all day."

Beauvoir tried to look disapproving but had to admit, she did look comfortable. She completed the look by having bed-head, though that was nothing new. Her hair always stuck out in all directions, probably where she ran her hands through it. And that would also account for the crumbs in there, and the flecks of paint.

He tried to think of something friendly to say, something that would lead her to believe he was there because he liked their company.

"Do you have your art show soon?"

"A couple of months." She took a long haul of her beer. "When I'm not practicing my interview for the *New York Times* and *Oprah* I try not to think about it."

"*Oprah?*"

"Yes. It'll be a huge tribute show, to me. All the top art critics will be there, weeping of course, overwhelmed by my insight, by the power of my images. Oprah will buy a few pieces for 100 million each. Sometimes it's 50 million, sometimes 150 million."

"So she's getting a bit of a bargain today."

"I'm feeling generous."

He laughed, surprising himself. He'd never had an actual conversation with Clara. With any of them. The Chief had. Somehow he'd managed to become friends with most of them but Beauvoir had never been able to pass through that membrane, to see people as both suspects and human. He'd never wanted to. The idea repulsed him.

He watched her take some mixed nuts and sip on her beer.

"Can I ask you something?" he said.

"Sure."

"Do you think Olivier killed the Hermit?"

Her hand stopped on its way for more nuts. He'd dropped his voice as he spoke, making sure they weren't overheard. She lowered her hand and thought for a good minute before answering.

"I don't know. I wish I could say absolutely he didn't, but the evidence is so strong. And if he didn't then someone else did."

She casually looked around the room, and he followed her gaze.

There was Old Mundin and The Wife. The handsome young couple was dining with the Parras. Old, despite his name, wasn't yet thirty and was a carpenter. He also restored Olivier's antiques and had been among the last people in the bistro the night the Hermit was killed. The Wife, Beauvoir knew, had an actual name though he'd forgotten what it was as had, he suspected, most people. What had started as a joke, the young couple mocking their married state, had become reality. She was The Wife. They had a young son, Charlie, who had Down syndrome.

Glancing at the child Beauvoir remembered that had been one of the reasons people considered Dr. Vincent Gilbert a saint. His decision to abandon a lucrative career to live in a community of people with Down syndrome, to care for them. From that experience he'd written the book *Being*. It was by most accounts a book of staggering honesty and humility. Staggering because it had been written by such an asshole.

Well, as Clara often told them, great works of creation often were.

Sitting with Old and The Wife were Roar and Hanna Parra. They'd been among the main suspects. Roar was cutting the paths through the woods and could have found the cabin with its priceless contents and shabby old occupant.

But why take the life and leave the treasure?

The same question held true for their son, Havoc Parra. Clara and

Beauvoir glanced over at him, waiting a table by the other fireplace. He'd worked late in the bistro the night the Hermit had been killed and had closed up.

Had he followed Olivier through the woods and found the cabin?

Had he looked inside, seen the treasures, and realized what it meant? It meant no more tips, no more tables, no more smiling at rude customers. No wondering what the future held.

It meant freedom. And all he'd have to do was knock a solitary old man on the head. But, again, why were most of the priceless treasures still in the cabin?

Across the room were Marc and Dominique Gilbert. The owners of the inn and spa. In their mid-forties they'd escaped high-paying, high-pressure jobs in Montreal, to come to Three Pines. They'd bought the wreck on the hill and turned it into a magnificent hotel.

Olivier despised Marc and it was mutual.

Had the Gilberts bought the run-down old home because the Hermit and the cabin came with it? Buried in their woods?

And finally there was the asshole saint Dr. Vincent Gilbert, Marc's estranged father who'd appeared at exactly the same time as the body. How could that have been a coincidence?

Clara's gaze returned to Beauvoir just as the bistro door slammed shut.

"Goddamned snow."

Beauvoir didn't have to look round to know who it was. "Ruth," he whispered to Clara, who nodded. "Still crazy?"

"After all these years," Clara confirmed.

"Jeez," Ruth appeared at Beauvoir's chair, a scowl on her deeply wrinkled face. Her cropped white hair lay flat on her head, looking like exposed skull. She was tall and stooped and walked with a cane. The only good news was that she wasn't in her nightgown.

"Welcome to the bistro," she snarled, giving Clara the once over. "Where dignity goes to die."

"And not just dignity," said Beauvoir.

She gave a barking laugh. "You find another body?"

"I don't follow bodies, you know. I have a life outside of work."

"God, I'm bored already," said the old poet. "Say something smart."

Beauvoir was silent, looking at her with disdain.

"Thought so." She took a swig of his beer. "Blech, this is crap. Can't you drink something decent? Havoc! Get him a Scotch."

"You old hag," Beauvoir murmured.

"Oh, banter. Very clever."

She intercepted his Scotch and stomped away. When she'd gotten far enough Beauvoir leaned across the table to Clara, who also leaned forward. The bistro was noisy with laughter and conversation, perfect for a quiet talk.

"If not Olivier," said Beauvoir, keeping his voice down and a sharp eye on the room, "who?"

"I don't know. What makes you think it wasn't Olivier?"

Beauvoir hesitated. Should he cross the Rubicon? But he knew he already had.

"This must go no further. Olivier knows we're looking into it, but I've told him to keep quiet. And you too."

"Don't worry, but why're you telling me this?"

Why indeed? Because she was the best of a bad lot.

"I need your help. You obviously know everyone way better than I do. The Chief's worried. Gabri keeps asking him why Olivier would move the body. It makes sense if he found the Hermit already dead but if you've just killed someone in a remote place you're almost certainly not going to advertise. The Chief thinks we might have gotten it wrong. What do you think?"

She was obviously taken aback by the question. She thought about it before slowly answering. "I think Gabri will never believe Olivier did it, even if he'd witnessed it himself, but I also think that's a good question. Where do we begin?"

We, thought Beauvoir, there is no "we." There's "me" and "you." In that order. But he needed her so he swallowed the retort, pasted a smile on his face and answered.

"Well, Olivier now says the Hermit wasn't Czech."

Clara rolled her eyes and ran her fingers through her hair which now stood out on both sides like Bozo. Beauvoir grimaced, but Clara neither noticed nor cared. Her mind was on other things. "Honestly, that man. Any other lies he's admitting to?"

"Not so far. He thought the Hermit was Québécois or perhaps

English but completely fluent in French. All his books were English and the ones he asked Olivier to find for him were also English. But he spoke perfect French."

"How can I help?"

He thought for a moment then made a decision. "I've brought the case file. I'd like you to read it."

She nodded.

"And since you know everyone here I'd like you to sometimes ask questions."

Clara hesitated. She didn't like the idea of being a spy but if he was right then an innocent man was in prison and a murderer was among them. Almost certainly in the room with them at that moment.

Myrna and Peter arrived and Beauvoir joined them for a bistro dinner, ordering the filet mignon with cognac blue cheese sauce. They chatted about various events in the village, the ski conditions at Mont Saint-Rémy, the Canadiens game the night before.

Ruth came by for dessert, eating most of Peter's cheesecake, then she limped off alone into the night.

"She misses Rosa terribly," said Myrna.

"What happened to her duck?" asked Beauvoir.

"Flew off in the fall," said Myrna.

The duck was smarter than it looked, thought Beauvoir.

"I dread the spring," said Clara. "Ruth'll be expecting her back. Suppose she doesn't come."

"It doesn't mean Rosa's dead," said Peter, though they all knew that wasn't true. Rosa the duck was raised from birth, literally hatched, by Ruth. And against all odds, Rosa had survived and thrived and had grown up, to follow Ruth everywhere she went.

The duck and the fuck, as Gabri called them.

And then last fall Rosa did what ducks do, what was in her nature to do. As much as she loved Ruth, she had to go. And one afternoon, as other ducks quacked and flew in formation overhead, heading south, Rosa rose up.

And left.

After dinner Beauvoir thanked them and got up. Clara walked him to the door.

"I'll do it," she whispered.

Beauvoir handed her the dossier and headed into the cold dark night. Walking slowly back to the B and B toward his warm bed, he stopped partway across the village green and looked at the three tall pine trees still wearing their multi-color Christmas lights. The colors bounced off the drifts of fresh snow. Looking up he saw the stars and smelled the fresh, crisp air. Behind him he heard people calling good night to each other and heard their scrunching steps in the snow.

Jean-Guy Beauvoir changed direction and arriving at the old clap-board home he knocked. The door was opened a crack.

"Can I come in?" he asked.

Ruth stepped back and opened her door.

Armand Gamache sat at Renaud's messy desk, bent over the diaries. For the past couple of hours he'd read them, making notes now and then. Like Champlain's diaries, Augustin Renaud's spoke of events but not feelings. They were really more of an agenda, but they were informative.

Sadly, while Renaud had made a note of the time of the Literary and Historical Society board meeting there was no indication why he was interested. And there was no mention of meeting anyone later in the day or that evening.

The next day was blank, though there was a notation for the following week. *SC at 1pm on the Thursday.*

The days stretched ahead, empty. Pages and pages, white and barren. A winter life. Not a lunch with a friend, not a meeting, not a personal comment. Nothing.

But what about his immediate past?

There were notations about books, page references, library references, articles. He'd made notes, done sketches of the old city, written addresses. Places, perhaps, he was considering for his next dig? All of them around the Notre-Dame Basilica.

It appeared he'd never considered any site outside a quite tight radius. Then what was he doing in the relative wilderness of the Lit and His? And if he was there simply to look for a book, as Émile had suggested, why was he in the basement, digging? And why ask to speak to the board?

Jean-Guy Beauvoir and Ruth Zardo stared at each other.

It felt like a cage match. Only one would emerge alive. Not for the first time in Ruth's company, Beauvoir felt an unpleasant retraction below his belt.

"What do you want?" Ruth demanded.

"I want to talk," snapped Beauvoir.

"Can't it wait, asshole?"

"No, it can't, you lunatic." He paused. "Do you like me?"

Her eyes narrowed. "I think you're anal, idiotic, cruel and perhaps slightly retarded."

"And I think the same of you," he said, relieved. It was as he thought, as he'd hoped.

"Well, glad we got that straight. Thank you for coming by, now, nighty night." Ruth reached for the doorknob.

"Wait," Beauvoir said, his hand out, almost touching her withered arm. "Wait," he said again, almost in a whisper. And Ruth did.

Gamache leaned closer to the diary, a small smile on his face.

Literary and Historical Society.

There it was. Written as bold as could be in Renaud's diary. Not for the day of the board meeting, the day he died, but a week earlier. And above it the names of four people he'd planned to meet there.

A Chin, a JD and two people named S. Patrick and F. O'Mara. Beneath that was a number 18-something. Gamache slid the desk lamp over so that the light pooled on the page. 1800, or maybe 1869 or 8.

"Or is it 1809?" Gamache mumbled to himself, squinting and flipping to the next page to see if, from the back, it was any clearer. It wasn't.

He took off his reading glasses and leaned back in the chair, tapping the glasses absently on his knee.

1800 would make sense. That would be a time, six in the evening. Most Québécois used the twenty-four-hour clock. But—

The Chief Inspector stared into space. It actually didn't make sense. The Lit and His closed at five in the afternoon. 1700 hours.

Why would Renaud arrange to meet four people there an hour after closing?

Maybe, thought Gamache, one of them had a key and would let them in.

Or, maybe Renaud didn't realize the library would be closed.

Or, maybe he'd arranged to meet someone else there, a Lit and His volunteer not named who would open the door.

Had Augustin Renaud been to the Literary and Historical Society before the day he died? It seemed so. Not walking in like any normal patron, that didn't seem Renaud's style. No, the man needed something more dramatic, clandestine. This was a man, after all, who'd managed to break into the Basilica and start digging. The Literary and Historical Society would pose no physical or moral barrier. No door was locked to Augustin Renaud in his Quixotic quest for Champlain.

Gamache looked at his watch. It was after 11 P.M. Too late to call Elizabeth MacWhirter or any of the other board members, or to drop by. He wanted to see their faces when he asked the question.

He turned back to the diary. What wasn't in question were Renaud's feelings about this rendezvous. He'd circled it a few times and even made a couple of exclamation marks.

The amateur archeologist seemed exultant, as though arranging the meeting had been a coup. Gamache found the phone book and looked up Chin. It sounded like a Chinese name and he remembered that Augustin Renaud had once, famously, dug through a wall looking for Champlain and ended up in the basement of a Chinese restaurant.

Could Chin be the name of the restaurant, or the owner?

But there was no Chin. Perhaps it was someone's first name. There weren't many Chinese in Quebec City, it wouldn't be hard to find out.

There were no O'Maras, but there was an S. Patrick living on rue des Jardins, in the old city. Gamache knew it. The small street wound along beside the Ursuline convent and ended right in front of the Notre-Dame Basilica.

And his address? 1809 rue des Jardins. 1809. Not a time then, but a street number. Were they to meet there first then head to the Lit and His?

There were a few other names in Renaud's diary, mostly, it seemed, officials he was arguing with or editors who'd turned down his manuscripts. Serge Croix, the Chief Archeologist, was mentioned a few times, always with the word *merde* as though his name was hyphenated. Serge Croix-Merde.

Booksellers, mostly used, figured large in Augustin Renaud's life. It seemed if he had a relationship with anyone it was with them. Gamache jotted down their names then looked at his watch.

It was almost midnight, and Beauvoir was sitting on a plastic garden chair in Ruth's kitchen. He'd never been in her home before. Gamache had, a few times, but Beauvoir had always begged off those interviews.

He disliked the wretched old poet immensely which was why he was there.

"OK, dick-head, talk."

Ruth sat across from him, a pot of watery tea on the white pre-formed table, and one cup. Her thin arms were strapped across her chest, as though trying to keep her innards in. But not her heart, Beauvoir knew. That had escaped years before, like the duck. In time all things fled Ruth.

He needed to talk to someone, but someone without a heart, without compassion. Someone who didn't care.

"You know what happened?" he asked.

"I read the papers you know."

"It wasn't all in the papers."

There was a pause. "Go on." Her voice was hard, unfeeling. Perfect.

"I was sitting in the Chief's office—"

"I'm bored already. Is this going to be a long story?"

Beauvoir glared at her. "The call came at 11:18 in the morning."

She snorted. "Exactly?"

He met her eyes. "Exactly."

He saw again the Chief's corner office. It was early December and Montreal was cold and gray through the windows. They'd been discussing a difficult case in Gaspé when the Chief's secretary opened the door. She had a call. It was the Inspector in Ste-Agathe. There'd been a shooting. An agent down and one missing.

But he wasn't missing, he was on the phone asking to speak to the Chief.

Things happened quickly after that, and yet seemed to go on for-ever.

Agents poured in, the tactical teams were alerted. Satellites, imaging, analysis. Tracing. All swung into action. Within moments there was a near frenzy of activity visible through the large window in the Chief's office. All going to a protocol Chief Inspector Gamache had designed.

But in his office there was quiet. Calm.

"I'm sorry, I'm so sorry," Agent Morin said, when connected to the Chief.

"It's not your fault. Are you hurt?" Gamache had asked.

By now Beauvoir was listening on the other line. For reasons he didn't yet understand they'd so far been unable to trace the call and the man who held Agent Morin and had shot the other agent seemed uncon-cerned. He'd handed the phone back to the young agent but not before making something clear.

He would neither let Morin go, nor would he kill him. Instead, he'd bind the young agent and leave him there.

"Thank you," said Gamache.

Through the glass Beauvoir could see agents at computers, record-ing, listening in, pin-pointing the location of the call. He could even see their fingers flying over the keys.

They'd know where Agent Morin was being held within moments. But Beauvoir felt a little uneasy. Why was it taking so long? This should be almost instantaneous.

"You'll follow me, I know you will," the farmer was saying. "So I need you not to."

"I won't," lied Gamache.

"Maybe," the man said in his broad country accent. "But I can't risk it."

Something stirred inside Beauvoir and he looked at Gamache. The Chief was standing, staring ahead, concentrating, listening, thinking. Trying not to make a mistake.

"What have you done?" Gamache asked, his voice hard, unyielding.

There was a pause. "I've tied your agent up and attached some-thing to him."

"What?"

"It's something I made myself." The man's voice was defensive, weak, explaining. It was a fearful voice and that meant unpredictable and that meant trouble. The worst possible hostage-taker to deal with, they could panic at any moment. Their reason had fled and they were going on nerves not judgment.

"What is it?" Gamache asked.

Beauvoir knew what the Chief was doing. He was trying to become the sturdy center, the thing a weak, fearful man would move toward. Something firm, solid, predictable. Strong.

"From fertilizer. I didn't want to but it's the only way you'll leave me alone."

The voice was becoming more and more difficult to understand. The combination of the thick accent and words muffled by desperation.

"It's set to go off in twenty-four hours. At 11:18 tomorrow morning."

Beauvoir wrote that down, though he doubted he'd forget it. And he was right.

He heard the Chief inhale sharply, then pause, trying to control his anger.

"This is a mistake," he said, his voice steady. "You must dismantle that bomb. You're making this worse for yourself."

"Worse? How could it be worse? That other agent's dead. I killed a Sûreté agent."

"We don't know that."

"I do."

"Then you know we'll find you eventually. You don't want to spend your whole life running, do you? Wondering where we are?"

There was a hesitation.

"Give yourself up," said Gamache, his voice deep and calm and reasonable. A smart friend with a good idea. "I promise you won't be hurt. Tell me where to meet you."

Beauvoir stared at the Chief and the Chief stared at the wall, at the huge map of Québec. Both willing the man to see reason.

"I can't. I need to go. Good-bye."

"Stop," Gamache called into the phone, then contained himself with great effort. "Stop. Wait. Don't do this thing. If you run you'll regret it the rest of your life. If you hurt Paul Morin you'll regret it."

His voice was barely more than a whisper, but even Beauvoir felt his skin grow cold from the threat in Gamache's voice.

"I have no choice. There's one other thing."

"What?"

Outside in the homicide offices more sophisticated equipment was being set up. Beauvoir could see Chief Superintendent Francoeur striding toward the Chief's door. Gamache also saw him and turned his back, fully focused on the voice at the other end of the line.

"I don't want you coming after me."

The door opened and Chief Superintendent Francoeur stepped in, his distinguished, handsome face determined. Gamache's back remained to him. Inspector Beauvoir took Francoeur by the arm.

"You need to leave, sir."

"No, I need to speak to the Chief Inspector."

They were outside the door now. "The Chief is on the line with the hostage-taker."

"With the murderer. Agent Bissonette died of his wounds five minutes ago."

He thrust his right hand into his jacket pocket. It was a signal they all knew, a sign the Chief Superintendent was agitated, angry. The room, previously a buzz of activity, grew still and silent except for the two voices, loud and clear. The Chief, and the killer, over the monitors.

"I'm taking over here," said Francoeur and made for the door again but Beauvoir blocked him.

"You might take over, I can't stop you, but this is Chief Inspector Gamache's private office and he needs privacy."

As the two men stared at each other they heard Gamache's voice.

"You have to stop this," said the Chief. "Give yourself up."

"I can't. I killed that cop." Now his voice had risen almost to hysterics.

"Then even more reason to surrender yourself to me. I'll guarantee your safety." The Chief sounded reasonable, convincing.

"I have to get away."

"Then why didn't you just leave? Why call me?"

"Because I needed to."

There was a pause. Beauvoir could see the Chief in profile now. He saw his eyes narrow and his brows lower.

"What have you done?" Gamache almost whispered.

Gamache packed up the diaries and left a scribbled receipt with his address and phone number on Renaud's desk, then he walked back through the streets.

It was past midnight and the revelers were just revving up. He could hear hoots on the plastic horns and unintelligible shouts a few streets over.

College kids, drunk and rowdy.

Gamache smiled. Some would end up in jail getting sober. It would make a great story one day, for disbelieving grandchildren.

A rowdy gang of young men rounded the corner and stumbled up rue Ste-Ursule. Then one spotted Gamache and stopped. The others, blind drunk, bumped into him and started shoving. A small skirmish broke out but the leader pulled them apart and nodded toward Gamache, who was standing in the middle of the road in front of them.

Watching.

They stared at each other, then Gamache smiled.

"*Bonne nuit*," he said to them, putting his large mittened hand on the leader's shoulder as he passed.

Really?" said Ruth. "You can make a bomb out of shit?" She seemed interested. "I don't believe it."

"Chemical fertilizer, not shit. And don't believe it. I don't care," said Beauvoir. In fact, he preferred it that way. There were times he didn't believe it himself. They were the best times. "Hag," he mumbled.

"Numb nuts," Ruth said, and poured him a cup of tea that looked like rancid water. She sat and rewrapped her torso with her arms. "So what was the other thing the crazy farmer said he'd done?"

Beauvoir still saw Gamache's face, would always see his face. The look of disbelief and surprise. Not yet dismay, not yet alarm. That would come in a moment.

"What have you done?" Gamache had asked.

"I've rigged it up."

"How?"

"I need you to be occupied, to give me time." Again the voice was wheedling, whiny, as though asking Gamache's permission, or understanding, or forgiveness.

Outside in the large common area of their division office, agents were bending over computer screens, tapping away, grabbing headphones. Giving and taking orders.

Chief Superintendent Francoeur stared at Beauvoir then turned and marched away. Beauvoir took a breath, unaware he'd been holding it, then quickly stepped back into the Chief's office.

"Tell me," said Gamache, his voice authoritative.

And the man did. Then he handed the phone back to Agent Paul Morin.

It was the last they ever heard from the man, though he might have been among the dead.

"I'm sorry," Agent Morin repeated. "I'm so sorry."

"It's not your fault. Are you hurt?" Gamache had asked.

"No." He sounded terrified and trying not to show it.

"Don't worry. We'll find you."

There was a pause. "Yes sir."

"But you still haven't answered my question," said Ruth, impatiently. "Do you think I have all night? What had the farmer done, besides the shit bomb?"

Jean-Guy Beauvoir looked down at the white, plastic garden table, feeling its rough edges. No doubt the demented old poet had found it by the side of some road or in a Dumpster.

Some piece of trash no one else wanted. She'd brought it home with her.

He stared for a very long time at the table, in a daze. No one had been told this, it hadn't been made public. And Beauvoir knew he shouldn't be saying anything now.

But he had to tell someone and who better than someone who didn't care? There'd be no sympathy, no pity, no real understanding. There'd be no awkwardness when they saw each other in the village, because while he'd bared his soul to her she wouldn't care.

"The bomb was wired to the phone line," he finally said, still staring at his hands and the expanse of white table. "It would go off if the line was cut."

"Okay," she said.

"And it would be cut if there was dead air. If they stopped talking for more than a few seconds."

There was silence then. "So you all took turns talking," said Ruth.

Beauvoir took a deep breath and sighed. There was something in the corner, by Ruth's chair, something he couldn't quite make out. A sweater she'd dropped or a dish towel.

"It didn't work that way. He needed Gamache tied to Morin, so he couldn't search for him."

"What do you mean, 'tied to Morin'?"

"There was voice recognition. It needed to be the two of them. Morin and the Chief."

"Oh, come on," laughed Ruth. "There's no such thing. You're making this up."

Beauvoir was silent.

"Well, okay, maybe you're not, but the farmer sure was. Are you telling me some backwoods bumpkin made a bomb, then a timer, then attached it to the phone line with, what did you call it? Voice recognition?"

"Would you risk it?" he growled, his eyes hard, daring her to go further. Hating her, as he knew he would, for seeing him so vulnerable. For not caring, for mocking. But he already hated her, what was a little more bile?

He pressed his lips together so hard he could feel his teeth cutting through.

In the office he watched his Chief as Gamache realized what this meant.

"I'm sorry, I'm so sorry," the young voice said down the phone line.

"I'm going to find you," the Chief promised.

"They talked the whole time?" Ruth asked.

"Every moment. For twenty-four hours. Until 11:18 the next morning."

Beauvoir glanced into the corner and knew what was curled there. It was a blanket, a soft, flannel blanket made into a nest. Ready. Just in case.

Armand Gamache woke, groggy, and looked at the bedside clock.

Three twenty in the morning.

He felt the chill of the night air on his face and the warmth of the sheets and duvet around him. Lyng there, he hoped maybe this time he'd fall back asleep but eventually he got up. Slowly, stiffly. Putting on one light he dressed. As he sat on the side of the bed gathering himself he stared at the small pill bottle on the bedside table. Beside him Henri watched, his tail swishing back and forth, his eyes bright, a fluorescent yellow tennis ball in his mouth. Gamache gripped the bottle in his large hand, feeling it there. Then he placed it in his pocket and walked quietly downstairs, making sure not to waken Émile. Gamache put on his parka, his scarf, his tuque and mitts. Lastly, he picked up the Chuck-it and they stepped out into the night.

Up the street they walked, their feet squeaking on the hard snow. At rue St-Louis they turned out the gate through the walls of the fortified and frozen city and past the ice palace. Bonhomme's palace.

Then onto the Plains of Abraham to toss the ball and contemplate a general's fatal mistakes. Henri, Chief Inspector Gamache and Agent Morin.

THIRTEEN

⌒

Armand Gamache slid the diary across the wooden table toward Émile Comeau.

"Look what I found last night."

Émile put on his reading glasses. As he examined the small book Gamache glanced out the window and patted Henri, sleeping beneath the table. They were having breakfast at Le Petit Coin Latin, a tiny restaurant on rue Ste-Ursule. It had been there forever and was a local favorite, with its dark wood interior, the fireplace, the simple tables. It was far enough off the main streets not to be found by accident. People went there on purpose.

The owner put their bowls of *café au lait* on the table and withdrew. Gamache sipped and watched the snow fall. It always seemed to snow in Quebec City. It was as though the New World was actually a particularly beautiful snow globe.

Finally Émile lowered the diary and removed his reading glasses.

"Poor man."

Gamache nodded. "Not many friends."

"None, as far as I can tell. The price of greatness."

"Greatness? You'd consider Augustin Renaud that? I was under the impression you and the other members of the Champlain Society considered him a kook."

"Aren't most great people? In fact, I think most of them are both brilliant and demented and almost certainly unfit for polite society. Unlike us."

Gamache stirred his coffee and watched his mentor.

He considered him a great man, one of the few he'd met. Great not in his singularity of purpose, but in his multiplicity. He'd taught his young protégé how to be a homicide investigator, but he'd taught him more besides.

Gamache remembered being shown into Chief Inspector Comeau's office his first week on the job, certain he was about to be fired for some mysterious transgression. Instead the wiry, self-contained man had stared at him for a few seconds then invited him to sit and told him the four sentences that lead to wisdom. He'd said them only once, never repeating them. But once had been enough for Gamache.

I'm sorry. I was wrong. I need help. I don't know.

He'd never forgotten them and when he took over as Chief Inspector, Gamache passed them on to each and every one of his agents. Some took them to heart, some forgot them immediately.

That was their choice.

But those four statements had changed Armand Gamache's life. Émile Comeau had changed his life.

Émile was a great man because he was a good man, no matter what was happening around him. Gamache had seen cases explode around his Chief, he'd seen accusations thrown, he'd seen internecine politics that would stagger Machiavelli. He'd seen his Chief bury his own beloved wife, five years earlier.

Strong enough to grieve.

And when, a few weeks ago, Gamache had marched in the achingly slow cortege behind the flag-draped coffins he had with each halting step remembered his agents and with each step remembered his first Chief. His superior then, his superior now and always.

And when, finally, Gamache could take the pain no longer he and Reine-Marie had come here. Not to be healed, but to be helped.

I need help.

The owner of the bistro brought their breakfasts of *omelettes*, fresh fruit and a croissant each.

"I respect people who have such passion," Émile was saying. "I don't. I have a lot of interests, some I'm passionate about, but not to the exclusion of everything else. I sometimes wonder if that's necessary for geniuses to accomplish what they must, a singularity of purpose. We mere mortals just get in the way. Relationships are messy, distracting."

"He travels the fastest who travels alone," quoted Gamache.

"You sound as though you don't believe it."

"It depends where you're going, but no, I don't. I think you might go far fast, but eventually you'll stall. We need other people."

"What for?"

"Help. Isn't that what Champlain found? All other explorers failed to create a colony but he succeeded. Why? What was the difference? Père Sébastien told me. Champlain had help. The reason his colony thrived, the reason we're sitting here today, was exactly because he wasn't alone. He asked the natives for help and he succeeded."

"Don't think they don't regret it."

Gamache nodded. It was a terrible loss, a lapse in judgment. Too late the Huron and Algonquin and Cree realized Champlain's New World was their old one.

"Yes," said Émile, nodding slowly, his slender fingers toying with the salt and pepper shakers. "We all need help."

He watched his companion. He'd been heartened by Gamache taking an interest in this case. It was somewhere else to put his mind, other than that scalded spot. But then early that morning, while everyone else slept, he'd heard Armand and Henri, quietly leaving. Again.

"It's not your fault, you know. So many lives were saved."

"And lost. I made too many mistakes, Émile." It was the first time he'd talked about the events to his mentor. "Right from the start."

"Like what?"

The farmer's voice, with its broad country accent, played again in Gamache's head. All the clues were there, right from the start. "I didn't put things together fast enough."

"No one else even came close. Jesus, Armand, when I think what might have happened if you hadn't done what you did."

Gamache took a deep breath and looked down at the table, his lips tight.

Émile paused. "Do you want to talk about it?"

Armand Gamache looked up. "I can't. Not yet. But thank you."

"When you're ready." Émile smiled, took a sip of strong, aromatic coffee, and picked up Renaud's diary again. "I haven't read it all, of course, but what strikes me immediately is that there seems very little new in this. Certainly nothing we haven't heard a million times before.

The places he'd marked as possible sites for Champlain's grave are all places we've known about. The Café Buade, rue de Trésor. But they've all been investigated and nothing's been found."

"Then why did he believe Champlain might be there?"

"He also thought Champlain was in the Lit and His, let's not forget. He saw Champlain everywhere."

Gamache thought for a moment. "There're bodies buried all over Québec from hundreds of years ago. How would you even know if you'd found Champlain?"

"That's a good question. It's had us worried for a long time. Would the coffin say Samuel de Champlain? Would there be a date, an insignia perhaps? Maybe by his clothes. He apparently wore a quite distinctive metal hat, Renaud always thought that's how he'd know him."

"When he opened the coffin he'd see a skeleton in a metal hat and decide it's the father of Québec?"

"Genius might have its limits," admitted Émile. "But scholars think there might be a few clues. All the coffins made back then were wood, with a few exceptions. Experts believe Champlain would be an exception. His coffin was almost certainly lined in lead. And it's easier these days to date remains."

Gamache looked unconvinced. "Père Sébastien at the Basilica said there were mysteries surrounding Champlain and his birth. That he might be a Huguenot or a spy for the King of France or even his illegitimate son. Was that just romanticizing or is there more to it?"

"It's partly romantic, the noble bastard son. But a few things feed that rumor. One is his own near maniacal secrecy. For instance, he was married but only mentions his wife of twenty-five years a couple of times, and even then not by name."

"They didn't have any children, did they?"

Émile shook his head. "But others were also pretty tight lipped about Champlain. A couple of the Jesuit priests and a Récollet lay brother mention him in their journals, but even then it was nothing personal. Just daily life. Why the secrecy?"

"What's your theory? You've studied the man most of your life."

"I think it was partly the time, less stress on the individual. There wasn't quite the culture of 'me' that there is now. But I also think there might've been something he was trying to hide and it made him a very private person."

"The unacknowledged son of a king?"

Émile hesitated. "He wrote prolifically, you know, thousands of pages. Buried in all those words, all those pages, was one sentence."

Gamache was listening closely, imagining Champlain bent over the paper with a quill pen and a pot of ink by candlelight in a Spartan home four hundred years and a few hundred yards away from where they were sitting.

"*I am obligated by birth to the King*," said Émile. "Historians for centuries have tried to figure out what that could mean."

Gamache rolled it around in his head. *I am obligated by birth to the King*. It was certainly suggestive. Then something occurred to him.

"If Champlain's body was found, and we knew beyond a doubt it was him, they could do DNA tests." He was watching Émile as he spoke. His mentor's eyes were on the table. Was it deliberate? Not wanting to make eye contact? Was it possible?

"But would it matter?" Gamache mused. "Suppose the tests proved he was the son of Henri IV, who cares today?"

Émile raised his eyes. "From a practical point of view it would mean nothing, but symbolically?" Émile shrugged. "Pretty potent stuff, especially for the separatists who already see Champlain as a powerful symbol of Québec independence. It would only add to his luster and the romantic vision of him. He'd be both heroic and tragic. Just how the separatists see themselves."

Gamache was quiet for a moment. "You're a separatist, aren't you Émile?"

They'd never talked about it before. It hadn't been exactly a dirty little secret, just a private subject they'd never broached. In Québec politics was always dangerous territory.

Émile looked up from his *omelette*. "I am."

There was no challenge, just acknowledgment.

"Then you might have some insight," said Gamache. "Could the separatist movement use this murder?"

Émile was quiet for a moment then put down his fork. "It's slightly more than a 'movement' Armand. It's a political force. More than half the population say they're Québec Nationalists. Separatists have formed the government many times."

"I didn't mean to belittle it," smiled Gamache. "I'm sorry. And I'm aware of the political situation."

"Of course you are, I didn't mean to imply you weren't."

Already the atmosphere was becoming charged.

"I've been a separatist all my adult life," said Émile. "From the late sixties to this very day. Doesn't mean I don't love Canada. I do. Who couldn't love a country that allows such diversity of thought, of expression? But I want my own country."

"As you say, many agree with you, but there're fanatics on both sides of the debate. Ardent Federalists who fear and distrust the French aspirations—"

"And demented separatists who'd do whatever it took to separate from Canada. Including violence."

Both men thought about the October Crisis decades earlier when bombs were going off, when Francophones refused to speak English, when a British diplomat was kidnapped and a Québec cabinet minister murdered.

All in the name of Québec independence.

"No one wants to return to those days," said Émile, looking his companion square in the eye.

"Are you so sure?" asked the Chief Inspector, gently but firmly.

The air bristled between them for a moment, then Émile smiled and picked up his fork. "Who knows what's hidden below the surface, but I think those days are dead and buried."

"*Je me souviens,*" said Gamache. "What was it René Dallaire called Québec? A rowboat society? Moving forward but looking back? Is the past ever really far from sight here?"

Émile stared at him for a moment, then smiled and resumed eating while Gamache gazed out the frosty window, his mind wandering.

If Samuel de Champlain was such a symbol of Québec nationalism, were the members of the Champlain Society all separatists? Perhaps. But did it matter? As Émile said, it was more common in Québec to be one than not, especially among the *intelligentsia*. Québec separatists had formed the government more than once.

Then another thought occurred to him. Suppose Samuel de Champlain was found and found not to be the son of the King? He would become slightly less romantic, slightly less heroic, a less powerful symbol.

Might the separatists prefer a missing Champlain to one found and flawed? Perhaps they too wanted to stop Augustin Renaud.

"Did you notice the entry from last week?" Gamache decided to change the subject. He opened the diary and pointed. Émile read then looked up.

"Literary and Historical Society? So last Friday wasn't his first visit there. And it says 1800. The time of the meeting?"

"I was wondering the same thing, but the library would have been closed."

Émile looked at the page once again. The four names, the blurry, scribbled number. 18-. He squinted closer. "Maybe it's not 1800."

"Maybe not. I haven't found any of the others but I did find an S. Patrick at 1809 rue des Jardins."

"There's your answer." Émile called for the bill and stood up. "Shall we?"

Gamache downed the last of his *café au lait* and stood. "I called and left a message on Monsieur Patrick's answering machine, saying we'd be there about noon. Before that I need to go to the Lit and His to ask them about that entry in Renaud's diary. Could you do something for me while I do that?"

"*Absolument.*"

Gamache nodded out the window. "See that building?"

"9¾ rue Ste-Ursule?" said Émile, squinting at the building. "Does it really say that? What does a three-quarter apartment look like?"

"Want to see? It's Augustin Renaud's."

The two men paid up and with Henri they walked across the snowy street and into the apartment.

"Good God," said Émile. "It looks like a bomb went off."

"Inspector Langlois and I spent much of last night putting it in order. You should have seen it before." Gamache wound between the piles of research.

"All about Champlain?" Émile picked up a sheet at random and scanned it.

"Everything I've found so far is. His diaries were stuffed behind that bookshelf."

"Hidden?"

"It seems so, but I'm not sure we can read much into that. He was pretty paranoid. Can you go through his papers while I go to the Lit and His?"

"Are you kidding?"

Émile looked like a kid loosed in the toy factory. Gamache left his mentor sitting at the dining table, reaching for a pile of papers.

Within minutes the Chief Inspector was at the old library, standing in the deserted hallway.

"May I tuna you?" Winnie asked from the top of the oak staircase.

"I was wondering if I could speak to you and whoever else is here." He spoke English in hopes the librarian would switch to her mother tongue.

"Meet we maybe in bookstore reunion?"

She hadn't taken the hint.

"Good idea," said Gamache.

"Bunny day," agreed Winnie and disappeared.

Gamache found Mr. Blake in the library and within minutes Winnie, Elizabeth and Porter had joined them.

"I have just a couple of questions," said the Chief. "We've found evidence that Augustin Renaud came here a week before he died."

He watched them as he spoke. To a person they looked surprised, interested, a little disconcerted, but none of them looked guilty. And yet one of them had almost certainly lied to him. One of them had almost certainly seen, perhaps even met, Renaud here. Let him in.

But why? Why had Renaud wanted to come here? Why had he brought four others?

"What was he doing here?" Gamache asked and watched as they first stared at him, then at each other.

"Augustin Renaud came to the library?" asked Mr. Blake. "But I didn't see him."

"Neither did I," said Winnie, surprised into English.

Elizabeth and Porter each shook their heads.

"He might have come after the library closed," said Gamache. "At six o'clock."

"Then he wouldn't have gotten in," said Porter. "The place would've been locked. You know that."

"I know you all have keys. I know it would be easy for one of you to let him in."

"But why would we?" asked Mr. Blake.

"Do the names Chin, JD, Patrick and O'Mara mean anything to you?"

Again they thought and again they shook their heads. Like the Hydra. One body, many heads. But of a mind.

"Members, perhaps?" he pressed.

"I don't know about JD, but the others aren't members," said Winnie. "We have so few I know their names by heart."

It struck Gamache for the first time what an interesting English expression that was. To commit something to memory was to know it by heart. Memories were kept in the heart, not the head. At least, that's where the English kept their memories.

"May I have a list of your members?" he asked. Winnie bristled and Porter jumped in.

"That's confidential."

"A library membership list? Secret?"

"Not secret, Chief Inspector. Confidential."

"I still need to see it."

Porter opened his mouth but Elizabeth jumped in. "We'll get it for you. Winnie?"

And Winnie, without hesitation, did what Elizabeth asked.

As he left, membership list folded in his breast pocket, Gamache paused on the top step to put his heavy gloves on. From there he looked across to St. Andrew's Presbyterian Church and the rectory facing the old library.

Who would have the easiest time letting someone into the Lit and His, unseen? And, if lights were turned on after closing time, who was most likely to see it?

The minister, Tom Hancock.

After first going to the stone home Gamache found the minister at his office in the church, a cluttered and comfortable back room.

"I'm sorry to disturb you, but I need to know if you saw Augustin Renaud at the Lit and His a week before he died."

If Tom Hancock was the one who'd let them in he would almost certainly deny it. Gamache wasn't expecting the truth, only hoping to surprise a fleeting look of guilt.

But he saw none.

"Renaud was there a week before he died? I didn't know that. How'd you find out?"

Alone among them Hancock hadn't tried to argue. He was simply, like the Chief, baffled.

"His diary. He was to meet four others there, after hours we think."

Gamache gave him the names but the minister shook his head. "Sorry, they mean nothing, but I can ask around if you like." He paused and examined Gamache closely. "Is there anything else I can help you with?"

Help. I need help. Gamache shook his head, thanked him, and left.

When he got back to 9¾ Ste-Ursule, Émile was still reading.

"Any luck?" He looked up.

Gamache shook his head and took off his coat, brushing snow from it. "You?"

"I was just wondering about these. Did you notice them?"

Gamache walked over to the table and looked down. Émile was pointing to the diary page, the one that mentioned the meeting at the Lit and His with the four men. At the bottom of the page, in very small but legible writing, were two numbers.

9-8499 and 9-8572.

"A bank account? A license plate maybe? They're not reference numbers," said Gamache. "At least, not Dewey Decimal numbers. I noticed them too, but he has so many numbers scribbled everywhere. The diary's littered with them."

They didn't seem to be phone numbers, certainly not for Québec. Map coordinates? Not like any he'd ever seen.

Gamache glanced at his watch. "I think it's time to visit Monsieur Patrick. Will you join me?"

Émile snapped the diary shut and stood, stretching. "It's amazing, all this paper and yet nothing new. All the research had been done by other people before him. You'd think in all those years Augustin Renaud might have found something new."

"Maybe he did. People aren't usually murdered because nothing's happened. Something happened in his life."

Gamache locked up and they made their way along the narrow streets with Henri.

"All this was forest in Champlain's time?" said Gamache, as they walked along Ste-Ursule. Émile nodded.

"The main settlement stopped at about rue des Jardins but it wasn't all that long after Champlain's death that the colony expanded. The Ursulines built the convent and more settlers came once they realized it wasn't going away."

"And that fortunes could be made," said Gamache.

"True."

They stopped at rue des Jardins. Like most of the streets in the old city, this one curved and disappeared around a corner. There was nothing even approaching a grid system, just a higgledy-piggledy warren of tiny cobbled streets and old homes.

"Which way?" Émile asked.

Gamache froze. It took him a moment to remember where that came from. The last time someone asked him that question. Jean-Guy. Staring down the long corridor, first in one direction then the other, then at him. Demanding to know which way?

"This way."

It had been a guess then and it was a guess now. Gamache could feel his heart thumping from the memory and had to remind himself it was just that. It was past, done. Dead and gone.

"You're right," said Émile, pointing to a gray stone building with an ornate, carved, wooden door, and the number above. 1809.

Gamache rang the doorbell and they waited. Two men and a dog. The door was opened by a middle-aged man.

"*Oui?*"

"Mr. Patrick," said Gamache, in English. "My name is Gamache. I left a message on your machine this morning. This is my colleague Émile Comeau. I wonder if I might ask you some questions?"

"*Quoi?*"

"Some questions," said Gamache more loudly, since the man seemed not to have heard.

"*Je ne comprends pas*," said the man, irritated, and began to close the door.

"No, wait," said Gamache quickly, this time in French. "*Désolé*. I thought you might be English."

"Everyone thinks that," said the man, exasperated. "My name's Sean Patrick." He pronounced it Patreek. "Don't speak a word of English. Sorry."

Once again he went to close the door.

"But, *monsieur*, that wasn't my question," Gamache hurried on. "It's about the death of Augustin Renaud."

The door stopped closing, then slowly opened again and Gamache, Émile and Henri were admitted.

Monsieur Patrick pointed them to a room.

Gamache ordered Henri to lie down by the front door then they took off their boots and followed Monsieur Patrick into the parlor, an old-fashioned word but one that fit. It certainly didn't seem to be a living room. Looking at the sofas Gamache could see no sign a body had ever touched those cushions, and weren't about to now. Monsieur Patrick did not invite them to sit down. Instead they clustered in the middle of the stuffy room.

"Lovely furniture," said Émile, looking around him.

"From my grandparents."

"Are those them?" asked Gamache, wandering over to the photos on the wall.

"Yes. And those are my parents. My great-grandparents lived in Quebec City too. That's them over there."

He waved to another set of photos and Gamache looked at two stern people. He always wondered what happened the instant after the shot was taken. Did they exhale, glad that was over? Did they turn to each other and smile? Was this who they really were, or simply a function of a primitive technology that demanded they stay still and stare sternly at the camera?

Though—

Gamache was drawn to another photo on the wall. It showed a group of dirty men with shovels standing in front of a huge hole. Behind them was a stone building. Most of the workers looked glum, but two were grinning.

"How wonderful to have these," said Gamache. But Patrick didn't look like it was wonderful, or terrible, or anything. Indeed, Gamache thought he probably hadn't looked at the sepia photos in decades. Perhaps ever. "How well did you know Augustin Renaud?" the Chief Inspector turned back into the room.

"Didn't know him at all."

"Then why did you meet him?"

"Are you kidding? Meet him? When?"

"A week before he died. He'd arranged to meet with you, Monsieur O'Mara and two others. A Chin and a JD."

"Never heard of 'em."

"But you do know Augustin Renaud," said Émile.

"Of him. I know of him. I don't know him."

"Are you saying Augustin Renaud never contacted you?" asked Gamache.

"Are you with the police?" Patrick had grown suspicious.

"We're helping the investigation," said Gamache, vaguely. Fortunately Monsieur Patrick wasn't very observant or curious, otherwise he might wonder why Gamache was there with an elderly man and a dog. A police dog, granted, but it was still unusual. But Sean Patrick didn't seem to care. Like most Quebeckers, he was simply fixated on Augustin Renaud.

"I hear the English killed him and buried him in the basement of that building."

"Who told you that?" asked Émile.

"That did." Patrick waved toward *Le Journaliste* on the table in the front hall.

"We don't know who killed him," said Gamache firmly.

"Come on," insisted Patrick. "Who else but the Anglos? They killed him to keep their secret."

"Champlain?" asked Émile, and Patrick turned to him, nodding.

"Exactly. The Chief Archeologist says Champlain isn't there, but he's almost certainly lying. Covering up."

"Why would he do that?"

"The Anglos bought him off." Patrick was rubbing his two fingers together.

"They did no such thing, *monsieur*," said Gamache. "Believe me,

Samuel de Champlain is not buried in the Literary and Historical Society."

"But Augustin Renaud was," said Patrick. "You can't tell me *les Anglais* didn't have something to do with that."

"Why was your name in Monsieur Renaud's diary?" Gamache asked and saw a look of astonishment on Patrick's face.

"My name?" Now Patrick was making a face, something between disdain and impatience. "Is this a joke? Can I see some ID?"

Gamache reached into his breast pocket and brought out his ID. The man took it, read it, stared at the name, stared at the photo and looked up at Gamache. Stunned.

"You're him? That Sûreté officer? Jesus. The beard threw me off. You're Chief Inspector Gamache?"

Gamache nodded.

Patrick leaned closer. Gamache didn't move, but grew even more still. A more observant man might have taken warning. "I saw you on TV of course. At the funerals." He examined Gamache as though he was an exhibit.

"*Monsieur*—" said Émile, trying to stop Patrick.

"It must have been horrible." And yet the man's eyes were gleaming, excited.

And still Gamache was silent.

"I kept the magazine, *L'actualité*, with you on the cover. You know, that photo? You can sign it for me."

"I will do no such thing."

Gamache's voice was low with a warning even, finally, Sean Patrick couldn't miss. Patrick turned at the door, an angry retort on his lips, and froze. Chief Inspector Gamache was staring at him. Hard. His eyes filled with contempt.

Patrick hesitated then colored. "I'm sorry. That was a mistake."

Silence filled the room and stretched on. Finally Gamache nodded.

"I have a few more questions," he said and Patrick, docile now, returned. "Has anyone mentioned Champlain to you or wanted to know the history of your home?"

"People are always interested in that. It was built in 1751. My great-grandparents moved here in the late 1800s."

"Do you know what was here before?" Émile asked.

Patrick shook his head.

"And these numbers," Gamache showed him the numbers from the diary page. 9-8499 and 9-8572. "Do they mean anything to you?"

Again Patrick shook his head. Gamache stared at him. Why was this man's name in a dead man's diary? He could swear that while insensitive, Sean Patrick wasn't lying. He seemed genuinely baffled when told Augustin Renaud had an appointment to meet him.

"What do you think?" Gamache asked Émile as they left. "Was he lying?"

"I actually don't think so. So either Renaud meant another S. Patrick, or he planned to meet them but never actually set up the appointment."

"But he seemed so excited about it. Why not follow through?"

They walked quietly for a few minutes, then Émile stopped. "I'm meeting some friends for lunch, would you like to join us?"

"*Non, merci.* I think I'll go back to the Literary and Historical Society."

"More digging?"

"Of a sort."

FOURTEEN

⁓

A few sightseers, of the more gruesome type of tourism, still hung round outside the Lit and His. What did they hope to see?

Gamache realized as he listened to them talk about Augustin Renaud and Champlain, about conspiracy theories, about *les Anglais*, that human nature hadn't changed in hundreds of years. Two hundred years ago a similar crowd would have stood exactly where they were, huddled against the biting cold. Waiting to see the convict led to that large opening above the door, put on a small balcony, a noose around his neck, and thrown off. To swing, dead or dying, before the crowd that had gathered.

The only difference today was that the death had already occurred.

Was it an execution too?

Chief Inspector Gamache knew that most killers didn't consider their act a crime. They'd somehow convinced themselves the victim had to die, had brought it on themselves, deserved to die. It was a private execution.

Was that what Renaud's killer had believed? The power of the mind, Gamache knew, could not be underestimated. A murder was never about brawn, it began and ended in the brain and the brain could justify anything.

Gamache looked at the people around him. Men and women of all ages staring at the building as though it might get up and do something interesting.

But was he any better? After leaving Émile, he and Henri had strolled the narrow, snowy streets, thinking about the case. But also about why he was still on it. Surely his obligation was discharged? Inspector Langlois was a competent and thoughtful man. He'd solve the case, Gamache was sure of it, and he'd make sure the English weren't unfairly targeted.

So why was he still poking around into the murder of Augustin Renaud?

Now there is no more loneliness.

"Suzanne and I have a dog, you know."

"Really? What sort?"

"Oh, a mutt," said Agent Morin.

As he talked, and listened, Chief Inspector Gamache sat at his desk in front of his computer following the progress of the search, or lack of progress.

It had been six hours and they still hadn't traced the call. More and more sophisticated equipment, more experts, were brought in, and still nothing.

One team was trying to trace the call, another was analyzing the farmer's voice, teams were combing the countryside and following leads on the ground. All coordinated by Chief Superintendent Francoeur.

Though there was no love lost between the two men, Gamache had to admit he was grateful to the Chief Superintendent. Someone had to take charge and he clearly couldn't.

Gamache's voice with Morin was calm, almost jovial, but his mind was racing.

Something was very wrong. It didn't make sense, none of this did. As Morin talked about his puppy Gamache was thinking, trying to put it together.

Then he had it. Leaning into his computer he fired off an instant message.

The farmer isn't a farmer. It was an act. Get the voice analysts to verify his accent.

They have, came Agent Isabelle Lacoste's response. *The accent's genuine.*

She was in Ste-Agathe, gathering information at the scene of the shooting.

Get them to look harder. He's not the bumpkin he wanted us to believe. He can't be. So what is he? In his ear he heard Morin talking about dog food.

What are you thinking? Beauvoir joined in. He was outside in the Incident Room, helping the investigation.

Suppose this wasn't an accident? wrote the Chief, his fingers pounding the keyboard, typing quickly as his thoughts raced. *Suppose he wanted to kill an agent and kidnap another? Suppose this was the plan all along.*

Why? asked Beauvoir.

There was a pause on the telephone line. "What's your dog's name?" Gamache asked.

"We call her Bois because she looks like a log." Morin laughed, as did the Chief.

"Tell me all about her."

I don't know, Gamache typed while Agent Morin told him about taking the dog home from the SPCA to Suzanne. *But let's say this is all planned, then that includes the timing. 11:18 tomorrow morning. They want us occupied until then. It's misdirection. They want us looking one way while they do something somewhere else.*

Something is planned to happen at 11:18 tomorrow morning? Both Beauvoir and Lacoste typed.

Or, typed the Chief, *something that ends at 11:18 tomorrow morning. Something that's going on right now.*

There was a pause. The cursor throbbed on Gamache's quiet screen while in his ears he heard about Bois's current habit of eating, and pooping, socks.

So what do we do? Beauvoir asked.

Gamache stared at his blinking cursor. What do they do?

You do nothing, appeared on the screen.

Who is this? typed Gamache quickly.

Chief Superintendent Francoeur, came the equally quick response. Gamache looked up and saw the Chief Superintendent in the Incident Room at a computer also staring at him through the window. *You, Chief Inspector, will continue to talk to your agent. That's your one and only job. Inspector Beauvoir and Agent Lacoste will continue to follow my orders. There can only be one leader of this investigation, you know that. We'll get your agent back, but you need to focus and follow a clear chain of command. Do not splinter off. That only helps the criminals.*

I agree, wrote Gamache. *But we need to consider other possibilities, sir. Including that this is all part of a well-organized plan.*

A plan? To alert every cop in North America? An agent's been killed, another kidnapped. Pretty crappy plan, wouldn't you say?

Gamache stared at the screen then typed. *This farmer isn't who he appears to be. We'd have found him by now. We'd have found Agent Morin. Something is going on.*

Your panicking isn't going to help, Chief Inspector. Follow orders.

He isn't panicking, wrote Beauvoir. *What he says makes sense.*

Enough. Chief Inspector Gamache, stay focused. We'll get Agent Morin back.

Chief Inspector Gamache watched the flashing cursor then looked over his screen. Francoeur was staring at him. Not angrily. Indeed, there seemed compassion in his stare, as though he had some idea how Gamache must be feeling.

And he might have. Gamache only wished the Chief Superintendent knew what he was thinking.

This was wrong. There were eighteen hours left to find Agent Morin and they were no closer. No ordinary farmer could bring all the resources and technology of the Sûreté to a halt. Therefore, this was no ordinary farmer.

Gamache nodded to the Chief Superintendent, who gave the Chief Inspector a grateful smile. This was not the time for the two leaders to clash and while Chief Superintendent Francoeur outranked Gamache, the Chief Inspector was the more respected.

No, a rift right now would be a disaster.

But so was ignoring what seemed to Gamache obvious. They were being led away from the truth. And with each passing minute they were getting further from it. From Agent Morin. From whatever larger plan was at work.

Gamache smiled back and paused. Should he do it? If he did, there was no going back. Careers and lives might be ruined. He stared through the window.

"You have a dog, don't you sir?"

"Yes. Henri. Also a foundling, like Bois."

"Funny how they get under your skin. I think there's something special about the ones we rescue."

"Yes," said Gamache decisively. He sat forward, jotted a note longhand and made eye contact with Inspector Beauvoir who got up, filled a pitcher with fresh water and wandered into the Chief's office, under the gaze of Chief Superintendent Francoeur.

Jean-Guy Beauvoir picked up the note and closed his hand over it.

Gamache's feet were growing numb with cold as he stared at the Literary and Historical Society. Beside him Henri was lifting first one paw then another. The snow and ice were so cold it actually, and ironically, burned.

Why was he still investigating the Renaud case? Was this his private misdirection? Was he trying to take his mind off something he might otherwise have to see? And hear? And feel? Was his whole career like that? Replacing one ghost with a fresher one? Racing one step ahead of his memory?

He yanked open the heavy wooden door and entered the Literary and Historical Society, where the Anglos kept and filed and numbered all their ghosts.

In the library Mr. Blake was just pouring himself a cup of tea and taking a cookie from the blue and white china plate on the long wooden table. He looked at Gamache and indicated the pot. Gamache nodded and by the time he'd taken off his coat and rubbed Henri's feet warm and dry there was a cup of tea and a cookie on the table for him.

Mr. Blake had gone back to reading and Gamache decided he might as well too. For the next hour he collected books, sipped the tea, nibbled his cookie and read, sometimes making notes.

"What're you reading?" Mr. Blake lowered his book, a slim volume on grasses in the Outer Hebrides. "Is it about the Renaud case?"

Armand Gamache marked his page with a slip of paper and looked across the sitting area to the elderly man, perfectly attired in gray flannels, a shirt, tie, sweater and jacket.

"No, I thought I'd give that a rest for an hour or so. This," he held up the book, "is just a curiosity of mine. It's about Bougainville."

Mr. Blake leaned forward. "As in bougainvillea? The flowering plant?"

"That's right."

They both imagined the exuberant, colorful plant, so common in the tropics.

"You're interested in botany too?" asked Mr. Blake.

"No, I'm interested in the Plains of Abraham."

"Not much bougainvillea there."

Gamache laughed. "Too true. But Bougainville was."

"Was what?"

"There," said Gamache. "At the Battle of the Plains of Abraham."

"Are we talking about the same man?" Mr. Blake asked. "The navigator? The one who brought bougainvillea back on one of his voyages?"

"The same. Most people don't realize he was one of Général Montcalm's *aides-de-camp*."

"Wait a minute," Mr. Blake said. "One of the greatest cartographers and navigators of his time fought at the Plains of Abraham?"

"Well, fought is debatable. That's what I'm looking into." More ghosts, thought Gamache. My life is filled with them. Mr. Blake was looking at him, astounded. He had reason to be. This was a little known and curiously little acknowledged historical fact.

"There's more." Now Gamache leaned forward. "The French under Montcalm lost the Battle of the Plains of Abraham. Do you know why?"

"Because the English under General Wolfe scaled the cliffs. It's now considered a brilliant tactic." The elderly gentleman lowered his voice so that the ghosts and the wooden statue above them wouldn't hear. "Between us? I think Wolfe was doped up on medicine and didn't know what in the world he was doing."

Gamache laughed, surprised. General Wolfe, the Anglo hero of the battle, had indeed been ill in the days leading up to that day.

"You don't think it was a dazzling strategy?"

"I think he was demented and just got lucky."

Gamache paused. "Maybe. There is another factor in the English victory, you know."

"Really? Was Montcalm also doped up?"

"He made some mistakes," said Gamache. "But that wasn't one of them. No, I was thinking of something else. When Montcalm realized where the actual attack was coming from, he did two things. He hurried to meet them and he sent a message to his *aide-de-camp*, Bougainville, to come at once. Then Montcalm engaged the English."

"Too quickly, if I remember correctly. Don't people say he should have waited for reinforcements?"

"Yes. One of his mistakes. He rushed into battle without enough men."

Gamache paused, gathering himself. Watching him, Mr. Blake wondered why this long lost battle should affect his companion so strongly. But it did.

"It cost Montcalm his life," said Blake.

"Yes, he died, though not on the field. General Wolfe died on the field, but not Montcalm. He was hit several times and was taken to the Ursuline convent inside the walls, not far from here, actually. The nuns tried to save him but he died the next morning and was buried along with some of his men, in their basement."

Mr. Blake thought for a moment. "What about the *aide-de-camp*? Bougainville? Where was he?"

"Exactly," said Gamache. "Where was he? He was waiting for the English further upriver. Everyone expected the first wave to come from there. But when Montcalm sent for Bougainville, desperate for reinforcements, why didn't he come?"

"Why didn't he?"

"I don't know. No one knows. He came, but slowly, and when he finally arrived he held back. His official explanation was that by that time he judged the battle already lost. He didn't want to destroy his army in a losing cause."

"Sensible."

"I agree, but is it likely? His general had ordered him back. He could see the slaughter. Would he have really stopped? Some historians say if Colonel Bougainville had engaged the enemy he'd almost certainly have won. The English were in disarray, most of their senior commanders dead or wounded."

"What's your theory? You do have one?" Mr. Blake's eyes were sharp.

"It's not likely to be very popular, probably not very accurate either. But there was someone on the English side also in the battle, someone not often mentioned in the histories and yet he's the most famous of all those present. World famous."

"Who?"

"James Cook."

"Captain Cook?"

"The very same. He went on to map most of South America, Australia, New Zealand and the Pacific. He was the most famous cartographer alive and still famous today. But before all that he commanded a ship that let off the soldiers, who scaled the cliffs and took Québec once and for all for the English. Québec would never again be in French hands."

"So what's your theory?"

"In my line of work you grow suspicious of coincidences. They happen, but not often. And when you see one you ask questions."

"And this is a big one," agreed Mr. Blake. "Two world-famous mapmakers fighting on opposite sides of the same battle in a far-flung colony."

"And one of them hesitates, perhaps disastrously."

"You think he did it on purpose, don't you." It wasn't a question.

"I think it's possible they knew each other, had communicated. I think it's possible Captain Cook, who was the more senior of the men, made a promise to Bougainville in exchange for a favor."

"A hesitation. A pause," said Mr. Blake. "It wouldn't seem much, but it cost the colony."

"And many lives, including Général Montcalm," said Gamache.

"And in exchange? What would Bougainville get?"

"Perhaps Cook pointed him toward the West Indies. Perhaps Cook turned his own blind eye and let Bougainville map and navigate some important places. I don't know. That's why I'm here." He held up his book. "I suspect I'm wrong and it really was just a coincidence."

"But it passes the time," said Mr. Blake. "And sometimes that's a blessing."

Avec le temps, thought Gamache. "And you?" he asked the elderly man.

Mr. Blake handed him the book on ancient Scottish grasses. "Ironically, now that I'm so near the end of my life I seem to have all the time in the world."

Gamache looked at the dry volume, trying to feign interest. Reading this would certainly make an hour seem an eternity. It would stretch, if not actually waste, time. He opened it. A first edition he noticed, but water damaged and so obscure it almost certainly wouldn't be worth anything. It was printed in 1845.

And there was something else, another number partly hidden beneath the library card.

"Do you know what this is?" He got up and showed it to Mr. Blake who shrugged.

"They're not important. This is the one that counts." Mr. Blake pointed to the Dewey Decimal catalog number.

"Still, I'd like to see the numbers underneath." Gamache looked round for assistance.

"Maybe we should get Winnie," said Mr. Blake.

"Good idea."

Mr. Blake picked up the phone and within minutes the librarian, tiny and suspicious, had arrived. After it was explained she turned to the Chief Inspector. "All right, come with me."

The three of them went through the corridors, twisting and turning, up some stairs, down others and finally they were in the large back office. Porter Wilson was there as was Elizabeth MacWhirter.

"Hello, Chief Inspector." Elizabeth came forward and shook hands, as did Porter.

Then, like a surgeon, Winnie bent over the book and with an X-Acto knife pried up the top of the card holder, glued to place a hundred years before.

And below it were the numbers, undamaged, clear as the day they were placed on the dreary first edition.

6-5923

"What does that number mean?" Gamache asked.

There was silence as they took turns looking at it. Finally Winnie answered him.

"I think it's the old cataloging system, don't you, Elizabeth?"

"I think you're right," said Porter, who clearly didn't have a clue.

"What old system?" asked the Chief Inspector.

"From the 1800s. We don't use it anymore," said Elizabeth, "but back when the Literary and Historical Society was first established this is how they marked items."

"Go on."

Elizabeth gave an embarrassed little laugh. "It wasn't actually much of a system. The Literary and Historical Society was founded in about 1820—"

"1824, actually," said Mr. Blake. "There's a charter somewhere around here."

He searched for it while Elizabeth talked.

"A call went out to the English community at the time to send in memorabilia, whatever people considered of historic importance," she laughed. "Apparently people took it as an excuse to empty their attics and basements and barns. They were given stuffed lizards, ball gowns, armoirs. Letters, shopping lists. Finally the Society refined its mandate so that it became mostly a library, and even then it was overwhelmed."

Gamache could imagine mountains of old, leather-bound books and even loose papers.

"As books came in they put on the year it arrived." She picked up the Scottish grasses volume and pointed. "That's the number 6 and the other was the number of the book. This one was the five thousandth, nine hundred and twenty-third."

Gamache was beyond baffled. "*Alors*, the first number, 6, means the year. But what decade? And was it the five thousandth book that year to arrive, or ever? I'm afraid I'm confused."

"Ridiculous system," sniffed Winnie. "Shocking. They obviously had no idea what they were doing."

"They were probably overwhelmed," said Elizabeth.

"And this sort of thing would just add to the confusion." Winnie turned to the Chief Inspector. "It takes hard work and some guessing to figure out the code. Since this book was published in 1845 we can assume it was donated in 1846. Or '56, or '66 and so on."

"But what about the 5923?" Gamache asked.

"That's even worse," admitted Winnie. "They started at number 1 and just kept adding."

"So this was the five thousandth, nine hundred and twenty-third book?"

"That would make too much sense, Chief Inspector, so no. When they got up to 10,000 they started back at 1," she sighed. This seemed painful for her to admit.

"They cataloged everything. Some ended up on shelves and some were eventually given Dewey Decimal numbers, some not," said Elizabeth. "It was and is, a mess."

"Found it," said Mr. Blake, holding a worn folder. "This is the wording of the original mandate." He read, *To discover and rescue from the unsparing hand of time the records which yet remain of the earliest history of Canada. To preserve, while in our power, such documents as may be found amid the dust of yet unexplored depositories, and which may prove important to general history and to the particular history of this province.*"

Gamache listened to the old voice reading the old words and was deeply moved by the simplicity and the nobility of them. He suddenly felt an overwhelming desire to help these people, to help save them from the unsparing hand of time.

"What might these mean?" He showed them the numbers found in Augustin Renaud's diary.

9-8499 and 9-8572.

"Was there a Dewey Decimal number too?" Winnie asked. He had the impression if she could snort Dewey numbers she'd get high. But he had to disappoint her.

"Just those. Do they tell you anything?"

"We could look them up in the catalog."

Gamache turned and stared at Mr. Blake.

"There's a catalog?" he asked.

"Well, yes. That's what a catalog number's for," said Mr. Blake with a smile. "It's over here."

The "it" turned out to be eight huge volumes, handwritten, collected by decade. They each took one and began looking. The first "hit" was in 1839. There Porter found both a 9-8499 and a 9-8572.

"The first is a travel journal around the horn of Africa, written by a Colonel Ephram Hoskins, and the 9-8572 is a book of sermons, donated by Kathleen Williams."

It didn't seem promising.

Gamache closed one catalog book and turned to another, his finger working down the long pages with the precise writing.

"Found one," said Elizabeth a few minutes later. "It's 9-8466 to 9-8594. Donated in 1899 by Madame Claude Marchand of Montreal."

"Nothing more specific?" Gamache asked, his heart sinking. Those were the only entries that might be what Augustin Renaud was interested in but he found it hard to believe a trip in the 1830s around Africa was of interest to the Champlain expert, or a collection of sermons. Even less promising was a lot of more than one hundred books given by a woman in Montreal. Still, it was the only lead.

"Are those books still in the library?"

"Let's see," said Winnie, taking the information over to their "modern" system. A card catalog. After a few minutes she looked up.

"The sermon book is in the library, though it hasn't been given a Dewey number yet. The horn of Africa one must still be in a box somewhere."

"And the Montreal lot?" Gamache asked.

"I don't know. All we have here is the lot number. It doesn't say what happened to the specific books."

"May I have the book of sermons, please?"

Winnie found it in the library and signed it out to him. He was the first to ever take it out. Gamache thanked them and left, walking with Henri back down the hill, their feet making prints side-by-side in the fluffy snow.

Once home he went onto his laptop and started searching. Émile returned and made a simple dinner of clay pot chicken and vegetables. After dinner Gamache went back to work, trying to track down Colonel Ephram Hoskins and Kathleen Williams. Colonel Hoskins died of malaria and was buried in the Congo. His book was considered important at the time then quickly fell into obscurity.

There was absolutely no connection to Champlain, Québec or Renaud.

Kathleen Williams turned out to be a steadfast benefactor of the Anglican Cathedral of Holy Trinity in old Québec. Her husband was a prosperous dry goods merchant and her son became a ship's captain. Gamache stared at the scant information, willing something to jump out at him, some connection he was missing.

Still sitting at the desk he scanned the book of sermons, a collection of stern Victorian lectures. Nothing about Québec, Champlain, or God as far as Gamache could tell.

Finally he searched Madame Claude Marchand of Montreal. It took him a while, even with the aid of the Sûreté computers but he finally found her.

"Coming to bed?" asked Émile.

Gamache looked up. It was almost midnight. "Not just yet. Soon."

"Don't strain your eyes."

Gamache smiled and waved good night, then went back to the search.

Madame Marchand was married to Claude Marchand. He died in 1925, she in 1937.

So why did they donate more than a hundred books back in 1899? Was it part of an estate? Had one of their parents died?

But why send the books to Québec? Surely that was a lot of trouble. And why to this little library? An English library when presumably the Marchands were French?

It was curious, Gamache had to admit.

After more searching through genealogical records he discovered neither Monsieur Marchand's parents nor Madame Marchand's parents died around 1899. So where did these books come from?

It had been a long time since the Chief Inspector had had to do research of this type. He generally assigned searches to agents or inspectors. It was the sort of thing Inspector Beauvoir in particular excelled at. Order, information.

They'd bring the facts to Gamache, scattered, disjointed often, and he'd try to make sense of it. See threads and connections, put them in order.

The Chief Inspector had almost forgotten the thrill of the information hunt, but as he tried this, then that, then the other lead he found himself getting lost in it, so that all else receded.

How did this couple come by the books? And why go to the effort and expense of having them shipped to Québec?

Gamache leaned back and stared at the screen, thinking.

The books were donated by her, not him, but he was alive at the time. What did that say? Gamache rubbed his still unfamiliar beard and stared.

What did it say?

It said that the books were hers to donate. They belonged not to them, but to her specifically. The census showed her as a housekeeper, though it didn't list her employer. But it did give her address.

A housekeeper, thought Gamache, in the late 1800s. There couldn't be that many who were literate, never mind owned a hundred books or more.

He leaned forward again and tapped on the keyboard, going here and there, trying to get information more than a century old on people who almost certainly had done nothing extraordinary. There was no reason for a record of them.

He tried down one route, then down another. The address wasn't very helpful. There were no phone books at the time, no electrical bills. Almost no paper trail, except, perhaps.

He started typing again. Insurance company records. And there he found it, the man who owned the home Madame Claude Marchand, housekeeper, had listed as an address in the census form.

Chiniquy. Charles Paschal Télesphore Chiniquy.

Who died in 1899.

Gamache threw himself back in the chair and grinned broadly.

He had it, he'd done it.

But what did it mean?

FIFTEEN

——

"Y ou were up late last night."

Émile Comeau found Armand setting a pot of coffee on the table along with a plate of croissants and jams. He was looking happy, Émile noticed. A spring in his step.

"I was."

"What were you up to?" Émile sipped the strong, aromatic coffee and reached for a croissant. A few flakes hit the wooden table as he broke it in two.

"I think I've figured out what those numbers in Renaud's journal mean."

"Is that so? What?"

"You were right, he wasn't looking for Champlain's body in the Literary and Historical Society. I think he was looking for books. Those are catalog numbers. They refer to books given to the Lit and His in 1899."

Émile lowered his croissant, his eyes gleaming. Once an investigator it never left the blood. The need to know.

"What books?"

"I don't know." Gamache took a sip of his coffee. "But I do know they were in a lot donated to the Literary and Historical Society by a Madame Claude Marchand. She was a housekeeper for a family named Chiniquy. Charles Paschal Télesphore Chiniquy. He died in 1899. It seems likely the books belonged to him."

"Chiniquy," said Émile slowly. "An unusual name."

Gamache nodded. "Extremely. I looked it up. There're no Chiniquys here now. Right after breakfast I'm going to access the census information, see if there were Chiniquys in Quebec City in the past."

"There were." Émile looked distracted. Not worried, exactly, but perplexed.

"Really?" asked Gamache, waiting while Émile thought.

"This doesn't make sense," said Émile at last. "You say Renaud was looking for books that belonged to Chiniquy?"

"I think so. He had their catalog numbers in his diary."

Émile scratched his neck and his eyes took on a faraway look as he searched for a timid answer. "It doesn't make sense," he mumbled again.

"You know the name?" Gamache finally asked.

"I know the name, but it's odd."

"How so?"

"Well, that Augustin Renaud should be interested in anything belonging to Chiniquy."

There was a pause while Émile thought.

"Who was this Chiniquy?" Gamache pressed. "How do you know of him? Was he a member of the Champlain Society too?"

"No, not that I know of. Almost certainly not. As far as I know he had nothing to do with Champlain."

"So who was he?"

"A priest," said Émile. "A blip in Québec history, but a loud one at the time. Quite a character. Famous for his temperance campaigns. This was back in the 1860s or 70s. He hated alcohol, thought it led to all sorts of social and spiritual ills. From what I remember he had only the one interest, getting poor Québécois laborers to quit drinking. He became quite famous for a while, but he also alienated the Catholic Church. I can't remember the details but he quit the church and became a fervent Protestant. Used to hang around bars and brothels on Petit-Champlain in the Lower Town trying to convince the drunks to give it up. Had a sanatorium outside the city for a while."

"Renaud was fixated on Champlain, and Chiniquy was fixated on temperance," said Gamache, almost to himself. Then he shook his head. Like his mentor he couldn't see a connection between the father of Québec in 1635, an 1800s teetotaler and a body three days ago in the Lit and His.

Except, maybe, the books. What were the books?

"Why would a Champlain scholar want books collected by a lapsed priest?" he asked, but got no answer. "Chiniquy showed no interest in Champlain?"

Émile shook his head and shrugged, flummoxed. "But I don't know much about the man and what I just told you might be wrong. Would you like me to look further?"

Gamache got up. "Please. But first, I'm going back to Renaud's apartment. Maybe the books are there. Would you like to come?"

"*Absolument.*"

As they put on their heavy winter parkas Émile realized how natural it felt to follow this man. Chief Inspector Émile Comeau had seen Gamache arrive, an eager young agent in homicide. Had watched his wavy dark hair thin and turn gray, his body thicken, his marriage, his children, his rise through the ranks. He'd promoted him to Inspector, had seen the young man take command, naturally. Had watched as older, more experienced agents ceded their place, turning to him for his opinion, his leadership.

But Émile knew something else. Gamache wasn't always right. No one was.

As they walked up the hill, their breaths puffing into the crisp air, Émile glanced at Armand, Henri walking at his side. Did he seem better? Was he getting better? Émile thought so, but he also knew it was the internal injuries that did the most damage. The worst was always hidden.

A few minutes later they were once again in the cramped and stuffy apartment, negotiating their way between piles of magazines, stacks of correspondence, and furniture littered with books and journals.

The two men got to work quickly, taking off their coats and boots and each taking a room.

Two hours later Émile wandered into the dining room, which almost certainly had never seen a dinner party. The walls were lined with shelves, packed two and three books deep. Gamache was halfway around the room, having taken down each book, examined and replaced it.

He was exhausted. An activity he could have done easily two months earlier was now almost too much for him, and he could see Émile was also flagging. He was leaning against the back of a chair, trying not to look done in.

"Ready for a break?" Gamache asked.

Émile turned a grateful face to him. "If you insist. I could go on all day but if you'd like to stop I guess I could."

Gamache smiled. *"Merci."*

Still, it surprised him how weak he still felt. He'd managed to fool himself into believing he was back to full strength. And he had improved, his energy was better, his strength was returning, even the trembling seemed to have diminished.

But when pushed, he faded faster than he'd expected.

They found a table by the window at Le Petit Coin Latin and ordered beers and sandwiches.

"What did you find?" Gamache asked, biting into a baguette stuffed with pheasant terrine, arugula and cranberry sauce. A micro-brewery beer was in front of him with a slight head of foam.

"Nothing I didn't expect to find. There were a couple rare books on Champlain the Society would love to get its hands on, but since you were there I chose not to steal them."

"How wise."

Émile inclined his head and smiled. "You?"

"The same. There was nothing that didn't relate directly to Champlain or the early 1600s. There was nothing on Chiniquy, on temperance, on anything to do with the 1800s. Still, we need to keep looking. I wonder where he got all his books."

"Probably from used bookstores."

"That's true." Gamache brought Renaud's diary out of his satchel and flipped through it. "He made regular visits to the local secondhand bookstores and the flea markets in the summer."

"Where else do you find old books? What is it?" asked Émile.

Armand Gamache had tilted his head to the side and narrowed his eyes. "Where do those used bookstores get their books?"

"From people who're moving or cleaning house. From estate sales, buying them in lots. Why?"

"I think when we're finished in the apartment we need to visit a few shops."

"What're you thinking?" asked Émile, and took a long sip of his beer.

"I'm remembering something Elizabeth MacWhirter told me." But now it was his turn to look at his companion. Émile Comeau was staring at the diary. Reaching out he turned it around so that it was right-side up for him. His slim finger rested on the page, below Augustin Renaud's clear printing. Below the words circled and underlined, below an assignation he had with a Patrick, and O'Mara, a JD and—

"Chin," said Gamache. "But there're no Chins in Quebec City. I thought I might ask at the Chinese restaurant on rue de Buade and find out if it's a—"

Gamache stared into the beaming eyes of his mentor. He closed his own eyes almost in pain. "Oh, no."

Opening them he looked down at the diary. "Is that it? Chin? Chiniquy?"

Émile Comeau was smiling and nodding. "What else?"

Jean-Guy Beauvoir took a soapy dish from Clara and dried it. He was standing in their large, open kitchen, doing the dishes. Something he rarely did at home, though he'd helped the Chief and Madame Gamache clean up a few times. It didn't seem like a chore with them. And it didn't, to his surprise, seem like a chore now. It was restful, peaceful. Like the village itself.

After lunch together, Peter Morrow had returned to his studio to work on his latest painting, leaving Clara and Jean-Guy to clean up after the soup and sandwiches.

"Did you get a chance to read the dossier?"

"I did," said Clara, handing him another dripping dish. "I have to say, it's a convincing case against Olivier. But let's say he didn't kill the Hermit, then someone else must have known the Hermit was hiding in the woods. But how would someone find him? We know he approached Olivier himself, to sell his things and because he wanted some companionship."

"And needed someone to do his errands, get things he needed from town," said Beauvoir. "He used Olivier and Olivier used him."

"A good relationship."

"People taking advantage of each other seems good to you?"

"Depends how you see it. Look at us. Peter's supported me financially all our married life, but I support him emotionally. Is that taking advantage of each other? I suppose it is, but it works. We're both happy."

Beauvoir wondered if that was true. He suspected Clara would be happy just about anywhere but her husband was another matter.

"Didn't seem equal to me," said Beauvoir. "Olivier brought the Hermit some groceries every two weeks and in exchange the Hermit gave Olivier priceless antiques. Someone was getting boned."

They carried their coffees into the bright living room. Unfiltered winter light streamed through the windows as they sat in large easy chairs by the hearth.

Her brow wrinkled as she looked into the mumbling fire. "But it seems to me the big issue, the only issue, is who else knew the Hermit was there? He'd been hiding in the forest for years, why was he suddenly killed?"

"Our theory was that Olivier killed him because the horse trail was getting close to the cabin. The Hermit and his treasure were about to be found."

Clara nodded. "Olivier didn't want anyone else discovering and maybe stealing the treasure, so he killed the Hermit. It was a spur of the moment thing, not planned. He picked up a menorah and hit him."

She'd heard it all at the trial and read it again last night.

She tried to imagine her friend doing that, and while her mind spun away from the image the truth was she could believe it. She didn't think Olivier would ever plan to kill someone, but she could see him doing it in a fit of rage and greed.

Olivier had then taken the menorah. Picked the bloody thing up from beside the dead man. He said he'd taken it because his fingerprints were all over it. He was afraid. But he also admitted the menorah was priceless. Greed and fear combined to drive him into a monumentally foolish act. An act of greed, not guilt.

Neither the judge nor the jury had believed him. But now Beauvoir had to at least consider the possibility Olivier had been stupid, but truthful.

"What changed?" Beauvoir mused. "Someone else must have found the Hermit."

"Someone who might've been looking for years, someone the Hermit stole from."

"But how'd he find him?"

"He either followed Olivier or followed the new horse trail," said Clara.

"That leads us to one of the Parras," said Beauvoir. "Either Roar or Havoc."

"Old Mundin could have done it. He's a carpenter and a carver, after all. He could have followed Olivier one night after picking up the broken furniture, and he could have carved that word, Woo, into the wood."

"But," said Beauvoir, "Old Mundin's a professional woodworker. I've seen his stuff. Woo was carved by an amateur, someone hacking away."

Clara thought. "Maybe it was someone new to the community, maybe that's what changed. The killer recently moved into Three Pines."

"The Gilberts," said Beauvoir. "They're the only new people."

Marc and Dominique Gilbert, Marc's mother Carole and his estranged father, Vincent. Saint Asshole, the famous doctor who now, curiously, lived in the Hermit's cabin. Beauvoir no longer wanted the murderer to be Dr. Vincent Gilbert but deep down he worried it might be.

"I think we need to talk to the suspects again," said Beauvoir. "I thought I might drop by the Mundins' place this afternoon, pretend I want to buy some furniture."

"Great, and I'll try to talk to some of the others." She hesitated. "There is another way the murderer could have found the Hermit."

"Yes?"

"Maybe he recognized the treasures when Olivier went to sell them. It says here," she tapped the manila file folder, "that Olivier sold a lot of the stuff on eBay. Well people all over the world could have seen it, including eastern Europe. Suppose someone recognized one of the items and tracked Olivier down."

"And followed him to the Hermit," said Beauvoir. "I'll look into it."

He was beginning to appreciate why the Chief Inspector insinuated himself into the communities they investigated. It had long perplexed Beauvoir and privately he didn't approve. It blurred the lines between investigator and investigated.

But he now wondered if that was such a bad thing.

As he stepped out of the small home the sun glared off the snow, blinding him. Beauvoir put his dark glasses on.

Ray-Ban. Old School. He liked them, made him look cool on cold days.

Getting in his car he let it warm up, feeling the heated seats grow warm under him. On a bitterly cold winter day it was almost as good as sex. Then he put the car in gear and headed up the hill and out of town.

Five minutes later he arrived at the old farm. The Sûreté team had last been there in late summer, when everything had been in bloom. Beyond bloom. It was going to seed, the leaves were turning color and the wasps fed drunkenly on over-ripe fruit.

But now it was all dead or dormant and the farm, once teeming with life, looked deserted.

But as he drove slowly up to the house the door opened and standing there was The Wife, holding little Charlie Mundin's hand.

As he got out of the car she waved and he noticed Old Mundin approaching the open door, wiping his large, expressive hands on a towel.

"Welcome," The Wife smiled, kissing him on both cheeks. He wasn't often greeted like that in a case, then he remembered, he wasn't on a case.

Like Old Mundin, The Wife was young, and like Old, she was stunning. Not in a *Vogue* sort of way, but her beauty came from her obvious good health and humor. Her dark hair was cut very short and her eyes were deep brown, large and warm. She smiled easily and readily, as did Old, as did Charlie.

"Come in, before you freeze," Old said, closing the door. "Would you like a hot chocolate? Charlie and I just got back from tobogganing and we sure could use one."

Charlie, his round face ruddy red from being outside, his eyes sparkling, looked up at Jean-Guy as though they'd known each other all their lives.

"I'd love one." Beauvoir followed them into their home.

"You'll have to excuse our place, Inspector," said The Wife, leading the way into the warm kitchen. "We're still renovating."

And the place certainly looked it. Some rooms weren't yet dry-walled, others had the plaster done, but no paint. The kitchen looked like something out of the 1950s, but not in a good way. Tacky, not retro-chic.

"It looks fine to me," he lied. What it did look, and feel, was comfortable. It felt like a home.

"You wouldn't know it," said Old, helping The Wife with the hot cocoa, "but we've actually done a lot of work. You should see the upstairs. It's wonderful."

"Old, I can't imagine the Inspector's come all this way to see our renovations," laughed The Wife. She returned to the kitchen table carrying steaming mugs of hot chocolate each with a large, melting, marshmallow.

"We saw you at the bistro the other night," said Old. "Gabri says you're here for a holiday. That's nice."

They looked at him with sympathy. It was gentle, it was meant to be supportive, but Jean-Guy wished it would stop, though he knew this young couple meant it kindly.

Fortunately, their sympathy also gave him the opening he needed.

"Yes, I haven't been back since the Hermit case. What a blow to the community."

"Olivier's arrest?" said The Wife. "We still can't believe it."

"You knew him quite well, as I remember," Beauvoir turned to Old. "Gave you your first job."

"He did. Restoring and repairing furniture."

"Show, show, show," said Charlie.

"Exactly," said The Wife. "*Chaud. Chocolat chaud.* He wasn't speaking six months ago but Dr. Gilbert's been coming once a week for dinner and working with him."

"Really? Vincent Gilbert?"

"Yes. You knew he used to work with children with Down syndrome?"

"*Oui.*"

"Boo," said Charlie to Beauvoir, who smiled and tried to ignore the child. "Boo," Charlie repeated.

"Boo!" said Beauvoir back, thrusting his head forward in a way he hoped was more playful than terrifying.

"He means wood. *Bois*," explained Old. "Yes Charlie, old son, we'll go soon. We whittle together in the evenings."

"Didn't Havoc Parra used to whittle toys for Charlie?" Beauvoir remembered.

"He did," said Old. "I'm afraid he's wonderful at cutting down trees but not so good at carving them, though he enjoys it. Comes here sometimes to help me with the furniture. I pay him a little."

"What does he do? Restore it?"

"No, that's way too specialized. He helps when I have some furniture to make. Mostly staining."

They chatted about local events, about renovation projects and the antiques waiting to be restored. Beauvoir pretended to be interested in seeing Old Mundin's furniture and almost bought a bookcase thinking he could pass it off as his own creation. But he knew even Enid wouldn't believe that.

"Would you like to stay for dinner?" The Wife asked when Beauvoir said he had to go.

"*Merci*, but no. I just wanted to stop by and see your furniture."

They stood by the back door, waving to him. He'd been tempted to accept their invitation to join their little family. As he drove away he thought again about what Old had said so innocently about Havoc and his skill as a whittler, which rivaled Charlie's. On arriving back in Three Pines he went across to the bistro and ordered a *tarte au sucre* and a cappuccino. Myrna joined him with her *éclair* and *café au lait*. They chatted for a few minutes then Beauvoir made notes and Myrna read the London *Sunday Times Travel Magazine*, moaning occasionally over the *éclair* and over the descriptions of the spa getaways.

"Do you think it's worth a twelve-hour flight to go here?" She turned the magazine round and showed him soft white beaches, thatched huts, nubile young men, shirtless, carrying drinks with fruit in them.

"Where is it?"

"Mauritius."

"How much?"

Myrna checked. "Five thousand two hundred."

"Dollars?" Beauvoir almost gagged.

"Pounds. But it includes the flight. My budget today is five thousand pounds so it's a little over that."

"Book business must be good."

Myrna laughed. "I could sell every book in my place and still not be able to afford that." She put her large hand on the shiny picture. Outside the frosted window, kids were arriving home from school. Parents waited for them to come down the snowy, icy road from where the bus dropped them off, all red faced, bundled up, distinguishable only by the color of their bulbous snowsuits. They looked like giant, colorful balls cascading down the hill.

"This is fantasy money for a fictional trip. Cheap, but fun."

"Did someone say cheap but fun?" Gabri joined them and Beauvoir closed his notebook. "Where're we going this week?"

"He's also fictional, you know." Myrna indicated Gabri with her head.

"I am sometimes made-up," Gabri admitted.

"I'm considering Mauritius." She handed a magazine to Gabri and offered one to Beauvoir. He hesitated then noticed the icicles hanging from the homes, the snow piled on the roofs, the people bent against the wind and rushing for warmth.

He took one.

"Vacation porn," whispered Gabri. "Complete with rubber suits." He flashed an image of a muscular man wearing a tight scuba outfit.

Beauvoir gave himself a fictional budget of five thousand dollars then lost himself in Bali, in Bora-Bora, in St. Lucia.

"Have you been on a cruise?" he asked Myrna.

"Was on one earlier in the week. Upgraded to the Princess Suites. Next time I think I might upgrade all the way."

"I'm considering the owner's suite."

"Can you afford it?"

"True, I might go fake broke but I think it's worth it."

"God, I could use a cruise," said Gabri, lowering his magazine.

"Tired?" Myna asked. Gabri looked it.

"*Très fatigué.*"

"It is true." Ruth plopped down in the fourth chair, knocking everyone with her cane. "He is a fatty gay."

The other two ignored her, but Beauvoir couldn't hide a small laugh. Before long the other two left, Myrna back to her quiet bookstore and Gabri to tend to a couple customers.

"So, why're you really here?" Ruth leaned forward.

"For your cheerful company, you old hag."

"Besides that, numb nuts. You never liked it here. Gamache does, I can tell. But you? You despise us."

Every hour of every day Jean-Guy Beauvoir searched for not just facts, but truth. He hadn't appreciated, though, how terrifying it was being with someone who spoke it, all the time. Well, her truth anyway.

"I don't," he said.

"Bullshit. You hate the country, you hate nature, you think we're hicks, idiots. Repressed, passive-aggressive and English."

"I know you're English," he laughed. She didn't.

"Don't fuck with me. I don't have that much time left and I refuse to waste it."

"Then go away if you think I'm such a waste of time."

They glared at each other. He'd opened up to her the other night, told her things few others knew. He'd been afraid that might lead to some awkwardness but sure enough, when they'd met the next morning she'd looked at him as though he was a stranger.

"I know why you're here," he said at last. "For the rest of the story. You just want to hear all the gory details. You feed on it, don't you? Fear and pain. You don't care about me or the Chief or Morin or anyone else, all you want from me is the rest of the story, you sick old crone."

"And what do you want?"

What do I want? he thought.

I want to tell it.

SIXTEEN

~

Jean-Guy glanced round. The bistro was quiet. Placing his hands on the arms of his chair he hauled himself forward. The chair felt warm from the fire. In the grate the large logs popped, sending embers bouncing against the screen to glow on the stone hearth then slowly die away.

The maple logs smelled sweet, the coffee was strong and rich, the aromas from the kitchen familiar.

Not of home but of here.

He leaned forward and stared into the cold, blue eyes across from him. Winter eyes in a glacier face. Challenging, hard, impenetrable.

Perfect.

He paused and in an instant he was back there, since "there" was never far away.

"My favorite season is autumn, I think," Gamache was saying.

"I've always loved winter," came the young voice over the monitors. "I think because I can wear thick sweaters and coats and no one can really see how skinny I am."

Morin laughed. Gamache laughed.

But that was all Inspector Beauvoir heard. He was out the door, through the Incident Room and into the stairwell. There he paused for a moment. Opening his fist he read the note Gamache had scrawled.

Find Agent Yvette Nichol. Give her this.

There was another note, folded, with Nichol's name on it. He opened it and groaned. Was the Chief mad? Because Yvette Nichol almost certainly was. She was the agent no one wanted. The agent who couldn't be fired because she wasn't quite incompetent or insubordinate enough. But she sure played around the cliff. And finally the chief had assigned her to telecommunications. Surrounded by things, not people. No interaction. Nothing major to screw up. No one to enrage. Just listening, monitoring, recording.

Any normal person would have quit. Any decent agent would have resigned. Like the witch trials of old. If she sank she was innocent, if she survived she was a witch.

Agent Nichol survived.

But still, he didn't hesitate. Down the stairs he ran, two at a time, until he was finally in the sub-basement. Yanking open a door he looked in. The room was darkened, and it took him a moment to make out the outline of someone sitting in front of green lights. On oval screens lines burst into a frenzy as words were spoken.

Then a face was turned to him. A green face, and eyes glowing green. Agent Yvette Nichol. He hadn't seen her in years and now he felt a tingling under his skin. A warning. Not to enter. This room. This person's life.

But Chief Inspector Gamache had wanted him to. And so he did. On the speaker he was surprised to hear the Chief's voice, talking now about various dog toys.

"Have you ever used a Chuck-it, sir?" Agent Morin asked.

"Never heard of it. What is it?"

"A stick thing with a cup on the end. It helps toss a tennis ball. Does Henri like balls?"

"Above all else," laughed Gamache.

"Idiotic conversation," came the female voice. A green voice. Young, ripe, filled with bile. "What do you want?"

"Have you been monitoring the conversation?" Inspector Beauvoir demanded. "It's on a secure channel. No one's supposed to have access to it."

"And yet you were about to ask me to start monitoring it, weren't you? Don't look so surprised, Inspector. Doesn't take a genius to figure that out. No one comes here unless they want something. What do you want?"

"Chief Inspector Gamache wants your help." He almost gagged on the words.

"And what the Chief Inspector wants, he gets. Right?" But she'd turned back into the room. Beauvoir felt on the wall and found the light switch. He turned it on and the room was flooded with bright fluorescent lights. The woman, who had seemed so menacing, so otherworldly, suddenly became human.

Staring at him now was a short, slightly dumpy, young woman with sallow skin marked by old blemishes. Her hair was dull and mousy and her eyes squinted to adjust to the sudden light.

"Why'd you do that?" she demanded.

"Sir," he snapped. "You're a disgrace but you're still a Sûreté officer. You'll call me 'sir' and the Chief Inspector by his full rank. And you'll do as you're ordered. Here."

He thrust the note at the agent who now looked very young, and very angry. Like a petulant child. Beauvoir smiled remembering his initial disquiet. She was pathetic. A sorry little person. Nothing more.

Then he remembered why he was there.

She might be a sorry little person, but Chief Inspector Gamache was risking his entire career in bringing her secretly into the investigation.

Why?

"Tell me what you know." She lowered the note and stared Beauvoir in the eye. "Sir."

It was a disconcerting look. Far smarter, far brighter, than he would have expected. A keen stare, and deep inside, still, a flash of green.

He bristled at her use of words. At that particular phrase. "Tell me what you know." It's what the Chief always asked when first arriving at a murder scene. Gamache would listen carefully, respectfully. Thoughtfully.

The antithesis of this willful, warped agent.

Surely she was mocking the Chief. But there were more important things than challenging her on that.

He told her what he knew.

The shooting, the kidnapping, the claims of the farmer to have attached a bomb. To go off the next morning at 11:18.

Instinctively they both glanced at the clock. Ten past six in the evening. Seventeen hours left.

"Chief Superintendent Francoeur believes the kidnapper's a

frightened backwoods farmer, probably with a small marijuana operation, who panicked. They think there's no bomb and no other plan."

"But Chief Inspector Gamache doesn't agree," said Agent Nichol, reading from the note. "He wants me to monitor closely." She looked up after a moment digesting the Chief's instructions. "They're monitoring closely upstairs I presume?"

She was unable, or unwilling, to rid her voice of bitterness. It was an annoying and annoyed little voice.

At a curt nod from Beauvoir she smiled and carefully folded the note. "Well I guess the Chief Inspector thinks I'm better."

Agent Nichol stared at Beauvoir, willing him to contradict her. He glared at her.

"Must be," he finally managed.

"Well, he's going to have to do more than talk about dog toys. Tell him to pause."

"Haven't you been listening? A pause and the bomb will go off."

"Does anyone really believe there's a bomb?"

"And you'd risk it?"

"Hey, I'm safe and warm here. Why not."

At a glare from Beauvoir she continued. "Look, I'm not asking him to go make a cup of coffee. Just a second here and there. Lets me record the ambient sound. Got it? Sir?"

Agent Yvette Nichol had started in homicide. Been chosen by Chief Inspector Gamache. Mentored by him. And had been a near complete failure. Beauvoir had begged the Chief to fire her. Instead, after many chances, he'd transferred her. To do something she needed to learn.

The one thing she clearly could not do.

Listen.

That was her job now. Her only job. And now Chief Inspector Gamache was putting his whole career, and perhaps Agent Morin's life, into these incompetent hands.

"Why haven't they traced the call yet?" Agent Nichol asked, swinging her seat back to the monitors and hitting some keys on her computer. The Chief's voice was crisper now, clear. As though he was standing with them.

"They can't seem to get a fix," said Beauvoir, leaning over her chair, staring almost mesmerized at the dancing waves on the screens. "When they do it shows Morin in a different place as though he's moving."

"Maybe he is."

"One moment he's by the U.S. border the next he's in the Arctic. No, he's not moving. The signal is."

Nichol made a face. "I think the Chief Inspector might be right. This doesn't sound like something rigged up by a panicked farmer." She turned to Beauvoir. "What does the Chief think it is?"

"He doesn't know."

"It would have to be something big," Nichol mumbled as she focused on the screen and the voices. "To kill an agent and kidnap another then to call the Chief Inspector."

"He needs to be able to communicate with us without Chief Superintendent Francoeur knowing," said Inspector Beauvoir. "Right now all his messages are monitored."

"No problem. Get me the code to his computer and I can set up a secure channel."

Beauvoir hesitated, examining her.

"What?" she demanded, then smiled. It was unattractive, and again Beauvoir felt a warning tingle. "You came to me remember. Do you want help or not? Sir?"

". . . Zora's a handful, apparently," came Gamache's voice. "Teething now. She loves the blanket you and Suzanne sent."

"I'm glad," said Morin. "I wanted to send a drum set but Suzanne said maybe later."

"Marvelous. Perhaps you could also send some caffeine and a puppy," laughed Gamache.

"You must miss them, sir. Your son and grandchildren."

"And our daughter-in-law," Gamache said. "Yes, but they're enjoying Paris. Hard to begrudge them that."

"Damn it. He needs to slow down," snapped Nichol, annoyed. "He has to give me pauses."

"I'll tell him."

"Well, hurry up," said Nichol. "And get that code." She turned her back on Inspector Beauvoir as he strode out the door.

"Sir," he muttered as he bounded back up the stairs. "Sir. Shit-head."

At the eighth floor he wheezed to a stop and gasped for breath. Opening the door a little he could see Chief Superintendent Francoeur not far away. Over the monitors came the familiar voices.

"Has anybody spoken to my parents?" the young man asked.

"We're giving them regular updates. I've sent an agent to be with your family and Suzanne."

There was a longer pause.

"Are you all right?" Gamache jumped in.

"Fine," came the voice, though it was thin and struggling. "I don't mind for myself. I know I'm going to be all right. But my mother—"

There was silence again, but before it could go on too long the Chief Inspector spoke, reassuring the young agent.

Chief Superintendent Francoeur exchanged glances with the Inspector beside him.

Across the room Beauvoir could see the clock.

Sixteen hours and fourteen minutes left. He could hear Morin and the Chief Inspector discussing things they wished had gone differently in their lives.

Neither of them mentioned this.

Ruth exhaled. "This story you just told me, none of that was in the news."

She said "story" as though it was a fairy tale, a children's make-believe.

"No," agreed Beauvoir. "Only a few know it."

"Then why're you telling me?"

"Who'd believe you if you said anything? They'd all just think you're drunk."

"And they'd be right."

Ruth cackled and Beauvoir cracked a tiny smile.

Across the bistro Gabri and Clara watched.

"Should we save him?" Clara asked.

"Too late," said Gabri. "He's made a deal with the devil."

They turned back to the bar and their drinks. "So, it's between Mauritius and the Greek Islands on the *Queen Mary*," said Gabri.

They spent the next half hour debating fantasy vacations, while several feet away Jean-Guy Beauvoir told Ruth what really happened.

Armand Gamache and Henri entered the third and last shop on their list, Augustin Renaud's list. The man while alive haunted the used bookstores in Quebec City buying anything that might have even a remote reference to Samuel de Champlain.

The little bell above the entrance tinkled as they entered and Gamache quickly closed the door before too much of the day crept in with him. It didn't take much, a tiny crack and the cold stole in like a wraith.

It was dark inside, most of the windows being "booked" off. Stacks of dusty volumes were piled in the windows, not so much for advertisement as storage.

Anyone suffering from claustrophobia would never get three steps into the shop. The already narrow aisles were made all the more cramped by bookcases so stuffed they threatened to topple over, and more books were stacked on the floor. Henri picked his way carefully along behind Gamache. The Chief's shoulders brushed the books and he decided it might be best to remove his parka before he knocked over all the shelves.

Getting the coat off proved quite an exercise in itself.

"Can I help you?"

The voice came from somewhere in the shop. Gamache looked round, as did Henri, his satellite ears flicking this way and that.

"I'd like to talk to you about Augustin Renaud," called Gamache to the ceiling.

"Why?"

"Because," said Gamache. Two could play that game. There was a pause then a clambering of feet on a ladder.

"What do you want?" the bookseller asked, taking small, quick steps out from behind a bookcase. He was short and skinny, his fisherman's sweater was pilled and stained. An almost white T-shirt poked out of the collar. His hair was gray and greasy and his hands were dark from dust. He wiped them on his filthy pants and stared at Gamache then he noticed Henri looking out from behind the large man's legs.

Hiding.

Though Gamache would never say it to Henri's face, they both knew he wasn't the most courageous of dogs. Nor, it must be said, was Henri very bright. But he was loyal beyond measure and knew what mattered. Din-din, walks, balls. But most of all, his family. His heart filled his chest and ran to the end of his tail and the very tips of his considerable ears. It filled his head, squeezing out his brain. But Henri, the foundling, was a humanist, and while not particularly clever was the smartest creature Gamache knew. Everything he knew he knew by heart.

"*Bonjour,*" the shopkeeper knelt in a totally involuntary movement and reached out to Henri. Gamache recognized it. He had it himself, as did Reine-Marie, when in the presence of a dog. The need to kneel, to genuflect.

"May I?" the man asked. It was the sign of an experienced dog owner, to always ask. Not only was it respectful, it was prudent. You never knew when a dog might not want to be approached.

"You run the risk of him never leaving, *monsieur,*" smiled Gamache as the shopkeeper produced a biscuit.

"Fine with me." He fed Henri the treat and rubbed his ears to groans from the dog.

It was then Gamache noticed the cushions on the floor and the name "Maggie" on the side of a food bowl. But no dog.

"How long ago?" Gamache asked.

"Three days," said the man, standing up and turning away. Gamache waited. He recognized this movement too.

"Now," the man finally said, turning back to Gamache and Henri. "You said you wanted to talk about Augustin Renaud. Are you a reporter?"

Gamache looked as though he might be, but not for the television or radio or even a daily paper. Perhaps for an intellectual, monthly magazine. One of those obscure university presses or journals specializing in dying ideas and the dead people who'd championed them.

He wore a shirt and tie under a cardigan the color of butterscotch. His slacks were charcoal gray corduroy. If the shopkeeper noticed the scar above Gamache's left temple he didn't mention it.

"*Non,* I'm not a reporter, I'm helping the police but in a private capacity."

Henri was now leaning against the little shopkeeper, whose hand was down by his side kneading the dog's head.

"Are you Alain Doucet?" Gamache asked.

"Are you Armand Gamache?" Doucet asked.

Both men nodded.

"Tea?" Monsieur Doucet asked. Within minutes the two men were sitting at the back of the tiny store in a cave of books, of words, of ideas and stories. And Monsieur Doucet, after pouring them fragrant cups of tea and offering his guest a digestive cookie, was telling his own story.

"Augustin came in once a fortnight at least, sometimes more often. Sometimes I'd call if I got in a book I knew he'd be interested in."

"What interested him?"

"Champlain, of course. Anything to do with the early colony, other explorers, maps. He loved maps."

"Was there anything he found here that particularly excited him?"

"Well, now, that's hard to say. Everything seemed to excite him, and yet he said almost nothing. I knew him for forty years but we never sat down like this, never had a conversation. He'd buy books and be animated and enthusiastic, but when I tried to ask him about it he'd get quiet, defensive. He was a singular man."

"He was that," said Gamache, taking a bite of his digestive cookie. "Did you like him?"

"He was a good client. Never argued about price, but then I never tried to take advantage."

"But did you like him?" It was funny, Gamache had asked this question of all the used-bookstore owners and all had been evasive.

"I didn't know him but I'll tell you something, I had no desire to get to know him better."

"Why not?"

"He was a fanatic and they scare me. I think he'd do just about anything if he thought it would get him an inch closer to Champlain's body. So, I was civil, but kept my distance."

"Do you have any idea who might have killed him?"

"He had a knack for annoying people, but you don't kill someone just because they're annoying. The place would be littered with bodies."

Gamache smiled and took a leisurely sip of his strong tea, thinking.

"Do you know if Renaud had a current idea? Some new theory about where Champlain might be buried?"

"You mean the Literary and Historical Society?"

"I mean any place."

Monsieur Doucet thought then shook his head.

"Did you buy books from them?"

"The Lit and His? Sure. Last summer. They had a big sale. I bought three or four lots."

Gamache put his mug down. "What was in them?"

"Frankly? I don't know. Normally I'd go through them but it was the summer and I was too busy with the flea market. Lots of tourists, lots of book collectors. I didn't have time to go through the boxes, so I just put them out at my stall. Renaud came by and bought a couple."

"Books?"

"Boxes."

"Did he go through them before buying?"

"No, just bought. People are like that, especially collectors. They want to go through them privately. I think that's part of the fun. I got another couple of lots from the Lit and His later, sometime this past fall, before they decided to stop the sale. I called Renaud and asked if he was interested. At first he said no then he showed up about three weeks ago asking if I still had them."

"Hmm." The Chief Inspector sipped and thought. "What does that tell you?"

Alain Doucet looked surprised. He had clearly thought nothing of it but now he did.

"Well, I guess it might mean he found something in that first lot and thought there might be more."

"Why the delay, though? If he bought the first couple boxes in the summer, why wait until after Christmas to contact you?"

"He's probably like most collectors. Buys loads of books meaning to go through them but they just sit there for months until he gets around to it."

Gamache nodded, remembering the rabbit warren that was Renaud's home.

"Do these numbers mean anything to you?" He showed Doucet the catalog numbers found in Renaud's diary. 9-8499 and 9-8572.

"No, but used books come in with all sorts of strange things written on them. Some are color-coded, some have numbers, some have signatures. Screws up their value, unless the signature is Beaudelaire or Proust."

"How'd he seem when he came by for the other lot?"

"Renaud? As always. Brusque, anxious. He was like an addict before a fix. Book freaks are like that, and not just old guys. Look at kids lining up for the latest installment of their favorite books. Stories, they're addictive."

Gamache knew that was true. But what story had Augustin Renaud stumbled on? And where were the two books? Not in his apartment, not on his body. And what happened to the other books in the lot? They weren't in the apartment either.

"Did he bring any books back?"

Doucet shook his head. "But you might ask the other used bookstores. I know he went to all of us."

"I've asked. You're the last, and the only one who bought the Literary and Historical Society books."

"Only one stupid enough to try to sell English books in old Quebec City."

The Chief's phone vibrated and he took it out. It was a call from Émile.

"Do you mind?" he asked and Doucet shook his head. "*Salut*, Émile. Are you at home?"

"No, I'm in the Lit and His. Amazing place. I can't believe I've never been before. Can you meet me here?"

"Have you found something?"

"I found Chiniquy."

"I'll be right there."

Gamache rose and Henri rose with him, ready to go wherever Gamache went.

"Does the name Chiniquy mean anything to you?" he asked as they walked to the front of the store. It was almost four P.M. and the sun had set. Now the shop looked cozy, lit by lamps, the books merely suggestions in the shadows.

Doucet thought about it. "No, sorry."

Time, thought Gamache as he stepped once more into the darkness, it covered over everything eventually. Events, people, memory. Chiniquy had disappeared beneath Time. How long before Augustin Renaud followed?

And yet Champlain had remained, and grown.

Not the man, Gamache knew, the mystery. Champlain missing was so much more potent than Champlain found.

Picking up his pace, he and Henri wove between the revelers carrying their hollow plastic canes filled with Caribou, wearing their Bonhomme pins on their down-filled parkas. They wore smiles and huge mittens and joyful fluffy, warm tuques, like exclamation marks on their heads. In the distance he heard the almost haunting blast on a plastic horn. A call to arms, a call to party, a call to youth.

Gamache heard it, but the call wasn't for him. He had another calling.

Within minutes he and Henri were standing outside the brightly lit Literary and Historical Society. The small crowd of gawkers had given up, perhaps called away by the horns to something more interesting. Called to life, not to death.

Gamache entered and found his old mentor in the library surrounded by small stacks of books. Mr. Blake had emigrated from his armchair to the sofa and the two elderly men were chatting. They looked over as the Chief Inspector entered, and waved.

Mr. Blake stood and indicated his place.

"No, please," said Gamache, but it was too late. The courtly man was already standing next to his habitual chair.

"We've been having a terrific talk, you know," said Mr. Blake. "All about Charles Chiniquy. Remarkable man. But then, we're likely to think that," he said with a laugh.

"Found another one, Monsieur Comeau," Elizabeth MacWhirter called down from the balcony, then spying Gamache she waved.

Gamache caught Émile's eye and smiled. He'd made a few conquests here.

Soon all four were sitting round the coffee table.

"So," said Gamache, looking at the three eager, elderly faces. "Tell me what you know."

"The first thing I did was call Jean," Émile said. "You remember him? He had lunch with us a few days ago at the Château Frontenac." Gamache remembered. The Laurel to René Dallaire's Hardy.

"A member of your Champlain Society."

"That's right, but he's also a student of Québec history in general. Most of the members are. He knew of Chiniquy, but not much more than I'd heard. Chiniquy was some sort of fanatic about temperance and had quit the Catholic Church and joined the Protestants. He's considered a bit of a nut. Did some good work then messed it up by going off the deep end himself.

"I was on my way home and just passing the Lit and His when I suddenly thought they might know Chiniquy here. After all, it is a Literary and Historical Society and presumably has links to Protestantism. So I came in."

Elizabeth picked up the thread. "He asked about Chiniquy. It's not a name I'm familiar with but I did find some books in our collection. He wrote quite a few. Then Mr. Blake came in and I directed Monsieur Comeau to him."

Mr. Blake leaned forward. "Charles Chiniquy was a great man, Chief Inspector. Much maligned and misunderstood. He should be considered one of the great heroes of Québec instead of forgotten or remembered only for his eccentricities."

"Eccentricities?"

"He was, it must be admitted, a bit of a showboat. Quite extravagant in his lifestyle and speeches. Charismatic. But he saved a lot of lives, built a sanatorium. At the height of his popularity tens of thousands took the pledge after listening to him speak. He was indefatigable. Ummm." Mr. Blake struggled a bit with the next part. "Then he went a bit far for the comfort of the Catholic Church. To be fair, they did give him a lot of warnings but finally he was stripped of his church. He quit in a rage and joined the Presbyterians."

"Didn't he claim Rome was conspiring to take over North America and had sent the Jesuits to kill Lincoln?" asked Émile.

"He might have mentioned that," said Mr. Blake. "Still, he did a great deal of good too."

"What happened to him?" asked Gamache.

"He moved to Illinois but annoyed so many people he soon left and ended his days in Montreal. Got married you know, and had two children, daughters I think. Died at the age of ninety."

"In 1899," said Gamache and when she looked surprised he explained.

"I looked it up last night, but the file had just his dates, no real information about the man."

"There was a huge obituary in the *New York Times*," said Mr. Blake. "He was considered a hero by many people."

"And a nut by many too," admitted Elizabeth.

"Why would Augustin Renaud be interested in Chiniquy?"

All three shook their heads. Gamache thought some more.

"The big Presbyterian church is right next door, and the Lit and His has a number of his books, is it fair to assume there might have been a connection? A relationship?"

"Between Charles Chiniquy and the Lit and His?" asked Elizabeth.

"Well, there was James Douglas, he'd be a connection," said Mr. Blake.

"And who is that?" asked Gamache. Both Elizabeth and Mr. Blake turned in their seats and looked out a window. Gamache and Émile also looked but in the dark they saw only their own reflections.

"That's James Douglas," said Mr. Blake. Still they stared, and still all they saw were their own baffled faces.

"The window?" asked Gamache finally, after waiting long enough for Émile to ask the nonsensical question.

"Not the window, the bust," said Elizabeth with a smile. "That's James Douglas."

Sure enough, on the deep windowsill there stood a white alabaster bust of a Victorian gentleman. They always looked disturbing to Gamache. It was the white, empty eyes, as though the artist had sculpted a ghost.

"He was one of the founders of the Literary and Historical Society," said Mr. Blake.

Elizabeth leaned forward and said to Émile beside her, "He was also a grave robber. Collected mummies, you know."

Neither Gamache nor Émile did know. But they wanted to.

SEVENTEEN

—

I'm afraid you'll have to explain yourself, *madame*," said Émile, with a smile. "Mummies?"

"Now, there was an original," Mr. Blake jumped in, warming to the subject. "James Douglas was a doctor, by all accounts a gifted physician. He could amputate a limb in less than ten seconds." On seeing their faces he continued, chastising them slightly. "It mattered back then. No anesthetic. Every moment must have been agony. Dr. Douglas saved a lot of people a lot of agony. He was also a brilliant teacher."

"Which is where the bodies come in," said Elizabeth, with more relish than they'd have expected. "He started off somewhere in the States—"

"Pittsburgh," said Mr. Blake.

"But was run out of town after he was caught grave robbing."

"It wasn't like it is today," said Mr. Blake. "He was a doctor and they needed bodies for dissection. It was common practice to take them from paupers' graves."

"But probably not common practice for the doctors themselves to dig them up," said Gamache to Elizabeth's muffled laugh.

Mr. Blake paused. "That is, perhaps, true," he conceded. "Still, there was never any question of personal gain. He never sold them, only used the corpses to teach his students, most of whom went on to distinguished careers."

"But he got caught?" Émile turned to Elizabeth.

"Made a mistake. He dug up a prominent citizen and the man was recognized by one of the students."

Now everyone grimaced.

"So he came to Québec?" asked Gamache.

"Started teaching here," said Mr. Blake. "He also opened a mental hospital just outside the city. He was a visionary, you know. This was at a time when the deranged were tossed into places worse than prisons, locked up for life."

"Bedlam," said Elizabeth.

Mr. Blake nodded. "James Douglas was considered more than a little strange because he believed the mentally ill should be treated with respect. His hospital helped hundreds, maybe thousands, of people. People no one else wanted."

"Must have been an extraordinary man," said Émile.

"He was, by most accounts," said Mr. Blake, "a miserable, opinionated, arrogant man. Wretched. Except, when dealing with the poor and displaced. Then he showed remarkable compassion. Strange, isn't it?"

Gamache nodded. It was what made his job so fascinating, and so difficult. How the same person could be both kind and cruel, compassionate and wretched. Unraveling a murder was more about getting to know the people than the evidence. People who were contrary and contradictory, and who often didn't even know themselves.

"But where do the mummies come in?" asked Émile.

"Well, he apparently continued to take bodies from graves in and around Quebec City," said Elizabeth. "Again, just for teaching. He seems to have stayed clear of digging up the premier minister or any archbishops but his fascination with bodies does seem to have spread beyond just teaching."

"He was simply curious," said Mr. Blake, a slight defensiveness in his voice.

"He was that," agreed Elizabeth. "Dr. Douglas was on vacation in Egypt and brought back a couple of mummies. Used to keep them in his home and would give talks in this very room on them. Propped them up against that wall," she waved to the far wall.

"Well," said Gamache slowly, trying to imagine it, "a lot of people were robbing graves back then. Robbing might be too strong a word," he said quickly, to assuage Mr. Blake's agitation. "It was the age when they were discovering all those tombs. King Tut, Nefertiti," he'd run out of Egyptian references. "And others."

Émile gave him an amused look.

"Show me a museum," said Mr. Blake, "and I'll show you treasures taken from graves. The British Museum stinks of tombs but where would we be without it? Thank God they took the things, otherwise they'd just be looted or destroyed."

Gamache remained silent. One civilization's courageous action was another's violation. Such was history, and hubris. In this case the famous Victorian ego that dared so much, discovered so much, desecrated so much.

"Whatever it was called," said Elizabeth, "it was strange. My grandparents went to Egypt on their Grand Tour and came back with rugs. Not a single body."

Émile smiled.

"One mummy was eventually sent to a museum in Ontario and then returned a few years ago to Egypt," Elizabeth continued, "when they discovered it was King Ramses."

"*Pardon?*" asked Gamache. "Dr. Douglas took the body of an Egyptian pharaoh?"

"Apparently," said Mr. Blake, struggling between embarrassment and pride.

Gamache shook his head. "So what does this remarkable Dr. Douglas have to do with Chiniquy?"

"Oh, didn't we say? They were good friends," said Mr. Blake. "While still a priest Chiniquy would go to Dr. Douglas's mental hospital to minister to the Catholics. It was Douglas who stirred Chiniquy to action. A number of the demented were also drunks. Dr. Douglas discovered if you locked them up, gave them good food and no alcohol they often returned to a state of sanity. But they had to stay sober or, better still, never have drunk to excess to begin with. He told Father Chiniquy about this and Chiniquy immediately grasped it. It became his life's work, his way to save souls, before they were damned."

"Temperance," said Gamache.

"The pledge," agreed Mr. Blake. "Get them to stop drinking, or never start. And tens of thousands did, thanks to Father Chiniquy. His public rallies became famous. He was the Billy Graham of his day, drawing people from all over Québec and the eastern United States. People couldn't sign up fast enough to take the pledge."

"All inspired by James Douglas," said Émile.

"They were lifelong friends," said Elizabeth.

A movement in the shadows caught Gamache's peripheral vision. He glanced up to the gallery but saw only the wooden statue of General Wolfe looking down on them, listening. But still, the Chief Inspector had the impression the General hadn't been alone. Someone else had been standing there, in the shadows. Hiding among the books, the stories. Listening. To the story of two inspired madmen, two old friends.

But there was another madman in the story. Augustin Renaud, who was also obsessed with the dead.

"The sale of books last year," Gamache began and immediately felt the shift in mood. Both Elizabeth MacWhirter and Mr. Blake became guarded. "I understand it wasn't very popular."

"No, within the English community it wasn't popular," admitted Elizabeth. "We eventually had to stop."

"Why?"

"Reactionaries," said Mr. Blake. "Perhaps not surprisingly the strongest opposition came from people who'd never even been in the Lit and His. They just hated the idea on principle."

"And what principle might that be?" asked Émile.

"That the Lit and His was created to preserve English history," said Elizabeth. "And any scrap of paper with English writing on it, every shopping list, every journal, every letter was sacred. By selling some off we were betraying our heritage. It just didn't feel right."

Feelings. As much as people tried to rationalize, tried to justify, tried to explain, eventually everything came down to feelings.

"Did anyone go through the books? How'd you decide what to sell?" Gamache asked.

"We started in the basement, ones that were deemed unimportant when they came in and so stayed in boxes. There were so many, I'm afraid we were overwhelmed and just sold them by the box load, happy to be rid of them."

"You had two sales?" asked the Chief.

"Yes. The first was in the summer, then we had a smaller, quieter one later. That was mostly to bookstores and people who seemed sympathetic to what we were doing."

"The books donated by Mrs. Claude Marchand back in 1899 were among the ones you sold," said Gamache.

"Is that right?" said Elizabeth.

"Is it significant?" asked Mr. Blake.

"We think so. Mrs. Marchand was Charles Chiniquy's housekeeper in Montreal. After his death they must have divided up his things and given her some of the books, or perhaps he asked that they be sent here. Either way, she must have known he had a relationship with the Literary and Historical Society and so sent them on. It seems when they arrived they were kept in boxes and probably put in your basement. People either didn't bother looking at them or didn't see their value."

"Are you saying we had a collection of Chiniquy's books and never even knew it?" asked Mr. Blake, getting quite agitated. "This is the very thing people were afraid of. That in our rush we'd sell off treasures. What were they?"

"We don't know," admitted Gamache. "But some were bought by Augustin Renaud and two books interested him in particular."

"Which ones?"

"Again, we don't know. We have the catalog numbers, but that's all. No titles, no idea what was in them."

"What could Father Chiniquy possibly have that Augustin Renaud would want?" Elizabeth asked herself. "Chiniquy wasn't interested in Champlain, at least not that we know of."

There were actually two questions, thought Gamache. What were those books? And why can't we find them?

Émile and Gamache paused outside the Lit and His.

"So, what do you think?" Émile asked, putting on his mitts and hat.

"I think if Chin is Chiniquy in Augustin Renaud's diary then JD must be James Douglas."

"And Patrick and O'Mara are long dead too," said Émile, his breath coming in puffs and his mouth already growing numb in the cold. Still the two men stood and talked.

Gamache nodded. "Renaud wasn't planning to meet those four men, he was making a note of a meeting they had. Here. More than a hundred years ago."

The men looked up at the building, rising behind them.

"And 18 whatever? The number in his diary?" Émile asked. "A time? A date?"

Gamache smiled. "We'll find out."

"We will," agreed Émile. It felt good to be working together again. "Coming?"

"I have a quick stop to make first. Can you take Henri home?"

Gamache watched Henri and Émile stepping carefully down rue St-Stanislas, making sure not to slip on the ice and snow.

The Chief Inspector walked the few meters to St. Andrew's Presbyterian Church. Trying the door he was somewhat surprised to find it unlocked. He poked his head into the church. The robin's egg blue ceiling was softly lit but the rest was in twilight.

"Hello," he called and his voice rattled round and finally disappeared. His intention was to speak to the young minister but he found himself drawn into the calm space. Taking his coat off he sat quietly for a few minutes, occasionally taking a deep breath and a long exhale.

Now there is no more loneliness.

Closing his eyes he let the voice loose, to play. To run around in his head, to laugh and tell him once again about breaking his first violin, a tiny one lent by the school. Worth more money than they had and his mother mending it and handing it back to the distraught boy reassuring him.

Things are strongest where they're broken. Don't worry.

"What a kind thing to say," Gamache said and meant.

"To a clumsy boy," Morin agreed. "I broke everything. Violins, vacuums, glasses, plates, you name it. I once broke a hammer. If I didn't break it I lost it."

Morin laughed.

Gamache felt himself almost nodding off in the warmth and the peace and the soft laughter in his head, and when he opened his eyes he was surprised to find he was no longer alone. The young minister was sitting quietly at the other end of the pew, reading.

"You seemed amused just now," Tom Hancock said.

"Did I? Something came to me. What're you reading?" Gamache asked, his voice not more than a whisper.

Tom Hancock looked down at the book in his hand.

"*Steer toward the third tall oak from the tip of Fischer's Point,*" he read. "*Once halfway across you must adjust your course, taking into account the current, the winds, the ice. And always steer for the ice floes, never to open water.*"

"A little known Gospel," said Gamache.

"Well, after the reforms they're harder to recognize," said the Reverend Mr. Hancock. He put a bookmark in, closed it and handed the old volume to his companion. Gamache accepted it and looked at the title.

DELIVERING THE MAIL ACROSS THE
MIGHTY SAINT LAWRENCE, IN WINTER.
A MANUAL.

Opening the cover he scanned the title page, and found the date. 1854.

"Obscure book." He handed it back. "Where'd you find it?"

"One of the perks of being so close to the Lit and His. You get to prowl the shelves. I think I'm the second person to take it out in 150 years."

"Have you found other interesting books there?"

"Some, most equally obscure. When I first arrived I'd check out books of old sermons, in the hopes some of my parishioners would be impressed but no one seemed to notice, so I stopped." He laughed. "This though is quite useful. Has strategies for crossing the river in winter."

"The ice canoe race? There must be easier pastimes."

"Are you kidding? Canoeing across a frozen river is a breeze compared to what I normally do."

Now Gamache shifted in the hard pew so that he was facing Tom Hancock. "That difficult?"

The young man grew somber. "At times."

"Have you heard of a Father Chiniquy?"

Tom Hancock thought then shook his head. "Who is he?"

"Was. He lived more than a hundred years ago. A famous Catholic priest who quit the church and joined the Presbyterians."

"Really? Chiniquy?" He thought about the name then shook his head. "Sorry. I should probably know who he was, but I'm not from here."

"Not to worry, not many know him now. I'd never heard of him."

"Is he important to the case?"

"I can't see how he can be, and yet his name's come up in Augustin Renaud's journal. Renaud seems to have bought a few of Chiniquy's books at the Lit and His sale."

The Reverend Mr. Hancock grimaced. "That sale haunts us."

"Were you in favor of it?"

"It seemed obvious. The place was in disrepair, it was a question of losing a few unused books to save the many. It should have been an easy decision."

Gamache nodded.

That was often the equation, give up the few to save the many. From a distance it seemed so simple, so clear. And yet, from a distance you might see the big picture, but not the whole picture, you missed the details. Not everything was seen, from a distance.

"Did the opposition surprise you?" Gamache asked.

Tom Hancock hesitated. "I was disappointed more than surprised. The English community is shrinking, but it needn't die out. It's on the cusp. It could go either way. It's crucial right now to keep the institutions alive. They're the anchors of any community." He hesitated a moment, not happy with his choice of words. "No, not the anchors. The harbors. The places people go and know they're safe."

Safe, thought Gamache. How primal that was, how powerful. What would people do to preserve a safe harbor? They'd do what they'd done for centuries. What the French had done to save Québec, what the English had done to take it. What countries do to protect their borders, what individuals do to protect their homes.

They kill. To feel safe. It almost never worked.

But Tom Hancock was speaking again. "It's vital to hear your own language, to see it written, to see it valued. That's one of the reasons I was so glad to be asked to sit on the Literary and Historical Society board. To try to save the institution."

"Do they share your concern?"

"Oh yes, they all know how precarious it is. The debate is really how best to keep the institutions going. The Lit and His, the Anglican cathedral, this church, the high school and nursing home. The CBC. The newspaper. They're all threatened."

The young minister turned earnest eyes on Gamache. Not the burning eyes of a zealot, not Renaud or Champlain or Chiniquy eyes, but the eyes of someone with a calling greater than himself. A simple desire to help.

"Everyone's sincere, it's just a question of strategy. Some think the enemy is change, some think change is what will save them, but they all know their backs are to the cliff."

"The Plains of Abraham, replayed?"

"No, not replayed. It never ended. The English only won the first skirmish, but the French have won the war. The long-range plan."

"Attrition?" asked Gamache. "Revenge of the cradle?"

It was a familiar argument, and a familiar strategy. The Catholic Church and politicians for generations demanded the Québécois have huge families to populate the huge territory, to squeeze the more modest Anglos out.

But finally it wasn't simply the size of the French population that did the English in, but their own hubris. Their refusal to share power, wealth, influence with the French majority.

If their backs were to the cliff it was an abyss of their own making and an enemy they'd created.

"If the English community is going to survive," said Tom Hancock, "it's going to have to make some sacrifices. Take action. Adapt." He paused, looking down at the book clasped in his hand.

"Change course?" asked Gamache, also glancing at the book in the minister's hand. "They're making for the open water? Trying the easy way first?"

Tom Hancock looked at Gamache and the tension seemed to break. He even laughed a little.

"*Touché.* I guess we all do. I think people see me as this muscular, young guy. Stunningly handsome even." He stole a glance at his amused companion. "But the truth is, I'm not strong at all. Every day frightens me. That's why I'm doing the canoe race. Ridiculous thing to do, really, paddle and run across a half-frozen river in minus thirty degree temperatures. You know why I'm doing it?" When Gamache shook his head the younger man continued. "So that people will think

I'm strong." His voice dropped, as did his eyes. "I'm not strong at all. Not where it counts. The truth is I'd rather be sweating and heaving a canoe over slush and ice than sitting one-on-one with a sick and dying parishioner. That terrifies me."

Gamache leaned forward, his voice as soft as the light. "What scares you about it?"

"That I won't know what to say, that I'll let them down. That I won't be enough."

I will find you. I won't let anything happen to you.

Yes sir. I believe you.

The two men stared into space, lost in their own thoughts.

"Doubt," said Gamache at last and the word seemed to fill the huge empty space around them. He stared straight ahead, seeing the closed door. The wrong door.

Tom Hancock watched his companion, let him sit in silence for a few moments.

"Doubt is natural, Chief Inspector. It can make us stronger."

"And things are strongest where they're broken?" asked the Chief, with a smile.

"They better be, I'm counting on it," said the Reverend Mr. Hancock.

Gamache nodded, thinking. "But still you do it," he said at last. "You sit with parishioners who are sick and dying. It scares you, but you do it every day. You don't run away."

"I have no choice. I have to aim for the ice, not the open water if I'm going to get where I want to go. And so do you."

"Where do you want to go?"

Hancock paused, thinking. "I want to get to shore."

Gamache took a deep breath and a long exhale. Hancock watched him.

"Not everyone makes it across the river," said Gamache quietly.

"Not everyone's supposed to."

Gamache nodded.

I believe you, whispered the young voice.

Gamache leaned forward in the pew, placing his elbows on his knees and lacing his strong fingers together, one hand clasping the other, which trembled just a little. Then he rested his chin on them.

"I made some terrible mistakes," he said at last, staring into the half light. "Not seeing the full picture, though all the clues were there. Not grasping it all until it was almost too late and even then I made a terrible mistake."

The corridor, the closed door. The wrong door, the wrong way. The seconds ticking down. The race back toward the other door, heart pounding.

Don't worry, son. It will be all right.

Breaking through the door and seeing him sitting there, his thin back to them, facing the wall. Facing the clock. That ticked down.

Yes sir, I believe you.

To zero.

Bringing himself back to the silent church Gamache looked over to Tom Hancock.

"Sometimes life goes in a direction not of our choosing," said the minister, softly. "That's why we need to adapt. It's never too late to change direction."

Gamache remained silent. He knew the young minister was wrong, sometimes it was too late. Général Montcalm knew that. He knew that.

"They should have sold all those boxes of books," said Tom Hancock, at last, lost in his own reverie. "Now, there's a symbol for you. The Lit and His cluttered with unwanted English words. Weighed down by the past."

"*Je me souviens,*" whispered Gamache.

"It'll drag them under," said the Reverend Mr. Hancock, sadly.

Gamache was beginning to understand this community and this case.

And himself.

EIGHTEEN

⁓

"Ten more."

Clara groaned and lifted her legs in unison.

"Keep your back flat!"

Clara ignored the order. This wasn't pretty. It certainly wasn't perfect, but she was going to damn well do it.

"One, grunt, two, groan, three . . ."

"Did I tell you about my day skiing at Mont Saint-Rémy?"

Pina, the exercise instructor, apparently didn't need to breathe. Her legs and arms seemed independent of the rest of her, moving in military precision while she lay on the mat chatting away as though at a slumber party.

Myrna was swearing and sweating freely and sometimes making other noises while Ricky Martin sang "Livin' la Vida Loca." Clara was always happy to exercise close to Myrna since any number of sins, and sounds, could be blamed on her. And she was easy to hide behind. The entire class could hide behind Myrna.

Myrna turned to Clara. "If you hold her down, I'll kill her."

"But how? We'd never get away with it." Clara had been giving it some thought. So far she'd done twelve leg lifts of the ten Pina announced, and now Pina was complaining bitterly about snowboarders while her own pneumatic legs went up and down.

"No one would say anything," said Myrna, lifting her legs a millimeter. "And if they threaten to, we kill them too."

It was as good a plan as Clara had heard.

"Where are we with the leg lifts?" Pina asked. "Three, four . . ."

"OK, Bugsy, I'm in," snorted Clara.

"So'm I," said Dominique Gilbert on Clara's other side, her voice almost as unrecognizable as her purple face.

"Dear God," said The Wife, across the room, "do it soon."

"Do what?" asked Pina, starting to bicycle her legs in mid-air.

"Murder you, of course," snapped Myrna.

"Oh, that," laughed Pina, never totally appreciating how close it came every class.

Twenty minutes later the class was over, after a last Tai Chi movement in which Clara meditated on murder. It was a good thing she adored Pina and needed the class.

Toweling off and rolling up her mat, Clara wandered over to the cluster of women who'd formed in the middle of the room. After a minute or so Clara managed to get the conversation around to where she wanted it.

"Did you see Inspector Beauvoir's back in the village?" she asked, nonchalantly, dabbing at a trickle of sweat down her neck.

"Poor guy," said Hanna Parra. "Still, he seems better."

"I think he's kinda cute," said The Wife. Her eyes were large, expressive and without guile. An earth mother, married to a carpenter.

"You don't," said Myrna with a laugh. "He's too skinny."

"I'd fatten him up," said The Wife.

"There's something about that Inspector. I want to save him," said Hanna. "Heal him, make him smile."

"Mr. Spock," said Clara, though this conversation wasn't exactly going as she'd hoped and she hadn't helped by just taking it off into outer space. "The Vulcan?" she explained when a few of the women looked perplexed. "Oh, for God's sake, you can't tell me you don't know *Star Trek*? Everyone had a crush on Mr. Spock because he was so cool and distant. They wanted to be the one to break down his reserve, to get into that heart."

"It's not his heart we want to get into," said Hanna and everyone laughed.

They put on their coats and ran across the snowy road to the inn and spa for the regular post-exercise tea and scones.

Clara was still amazed every time she entered the inn and spa, remembering it as the crumbling old Hadley house before Dominique and her husband Marc had bought it. Now their hostess sat relaxed and elegant, smiling and pouring tea.

Had Dominique killed the Hermit? Clara couldn't see it. No, if Clara was being honest, the most likely suspect months ago, and the most likely one still, was Marc Gilbert. Dominique's husband.

Clara brought the conversation around to murder once again.

"Hard to believe Olivier's been gone almost six months," she said, accepting a fragrant cup of tea from Dominique. Out the window she could see the clear blue day, always the coldest. Snow caught up in a whirlwind swirled by the window, making a slight sprinkling sound, like sand against the glass.

Inside the inn and spa it was peaceful. The room was filled with antiques, not cumbersome Victorian oak, but simple pine and cherry pieces. The walls were painted pastel shades and felt restful, serene. A fire was lit and the place smelled delicately of maple wood smoke, moisturizers and tisanes. Chamomile, lavender, cinnamon.

A young woman arrived with a plate of warm scones, clotted cream and homemade strawberry jam. This was Clara's favorite part of exercise class.

"How's Olivier doing?" The Wife asked.

"He's trying to adjust," said Myrna. "I saw him a few weeks ago."

"He still insists he didn't kill the Hermit," said Clara, watching everyone closely. She felt a fraud, pretending to be a homicide investigator, play-acting. Still, there were worse stages. Clara smoothed clotted cream on her warm scone, then strawberry jam.

"Well, if he didn't do it, who did?" Hanna Parra was a stout, attractive pillar. Clara had known her for decades. Could she be party to a murder? Might as well ask.

"Could you kill anyone?"

Hanna looked at her with some surprise, but no anger or suspicion.

"Now there's an interesting question. I know for sure I could."

"How can you be so sure?" asked Dominique.

"If someone broke into our home and threatened Havoc or Roar? I'd kill them in a second."

"Kill the women first," said The Wife.

"I beg your pardon?" asked Dominique. She sat forward and placed her delicate teacup on its saucer.

"It's a training booklet put out by the Mossad," said The Wife. Even the therapists who were giving Myrna and Hanna pedicures stopped what they were doing to stare at this lovely young woman who'd said the ugliest thing.

"How would you know that?" asked Myrna.

The Wife smiled fully. "Got you scared, don't I?"

They all laughed, but the truth was, they were thrown off a little. The Wife let them stew for a moment then laughed.

"I heard it on CBC Radio. A show on terrorism. The theory is that women almost never kill. It takes a great deal to get a woman to murder, but once she decides to, she won't stop until it's done."

There was silence as they thought about that.

"Makes sense to me," said Myrna, at last. "When a woman commits to something she does it with both her heart and her head. Very powerful."

"That was the point of the interview," said The Wife. "Women rarely join terrorist cells, but Mossad agents are told if they raid a cell and there's a female terrorist, kill her first because she'll never surrender. She'll be the most vicious one there. Merciless."

"I really hate that thought," said Dominique.

"So do I," admitted The Wife. "But I think it might be true. Almost nothing could get me to hurt anyone, physically or emotionally, but I can see if I had to, I could. And it'd be awful."

The last sentence was said with sadness, and Clara knew it to be the truth.

Had one of these women killed the Hermit after all? But why? What could have driven them to it? And what did she really know about them?

"Did you know Charlie's speaking now?" said The Wife, changing the subject. "Thanks to Dr. Gilbert. He comes by once a week and works with him."

"How kind." A man's voice spoke from the doorway. They looked over.

Marc Gilbert stood there, tall, lanky, his blond hair was cut to his scalp and his blue eyes were intense.

"Charlie can now say 'boo' and 'shoo,'" said The Wife with enthusiasm.

"Congratulations," Marc smiled. There was sarcasm there, and amusement.

Clara felt her back go up. How easy it was to dislike this smiling man.

She'd tried to like him, for Dominique's sake, but it was a losing battle.

"I remember, my first word was 'poo,'" she said to The Wife, who was looking at Marc, perplexed.

"Poo?" asked Myrna, jumping into the awkward silence. "Should I ask?"

Clara laughed. "I was trying to say 'puppy.' Came out as 'poo.' Then it became my nickname, everyone called me that for years. My father still does, sometimes. Did your father have a nickname for you, growing up?" Clara asked Marc, trying to break some of the tension.

"He was never around. Then he took off and that was that. So, no."

The tension in the room rose.

"And now, it seems he's found another family." Marc stared at The Wife.

So that was it, thought Clara. Jealousy.

The Wife stared at Marc and Clara could see a flush spreading up her neck. Marc smiled, turned on his heels, and left.

"I'm sorry—" Dominique started to say to The Wife.

"It's all right, he has a point actually. Old worships your father-in-law. I think he sees him as a sort of surrogate grandfather for Charles."

"His own father doesn't visit?"

"No. He died when Old was a teenager."

"Must have been a fairly young man when he died," said Myrna. "An accident?"

"He walked out onto the river one spring. The ice wasn't as solid as he thought."

She left it at that and it was far enough. Everyone in the room knew what must have happened. The cracking underfoot, the web of lines, the man looking down. Stopping. Standing still.

How far away the shore must seem when you're on thin ice.

"Did they ever find him?" Myrna asked.

The Wife shook her head. "I think that's the worst. Old's mother's still waiting for him."

"Oh, God," moaned Clara.

"Does Old?" Myrna asked.

"Think he's still alive? No, thank God, but he doesn't think it was an accident."

Neither did Clara. It sounded deliberate to her. Everyone knew that walking on ice in spring was courting death.

And sure enough, the ice had broken under the father, as he knew it would, but his son had also lost his footing that day. And Vincent Gilbert had righted him. The Asshole Saint had stepped in and was helping Charlie, and helping Old. But at what cost?

Was that what she'd heard a few minutes ago in Marc Gilbert's voice? Not sarcasm, but a small crack?

"What about you Clara?" Dominique asked, pouring more tea. "Are your parents still alive?"

"My father is. My mother died a few years ago."

"Do you miss her?"

There was a question, thought Clara. Do I miss her?

"At times. She had Alzheimer's at the end." Seeing their faces she hurried to reassure them. "No, no. Strangely enough the last few years were some of our best."

"When she was demented?" asked Dominique. "I begin to see why they called you Poo."

Clara laughed. "It was actually a bit of a miracle. She forgot everything, her address, her sisters. She forgot Dad, she even forgot us. But she also forgot to be angry. It was wonderful," Clara smiled. "Such a relief. She couldn't remember her long list of grievances. She actually became a delightful person."

She'd forgotten to love, but she also forgot to hate. It was a trade-off Clara was happy to accept.

The women in the room chatted about love, about childhood, about losing parents, about Mr. Spock, about good books they'd read.

They mothered each other. And by lunch they were ready to meet the winter's day. As Clara walked home, scone crumbs in her hair, the taste of chamomile on her lips, she thought of Old's father, frozen in time. And the look on Marc Gilbert's face as the crack had appeared.

Armand Gamache sat in the Paillard bakery on rue St-Jean and stared at Augustin Renaud's diary. Henri was curled up under the table while outside people were trudging head down through the snow and the cold.

How could Chiniquy, the fallen priest, and Augustin Renaud, the amateur archeologist be connected? Gamache stared at Renaud's excited markings, the exclamation marks, the swirls around the names of the four men. Chin, JD, Patrick, O'Mara. Swirls of ink so forceful the pen had almost ripped the paper. And below the entry were the catalog numbers.

9-8499

9-8572

Almost certainly the numbers related to books sold by the Literary and Historical Society and, equally certainly, they were from the lot donated by Chiniquy's housekeeper and left in their boxes in the basement for more than a century.

Until Augustin Renaud had bought them from the secondhand bookseller, Alain Doucet. In two lots. First in the summer, then the last lot just a few weeks ago.

What was in those books?

What did Chiniquy have that excited Augustin Renaud?

Gamache took a sip of hot chocolate.

It had to have something to do with Champlain, and yet the priest had shown absolutely no interest in the founder of Québec.

Chin, Patrick, O'Mara, JD. 18-something.

If Chiniquy was ninety when he died in 1899, that meant he was born in 1809. Could the number be 1809? Or 1899? Maybe. But where did that leave him?

Nowhere.

His eyes narrowed.

He looked at 1809 closely then snapping his notebook shut he drained his drink, put money on the table then he and Henri hurried into the cold. Taking long strides he saw the Basilica getting larger and larger as he approached.

At the corner he paused, in his own world, where snow and biting cold couldn't touch him. A world where Champlain was recently dead and buried, then reburied.

A world of clues over the centuries, as buried as the body.

He turned and walked briskly up des Jardins, stopping in front of the beautiful old door, with the wrought-iron numerals.

1809.

He rapped and waited. Now he felt the cold and beside him Henri leaned against his legs for warmth and comfort. Gamache was about to turn away when the door opened a crack, then all the way.

"*Entrez*," said Sean Patrick, stepping back quickly, out of the way of the biting wind as it invaded his home.

"I'm sorry to bother you again, Monsieur Patrick," said the Chief Inspector as they stood in the dark, cramped entrance. "But I have a couple of questions. May I?" He motioned toward the interior of the home.

"Fine," said Patrick, walking reluctantly ahead. "Where to?"

"The living room, please."

They found themselves in the familiar room, surrounded by censorious Patricks past.

"These are your great-grandparents, correct?" Gamache looked at a couple posing in front of this home. It was a wonderful picture, two stern sepia people in what looked like their Sunday best.

"It is. Taken the year they bought this place."

"In the late 1800s you told us last time we talked."

"That's right."

"Do you mind?" Gamache reached to take the photo off the wall.

"Please yourself." It was clear Patrick was curious.

Turning the picture over Gamache found it was sealed at the back with brown paper. There was a photographer's shop sticker, but no date. And no names.

Gamache put his reading glasses on and peered closely at the photo. And there, poking out from under the frame in the lower right-hand corner was what he was looking for.

A date.

1870.

Replacing the photo, he moved down the wall and stopped in front of another picture of great-grandfather Patrick. In this one he was with a group of other laborers, standing in front of a big hole. The building behind was barely visible.

Great-grandfather Patrick was smiling and so was another man, standing next to him. But everyone else in the photo looked grim. And why not? Their lives, like their fathers' before them, would have been miserable.

Irish immigrants, they'd come to Canada for a better life only to die of plague in the crowded ships. Those that survived spent their lives in menial labor. Living in squalor in the Basse-Ville, the Lower Town, in the shadow of the cliffs, below the mighty Château Frontenac.

It was a life of near despair. So why were these two men smiling? Gamache turned the photo around. It too was sealed.

"I'd like to take this backing off. Do you mind?"

"Why?"

"I think it might help us with the case."

"How?"

"I can't tell you, but I promise not to harm the photo."

"Is this going to get me into trouble?"

Patrick searched Gamache's face and rested on his thoughtful eyes.

"Not at all. Indeed, I'd consider it a favor."

After the briefest pause, Patrick nodded.

"*Bon, merci.* Can you turn on all the lights and get me your sharpest knife?"

Patrick did all that and the two men and a dog leaned over the table, the knife in Gamache's hand. It shook slightly and Gamache gripped it tighter. Patrick glanced at the Chief Inspector, but said nothing. Gamache lowered the knife and carefully pried the brittle old paper away from the frame. Little by little it came up.

Resisting the temptation to rip it off in one go, they carefully teased it up until it was off and the back of the photograph was exposed to sunlight for the first time since it was sealed more than a century earlier. And there, in precise, careful writing, were the names of the men, including the two who were smiling.

Sean Patrick and Francis O'Mara.

1869.

Gamache stared.

The note in Augustin Renaud's diary didn't say 1809. It said 1869.

Chiniquy met with this Patrick and this O'Mara and James Douglas in 1869.

Why?

Gamache looked over at the wall of ancestors standing outside this home. A great distance from the Basse-Ville, a universe away from there. Much further than the distance between Ireland and Canada, this was the unbridgeable gap between Us and Them.

A rough Irish laborer in a fine Upper Town home, in 1870. It should not have been. And yet, it was.

Gamache looked back down at the smiling men in the photograph, standing in front of a building. O'Mara and Patrick. What were they so happy about?

Gamache could guess.

NINETEEN

⌒

"Dr. Croix?"

Gamache saw the man's back stiffen. It was an eloquent little movement, involuntary and habitual. Here was a man engrossed in what he was doing, not pleased with the interruption. That, Gamache knew, was understandable. Who didn't feel that way occasionally?

What was even more telling, though, was the long pause. Gamache could almost see the armor going on, the plates snapping down the archeologist's back, the spikes and prickles and chains clicking into place. And then, after the armor, the weapon.

Anger.

"What do you want?" the stiff back demanded.

"I'd like to speak with you, please."

"Make an appointment."

"I don't have time."

"Neither do I. Good day." Serge Croix leaned further over the table, examining something.

There was a reason, Gamache knew, Québec's Chief Archeologist chose to work with clay and shards of pottery, with arrowheads and old stone walls. He could question them and while they might, occasionally, contradict him it was never messy, never emotional, never personal.

"My name is Armand Gamache. I'm helping to investigate the murder of Augustin Renaud."

"You're with the Sûreté. You have no jurisdiction here. Go mind your own business."

Still the stiff back refused to move.

Gamache contemplated him for a moment. "Do you not want to help?"

"I have helped." Serge Croix turned round and glared at Gamache. "I spent an entire afternoon with Inspector Langlois digging in the basement of the Literary and Historical Society. Gave up my Sunday for that and you know what we found?"

"Potatoes?"

"Potatoes. Which is more than Augustin Renaud ever found when digging for Champlain. Now, I don't mean to be rude but go away, I have work to do."

"On what?" Gamache approached.

They were in the basement of the chapel of the Ursuline convent. It was lit with industrial lamps and long examination tables were set up in the center of the main room. Dr. Serge Croix stood beside the longest table.

"It's an ongoing dig."

Gamache looked into a hole by one of the rough stone walls. "Is this where Général Montcalm and his men were buried?"

"No, they were found over there." Croix motioned into another part of the basement and went back to his work. Gamache took a few strides and peered in. He'd never been in that basement before, but had read about it since he was a schoolboy. The heroic Général riding up and down on his magnificent horse, inspiring the troops. Then the fusillade, and the Général was hit, but still he clung to his mount. When it was clear the battle was lost, when it was clear Bougainville was not going to arrive, the French forces had retreated into the old city. Montcalm had ridden there, supported on either side by foot soldiers. Taken to this very spot, to die in peace.

He'd hung on, remarkably, until the next day when he finally succumbed.

The nuns, afraid the English might desecrate the body, afraid of reprisals, had buried the Général where he'd died. Then, at some later date, the sisters had dug up his skull and a leg bone and put it into a crypt in the chapel, to be protected and prayed to privately.

A relic.

These things had power in Québec.

Général Montcalm had only recently been reunited with the men he'd died with. His remains had been reburied in a mass soldiers' grave a few years ago, a grave that contained the bodies of all the men who died in one terrible hour on the fields belonging to the farmer Abraham.

French and English, together for eternity. Long enough to make peace.

Gamache watched the Chief Archeologist bend over a piece of metal, brushing the dirt free. Was this grave robbing? Could they never let the dead be? Why dig up the Général and rebury him with great ceremony and a huge monument a couple hundred yards away? What purpose was served?

But Gamache knew the purpose. They all did.

So that no one would ever forget, the deaths and the sacrifice. Who had died and who had done it. The city might have been built on faith and fur, on skin and bones, but it was fueled by symbols. And memory.

Gamache turned and saw that Dr. Croix was staring in the same direction, to where the Général had been buried and dug up.

"*Dulce et Decorum est,*" the archeologist said.

"*Pro patria mori,*" Gamache finished.

"You know Horace?" Croix asked.

"I know the quote."

"It is sweet and right to die for your country. Magnificent," said Croix, gazing beyond Gamache.

"You think?"

"Don't you, *monsieur?*" Croix turned suspicious eyes on the Chief Inspector.

"No. It's an old and dangerous lie. It might be necessary, but it is never sweet and rarely right. It's a tragedy."

The two men glared at each other across the dirt floor.

"What do you want?" Croix demanded.

He was tall and slender, hard and sharp. A hatchet. And he was aimed at Gamache.

"Why would Augustin Renaud be interested in some books belonging to Charles Chiniquy?"

Not surprisingly Dr. Croix looked at Gamache as though he was mad.

"What's that supposed to mean? I don't even understand the question."

"Not long before he was murdered Renaud found two books that excited him. Books that came from the Literary and Historical Society, but that had once belonged to Father Chiniquy. You know who I mean?"

"Of course I know. Who doesn't?"

The entire world out there, thought Gamache. It was funny how obsessed people believed others equally obsessed, or even interested. And for archeologists and historians, gripped by the past, it was inconceivable others weren't.

For them, the past was as alive as the present. And while forgetting the past might condemn people to repeat it, remembering it too vividly condemned them to never leave. Here was a man who remembered, vividly.

"What connection could Charles Chiniquy have had to Champlain?" Gamache asked.

"None."

"Think, please." Gamache's voice, while still pleasant, now held an edge. "Chiniquy possessed something that excited Augustin Renaud. We know Renaud had only one passion. Champlain. Therefore, in the late 1800s Charles Chiniquy must have found something, some books, about Champlain and when Renaud found them he felt they'd lead him to where Champlain is buried."

"Are you kidding? Birds led him there. Little voices in his little head led him there, rice pudding led him there. He saw clues and certainties everywhere. The man was a lunatic."

"I don't say the Chiniquy books really did answer the mystery of Champlain," Gamache explained. "Only that Renaud believed they did."

Croix's eyes narrowed but Gamache could see he was no longer dismissing the question. Finally he shook his head.

"I have another question," said the Chief Inspector. "Chiniquy and James Douglas were friends, correct?"

Croix nodded, interested in where this might be going.

"Why would they meet two Irish immigrant laborers in 1869?"

"The workers were either drunk or insane or both. No big mystery there."

"Except there is. They met at the Literary and Historical Society."

That gave Croix pause.

"Now, that is a mystery," he admitted. "The Irish hated the English. There's no way they'd have gone to the Literary and Historical Society voluntarily."

"You mean, it wouldn't have been their idea?"

"I frankly doubt they could even read and write. Probably didn't know the Literary and Historical Society existed and if they did, the last place they'd want to go is into the heart of the Anglo establishment."

"And yet they did. To meet with Father Chiniquy and Dr. James Douglas. Why?"

When no answer came Gamache fished into his breast pocket and brought out the old photograph.

"These are the workers, the ones smiling. Shortly after this was taken that man," Gamache placed his finger on the figure of Sean Patrick, "bought a home in the Upper Town, just around the corner from here on des Jardins."

"Impossible."

"Fact."

Croix searched Gamache's face then returned to the photograph.

"Do you know what digging work was going on at the time?"

"In 1869? Lots I'd imagine."

"It would be the summer, judging by what they're wearing and probably in the old city. Look at the stonework."

Croix examined the grainy photo and nodded.

"I can try to find out."

"*Bon*," said Gamache, holding out his hand for the picture. Croix seemed reluctant to let it go but eventually gave it back.

"How did you find out about this meeting between Chiniquy, Douglas and the laborers?" Croix asked.

"From Renaud's diary. I have no idea how he knew about it. Presumably it's in one of the books he found. He bought the Chiniquy collection from the Literary and Historical Society. There was something in them, but we can't find the books. Renaud seems to have hidden them. What could hundred-year-old books contain that someone was willing to kill for them?" Gamache wondered.

"You'd be surprised. Not everything buried is actually dead," said the archeologist. "For many the past is alive."

What putrid piece of history was walking among them? Gamache wondered. What had Augustin Renaud disturbed?

He remembered an entry in Renaud's diary. Not the one circled and exclaimed over but a quieter entry, a meeting he would never make. With an SC.

The Chief Inspector slowly returned the photograph to his pocket, watching Croix, who was walking back to his work table.

"Were you going to meet Augustin Renaud?"

Croix stopped, then turned and stared.

"What?"

"Thursday at one o'clock. Augustin Renaud had an appointment with an SC."

"SC? That would be anyone."

"With the initials SC, yes. Was it you?"

"Me, have lunch with Renaud? I wouldn't be seen in the same room with the man if I could help it. No. He was always asking, demanding, to meet with me, but I never agreed. He was a nasty little piece of work who thought he knew better than anyone else. He was vindictive and manipulative and stupid."

"And maybe, finally, he was right," said Gamache. "Maybe he found Champlain. Was that what you were afraid of? That he might actually succeed? Is that why you tried to stop him at every turn?"

"I tried to stop him because he was a bumbling idiot who was ruining perfectly good and valuable archeological digs with his fantasies. He was a menace."

Serge Croix's voice had risen so that the harsh words bounced and throbbed off the hard stone walls, coming back at the two men. Filling the space with rage that echoed and grew.

But the last sentence was rasped out. Barely audible, it scraped along the dirt floor and gave Gamache a chill.

"You tried to stop him. Did you finally succeed?"

"You mean did I kill him?"

They glared at each other.

"I didn't arrange to meet him, and I certainly didn't kill him."

"Do you know where Champlain is buried?" Gamache asked.

"What did you just ask?"

"Do you know where Samuel de Champlain is buried?"

"What do you mean by that?" Croix's voice was low and his look filthy.

"You know what I mean. The question is clear."

"You think I know where Champlain is buried and am keeping it a secret?"

Croix invested each and every word, every syllable, with scorn.

"I think it's almost inconceivable that we know where minor clerics, where war heroes, where farmers are buried," said Gamache, not taking his eyes off the archeologist. "But not the founder of this country, the father of this country. I think you and the archeological establishment heaped derision onto Augustin Renaud, not because he was so laughable, but because he wasn't. Was he getting close? Had he actually found Champlain?"

"Are you mad? Why would I hide the greatest archeological find in the nation? It would make my career, make my reputation. I'd be forever remembered as the man who gave the Québécois the one piece missing in their history."

"That piece isn't missing, *monsieur*, just the body. Why?"

"There was a fire, the original church burned, documents burned—"

"I know the official history but that doesn't explain it and you know that. Why hasn't his body been found? It makes no sense. So I ask myself the other question. Not why hasn't he been found, but suppose he has? Why cover it up?" Gamache moved closer to the Chief Archeologist with each word until they were almost nose to nose. And Gamache whispered, "To the point of murder."

They stared and finally Croix leaned back.

"Why would someone want to do that?" asked Croix.

"There's only one reason, isn't there," said Gamache. "Champlain wasn't what he seemed. He wasn't quite the hero, the father figure, the great man. Champlain's become a symbol of the greatness of the Québécois, a potent symbol for the separatists of what the settlement might have been, had the English not taken over. Champlain hated the English, derided them as brutes. On every level Champlain is the perfect tool for Québec separatists. But suppose this wasn't true?"

"What're you saying?"

"A lot of what we know to be history isn't," said Gamache. "You know that, I know that. It serves a purpose. Events are exaggerated, heroes fabricated, goals are rewritten to appear more noble than they actually were. All to manipulate public opinion, to manufacture a common purpose or enemy. And the cornerstone of a really great movement? A powerful symbol. Take away or tarnish that and everything starts to crumble, everything's questioned. Can't have that."

"But what could be so bad about Champlain?" Croix asked.

"When was he born?"

"We don't really know."

"What did he look like?"

Croix opened his mouth then shut it again.

"Who was his father?"

Now Croix was silent, not even trying.

"Was he a spy? He was an expert mapmaker and yet many of the maps showed ridiculous creatures and claimed events that were clearly lies."

"It was the style of the time."

"To lie? Is that ever a style? We know who would want him found, Dr. Croix, but who wants him to remain buried?"

As Gamache left he wished the meeting with the Chief Archeologist could have been more cordial, if such a thing was possible with Serge Croix. He'd have loved to poke around that storied basement, loved to ask about the Battle of the Plains of Abraham, about the cannonballs still found in trees in old Quebec City.

He'd have loved to ask him about the strange coincidence of Captain Cook and Bougainville fighting in the same battle, on opposite sides, and Bougainville's almost inconceivable decision not to help his Général.

But those were questions that would have to wait and for which there might be no answer.

Just before plunging back into the Québec winter he called Inspector Langlois and made an appointment. Ten minutes later he was walking through the corridors of police headquarters looking for Inspector Langlois's offices, a visiting professor perhaps, an academic called in to consult.

"Chief Inspector." Langlois advanced, his hand out. Others in the large room got to their feet as Gamache entered. He nodded to them and smiled briefly then Langlois showed him into his private office.

"You must be used to it by now," said Langlois.

"The staring? Goes with the position, so yes, I'm used to it." Gamache handed Langlois his coat. "But it's changed of course, since the kidnapping and the other events."

No use pretending otherwise.

Inspector Langlois hung up the Chief's parka.

"I've been following the fall-out from it all, of course. The main question seems to be why we didn't realize the attack was coming."

Langlois searched Gamache's face, anxious for an answer. But he'd find none there.

"The people who did this were patient. The plan a long time in the making," said the Chief at last. "It moved so slowly as to be invisible."

"But something that big—" Inspector Langlois's question was the same as everyone else's. How could they have missed it?

Misdirection. And cunning. And the ability of the attackers to adapt. That was how, thought Gamache.

He accepted the chair indicated but said nothing.

Langlois sat across from him. "When did you realize it was more than a simple kidnapping?"

Gamache was quiet. He saw again Inspector Beauvoir returning from seeing Agent Nichol in the basement of Sûreté headquarters. Where Chief Inspector Gamache had placed her a year or more ago. A job he knew she'd hate, but needed to learn. Listening to other people. And not talking.

She needed to learn to be quiet.

Beauvoir had not been happy at bringing Agent Nichol in. Neither had he, for that matter. But he could see no other option. Chief Superintendent Francoeur was off chasing the kidnappers, down paths Gamache was more and more convinced were being laid out by the kidnappers themselves. Leading the Sûreté here and there. Morin's transmissions appearing to pop up all over the vast province. The trace a farce.

No. They needed help. And the embittered young agent in the basement was the only one he could turn to.

Chief Superintendent Francoeur would never think of her. No one ever did. And so Gamache could operate quietly, through her.

She says she needs the password for your computer, Beauvoir scrawled longhand. *So that nobody else will see our messages. She also wants you to pause as long as possible when speaking with Morin so she can get some ambient sound.*

Gamache nodded and without hesitation handed over his private password. He knew he was giving her access to everything. But he also knew he had no choice. They were blind. Not even Morin could help them. He was tied up facing a wall, and a clock. He'd done the best he could, describing his surroundings. The concrete floors, the dirt, the impression he had that wherever he was, it was abandoned. Paul Morin described the silence.

But he'd been wrong. The place wasn't abandoned. Nor was it silent. Not quite. He'd been fooled by the headset, which made clear Gamache's voice from miles away, but muffled any sound just feet away.

But Agent Nichol had found it. Slight sounds in the silence.

"The *premier* seems relieved it hasn't reached the political level, yet," said Langlois, crossing his legs. "The damage has been contained."

Seeing Gamache's blank face he immediately regretted his comment.

"*Désolé*, I didn't mean that. I was in the funeral cortège. Far behind you, of course."

Gamache smiled slightly. "It's all right, it's hard to know what to say. I suspect there's no right thing. Don't worry about it."

Langlois nodded then, making up his mind, he leaned forward. "When did you realize what was going on?"

"You don't really expect me to answer that, do you?" It was said with some humor, just enough to cut the edge off the words.

"I suppose not. Forgive me. I know you've given your depositions but as a cop I'm just curious. How did we all miss it? Surely it was obvious? The planned attack was so," Langlois searched for a word.

"Primitive?" asked Gamache at last.

Langlois nodded. "So simple."

"And that's what made it effective," said Gamache. "We've spent years looking for a high-tech threat. The latest bomb. Bio-industrial, genetic, nuclear. We searched the Internet, used telecommunication. Satellites."

"But the answer was right there all along," said Langlois, shaking his head in amazement. "And we missed it."

I'll find you. I won't let anything happen to you.

I believe you, sir.

In the brief pauses Gamache provided in his conversation with Paul Morin they'd picked up distant sounds, like the whispers of ghosts deep in the background.

Agent Morin wasn't alone. The "farmer" hadn't abandoned him after all. Others were there, speaking softly, softly. Walking softly, softly. Making almost no noise. But some. Enough for the delicate equipment and surprisingly sensitive ears to find.

And the words they'd spoken? It had taken hours, precious hours, but Nichol had finally isolated one crucial phrase.

La Grande.

Over and over she'd played it for Beauvoir, examining each syllable, each letter. The tone, the breath. Until they'd reached a conclusion.

La Grande. The power dam that held back trillions of tons of water. The giant dam that was ten times the size of any other in North America. That provided hydroelectricity for millions, hundreds of millions, of people.

Without it much of Canada and the States would be plunged into a dark age.

The La Grande dam was in the middle of nowhere, near impossible to get to without official permission.

Gamache had looked at his watch at that moment, when Beauvoir and Nichol had written him from the basement. Sent him the sound bite so he could hear what they'd found.

It was three in the morning. Eight hours left. He and Morin had been discussing paint samples and names. Banbury Cream. Nantucket Marine. Mouse Hair.

In a few strides Gamache was over at the huge ordinance map of Québec on his wall. His finger quickly found the La Grande River, and the slash across it that had diverted and dammed the flow, killing thousands of acres of old-growth forest, herds of caribou and deer and moose. Had stirred up mercury and poisoned native communities.

But it had also been a miracle of engineering and continued to provide power decades later. And if it was suddenly removed?

Chief Inspector Gamache's finger made its dreadful way south, tracing the torrent that would be created when all that water was suddenly released, all that energy suddenly released. It would be like nuclear bombs tumbling down the length of the province.

His finger hit Cree villages then larger and larger towns and cities. Val-d'Or. Rouyn-Noranda.

How far down would the water get before it petered out, before it dissipated? Before all its energy was spent? How many bodies would be swept down with it?

Now Paul Morin was talking about the family cat peeing in his father's printer.

Had Morin been taken there? Was he being held at the dam?

I'll find you.

I believe you, sir.

"Sir?"

Gamache looked up into the face of Inspector Langlois.

"Are you all right?"

Gamache smiled. "Just fine. My apologies."

"What can I do for you?"

"It's about the Renaud case. Have you found any boxes of books that might have belonged to Renaud that weren't in his apartment?"

"His ex-wife has some. He'd taken them over to her basement a few weeks ago. What is it?"

Gamache sat forward and brought out his notebook. "May I have her address please?"

"Certainly." He wrote the address down and handed it to the Chief Inspector. "Anything else?"

"No, this is perfect. *Merci.*" Gamache folded the note, put on his coat, thanked the Inspector and left, his boots echoing with purpose down the long corridor and out the door.

Hopping into a cab he called Émile then had the cab swing by his home and together they drove out the old gates, along Grande-Allée with its merrily lit bars and restaurants. The cab turned right onto Avenue Cartier then right again onto a small side street. Rue Aberdeen.

From the taxi Gamache had called Madame Renaud to make sure she was home. A moment later she opened the door and the two men entered. It was a main-floor flat in the gracious old row houses, each with wrought-iron stairs outside, leading to the apartments above.

Inside, the floors were dark wood and the rooms were generous and beautifully proportioned. Wide original crown molding swept around where the walls met the high ceiling. Each chandelier had a plaster rosette. These were genteel homes in a much sought-after *quartier* of Québec. Not everyone wanted to live within the walls, where life tended to be cramped and dictated by planners long dead. Here the streets were wider, planted with soaring old trees and each home had a modest front garden, when not buried under feet of snow.

Madame Renaud was short and cheerful. She took their coats and offered them a cup of coffee which both men declined.

"We're sorry for your loss, *madame*," said Gamache, taking a seat in the inviting living room.

"*Merci*. He was unbearable, of course. A pig-headed man, totally self absorbed. And yet—"

Gamache and Émile waited while she composed herself.

"And yet now that he's gone life feels emptier, less vibrant. I envied him his passion. I don't think I've ever felt that strongly about anything. And he wasn't a fool, you know, he knew the price he paid, but he was willing to pay it."

"And what was that price?" Émile asked.

"He was mocked and ridiculed, but more than that, no one liked him."

"Except you," said Gamache.

She said nothing. "He was lonely, you know, in the end. But still he couldn't stop, couldn't trade a dead explorer for living friends."

"When did he bring these books to you?" Gamache asked.

"About three weeks ago. There're four boxes. He said his apartment was too crowded."

Émile and Gamache exchanged a quick glance. Renaud's apartment was certainly cramped, but it was already a disaster, four more boxes would have made no difference.

No. He'd brought them to his wife for another reason. For safekeeping.

"Did he bring you anything else?" Émile asked.

She shook her head. "He was secretive by nature, some might say paranoid," she smiled. She was a woman of good cheer and Gamache wondered at Augustin Renaud, who'd chosen her as his wife. For a few bright years had he known happiness? Had that been his one shining attempt to change course? And find a place on the shore with this jovial, kind woman? But he couldn't, of course.

Gamache watched Madame Renaud chat with Émile. She still loved him, despite all that, thought Gamache. Was that a blessing or a curse?

And he wondered if that would go away, with time. Would the voice fade, the features blur? Would the memories recede and take their place with other pleasant, but neutral events from the past?

Avec le temps. Do we love less?

"Do you mind if we go through the boxes?" Gamache asked.

"Not at all. The other officers took a look but didn't seem very interested. What are you looking for exactly?"

"Two books," said Gamache. They'd walked to the back of the apartment, into the large, old-fashioned kitchen. "Unfortunately we don't know what they are."

"Well, I hope you find them here." She opened a door and turned on a light.

Gamache and Émile saw wooden steps going straight down into a dark cellar with a dirt floor. A slight musky aroma met them, and as they headed down the stairs it felt a bit like wading into water. Gamache could feel the cool air creep up his legs until it was at his chest, his head and he was submerged in the dank and the chill.

"Watch your heads," she called but both men were familiar with these old homes and had already ducked. "The boxes are over by the far wall."

It took a moment for Gamache's eyes to adjust, but finally they did and he saw the four cardboard boxes. Walking over he knelt at one while Émile took another.

Gamache's box contained a variety of books in different sizes. First he checked their catalog numbers. All were from the Literary and Historical Society, a few even had the name Charles Chiniquy written in but none matched the numbers in the diary. He moved to another box.

That box was filled with bound sermons, reference books and old family bibles, some Catholic, some Presbyterian. He opened the first book and checked the number. 9-8495. His heart quickened. This was the box. Opening the next book and the next, the numbers mounted. 9-8496, 8497, 8498. Gamache brought out the next book, a black leather collection of sermons and opened it. 9-8500.

He stared at it, willing the numbers to change, then he carefully, slowly opened again and replaced each of the twenty books in the box. One was indeed missing.

9-8499.

It had sat between that book of sermons and Chiniquy's confirmation bible.

"*Maudits*," Gamache swore under his breath. Why wasn't it there?

"Any luck?" He turned to Émile.

"Nothing. The damned book should be right here," Émile shoved a finger between two volumes. "But it's gone. 9-8572. Do you think someone got here first?"

"Madame Renaud said only Langlois's team has been."

"Still, what is here might be helpful," said Émile.

Gamache peered into the box. It contained a series of black leather volumes, spine out, all the same size. Gamache took one out and examined it. It was a diary. Émile's box contained the diary and journals of Charles Paschal Télesphore Chiniquy.

"Each book is a year," said Émile. "The missing one is for 1869."

Gamache sat back on his haunches and looked at his mentor, who was smiling.

Even in the dim light of the basement Gamache could see Émile's eyes were bright. "Well, Chief?" said Émile, straightening up. "What next?"

"There's only one thing to do now, Chief," smiled Gamache. He picked up the box of Chiniquy journals. "Go for a drink."

The two men returned upstairs and with Madame Renaud's permission they left with the box. Just around the corner was the Café Krieghoff and a chilly minute later they were there, sitting at a corner table by the window, away from other patrons. It was six in the evening and the work crowd was just arriving. Civil servants, politicians from the nearby government offices, professors, writers and artists. It was a bohemian hangout, a separatist haunt, and had been for decades.

The waitress, clad in jeans and a sweater, brought them a bowl of nuts and two Scotches. They sipped, nibbled the nuts, and read from Chiniquy's journals. It was fascinating stuff, insight into a mind both noble and mad. A mind with absolutely no insight into itself, a mind filled with purpose and delusion.

He would save souls and screw his superiors.

Gamache's phone vibrated and he took the call.

"Chief?"

"*Salut* Jean-Guy. How are you?"

The question was no longer simply *politesse* but was asked with sincerity.

"I'm actually doing well. Better."

And he sounded it. There was an energy to the younger man's voice Gamache hadn't heard in months.

"You? Where are you? I hear lots of noise."

"Café Krieghoff."

Beauvoir's laugh came down the telephone line. "Deep into a case, I see."

"*Bien sûr.* And you?" He could hear sounds as well.

"The bistro. Research."

"Of course. Poor one."

"I need your help," said Beauvoir. "About the murder of the Hermit."

TWENTY

It took Chief Inspector Gamache a moment to tear himself away from the 1860s Québec of Charles Chiniquy's journals to the quaint village of Three Pines today.

And yet, it wasn't that much of a leap. He suspected Three Pines probably hadn't changed all that much in the last 150 years. Had Father Chiniquy chosen to visit the tiny hamlet he'd have seen the same old stone houses, the clapboard homes with dormers and smoking chimneys. He'd have walked across the village green to the shops made of faded rose brick, pausing perhaps to admire the trinity of trees at the very center of the community.

Only the people had changed in Three Pines in the past 150 years, with the possible exception of Ruth Zardo. Gamache could only imagine how Ruth would have greeted Father Chiniquy. He smiled at the thought of the drunken mad poet meeting the sober mad minister.

Well, take this then. Ruth had written. *Have some more body.*
Drink and eat.
You'll just make yourself sick. Sicker.
You won't be cured.

Would Chiniquy have cured her? Of what? Her drinking, her poetry? Her wounds? Her words?

"How can I help?" he asked Beauvoir, picturing his second in command sitting in the bistro in front of the fire with a micro-brewery beer and a bowl of salty chips.

"If Olivier didn't kill the Hermit it comes down to five other suspects," said Beauvoir. "Havoc Parra and his father Roar. Vincent Gilbert and his son Marc or Old Mundin."

"Go on." Gamache looked out the window of the Café Krieghoff to the cars crawling along the snowy evening street and the cheerful holiday lights still up. The capital had never looked prettier.

"There are two questions. Who had the opportunity and who had the motive? From what I can see, Roar, Havoc and Marc had the opportunity. Roar was cutting the trails that led right to the Hermit. The cabin was on Marc's land and he could have walked those trails at any time and found it."

"*C'est vrai*," said the Chief, nodding as though Beauvoir could see him.

"Havoc worked late every Saturday and could have followed Olivier to the cabin."

Gamache paused, remembering the case, remembering the night the Hermit had been killed. "But it wasn't just Havoc in the bistro, Old Mundin also came in every Saturday night around closing time to get furniture to repair. He was there the night of the murder."

"That's true," agreed Beauvoir. "Though he mostly went straight home before the bistro was locked up. But, yes, he's a possibility."

"So that's Roar and Havoc Parra, Old Mundin and Marc Gilbert. All could have found the cabin and killed the Hermit. So why is Vincent Gilbert still a suspect? As you say, he doesn't seem to have had the opportunity to find the cabin."

Beauvoir paused. "It just seems too pat. His son buys a derelict old home no one wanted. They move here, then the Hermit is murdered and Marc's estranged father shows up at almost exactly the same moment."

"But you have no proof," said Gamache, pushing slightly, "beyond a feeling."

He could sense his second in command bristle. Jean-Guy Beauvoir had no truck with "feelings," with "intuition." Gamache, on the other hand, did.

"But you might be right," said the Chief. "And what about motive?"

"That's more difficult. We know why Olivier might have wanted the Hermit dead, but why would anyone else? If the motive was robbery the killer made a pretty poor job of it. From what we can make out, nothing was stolen."

"What other motives could there be?" asked Gamache.

"Revenge. The Hermit did something terrible and the murderer found him and killed him for it. Might have been hunting him for years. That would also explain why the Hermit was a hermit. He was hiding. Those treasures had to come from somewhere. He almost certainly stole them himself."

"Then why didn't the murderer take them after he'd killed the Hermit? Why leave everything there?"

Gamache saw again the home buried in the wilderness. From the outside it seemed just a rustic log cabin, with window boxes of flowers and herbs, a vegetable garden, a fresh stream behind the home. But inside? Signed first editions, ancient pottery, tapestries, a panel from the famous Amber Room, leaded crystal and gold and silver candlesticks. And the violin.

And he saw young Agent Morin standing in the cabin, so awkward, like a wooden puppet, all gangly arms and legs. But as soon as he'd played that priceless violin his body had changed.

The haunting first notes of "Colm Quigley" returned to Gamache.

"There's another possibility," said Beauvoir. "The murder wasn't about the treasure but something else the Hermit had done."

"Your theory then is that the treasure distracted us. Distracted me."

"No one who walked into that cabin believed the motive was anything other than the treasure. It seemed so obvious."

But Gamache knew Beauvoir was being uncharacteristically tactful. He, Gamache, had been in charge of the investigation. He'd assigned the agents and investigators and he'd followed his own instincts, often in the face of strong protests on the part of Inspector Beauvoir who'd insisted all along both the murderer and the motive were in Three Pines.

Gamache now believed Beauvoir was right, and he'd been wrong. And perhaps had put an innocent man in prison.

"Okay, let's suppose the treasure had nothing to do with the murder," said the Chief Inspector. "Suppose the only thing of value the murderer wanted was the Hermit's life and once taken he left."

"So," said Beauvoir, slinging his leg over the side of the easy chair and burrowing into the wing. He was hidden from view of the rest of the bistro, only his casual leg visible. No one could see him, but neither could he see anyone. "Take away the treasure but that still leaves us with other clues. The repetition of the word 'Woo' whittled into that chunk of red cedar, and woven into the web. It must mean something. And Charlotte, that name kept popping up, remember?"

Gamache did remember. It had sent him rushing across the continent to a mist-covered archipelago in northern British Columbia, on what now appeared to be a fool's errand.

"There's something about your list of suspects," said Gamache after going over each one again in his head.

"*Oui?*"

"They're all men."

"Are you afraid the Equal Opportunity Bureau's going to complain?" laughed Beauvoir.

"I just wonder if we should be considering some of the women," said Gamache. "Women have patience. Some of the most vicious crimes I've seen have been committed by women. It's more rare than men, but women are more likely to bide their time."

"That's funny, Clara was saying the same thing this afternoon."

"How so?" Gamache leaned forward. Anything Clara Morrow had to say was, in the Chief's opinion, worth listening to.

"She spent the morning with a bunch of women from the village. Apparently Old's wife said something odd. She quoted some instruction manual that advised anti-terrorism squads to kill the women first."

"The Mossad," said Gamache. "I've read it."

Beauvoir was silent. The Chief Inspector often surprised him. Sometimes it was with incomprehensible bits of Ruth's poetry but mostly it was with things like this, with what he knew.

"So you know what it refers to," said Beauvoir. "A woman's capacity to kill."

"Yes, but mostly it's about her dedication. Once committed some women will never give up, they'll be merciless, unstoppable." Gamache was silent for a moment, staring out the window but no longer seeing the flow of people bundled against the biting cold. "In what context were they talking about this? Why did The Wife say it?"

"They were talking about the case. Clara had asked Hanna Parra if she could kill."

"Clara needs to be more careful," said the Chief. "Did anyone particularly respond to that?"

"Clara said they all did, but after some discussion they reluctantly agreed the Mossad might have had it right."

Gamache frowned. "What else did the women talk about?"

Beauvoir looked at his notes and told Gamache about the rest of the conversation. About fathers and mothers, about Alzheimer's, about Charlie Mundin and Dr. Gilbert.

"There was something else. Clara thinks Marc Gilbert is desperately jealous of Old Mundin."

"Why?"

"Apparently his father's spending a lot of time at the Mundins'. The Wife admitted Old has developed a sort of bond with Dr. Gilbert. A substitute father."

"Jealousy's a powerful emotion. Powerful enough to kill."

"But the wrong victim. Old Mundin isn't dead."

"So how could this play into the death of the Hermit?" the Chief asked and waited while there was a long pause. Finally Beauvoir admitted he didn't see how it could.

"Both Carole Gilbert and Old Mundin are originally from Quebec City. Could you ask around about them?" When the Chief agreed Beauvoir paused before asking his last question. "How are you?"

He hated to ask, afraid that maybe the Chief would one day tell him the truth.

"I'm at the Café Krieghoff with Émile Comeau, a bowl of nuts and a Scotch. How bad can it be?" Gamache asked, his voice friendly and warm.

But Jean-Guy Beauvoir knew exactly how bad it could be and had been.

Hanging up, an image stole into his mind, uninvited, unexpected, unwanted.

Of the Chief, gun in hand, suddenly being lifted off his feet, twisting, turning. Falling. To lie still on the cold cement floor.

Gamache and Émile hailed a cab and took the diaries home. As Émile prepared a simple supper of warmed-up stew Gamache fed Henri then took him for a walk to the bakery for a fresh baguette.

Once home the men sat in the living room, a basket of crusty bread on the table, bowls of beef stew in front of them and the Chiniquy diaries piled on the sofa between them.

They spent the evening eating and reading, making notes, occasionally reading each other a particularly interesting, moving or unintentionally amusing passage.

By eleven Armand Gamache took off his reading glasses and rubbed his weary eyes. So far while historically fascinating the Chiniquy journals hadn't revealed anything pertinent. There was no mention of the Irish laborers, Patrick and O'Mara. And while he did talk about James Douglas in the earlier diaries, the later ones mentioned him only in passing. Eventually there was an entry Émile read Gamache about Douglas packing up his three mummies and heading down to Pittsburgh, to live with his son.

Gamache listened and smiled. Chiniquy had made it sound petty, like a kid picking up his marbles and going home. Had Father Chiniquy done that on purpose, to diminish Dr. Douglas? Had there been a falling out? Did it matter?

An hour later he glanced at Émile and noticed the older man had fallen asleep, a journal splayed open on his chest. Gently raising Émile's hand he removed the book, then put a soft pillow under Émile's head and covered him with a comforter.

After quietly placing a large cherry log on the fire Gamache and Henri crept to bed.

The next day, before breakfast, he found an email from the Chief Archeologist.

"Something interesting?" Émile asked.

"Very. Sleep well?" Gamache looked up from his message with a smile.

"Wish I could say that was the first time I'd nodded off in front of the fire," Émile laughed.

"So it wasn't my stimulating conversation?"

"No. I never listen to you, you know that."

"My suspicions confirmed. But listen to this," Gamache looked back down to his email. "It's from Serge Croix. I asked him to find out what digging work was being done in the old city in the summer of 1869."

Émile joined his friend at the table. "The year Chiniquy and Douglas met the Irish workers."

"Exactly, and the year covered in the missing journal. Dr. Croix writes to say there were three big digs. One at the Citadelle, to reinforce the walls, one to expand the Hôtel-Dieu hospital and the third? The third was to dig a basement under a local restaurant. The Old Homestead."

Émile sat for a moment then leaned back in the chair and brought a hand up to his face, thinking. Gamache got to his feet.

"I think I'll treat you to breakfast, Émile."

Comeau got up, his eyes bright now too. "I think I know where."

Within twenty minutes they'd climbed the steep and slippery slope of Côte de la Fabrique, pausing for breath and to stare at the imposing Notre-Dame Basilica. Where the original little church had stood, built by the Jesuit priests and brothers and supported by Champlain. A modest New World chapel dedicated to the Virgin Mary to celebrate the return of Québec from the English in their see-saw battle for possession of the strategic colony.

This was where the great man's funeral had been held and where he'd been buried, albeit briefly. At one time Augustin Renaud had been convinced he was still there in the small chapel of St. Joseph, where the amateur archeologist had found a lead-lined coffin and some old coins. And had started digging without permission, igniting a storm that had engulfed even the church. Père Sébastien had sided with Renaud, to the fury of the Chief Archeologist.

Still, nothing had been found. No Champlain.

Though, strangely, that coffin had never been opened. All had agreed it couldn't possibly be Champlain. It was a rare show of respect for the dead, by the archeologists, by Renaud and by a church more than happy to dig up Général Montcalm but not this anonymous corpse.

So, Gamache thought as he continued his walk, suppose Champlain hadn't originally been buried in the chapel but in the graveyard. The records showing the exact resting place of the father of Québec had been lost in the fire, even the exact position of the cemetery was just a guess. But if it was beside the chapel that could put the cemetery right about—

Here.

Gamache stopped. Above him loomed the Château Frontenac and

off to the side Champlain himself, imposing and impossibly heroic, staring out across the city.

And in front of the Chief? The Old Homestead, now a restaurant.

Taking off his gloves he reached into his jacket and took out the sepia photo taken in 1869.

The Chief Inspector backed up a few paces, walked a couple to the right, then stopped. Looking from the photo to the reality and back again. His bare fingers were red and burning from the cold, but still he held the photo, to be sure.

Yes.

This was it, this was the exact spot where Patrick and O'Mara had stood 150 years earlier, on a sweltering summer day.

They'd been digging beneath the Old Homestead and something they found made the normally sullen men smile. Before it had been a restaurant the Homestead had been, as it sounded, a private home. And before that? It was a forest, or a field.

Or maybe, a graveyard.

The Old Homestead was now a greasy spoon. It had seen better days. Even bombardment by English cannons would have been better than what had become of it in recent years.

Waitresses, gamely wearing vaguely period costume, poured weak coffee into mass-produced white mugs. Hard, uncomfortable wooden chairs, made to look olde worlde, held tourists who'd hoped the charming exterior was a promise of a charming interior.

It wasn't.

Mugs with coffee slurping over the rims were placed in front of Émile and Gamache. They'd managed to get a banquette of worn red Naugahyde, rips and tears repaired with shiny silver duct tape.

Gamache caught Émile's eye. Both felt slightly ill as they looked at what had been done to a landmark. Old Quebec City had been fought over, the French valiantly defending their heritage, their *patrimoine*. They'd ripped it from the hands of the English time and again, only to ruin it themselves centuries later.

Still, it wasn't what was inside that mattered to them now. It wasn't even what was outside. What mattered to them was what lay beneath it. After ordering a simple breakfast of bacon and eggs the two men talked about the various theories. Their breakfast arrived, with a side order of home fries and baked beans. Surprisingly, the eggs were perfectly cooked, the bacon crispy and the *pain de ménage* actually homemade, warm and tasty. Once they'd finished and paid the waitress Gamache called her over again.

"I have one more request."

"What is it?"

She was impatient. She had her tip and needed to go work for another, and another and enough to put a modest roof over her head and feed her children. And these well-off men were delaying her, with their nice clothes and aromas of soap and something else.

Sandalwood, she recognized. It was a nice fragrance and the larger man had kind eyes, thoughtful eyes, and was smiling at her. Still, she couldn't pay the landlord with smiles, though God knows she'd tried. Couldn't feed her kids the kindness of strangers. She needed these men gone and new bums on the seats.

"Can we speak to the manager, please." Gamache saw her alarm and hastened to reassure her. "No complaints, not at all. We have a favor to ask. In fact, perhaps you could help too. Did you know Augustin Renaud?"

"The Champlain guy, the one who was killed? Sure."

"But did you know him personally?"

"What's that supposed to mean?"

"Did he ever come into the restaurant?"

"A few times. Everyone knew him. I waited on him once, a few weeks ago."

"Was he alone, or was someone else with him?"

"Always alone."

"Do you remember all your customers?" Émile asked and was treated to her scrutiny.

"Not all," she said dismissively. "Only the memorable ones. Augustin Renaud was memorable. A local celebrity."

"But he only started coming in recently?" asked Gamache.

"Last few weeks I guess. Why?"

"Did he ever speak to the manager?"

"You can ask her yourself." She pointed with the coffee pot to a young woman by the cash register.

Gamache gave her a twenty-dollar tip then they walked over to introduce themselves. The manager, a polite young woman, answered their questions. Yes, she remembered Augustin Renaud. Yes, he'd asked to see their basement. She'd been afraid he'd wanted to dig down there.

"Did you show it to him?" Émile asked.

"I did." Her eyes were wary, a naïve young woman afraid of doing the wrong thing and slowly realizing someone would always take exception.

"When was this?" Émile asked, his voice relaxed, disarming.

"A few weeks ago. Are you with the police?"

"We're helping with the investigation," said Gamache. "May we see your basement, please?"

She hesitated, but agreed. He was glad he didn't need to get a search warrant, or ask Émile to fake a stroke while he snuck down unseen.

The basement was low and once again they had to duck. The walls were cinder block and the floor was concrete. Boxes of wine and cases of beer were piled in cool corners, broken furniture was stacked in the back rooms.

Like skeletons, but not skeletons. There was no sign that this had ever been anything other than the basement of a dreary restaurant. Gamache thanked her and as she disappeared upstairs and Émile was halfway up, he paused.

"What is it?" Émile asked.

Gamache stood quietly. For all the fluorescent light, for the smell of beer and cardboard and cobwebs, for the weary feel of the place, Gamache wondered.

Could this have been it? Was this where Champlain had been buried? Émile came back down the stairs. "What is it?" he repeated.

"Can I speak to your Champlain Society?"

"Of course you can. We're meeting today at one thirty."

"Wonderful," said Gamache and headed for the stairs, energized. At the top, just before turning off the lights he looked down into the basement again.

"We meet in the room right beside the St-Laurent Bar, in the Château," Émile said.

"I didn't know there was such a room."

"Not many do. We know all the secrets."

Perhaps not all, thought Gamache as he snapped off the lights.

TWENTY-ONE

⌒

The men split up just outside the Old Homestead, with Émile going about his errands and Gamache turning right toward the Presbyterian church. He was tempted to go inside, to be in the calm interior and to speak with the young minister who had more to offer than he realized.

Gamache liked Tom Hancock. In fact, thinking about it as he walked, he liked everyone in this case. All the members of the Literary and Historical Society board, the members of the Champlain Society, he'd even liked, or at least understood, the Chief Archeologist.

And yet, one of them was almost certainly a murderer. One of them had taken a shovel to the back of Augustin Renaud's head, burying him in the basement in the hopes and expectation the body would be cemented over. If the phone line hadn't been severed Augustin Renaud might have disappeared as completely as Champlain.

Gamache paused for a moment to contemplate the façade of the Lit and His and think about the case.

Motive and opportunity, Beauvoir had said, and of course, he was right. A murderer had to have both a reason to kill and a chance to do it.

He'd been wrong in the Hermit case, had been blinded by the treasure, had seen just the façade of the case and had failed to see what was hiding beneath it.

Was he making the same mistake with this case? Was Champlain's grave the big, shiny, obvious motive, that was wrong? Maybe this had nothing to do with the search for the founder of Québec. But if not, what else was there? Renaud's life was consumed by only one thing, surely his death was too.

Walking up the steps he tried the door to the Lit and His only to discover it locked. He looked at his watch. It wasn't yet nine in the morning, of course it'd be locked. Now he was at a loss and, perversely, he felt even more strongly the need to get in.

Pulling out his phone he dialed. After the second ring a woman answered, her voice strong and clear.

"*Oui allô?*"

"Madame MacWhirter, it's Armand Gamache. *Désolé*, I hope I'm not disturbing you so early."

"Not at all, I was just sitting down to breakfast. What can I do for you?"

Gamache hesitated. "Well, it's a little embarrassing, but I'm afraid I've been overly ambitious with time. I'm outside the Literary and Historical Society but, of course, it's locked."

She laughed. "We've never had a member so anxious to get in. It's a novel experience. I have a key—"

"I don't want to disturb your breakfast."

"Well, you can't just stand on the stoop waiting, you'll freeze to death."

And Gamache knew that wasn't just a figure of speech. Every winter scores of people did just that. They were out in the cold too long, had exposed too much of themselves. And it killed them.

"Come over here, have a coffee and we'll head back together in a few minutes."

Gamache recognized a command when he heard it. She gave him her address, a home just around the corner on rue d'Auteuil.

When he arrived a couple minutes later he stood outside and marveled. It was as magnificent as he'd expected. In old Quebec City, "magnificent" wasn't measured in square feet, but in details. The blocks of gray stone, the carving over the doors and windows, the simple, clean lines. It was a gracious and elegant row of homes.

He'd walked up and down rue d'Auteuil many times in the past. It was a particularly beautiful street in a city thick with them. It followed the line of the old stone walls that defended the capital, but was set back, a ribbon of parkland between the street and the walls. And on the other side of the street, these homes.

This was where the first families of Québec lived, French and English. The *premier ministres,* the industrialists, the generals and archbishops, all lived in this row of elegant houses looking over the walls as though daring their enemies to attack.

Gamache had been to cocktail parties in some of the homes, a few receptions and at least one state dinner. But he'd never been into the one he stood in front of now. The stone was beautifully pointed, the wood painted, the iron work kept up and repaired.

As he stood on the stoop the door opened. He stepped in quickly, bringing the chill with him. It clung to him as he stood in the dark wood entrance but slowly the cold, like a cloak, slid off.

Elizabeth took his coat and he removed his boots. A neat rank of velvet slippers, some for men, some for women, was lined up in the entrance.

"Take whichever fits, if you'd like."

He found a pair and wondered how many feet, over how many generations, had used the slippers. They looked Edwardian and felt comfortable.

The walls were papered in a William Morris print, rich, ornate, beautiful. Gleaming mahogany panels went a third of the way up the walls.

On the fine wood floors Indian rugs were scattered.

"Follow me. I eat in the morning room."

He followed her into a bright and airy room, a fire lit in the hearth, bookcases along a wall, *jardinières* filled with healthy ferns and Christmas cacti. And a breakfast tray on a hassock in front of the fire. Toast and jam and two bone china coffee cups.

"May I?" she asked.

"Please."

She poured him a cup and he added a touch of cream and sugar. As he sat in a comfortable chair across from the sofa where she sat, he noticed books on the floor and three newspapers. *Le Devoir, Le Soleil* and the *Gazette.*

"What brings you to the Lit and His so early, Chief Inspector?"

"We're getting closer to knowing what the books were that Augustin Renaud got from your sale."

"That's a little awkward," she smiled slightly. "Our critics right. Most embarrassing. Did we sell books that should never have left us?"

Gamache looked into her eyes. They were steady, unwavering, dreading the answer, perhaps, but wanting to hear it anyway. As he watched her he noticed a few things, details that caught his eye. The faded and even frayed upholstery of the sofa and his own chair. A few floorboards heaved slightly, out of alignment. They could be easily nailed back to place. A handle missing from one of the doors of a cupboard.

"I'm afraid you did. They were Father Chiniquy's personal journals and diaries."

She closed her eyes but did not lower her head. When she opened them again a moment later her eyes were still steady but perhaps a little sad.

"Oh dear, that's not good news. The board will have to be told."

"They're evidence now but I suspect if you speak with Monsieur Renaud's widow she might sell them back at a reasonable price."

She looked relieved. "That would be wonderful. Thank you."

"But one is missing. From 1869."

"Really?"

"It was one of the books we were looking for, one of the books Augustin Renaud makes reference to in his own journals."

"Why 1869?"

"I don't know." And that was true, to a point. He actually had a very good idea why, but wasn't going to talk about it just yet.

"And the other book?"

"Missing too. We've found the lot it was bought with, but it could be anything." He put his cup down carefully on the tray. "Did you ever hear of a meeting in the Literary and Historical Society between Father Chiniquy, James Douglas and two Irish workers?"

"In the late 1800s?" She was surprised. "No. Irish workers you say?" Gamache nodded. She said nothing, but frowned.

"What is it?"

"It's just unlikely the Irish would have come to the Lit and His back then. Nowadays, yes, we have lots of members who are Irish. There isn't such a distinction, thank God. But I'm afraid back then there was a lot of animosity between the Irish and the English."

That was the weakness, Gamache knew, about New Worlds. People brought old conflicts.

"But feelings aren't so bad today?"

"No, with the passage of time things got better. Besides, we're too small, can't afford to fight."

"The lifeboat?" he smiled, picking up his coffee.

"You remember the analogy? Yes, that's exactly it. Who'd be foolish enough to rock a lifeboat?"

And what would the passengers do to keep the peace, wondered the Chief Inspector. He sipped his coffee and took in the room. It was faded and comfortable, a room he would choose to live in. Did she not notice, though, the worn fabric, the chipped paint? The small repairs adding up? He knew when people lived in a place for a long time, a lifetime, they stopped seeing it as it is, instead always seeing it as it was.

And yet, the outside of the home had been kept up. Painted, repaired.

"Speaking of small communities, do you know the Mundin family?"

"The Mundins? Yes, of course. He ran a successful antique shop on Petit-Champlain for years. Had beautiful things. I've taken a few things there."

Gamache looked at her quizzically.

"To sell, Chief Inspector."

It was said without flinching, without blushing, without apology. A statement of fact.

And he had his answer. She noticed everything but used her modest income to only repair the outside. The façade, the public face. The famous MacWhirter fortune had disappeared, become a fiction, one she chose to keep up.

This was a woman for whom appearances mattered, façades mattered. What would she be willing to do, to keep it in place?

"There was a tragedy, I hear," he said. "With the Mundin family."

"Yes, very sad. He killed himself one spring. Walked out onto the river and fell in. They called it an accident, but we all knew."

"Thin ice."

She smiled slightly. "Just so."

"And why did he do it, do you think?"

Elizabeth thought about it then shook her head. "I can't imagine. He seemed happy, but then things aren't always as they seem."

Like the gleaming paint, the pointed stones, the perfect exterior of this home.

"Had a couple of children though I only met the one. His son. Adorable, with curly blond hair. Used to follow his father everywhere. He had a nickname for him. Can't remember it now."

"Old."

"Pardon?"

" 'Old' was the nickname."

"Yes, that's right. 'Old son,' his father would say. I wonder what became of the boy."

"He lives in a village called Three Pines, making and restoring furniture."

"The things we learn from our parents," said Elizabeth with a smile.

"My father taught me the fiddle," said Agent Morin. "Did your father teach you an instrument?"

"No, though he used to love to sing. My father taught me poetry. We'd go for long walks through Outremont and onto Mont Royal, and he'd recite poetry. I'd repeat it. Not well, most of the words meant nothing to me, but I remembered it all, every word. Only later did I realize what it meant."

"And what did it mean?"

"It meant the world," said Gamache. "My father died when I was nine."

Morin paused. "I'm sorry. I can't imagine losing my father, even now. It must have been terrible."

"It was."

"And your mother? It must have been awful for her."

"She died too. It was a car accident."

"I'm sorry," said the voice, small now, in pain for the large man sitting comfortably in his office while the young agent was all alone, tied to a hard chair, strapped to a bomb, facing a wall with a clock.

Counting down. Six hours and twenty-three minutes left.

And on Gamache's computer the rapid instant messages from his team, covertly following leads.

It was clear now the young agent wasn't being held at the La Grande dam. Agent Nichol and Inspector Beauvoir couldn't pick up the sounds of the massive turbines. But they could pick up other sounds. Trains. Some freight according to Nichol. Some passenger. Planes overhead.

Agent Nichol stripped back layer after layer of sound. Isolating bits and pieces.

We can't trace the call because it's embedded, her message had said.

What does that mean? Gamache had written.

It's like a hobo, riding along on a telecommunication line. Popping up here and there. That's why he seems to be everywhere at once.

Can you find which line?

Not enough time, Nichol replied.

Six hours left. Then two things would happen, simultaneously. A bomb would destroy the biggest dam in North America. And Agent Paul Morin would be executed.

As the moments ticked down Chief Inspector Armand Gamache knew a terrible decision was racing toward them. A choice.

"Is Mundin's son happy?" Elizabeth asked.

It took Gamache a moment, a heart beat, to come back. "I think so. Has a son of his own. Charlie."

"Charlie," she smiled. "I always think it's nice when a child is named for a parent."

Elizabeth got up, clearing the breakfast things. Gamache carried the tray to the old kitchen.

"There's someone else I wanted to ask you about," said Gamache, drying the dishes. "Do you know Carole Gilbert?"

"As in Vincent Gilbert?"

"*Oui*," though he couldn't believe Madame Gilbert would like to be defined by her estranged and exacting husband.

"I knew her slightly, we belonged to the same bridge club. But I think she's moved away. Quebec City is quite small, Chief Inspector. And old Québec even smaller, within the walls."

"And social circles smaller still?" smiled the Chief.

"Exactly. Some defined by language, some by economics and social standing, some by common interests. And often they overlap, and most people belong to more than one circle of friends and acquaintances. Carole Gilbert was an acquaintance, of the bridge variety."

She smiled at him warmly as they walked to the front hall. "But why do you ask?"

They put on their heavy winter coats, boots, hats and scarves, so that by the time they were finished there wasn't all that much to distinguish the Chief Inspector of homicide for Québec from the seventy-five-year-old woman.

"There was a case a few months back, in a village called Three Pines. Carole Gilbert lives there now. So does Old Mundin."

"Really?" But she didn't seem all that interested. Polite, but hardly riveted. Heading out into the sunshine they walked side-by-side down the middle of the narrow streets. Ahead they could see the young mountaineers strapped and harnessed thirty feet above the ground. They labored all winter shoveling snow from the steep metal roofs. It was harrowing to watch as they swung their axes and picks, hacking away at the feet of ice and snow that had accumulated, threatening to collapse the roofs.

Every winter roofs did collapse and every winter snow and ice slid off to the sidewalk below, crushing unfortunate pedestrians. There was a sound sliding ice made, a sound like no other, a cross between a slow, deep moan and a shriek. Every Québécois knew it, like buzz bombs in the Blitz.

But hearing it, and being able to do anything were two different things. The sound echoed off the old stone buildings, disguising location. It might be right above you, or it might be streets away.

True Québécois walked in the middle of the road. Tourists often thought the Québécois gracious, to cede the sidewalk to them, until the sound began.

"Would they have known each other here in Quebec City?" he asked.

"It's possible. She might have bought some antiques from Monsieur Mundin, or sold some I suppose. She had marvelous things, as I remember. An old Québec family, you know."

"The Gilberts?"

"No, Madame Gilbert's family. The Woloshyns."

They were approaching the Literary and Historical Society.

"I always liked Carole. Very sensible," said Elizabeth as she brought out the key, warm from being carried in her glove. "It was a pleasure to play bridge with her. She'd never do anything foolish. Very patient, very calm, great strategist."

Once inside Gamache helped Elizabeth turn on the lights and turn up the heat, then she went to her office leaving the Chief Inspector alone in the magnificent library. He stood for a moment, like a miser at the bank. Then walking over to the circular iron staircase he hauled himself up. At the top he paused again. It was quiet, as only an old library can be and he was left alone with his thoughts.

"La Grande? Are you fucking kidding me?" Chief Superintendent Francoeur demanded.

Inspector Beauvoir had joined the Chief Inspector in his office, bringing with him the evidence he and Agent Nichol had collected. It was sparse, but enough. They thought. They hoped. Beauvoir had again taken the stairs two at a time, preferring to arrive unannounced, by the back way. From the stairwell door he'd once again seen the Chief Superintendent leading the search operations. Monitoring. Issuing orders. Giving every impression of doing his best.

And he probably was doing his best. But his best was not, Beauvoir knew, good enough.

He could hear over the speakers Chief Inspector Gamache talking about his days at Cambridge University. How he'd arrived with almost no English. Only the phrases he'd picked up off the English television programs beamed into Québec in the 1960s.

"Like what?" Paul Morin asked. His voice dragged, each word forced out.

"Fire on the Klingons," said the Chief Inspector.

Agent Morin laughed, perking up. "Did you actually say that to anyone?"

"Sadly, I did. It was either that or, 'My God, Admiral, it's horrible.'"

Now Agent Morin whooped with laughter and Beauvoir saw smiles on the faces of the men and women in the Incident Room, including Chief Superintendent Francoeur. Smiling himself Beauvoir turned his attention to the Chief Inspector.

Through the glass he saw the Chief. His eyes closed, gray stubble on his face. And then Gamache did something Beauvoir had never seen him do before. In all the years, all the cases, all the death and despair and exhaustion of past cases.

Chief Inspector Gamache lowered his head into his hands.

Just for a moment, but it was a moment Inspector Beauvoir would never forget. As young Paul Morin laughed, Chief Inspector Gamache covered his face.

Then he looked up, and met Inspector Beauvoir's eyes. And the mask reappeared. Confident. Energetic. In command.

Jean-Guy Beauvoir entered the Chief's office with the evidence. And at Gamache's request, invited Chief Superintendent Francoeur in and played him the tape.

"Are you fucking kidding?"

"Does it look like I'm kidding?"

The Chief was on his feet. He'd asked Paul Morin to carry the conversation, to keep speaking. And had whipped his headphone off, covering the microphone with his hand.

"Where'd you even get that recording?" Francoeur demanded. In the background Paul Morin was talking about his father's vegetable garden and how long it took to grow asparagus.

"It's background sound, from where Morin's being held," said Gamache.

"But where did you get it?" Francoeur was annoyed.

"It can't possibly matter. Are you listening?" Gamache replayed the fragment Agent Nichol had found. "They mention it two or three times."

"La Grande, yes I hear, but it could mean anything. It could be what they call whoever's behind the kidnapping."

"La Grande? As in La Grande Fromage? This isn't a cartoon." Gamache took a long breath and tried to control his frustration. On the speakers they could hear that Morin had moved on to a monologue on heirloom tomatoes.

"This is what I think, sir," said Gamache. "The kidnapping wasn't done by a frightened backwoods farmer with a marijuana crop. This was planned all along—"

"Yes, you've mentioned that before. There's no evidence."

"This is evidence." With a mighty effort Gamache stopped himself from shouting, instead lowering his voice to a growl. "The farmer has not left Morin alone as he said he would. In fact, not only is Morin clearly not alone, there're at least two, maybe three others with him."

"So, what? You think he's being held at the dam?"

"I did at first, but there're no turbine sounds in the background."

"Then what's your theory, Chief Inspector?"

"I think they're planning to blow the dam and they kidnapped Agent Morin to keep us occupied elsewhere."

Chief Superintendent Francoeur stared at Gamache. It was a scenario the Sûreté had practiced for, had protocols for. Dreaded. A threat against this mighty dam.

"You're delusional. Based on what? Two words barely heard far in the background. It might even be crossed wires. You think that in what"—Francoeur turned to look at the clock—"six hours someone's going to destroy the La Grande dam? And yet, they're not even there? They're sitting with your young agent somewhere else?"

"It's misdirection. They wa—"

"Enough," snapped Chief Superintendent Francoeur. "If it's misdirection it's one you've fallen for. They want you to hare off after a ridiculous clue. I thought you were smarter than that. And who are this mysterious 'they' anyway? Who'd want to destroy the dam? No, it's absurd."

"For God's sake, Francoeur," said Gamache, his voice low and hoarse with fatigue, "suppose I'm right?"

That stopped the Chief Superintendent as he made for the door. He turned and stared at Chief Inspector Gamache. In the long silence between the men they heard a small lecture on cow versus horse compost.

"I need more evidence."

"Agent Lacoste is trying to collect it."

"Where is she?"

Chief Inspector Gamache glanced quickly at Inspector Beauvoir. They'd dispatched Agent Lacoste two hours ago. To a remote Cree community. To the settlements closest to the great dam. Most affected by it going up. And most affected were it to suddenly, catastrophically, come down. There she'd been told to visit an elderly Cree woman Gamache had met years earlier. On a bench. Outside the Château Frontenac.

They'd hoped to have her evidence by now. To convince Chief Superintendent Francoeur to stop his high-tech search and lower his sights. To change course. To stop looking at the present and look to the past.

But so far, nothing from Agent Lacoste.

"I'm begging you, sir," said Gamache. "Just put a few people on it. Quietly alert security at the dam. See what the other forces might have."

"And look like a fool?"

"Look like a thorough commander."

Chief Superintendent Francoeur glared at Gamache. "Fine. I'll do that much."

He left and Gamache saw him speaking with his own second in command. While he suspected Francoeur of many things, the murder of tens of thousands of Québécois wasn't among them.

He slipped the headphones back on and rejoined Agent Morin, describing an argument he and his sister once had that resulted in fresh peas being thrown. His voice was once again slow, exhausted.

Gamache picked up the conversation, telling Morin about arguments between his own children, Daniel and Annie, when they were young. How Daniel was the more sensitive, more measured of the two. How Annie, young and bright, could always best her brother. And about the competition between them that had settled, with time, into a deep affection.

But as he spoke he knew two things.

In just under six hours, at 11:18, the La Grande Hydro Electric Dam would be blown up. And Agent Paul Morin would be executed. And Chief Inspector Gamache knew something else. If it was possible to stop only one of those acts, he knew which it would have to be.

"How's your friend?"

"Friend?" Gamache turned to see Elizabeth bringing a few books into the library and placing them on the "returns" cart.

"Monsieur Comeau," she said. "Émile." She leaned over the cart, sorting books, not looking at Gamache.

"Oh, he's fine. I'm seeing him in a few hours at the Château. There's a meeting of the Société Champlain."

"Interesting man," she said then left, leaving Gamache alone in the library once again. He waited until he heard her steps disappear then looked around at the acres of books. Where to start?

"Are you close? Are you going to make it?"

Fatigue had finally worn Morin down, so that his fear, contained for so long, boiled out through frayed nerves and down the telephone line.

"We'll make it. Trust me."

There was a pause. "Are you sure?" The voice was strained, almost squeaky.

"I'm sure. Are you afraid?"

There was no answer, just silence and then a keening.

"Agent Morin," said Gamache, standing up at his desk. He waited and still there was no reply, except the sound which said it all.

Gamache talked for a few minutes, soothing words about nothing in particular. About spring flowers and wrapping presents for his grand-children, about lunches at Leméac Bistro on rue Laurier and his father's favorite song. And in the background was a wailing, a sobbing and coughing, a howling as Agent Morin finally broke down. It surprised Gamache the young man had been able to hold his terror in so long.

But now it was out, and fled down the phone line.

Chief Inspector Gamache talked about skiing at Mont Saint-Rémy and Clara Morrow's art and Ruth Zardo's poetry and slowly, in the background, the howling became a sob and the sob became a shudder-ing breath and the breath became a sigh.

Gamache paused. "Are you afraid?" he asked again.

Outside the office, through the large glass window, the agents, ana-lysts, special investigators and Chief Superintendent Francoeur all stopped and stared at the Chief Inspector, and listened to the agent who had been so brave and was now falling apart.

Down in her dim studio Agent Yvette Nichol recorded it all and, glowing green, she listened.

"Are you with me, Agent Morin?"

"Yes sir." But the voice was small, uncertain.

"I will find you in time." Each word was said slowly, deliberately. Words made of rock and stone, firm words. "Stop imagining the worst."

"But—"

"Listen to me," the Chief commanded. "I know what you're doing. It's natural, but you must stop. You're imagining the clock reaching zero, imagining the bomb going off. Am I right?"

"Sort of." There was panting, as though Morin had run a race.

"Stop it. If you have to look ahead think about seeing Suzanne again, think about seeing your mother and father, think of the great stories you can bore your children with. Control your thoughts and you can control your emotions. Do you trust me?"

"Yes sir." The voice was stronger.

"Do you trust me, Agent Morin?" insisted the Chief.

"Yes sir." The voice more confident.

"Do you think I'd lie to you?"

"No sir, never."

"I will find you in time. Do you believe me?"

"Yes sir."

"What will I do?"

"You'll find me in time."

"Never, ever forget that."

"Yes sir." Agent Morin's voice was strong, as certain as the Chief Inspector's. "I believe you."

"Good." Gamache spoke and let his young agent rest. He talked about his first job, scraping gum off the Montreal Metro platforms and how he met Madame Gamache. He talked about falling in love.

Now there is no more loneliness.

As he spoke he followed all the instant messaging. The information. From Inspector Beauvoir and Agent Nichol as they isolated the recordings and reported on their findings. Sounds hidden in the background. Planes, birds, trains. Echoes. And things not heard. Cars and trucks.

Agent Lacoste finally reporting in from the Cree community. Leads she was following on the ground. Getting them closer to the truth.

He looked at the clock. Four hours and seventeen minutes left.

In his ear, in his head, Paul Morin talked about the Canadiens and their hockey season. "I think we finally have a shot at the cup this season."

"Yes," said Gamache. "I think we finally have a chance."

In the gallery of the Literary and Historical Society, Armand Gamache reached for the first book. Over the next few hours the library opened, the volunteers arrived and went about their work, Mr. Blake showed up and took his seat. A few other patrons appeared, found books, read periodicals, and left.

And all the while on the gallery the Chief Inspector pulled out books, examining them one at a time. Finally, just after noon he took his seat across from Mr. Blake. They exchanged pleasantries before both men subsided into their reading.

At one o'clock Armand Gamache rose, nodded to Mr. Blake then left, taking two books hidden in his satchel with him.

TWENTY-TWO

—

M yrna handed Clara a book.

"I think you'll like it. It's one of my favorites."

Clara turned it over. Mordecai Richler, *Solomon Gursky Was Here.*

"Is it good?"

"No, it's crap. I only sell crap here, and recommend it of course."

"So Ruth was right," said Clara. She tipped the book toward Myrna. "Thank you."

"Okay," said Myrna, sitting across from her friend. "Spill."

The woodstove was heating the bookstore and keeping the perpetual pot of tea warmed. Clara sipped from her favorite mug and read the back of the book as though she hadn't heard her friend.

"What's going on?" Myrna persisted.

Clara raised innocent eyes. "With what?"

Myrna gave her a withering look. "Something's up. I know you, what was all that at Dominique's yesterday after exercise class?"

"Sparkling conversation."

"It wasn't that." Myrna watched Clara. She'd been wanting to ask for several days, but the episode at the inn and spa convinced her.

Clara was up to something.

"Was it obvious?" Clara put the book down and looked at Myrna, her eyes worried.

"Not at all. I doubt anyone noticed."

"You did."

"True, but I'm very smart." Her smile faded and she leaned forward. "Don't worry, I'm sure no one else found it strange. But you were asking some unusual questions. Why were you talking about Jean-Guy and Olivier and all that?"

Clara hesitated. She hadn't expected to be asked and had no lie prepared. Foolish, really. What were her regular lies?

I'm busy that night. The art world's just too conservative to appreciate my work. The dog did it or, as a variation, it's Ruth's fault. That covered everything from smells, to missing food, to dirt through the house. To, sometimes, her art.

It didn't, however, seem to cover this.

"I think having the Inspector here just reminded me of Olivier, that's all."

"Bullshit."

Clara sighed. She'd really messed up. The one promise she'd made to Beauvoir she was about to break. "You can't tell anyone."

"I won't."

And Clara believed Myrna but then, Beauvoir had believed her. Oh well, his mistake.

"Inspector Beauvoir's not here to recover from his injuries. He came down to unofficially reopen Olivier's case."

Myrna smiled. "I'd hoped that might be it. The only other explanation was that you'd lost your mind."

"And you weren't sure which it was?"

"It's so hard to tell." Myrna's eyes were bright. "This is the best news. So they think maybe Olivier didn't kill the Hermit? But then, who did?"

"That's the question. Seems it comes down to Roar, Havoc, Marc, Vincent or Old Mundin. And I have to say, what The Wife said about killing was pretty strange."

"That's true," said Myrna. "But—"

"But if she or Old were really involved she'd never have talked about killing. She'd have kept quiet."

"There you are."

The two women looked up with a guilty start. Inspector Beauvoir was standing in the doorway that connected the bookstore to the bistro.

"I was looking for you." He gave them a mighty frown. "What're you talking about?"

Unlike Gamache, who could make an interrogation sound like a pleasant conversation, Beauvoir managed to make niceties sound like accusations.

Though, both women knew, he had good reason.

"Tea?" Myrna offered and busied herself pouring another cup and putting more hot water and another bag into the Brown Betty on the woodstove. This left Clara trying not to catch Beauvoir's eye. He sat beside Clara and glared at her.

The dog did it, the dog did it.

"I told Myrna everything." Clara paused. "It's Ruth's fault."

"Everything?" Beauvoir lowered his voice.

"So, I hear we still have a murderer among us," said Myrna, handing the mug to Beauvoir and taking her seat.

"Just about," said Clara.

Beauvoir shook his head. Still, it wasn't perhaps unexpected, nor was it necessarily a bad thing. Myrna had helped the Chief in the past and while Beauvoir had never, until now, wanted to ask for help from the villagers he suspected they actually had some to give. And now he had no choice.

"So what do you think?" he asked.

"I'd like to hear more. Have you found out anything new?"

He told them about his conversation with Gamache and what the chief had found out in Quebec City about Old Mundin's family and Carole Gilbert.

"Woloshyn?" Clara repeated. "Woo?"

"Perhaps," Beauvoir nodded.

"The inn and spa has a lot of antiques," said Myrna. "Could they have found them on rue Notre-Dame?"

"In the same store where Olivier sold the Hermit's things?" said Beauvoir. "You're thinking if they went in, they might have recognized some of Olivier's items?"

"Exactly," said Myrna. "All Carole Gilbert would have to do is casually ask how the owner got them. He would have directed her to Olivier and Three Pines, and *voilà*."

"No, it doesn't work," said Beauvoir.

"Of course it does. It's perfect," said Clara.

"Think about it," Beauvoir turned to her. "Olivier sold those things to the antique shop years ago. If Carole Gilbert found them why'd they wait almost ten years to buy the old Hadley house?"

The three sat there, thinking. Eventually Clara and Myrna started batting around other theories, but Beauvoir remained lost in his own thoughts.

Of names. Of families. And of patience.

Armand Gamache folded back the sleeve of his parka so that he could see his watch.

Quarter past one. A little early for the meeting. He dropped his arm over the satchel, protecting it.

Instead of heading straight in to the Château Frontenac he decided to stroll along the Dufferin Terrace, the long wooden boardwalk that swept in front of the hotel and overlooked the St. Lawrence River. In the summer it was filled with ice cream carts and musicians and people relaxing in the pergolas. In the winter a bitter damp wind blew down the St. Lawrence River and hit pedestrians, stealing their breaths and practically peeling the skin off their faces. But still people walked along the outdoor *terrasse*, so remarkable was the view.

And there was another attraction. *La glissade*. The ice slide. Built every winter it towered above the promenade. As he turned the corner of the Château the wind hit Gamache's face. Tears sprung to his eyes and froze. Ahead, midway along the *terrasse*, he could see the slide, three lanes wide with stairs cut into the snow at the side.

Even on this brittle day kids were lugging their rented toboggans up the steps. In fact, the colder the day the better. The ice would be keen and the toboggans would race down the steep slope, shooting off the end. Some toboggans were going so fast and so far pedestrians on the *terrasse* had to leap out of their way.

As he watched he noticed it wasn't just kids climbing to the top, but adults as well including a few young couples. It was as effective as a scary movie to get a hug, and he remembered clearly coming to the slide with Reine-Marie early in their relationship. Climbing to the top, dragging the long toboggan with them, waiting their turn. Gamache, deathly afraid of heights, was still trying to pretend otherwise with this girl who'd stolen his heart so completely.

"Would you like me to sit in front?" she'd whispered as the people in front of them shoved off and plummeted down the slide.

He'd looked at her, a protest on his lips, when he realized here was a person he needn't lie to, needn't pretend with. He could be himself.

Their toboggan hurtled toward the Dufferin Terrace below, though it looked as though they were heading straight into the river. Armand Gamache shrieked and clutched Reine-Marie. At the bottom they laughed so hard he thought he'd ruptured something. He never did it again. When they'd brought Daniel and Annie it had been their mother who'd taken them while Dad waited at the bottom with the camera.

Now Chief Inspector Gamache stood and watched the kids, the couples, an elderly man and woman walk up the narrow snow steps and then shoot back down.

It comforted him slightly to hear that they too screamed. And laughed.

As he watched he heard another shout but this wasn't from the direction of the ice slide. This came from over the side of the terrace, from the river.

He wasn't the only one to notice. A few people drifted to the handrail. Gamache walked over and wasn't surprised to see teams of canoeists out on the ice practicing. The race was Sunday, two days away.

"Stroke, stroke," came the command. While there were three boats out there, only one voice was heard, loud and clear.

"Left, stroke, left, stroke." An English voice.

Gamache strained but couldn't make out which boat it was, nor did he recognize the voice. It wasn't Tom Hancock. Nor did he think it was likely to be Ken Haslam. A telescope was available, and though it was all but frozen, as was he, Gamache put some money in and trained it on the river.

Not the first boat.

Not the second, though he could see the leader's mouth moving he couldn't hear the words.

He trained the telescope on the furthest boat. Surely not. Not from so far away. Was it possible the piercing voice had traveled this far?

The boat was way out there in the middle of the river, six men sitting down, rowing. The boats could be paddled or rowed, could be in water or dragged over ice. This team was just clearing open water and heading upstream toward an ice floe.

"Stroke, stroke," came the command again. And now, because the racers were heading forward but facing backward, Gamache could see who it was.

He stared through the lens, not daring to touch his forehead to the metal telescope in case it froze there.

The booming, clear voice belonged to Ken Haslam.

Walking back to the Château, Gamache thought about that. Why would a man whisper all through his life, in every circumstance but be able, in fact, to shout?

Louder than anyone else out there. His voice had been piercing.

Was Haslam as surprised as Gamache? Had Haslam, in his sixty-eighth year, found his voice on the ice of Québec, doing something few others would attempt?

It was always a relief to get indoors, and even more wonderful when that indoors was the Château Frontenac. In the magnificent front lobby Gamache took off his mitts, coat, hat and scarf and checked them. Then, still protecting his satchel with his arm, he walked down the long, wide corridor to the double glass doors at the far end, with the light streaming through.

Inside the St-Laurent Bar he paused. Ahead of him was the circular wooden bar and around it tables and the huge windows. Open fires roared in the two hearths.

But this wasn't where he was expected.

Glancing to his right Gamache was surprised to see a door, one he'd never noticed before. Opening it he walked into a bright and airy side room, almost a solarium, with its own lit fireplace.

Whoever had been talking stopped as he entered. A dozen faces looked at him. All elderly, all white, all male. They were seated on the comfortable floral sofas and in wing chairs and armchairs. He'd been expecting something more formal, a boardroom, a long table, a lectern.

He'd also been expecting that the meeting wouldn't have started. It was 1:25. Émile had said they started at 1:30 but it seemed clear the meeting was well under way.

Gamache glanced at Émile, who smiled then broke eye contact.

"*Bonjour*," said the Chief Inspector. "I hope I'm not disturbing you."

"Not at all." René Dallaire, as large and affable as the last time they met, greeted him. Others got to their feet as well. Gamache made the rounds, shaking hands, smiling greetings.

Everyone was cordial, pleasant, and yet he had the impression there was tension in the room, as though he'd interrupted an argument.

"Now, you wanted to speak with us?" Monsieur Dallaire said, indicating a large chair.

"Yes. It will come as no surprise that it's about the death of Augustin Renaud." Gamache sat down. There were sympathetic nods from some, others just stared, wary. While this wasn't exactly a secret society, it did seem secretive.

"Actually, I'd like to start off by talking about Charles Chiniquy."

That brought the reaction he was expecting. A few sat up in their seats, more than a few looked at each other then back to Gamache with some annoyance.

Once again René Dallaire took the lead. "Forgive me, Monsieur Gamache, but you do realize we're not a general historical society?"

"*Oui, merci*, I know that you're the Société Champlain." As he said it something twigged. The Société Champlain. "But my story begins neither with Samuel de Champlain nor with Augustin Renaud, but somewhere in between. In 1869, to be exact, with Father Chiniquy."

"He was a nut," one elderly man said from the back.

"So you do know him," said Gamache. "Yes, he was a nut to some, a hero to others. He was something else entirely in our story."

Gamache glanced at Émile, who was looking out the window. Distancing himself from what was about to happen? Gamache wondered.

"Father Chiniquy was famous for one thing," said the Chief. "He wanted to save alcoholics. To do that he went to where he'd find them. In the Québec of the 1860s that was rue du Petit-Champlain, directly below us."

Indeed, if he could throw himself out that window with enough force he'd sail over the Dufferin Terrace and land on rue du Petit-Champlain below. Now a charming, cobbled street filled with lace stores and cafés and tourist shops, but back then it was the notorious Basse-Ville. Filled with drunks and blackguards and prostitutes, filled with sewage and disease.

Filled with poor French workers and Irish immigrants. And a fallen priest determined to save them and maybe himself.

"One summer's evening Chiniquy was in a bar scouting souls when he overheard a conversation between two Irishmen. Patrick and O'Mara. They'd been hired as diggers in the Upper Town to hack out a basement under an old building. There were more than twenty laborers on the site, but it was Patrick and O'Mara who made the discovery. They found something they believed might be valuable."

Despite themselves the members of the Société Champlain had grown interested. A few still looked annoyed and impatient but even they were listening. Only Émile continued to stare out the window.

What was he thinking? Gamache wondered. Did he see what was coming, know what was coming?

But it didn't matter. It was too late.

"Chiniquy listened to the two men and as he listened he grew more interested. Finally he joined them. The men, knowing who Chiniquy was, weren't overly welcoming at first but once the priest offered to buy them drinks they warmed up. And after a few more drinks they told him what they'd found.

"It was a coffin. At first Chiniquy was disappointed. Old Quebec City was practically built on coffins, built on bones. Not finding one would have been unusual. Surely these workers knew that. But this one was different, they said, it was heavy.

"The two men figured this was not only unusual but perhaps even valuable. They'd dragged it from the work site down the hill to Patrick's home. His wife refused to have it inside. He insisted, but knew he couldn't keep it there for long. The home was little more than a shack, and already crowded with Patrick, his wife and six kids. Now there was also a dead man."

Gamache examined his audience. They were all listening now, including Émile. They could see the scene, as could Gamache. The trampled and discouraged Irish woman. Having survived the harrowing voyage to her New World, she'd found it even worse than the humiliation and famine she'd fled and, as though life wasn't difficult enough, her husband had brought a corpse home from work.

"The men set about opening it, carefully prying the sealed lid off," Gamache continued the story. "Imagining why it was so heavy. It must, they felt, be filled with gold, with jewelry, with silver. This must be the coffin of a very rich person. But once opened, they were sorely disappointed. There was nothing inside except a ratty old book, a bible, and some remains. Bones and bits of clothing. It was heavy because it was lead-lined."

There was a small stir in the room. Did they know where this was headed?

"Patrick and O'Mara had been in the bar discussing how best to strip the lead, sell it then dump the body into the river, the bible with it. They couldn't read, so it was useless. Chiniquy asked to see the bible. At that stage the men grew wary. Then the priest tried another tack. If they would bring the coffin and the bible to the Literary and Historical Society the next night, Chiniquy could promise them a small reward.

"Why? the men had asked.

"Because they collect everything historic, especially books. This coffin might be old, Chiniquy reasoned.

"Patrick and O'Mara were already half drunk and didn't really care. If there was money they'd be there. The next night they showed up and were met by Father Chiniquy and another man. James Douglas."

"Is there a point to this?" one of the members of the Société Champlain asked.

"Please, Benoît," René Dallaire looked pained. "Civility."

"I'll be civil when he stops wasting my time."

"There is a point, *monsieur*, and we're almost there," said Gamache. He could feel his phone buzzing but couldn't very well look at it now. "I'm sure you've heard of Dr. Douglas?"

There were nods.

"He opened the coffin and examined the contents while Father Chiniquy looked at the bible. Then James Douglas made a mistake. He offered Patrick and O'Mara five hundred dollars each. Chiniquy was furious, but said nothing. The workers immediately knew something was up. That was a small fortune, way too much for the remains of some long-dead guy and a ratty old bible.

"They refused, insisting on one thousand dollars each, and they got it but only after Douglas had secured their pledge of secrecy and found out where they lived. The Irishmen, who hated the English, also feared them. They knew what lay behind the civilized veneer. They knew what an Englishman was capable of, if crossed. Patrick and O'Mara agreed, then carried the coffin to the basement and left."

His phone buzzed again. Still Gamache ignored it.

"How do you know all this?" someone asked.

"Because I found this."

Gamache bent down to his satchel and removed a black leather book. As he held it he looked at Émile who looked surprised, and something else. Was that a small smile? A grin or a grimace?

"It's Father Chiniquy's journal for the year 1869. Augustin Renaud found it and recognizing its significance he hid it."

"Where was it?" Émile asked.

"The library of the Literary and Historical Society," said Gamache, staring at his mentor.

"Augustin Renaud hid the journal in a library?" asked René Dallaire.

"No," clarified Gamache. "His murderer did."

"Why're you telling us all this?" Jean Hamel, slender and contained and sitting next to René Dallaire as always, asked.

"I think you know why," said Gamache, looking the man directly in the eyes until Hamel lowered his.

"Where did you say the Irish workers were digging?" a member asked.

"I didn't, but I can tell you. It was under the Old Homestead."

The room grew very quiet. Everyone stared at Gamache.

"You found the other book, didn't you," said Émile into the silence.

"I did."

Gamache reached into the satchel, now on his lap. The satchel he'd spent the last few hours protecting.

"Last year the Literary and Historical Society sold a number of boxes of books, boxes they hadn't bothered to examine. Augustin Renaud bought some of them. When he went to see what he had he found they were from the collection of Father Charles Chiniquy. Not very promising, for a Champlain scholar—"

The use of the word "scholar" brought some harrumphs.

"—so he didn't hurry to read them. But eventually, scanning them, he came across something extraordinary. He made mention of it in his own diary, but in true Renaud fashion he was"—Gamache searched for the word—"guarded."

"Don't you mean demented?" asked Jean Hamel. "Nothing he said or wrote can be trusted."

"No, I mean guarded. And he was quite right. What he'd found was staggering."

Gamache withdrew another black leather book. This one was larger, thicker than the first. Frayed and brittle, but in good condition. It had not seen the sun for hundreds of years then, dug up, it had sat anonymously on the bookshelves of Father Chiniquy's home for thirty years until his death.

"This," Gamache held up the book, "was Father Chiniquy's secret, and in the end the secret had died with him so that when his housekeeper packaged up his books and sent them to the Lit and His more than a century ago, no one knew what treasures they contained.

"In reading Chiniquy's journals Augustin Renaud found the report of the fateful encounter one July evening in 1869. And among the many religious books, the hymnals, the sermons, the family bibles in the box of used books he found this."

Gamache laid his large hand on the plain leather cover, barely recognizable for what it was.

Once again his phone buzzed. It was his private line. Few knew the number, but it hadn't stopped ringing for the past ten minutes.

"May I?" Émile reached out.

"Oui." Gamache stood and handed the book to his mentor and watched as Émile did exactly what he himself had done an hour earlier. Exactly what he imagined Augustin Renaud had done a month ago. What Father Chiniquy had done a century ago.

Émile opened the simply tooled leather book to the inscription page.

There was a sharp intake of breath then Émile sighed and with the sigh two words escaped. "Bon Dieu."

"Yes," said the Chief. "Good God."

"What is it?" Jean Hamel asked, stepping out from the convenient shadow of his friend René. It was clear now who was the real leader of the Société Champlain.

"They'd found Champlain," said Émile, staring at Gamache. It wasn't a question, it was beyond question. "It was Champlain's coffin the Irish workers found beneath the Old Homestead."

"Ridiculous," said the ornery member. "What would Champlain be doing buried under the Old Homestead? We all know he was either buried in the chapel, which burned, or in the cemetery, not hundreds of yards away in a field."

"Champlain was a Huguenot," said Émile, his voice barely audible. "A Protestant." He held out the book. A bible.

"But that's impossible," snapped Jean. There was a hubbub of agreement. Hands snatched at the bible and the uproar subsided as it made the rounds and the men saw the evidence.

Samuel de Champlain, inscribed in ink. The date, *1578*.

It was an original Huguenot bible, a rare find. Most had been destroyed in the various Inquisitions, burned along with their owners. It was a dangerous book, to the church and to whoever possessed it.

Champlain must have been a devout man indeed to have kept such a thing, and to have been buried with it.

The room was quiet, just the mumbling and crackling of the fire. Gamache took the bible back and replacing it in his satchel along with Chiniquy's journal he said, *"Excusez-moi,"* to the group lost in their own thoughts, and left the room.

Outside he took the call and noticed there'd been twenty-seven calls from a variety of people. Reine-Marie, his son Daniel and daughter Annie. From Superintendents Brunel and Francoeur and Agent Isabelle Lacoste. From various friends and colleagues, and from Jean-Guy Beauvoir whose call was now coming in.

"Bonjour, Jean-Guy. What's happened?"

"Chief, where've you been?"

"In a meeting, what's going on?"

"There's a video, gone viral on the Internet. I just heard about it from Peter Morrow, then Lacoste called and a few friends. More calls are coming in. I haven't seen it yet."

"What is it?" But even as he asked he could guess, and felt a sickening feeling in his stomach.

"It's from the tapes, the ones recorded at the raid."

Everyone had worn tiny cameras integrated into their headsets, to record what happened. Investigators had long realized a verbal debrief wasn't enough. Even well-intentioned cops would forget details, especially in the heat of the moment, and if things went badly, as they often did, cops could stop being "well intentioned" and start lying.

This made lying harder, though not impossible.

Each camera showed what each officer saw, and what each officer did, and what each officer said. And, like any film, it could be edited.

"Chief?" Beauvoir asked.

"I see." He felt like Beauvoir sounded. Upset, suddenly exhausted, bewildered that anyone would do this and that anyone would want to see such a thing. It was a violation, especially for the families. His officers' families.

"I'll call," he said.

"I can, if you'd like."

"No, *merci*. I'll do it."

"Who would do this?" Beauvoir asked. "Who even has access to the tapes?"

Gamache lowered his head. Was it possible?

He'd been told there were three gunmen. But there'd been more, many more. Gamache had assumed it was a mistake. Dreadful, but unintentional.

He'd doubled the number of suspects, and assumed instead of three there were six.

Knowing that to be on the safe side.

He'd been wrong.

He'd brought six agents with him. Chosen them. Handpicked. And he'd brought Inspector Beauvoir. But not Agent Yvette Nichol. She'd stood there, her tactical vest already on. Her pistol on her belt. Her eyes keen. She would go with them into the factory. The place she'd found by following the sounds. By listening more closely than she'd ever listened in her life.

To the trains. To their frequency. To their cadence. Freight trains. A passenger train. A plane overhead. A hoot in the background. A factory.

And whispers. Ghosts in the background.

Three of them, she'd said.

With Inspector Beauvoir's furious help they'd narrowed and narrowed. Winnowed, whittled. Pored over train timetables, over flight paths, over factories old enough to still use whistles.

Until they knew where Agent Paul Morin was being held.

But there was another goal. The La Grande dam. To save the young agent would be to alert the suspects that their plot against the dam had been discovered. And if they realized that they might destroy it right away, before the tactical squad could be moved into place.

No. A choice had to be made. A decision had to be made.

Gamache could see Agent Nichol standing by the door. Ready. And her rage when told his decision.

"Are you going to watch?" Beauvoir asked.

Gamache thought. "Yes. You?"

"Maybe." He also paused. "Yes." There was a silence as both men considered what that meant. "Oh, God," sighed Beauvoir.

"When you do, don't be alone," said Gamache.

"I wish—"

"So do I," said Gamache. They both wished the same thing. That if they had to relive it, they could at least be together.

Sitting heavily in one of the leather wing chairs of the St-Laurent Bar, Chief Inspector Gamache asked for a glass of water and called Reine-Marie.

"I was trying to get you." She sounded stressed, upset.

"I know, I'm sorry, I've been in a meeting. Jean-Guy just told me. How did you hear?"

"Daniel called from Paris. A colleague told him. Then Annie called. It apparently appeared about noon and has gone wild. Journalists have been calling for the past half hour. Armand, I'm so sorry."

He heard the strain in her voice and he could have happily killed whoever had done this. Forcing Reine-Marie to relive it, forcing Annie and Daniel and Enid Beauvoir. And worse. The families of those who died.

He wanted to reach down the line and hold Reine-Marie, hug her to him. Rock her and tell her it would be all right, that this was just a phantom from the past. The worst was over.

But was it?

"When will you be home?"

"By tomorrow."

"Who would do this, Armand?"

"I don't know. I need to watch it, but you don't. Can you wait until I come home? If you still want to see it we can watch together."

"I'll wait," she said. She could wait.

She remembered fragments of that day. Armand hadn't been home. Isabelle Lacoste had contacted her and explained the Chief was working on a case and couldn't even, in fact, speak with her. Not for a day.

She'd never gone twenty-four hours without hearing her husband's voice. Not once, in more than thirty years together. Then, next morning, at just after noon a coworker at the Bibliotheque Nationale arrived at work, her face stricken.

A bulletin on Radio-Canada. A shootout. Officers of the Sûreté among the dead, including a senior homicide officer. The race to the hospital, not listening to the reports. Too afraid. The world had collapsed to this imperative. To get there. To get there. Get there. Seeing Annie in the emergency room, just arrived.

The radio said Dad—

I don't want to hear it.

Comforting each other. Comforting Enid Beauvoir, Jean-Guy's wife, in the waiting room. And others arriving she didn't know. The grotesque pantomime, strangers comforting each other while secretly, desperately, shamefully praying the other will be the one with bad news.

A paramedic appearing through the swinging doors from the emergency room, looking at them, looking away. Blood on his uniform. Annie grabbing her hand.

Among the dead.

The doctor, taking them aside, away, separating them from the rest. And Reine-Marie, light-headed, steeling herself to hear the unbearable. And then those words.

He's alive.

She didn't really take in the rest. Chest wound. Head wound. Pneumothorax. A bleed.

He's alive was all she needed to know. But there was another.

Jean-Guy? she'd asked. Jean-Guy Beauvoir?

The doctor hesitated.

You must, tell us, Annie said, far more insistent than Reine-Marie expected.

Shot in the abdomen. He's in surgery now.

But he'll be all right? Annie demanded.

We don't know.

My father, you said a bleed, what does that mean?

From the head wound, a bleed into his head, the doctor had said. A stroke.

Reine-Marie didn't care. He's alive. And she repeated that to herself now as she had every hour of every day since. It didn't matter what the damned video showed. He's alive.

"I don't know what could be on it," Gamache was saying. And that was the truth. He'd forced himself to remember, for the inquiry, but mostly what he was left with were impressions, the chaos, the noise, the shouting and screams. And gunmen, everywhere. Far more than expected.

The rapid gunshots. Concrete, wood exploding from the bullets all around. Automatic weapons fire. The unfamiliar feel of his tactical vest. An assault weapon in his hands. The people in his sights. The report as he fired. Aiming to kill.

Scanning for gunmen, issuing orders. Keeping order even in the storm.

Seeing Jean-Guy fall. Seeing others fall.

He woke at night with those images, those sounds. And that voice.

"I'll find you in time. Trust me."

"I do. I believe you, sir."

"I'll be home tomorrow," Gamache said to Reine-Marie.

"Be careful."

That was also something she never said before. Before all this happened. She'd thought it, he knew, every time he left for work, but never said it. But now she said it.

"I will. I love you." He hung up, pausing to gather himself. In his pocket he felt the bottle of pills. His hand went to it, closing over it.

He closed his eyes.

Then taking his empty hand from his pocket he started calling the officers who'd survived, and the families of those who hadn't.

He talked to their mothers, their fathers, their wives and a husband.

In the background he could hear a young child asking for milk. Over and over he called, and listened to their rage, their pain, that someone could release a video of this event. Not once did they blame him, though Armand Gamache knew they could.

"Are you all right?"

Gamache looked up as Émile Comeau lowered himself into the seat opposite.

"What's happened?" Émile asked, seeing the look on Gamache's face.

Gamache hesitated. For the first time in his life he was tempted to lie to this man who had lied to him.

"Why did you say the Société Champlain meets at one thirty when it clearly meets at one?"

Émile paused. Would he lie again? Gamache wondered. But instead the man shook his head.

"I'm sorry about that Armand. There were things we needed to discuss before you came. I thought it was better."

"You lied to me," said Gamache.

"It was just half an hour."

"It was more than that, and you know it. You made a choice, chose a side."

"A side? Are you saying the Champlain Society is on a different side than you?"

"I'm saying we all have loyalties. You've made yours clear."

Émile stared. "I'm sorry, I should never have lied to you. It won't happen again."

"It already has," said Gamache getting to his feet and putting down a hundred dollars for the water and the use of the quiet table by the fireplace. "What did Augustin Renaud say to you?"

Émile got to his feet too. "What do you mean?"

"SC in Renaud's journals. I'd taken it to mean an upcoming meeting with someone, maybe Serge Croix. A meeting he'd never make because he was murdered. But I was wrong. SC was the Société Champlain, and the meeting was for today at one. Why did he want to meet the Society?"

Émile stared, stricken, but said nothing.

Gamache turned and strode down the long corridor, his phone buzzing again and his heart pounding.

"Wait, Armand," he heard behind him but kept walking, ignoring the calls. Then he remembered what Émile had meant to him and still did. Did this one bad thing wipe everything else out?

That was the danger. Not that betrayals happened, not that cruel things happened, but that they could outweigh all the good. That we could forget the good and only remember the bad.

But not today. Gamache stopped.

"You're right. Renaud wanted to meet with us," said Émile, catching up to Gamache as he retrieved his parka from the coat check. "He said he'd found something. Something we wouldn't like but he was willing to bury, if we gave him what he wanted."

"And what was that?"

"He wanted to join the Société and have all the credibility that went with it. And when the coffin was found he wanted us to admit he'd been right all along."

"That was all?"

"That's it."

"And did you give it to him?"

Émile shook his head. "We decided not to meet him. No one believed he'd actually found Champlain, and no one believed he'd found anything compromising. It was felt that having Augustin Renaud in the Société would cheapen it. He was blackballed."

"An elderly man comes to you wanting acceptance, just acceptance, and you turn him away?"

"I'm not proud of it. That's what we needed to discuss privately. I wanted them to tell you everything and said if they didn't I would. I'm so sorry Armand. I made a mistake. It's just that I knew it couldn't matter to the investigation. No one believed Renaud. No one."

"Someone did. They killed him."

The meeting of the Société Champlain had been filled with elderly Québécois men. And what held them together as a club? Certainly their fascination with Champlain and the early colony, but did that explain a lifetime's loyalty? Was it more than that?

Samuel de Champlain wasn't simply one more explorer, he was the Father of Québec, and as such he'd become a symbol for the Québécois of greatness. And freedom. Of New Worlds and new countries.

Of sovereignty. Of separation from Canada.

Gamache remembered the extremes of the late 1960s. The bombs, the kidnappings, the murders. All done by young separatists. But the young separatists of the 1960s became elderly separatists, who joined societies and sat in genteel lounges and sipped aperitifs.

And plotted?

Samuel de Champlain was found and found to be a Protestant. What would the church make of that? What would the separatists make of that?

"How did you find the books?" Émile asked, dropping his eyes to the bag at Gamache's side.

"It was his satchel. Why carry it just for a small map? There must have been something else in it. Then when we couldn't find the books I realized he probably kept them with him. Augustin Renaud would have refused to let them out of his possession, even for a moment. He must have taken them to the Literary and Historical Society when he met his murderer. But they weren't on his body. That meant the killer must have taken them. And done what?"

Émile's eyes narrowed, his mind moving along the path Armand had laid out. Then he smiled. "The murderer couldn't take them home with him. If they were found in his possession they'd incriminate him."

Gamache watched his mentor.

"He could have destroyed them, I suppose," Émile continued, thinking it through. "Thrown them into a fireplace, burned the books. But he couldn't bring himself to do that. So what did he do?"

The two men stared at each other in the crowded hall of the hotel. People swirled around them like a great river, some bundled against the cold, some in formal wear off to a cocktail party. Some in the color-ful, traditional sashes of the Carnaval, *les ceinture fléchée*. All ignoring the two men, standing stock-still in the current.

"He hid them in the library," said Émile, triumphantly. "Where else? Hide them among thousands of other old, leather, unread, unap-preciated volumes. So simple."

"I spent this morning looking and finally found them," said Gamache.

The two men walked out of the Château, gasping as the cold hit their faces.

"You found the books, but what happened to Champlain?" Émile asked, blinking his eyes against the freezing cold. "What did James Douglas and Chiniquy do with him?"

"We're about to find out."

"The Lit and His?" Émile asked, as they turned left past the old stone buildings, past the trees with cannonballs still lodged in them, past the past they both loved. "But why didn't the Chief Archeologist find Champlain when he looked a few days ago?"

"How do you know he didn't?"

TWENTY-THREE

———

When the Chief Inspector and Émile Comeau arrived at the Literary and Historical Society, Elizabeth, Porter Wilson, tiny Winnie the librarian and Mr. Blake were assembled in the entrance hall, waiting.

"What's going on?" Porter launched right into it before Gamache and Émile had even closed the door behind them. "The Chief Archeologist is back with some technicians and that Inspector Langlois is also there. He's ordered us to stay away from our own basement."

"Had you planned to go down there?" Gamache asked, taking off his coat.

"Well, no."

"Do you need to go down there?"

"No, not at all." The two men stared at each other.

"Oh, for God's sake, Porter, this is embarrassing," said Elizabeth. "Let the men do their work. But," she turned to Armand Gamache, "we would appreciate some information. Whatever you can give us."

Gamache and Émile exchanged glances. "We think Augustin Renaud might have been right," said the Chief Inspector.

"About what?" snapped Porter.

"Don't be a fool," said Mr. Blake. "About Champlain, what else?" When Gamache nodded Mr. Blake frowned. "You believe Samuel de Champlain is in our basement and has been all this time?"

"For the last 140 years anyway, yes. *Pardon*."

The men squeezed past the gathering and made their way through the now familiar halls to the trap door into the first basement, then down another steep metal ladder to the final level.

Through the floorboards of the level above they could see glaring light, as though the sun was imprisoned down there. But once down they recognized it for what it was, a series of brilliant industrial lamps trained, once again, on the dirt and stone basement.

The Chief Archeologist was standing in the center of the room, his long arms hugging his chest perhaps trying, unsuccessfully, to contain his anger. The same two technicians who'd accompanied him before were there again, as was Inspector Langlois, who immediately took Gamache aside.

"I can explain," Gamache began before being interrupted.

"I know you can, it's not that. Let Croix stew for a while, he's an asshole anyway. Have you heard?"

Langlois searched the Chief Inspector's face.

"About the video? *Oui.* But I haven't seen it." Now it was Gamache's turn to examine his companion. "Have you?"

"Yes. Everyone has."

It was, of course, an exaggeration but not, perhaps, by much. He continued to examine Langlois's face for clues. Was there a hint of pity?

"I'm sorry this has happened, sir."

"Thank you. I'll be watching it later this afternoon."

Langlois paused, as though he wanted to say something, but didn't. Instead he turned swiftly to look back at the Chief Archeologist.

"What's this all about, *patron?*"

"I'll tell you," smiled Gamache, touching the man on the arm and guiding him back to the larger room and the gathering. He spoke to Serge Croix.

"You were here almost a week ago, I know, to see if maybe Augustin Renaud's wasn't the only body in this basement. To see if the man you considered a menace might actually have been right, that Champlain was buried here. Not surprisingly, you found nothing."

"We found root vegetables," said Croix to the snickers of the technicians behind him.

"I'd like you to look again," said the Chief, smiling too, and staring at the archeologist. "For Champlain."

"Not here I'm not. It's a waste of time."

"If you don't, I will." Gamache reached for a shovel. "And you must know, I'm even less of an archeologist than Renaud."

He took his cardigan off and handed it to Émile then, rolling up his sleeves, he looked around the basement. It was pocked with fresh-turned earth, where holes had been dug and filled back in.

"Maybe I'll start here." He put the shovel in the earth and his boot on it.

"Wait," said Croix. "This is absurd. We searched this basement. What makes you think Champlain would be here?"

"That does."

Gamache nodded to Émile, who opened the satchel and handed the old bible to Serge Croix. They watched as the Chief Archeologist's life changed. It began with the tiniest movement. His eyes widened, fractionally, then he blinked, then he exhaled.

"*Merde*," he whispered. "Oh, *merde*."

Croix looked up from the bible and stared at Gamache. "Where did you find this?"

"Upstairs, hiding where you'd hide a precious old book. Among other old books, in a library no one used. It was almost certainly put there by the murderer. He didn't want to destroy it, but neither could he keep it himself, so he hid it. But before that it was in Renaud's possession and before that it belonged to Charles Chiniquy."

Gamache could see the man's mind racing. Making connections, through the years, through the centuries. Connecting movements, events, personalities.

"How'd Chiniquy find this?"

"Patrick and O'Mara, those two Irish laborers I told you about, found it and sold it to Chiniquy."

"You asked me to find out about digging sites in 1869, is this what that was about? They were working at one of the sites?"

Gamache nodded and waited for Croix to make the final connection.

"The Old Homestead?" the Chief Archeologist finally asked, then brought his hand to his forehead and tilted his head back. "Of course. The Old Homestead. We'd always dismissed it because it was outside the range we considered reasonable for the original hallowed ground.

But Champlain wouldn't have been buried in hallowed ground. Not if he was a Huguenot."

Croix gripped the bible and seemed himself in the grip of something, a great excitement, a sort of fugue.

"There'd been rumors, of course, but that's the thing with Champlain, so little's known about the man, there were rumors about everything. This was just one more, and a not very likely one, we thought. Would the King put a Protestant, a Huguenot in charge of the New World? But suppose the King didn't know? But no, it's more likely he did and this would explain so much."

The Chief Archeologist was now like a teenager with his first crush, giddy, almost babbling.

"It would explain why Champlain was never given a royal title, why he was never officially recognized as the Governor of Québec. Why he was never honored for his accomplishments, while others were honored for much less. That's always been a mystery. And maybe it explains why he was sent here in the first place. It was considered almost a suicide mission and maybe Champlain, being a Huguenot, was expendable."

"Would the Jesuits have known?" one of the technicians asked. It was a question that had puzzled Gamache as well. The Catholic Church played a powerful role in the establishment of the colony, in converting the natives and keeping the colonists in line.

The Jesuits were not famous for tolerance.

"I don't know," admitted Croix, thinking. "They must have. Otherwise they'd have buried him in the Catholic cemetery, not outside it."

"But surely the Jesuits would never have allowed him to be buried with that." Gamache pointed to the Huguenot bible, still in Croix's grip.

"True. But someone must have known," said Croix. "There're all sorts of eyewitness accounts of Champlain being buried in the chapel, a chapel he himself had supported. Left half his money to them."

The Chief Archeologist stopped, but they could see his mind racing.

"Could that be it? Was the money a bribe? Did he leave half his fortune to the church here so they'd give him a public burial in the chapel then later, let him be reburied beyond the Catholic cemetery, in a field? With this?" He held up the bible.

Gamache listened, imagining this great leader dug up in the dead of night, his remains lugged across the cemetery, across hallowed ground, and beyond.

Why? Because he was a Protestant. All his deeds, all his courage, all his vision and determination and achievements finally stood for nothing. In death he was only one thing.

A Huguenot. An outsider, in a country he'd created, a world he'd built. Samuel de Champlain, the humanist, had been lowered into the New World, in ground unblessed, but unblemished too.

Had Champlain come here hoping it would be different? Gamache wondered. Only to find the New World exactly like the Old, only colder.

Samuel de Champlain had lain in his lead-lined coffin with his bible until two Irish workers, living in squalor and despair had dug him up. He'd made their fortune. One, O'Mara, had left the city. The other, Patrick, had left lower Québec, buying a home on des Jardins among the affluent.

Had he been happier there?

"And now you think he's here?" Serge Croix turned to Gamache.

"I do." And Gamache told them the rest of the story. Of the meeting with James Douglas, of the payoff.

"So Chiniquy and Douglas buried him here?" Croix asked.

"That's what I think. Champlain was too powerful a symbol for French Québec, a rallying point. Better never found. 1869 was only two years after Confederation. A lot of French Québec wasn't happy about joining Canada, there were calls for separation even then. Finding Champlain would do no good to the Canadian cause, and might do a great deal of harm. Chiniquy probably didn't care greatly, but I suspect Dr. Douglas did. He was aware of the political forces, and a conservative by nature, the less fuss the better."

"And the remains of Champlain would cause a fuss," said Inspector Langlois, nodding. "Better to bury the dead, and leave it be."

"But the dead had a habit of leaving the grave," said Croix. "Especially around James Douglas. You're familiar with his activities?"

"As a grave robber?" said Gamache. "Yes."

"And the mummies," said Croix.

"Mummies?" Langlois asked.

"Another time," said the Chief Inspector. "I'll tell you all about it. Now we have another body to find."

For the next hour the archeologist and his technicians searched the basement again, finding more tin boxes, more vegetables.

But under the stairs, exactly where the metal steps landed, they found something else. Something dismissed in their first sweep earlier in the week as just the blip from the stairs themselves but now, examined closer, proved to be something else.

Digging carefully but without enthusiasm or conviction, the technicians hit something, something larger than the tin boxes. Something, indeed, not tin at all but wood.

Digging more carefully now, excavating, taking photographs and recording the event, they slowly, painstakingly, uncovered a coffin. The men gathered round and by rote crossed themselves.

The Inspector called his forensics team and within minutes the investigators had arrived. Samples were taken, more photographs, prints.

Cameras recording, the coffin was raised and the Chief Archeologist and his head technician pried up the nails, long and rusty red. With a slow shriek they came out of the wood, reluctant to leave, reluctant to reveal what they'd hidden for so long.

Finally freed of the nails the lid was ready to be lifted. Serge Croix reached out then hesitated. Looking over at Gamache he gestured, beckoning him forward. Gamache declined, but when the Chief Archeologist insisted he agreed.

Armand Gamache stood before the worm-eaten coffin. A simple maple wood, made from the ancient forests hacked down to build Québec four hundred years earlier. Gamache could feel the tremble in his right hand, and knew it showed.

He reached out and touched the coffin, and the tremble stopped. Resting his hands there he considered what was about to happen. After centuries of hunting, after lifetimes spent in the singular search for the Father of Québec, after his own childhood spent reading about it, dreaming about it, reenacting it with friends. A stick in his hand, he'd stood astride rocks in Parc Mont Royal, commanding the great ship, fighting noble battles, surviving terrible storms. Valiant. Along with every other school child in Québec his hero had been Samuel de Champlain.

Exploring, mapping. Creating. Québec.

Gamache looked down at his large hands, resting gently on the old wood.

Samuel de Champlain.

Gamache stepped aside and gestured to Émile to take his place. The elderly man shook his head but Gamache walked over and led him to the coffin then stepped back and smiled at his mentor.

"*Merci*," Émile mouthed. Together he and the Chief Archeologist slowly, carefully, raised the heavy, lead-lined lid.

A skeleton lay there. Finally, found.

After a long silence the Chief Archeologist, gazing into the coffin, spoke.

"Unless Champlain had another big secret, this isn't him."

"What do you mean?" Gamache asked.

"It's a woman."

Something had changed. Jean-Guy Beauvoir could feel it. It was the way people looked at him. It was as though they'd seen him naked, as though they'd seen him in a position so vulnerable, so exposed it was all they could see now.

Not the man he really was. An edited man.

They'd seen the video, all of them. That much was obvious. He was the only one in Three Pines who hadn't, he and maybe Ruth, who was barely out of the stone ages.

But while the people of Three Pines might know something about him, he knew something about them, something no one else knew. He knew who'd killed the Hermit.

It was late Friday afternoon. The sun had long since set and the bistro was clearing out, people heading home for dinner after a drink.

Beauvoir looked round. Clara, Peter and Myrna were sitting with Old Mundin and The Wife, who held a sleeping Charles. At another table Marc and Dominique Gilbert sipped beer while Marc's mother, Carole, had a white wine. The Parras were there, Roar and Hanna. Their son Havoc was waiting tables.

Ruth sat alone and Gabri stood behind the bar.

The door opened and someone else blew in, batting snow off his hat and stomping his feet. Vincent Gilbert, the asshole saint, the doctor who'd been so tender with Beauvoir and so cruel with others.

"Am I late?" he asked.

"Late?" said Carole. "For what?"

"Well, I was invited. Weren't you?"

Everyone turned to Beauvoir then to Clara and Myrna. Old and The Wife had been invited for drinks by the two women, as had the Parras. The Gilberts had come at Beauvoir's invitation and Ruth was just part of the décor.

"*Patron*," said Beauvoir, and Gabri locked the front door then closed the side entrances from the other shops.

"What's all this about?" Roar Parra asked, looking perplexed but not alarmed. He was short and squat and powerful and Beauvoir was glad he wasn't alarmed. Yet.

They stared at Beauvoir.

He'd quietly had a word with Gabri earlier and asked him to ask the other patrons to leave, discreetly, so that only these few remained. Outside snow was falling and beginning to blow about, visible in the glow from the homes. The cheery Christmas lights on the three pine trees on the village green bobbed in the wind. They'd be battling a small blizzard by the time they left.

Inside, it was snug and warm and though the wind and snow swirled against the windows it only increased their sense of security. Fires were lit in the hearths and while they could hear the wind outside the sturdy building never even shuddered.

Like the rest of Three Pines, and its residents, it took what was coming and remained standing. And now, together, they stared at him.

With just a touch of pity?

"OK, numb nuts, what's all this about?" asked Ruth.

Armand Gamache sat in the library of the Literary and Historical Society marveling that a week ago he barely knew it, barely knew the people, and now he felt he knew them well.

The board had assembled one more time.

Tense, suspicious Porter Wilson at the head of the table, even if he wasn't a natural leader. The real leader sat beside him and had all their lives, quietly running things, picking up pieces dropped and broken by Porter. Elizabeth MacWhirter, heir to the MacWhirter shipyard fortunes, a fortune long faded away until all that remained were appearances.

But appearances mattered, Gamache knew, especially to Elizabeth MacWhirter. Especially to the English community. And the truth was, they were at once stronger and weaker than they appeared.

The English community was certainly small, and diminishing, dying out. A fact lost on the Francophone majority who, despite every evidence, still saw the Anglos, if they saw them at all, as threats.

And why not, really? Many of the Anglos still saw themselves as wielding, and deserving, of power. A manifest destiny, a right conferred on them by birth and fate. By General Wolfe, two hundred years earlier on the field belonging to the farmer Abraham.

Like whites in South Africa or the Southern states who knew that things had changed, who even accepted the changes, but who couldn't quite shake the certainty deeply, diplomatically, hidden, that they should still be in charge.

There was Winnie, the tiny librarian who loved the library and loved Elizabeth and loved her work among things and ideas no longer relevant.

Mr. Blake was there, in suit and tie. A benign older gentleman, whose home had shrunk from the entire city, to a house, and finally to this one magnificent room. And what, Gamache wondered, would someone do to defend their home?

Tom Hancock sat quietly, watching. Young, vital, wise, but not really one of them. An outsider. But that gave him clarity, he could see what was only visible from a distance.

And finally, Ken Haslam. Whose voice was either silent or shrieking. No middle ground, a man of extremes, who either sat quietly in his chair or fought his way across a frozen river.

A man whose wife and daughter were buried in Québec but who was not considered a Québécois, as though even more could be expected.

They'd adjourned to the library once the coffin had been removed and the others had gone, leaving Émile, Gamache and the board.

Gamache looked at the board members, resting finally on Porter Wilson. Expecting an outburst, expecting a demand for information, tinged perhaps with a slight accusation of unfairness.

Instead they all simply looked at the Chief Inspector, politely. Something had changed, and Gamache knew what.

It was the damned video. They'd seen it, and he hadn't. Not yet.

They knew something he didn't, something about himself. But he knew something they didn't, something they wanted to know.

Well, they'd have to wait.

"You were out practicing this afternoon, I believe," said Gamache to the Reverend Mr. Tom Hancock.

"We were," he agreed, surprised by the topic.

"I saw you." The Chief turned to Ken Haslam.

Haslam smiled and mouthed something Gamache couldn't make out. There was a nodding of heads. The Chief turned to the others.

"What did Mr. Haslam just say?"

Now several faces blushed. He waited.

"Because," he finally said, "I didn't hear a word and I don't think you did either." He turned again to the upright, distinguished man. "Why do you whisper? In fact, I don't think it can even be called a whisper."

Gamache had spoken respectfully, quietly, without anger or accusation but wanting to know.

Haslam's lips moved and again no one heard anything.

"He speaks—" began Tom Hancock before Gamache put up a hand and stopped him.

"I think it's time Mr. Haslam spoke for himself, don't you? And you, perhaps uniquely, know he can."

Now it was the Reverend Mr. Hancock's turn to blush. He looked at Gamache but said nothing.

Gamache leaned forward, toward Haslam. "I heard you out on the ice calling the strokes. No other crew could be heard, no other person. Just you."

Ken Haslam looked frightened now. He opened his mouth, then shook his head, practically in tears.

"I can't," he said, his voice barely registering. "All my life I've been told to be quiet."

"By whom?"

"Mother, Father, brothers. My teachers, everyone. Even my wife, God bless her, asked me to keep my voice down."

"Why?"

"Because."

The word was spoken clearly, too clearly. It wasn't so much piercing as all enveloping, filling the space. It was a voice that carried, boomed, and drove all before it. No other voice could exist, but that one. An English voice, drowning out all others.

"And so you learned to be silent?" asked Gamache.

"If I wanted friends," said Haslam, his words slamming into them. Was it some quirk of palate and brainpan and voice box so that the sound waves were magnified? "If I wanted to belong, yes, I learned never to raise my voice."

"But that meant you could never speak at all, never be heard," said Gamache.

"And what would you choose?" Haslam asked, his loud voice turning a rational question into an attack. "To speak up but chase people away, or to be quiet in company?"

Armand Gamache was silent then, looking down the long table at the solemn faces, and he knew Ken Haslam wasn't the only one who'd faced that question, and made the same choice.

To be silent. In hopes of not offending, in hopes of being accepted.

But what happened to people who never spoke, never raised their voices? Kept everything inside?

Gamache knew what happened. Everything they swallowed, every word, thought, feeling rattled around inside, hollowing the person out. And into that chasm they stuffed their words, their rage.

"Perhaps you could explain the coffin in our basement," Elizabeth broke the silence.

It seemed a reasonable request.

As you know I came here to recover from my wounds." Beauvoir wouldn't let them think he didn't know what they knew. A few villagers lowered their eyes, a few blushed as though Beauvoir had dropped his pants, but most continued to look at him, interested.

"But there was another reason. Chief Inspector Gamache asked me to look into the murder of the Hermit."

That caused a stir. They looked at each other. Gabri, alone among them, stood up.

"He sent you? He believed me?"

"Hasn't that case been solved?" said Hanna. "Haven't you caused enough harm?"

"The Chief wasn't satisfied," said Beauvoir. "At first I thought he was wrong, that perhaps he'd been persuaded by the wishful thinking of Gabri here, who every day since Olivier was arrested sent the Chief a letter, containing the same question. Why did Olivier move the body?"

Gabri turned to Clara. "It was my query letter."

"And we all know you're quite a query," said Ruth.

Gabri was bursting, beaming. No one else was.

"The more I investigated the more I began to think Olivier might not have killed the Hermit. But if not Olivier, then who?"

He stood with his hands on the back of a wing chair for support. Almost there. "We believed the motive had to do with the treasure. It seemed obvious. And yet, if it was the motive, why hadn't the murderer taken it? So I decided to take a different tack. Suppose the treasure had very little to do with the killing of the Hermit? Except for one crucial feature. It led the murderer here, to Three Pines."

They all stared at him, even Clara and Myrna. He hadn't shared his conclusions with them. This close to trapping the killer he couldn't risk it.

"If he hid all those things in his cabin, how could they lead anyone to Three Pines?" Old Mundin asked from the back of the room.

"They didn't stay hidden," Beauvoir explained. "Not all of them. The Hermit began to give some to Olivier in exchange for food and company and Olivier, knowing what he had, sold them. Through eBay, but also through an antique shop in Montreal on rue Notre-Dame."

He turned to the Gilberts. "I understand you bought some things on rue Notre-Dame."

"It's a long street, Inspector," said Dominique. "A lot of stores."

"True, but like butchers and bakers, most people develop a loyalty for a specific antique shop, they go back to the same one. Am I right?"

He looked around. Everyone, except Gabri, dropped their eyes.

"Well, not to worry. I'm sure the owner will recognize your photographs."

"All right, we used Le Temps perdu," said Carole.

"Le Temps perdu. Popular place. It happens to be where Olivier sold the Hermit's things." Beauvoir wasn't surprised. He'd already spoken to the owner about the Gilberts.

"We didn't know that's where he went," said Dominique, her voice sounding squeezed, sharp. "It just had nice things. Lots of people go there."

"Besides," said Marc. "We only bought the home here in the last year. We didn't need antiques before that."

"You might have gone in to look. People window-shop up and down rue Notre-Dame all the time."

"But," said Hanna Parra, "you said the Hermit wasn't killed for his treasure. Then why was he killed?"

"Exactly," said Beauvoir. "Why? Once I set aside the treasure other things took on more importance, mostly two things. The word 'Woo,' and the repetition of another word. 'Charlotte.' There was *Charlotte's Web*, Charlotte Brontë, the Amber Room was made for a Charlotte, and the violin's maker, his wife and muse was named Charlotte. We might, of course, be reading more into it than it deserved, but at the very least it deserved another look."

"And what did you find?" The Wife asked.

"I found the murderer," said Beauvoir.

Armand Gamache was tired. He wanted to go home to Reine-Marie. But now wasn't the time to show weakness, now wasn't the time to flag. Not when he was so close.

He'd told them about Chiniquy, he'd told them about James Douglas. About Patrick and O'Mara. And he showed them the books, the ones they'd unwittingly sold from their collection.

Including perhaps the most valuable volume in Canada today.

An original Huguenot bible belonging to Samuel de Champlain.

That had brought groans from the board members, but no recriminations. They were beginning to band together, to shore up their differences.

Things are strongest when they're broken, Agent Morin had said, and Armand Gamache knew it to be true. And he knew he was witnessing a broken community, fractured by unkind time and events, and a temperament not, perhaps, best suited to change.

But it was pulling together, mending, and it would be very strong indeed because it was so broken. As Ken Haslam had been broken, by years of hushing. As Elizabeth MacWhirter had been worn down by years of polishing the façade. As Porter Wilson and Winnie and Mr. Blake had been shattered watching family, friends, influence, institutions disappear.

Only young Tom Hancock was unscathed, for now.

"So when Augustin Renaud came to speak to us a week ago he wanted to dig?" asked Mr. Blake.

"I believe so. He was convinced Champlain was buried in your basement, put there by James Douglas and Father Chiniquy."

"And he was right," said Porter, all bravado gone. "What'll they do to us when they find out we've been hiding Champlain all these years?"

"We didn't hide him," said Winnie. "We didn't even know he was there."

"Try convincing the tabloids of that," said Porter. "And even if most believe us, the fact is, it was still an Anglo conspiracy."

"A conspiracy of two," said Mr. Blake. "More than a hundred years ago. Not the whole community."

"And you think if James Douglas had asked the community they'd have disagreed?" demanded Porter, making a more coherent argument than Gamache had thought him capable of. One thing was certain, he knew his community, as did Mr. Blake, who accepted that Porter, finally, was right.

"This is a disaster," said Winnie and no one contradicted her, except Gamache.

"Well, not entirely. The coffin was Champlain's, but the body inside wasn't."

Now they gaped at him. Dying men thrown a rope, a slender hope.

They were hushed. And finally Ken Haslam spoke, his voice filling the room, squeezing them all into the corners.

"Who was he?"

"She. The body in the coffin appears to be female."

"She? What was she doing in Champlain's coffin?" Haslam shouted.

"We don't know, but we will."

Beside him Émile's eyes slid from Haslam to Elizabeth MacWhirter. She looked sad and frightened. Her veneer cracking. Émile smiled at her slightly. An encouraging look from someone who knew what it felt like to be shattered.

"Things are strongest where they're broken," Agent Morin laughed. "Good thing too, since I'm always dropping things. Suzanne's pretty clumsy too, you know. We're going to have to put our babies in bubble wrap. Babies bounce, right?"

"Not twice," said Gamache and Morin laughed again.

"Oh well, I guess we'll have strong kids."

"Without a doubt."

I started with the assumption that the killer had found one of the Hermit's treasures in the antique shop," said Beauvoir, "and traced it back here to Three Pines."

The only sounds now in the bistro were the crackling of the log fire and snow hitting the windows.

Inside, the fireplaces threw odd shadows against the walls but none of them threatening. Not to Beauvoir, but he suspected at least one person in this room was beginning to find it close, tight, claustrophobic.

"But who could it be? The Gilberts had bought a lot of antiques from that very store. The Parras? They'd inherited a lot of things from their family in the Czech Republic and managed to get them out when the wall came down. By their own admission, they'd sold most of it to pay for their new home. Perhaps they sold the things through Le Temps perdu. Old Mundin? Well, he restores antiques. Wouldn't he also be drawn to the terrific shops on rue Notre-Dame?

"It hardly seemed to narrow the suspects, so I looked at another clue. Woo. Olivier had described the Hermit whispering the word when he was particularly distressed. It was upsetting to him. But what did 'woo' mean? Was it a name, a nickname?"

He looked over to the Gilbert table. Like the rest they were staring, entranced and guarded.

"Was 'woo' short-form for a name that was hard to say, particularly for a child? That's when most nicknames are given, isn't it? In childhood. I was at the Mundins' and heard little Charlie speaking. Shoo, for *chaud*. Kids do that, trying to get their tongues around hard words. Like Woloshyn. Woo."

Clara leaned in to Myrna and whispered, "That's what I was afraid of. As soon as I heard her maiden name was Woloshyn."

Myrna raised her brows and turned, with the rest of them, to look at Carole Gilbert.

Carole didn't move but Vincent Gilbert did. He rose to his full height, his towering personality filling the room.

"Enough with these insinuations. If you have something to say come out with it."

"And you," Beauvoir rounded on him. "Sir. The magnificent Dr. Gilbert. The great man, the great healer." As he spoke he knew the Chief Inspector would be handling this differently, would never employ sarcasm, would rarely lose his temper, as Beauvoir could feel himself doing. With an effort he pulled back from the edge. "One of the great mysteries of this case has always been why the murderer didn't steal the treasure. Who could resist it? Even if it wasn't the motive for murder, it was just sitting there. Who wouldn't pick up a trinket? A rare book? A gold candlestick?"

"And what was your brilliant conclusion?" Dr. Gilbert asked, his voice filled with contempt.

"There seemed only one. The killer had no need of it. Did that apply to Olivier? No. He was about as greedy as they come. Marc, your son? Same thing. Greedy, petty. He'd have stripped the cabin."

He could see Marc Gilbert struggling, wanting to defend himself, but recognizing that these insults actually helped clear him of suspicion.

"The Parras? A landscaper, a waiter? Not exactly rolling in money. Even one of the Hermit's pieces would make a huge difference in their lives. No, if one of them had killed the Hermit they'd have stolen something. Same with Old Mundin. A carpenter's income is fine for now, but what happens when Charlie gets older? He'll need to be provided for. The Mundins would have stolen the treasure if not for themselves then for their son."

Now he turned back to Vincent Gilbert.

"But one person, sir, didn't need the treasure. You. You're already wealthy. Besides, I don't think money's important to you. You have another motivation, another master. Money was never the currency that counted. No. It's compliments you collect. Respect, admiration. You collect the certainty that you're better than anyone else. A saint, even.

It's your ego, your self-esteem that needs feeding, demands feeding, not your bank account. You alone among all the suspects would have left the treasure, because it meant nothing to you."

If Dr. Gilbert could have ripped Beauvoir's life away with a look, the young Inspector would have dropped dead right there. But instead of dying, Inspector Beauvoir smiled and continued his story, his voice suddenly calm, reasonable.

"But there was another mystery. Who was the Hermit? Olivier started off saying he was Czech and his name was Jakob but he's since admitted he was lying. He had no idea who the man was except that he wasn't Czech. More likely French or English. He spoke perfect French, but seemed to prefer to read English."

Beauvoir noticed Roar and Hanna Parra exchange relieved glances.

"The only clue we had led us back to the antiques and antiquities in his cabin. I don't know antiques, but people who do said these were amazing. He must have had an eye for it. He didn't pick the stuff up at flea markets and garage sales."

Beauvoir paused. He'd seen Gamache do this time and again, reeling in the suspect then letting him run, then reeling some more. But doing it subtly, carefully, delicately, without the suspect even realizing it. Doing it steadily, without hesitation.

It would be terrifying for the murderer when it dawned on him what was happening. And that terror was what the Chief counted on. To wear the person down, to grind them down. But it took a strong stomach, and patience.

Beauvoir had never appreciated how difficult this was. To present the facts in such a way so that the murderer would eventually know where it was heading. But not too soon as to be able to wiggle away, and not too late to have time to fight back.

No, the point was to wear the murderer's nerves wire thin. Then give him the impression he wasn't a suspect, someone else was. Let him breathe, then move in again when his guard was down.

And do that, over and over. Relentlessly.

It was exhausting. Like landing a huge fish, only one that could eat the boat.

And now Beauvoir moved in again, for the last time. For the kill.

"The truth, for we know it now, is that the treasure played a role. It was the catalyst. But what drove the final blow wasn't greed for a treasure lost but for something else lost. Something more personal, more valuable even than treasure. This wasn't about the loss of family heirlooms, but the family itself. Am I right?"

And Beauvoir turned to the murderer.

The killer stood and everyone in the room stared, bewildered.

"He killed my father," said Old Mundin.

TWENTY-FOUR

⌒

The Wife pushed away from the table and gaped.

"Old?" she whispered.

It was as though the bitter wind had found a way in and frozen everyone in place. Had Beauvoir accused the mantelpiece of murder they could not have been more astonished.

"Oh, God, Old, please," The Wife begged. But a hint of desperation had crept into her eyes, slowly replacing disbelief. Like a healthy woman told she had terminal cancer, The Wife was in a daze. The end of her life was in sight, her simple life with a carpenter, making and restoring furniture, living in the country in a modest home. Raising Charles, and being with the only man she ever wanted to be with, the man she loved.

Over.

Old turned to her and his son. He was impossibly beautiful and even the vile accusation couldn't tarnish that.

"He killed my father," Old repeated. "I came to Three Pines to find him. He's right," he jerked his head toward Beauvoir. "I was working in Le Temps perdu, restoring furniture when a walking stick came in. It was very old, handmade. Unique. I recognized it right away. My father had shown it to me and pointed out the inlaying, how the woodworker had designed it around the burling. It appeared to be just a simple, rustic walking stick, but it was a work of art. It had been my father's and had been stolen after he died. Had been stolen by his murderer."

"You found out from the shop records who had sold it to Le Temps perdu," said Beauvoir. This was supposition now, but he needed to make it sound as though he knew it to be true.

"It was from an Olivier Brulé, living in Three Pines." Old Mundin breathed deeply, prepared to take the plunge. "I moved here. Got a job repairing and restoring Olivier's furniture. I needed to get close to him, to watch him. I needed proof he'd killed my father."

"But Olivier could never do that," said Gabri, quietly but with certainty. "He could never kill."

"I know," said Old. "I realized that the more I got to know him. He was a greedy man. Often a little sly. But a good man. He could never have killed my father. But someone did. Olivier was getting my father's things from someone. I spent years following him all over the place, as he did his antiquing. He visited homes and farms and other shops. Bought antiques from all over the place. But never did I see him actually pick up one of my father's things. And yet, they kept appearing. And being sold on."

Perhaps it was the atmosphere, the warm and snug bistro. The storm outside. The wine and hot chocolate and lit fires, but this felt unreal. As though their friend was talking about someone else. Telling them a tale. A fable.

"Over the years I met Michelle and fell in love," he smiled at his wife. No longer The Wife. But the woman he loved. Michelle. "We had Charles. My life was complete. I'd actually forgotten about why I'd come here in the first place. But one Saturday night I was sitting in the truck after picking up the furniture and I saw Olivier close up and leave the bistro. But instead of heading home he did something strange. He went into the woods. I didn't follow him. I was too surprised. But I thought about it a lot and the next Saturday I waited for him, but he just went home. But the following week he went into the woods again. Carrying a bag."

"Groceries," said Gabri. No one said anything. They could see what was happening. Old Mundin in his truck. Watching and waiting. Patient. And seeing Olivier disappear into the woods. Old quietly getting out of the vehicle, following Olivier. And finding the cabin.

"I looked in through the windows and saw—" Old's voice faltered. Michelle reached out and quietly laid her hand on his. He slowly regained himself, his breathing becoming calmer, more measured, until he was able to continue with the story.

"I saw my father's things. Everything he'd kept in the back room. The special place for his special things, he'd told me. Things only he and I knew about. The colored glass, the plates, the candlesticks, the furniture. All there."

Old's eyes gleamed. He stared into the distance. No longer in the bistro with the rest of them. Now he was back at the cabin. On the outside looking in.

"Olivier gave the bag to the old man and they sat down. They drank from china my father let me touch, and ate off plates he said came from a queen."

"Charlotte," said Beauvoir. "Queen Charlotte."

"Yes. Like my mother. My father said they were special because they would always remind him of my mother. Charlotte."

"That's why you named your son Charles," said Beauvoir. "We thought it was after your father, but it was your mother's name. Charlotte."

Mundin nodded but didn't look at his son. Couldn't look at his son, or his wife now.

"What did you do then?" Beauvoir asked. He knew enough now to keep his voice soft, almost hypnotic. To not break the spell. Let Old Mundin tell the story.

"I knew then I was looking at the man who'd killed my father fifteen years ago. I never believed it was an accident. I'm not a fool. I know most people think it was suicide, that he killed himself by walking onto the river. But I knew him. He would never have done that. I knew if he was dead he'd been killed. But it was only much later I realized his most precious things had been taken. I talked to my mother about it but I don't think she believed me. He'd never shown her the things. Only me.

"My father had been murdered and his priceless antiques stolen. And now, finally, I'd found the man who'd done it."

"What did you do, Patrick?" Michelle asked. It was the first time any of them had heard his real name. The name she reserved for their most intimate moments. When they were not Old and The Wife. But Patrick and Michelle. A young man and woman, in love.

"I wanted to torment the man. I wanted him to know someone had found him. One of our favorite books was *Charlotte's Web*, so I made a web from fishing line and snuck into the cabin when he was working on his vegetable garden. I put it in the rafters. So that he'd find it there."

"And you put the word 'Woo' into it," said Beauvoir. "Why?"

"It was what my father called me. Our secret name. He taught me all about wood and when I was small I tried to say the words but all I could say was 'woo.' So he started calling me that. Not often. Just sometimes when I was in his arms. He'd hug me tight and whisper, 'Woo.'"

No one could look at the beautiful young man now. They dropped their eyes from the scalding sight. From the eclipse. As all that love turned into hate.

"I watched from the woods, but the Hermit didn't seem to find the web. So I took the most precious thing I own. I kept it in a sack in my workshop. Hadn't seen it in years. But I took it out that night and took it with me to the cabin."

There was silence then. In their minds they could see the dark figure walking through the dark woods. Toward the thing he had searched for and finally found.

"I watched Olivier leave and waited a few minutes. Then I left the thing outside his door and knocked. I hid in the shadows and watched. The old man opened the door and looked out, expecting to see Olivier. He looked amused at first, then puzzled. Then a little frightened."

The fire crackled and cackled in the grate. It spit out a few embers that slowly died. And Old described what happened next.

The Hermit scanned the woods and was about to close the door when he saw something sitting on the porch. A tiny visitor. He stooped and picked it up. It was a wooden word. Woo.

And then Old had seen it. The look he'd dreamed of, fantasized about. Mortgaged his life to see. Terror on the face of the man who'd killed his father. The same terror his father must have felt as the ice broke underneath him.

The end. In that instant the Hermit knew the monster he'd been hiding from had finally found him.

And it had.

Old separated himself from the dark forest and approached the cabin, approached the elderly man. The Hermit backed into the cabin and said only one thing.

"Woo," he whispered. "Woo."

Old picked up the silver menorah and struck. Once. And into that blow he put his childhood, his grief, his loss. He put his mother's sorrow and his sister's longing. The menorah, weighed down with that, crushed the Hermit's skull. And he fell, Woo clutched in his hand.

Old didn't care. No one would find the body except Olivier and he suspected Olivier would say nothing. He liked the man very much, but knew him for what he was.

Greedy.

Olivier would take the treasure and leave the body and everyone would be happy. A man already lost to the world would be slowly swallowed by the forest. Olivier would have his treasure, and Old would have his life back.

His obligation to his father discharged.

"It was the first thing I ever made," said Old. "I whittled Woo and gave it to my father. After he died I couldn't bear to look at it anymore so I put it in the sack. But I brought it out that night. One last time."

Old Mundin turned to his family. All his energy spent, his brilliance fading. He placed his hand on his sleeping son's back and spoke.

"I'm so sorry. My father taught me everything, gave me everything. This man killed him, shoved him onto the river in spring."

Clara grimaced, imagining a death like that, imagining the horror as the ice began to crack. As it did now beneath The Wife.

Jean-Guy Beauvoir went to the bistro door and opened it. Along with a swirl of snow two large Sûreté officers entered.

"Can you leave us, please?" Beauvoir asked of the villagers, and slowly, stunned, they put their winter coats on and left. Clara and Peter took The Wife and Charles back to their home, while Inspector Beauvoir finished the interview with Old Mundin.

An hour later the police cars drew away, taking Old. Michelle accompanied him, but not before stopping at the inn and spa to hand Charles over to the only other person he loved.

The asshole saint. Dr. Gilbert. Who tenderly took the boy in his arms and held him for a few hours, safe against the bitter cold world pounding at the door.

Hot toddy?"

Peter handed one to Beauvoir, who sat in a deep, comfortable chair in their living room. Gabri sat on the sofa in a daze. Clara and Myrna were also there, drinks in their hands, in front of the fireplace.

"What I don't get," said Peter, perching on an arm of the sofa, "is where all those amazing antiques came from in the first place. The Hermit stole them and took them into the woods, but where did Old's father get them to begin with?"

Beauvoir sighed. He was exhausted. Always happier with physical activity, it constantly amazed him how grueling intellectual activity could also be.

"For all that Old Mundin loved his father, he didn't know him well," said Beauvoir. "What kid does? I think we'll find that Mundin made some trips to the Eastern Bloc, as communism was falling. He convinced a lot of people to trust him with their family treasures. But instead of keeping them safe, or sending people the money, he just disappeared with their treasures."

"Stole them himself?" Clara asked.

Beauvoir nodded.

"The Hermit's murder was never about the treasure," said Beauvoir. "Old Mundin could care less about it. In fact, he came to hate it. That's why it was left in the cabin. He didn't want the treasure. The only thing he took was the Hermit's life."

Beauvoir looked into the fire and remembered his interrogation of Old, in the deserted bistro, where it had all begun months ago. He heard about the death of Mundin's father. How Old's heart had broken that day. But into that crack young Old had shoved his rage, his pain, his loss but that wasn't enough. But once he placed his intention there his heart beat again. With a purpose.

When Olivier had been arrested Old Mundin had wrestled with his conscience, but had finally decided this was fate, this was Olivier's punishment for greed, for helping a man he knew very well was at best a thief and at worst, worse.

"You play the fiddle?" Beauvoir had asked Old, when they were alone in the bistro, after the others had left. "I understand you perform at the Canada Day picnics?"

"Yes."

"Your father taught you that too?"

"He did."

Beauvoir nodded. "And he taught you about antiques and carpentry and restoration?"

Old Mundin nodded.

"You lived in old Quebec City, at number sixteen rue des Ramparts?"

Mundin stared.

"And your mother used to read *Charlotte's Web* to you and your sister, as children?" Beauvoir persisted. He didn't move from his seat, but it felt as though with each question he was approaching Mundin, getting closer and closer.

And Mundin, baffled, seemed to sense that something was approaching. Something even worse than what had already happened.

The lights flickered as the blizzard threw itself against the village, against the bistro.

"Where did you get your name?" Beauvoir asked, staring at Old Mundin across the table.

"What name?"

"Old. Who gave you that name? Your real name is Patrick. So where did Old come from?"

"Where everything I am came from. My father. He'd call me old son. 'Come along, old son,' he'd say. 'I'll teach you about wood.' And I'd go. After a while everyone just called me Old."

Beauvoir nodded. "Old. Old son."

Old Mundin stared at Beauvoir, his face blank then his eyes narrowed as something appeared on the horizon, very far off. A gathering. Terror, the Furies. Loneliness and Sorrow. And something else. Something worse. The worst thing imaginable.

"Old son," Beauvoir whispered again. "The Hermit used that expression. Called Olivier that. 'Chaos is coming, old son.' Those were his words to Olivier. And now I say it to you."

The building shuddered and cold drafts stole through the room.

"Chaos is coming, Old son," Beauvoir said quietly. "The man you killed was your father."

He killed his own father?" Clara whispered. "Oh, dear God. Oh my God."

It was over.

"Mundin's father faked his death," said Beauvoir. "Before that he'd built the cabin and moved the treasures. Then he returned to Quebec City and waited for spring, and a stormy day to cover his tracks. When the perfect conditions came he put his coat by the shore and disappeared, everyone assumed into the St. Lawrence River. But in fact, into the forest."

There was silence then, and in that silence they imagined the rest. Imagined the worst.

"Conscience," said Myrna, at last. "Imagine being pursued by your own conscience."

And for a terrible moment they did. A mountain of a conscience. Throwing a lengthening shadow. Growing. Darkening.

"He had his treasure," said Clara, "but finally all he wanted was his family."

"And peace," said Myrna. "A clear and quiet conscience."

"He surrounded himself with things that reminded him of his wife and kids. Books, the violin. He even carved an image of what Old might look like as a young man, listening. It became his treasure, the one thing he could never part with. He carved it, and scratched 'Woo' under it. It kept him company and eased his conscience. A bit. When we first found it we thought the Hermit had made a carving of Olivier. But we were wrong. It was of his son."

"How's Old?" Clara asked.

"Not good."

Beauvoir remembered the look of rage on the young man's face when the Inspector had told him the Hermit was in fact his father. He'd murdered the very man he meant to avenge. The only man he wished was alive, he killed.

And after the rage, came disbelief. Then horror.

Conscience. Jean-Guy Beauvoir knew it would keep Old Mundin company in prison for decades to come.

Gabri held his head in his hands. Muffled sobs came from the man. Not great dramatic whoops of sorrow, but tired tears. Happy, confused, turbulent tears.

But mostly tears of relief.

Why had Olivier moved the body?

Why had Olivier moved the body?

Why had Olivier moved the body?

And now, finally, they knew. He'd moved the body because he hadn't killed the Hermit, only found him already dead. It was a revolting thing to do, disgraceful, petty, shameful. But it wasn't murder.

"Would you like to stay for dinner? You look exhausted," Beauvoir heard Clara say to Gabri. Then he felt a soft touch on his arm and looked up.

Clara was talking to him.

"It'll be simple, just soup and a sandwich, and we'll get you home early."

Home.

Perhaps it was the fatigue, perhaps it was the stress. But he felt his eyes burning at the word.

He longed to go home.

But not to Montreal.

Here. This was home. He longed to crawl under the duvet at the B and B, to hear the blizzard howl outside and do its worst and to know he was warm, and safe.

God help him, this was home.

Beauvoir stood and smiled at Clara, something that felt at once foreign and familiar. He didn't smile often. Not with suspects. Not at all.

But he smiled now, a weary, grateful grin.

"I'd like that but there's something I have to do first."

Before he left he went into the washroom and splashed cold water onto his face. He looked into the reflection and saw there a man far older than his thirty-eight years. Drawn and tired. And not wanting to do what came next.

He felt an ache deep down.

Bringing the pill bottle out of his pocket he placed it on the counter and stared at it. Then pouring himself a glass of water he shook a pill into his palm. Carefully breaking it in half he swallowed it with a quick swig.

Picking up the other half from the white porcelain rim of the sink he hesitated then quickly tossed it back in the bottle before he could change his mind.

Clara walked him to the front door.

"Can I come by in an hour?" he asked.

"Of course," she said and added, "bring Ruth."

How did she know? Perhaps, he thought as he plunged into the storm, he wasn't as clever as all that. Or perhaps, he thought as the storm fought back, they know me here.

"What do you want?" Ruth demanded, opening the door before he knocked. A swirl of snow came in with him and Ruth whacked his clothing, caked in snow. At least, he thought that was why she was batting away at him, though he had to admit the snow was long gone and still she hit him.

"You know what I want."

"You're lucky I have such a generous spirit, dick-head."

"I'm lucky you're delusional," he muttered, following her into the now familiar home.

Ruth made popcorn, as though this was trivial. Entertainment. And poured herself a Scotch, not offering him one. He didn't need it. He could feel the effects of the pill.

Her computer was already set up on the plastic garden table in her kitchen and they sat side-by-side in wobbly pre-formed plastic chairs.

Ruth pressed a button and up came the site.

Beauvoir looked at her. "Have you watched it?"

"No," she said, staring at the screen, not at him. "I was waiting for you."

Beauvoir took a deep ragged breath, exhaled, and hit play.

"Too bad about Champlain," said Émile as they walked down St-Stanislas and across rue St-Jean, waiting for revelers to pass like rush-hour traffic.

It was beginning to snow. Huge, soft flakes drifted down, caught in the street lamps and the headlights of cars. The forecast was for a storm coming their way. A foot or more expected overnight. This was just the vanguard, the first hints of what was to come.

Quebec City was never lovelier than in a storm and the aftermath, when the sun came out and revealed a magical kingdom, softened and muffled by the thick covering. Fresh and clean, a world unsullied, unmarred.

At the old stone home Émile got out his key. Through the lace curtains on the door they could see Henri hiding behind a pillar, watching.

Gamache smiled then brought his mind back to the case. The curious case of the woman in Champlain's coffin.

Who was she, and what happened to Champlain? Where'd he go? Seemed his explorations didn't end with his death.

Once inside Gamache took Henri for a walk and when he returned Émile had set the laptop on the coffee table, put out a bottle of Scotch, lit the fire and was waiting.

The elderly man stood in the center of the room, his arms at his side. He looked formal, almost rigid.

"What is it, Émile?"

"I'd like to watch the video with you."

"Now?"

"Now."

All through the walk the Chief Inspector had been preparing himself for this. The cold flakes on his face had been refreshing and he'd stopped and tilted his face up, closing his eyes and opening his mouth, to catch them.

"I love doing that," Morin said. "But the snow has to be just right."

"You were a connoisseur?" the Chief asked.

"Still am. The flakes have to be the big, fluffy kind. The ones that just drift down. None of the hard, small flakes you get in storms. That's no fun. They go up your nose and get in your ears. Get everywhere. No it's the big ones you want."

Gamache knew what he meant. He'd done it himself, as a child. Had watched Daniel and Annie do it. Children didn't need to be taught, it seemed instinctive to catch snowflakes with your tongue.

"There's a technique, of course," said Morin in a serious voice, as though he'd studied it. "You have to close your eyes, otherwise the snow gets in them, and stick out your tongue."

There was a pause and the Chief Inspector knew the young agent was sitting, bound to the chair, his head tilted back, his eyes closed, his tongue out. Catching snowflakes.

"Now," agreed Gamache and after bending down to release Henri, he walked to the sofa and sat before the laptop.

"I found the site." Émile sat and looked over at Armand in profile. The trim beard suited the man, now that Émile had gotten used to it. Gamache's eyes were steady, staring at the screen, then he turned and looked directly at his mentor.

"*Merci.*"

Émile paused, taken by surprise. "What for?"

"For not leaving me."

Émile reached out and touched Gamache on the arm, then clicked the button and the video started to play.

Beauvoir stared at the screen. As he suspected, the images were cobbled together from the tiny cameras attached to the headsets of each Sûreté officer. What he hadn't expected was the clarity. He'd thought it'd be grainy, hard to distinguish the players, but it was clear.

As were their voices.

"Officer down!" Gamache called above the gunfire.

"Go, go, go," Beauvoir shouted, pointing to a gunman on the gallery above. Rapid fire shots, the camera swinging wildly, then dropping. Then another view, of the officer on the ground. And blood.

"Officer down," shouted one of the team. "Help him."

Two forms moved forward, automatic weapons firing, laying down cover for a third. Someone grabbing the downed officer, dragging him away. Then a cut to a corridor, racing, chasing the gunmen down darkened halls and into cavernous rooms. Explosions, shouts.

The Chief leaning against a wall, wearing a black tactical vest, automatic rifle in his hands. Firing. It looked so strange to see Gamache with a gun, and using it.

"We have at least six shooters," someone called.

"I count ten," said Gamache, his voice clipped, precise, clear. "Two down. That leaves eight. Five on the floor above, three down here. Where're the medics?"

"Coming," came Agent Lacoste's voice. "Thirty seconds away."

"We need a target alive," the Chief ordered. "Take one alive."

All hell was breaking loose as bullets slammed into walls, into bodies, into the floor and ceiling. Everything became gray, the air filled with dust and bullets. Shouts and screams. The Chief issuing orders as they pushed the gunmen from one room into another. Cornering them.

Then Beauvoir saw himself.

He stepped out from the wall and shot. Then he saw himself stagger, and fall.

Hitting the floor.

"Jean-Guy!" the Chief yelled.

He saw himself splayed on the ground, legs collapsed beneath him. Unmoving.

Gamache ran, calling, "Where are those medics!"

"Here, Chief, here," called Lacoste. "We're coming."

Gamache grabbed Beauvoir's jacket, dragging him behind the wall, shots ringing out. Now, with the sounds of explosions all round, the scene was suddenly intimate. The Chief's worried face, in close up, staring down.

Armand Gamache watched, unblinking, though all he wanted to do was look away. Close his eyes, cover his ears, curl into a ball.

He could smell again the acrid gunpowder, the burning, the concrete dust. He could hear the violent report of the weapons. Feel the rifle in his own hands, pounding out bullets. And weapons firing at him.

Bang, bang, bang, exploding all round. The bullets hitting and bouncing, ricocheting, thudding. The riot of sensations. It was near impossible to think, to focus.

And for an instant he felt again the jolt of seeing Beauvoir hit.

On the screen he saw himself staring down at Beauvoir, searching his face. Feeling for a pulse. The camera catching not just the events, but the sensations, the feelings. The anguish in Gamache's face.

"Jean-Guy?" he called and the Inspector's eyes fluttered and opened, then rolled closed.

Bullets splayed their position and the Chief ducked over Beauvoir, pulling him further behind the wall and propping him up. He opened Jean-Guy's vest, his eyes sweeping down the Inspector's torso, stopping at the wound. The blood. Ripping open a pocket in his own vest he brought out a bandage and pressed it into Beauvoir's hand then pressed the hand to the wound.

Leaning forward he whispered in Beauvoir's ear.

"Jean-Guy, you have to hold your hand there, can you do it?"

Beauvoir's eyes fluttered open again, fighting for consciousness.

"Stay with me," the Chief commanded. "Can you stay conscious?"

Beauvoir nodded.

"Good." Gamache looked up, at the fighting ahead and overhead, then looked back down. "Medics are on their way. Lacoste's coming, she'll be here in a moment." He paused and did something not meant to be seen by anyone else, and now seen by millions. He kissed Beauvoir on the forehead. Then smoothing Beauvoir's hair, he left.

Beauvoir watched the screen through his fingers clutched to his face, his eyes wide. He'd expected the video to have captured, imperfectly, the events. It hadn't occurred to him it would also capture how it felt.

The fear and confusion. The shock, the pain. The searing pain as he clutched at his abdomen. And the loneliness.

On the screen he saw his own face watching, pleading, as Gamache left him. Bleeding and alone. And he saw Gamache's agony, at having to do it.

The view changed and they followed the team, chasing gunmen through corridors. Exchanging fire. A Sûreté officer wounded. A gunman hit.

Then Gamache taking the stairs two at a time, in pursuit, the man turning to fire. Gamache throwing himself at him and the two struggling, fighting hand to hand. From the screen came a confusion of arms and torsos, gasps, as they fought. Finally the Chief grabbed for the weapon that had been knocked out of his hand. Swinging it at the terrorist he caught him with a terrible crunch to the head. The man dropped.

As the cameras watched, Gamache collapsed to his knees beside the man and felt for a pulse, then he cuffed him and dragged him down the stairs. At the bottom the Chief staggered a bit, catching himself. Struggling to stand upright, Gamache turned. Beauvoir was sprawled against the wall across the room. A bloody bandage in one hand and a gun in the other.

There was a rasping, gasping.

"I . . . have . . . one," Gamache was saying, trying to catch his breath.

Émile hadn't moved since the video began. He'd only twice in his career had to fire his gun. Both times he'd killed someone. Hadn't wanted to, but he'd meant to.

And he'd taught his officers well. It was an absolute, you never, ever take out your gun unless you mean to use it. And when you use it, aim for the body, aim to stop. Dead, if need be.

And now he watched Armand, his face bloody from the fight, sway a bit, then step forward. From his belt he grabbed his pistol. The gunman was unconscious at his feet. Shots continued all round. Émile saw the Chief Inspector turn, react to shooting above him. Gamache took another step forward, raised his gun and took shots in quick succession. A target was hit. The shooting stopped.

For a moment. Then there was a rapid fire.

Gamache's arms lifted. His whole body lifted. And twisted. And he fell to the ground.

Beauvoir held his breath. It was what he'd seen that day. The Chief lying, unmoving, on the floor.

"Officer down," Beauvoir heard himself rasp. "The Chief's down."

It seemed forever. Beauvoir tried to move, to drag himself forward, but he couldn't. Around him he heard gunfire. In his headphones officers were calling to each other, shouting instructions, locations, warnings.

But all he saw was the still form in front.

Then there were hands on him and Agent Lacoste kneeling, bending over him. Her face worried and determined.

He saw her eyes move down his body, to his bloody hand clutching his abdomen. "Here, over here," she shouted and was joined by a medic.

"The Chief," Beauvoir whispered and motioned. Lacoste's face fell as she looked.

As medics leaned over Beauvoir, putting pressure bandages on his wound, sticking needles into him, calling for a stretcher, Beauvoir watched Lacoste and a medic run to the Chief. They moved toward him but shooting erupted and they had to take cover.

Gamache lay motionless on the concrete floor just beyond their reach.

Finally Lacoste raced up the stairs and from her camera they saw her trace the shots to a gunman in a doorway above. She engaged him, eventually hitting him. Grabbing his gun she shouted, "Clear!"

The medic ran to Gamache. Across the floor Beauvoir strained to see.

Émile watched as the medic leaned over Gamache.

"*Merde*," the medic whispered. Blood covered the side of the Chief Inspector's head and ran into his ear and down his neck.

The medic looked up as Lacoste joined him. The Chief was coughing slightly, still alive. His eyes were half closed, glazed, and he gasped for breath.

"Chief, can you hear me?" She put her hands on either side of his head and lifted it, looking into his eyes. He focused and struggled to keep his eyes open.

"Hold this." The medic grabbed a bandage and put it over the wound by Gamache's left temple. Lacoste pressed down, holding it there, trying to stop the bleeding.

The Chief stirred, tried to focus, fighting for breath. The medic saw this, his brow furrowed, perplexed. Then he ripped open the Chief's tactical vest and exhaled.

"Christ."

Lacoste looked down. "Oh, no," she whispered.

The Chief's chest was covered in blood. The medic tore Gamache's shirt, exposing his chest. And there, on the side, was a wound.

From across the room Beauvoir watched, but all he could see were the Chief's legs, his polished black leather shoes on the floor moving slightly. But it was his hand Beauvoir stared at. The Chief's right hand, bloody, tight, taut, straining. And in the headset he heard gasping. Struggling for breath. Gamache's right arm outstretched, fingers reaching. His hand grabbing, trembling, as though the breath was just out of reach.

As medics lifted Beauvoir onto a stretcher he whispered over and over again, pleading, "No, no. Please."

He heard Lacoste shout, "Chief!"

There was more coughing, weaker. Then silence.

And he saw Gamache's right hand spasm, shudder. Then softly, like a snowflake, it fell.

And Jean-Guy Beauvoir knew Armand Gamache was dying.

On the uncomfortable plastic chairs, Beauvoir let out a small moan. The video had moved on. Shots of the squad engaging the remaining gunmen.

Ruth stared at the screen, her Scotch untouched.

Chief!" Lacoste called again.

Gamache's eyes were open slightly, staring. His lips moved. They could barely hear what he was saying. Trying to say.

"Reine . . . Marie. Reine . . . Marie."

"I'll tell her," Lacoste whispered into his ear and he closed his eyes.

"His heart's stopped," the medic called and leaned over Gamache, preparing for CPR. "He's in cardiac arrest."

Another medic arrived and kneeling down he grabbed the other's arm.

"No wait. Get me a syringe."

"No fucking way. His heart's stopped, we need to start it."

"For God's sake do something," Lacoste shouted.

The second medic rifled through the medical kit. Finding a syringe he plunged it into the Chief's side and broke the plunger off.

There was no reaction. Gamache lay still, blood on his face and chest. Eyes closed.

The three stared down. He didn't move. Didn't breathe.

Then, then. There was a slight sound. A small rasp.

They looked at each other.

Émile finally blinked. His eyes felt dry as though they'd been sand-blasted and he took a deep breath.

He knew the rest of the story, of course, from calls to Reine-Marie and visits to the hospital. And the Radio-Canada news.

Four Sûreté officers killed, including the first by the side of the road, four others wounded. Eight terrorists dead, one captured. One critically wounded, not expected to survive. At first the news had reported the Chief Inspector among the dead. How that leaked out no one knew. How any of it leaked out no one knew.

Inspector Beauvoir had been badly hurt.

Émile had arrived that afternoon, driving straight from Quebec City to Hôtel-Dieu hospital in Montreal. There he found Reine-Marie and Annie. Daniel was on a flight back from Paris.

They looked wrung out, nothing left.

"He's alive," Reine-Marie had said, hugging Émile, holding him.

"Thank God for that," he'd said, then seen Annie's expression. "What is it?"

"The doctors think he's had a stroke."

Émile had taken a deep breath. "Do they know how bad?"

Annie shook her head and Reine-Marie put her arm around her daughter. "He's alive, that's all that matters."

"Have you seen him?"

Reine-Marie nodded, unable now to speak. Unable to tell anyone what she'd seen. The oxygen, the monitors, the blood and bruising. His eyes closed. Unconscious.

And the doctor saying they didn't know the extent of the damage.

He could be blind. Paralyzed. He could have another one. The next twenty-four hours would tell.

But it didn't matter. She'd held his hand, smoothed it, whispered to him.

He was alive.

The doctor had also explained the chest wound. The bullet had broken a rib which had punctured the lung causing it to collapse and collapsing the second. Crushing the life out of him. The wound must have happened early on, the breathing becoming more and more difficult, more labored, until it became critical. Fatal.

"The medic caught it," the doctor said. "In time."

He hadn't added "just," but he knew it to be the case.

Now the only worry was the head wound.

And so they'd waited, in their own world of the third floor of Hôtel-Dieu. An antiseptic world of hushed conversations, of soft fleet feet and stern faces.

Outside, the news flew around the continent, around the world.

A plot to blow up the La Grande dam.

It had been a decade in the planning. The progress so slow as to be invisible. The tools so primitive as to be dismissed.

Canadian and American government spokesmen refused to say how the plan was stopped, citing national security, but they did admit under close questioning that the shootout and deaths of four Sûreté officers had been part of it.

Chief Superintendent Francoeur was given, and took, credit for preventing a catastrophe.

Émile knew, as did anyone who'd had a glimpse inside the workings of major police departments, that what was being said was just a fraction of the truth.

And so, as the world chewed over these sensational findings, on the third floor of Hôtel-Dieu they waited. Jean-Guy Beauvoir came out of surgery and after a rocky day or so, began the long, slow climb back.

And after twelve hours Armand Gamache struggled awake. When he finally opened his eyes he saw Reine-Marie by his side, holding his hand.

"La Grande?" he rasped.

"Safe."

"Jean-Guy?"

"He'll be fine."

When she returned to the waiting room where Émile, Annie, her husband David and Daniel sat, she was beaming.

"He's resting. Not dancing yet, but he will."

"Is he all right?" Annie asked, afraid yet to believe it, to let go of the dread too soon in case it was a trick, some jest of a sad God. She would never recover from the shock of being in her car, listening to Radio-Canada and hearing the bulletin. Her father . . .

"He will be," said her mother. "He has some slight numbness down his right side."

"Numbness?" asked Daniel.

"The doctors are happy," she assured them. "They say it's minor, and he'll make a full recovery."

She didn't care. He could limp for the rest of his days. He was alive.

But within two days he was up and walking, haltingly. Two days after that he could make it down the corridor. Stopping at the rooms, to sit by the beds of men and women he'd trained and chosen and led into that factory.

Up and down the corridor he limped. Up and down. Up and down.

"What are you doing, Armand?" Reine-Marie had asked quietly as they walked, hand in hand. It had been five days since the shooting and his limp had all but disappeared, except when he first got up, or pushed too hard.

Without pausing he told her. "The funerals are next Sunday. I plan to be there."

They took another few paces before she spoke. "You intend to be at the cathedral?"

"No. I intend to walk with the cortege."

She watched him in profile. His face determined, his lips tight, his right hand squeezed into a fist against the only sign he'd had a stroke. A slight tremble, when he was tired or stressed.

"Tell me what I can do to help."

"You can keep me company."

"Always, *mon coeur*."

He stopped and smiled at her. His face bruised, a bandage over his left brow.

But she didn't care. He was alive.

The day of the funerals was clear and cold. It was mid-December and a wind rattled down from the Arctic and didn't stop until it slammed into the men, women and children who lined the cortege route.

Four coffins, draped in the blue and white fleur-de-lys flag of Québec, sat on wagons pulled by solemn black horses. And behind them a long line of police officers from every community in Québec, from across Canada, from the United States and Britain, from Japan and France and Germany. From all over Europe.

And at the head, walking at slow march in dress uniform, were the Sûreté. And leading that column were Chief Superintendent Francoeur and all the other top-ranking officers. And behind them, alone, was Chief Inspector Gamache, at the head of his homicide division. Walking the two kilometers, only limping toward the very end. Face forward, eyes determined. Until the salute, and the guns.

He'd closed his eyes tight then and raised his face to the sky in a grimace, a moment of private sorrow he could no longer contain. His right hand clamped tight.

It became the image of grief. The image on every front page and every news program and every magazine cover.

Ruth reached out and clicked the video closed. They sat in silence for a moment.

"Well," she finally said. "I don't believe a word of it. All done on a soundstage I bet. Good effects, but the acting sucked. Popcorn?"

Beauvoir looked at her, holding out the plastic bowl.

He took a handful. Then they walked slowly through the blizzard, heads bowed into the wind, across the village green to Peter and Clara's home. Halfway across, he took her arm. To steady her, or himself, he wasn't really sure.

But she let him. They made their way to the little cottage, following the light through the storm. And once there, they sat in front of the fireplace and ate dinner. Together.

Armand Gamache rose.

"Are you all right?" Émile got up too.

Gamache sighed. "I just need time alone." He looked at his friend. *"Merci."*

He felt nauseous, physically sickened. Seeing those young men and women, shot. Killed. Again. Gunned down in dark corridors, again.

They'd been under his command. Hand-picked by him against Chief Superintendent Francoeur's protests. He'd taken them anyway.

And he'd told them there were probably six gunmen in the place. Doubling what he'd been told. What Agent Nichol had told him.

There're three gunmen, the message had said.

He'd taken six officers, all he could muster, plus Beauvoir and himself. He thought it was enough. He was wrong.

"You can't do this," Chief Superintendent Francoeur had said, his voice low with warning. The Chief Superintendent had burst into his office as he'd prepared to leave. In his ear Paul Morin was singing the alphabet song. He sounded drunk, exhausted, at the end.

"Once more please," Gamache said to Morin then whipped off his headset and Chief Superintendent Francoeur immediately stopped talking.

"You have all the information you need," the Chief Inspector glared at Francoeur.

"Gleaned from an old Cree woman and a few sniff-heads? You think I'm going to act on that?"

"Information gathered by Agent Lacoste, who's on her way back. She's coming with me, as are six others. For your information, here are their names. I've alerted the tactical squad. They're at your disposal."

"To do what? There's no way the La Grande dam is going to be destroyed. We've heard nothing about it on the channels. No one has. Not the feds, not the Americans, not even the British and they monitor everything. No one's heard anything. Except you and that demented Cree elder."

Francoeur stared at Gamache. The Chief Superintendent was so angry he was vibrating.

"That dam is going to be blown up in one hour and forty-three minutes. You have enough time to get there. You know where to be and what to do."

Gamache's voice, instead of rising, had lowered.

"You don't give me orders," Francoeur snarled. "You know nothing I don't and I know no reason to go there."

Gamache went to his desk and took out his gun. For an instant Francoeur looked frightened, then Gamache put the pistol on his belt and walked quickly up to the Chief Superintendent.

They glared at each other. Then Gamache spoke, softly, intensely.

"Please, Sylvain, if I have to beg I will. We're both too old and tired for this. We need to stop this now. You're right, it's not my place to give you orders, I apologize. Please, please do as I ask."

"No way. You have to give me more."

"That's all I have."

"But it doesn't make sense. No one would try to blow up the dam this way."

"Why not?"

They'd been over this a hundred times. And there was no time left.

"Because it's too rough. Like throwing a rock at an army."

"And how did David slay Goliath?"

"Come on, this isn't biblical and these aren't biblical times."

"But the same principle applies. Do the unexpected. This would work precisely because we won't be expecting it. And while you might not see it as David and Goliath, the bombers certainly do."

"What are you? Suddenly an expert in national security? You and your arrogance, you make me sick. You go stop that bomb if you really believe hundreds of thousands of lives are at stake."

"No. I'm going to get Paul Morin."

"Morin? You're saying you know where he is? We've been looking all night," Francoeur waved to the army of officers in the outer office, trying to trace Morin. "And you're telling me you know where he is?"

Francoeur was trembling with rage, his voice almost a scream.

Gamache waited. In his peripheral vision he could see the clock, ticking down.

"Magog. In an abandoned factory. Agent Nichol and Inspector Beauvoir found him by listening to the ambient sound."

By listening to the spaces between words they'd found him.

"Please, Sylvain, go to La Grande. I'm begging you. If I'm wrong I'll resign."

"If we go there and you're wrong I'll bring you up on charges."

Francoeur walked out of the office, out of the incident room. And disappeared.

Gamache glanced at the clock as he made for the door. One hour and forty-one minutes left. And Armand Gamache prayed, not for the first time that day, or the last.

It could've been worse," said Émile. "I mean, who knows who made this video? They could've made the entire operation look like a catastrophe. But it doesn't. Tragic, yes. Terrible. But in many ways heroic. If the families have to watch, well . . ."

Gamache knew Émile was trying to be kind, trying to say the editing could have made him out to be a coward or a bumbling idiot. Could have looked like those who died had squandered their lives. Instead everyone had looked courageous. What was the word Émile used?

Heroic.

Gamache slowly climbed the steep stairs, Henri at his heels.

Well, he knew something Émile didn't. He suspected who had made the video. And he knew why.

Not to make Gamache look bad, but to make him look good, too good. So good the Chief would feel as he did. A fraud. A fake. Lionized for nothing. Four Sûreté officers dead and Armand Gamache the hero.

Whoever had done this knew him well. And knew how to exact a price.

In shame.

TWENTY-FIVE

The storm blew in to Quebec City a few hours later and by two in the morning the capital was lashed by high winds and blowing snow. Highways were closed as visibility fell to zero in white-out conditions.

In the garret of the old stone home on St-Stanislas, Armand Gamache lay in bed, staring at the beamed ceiling. Henri, on the floor beside him, snored, oblivious to the snow whipping the windows.

Quietly, Gamache rose and looked out. He couldn't see the building across the narrow street and could just barely make out the street lamps, their light all but blotted out by the driving snow.

Dressing quickly, he tiptoed down the stairs. Behind him he heard the clicking of Henri's nails on the old wooden steps. Putting on his boots, parka, tuque, heavy mitts and wrapping a long scarf around his neck Gamache bent down and petted Henri.

"You don't have to come, you know."

But Henri didn't know. It wasn't a matter of knowing. If Gamache was going, Henri was going.

Out they went, Gamache gulping as the wind hit his face and took away his breath. Then he turned his back and felt it shoving him.

Perhaps, he thought, this was a mistake.

But the storm was what he needed, wanted. Something loud, dramatic, challenging. Something that could blot out all thought, white them out.

The two struggled up the street, walking in the middle of the deserted roads. Not even snow plows were out. It was futile to try to clear snow in the middle of a blizzard.

It felt as though the city was theirs, as though an evacuation notice had sounded and Gamache and Henri had slept through it. They were all alone.

Up Ste-Ursule they trekked, past the convent where Général Montcalm had died. To rue St-Louis, then through the arched gate. The storm, if possible, was even worse outside old Quebec City. With no walls to stop it, the wind gathered speed and snow and slammed into trees, parked cars, buildings, plastering itself against whatever it hit. Including the Chief Inspector.

He didn't care. He felt the cold hard flakes hit his coat, his hat, his face. And he heard it pelting into him. It was almost deafening.

"I love storms," Morin said. "Any kind of storm. Nothing like sitting in a screen porch in summer in the middle of a thunderstorm. But my favorite are blizzards, as long as I don't have to drive. If everyone's safe at home, then bring it on."

"Do you ever go out in them?" Gamache asked.

"All the time, even if it's just to stand there. I love it. Don't know why, maybe it's the drama. Then to come back in and have a hot chocolate in front of the fire. Doesn't get any better."

Gamache trudged forward, his head down, looking at his feet as he plowed his way slowly through the knee-high drifts. Excited, Henri leapt up and down in the trail made by Gamache.

They made slow progress but finally found themselves in the park. Lifting his head the Chief was briefly blinded by the snow, then squinting he could just make out the shapes of ghostly trees reeling against the wind.

The Plains of Abraham.

Gamache looked behind and noticed his boot prints had filled in, disappearing almost as quickly as he made them. He wasn't lost, not yet, but he knew he could be if he went too far.

Henri abruptly stopped his dancing and stood still, then he started to growl and slunk behind Gamache's legs.

This was a sure sign nothing was there.

"Let's go," said Gamache. He turned and came face-to-face with someone else. A tall figure in a dark parka also plastered with snow.

His head was covered in a hood. He stood quietly a few feet from the Chief.

"Chief Inspector Gamache," the figure spoke, his voice clear and English.

"Yes."

"I hadn't expected to find you here."

"I hadn't expected to find you either," Gamache shouted, struggling to make himself heard above the howling wind.

"Were you looking?" the man asked.

Gamache paused. "Not until tomorrow. I was hoping to speak to you tomorrow."

"I thought so."

"Is that why you're here now?"

There was no answer. The dark figure just stood there. Henri, emboldened, crept forward. "Henri," Gamache snapped. *"Viens ici."* And the dog trotted to his master's side.

"The storm seemed fortuitous," said the man. "It makes it easier, somehow."

"We need to talk," said Gamache.

"Why?"

"I need to talk. Please."

Now it was the man's turn to pause. Then he indicated a building, a round stone turret built on the knoll, like a very small fortress. The two men and one dog trudged up the slight hill to the building and trying the door Gamache was a bit surprised to find it unlocked, but once inside he knew why.

There was nothing to steal. It was simply an empty, round, stone hut.

The Chief flicked a switch, and an exposed light bulb overhead came on. Gamache watched as his companion lowered his hood.

"I didn't expect to find anyone out in this storm." Tom Hancock whacked his snow-caked hat against his leg. "I love walking in storms."

Gamache raised his head and stared at the young minister. It was almost exactly what Agent Morin had said.

Looking round he noticed there were no seats but he indicated the floor and both men sat, making themselves comfortable against the thick stone walls.

They were silent for a moment. Inside, without a window, without an opening, they could have been anywhere, anytime. It could have been two hundred years earlier, and outside not a storm but a battle.

"I saw the video," Tom Hancock said. His cheeks were brilliant red and his face wet with melted snow. Gamache suspected he looked the same only, perhaps, not quite so young and vital.

"So did I."

"Terrible," said Hancock. "I'm sorry."

"Thank you. It wasn't quite as it looked, you know. I—" Gamache had to stop.

"You?"

"It made me look heroic and I wasn't. It was my fault they died."

"Why do you say that?"

"I made mistakes. I didn't see the magnitude of what was happening until it was almost too late. And even then I made mistakes."

"How so?"

Gamache looked at the young man. The minister. Who cared so much for hurt souls. He was a good listener, Gamache realized. It was a rare quality, a precious quality.

He took a deep breath. It smelled musky in there, as though the air wasn't meant to be breathed, wasn't meant to sustain life.

Then Gamache told this young minister everything. About the kidnapping and the long and patient plot. Hidden inside their own hubris, their certainty that advance technology would uncover any threat.

They'd been wrong.

Their attackers were clever. Adaptable.

"I've since discovered that security people call it an 'asymmetrical approach,'" Gamache smiled. "Makes it sound geometric. Logical. And I guess in some ways it was. Too logical, certainly too simple for the likes of us. The plotters wanted to destroy the La Grande dam, and how would they do it? Not with a nuclear bomb, not with cleverly hidden devices. Not by infiltrating the security services or using telecommunications or anything that left a signature that could be found and traced. They did it by working where they knew we wouldn't look."

"And where was that?"

"In the past. They knew they could never compete with us when it came to modern technology, so they kept it simple. So simple it was invisible to us. They relied on our hubris, our certainty that state-of-the-art technology would protect us."

The two men's voices were low, like conspirators, or storytellers. It felt as it must have millennia ago, when people sat together across fires and told tales.

"What was their plan?"

"Two truck bombs. And two young men willing to drive them. Cree men."

Tom Hancock, who had been bending forward toward the story and the storyteller, leaned slowly away. He felt his back against the cold stone wall. A wall built before the Cree knew of the disaster approaching. A disaster they would even assist, guiding the Europeans to the waterways. Helping them collect the pelts.

Too late, the Cree had realized they'd made a terrible mistake.

And now, hundreds of years later some of their descendents had agreed to drive huge trucks filled with explosives along a perfectly paved ribbon of road through a forest that had once been theirs. Toward a dam thirty stories high.

They would destroy it. And themselves. Their families. Their villages. The forests, the animals. The gods. All gone. They would unleash a torrent that would sweep it all away.

In the hopes that finally someone would hear their calls for help.

"That's what they were told, anyway," said the Chief, suddenly weary, wishing now he could sleep.

"What happened?" whispered Tom Hancock.

"Chief Superintendent Francoeur got there in time. Stopped them."

"Were they—?"

"Killed?" Gamache nodded. "Yes. Both shot dead. But the dam was saved."

Tom Hancock found himself almost sorry to hear that.

"You said these young Cree men were used. You mean this wasn't their idea?"

"No, no more than it was the truck's idea. Whoever did this chose things ready to explode. The bombs made by them and the Cree made by us."

"But who were they? If the two Cree men were used by the bombers, then who planned all this? Who was behind it?"

"We don't know for sure. Most died in the raid on the factory. One survived and is being questioned but I haven't heard anything."

"But you have your suspicions. Were they native?"

Gamache shook his head. "Caucasian. English speaking. All well trained. Mercenaries, perhaps. The goal was the dam, but the real target seems to have been the eastern seaboard of the United States."

"Not Canada? Not Québec?"

"No. In bringing down La Grande they would have blacked out everything from Boston to New York and Washington. And not just for an hour, but for months. It would have blown the whole grid."

"With winter coming too."

They paused to imagine a city like New York, millions of frightened, angry people freezing in the dark.

"Home-grown terrorists?" asked Hancock.

"We think so."

"You couldn't have seen this coming," said Hancock at last. "You speak of hubris, Chief Inspector. Perhaps you need to be careful yourself."

It was said lightly, but the words were no less sharp.

There was a slight pause before Gamache responded. It was with a small chuckle. "Very true. But you mistake me, Mr. Hancock. It wasn't the threat I should have seen coming, but once it was in motion I should have known the kidnapping wasn't so simple much sooner. I should have known the backwoods farmer wasn't that. And—"

"Yes?"

"I was in over my head. We all were. There was almost no time and it was clear something massive was happening. As soon as Agent Nichol isolated the words 'La Grande' I knew that was it. The dam is in Cree territory so I sent an agent there to ask questions."

"Just one agent? Surely you should have sent everyone." Only then did Hancock stop himself. "If you need any more suggestions on tactics, come to me. They teach it, you know, at the seminary."

He smiled and heard a small guffaw beside him. Then a deep breath.

"The Cree have no love of the Sûreté. Nor should they," said Gamache. "I judged one smart agent was enough. We have some contacts there, among the elders. Agent Lacoste went to them first."

As the hours passed her reports had started to come in. She moved from community to community, always accompanied by the same elderly woman. A woman Chief Inspector Gamache had met years ago, sitting on a bench in front of the Château Frontenac. A woman everyone else had dismissed as a beggar.

He had helped her then. And she helped him now.

Agent Lacoste's reports started to form a picture. Of a generation on the reserves without hope. Drunk and high and lost. With no life and no future and nothing to lose. It had all been taken. This Gamache already knew. Anyone with the stomach to look saw that.

But there was something he didn't know. Lacoste had reports of outsiders arriving, teachers. White teachers, English teachers. Insinuating themselves into the communities years earlier. Most of the teachers were genuine, but a few had an agenda that went far beyond any alphabet or times table. Their curriculum would take time to achieve. The plan had started when the young men were boys. Impressionable, lost, frightened. Hungry for approval, acceptance, kindness, leadership. And the teachers had given them all that. Years it had taken to win their trust. Over those years the teachers taught them how to read and write, how to add and subtract. And how to hate. They'd also taught their students that they need not be victims any longer. They could be warriors again.

Many young Cree had toyed with the attractive idea, finally rejecting it. Sensing these were simply more white men with their own aims. But two young men had been seduced. Two young men on the verge of doing themselves in anyway.

And so they would go out in glory. Convinced the world would finally take notice.

At 11:18.

The La Grande dam would be destroyed. Two young Cree men would die. And, miles away, a young Sûreté agent would be executed.

Armed with this evidence Gamache had presented it, yet again, to Chief Superintendent Francoeur. But when Francoeur had again balked, instead of reasoning with the man Gamache had allowed his temper to flare. His disdain for the arrogant and dangerous Chief Superintendent to show.

That had been a mistake. It had cost him time. And maybe more.

"What happened?"

Armand Gamache looked over, almost surprised to find he wasn't alone with his thoughts.

"A decision had to be made. And we all knew what that was. If Agent Lacoste's information was right we had to abandon Agent Morin. Our efforts had to go into stopping the bombing. If we tried to save Morin the bombers would be warned and might move sooner. No one could risk that."

"Not even you?"

Gamache sat still for a very long time. There was no sound outside or inside. How many others had hidden in there against a violent world? A world not as kind, not as good, not as warm as they wished. How many fearful people had huddled where they sat? Taken refuge? Wondering when it might be safe to go out. Into the world.

"God help me, not even me."

"You were willing to let him die?"

"If need be." Gamache stared at Hancock, not defiantly but with a kind of wonder that decisions like that needed to be made. By him. Every day. "But not before I'd tried everything."

"You finally convinced the Chief Superintendent?"

Gamache nodded. "With a little under two hours to go."

"Good God," exhaled Hancock. "That close. It came that close."

Gamache said nothing for a moment. "We knew by then that Agent Morin was being held in an abandoned factory. Agent Nichol and Inspector Beauvoir found him by listening to the sounds and cross-referencing plane and train schedules. It was masterful investigating. He was being held in an abandoned factory hundreds of kilometers from the dam. The plotters kept themselves at a safe distance. In a town called Magog."

"Magog?"

"Magog. Why?"

The minister looked bemused but also slightly disconcerted. "Gog and Magog?"

Gamache smiled. He'd forgotten that biblical reference.

"*You will make an evil plan,*" the minister quoted.

Once again Gamache saw Paul Morin at the far end of the room, bound to the chair, staring at the wall in front of him. At a clock.

Five seconds left.

"You found me," said Morin.

Gamache took off across the room. Morin's thin back straightened.

Three seconds left. Everything seemed to slow down. Everything seemed so clear. He could see the clock, hear the second hand thud closer to zero. See the hard metal frame chair and the rope strapped around Paul Morin.

There was no bomb. No bomb.

Behind Gamache, Beauvoir and the team rushed in. Gunshots exploded all round. The Chief leapt, to the young agent who sat up so straight.

One second left.

Gamache gathered himself. "I made one final mistake. I turned left when I should have turned right. Paul Morin had just described the sun on his face, but instead of heading to the door with light coming through, I headed for the darkened one."

Hancock was silent then. He'd seen the video and now he looked at the solemn, bearded man sitting on the cold stone floor with him, his dog's head with its quite extravagant ears resting on Gamache's thigh.

"It's not your fault."

"Of course it's my fault," said Gamache angrily.

"Why are you so insistent? Do you want to be a martyr?" said Hancock. "Is that why you came out in a blizzard? Are you enjoying your suffering? You must be, to hold on to it so tightly."

"Be careful."

"Of what? Of hurting the great Chief Inspector's feelings? If your heroism doesn't put you beyond us mere mortals then your suffering does, is that it? Yes it was a tragedy, it was terrible, but it happened to them, not you. You're alive. This is what you've been handed, nothing's going to change that. You have to let it go. They died. It was terrible but unavoidable."

Hancock's voice was intense. Henri lifted his head to stare at the young minister, a slight growl in his throat. Gamache put a calming hand on Henri's head and the dog subsided.

"It is sweet and right to die for your country?" asked the Chief.

"Sometimes."

"And not just to die, but to kill as well?"

"What does that mean?"

"You'd do just about anything to help your parishioners, wouldn't you?" said Gamache. "Their suffering hurts you, almost physically. I've seen it. Yes, I came out into the blizzard in hopes it would quiet my conscience, but isn't that why you signed up for the ice canoe race? To take your mind off your failings? You couldn't stand to see the English suffer so much. Dying. As individuals, but also as a community. It was your job to comfort them but you didn't know how, didn't know if words were enough. And so you took action."

"What do you mean?"

"You know what I mean. Despite a city filled with people he'd alienated, only six people could have actually murdered Augustin Renaud. The board of the Literary and Historical Society. Quite a few volunteers have keys to the building, quite a few knew the construction schedule and when the concrete was to be poured, quite a few could have found the sub-basement and led Renaud there. But only the six board members knew he'd visited, knew he'd demanded to speak with them. And knew why."

The Reverend Mr. Hancock stared at Gamache in the harsh light of the single, naked bulb.

"You killed Augustin Renaud," said Gamache.

There was silence then, complete and utter silence. There was no world outside. No storm, no battlefield, no walled and fortified and defended city. Nothing.

Only the silent fortress.

"Yes."

"You aren't going to deny it?"

"It was obvious you either knew already or would soon find out. Once you found those books it was all over. I hid them there, of course. Couldn't very well destroy them and couldn't risk having them found in my home. Seemed a perfect place. After all, no one had found them in the Literary and Historical Society for a hundred years."

He looked closely at Gamache.

"Did you know all along?"

"I suspected. It could really only have been one of two people. You or Ken Haslam. While the rest of the board stayed and finished the meeting you headed off for your practice."

"I went ahead of Ken, found Renaud and told him I'd sneak him in that night. I told him to bring whatever evidence he had, and if I was convinced, I'd let him start the dig."

"And of course he came."

Hancock nodded. "It was simple. He started digging while I read over the books. Chiniquy's journal and the bible. It was damning."

"Or illuminating, depending on your point of view. What happened?"

"He'd dug one hole and handed me up the shovel. I just swung it and hit him."

"As simple as that?"

"No it wasn't as simple as that," Hancock snapped. "It was terrible but it had to be done."

"Why?"

"Can't you guess?"

Gamache thought. "Because you could."

Hancock smiled a little. "I suppose so. I think of it more that no one else could. I was the only one. Elizabeth never could do it. Mr. Blake? Maybe, when he was younger, but not now. Porter Wilson couldn't hit himself on the head. And Ken? He gave up his voice years ago. No, I was the only one who could do it."

"But why did it need to be done?"

"Because finding Champlain in our basement would have killed the Anglo community. It would have been the final blow."

"Most Québécois wouldn't have blamed you."

"You think not? It doesn't take much to stir anti-Anglo sentiment, even among the most reasonable. There's always a suspicion the Anglos are up to no good."

"I don't agree," said Gamache. "But what I think doesn't matter, does it. It's what you believe."

"Someone had to protect them."

"And that was your job." It was a statement, not a question. Gamache had seen that in the minister from the first time he'd met him. Not a fanaticism, but a firm belief that he was the shepherd and they his flock. And if the Francophones harbored a secret certainty the Anglos were up to no good, the Anglos harbored the certainty the French were out to get them. It was, in many ways, a perfect little walled society.

And the Reverend Tom Hancock's job was to protect his people. It was a sentiment Gamache could understand.

But to the point of killing?

Gamache remembered stepping forward, raising his gun, having the man in his sights. And shooting.

He'd killed to protect his own. And he'd do it again, if need be.

"What are you going to do?" Hancock asked, getting to his feet.

"Depends. What are you going to do?" Gamache also rose stiffly, rousing Henri.

"I think you know why I came here tonight, to the Plains of Abraham."

And Gamache did. As soon as he knew it was Tom Hancock in the parka he'd known why he was there.

"There would at least be a symmetry about it," said Hancock. "The Anglo, slipping back down the cliff, two hundred and fifty years later."

"You know I won't let you do that."

"I know you haven't a hope of stopping me."

"That's probably true and, it must be admitted, this one won't be any help," he indicated Henri. "Unless the sight of a dog whimpering frightens you into surrendering."

Hancock smiled. "This is the final ice floe. I have no choice. It's what's been handed me."

"No, it isn't. Why do you think I'm here?"

"Because you're so wrapped up in your own sorrow you can barely think straight. Because you can't sleep and came here to get away, from yourself."

"Well, that too, perhaps," smiled Gamache. "But what are the chances we'd meet in the middle of the storm? Had I come ten minutes earlier or later, had we walked ten feet apart, we'd have missed each other. Walked right by without seeing, blinded by the blizzard."

"What are you saying?"

"I'm saying, what are the chances?"

"Does it matter? It happened. We met."

"You saw the video," Gamache said, lowering his voice. "You saw what happened. How close it came."

"How close you came to dying? I did."

"Maybe this is why I didn't."

Hancock regarded Gamache. "Are you saying you were spared to stop me from jumping over the cliff?"

"Maybe. I know how precious life is. You had no right to take Renaud's and you have no right to take your own now. Not over this. Too much death. It needs to stop."

Gamache stared at the young man beside him. A man, he knew, drawn to seawalls and jagged cliff faces and to the Anglos of Québec, standing just off shore where the ice was thinnest.

"You're wrong you know," Gamache finally said. "The English of Québec aren't weak, aren't frail. Elizabeth MacWhirter and Winnie and Ken and Mr. Blake, and yes, even Porter, couldn't kill Augustin Renaud, not because they're weak but because they know there's no need. He was no threat. Not really. They've adapted to the new reality, to the new world. You're the only one who couldn't. There'll be Anglos here for centuries to come, as there should be. It's their home. You should have had more faith."

Hancock walked up to Gamache.

"I could walk right by you."

"Probably. I'd try to stop you, but I suspect you'd get by. But you know I'd follow you, I'd have to. And then what? A middle-aged Francophone and a young Anglo, lost in a storm on the Plains of Abraham, wandering, one in search of a cliff, the other in search of him. I wonder when they'd find us? In the spring, you think? Frozen? Two more corpses, unburied? Is that how this ends?"

The two men looked at each other. Finally Tom Hancock sighed.

"With my luck, you'd be the one to go over the cliff."

"That would be disappointing."

Hancock smiled wearily. "I give up. No more fight."

"*Merci*," said Gamache.

At the door Hancock turned. Gamache's hand, with a slight tremble, reached for the latch. "I shouldn't have accused you of trading on your grief. That was wrong."

"Perhaps not so far off," smiled Gamache. "I need to let it go. Let them go."

"With time," said Hancock.

"Avec le temps," Gamache agreed. "Yes."

"You mentioned the video just now," said Hancock, remembering another question he had. "Do you know how it got onto the Internet?"

"No."

Hancock looked at him closely. "But you have your suspicions."

Gamache remembered the rage on the Chief Superintendent's face when he'd confronted him. Theirs was a long battle. An old battle. Francoeur knew Gamache well enough to know what would hurt him most wouldn't be criticism over how he handled the raid, but just the opposite. Praise. Undeserved praise, even as his people suffered.

Where a bullet had failed to stop the Chief Inspector, that might.

But he saw, now, another face. A younger face. Eager to join them. And denied, yet again. Sent back into her basement. Where she monitored everything. Heard everything. Saw everything. Recorded everything.

And remembered, everything.

TWENTY-SIX

~

"Give Reine-Marie my love," said Émile.

He and Armand stood by the door. Gamache's Volvo was packed with his suitcase and assorted treats from Émile for Reine-Marie. Pastries from Paillard, paté and cheese from J.A. Moisan, chocolate made by the monks, from the shop along rue St-Jean.

Gamache hoped most of it made it back to Montreal. Between him and Henri, he had his doubts.

"I will. I'll probably be back in a few weeks to testify, but Inspector Langlois has all the evidence he needs."

"And the confession helps," said Émile with a smile.

"True," agreed Gamache. He looked around the home. He and Reine-Marie had been coming for many years, since Émile had retired and he and his wife moved back to Quebec City. Then, after Alice died, they came more often, to keep Émile company.

"I'm thinking of selling," said Émile, watching Armand look around.

Gamache turned to him and paused. "It's a lot of house."

"The stairs are getting steeper," agreed Émile.

"You're welcome to come live with us, you know."

"I do know, *merci*, but I think I'll stay here."

Gamache smiled, not surprised. "You know, I suspect Elizabeth MacWhirter is finding the same thing. Difficult living in a large home alone."

"Is that right?" said Émile, looking at Gamache with open suspicion.

Armand smiled and opened the door. "Don't come out, it's cold."

"I'm not that frail," snapped Émile. "Besides, I want to say good-bye to Henri."

At the sound of his name the shepherd looked at Émile, ears forward, alert. In case there was a biscuit involved. There was.

The sidewalk was newly plowed. The blizzard had stopped before dawn and the sun rose on a white, unblemished landscape. The city glowed and light sparkled off every surface making it look as though Québec was made of crystal.

Before opening the car door Gamache scooped up some snow, pressed it into his fist and showed Henri the snowball. The dog danced, then stopped, intent, staring.

Gamache tossed it into the air and Henri leapt, straining for the ball, believing this time he'd catch it, and it would remain perfect and whole in his mouth.

The snowball descended, and Henri caught it. And bit down. By the time he landed on all fours he had only a mouthful of snow. Again.

But Henri would keep trying, Gamache knew. He'd never give up hope.

"So," said Émile, "who do you think the woman in Champlain's coffin was?"

"I'd say an inmate of Douglas's asylum. Almost certainly a natural death."

"So he put her into Champlain's coffin, but what did he do with Champlain?"

"You already know the answer to that."

"Of course I don't. I wouldn't be asking if I did."

"I'll give you a hint. It's in Chiniquy's journals, you read it to me the other night. I'll call you when I get home, if you haven't figured it out I'll tell you."

"Wretched man." Émile paused, then reached out and laid his hand briefly on Gamache's as it held the car door.

"*Merci*," said Gamache. "For all you've done for me."

"And you for me. So you think Madame MacWhirter might need a little help?"

"I think so." Gamache opened the car door and Henri jumped in. "But then, I also think the night might be a strawberry."

Émile laughed. "Between us? So do I."

At home three hours later, Gamache and Reine-Marie sat in their comfortable living room, a fire crackling away in the grate.

"Émile called," said Reine-Marie. "He asked me to give you a message."

"Oh?"

"He said 'Three mummies.' Does that mean anything to you?"

Gamache smiled and nodded. Three mummies were taken to Pittsburgh but Douglas had only brought two back from Egypt.

"I've been thinking about that video, Armand."

He took off his half-moon glasses. "Would you like to see it?"

"Would you like me to?"

He hesitated. "I'd rather not, but if you need to I'd watch it with you."

She smiled. "*Merci*, but I don't want to see it."

He kissed her softly then they went back to reading. Reine-Marie glanced over her book at Armand.

She knew all she needed to know.

Gabri stood behind the bar of the bistro, dish towel in hand, wiping a glass clean. Around him his friends and clients chatted and laughed, read and sat quietly.

It was Sunday afternoon and most were still in their pajamas, including Gabri.

"I'd love to go to Venice," said Clara.

"Too many tourists," Ruth snapped.

"How do you know?" Myrna asked. "Have you been?"

"Don't need to go. Everything I need is here." She took a sip of Peter's drink and screwed up her face. "Dear God, what is that?"

"Water."

The friends drifted over to the fireplace to chat to Roar and Hanna Parra while Gabri took a handful of licorice allsorts from the jar on the bar and scanned the room.

His eyes caught a movement outside the frosted window. A familiar car, a Volvo, drove slowly down du Moulin into the village. The sun gleamed off the fresh snow banks and kids skated on the frozen pond on the village green.

The car stopped halfway through the village and two men got out.

Jean-Guy Beauvoir and Armand Gamache. They paused beside the car then the back door opened.

Clara turned at the sound of soft thudding at the bar. Allsorts were spilling from Gabri's hand. The conversation in the bistro dropped then disappeared as patrons first looked at Gabri, then out the window.

Gabri continued to stare.

Surely not. He'd imagined, fantasized, pretended so many times. Had seen it clearly only to have to come back, alone, to the real world. Not taking his eyes off the sight, he walked from behind the bar. Patrons parted, making way for the large man.

The door opened, and Olivier stood there.

Gabri, unable to speak, opened his arms and Olivier fell into them. The two men hugged and rocked and wept. Around them villagers applauded and cried and hugged each other.

After a time the two men parted, wiping tears from each other's faces. Laughing and staring at each other, Gabri afraid to look away in case it was taken away, again. And Olivier overwhelmed by all that was so familiar and beloved. The faces, the voices, the sounds he knew so well and hadn't heard in what seemed a lifetime. The scent of maple logs in the fire, and buttery croissants, and roasted coffee beans.

All the things he remembered, and ached for.

And Gabri's scent, of Ivory soap. And his strong, certain arms around him. Gabri. Who'd never, ever stopped believing in him.

Gabri dragged his eyes from Olivier and looked behind his partner to the two Sûreté officers.

"Thank you," he said.

"Inspector Beauvoir deserves the thanks," said the Chief Inspector. The place was quiet again. Gamache turned to Olivier. He needed to say this for everyone to hear. In case there were any lingering doubts.

"I was wrong," Gamache said. "I'm so sorry."

"I can't forgive you," Olivier rasped, struggling to keep his emotions in check. "You have no idea what it was like." He stopped, regained his composure then continued. "Maybe, with time."

"*Oui*," said Gamache.

As everyone celebrated, Armand Gamache walked out into the sunshine, into the sound of children playing hockey, and snowball fights, and tobogganing down the hill. He paused to watch but saw only the young man in his arms. Bullet wounds through his back.

Found, but too late.

Armand Gamache hugged Paul Morin to him.

I'm so sorry. Forgive me.

There was only silence then and, from very far away, the sound of children playing.

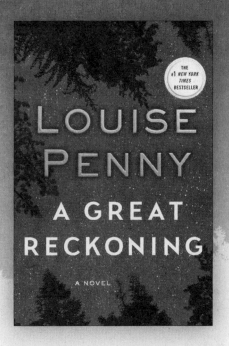
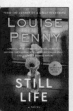

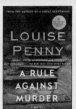

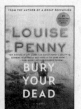
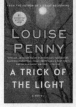
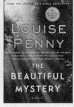
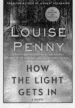

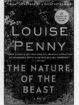